Blue Shaman Trilogy
by Hugh Malafry

Book 1: Stone of Sovereignty

Book 2: Caverns of Ornolac

Book 3: Master of Hallows

Master of Hallows
Hugh Malafry

Book Three

of

Blue Shaman Trilogy

authorHOUSE®

AuthorHouse™
1663 Liberty Drive
Bloomington, IN 47403
www.authorhouse.com
Phone: 1 (800) 839-8640

© 2017 Hugh Malafry. All rights reserved.

No part of this book may be reproduced, stored in a retrieval system, or transmitted by any means without the written permission of the author.

Published by AuthorHouse   08/03/2017

ISBN: 978-1-5462-0253-0 (sc)
ISBN: 978-1-5462-0252-3 (e)

Print information available on the last page.

Any people depicted in stock imagery provided by Thinkstock are models, and such images are being used for illustrative purposes only. Certain stock imagery © Thinkstock.

This book is printed on acid-free paper.

Because of the dynamic nature of the Internet, any web addresses or links contained in this book may have changed since publication and may no longer be valid. The views expressed in this work are solely those of the author and do not necessarily reflect the views of the publisher, and the publisher hereby disclaims any responsibility for them.

...Without father, without mother, without descent, having neither beginning of days, nor end of life; but made like unto the Son of God; abideth a priest continually...

Chapters

Epiphany 1
Dragon Weather 5
Sun-Wheel 22
Backwash 39
Sun Temple 54
Desert Solitaire 67
The Fates 80
The Shades 95
Irkala 106
Desert Fathers 119
Left Hand Path 130
Oasis 139
Sanctuary 154
Garden Grove 170
Carnival 183
Cross Currents 196
Beast of Ulcinj 215
Amour 232
Dark Mirror 253
Charade 274
Cockaigne 289
Black Tower 306

Rose Window	325
The Play's the Thing	338
Heaven and Earth	352
Brethren of the Free Spirit	362
Castle of Women	376
Shadow and Substance	391
Chapel of Angels	405
Chapel of Tears	416
Thresholds	425
Facade	433
Blue Shaman	448
Elysium	461
What Lies Beneath	476
Ruin	486
The Mind on Fire	497
The Choice	506
The Fifth Gate	518
Sovereignty	528

1

Epiphany

"Dark and devious are the ways of men… Wherefore, let there be light."

Caron watched Flegetanis taken in a blaze of light, linger a moment in a cloud of glory, and dissolve on a flood of radiance.

The capstone of the pyramid kindled a blue sun, illumining the desert and for a moment lighting the heavens as day.

His love for the old sage kindled the phoenix-flame. Sheath upon sheath of veiling substance fell away from Caron's soul, until in light body alone he was loosed in falcon's flight.

Borne upon the winds, lifted up among the stars, he felt the draw of the great river below flowing to the sea. But Caron was called, and turning to the source of the river flew to the one who awaited him in the First Time.

"Betake yourself to the waterway; fare upstream, travel about Abydos in this spirit-form of yours, which the gods command to belong to you."

Drawn by love the sun-bird flew to the end of the night, to the wellsprings of the shining river and fountainhead of creation, until he came again to the temple of a million years, the memory and the commission that informed his way now full upon him. And there he communed with the lord of truth incarnate in Osiris; at his hand Nephthys and Isis, dusk and dawn.

But for Flegetanis, who walked into the light, time slowed. A sun kindled in him: forces, rays and affinities measured in graceful articulation to inform his soul. In a place unravished by time he was transfigured, suspended between worlds in that first flesh made for man, before he cloaked himself in the dust of the earth.

He had come as bidden - not that he would have chosen otherwise – and found he sat silently upon a curved stone bench before a reflecting pool under a flowering tree. He looked toward a stair that led up to a small tiered pyramid of lapis blue stone, and knew at once he was in the final height of the sun temple on the peak of Whiter Morn. Here was the apex of the Archaeus, capstone to the realms of earth it informed, its highpoint a four-tiered altar before a dolmen arch framing an azure sky.

He waited and watched the light intensify between the pillars, marking the threshold of the realms of earth to the realms of light in the kingdom of the sun. In the light of Whiter Morn he could apprehend it all: the margin of the given world, the islands of the sea, the ring of bright water, the three peaks that defined the realm, and on to the very edge of uncreated darkness.

And still Flegetanis waited, expecting momentarily an invitation to enter in and cross over into the realms of light, but none came. Instead, the flame on the four-tiered altar burned brighter and within the dolmen arch appeared a being of light.

The vision of the Aton-Re was first too intense to endure and Flegetanis turned away. But the lord of the crossing, gentling his radiance, bade Flegetanis turn and face him. And still he fell to his knees before the shining one, his senses overwhelmed. Dazzling colours, intoxicating scents, vibrant tones, and intense passions all mounted in his mind. But he kept his focus in the shining one, and all gave way at last to silence and the all-encompassing tone of the celestial Aum.

"I have home in my heart," Flegetanis ventured. "Do but bid me enter in and come to you."

"Have you ever left us?"

"Forgive, Master, what clings like rust and soils; though I am here, in the residue of my existence I am still somewhat in the world."

The Aton-Re came closer, more substantial in light body and the undying flesh of Whiter Morn. Thus cloaked his radiance was more readily borne, and in this wise the shining one laid his hand on Flegetanis' shoulder. In the substance that rose in response to the hand of the Aton-Re, Flegetanis was refreshed and restored. At once he understood. "It is not yet my time," he whispered.

"We would have you bide yet a little while, to keep the way of the crossing of the worlds."

In the light of the wonderful one it was made plain what he had begun to suppose. Maia and all she contrived was unfinished business, and Caron was not fully accomplished. "You have awakened him from his long sleep," the Aton-Re confirmed. "Now, you must teach him to come into my presence."

But there was more, and Flegetanis felt it impressed upon his soul as certain as any commission. A decision was made and the days of man were numbered, until there would come a time when there was time no more. Again the Aton-Re confirmed.

"Even from the time of the great transgression man has denied the open hand of opportunity given him to return, to rise up in the light of the wonderful one.

"Once more chance shall be given to rebuild the altar of life that was broken down, and restore the oneness of the worlds. He will be shown again the way to awaken to the lords of light that man in divine identity be restored, and the abomination of desolation cleansed from the earth."

"And if he will not?"

"Whether he will or no the radiance of the realms of light shall intensify in the flesh of the earth. Those who fight against it shall fail, and falling into their own degenerate natures will bring an end, and perish in the flesh."

"And for those who answer true?"

"They who rise up in the quickening shall birth a new heaven and a new earth. You know whereof I speak and the way of intensification in the light, for the essence is written in you."

"How long?"

"In these times a beginning is made. It may yet be an age before the consummation is wrought, but the issue of the earth moves on."

"Full of years I cannot return as once I was."

"I have lifted some burden of years from your flesh that you might endure, until your time of renewing is come. And I will magnify in you the gift of the shining ones to veil appearance, that as needful you may be hidden from the eyes of men."

"It is well," Flegetanis agreed. "I have come too far not to see the beginning and the end of it."

In a moment it was done. Flegetanis knelt once more on the cold, stone floor of the King's Chamber, facing west to the empty tomb. At his side Caron knelt deep in trance; at rest in this world, his consciousness in flight through the seasons of suns.

Feeling a burden of years lifted from him Flegetanis arose, knowing what must be done. For a moment he rested his hand on Caron's shoulder. "You must go a journey you never thought possible," he said softly. "Never alone, others will uplift you in the way, old friend, until in an hour ordained we shall meet again.

"Seek out the sage, Origen. He dwells in the monastery of Alba on the Red Sea Shore. He will teach you to awaken to who you are. He will instruct you in the way you must go."

With a tender glance back, Flegetanis gathered up his cloak and carefully retraced his steps down the Grand Gallery, past the Queen's Chamber to the parting of the ways, until he emerged in starshine of the celestial Nile in the shadow of the Great Pyramid. Beneath the stars he paused a moment looking up into the night sky before walking off into the silent desert.

2

Dragon Weather

And when he had communed with the lord of Osiris, taken council with that one who ordained the shining ones of the First Time; loosed in the light of the rising sun from the heart of the lord of truth, in falcon flight Caron took the wings of the morning.

But even as he rose in the light the east wind whispered remembrance: *"As for him who knows the spell of it; he himself is a god in the wise of Thoth, and will go down to any sky he wishes to go down to."*

Caron knew then before entering again into the flesh of the fallen world, he must awaken to what was lost in the forgotten time that left him only with intuitions of who and what he is. So he asked it of the lord of truth who answers with light. And seeing the way he must go let the currents of river and air, and the reigning wisdom of the sun within, guide his flight in the earth, for well he knew the spell of all things is written in the sacred four.

Curiously, the sky that opened before him arced over neither the red land nor river of time, or the black earth of Kemet. Instead, in falcon flight he flew over the flowering meadows of a realm once known as Caer

Myrddin; in a time now forgotten when the worlds touched, obscured by the veil of the human heart. And on that fair field on that day armies gathered in splendid array; to battle over who should possess the sovereignty and govern the threshold of the worlds. He stayed not but drawn swiftly flew on over the sea cliffs toward three men and a youth, who in the eye of the wind sailed in a craft called Swiftsure, and sailors eager to be home.

"These are Myrddin, Taliesin and Manawyddan returned from Álfalan."

"And you on that fateful day," a voice, carried on a whisper of wind, confirmed.

In his name of *Ka* Caron rode high upon crest of the sea wind, watched the men below take hurried leave of one another, and the little ship turn again to sea and sail northwest toward Manannán's Isle, leaving Myrddin and his youthful apprentice at the foot of the seven hundred stairs that straddled the cliffs from the sea to the fields of Caer Myrddin.

Pressed by the rising winds, eager to be home again, they seemed blissfully unaware of the impending clash of armies in the fields above. But the old sage paused in the ascent and pointed out to the youth an apparition in the heavens; its comet tail blown by invisible winds undulating as if some scintillating serpent made its way across the sky, glittering over the sea in the full of day.

Caron felt the storm gather like electricity in the air, and sensing danger to the old sage flew in pursuit of the little vessel scudding across the white, foam sea. "*Ka Ra Na,*" the voice whispered: "bring back Manawyddan and Taliesin; bring them to Caer Myrddin." With a flare of feathers the windhover wheeled on the wind, dove on the little ship already running far from the land, and hung motionless upon a crest of wind before Manawyddan, who stood forward of the mast seeing the way they must go. The eyes brightened with delight in the falcon's flight before him. Caron gazed into them. It was a familiar face looked back at him.

"Taliesin, come and see." The bard stood with Manawyddan and watched the windhover. "A spirit loosed in air."

"Is it Myrddin?" Taliesin asked.

"He would speak to us."

"Unless something is amiss and cannot."

The falcon cried out, piercing the wind with his call for help, whether they could hear or not under this sky. Perhaps what was done could not be undone; only seen again. The wind like a wave bore down upon them; he turned on a flare of a tail and feather's tip, caught the curl and soared. And Manawyddan did likewise, ordering Swiftsure brought about turning again toward Caer Myrddin.

The falcon found the sage Myrddin with his apprentice toward the top of the stone stair, stopping to rest. "Wait on an old man," he asked. Myrddin rested and gazed out over the sea to find the little boat now a speck on the horizon. As he looked it seemed the vessel came about on the wind, but then his eyes were old and he was unsure. Perhaps it was on the tack. He had invited them to stay but after two years they were as anxious as he to be home to their own.

Myrddin took the blue stone men called sovereignty out of his scrip and held it to the sun. Months past Myrddin felt patterns shift and intensify within and knew a crisis was at hand. And a month ago in the dead of night he had seen its sign in the heavens: the rider of the storm returned, though this time it appeared on a path less likely to trouble the earth. He had spoken of it with Taliesin and Manawyddan and together and they agreed that returning to their own before it came upon them was best. Fear and panic ran before the rider of the storm; madness followed in its wake.

"Can I hold it?"

Myrddin put the stone cautiously in the youth's outstretched hand. "What do you feel?"

"What do you mean, feel?"

"Well, things like courage, strength, and confidence - the virtues of a young man's heart - do you feel those?"

"Yes," the youth said thoughtfully. "Those are there."

"And something more?"

"Like fresh water," he said: "as light as a bird's feather; like apple blossom; bright as fire."

"I should have sent you with Taliesin. Can you find one word?"

"Clean?"

"Manawyddan was right; your name shall be Caron." Myrddin took a little white stone he had carried form the shores of Álfalan out of his scrip. "You may keep this one."

"What does it mean, this use name, Caron?" The youth looked from one stone to the other.

Myrddin closed the boy's hand about the white stone. "In the language of these people it means pure." He held his hand closed tightly for a moment about hand and stone. "Blessed are the pure in heart. There, I have written the word within for remembrance." Caron kept the white stone and carefully Myrddin turned the blue stone into his own scrip.

"And what is the name of the blue stone?"

"Some call it sovereignty; others, the Aton, Orion, Osiris, or in the old tongue, *Uru An-Na*. But always its name is light of Heaven, after the star whose patterns inform this world. When you have learned to read what is written in the white stone, you will know how to read what is written in the *Uru An-Na*."

Caron gazed a moment on the white pebble Myrddin gave him, then put it carefully in his scrip, as surely as if it was the most precious jewel in creation.

"And will you teach me how to read?"

Myrddin looked once more out to sea and clearly the ship was returning. He was not, however, about to wait for them here upon the stair; for now he felt the urgency of his return. He turned to climb when a whistle, swoosh and whir of wings on the air startled him into looking up. The falcon rode the rising air and hung arm's length off the stairs over the crags below.

Myrddin stretched out his hand and the bird lighted upon it. The kestrel ruffled up, straightened a pin feather that was sticking him, then alert turned his head and peered into Myrddin's eyes. "You come as messenger. I would have a little joy in my life before taking up new burdens."

Caron made the link, and it was indeed as if meeting an old friend, but he felt Myrddin weary, resigned to things to come he could do nothing about. The old man smiled, looked curiously a moment to the youth. "You have an avatar, Caron." He turned again to the bird: "I have seen the great king come and gone and the end of the matter when he shall come again. But so much lies between, and I am weary and would return to my own. But mind me not, spirit," he said, with another glance to the youth, and then again the bird. "Welcome, bright spirit. What sky do you come down from? Are you my past or my future; your message a reminder of what has been or a warning of what shall be?"

He whispered warning but the old sage seemed not to hear. "I think he has come to warn us of something yet to come," Caron said. And at his word the falcon took flight and rose in the sun. Myrddin watched it catch the wind and spiral up into the light.

"You come to me I think from the lord of truth in the First Time," Myrddin said. "Light streamed into the sage's soul. He stood entranced, his face lifted to the sun, head resting on the rock. Yes, it was for warning the falcon had come. The storm gathered and the spoiler was at it again. "I fear we face yet another bloody battle over a worthless sovereignty."

"Are you well old father?"

"Well enough to beat you to the top of these stairs." The youth ran ahead and Myrddin followed, climbing the stairs to the plain of Caer Myrddin and the castle above.

This time it began a tournament. Rhydderch Hael, the generous, refusing the hospitality of king Gwenddolan, Myrddin's temporal lord, encamped his following in the meadows of Caer Myrddin. Hael then challenged Gwenddolan to a contest over sovereignty of the realms; for, though there were those who said Myrddin's return was immanent, so long was he gone Hael felt sure he would never more.

Gwenddolan was to forsake the way of Myrddin and the old order and accept his own, or suffer siege and the wrath of the sword Dyrnwyn that drawn in battle burst into flame. To this end, Hael brought seven black cloaks of the new religion with him, to legitimize his right to convert and claim sovereignty over Gwenddolan's lands and subjects.

To impress upon Gwenddolan the seriousness of his challenge, a priest of the old powers in robes of dark blue came likewise to challenge should the absent mage magically reappear. That one stood aloof with his red haired mistress, the witch Nemain, at his side to observe the outcome. In truth Hael cared not for the new religion or the old; only to magnify his kingdom.

King Gwenddolan refused to yield sovereignty without consulting Myrddin, but honour required a response and a tournament was arranged to play out the forces for diplomacy is always preferable to bloodshed. So it was two armies were set in array in the meadows of Caer Myrddin. Pavilion tents were raised and the tournament began with feasting and display of all finery and art each to be met in kind by the other. It was to span three days, and Gwenddolan, host by virtue of having it thrust upon him, was to choose the manner of the first day. Gwenddolan was a peaceful man and so he chose the poets who had gathered to Caer Myrddin to await Myrddin's return; the mage had gone a great journey and his fate was a matter of some importance to them for the shaping of their songs.

So, on the first day the poet priests appeared, dressed in coloured robes with their sash of rank in the Druid College, to engage the host of Rhydderch Hael. They told the tales of the ancients, of the defeating the one-eyed Formorian giants who invaded when the lands in the western sea were lost beneath the waves and here laid out the pattern of the sacred land.

The black priests responded by telling the stories of God's creation of heaven and earth; the making of a garden of a paradise lost, in which man and woman once dwelt in perfection. And they filled their tales with the longings of the heart that it might be so again. Some of Gwenddolan's bards wished in turn to tell of *Tír inna n-Óc*, the land of eternal summer where Myrddin had gone, but it was agreed the tales were well told and should move on.

Then Gwenddolan's poets turned to tales of heroes and sang of how the nobles of the Goddess Danu journeyed to the holy isles bearing the Hallows; they sang of Magh Tuiredh when Lugh, son of light, fought for the wounded king Nuada; and of the day when the Fir Bholg came against the Tuatha de Danu. In battle, bright and beautiful in his array, Lugh, son of the Great Father and the Great Mother, slew the Fir Bholg leader, his own grandfather Balor of the baleful eye, whose glance no man could survive, by piercing the single great eye with his spear of light. Balor's sight turned in upon itself, by his own gaze he perished as always evil must at the last destroy itself.

In reply the black priests told the tale of Jesus of Nazareth, the son of God who was the light of the world, and how he lay down his life for all who called him friend; giving himself not to human corruption but to God overcoming the son of perdition who contrived his destruction, and enslavement of all mankind.

Again it was agreed these were good tales all, and that no judgment might be made favoring one over the other, so at length the issue turned to prophecy. Gwenddolan's poets sang of Mórrígan, the phantom, raven-haired goddess of war, and the prophecies made after the battle of Magh Tuiredh, where she fought for the Tuatha de Danu. Her first prophecy was of a world of cosmic order and prosperity to come; her second a warning of chaos and the end of the world. The black priests argued much among themselves which of the two should be addressed as true prophecy, and chose frightening tales of the apocalypse and the end of time, when the world would be judged and cleansed of sin and a new heaven and new earth ushered in.

A third time it was agreed, though for art the poets had the advantage in the telling, that the tales were well told, and so after much feasting a second form of contest over the weaving of spells was suggested. The black priests resisted the challenge saying God did not involve himself in nature by the weaving spells, but had set everything after its own seed. The poets asked *which* God did not, and argument followed over the number of gods. The black robes suggested instead a contest of prayers to God for a speedy resolution to this strife engendered by Gwenddolan's unwillingness to yield sovereignty to a Christian lord.

The poets in turn were confused with wondering why one would frame pleas to a God who had given the world and the skills to shape what was needful by arts and spells, and so the argument went full circle and the invitation to compete in prayers was declined. The suspicion grew that they were competing on different grounds, and that there was a gulf between them that no contest of wits could resolve. And so it was agreed to defer this contest to another day when the magical powers of each should be demonstrated. The black robes again objected they did not use magic. But they were silenced when one of the poets suggested a demonstration of the art of changing bread and wine into the flesh and blood of God, as the black priests were said to do, would serve.

This contest of wits at an end, the tournament moved on to feats of skill in the arts of war as the mighty men of each camp tested each other, found each other worthy, and parted amicably. The day nearly came to blows, however, when the battle crone intervened in a match, took the sword of one young warrior, and chastised him for not learning well the skills she had taught him. She proceeded to demonstrate her lesson in sword magic by immediately disarming his opponent, and two others who came after to test her skill. When all three attacked her she cast a spell changing them into swine. They ran squealing through the crowds, to the horror of the black robes who ran after to lift the curse upon them; though what they saw was in their minds only.

Rhydderch's Hael's men rattled their swords upon their shields and urged battle over the insult, when the whisper went round that within the old one dwelled the Mórrígan, and it was the doom of men they did not know her. Then were the hosts of Rhydderch Hael silenced with thought of what they faced, for despite the new religion they still feared death. The black robes were further confused when the three heroes returned sodden from the lake into which they plunged, and argued because of trickery the day should be theirs. But they were quickly silenced when the identity of the battle crone was whispered.

Frustrated in their efforts to win the day, Hael's nobles urged him to do personal battle with Gwenddolan to settle their cause. Did he not they argued possess one of the thirteen treasures of Britain, the sword Dyrnwyn, forged by the Norse smith Wayland, which in the hands of a noble burst into flames in battle? But Hael, despite his agreements with the black robes, refused: he was not about to try to claim personal victory in battle over an order not only said to possess the stone of sovereignty, but one whom the goddess of war appeared to favour. He was confused. It was well known that to take the stone by force was lethal, but until the Mórrígan appeared to fight for Gwenddolan's court, he was sure he held sway and the stone by rights his to possess.

Now he realized the heavens did not favour him, and was prepared to cede the field for another day. And so to consider what should come next, it was agreed each side should retire to its own solemn feasts. Frustrated with the deadlock Rhydderch Hael went apart alone to take drink and contemplate what he must do to make amends to Gwenddolan for his false challenge. As he sat within his tent the weather shifted; clouds gathered and the sun-shot sky was full of moods as the apparition they feared once again appeared in the heavens. It was then Hael's mistress, Nemainn, came to him and suggested the tournament of chess. And it was on that day Myrddin returned.

Guardian of the stone of sovereignty, the lord Gwenddolan also possessed another of the thirteen treasures of the isle of Britain; a marvelous chessboard of gold with pieces of silver, that set to an issue of consequence were said to play themselves. It was called the Chessboard of the Empress, because the goddess of sovereignty revealed her will through the movement of the pieces. While they were comfortable with the mystique of the sword Dyrnwyn, so long as it served their purpose, the very existence of an enchanted chessboard said to reveal the will of the goddess was an offense to the black cloaks; let alone the suggestion it should decide the outcome of the tournament. But in an afternoon of uncertain weathers, when the sun shone now brilliant, now masked behind ranges of dark clouds, a match was set up between the two hosts, and Gwenddolan unveiled the Chessboard of the Empress.

Champions were chosen, for like Dyrnwyn that once drawn burst into flame only in the hands of a noble, the Chessboard of the Empress would not play itself, except players key to the outcome of the match faced off one from another. It was assumed Rhydderch Hael and Gwenddolan should play, but though for thirty tense minutes they sat across the board taking measure of each other nothing happened. And this to the relief of the black robes who were secretly afraid what was said of the chessboard was true, that it played itself, for they feared holy relics. At this point everyone on both sides began to feel that the contest as a whole was ill favored, and that the tournament would prove inconclusive and only battle would resolve what arts had not.

At length Gwenddolan rose from the table: "It is simple enough to understand," he said. "The goddess has forbidden this match. It is not for me to wager the stone of sovereignty over your claim to a kingdom. Even now it is in Myrddin's possession and not mine, and it is for him to read what is written therein; him to part with it should he see fit.

"Be at peace Rhydderch Hael and let us go our ways. We shall await Myrddin's return, and if he yields the sovereignty to this new order, I shall in no wise resist him."

"And if he never comes again?"

"Then I fear we shall each inherit a kingdom of blood. But I know he lives and shall return."

Rhydderch Hael took counsel with his lords and with the black robes in attendance. The priests persuaded him the power of the old ways was to be overcome by faith, as evidenced by the failure of the enchanted chessboard, and urged him to seek the conversion of the heathen forces of Gwenddolan to the sovereignty of the church, or failing that do righteous battle with them. Hael was unconvinced; he had seen the power of the battle crone; he was afraid of the raven-haired Mórrígan.

It was then his mistress Nemain came forward and suggested a noble woman of each power face off over the contest. And, as all sovereign women are the goddess' own, in one or another transmutation, it should be seen whom she favored; this seemed eminently sensible to both parties. And so Gwenddolan choose Myrddin's wife, Gwendolena, who in his court awaited her husband's return.

Younger than her husband by more than thirty years, Gwendolena remained true to her lord in his absence, and lost nothing of her youthful beauty but for mourning it. Indeed, a murmur of appreciation went up from Rhydderch's Hael's host when she appeared, blithe and fair in soft green and yellow gown to take up the challenge of the tournament. But the appreciation turned to awe when she sat before the chessboard, and immediately the white ivory and silver pieces at her hand trembled and came to life, while the ebony and silver forms remained inert. Rhydderch was distressed, not knowing how to answer; and were it possible, the black cloaks were blacker yet, and gathered together like a court of crows to croak over the conundrum.

Rhydderch Hael as yet had no queen but against her will had taken a mistress, Nemain, spoil of battle from an Irish king. She longed to go home but Rhydderch Hael intended, when she truly warmed to him, to make her his queen. Red haired Nemain stood with the druid who urged her now to go to Rhydderch Hael and take his part, and affectionately took his arm in hers. "The pieces will move for me," she said. "I can give you Gwendolena and so with or without the stone sovereignty of her and a kingdom."

"Ask what you will for it."

"Leave to return to my people."

As they had for Gwendolena, the pieces came to life when Nemain sat at the golden chessboard. Three matches were proposed: to begin with wagers made between the players and the hosts of Gwenddolan and Rhydderch Hale, bearing on the rights of possession and rule leading to the final match for sovereignty. Horses, arms, precious stones, lands and women were wagered as the two sat down to play. They made a pair that no man's eyes could resist: fair-haired, blue-eyed Gwendolena, wife of Myrddin; red-haired, green-eyed Nemainn, over whose fatal beauty wars were fought.

The first game went to Gwendolena, but as the pieces played themselves and the two women watched the drama unfold, it was not a matter of skill but a sense of the right that was nurtured. At behest of the black robes, in the name of their God, Rhydderch Hael had come challenging a lawful king. But he was steeped enough in the ways of his forbears to know the goddess of sovereignty was a power to be reckoned with. And the chessboard revealed, not only to him but to his host, that despite the black robes they did not have her blessing of right to rule. Many goods changed hands, though Gwendolena had been willing to wager only trifles, jewels and clothing; to barter in souls of men ran counter to her nature. Nemain grew darker like the skies above as the game unfolded, for she promised Rhydderch Hael victory, and on that her freedom.

By the time of the third match the winds had come up and the pavilion tent flapped in the gusts. The blood of the hosts was up, too, for Rhydderch's men sensed a decisive end that cost them dearly in possessions. Even still pride would not let them back off and they wagered heavily against the outcome. But for his honour and fear of the Mórrígan, who he was now sure had taken a hand in this, Rhydderch Hael would have then broken off the match for, win or lose, she punished cowardice and an ungenerous spirit.

"She has spoken twice. By rights I have bested you," Gwenddolan said. "I claim nothing of you, but your friendship and loyalty. You shall live in your way, and I shall live in mine. Let no blood be shed for pride between us by pressing this further."

Rhydderch Hael turned to Nemain. "What say you?"

"These matches have been for goods and chattel; not anything the lady cares for, and not the sovereignty of her lord. This is the Chessboard of the Empress; we offend her to play for trifles skirting the purpose of the match."

"Then play outright for the stone of sovereignty," Hael demanded. "I will wager the sword Dyrnwyn and my fealty against it."

"It cannot be," Gwenddolan said. "It is not mine to wager but with

Myrddin, who journeys to the Otherworld to heal the great king given to rule over us one and all."

"And yet there is a way between women," Nemain said. "Dare I speak of it?" The men agreed they should hear of it. "Gwendolena," Nemain asked, "you have the advantage of me, but shall we test our resolve with a wager between us?"

A rumble of thunder distracted Gwendolena before she could reply. The wind gusted smelling of the sea, and there was a whir of wings on the wind. A windhover hung over the pavilion tent just beyond her. Nemain started at the bird, and grasped a silver piece from the chessboard to hurl at it, but like a bee the piece stung her, and she dropped it. Gwendolena picked it up and replaced it carefully. Dismissing the bird, Nemain urged Hael to shoot it from the sky, and seeking Gwendolena's eye returned to the game. "Shall we have a woman's wager?"

But Gwendolena was distracted. From where she sat she saw two figures coming across the meadow from the sea cliffs toward Caer Myrddin, one the likeness of her husband, Myrddin.

"Gwendolena," Nemainn insisted, fixing her eye. "It is a matter of honour. Will you?"

"Yes, we shall have our wager," Gwendolena said, absently. "What will it be?"

"Lord against lord for the sovereignty."

"Is that not now the wager?"

"If you win, Rhydderch Hael will yield his sword, Dyrnwyn. And in body and soul offer me and fealty to Gwenddolan. If I win, you and King Gwenddolan will yield sovereignty, body and soul, to Rhydderch Hael."

"It cannot be. I am wed to my lord Myrddin."

"He has been gone two years," Nemainn said. "He shall never return. But to be generous, shall we say, with one year and a day it shall be resolved thus: if Myrddin does not by then return, only then shall you and Gwenddolan yield sovereignty to Rhydderch Hael's will for you."

Gwendolena watched her husband coming across the meadow toward her. She was sure it was him. Falcon, rider of the wind, hovered over the sage as he came. Myrddin was come home. Her husband already returned she had already won, and none but she had seen it. It was her chance to bring peace where there had been threat of war, to his homecoming.

"It would not please the goddess that you distrust her in this, for if your love be true you cannot fail this game. Do you fear the wager?"

"No, you have your wager."

"So be it," Nemain said, sitting back satisfied. "I have said, one year from tomorrow."

"Then you have lost also the third match, Nemain," she said, rising to meet Myrddin, "for my husband even now returns from Álfalan."

Nemainn turned startled to see Myrddin come across the field, and the host of Gwenddolan bow like grass in the wind before him. But Rhydderch Hael cuffed Nemainn across the face so that her lip bled, and she shuffled off to shelter within the cloak of the Druid priest who watched fate unfold before him, for if his power over Rhydderch Hael was to be challenged it would be now.

Fear at the sight of Myrddin like a wave washed over the host of Rhydderch Hael, but there was jubilation in the host of Gwenddolan. Gwendolena rushed to her husband's arms. He embraced her silently, even as the weather failed and huge banks of rumbling cloud mounted over the hills converging on the meadow of tents and pennants. The youth Caron who ran after the old mage struck with the power of the gathered hosts gazed distracted over the colorful scene, exalting in the gathering storm.

Myrddin took his fair wife by the hand and turned to the chessboard. "What is this?" Gwendolena explained what had come to pass, but Myrddin had already read it in the board. Gwenddolan greeted the sage, and the host of Gwenddolan stood silent by to see what was to come. The host of Rhydderch Hael banged their swords on their shields for courage, and Hael came forward to pay his respects to Myrddin. The falcon hovered on the air. The sky grew dark with squalls of rain.

"You have wagered and won twice for Gwenddolan?"

"She has wagered thrice, and the third match is yet to be played," Nemain said boldly.

Myrddin turned to the red haired witch who bartered with his wife. He studied her for a moment, held out his hand, and the falcon dove from the winds and lighted upon it. When they touched Caron found himself suspended on a flow of thought, seeing through Myrddin's eyes. "Do you see what I see?"

Caron saw Maia, the lady of illusions, searching to find a way into the sage's soul. But he was aware of her, hedged her out, and she could not enter.

"Mórrígan, in one guise or another," Myrddin said to Nemain. "As usual you enter into both sides of dispute to beguile and take blood sacrifice of your wiles from each.

"I seek advantage where it may be found."

"What hatred compels you now to strive against our peace, to beguile and pit these priests of the prince of peace against us?"

"These are nothing to me, Myrddin. It is but a game I play here for the mastery."

"You would not have come but for carnage."

"I have had my fill of prating poets, the strutting of fools, pleas of supplicants, and the tawdry honour of men: I will strip the veil from these. I will have blood."

"Mórrígan," Rhydderch shouted his boast, and drew the sword Dyrnwyn. "She plays for us."

"Only a noble soul in a noble cause," Myrddin said, passing his hand over the blade, "kindles Dyrnwyn." The sword flickered but would not burst into flame, and then as dull as lead. A shadow fell over them, and the clouds spilled down in slow, undulant waves over the meadows and covered the sun. The apparition stopped in its motion across the sky and swelled toward the earth.

"He brings the heavens against us." A cry went up among the host of Rhydderch Hael. Myrddin looked about and beckoned to those who stood by to gather to him, but none moved for fear.

"Come to me, Caron," Myrddin drew the boy close, and for the moment everything froze around them and they communed in a time out of time. "The hedge is breached," Myrddin said, "the pattern broken, and I must see it through, but thou…" The old sage pressed the pouch with the blue stone in the youth's hand. "Hide in the woods. I will come to you." Caron resisted, reluctant to turn away. "There will be another day," Myrddin insisted, raising his arm urging the falcon into flight, but like the youth the bird would not flee and hovered on the wind above him. "Nobody listens to me," he complained.

The moment past and Myrddin turned to his wife. "What have you wagered this mistress of illusions in your game of chess?"

"The goddess has given us the victory."

"What have you wagered, Gwendolena?"

"It is done and won," she said. "Rhydderch will yield the sword Dyrnwyn and sovereignty to Gwenddolan."

"And if Nemain wins?"

"She lost two matches," Gwendolena said, "and with your return a third."

The clouds boiled over the field and water and air mingle din a fire that burned with a lurid light like an open furnace within them. The horses cried and the host watched dumbly and darting arrows of flame shot through the darkness that fell over the land. "What did you wager? What did you promise her?"

"Should you not return within the year, Gwenddolan was to yield sovereignty and I give myself to the pleasure of Rhydderch Hael. But she could not win, beloved," she said tearfully, "I saw you coming across the meadows to me."

"You wagered the sovereignty of our love. Nemain has already taken what she wants, and we are lost for it."

"Nothing has changed."

"Everything is changed. We dwell where intent is as the deed, and you have betrayed truth to a wager. The world you opened to me, and all engendered between us you have given Rhydderch Hael, as if it were the very deed.

"This one would now vanquish by betraying me to fight to bring you back and draw substance from me to her blood lust. And I will not, Gwendolena. Henceforth, I will receive you as a friend, but the field abandoned is lost, and I have no power here."

The black cloaks came across the space between the ranks to the pavilion tent, their robes floating in the air like crows laboring in a heavy wind. But Rhydderch Hael's druid stood off and watched. The falcon dived on them screeching, and they fell to their knees holding their hands aloft to fend off the devil bird. The sky erupted. Thunder rattled the earth. It shook and cracked open the cliffs over the sea. The wet grass burned and the air stung electric. Tents were blown aside like chaff before the brutal wind that swept the encampments, driving ashes and sparks before it.

19

"Come now fear and panic," Myrddin said. "Flee Caron" he urged the youth who still held back, "flee to the forest."

Enraged with surging passions he could not comprehend, Hael thrust his blind sword into Gwenddolan's belly. The ranks of those left standing erupted; Gwenddolan's host surged forward to their fallen lord. Bloodied sword raised high above his head, enraged with shame it would not burn, Rhydderch Hael gathered his men to him. He counted the black priests nothing, fearing now he had forever lost honour and the power of his sword; except in battle he impress the Mórrígan and prevail against Myrddin's enchantments. The women screamed and ran, blown like loose skeins of silk across the field. But Nemainn stood still in the midst of the carnage, red hair streaming in the wind, shouting frenzy: "fools, fools, I am courted by fools."

Myrddin fell to his knees with the youth sheltering him, and looked heavenward. "Old Father," the sage said, "when we should rise to meet you we are unprepared, and again the rider of the storm is come upon us." The apparition appeared in the heavens, now a whirlpool that drew streamers of torn and bloodied cloud into itself, concentrating in a single, gory red eye in a mass of darkness that obscured the sun. Arrows of ice fell from the sky; long shining spears of flame flashed, darted and flung their deadly points into the scattered hosts." From what forgotten realms do you now come and what to awaken in us?" Myrddin prayed.

Men fell to the fiery shafts cast down from the clouds, in a din like the rumble of cavalry advancing and the grinding of steel of combat. "Oh Lord thou comest to slay the wicked," the black robes shouted to the heavens. "Fall upon the heathen; smite them with your mighty sword. Visit your justice upon them, and make the memory of their name an abomination in the earth."

But the heavens rained down alike upon the just and the unjust; the fiery lances piercing them where they knelt; the thousands who fought with anguish so ancient it was nameless, roused up, come round again to feed this fire with fuel. Fiery stones mingling with ice and hail smashed down upon them and set the fields ablaze, as men who feasted together and but days before called each other friend murdered one another never knowing why.

"*Ka Ra Na*," the voice within urged, "fly, fly, fly." Lifted on the winds the falcon rose in a flurry of bright feathers tossed and tumbling on the air in search of the sun, until swept up in the last remaining light was gone.

In the tales that were told thereafter of rage and war and pestilence, it was said six months the battle burned from drawing of first blood. In fact it was not so long for almost at once it was done; a thunderbolt from the dark eye of the apparition shook the earth, striking insensible the host of men and women who fell unconscious upon the plain of Caer Myrddin awakening to carnage and vague memories how it had come to this.

In that day, too, the sky kindled with light too great for human sense to endure, blinding any who dared look into it. And so was it for seven days the specter hung in the heavens glowering over the earth, and the hosts left standing from the heat and the hot breath of it scattered on the winds like ashes.

And the sorrows of Caer Myrddin were not theirs alone, for the coming again of the rider of the storm marked the beginning of a dark age of endless winters and famine in diverse places; a dragon age of rock and ice and fire, unspoken of for fear evoked it shall come again, even as Myrddin then knew it must.

Caron would not run. But seeing Myrddin in the midst of the slaughter, overcome with distraction as the weave of the pattern the shining ones wove came undone, alone and with truest instinct the youth led Myrddin from the field, fleeing into the great forest. It is said Rhydderch Hael won the day of battle, and the sovereignty and Myrddin's wife Gwendolena. He lived, but truth be told all he possessed was but for a moment, gone in the twinkling of an eye.

Caron and Myrddin endured. And in time, returned to his senses, the old wizard hid himself from the sight of men and began the work anew. But a veil obscured Caron's consciousness from all that had befallen him until he should awaken again. And under Myrddin's watchful eye he endured the centuries, through the seasons of the renewing in the shining ones, until the hour of his ascent with Flegetanis in the great pyramid, into the secret place of the most high.

His flight accomplished, Caron opened eyes and found himself alone in the silence of the King's Chamber, illumined yet by the soft afterglow of transfiguration that took Flegetanis. And if he knew not yet precisely who he was, he knew now what he was.

3

Sun-Wheel

Her impulse was to sacrifice the child. That was the old way when a birth was inconvenient and offense against a daughter of the Order, lest the blood be corrupted. But the Masters of Hallows counseled against it and she at last must reluctantly agree, but not gracefully. She scolded them for resisting her will and left them feeling stripped flesh from bone, raw nerves exposed to her elemental rage. And when they had suffered her - they needed to know whence their authority derived - she made up with them.

But there was more: they balked when she demanded the masters contrive to curse Caron. "Make all his paths crooked; his works come to naught. Confine, constrain and strip from him all joy in life. Let him be deceived and denied by those he would trust. Set stumbling blocks before him, delivering him into the hands of his enemies that he never again plagues me."

The Masters of Hallows took counsel together, and as it was Telgesinus' time to govern he made reply for them. "Let it be as you have said, but we must speak plainly to our condition in these times: our influence is much diminished. In the burning time we were unable to shape a pattern to stand against the slaughter of Cathar and Templar. Our failure diminished the faith of the temporal lords in us and so our powers.

"And late the breaking of the hedge and assault upon the daughters of the Blood Royal provokes questions of your ability to govern the Order. The lords believe you weak, the power of their realms declining, and because of you their future in doubt."

Magda was incensed. "In those days I was deceived; ravished against my will. It was that wicked necromancer Caron who perverted the power of the stone to harm us."

"Our inability to master Caron and to possess the stone of sovereignty is a great failing," Telgesinus whinged. "It puts the very future of the Order in question."

She wanted to scold that they should question her, but if she lost them the powers locked in her breast would perish in rancor and never flower. And so turning to wiles she softened. "Then we are agreed concerning Caron. He must be overcome. You are my counselors. Say what is to be done."

And so they took counsel together, but not Flegetanis for he was yet in Egypt. And when they were done Blaise, most accomplished of the three, spoke for them. "Milady," he began cautiously, "I have this day received a letter from Bran, Lord of Caer Myrddin. He invites you to appear there on the equinox one year from this September month for the *Troth*, where you will undergo your trial of investiture as Domina of the Blood Royal. Others will be summoned to bear witness to this rite of passage."

"We are summoned?"

"We have spoken to you of the investiture. It is ritual but the force of it very real. Except you are confirmed Domina by the Guardian of the Blood Royal your powers will not come full upon you, and your right to rule will be subject to challenge."

"I am heir, chosen of the Cailleach."

"Heir apparent, and until it is done may face a challenge."

"It will be Gwenhwyfar," Magda said. "This rite of passage; what must I do?"

"It is the same for all who went before," Blaise said. "You must prepare to walk a full cycle of the sun-wheel at Caer Myrddin to confirm, correct and restore the foundational cycles of the Order. Your trial is to focus those forces that pertain to the Domina, master the passage in a problem set for you, and so doing affirm your right to rule."

"How shall I prepare for this?"

"I will see to your readiness."

"Not Telgesinus?"

"No, milady," Telgesinus answered. "It is the Guardian's will that Blaise attend to you in this."

"The Guardian's will: very well," she said, reluctantly.

"At Green Chapel we shall initiate the cycle of what is to come," Blaise said. "Thereafter we shall journey to gather up such response of the temporal lords we may be assured of, as we move to consummation at Caer Myrddin. And we must send for the Master Flegetanis to attend us at Caer Myrddin; to bear witness to the power of the Grail Hallows."

Telgesinus darkened at thought of Flegetanis returning. Magda balked, too, for his powers were beyond all theirs combined, and she feared him; her *genius* warned against him. What's more, he would never support the curse she would inflict upon his protégé. "Must Flegetanis come? It was he who instructed Caron in the arts of magic turned black. It may be he still holds with this necromancer."

"He is a master of masters, and true to what he is. You will find in him only support for the truth of what you are."

"The Cailleach trusted and he never failed her," she mused. "Nevertheless, if he fails me in this I will have his life."

Despite his enmity Telgesinus was jealous for his own powers and troubled by Magda's tone; it took the four masters to make a whole. "We must temper our moods," Telgesinus counseled. "We must gather up all that is our due and restore our weave of influence, or diminished in all our affairs."

"Who is Guardian of our Order?" She had heard it spoken of before that there was one, to whom the Order was responsible; she did not care to think she was not its ultimate authority.

"He who stands on the threshold of the worlds shall come to Caer Myrddin to try the heart: to guide, protect, and uplift you in the way." Of him Blaise would say no more, for he was present at the trials and investiture of the Domina Branwyn and these things must await their timely revelation.

She stilled, come to the eye of the storm. It was legend that once departed, they who shaped the Order abode in another realm close at hand to guide its mistress' way. And because of the one who watched over her, Magda knew it to be so; one so skilled in the arts of shaping she might weave water into knots, And this genius who from time to time attended her, who came to her in visions of the night promising to guide her path to power, she called Maia. Surely, her attendant spirit was the one they spoke of as Guardian of the Order. The thought of it being a man appalled her.

"Through the power of the stone Caron has become a powerful necromancer to raise up even the powers of the dead to his purpose," Magda said, firmly. "He conjured up the spectral wind, let loose the riders of the storm, incited rough men to rape the daughters of the Blood Royal. Unrestrained he will return to challenge our power.

"With what powers remain to us we must contrive a pattern to restore this lost hallow of our Order. And as it is Caron who stands in our way, you must destroy this evil necromancer. Shape what pattern you will to this end, and I will empower it with all the influences I can muster."

They begged time to consider the cost in influence the curse she would contrive for she must play her part without distraction in what lay ahead. After a week they assented but urged her to begin at once to prepare for Caer Myrddin. So it was agreed, and to that end she rode forth alone in the rain on the appointed day. She had much to ponder in the matter of restoring the Order, in finding the way forward; and it turned on her mastering the sun-wheel at Green Chapel to prepare for the *Troth* at Caer Myrddin.

An hour's ride through driving rain she came to the cleft in the mountain that led to the sanctum within; the ceremonial gathering place of the Blood Royal. She dismounted and led her horse into the darkness, following the wall along a familiar path, her horse dutifully after. At length they turned the corner into the light: it broke in upon her with the full force of a revelation; emerging within a ring of sheer canyon walls under lofty peaks, encompassing the oval amphitheatre they called Green Chapel. And there she stood alone in the rain lamenting what had become of her.

The vale was a holy place, the center of her world and ceremonial life; indeed, her identity from youth. Sheer mountain walls hedged the hidden valley, its hillsides in flowering shrub and trees, and on the lower slopes stone benches carved in a tiered amphitheatre centering on the green. Four menhirs portioned out the vale of Green Chapel, each quadrant apportioned to one of the four houses of the Blood Royal, each to its quadrant where in times of ceremony they set their pavilions and flew their colours. Southeast of the valley, midway between first and second quadrants, a dolmen arch opened from a mountain cavern onto the green. Out of this sanctum all ceremonial processions emerged; it was for what lay within beyond that arch she came.

It was a raw March day. In the vale she was somewhat sheltered from the wind, though it moaned in the mountain tops driving dark streaming clouds against the sky. She was comfortable enough in her woollen cloak, but her heart was raw with winter still, and she struggled to let go. The day the Cailleach died, that day of the Gathering here in Green Chapel, should have been the day of her triumph but for Caron's refusal to yield the stone of sovereignty. And the Cailleach agreed. In a moment all that was rightly hers turned to dust and ashes. Gone was the sweetness and light, and in its stead come ferocity of purpose. Relentless rain fell from the troubled sky plashing upon her face, covering her tears, and she took comfort in the thought nature wept with her.

Urged on by the powers informing her, Magda was determined to dazzle with her mastery of the great sun-wheel. She would put these petulant servants who proclaimed themselves masters in their place, for without her they were nothing. She stood between the menhirs of the dolmen arch the rain soaked green before her, the dark at her back, and rebuked the Master Blaise: "You do not tell me what I may do old man. I know full well what I must do."

Still, she stood another moment in the rain lamenting how it had come to this and dwelt on the unwanted child and the indignities heaped upon her. It was a female infant, fair hair, elegant in form, blue eyes like the twilight sky - Caron's daughter born at Imbolc - she at once determined the child should never supplant her, and swore those who knew of it to secrecy at peril of their lives. In time she would treat of them as they deserved, and in this matter of the child she had yielded not out of any conviction but that it might easily be undone later. And so she had sent word to a family of minor nobility in Norway; they should obtain and raise the child as their own, never revealing whence she came.

For now there were other more pressing matters. In youth she was tutored and excelled above all the daughters of the Blood Royal in the art of shaping patterns in the forces of the sun-wheel. The Lady Gwen had shown talent as well, and always two were trained together lest some ill fate befall one or the other. And so she was paired with Gwenhwyfar through those years of preparation, until at last the Cailleach named Magda heir apparent.

The sanctum of the Sonnenrad – the sun-wheel of Green Chapel - was one of three known to the Blood Royal. It was said hidden there were yet four more; their mysteries revealed only to those who first mastered the essences of the three. And so she entered with the reverence due the dignity of her office, pausing a moment at the threshold to let the pattern open in her, and stepped into the court of the holy place.

At the threshold was a seven tiered fountain, each basin brimming and overflowing into the next, purling down into a pool that returned into the rock from which it had sprung. Magda loosed her ankle boots, stepped down into the pool to enter bare footed into the sanctuary. She turned to the third font of fresh water to wash her hands, pausing at last to sprinkle a little water from the fourth upon her temple. This she did for ritual cleansing of thought, word, and deed; for the purification of her heart. She had come burdened, and well she knew the influence of what lay within on those who came soiled of the world.

"Peace, be still." She let her firefly thoughts settle, and the tranquility of the sanctuary enter her. Whatever her feelings about the past, she was on the threshold of destiny. She must refresh her understanding and deepen her mastery of the art of shaping, as all who reigned before her. She must master the harmony of these forces that focused in the sun-wheel, for they would magnify and fulfill in form what in her soul was wrought in essence.

The makers of old who wrought the sun-wheel likewise shaped and smoothed the chamber walls, and cut baffled flues in stone to let soft currents of air refresh the sanctum, and set gateways to what lay within. A number of passages led off from the central chamber into darkness. She understood beyond was the demesne of the Masters of Hallows, forbidden to all others, and known only to the Cailleach before her. It was said the vaults and secrets of the Hallows, and as well records of the Order lay deep within; in good time they must acquaint her as they had her forebears with their mysteries.

But facing her now was mystery enough to hold her. The Sonnenrad of old was taken as emblem of the House of Mérovée, and in shape an exquisite work of art. This one comprised three concentric circles; inlaid in blue lapis about a dark obsidian core, like the eye of a daisy on a pavement of creamy yellow marble: a Black-eyed Susan or Sunflower, she'd often thought. And in the dark obsidian fire pit at its core; fed by igneous vapors rising through a vein in rock from some plutonic realm, burned an eternal flame.

It was a splendid artifice but more: the symbol of a zone of power and containment, a creative field engaging those invisible forces that inform all that is made. To the unresponsive one caught up in sensual sleep, it revealed nothing. To the awakening it revealed what lay within and the way one must go. To the ascending ones it was an instrument of creation, the gift of the Makers.

The old masters taught the sun-wheel was fashioned in field and force after the Word of Shekinah - after the light of revelation, the fire of purification, and the glorification of radiant life. And this they taught that whosoever masters the right hand path, and enters in to the presence of the one who dwells in the midst of the flame, his divine identity is revealed. For all this lore the new masters tended to speak of it only as a mnemonic device.

The third and outer circle was the periphery of the sun-wheel; its coronal cloud of glory, the shaper's field of force radiant with life overflowing the boundaries of the arc of creation to inform the yet unformed. Equidistant from the center to the periphery, the second circle was a zone of revelation. And of this they taught that it here the weave of design and control that shape creative endeavor in harmony with the whole comes to focus.

It was in the zone of revelation the greatest difficulty in transiting the cycle of the sun-wheel oft arose. Illumination is learning to let go in the light, and few were willing to let go of self-determination to learn the art of tending and keeping a creative field; to let what is sown of life come to fulfillment without forcing arbitrary outcomes.

As for the first and inner circle of the sun-wheel, this was likened to the fire that burns at the heart of Shekinah, a realm of suspended substance at the core of creation: the flame a blending of the love of the wonderful one and the current of answering response rising like passion from those who entered in. There is a measure appointed to everything in creation, and all that approaches the fire must be purified of fire to dwell therein, for nothing wrought of the passage of the sun-wheel long endures if the seed of destruction is in it.

From its core twelve rays radiate to the periphery of the sun-wheel, each marked by a runic symbol. These were inlaid in a pavement about the wheel, some 48 feet in diameter, in a secret language only the Masters of Hallows know. And it is said of that language it was the cipher of the Word of God in man before the time of the confusion of tongues, and that to speak the name of the rune was to evoke the power of its ray.

Taken together these outward elements of design comprise a path, a revelation in form of the creative field that informs the flesh of humankind with the radiant essences of the Creator. And this they taught, that in harmony with the one law of creation, the law of positive radiation and negative response, learning to walk the right hand path through the stations of the sun-wheel leads into a realization of the divine design and the way of bringing forth heaven on earth in the revelation of the union of the worlds in the Shekinah made flesh.

And so coming here now, her thoughts turned to the day the mystery was first revealed to her. "Why must it always begin with water?" She was young, impetuous and realized not to whom she spoke.

"Because it does," the Master Flegetanis said. "It is the way it is: Except it begin with water, you will perish in the fire."

The memory of all that came back to her now, and still there were men telling her what to do. She whispered resentment and stepped cautiously to the margin of the sun-wheel. "The years have come and gone. I have mastered your arts old man, and so you," she said aloud. Then she looked up and saw the Master Blaise standing silently across the chamber. She did not think he had heard for he did not approach but simply watched her reacquaint herself with the wonder. It all came back to her as she stepped cautiously across the periphery, where despite her objection that every cycle of the sun-wheel begin with water, she must begin.

She knew and must acquiesce to the truth of it: water, air, earth, and fire were the great architects; the four forces that informed the shaping.

Water stilled consciousness, soothed fevered thought and troubled heart; extinguished fiery desire to impose a resolution. Like a cool spring rising on a sweltering day to assuage the thirst; like the falling of the latter rain upon the dusty earth, water eased and opened heart and mind to what might be.

And when one was still in the silence of the waters, the one who dwelled, obscured by the noise of the world, came forth and moving upon the face of the still waters of one's soul initiated an ascending cycle of the sacred four, consummating in the fire of love. And of this act of creation what was shaped in the invisible heaven would in the days of our tomorrows be brought forth in tangible form. At least that was what the masters taught, and by this art she reasoned they were well able to set her curse upon Caron.

She remembered how in the first time she came to the sun-wheel her mentor then was the Master Gisors, tasked with the initial instruction of the daughters of the Blood Royal. They were young girls, on this occasion eight in number, from noble families; but especially the Lady Gwenhwyfar of Wales a niece of the Domina Branwyn, for they were inseparable.

"What is wrought here is a sacred art to tone the soul." Gisors began in his ever sententious manner. His voice had a quaver in it, even in younger years, and he was oft times distracted to the girls' amusement, but that day keen wit prevailed. "All your senses will be heightened." That sounded promising. "What has been only reflective in your soul, within the corona of the sun-wheel comes alive. Radiant touch, taste, smell, sound and sight: all illumined from within will enliven your passions, and you must master these sensations of intense influence in you. Mark me well: these are given not to indulge, but to reveal the hidden life."

They had looked at each other and wondered what that might mean. The first part seemed quite intriguing. As for knowledge of the hidden self that seemed a little too much of an abstraction to appeal to lively animal spirits. Gisors caught the glance. "It will stir things up, my dears, you did not know existed. So, when first you walk the path we four shall guide you that you stray not in your hearts."

They had all begun with a kind of holy dread, wondering what might occur. And in fact all were touched by something, but through a general unwillingness to speak to it, hard to say just what. For Magda her step into the unknown began with a cool, refreshing sensation like a wash of rain and the scent of leaves breaking the heat of day. She had few thoughts in her passage about the circumference, but felt the rain turned to feather light drops of wistfulness, soft melody bearing breezes, and the heady scent of flowering and fertile earth, the prayer of their being.

And as these forces fulfilled themselves in her, there was first a bud of fire in the heart, then a bloom, and gentle surge of passion that touched her with the wonder of existence and longing of the heart so very personal she had no wish to speak of it. That was her first experience of walking the right hand path and she had never forgotten. Now she looked back with something akin to longing; to know it just that way again, when the passage was all friendship and innocence.

"You might walk this path a thousand times," Gisors said, "and ever will it stir up memory in you, tease out intuitions, try your spirits, search your minds and hearts provoking and evoking a thousand sensations you have not dreamed of; always leading you toward realization of your being, and in God's good time resolution of the issues you bring into your meditation.

"For now this is all we ask of you. And yet one day for some of you, the way that opens before you will be in another dimension of experience, and if you are able to rise to it, you will be invited to come closer to learn of us, for from that day forward what you bring forth in the cycle of your days and seasons of your life will light your way, or scorned destroy you."

The lesson that day was Gisors' but unannounced the Masters Blaise and Flegetanis appeared on the threshold, and with them the Lady Branwyn of Wales, Domina of the Blood Royal. And as they entered in, the sanctuary filled with profound peace and much excitement for the Master Flegetanis was said to be the master of masters, much revered but seldom seen. Gisors at once deferred to him but it was Blaise, Master of Sword Hallows, who stepped forward in his stead. And with him came utter silence, for it was well known you would have nothing of Blaise until you entered into his peace. He took up where Gisors left off; his tone free of stricture, filled with the virtue of an understanding heart.

"Shall I initiate you in a cycle of the sun-wheel," Blaise asked. Of course there was no question. "Everything depends on the clarity of your response to what unfolds in the light that illumines the initiation of the cycle," he continued. "The more intense your engagement, the more substantial the force loosed in you; the greater your influence for creation or destruction in the cycles you set in motion.

"Think of this threshold force of water as the water of truth, the very same waters as those upon which the Spirit of God moves in every beginning; waters stilled to respond to His influence, and to bring forth whatsoever He will in you. We speak of this first of forces as water because the vibrational force itself is in some wise reflected in the material properties of water in its varied manifestations. So is it with the other forces, but let us begin with water.

"In the beginning let the cool waters refresh and still your troubled hearts and minds, as you open to a beginning realization of your own divine identity. Where there was darkness there will be light to guide you in a careful and thoughtful fashion on the right hand path.

"Be vigilant over what rises from the depths of your heart into awareness. Try the spirits and let your response be to the one who dwells in the light, desiring only what comes through you be a blessing to all who will receive it."

As Blaise led the daughters through their initial passage of the sun-wheel, Flegetanis and the Domina Branwyn looked on. She stood beside him with the reverence of a loving sister, wife or daughter – Magda could not say – but reverence it was and from one who crowned the Order. And, indeed, Flegetanis did inspire reverence, for a high seriousness gathered like a cloak about him, making words seem trivial to the unspoken experience of just being near him. They were in awe for all had heard he attained beyond all the Masters; that he had opened up levels of the sun-wheel of which they were unaware, and it was in him chiefly the Domina of the Blood Royal rested and took counsel.

"It is not a children's game," Blaise said at last. "You are learning the elementals of the science of Mazzaroth; the principles of creation in the realms of light that inform this world. We are dealing with invisible forces in the place of shaping before ever they are in the earth. We are learning we have sensibilities capable of attuning with them, and as we mature our perception of these will become more acute." And when he was done he turned to Flegetanis that if he were willing he might have a word.

"If you remember nothing else, remember this." It seemed to Magda Flegetanis looked straight at her; she was flattered he would pay her such attention, for then she did not see herself as Domina of the Blood Royal, but rather imagined that honour would fall to Gwenhwyfar.

"Do not contrive to walk the left hand path about the sun-wheel," Flegetanis said, sternly. Do not contrive to enter into the cycle of the sacred four by fire.

"Some there are who seek to walk the left hand path in search of ecstasy, pleasures of the flesh, aspiring to power, wealth, destruction, whatever seems good to them to possess: some even for the heart's longing to see God. But the last it all comes to corruption and self-destruction, for as was said long ago: *Except the Lord builds the House they labor in vain who build it.*

"Only they who harmonize their lives with the cycles of the sacred four, who drink deep of the waters of truth, shall enter in and know the fire of love as it was meant to be, after God's own heart.

"They who seek to enter in any other way are thieves and robbers, and with the very intensity they would grasp to possess the fire, so will the passage of their lives come to ruin."

One moment he was there his presence filling the chamber; the next he was gone, leaving longing and holy fear upon the air, as if his words were written in the substance of the sanctum. And so it went, but Magda fascinated and eager to cultivate the art, unable to get past the thought that the left hand path was so sternly forbidden, must speak up. "Why should ills befall one who has chosen to walk the left hand path? What will become of the one who does?"

Blaise had shifted uneasily for Magda was already spoken of as possible heir apparent to the Cailleach, and must not be humiliated in the presence of her sisters. And so he answered with punctilious precision.

"Who walks the left hand path puts feeling before truth. He falls into manipulating one and all to gain the object of his passions, and will sacrifice the lives of others to attain what he deems fulfillment.

"The left hand path is the way of the impure heart. And all the while justifying what is done as righteous, leads on to annihilation of the soul."

The Lady Gwenhwyfar chimed in to support her friend. "But to lead from passion is the way of the world."

"It is the way of the blind leaders of the blind who rule by exploiting the fallen, generation after generation bring the world to destruction.

"These beguile the ignorant; they mine their grievances in life, enflame their hurt hearts with visions of power, exploit their weakness and promise the fulfillment of their heart's desires in return for their allegiance. And at the last it all comes to dust and ashes."

"I am passionate. My feelings matter to me," Magda urged, pleased that all the women agreed in her, for well she knew above all they cherished their feelings.

"Let those passions be centered in truth," Blaise answered mildly. "So doing, beyond that sad simulacrum of love that bedevils the human heart, you will come to know the truth of love."

"How can you deny our passions?"

She hadn't heard and it was of some concern to him for she had the response of the others. "Wisdom is the principle thing, Magda," he said, "and on the right hand path the way that leads to the truth of love, likewise reveals the fitness of things.

"We do not deny passion or any other gift of the soul, but let that passion be the fire of God's love that fills your heart. And the way that unfolds to that end is the right hand path, and begins with the waters in the responsiveness of your heart and mind, and your passion for the truth.

"Let your heart be a hearth that burns bright to warm a home; not fire rampant that destroys house and home and all who would dwell therein.

"As for all of you," he said, addressing the young women, "for one raised in the House of the Blood Royal, knowing the intensification of power that comes of walking the right hand path, let her beware. If ever she shall revert to the way of the left hand path, it will be to her destruction."

"And yet the path exists? It must have a use."

"If so," Blaise said cautiously, "it is known only to a master of the path and forces of creation; to an end you never need concern yourself."

"Why, because I am a woman?" she persisted.

"Simply, because it is not given you," he answered.

"And is there, then, such a master to whom it is given?" She calculated she still had the women's response.

"I think only Flegetanis capable of this and you have heard his warning. For my part I must keep the straight and narrow way that leads to life everlasting. And so must you."

Thereafter Magda desired nothing but to attain as Flegetanis, for of all the masters he alone was fully accomplished, and she knew if anyone understood the left hand path it was he. And so again and again she had come to Green Chapel to walk the pattern of the sun-wheel, working with herself, until she felt each time she entered the pattern the influence of the powers that informed it grow in her.

And each time she came alone with none to see, she took tentative steps to test the influence of the left hand path in the substance of her soul. And each time, when she could no longer bear the conflagration of emotions that rose in her, she must return to the cooling waters; the way the sages said led in season to understanding and fulfillment in the truth of love.

Then one day she was summoned into the chambers of the Domina Branwyn, and there sat across from her before her fire was Flegetanis, Master of Grail Hallows. Branwyn rose, bade Magda sit across from the sage and without a word left the room leaving them alone together. For the longest time he said nothing but she felt his presence searching her, warm like the fire on the hearth, until she settled into his comfort. "This is the first time we've spoken, person to person," he said at last.

"I have looked to this moment," she replied, confidently.

"Have you, indeed," he replied, gently. "Magda, as Master of the Grail Hallows, there is a question I must ask of each daughter of the Blood Royal, if she is to comprehend her influence and come into her power."

She felt passion rise like a melody in her, as if every word he spoke plucked some tuned string of her soul and set her vibrating.

"How old are you?" he asked, gently.

"Seventeen," she replied released, and as the voice stream flowed again she gushed: "what is the question?"

"Each must answer to whom the Grail serves." As he said it he rose and stood looking into the fire; tall, somewhat gaunt she thought, an older man but youthful and limber yet and not unattractive to her. Then Flegetanis turned to her, the fire at his back. "Blessed are the poor… in the spirit of this world," he said, "for theirs is the kingdom of heaven. And so begins the cycle of ascension.

"There must be space in each one of us for the things of God. When we are filled with the things of the world there is no room for the wonderful one. Blessed are the meek, blessed are the merciful, blessed are the pure in heart... this is the path to divine and the realization of spiritual powers in the way of the Masters."

She would answer him but her breast tightened, her breath faltered and she was at a loss to say. And he said no more, but another long silence between them. And as she thought the interview was over, she rose, too. That was the impulse, but not how it fulfilled itself in her.

A moment later, unbidden, she found herself in his arms, a motion so swift and uncontrived she could account for none of it other than she was at once enveloped in a cool peace such as the sages say passeth all understanding. All the fevered emotions of her impetuous youth were gone. She felt no grand passion, only the bliss of being completely still resting her head on his heart. She was utterly content, but it was not to end there. Her peace turned to yearning, like that evening hour in a garden when a certain slant of light and fragrance on the air touches the soul with ineffable longing. And with that she felt herself enveloped in an aura like the lustre that gathers to the unfolding rose, and like the heady scent of roses dissolve like dew in light and air.

"Blessed are the pure in heart," he said, "for they shall see God."

She let go, lifted up on a brimming current of life that rose within her until her heart overflowed, her senses kindled, and passion transfigured her flesh. She gave way to sweet essences permeating her flesh, until her body like a hard and brittle seed gave way to the very life that would kindle her into being. Then she was beside herself, in some flesh, tender like the petals of rose to which her old body if youthful still seemed but a husk. It was ecstasy, but for all that he took no advantage of her, but what followed was ineffable.

She was enfolded in the embrace of a presence, as if she dwelled in some sacred sanctuary, under the overarching wings of a great, solemn power, where ecstasy was the very garment of her life. And still she felt the quiet presence of the master who held her in his arms; there was passion but not the raging of a fire, for he burned silently like a cool, blue flame wherein sanctuary from the conflagration of the world. She was awake in the light, at peace with creation.

"It is the ascending way," he said, gently releasing her embrace. "Hunger and thirst after righteousness and you shall be filled. I have shown you this so when the question is put to you of the others, you will know how to answer. Walk the right hand path, Magda. In it is the glorious freedom of the sons and daughters of God."

But she was impetuous. From that day she'd had many lovers, always striving for a moment of rapture, but never again the ecstasy of the master's embrace. And in some way she resented him for it. For all that he showed her in a moment, it had come to this. Here she stood diminished in substance and influence as she sought to overcome the maelstrom of feeing that overwhelmed her; again limited to the threshold experience common to all, and confined to bland meditations on the state of her consciousness.

The starting point on the path back was before her. She took a great step from the periphery of the sun-wheel toward the sun at the core, its first ray immediately at her feet, and there she stood silently for full five minutes, trying to let all that troubled her heart and bedeviled her mind settle; unable to move forward. Through the solid rock of the mountain she felt the weather without muddying the earth, staining the rock; wind beating at the skeletal trees, feeling at once the weather without and within. "I am wind and rain and rock," she whispered, feeling forces at work within her, "restless like the squalls through which I rode, I am come here to remember and take little pleasure in it."

And still she was unable to find in herself what stood in her way. It was unbelievable the right hand path should be closed to her. The forces that would buoy her up resisted what she would impose upon the pattern. She fought with life over changes that should be wrought in her. She knew it well enough. "To walk the right hand path," she said, "I must keep the straight and narrow way."

Suddenly remembering she was not alone, she turned again to Blaise who watched silently across the arc of the sun-wheel. Still, she would not back down but paused a petulant moment. "It is well I have woven a pattern that purposes his death," she said intent on Blaise. The thought of it overwhelmed her with feeling. "No matter," she said, "I know what I must do, even if you will not join with me in this."

"You have suffered setback," Blaise said, encouraging. "You can and must master the cycle again to depths you once knew. But today you will proceed no further; not with a mind in turmoil and resentful heart. Let the waters cool your passions, still your mind."

She let go the effort and stepped out of the circle, and Blaise nodded assent. "It has been some time since I walked the pattern; I must refresh my soul in this matter."

"Return each day until this is resolved and prepared for the rite of passage at Caer Myrddin."

"What kind of rite?" She was feeling defeated.

"What factors you may face I do not know. But the trial is always the same: to set to rights a pattern distorted by time and human machinations. So doing, you initiate the cycle of your tenure as Domina of the Blood Royal, and serve the mandate of the Order to restore the cycles of creation to the divine design."

"Then you shall guide me in this. Tomorrow," she said. She cared little for Blaise, but he was the most accomplished of the masters remaining to her; Flegetanis aloof and dwelling in Egypt. With Blaise's help, she would return here again and again, until there was no doubt of her mastery of the sun-wheel.

She left the sanctuary into the grey light of a storming evening; stood alone in the rain until soaked through, thoroughly humiliated by what had come upon her. She must submit to a rite of passage and trial of her arts, making herself accountable to the judgment of those who should serve her; accountable to the one they called the Guardian; one she feared she knew not.

4

Backwash

Siduri was inconsolable, her eyes black with wrath. She struck out, smote Caron hard upon the cheek and with fists clenched pushed him away from her. "You let him die," she raged, her chest crushed and fighting for breath, overcome with cold fury. "You let him die."

How could he tell her what had become of her father in the chamber of the empty tomb? She was too distraught to listen let alone understand, and Shirazi utterly bewildered. For his own part Caron was drained and unable to resist her emotional onslaught. He was disoriented. Eons of time in a moment rendered nothing, by a timeless event he could not begin to grasp with his mind. A window in heaven opened, and beyond the frayed and fragile coverings of form he gazed a moment into the heart of light. Returned to a world of troubled hearts and minds striving with eternity, he was caught up in a swirl of motion and sense awash in Siduri's emotions. How could he explain? And yet he must try.

"He is not dead," Caron assured her.

"Then where is he?"

Caron looked helplessly to Shirazi who stared blankly back at him.

"Gone," Caron said, "Flegetanis is gone. Did he not explain these things to you? What did you think the nature of our journey; of my journey of all these years to return the sun stone?"

She was at once all ice and fire. "As you did him," she whispered, "thee, I give to death."

"He walked into the light and the light took him. It is the way of the shining ones."

"The very light that restored your youth took his life. In that you failed him. You were transformed; he is no more."

"It was not that way this time." Truly it was said, hell hath no fury like a woman's rage.

"The stone is cursed." She pushed at him as a man might provoke another, seeking a fight. He backed away; she came at him again. He caught her wrist and held it firmly in his grasp.

"Give the cursed stone to me," she hissed. I will drown it in the waters of the Nile."

"Your father lives. For such an one there is no death."

She turned away fiercely; inconsolable, she retreated to her rooms. She did not return or cease from weeping until day had turned again into day, and when she finally came forth into the company of the villa she found Shirazi sat alone in her father's courtyard near the fountain, with a plate of oranges and dates, and a cup of dark coffee steaming in the morning air.

"Are we alone?"

"If you mean, is Hugues about…" Shirazi said, pouring a careful coffee for her: "no he is not."

"I care not where he is."

"He has gone into the desert, alone."

"He has much on his conscience."

"I have no reason to believe he will return."

Siduri's hand trembled and she spilled her coffee on the marble table. It pooled and ran into her lap. She stood angrily and brushed the dark stain off her morning robes. "It is still that cursed stone. It took my father's soul; it still possesses his."

"When his need was as great as your own," Shirazi said carefully, "you gave him nothing of yourself but rancor."

Siduri's eyes narrowed, and even in the morning light Shirazi watched as darkness gathered about her. "By the goddess Nephthys, I will bring an end to this."

Shirazi looked at her curious where that had come from. He beckoned her to sit and refilled her cup. "If you want my advice," he said kindly, "before you begin, look first to your own heart."

She said nothing but drank her coffee looking silently into the dark brew and heard not another word.

In the day the veil between the heavens and the earth shall dissolve at last; on that day the band of dark cloud that cloaks the three highest peaks of Whiter Morn will dissipate, and the temple of the sun shall be clearly seen. And until that day, the veil that obscures the summit reflects back upon the world the darkness of the human heart; though the view from the mountaintop is clear as daylight, and nothing hidden from the wonderful one.

So it was written, and the Elders understood. Each who now dwelled in Whiter Morn had served in the world for the day when the realms would again be one as they were in the First Time. And among these there were those, too, who had walked the path within the mountain, ascended to the highest peak of the worlds of the Archaeus, and communed with the *Aton-Re*, Lord of the crossing.

He it was who kept the way of the realms of light at the summit of the created worlds, and upheld the works of the watchers of Whiter Morn. These knew what man had lost, understood how it was the radiance of the wonderful one was restrained lest no flesh survive; and must be so, until man turns away from destruction to bear again the light of creation.

But this morning's light troubled even these, for in the rising sun were heard voices whispering in the heights, rumbling in the mountain valleys, and in a dark swaddling band of cloud that obscured the peaks of Whiter Morn, lightnings and thunderings. Underfoot, quakes shook the firmament of the Archaeus itself, and with the dark of another night came the thunder snow: a storm of wind, hail, and forked lightning, descending from the heights; giving way to a wet heavy fall like snowy ash that cloaked the summer land.

"Portents," they whispered, for all begins and ends in Whiter Morn, and future events cast their shadows before. And, if so on Whiter Morn where all is essence and that essence moved to this, what shall it mean for the realm of earth? And so they gathered in council to review and if need be amend those patterns they shaped, to understand how it came to this. Still it remained unclear what was not done they ought to have done; what they had not they ought to have done, as the word goes.

Other than Lord of the crossing there was but one in Whiter Morn who understood the pattern as a whole, and Innkeeper had precious little to say; always more inclined to ask questions than answer them. He rarely took part in the gatherings of the Elders, though he would from time to time discreetly appear to measure their considerations. Even so, he alone moved freely throughout the realms of the Archaeus, and to him the principals of Whiter Morn came when they sought counsel. Otherwise, they continued about the business of tending and keeping the pattern given into their care; keeping the holy norm shaped in the ordinances of heaven, until the process of events brought them into his presence.

This was such a juncture and so a delegation of Elders came to speak with Innkeeper, for it was understood he kept the way of the crossing between the Archaeus and realms of earth, even as the Aton-Re the way of the crossing between the realms of light and Whiter Morn. Innkeeper was known to say very little, and so it was when the delegation came he reminded them simply how it is when the way is obscured. "The truth is true and all is well," he said: "unconquerable life prevails." There followed a long silence as he waited until they settled in him.

"I have seen it," he said at last, almost casually. "Something new is in the light. Changes in the Heavens can abide no more the fallen state. An end shall be made."

"What is to be done?"

"Keep steadfast watch over patterns in your care. Mark me: force nothing," he counseled: "Commune in the light, keep the balance of forces in their season; let all things unfold to perfection.

"And man shall answer the question put to him: Wilt thou be made whole? In the way of shaping, sowing and reaping in the substance of the earth - in the measure of every thought, word, and deed - the world will respond, embrace, and rise up in the light - or in reaction perish, by reason of this one unalterable law of radiation and response."

"Will you speak for us to the Lord of the crossing?"

"I will, if he bids me come to him."

And so they went home to their own dominions pondering what this meant for Whiter Morn and all the realms of the Archaeus. And when they were gone Innkeeper returned to the silent study of his chessboard and the state of the match.

For her part, Maia felt sure she knew what the portents meant; it was all about her. She'd given herself to Morgon Kara and yielded influence to fashion change in the earth. So doing she'd challenged Innkeeper in his game of chess with the world and lost. She was a queen and proved herself a pawn; her gamble lost, her king taken, the game done. She'd failed and was diminished to animus she could not overcome, and had no place in Whiter Morn. And still her heart ached for a world caught in a dark age with no way forward.

Morgon Kara's failure to master Caron cost him his life. Innkeeper would not admit it but she knew he watched over the man who thwarted her intentions, and she despised him for it. Full of ire she felt her substance drawn into the dark mass of cloud that hid the summit of Whiter Morn, and knew there were consequences for empowering the shaman and challenging Innkeeper. She should go to him and set this to rights but her pride would not allow. Instead, she withdrew to Eleleth of the Archaeus and dwelled isolate in her own realm. Her sisters, whose influences inform the earth, came to entreat her to resolve the dissonance, but she turned them away.

At length an invitation came. She was to grace Innkeeper with her presence and no doubt trade question for question, if that was his humor. Should she go as she had before; to come late and sit with him by his fire to discuss what transpired between them? For a moment it seemed much to be desired, but then her heart rebelled. And why should she go? She was no less than any other in these realms. Each was a focus of force, power and principle in his or her own dominion; each was born of the realms of light; each a differentiation of the spectrum of light which illumined, sustained and informed the whole within the body of the sun, its many realms and attendant spheres of influence.

Was it possible to say who was the greatest in Whiter Morn? Each kept and tended his garden with discreet care. The Watchers, Guardians and Shapers were each given in their own way to sustain the realms of earth, guide it back from the abyss, and restore the realms of form to the realms of light, they lived to serve. And as was oft said, the greatest among them was the servant of all.

Truth was in Whiter Morn you became aware of what was unfolding under another's hand only when the currents of creation drew you into attunement with that pattern to let some wonder form. It was impossible to say in such a complex weave of factors that touched on all the forces that sustained the earth what was less important, or could be left out without dire consequences. And yet there were distinctions to be made, even if Maia was unable to articulate them; it irked her that it was so for now she knew these same distinctions isolated her. She was determined to refuse being summoned by one who had thwarted her designs over a silly game of chess he believed he played in the forces of the world.

The more she resisted the more she felt her powers wane, her radiance fade, until at length she began to feel like one who has fasted too long, it was finished with her. Even in Whiter Morn there are times and seasons, and she began to feel resigned to relinquishing her part; to be done with her commission and cross over as others had done before her into what - the clear light of the void? For, unlike others who had walked into the light, Maia doubted there was anything in the light but uncreated darkness and come to this she welcomed oblivion.

Refusing Innkeeper's invitation, Maia sank deeper into loneliness; her realm more isolated it reflected in all about her. When she walked in her garden in early morn forlorn, nothing rose to meet her. No bird sang; no fragrance of distant shores, fields or mountain groves on the wind; the flowers gave no scent but plain as paper, they shied closed and turned away from her as she walked among them. The virtue had gone out of her and with her failing influence and in some wise everything she touched. Her ever flowering land had begun to reflect her dissipation, and with it a long, slow brooding storm gathered over the world.

But how was it her fault? All she could think was how, through the meddling of others, Morgon Kara perished. And yet within her discouragement came thoughts of how this might yet turn advantage, for not overnight it had all come to this and she was not alone responsible.

Maia knew the old stories. She sat by her garden fountain in the pale morning light pondering what it all might mean to her now. A small bird, a little flash of light, spritely down and whorl of colour, lit on the fountain edge, flit onto her outstretched hand and tilted head to eye, questioning. It took heed of her, and she teared at its moment of caring before it was carried off in a stream of melody on scented air and gone. Much was lost but something remained.

Maia folded her hands in her lap trying to remember how it was in the time before the great transgression; how it must be again when the world is shaped anew, and grew impatient with thought that would not flow freely. There were recollections, of course; something in her yet remembered how in the day the foundations of the earth were laid, the morning stars sang together and all the sons and daughters of God shouted for joy. And still her memories were incomplete; not altogether her own these were, but written in the vibratory record and substance of the Archaeus.

Others who had been here from the beginning, the few who must abide until all is resolved, had more complete memories of what had been and sometimes they spoke together of it. Mostly, all in the realms of the Archaeus went about their business with firmness of purpose toward the day of resolution; knowing that in that day the veil between the worlds shall dissolve, and the veil of clouds that cloak the summit of Whiter Morn will dissipate in the intensified radiance of the realms of light. Then shall come the revelation of the seven dimensional world; knowledge held in trust in the Lord of the crossing, who dwells in the temple of the sun on the highest peak of Whiter Morn.

What Maia remembered were records from the time of the great transgression, some 20,000 years past as men reckon time. Thereafter, for eight thousand years the world was held in precarious balance by those who yet dwelled in the earth to keep the way of the First Time. It is recorded in the Archaeus there came a time - with a measure of creative power still within their grasp - despite dire warnings the fallen ones incarcerated themselves the flesh of the world, and cohabiting with their creations shaped abominations in the earth. At length the divine design in the realms of earth could be sustained no more. It was then under the hand of the Lord of the crossing the Shapers, the Watchers and the Guardians made a hedge in the earth to separate fallen man from those who dwelled in the light, and shaped these realms of the Archaeus and of Whiter Morn.

And these are they who dwelled now in Whiter Morn, entering betimes into the earth, for the restoration of the world to the divine design. And to each the Aton-Re, Lord of the crossing, has given a portion, a realm within the Archaeus to watch over and guide toward the hour when the heavens and the earth shall again be one restored to the patterns of the First Time. This she knew for it was writ in the Archaeus and in the memories of those who from age to age serve in the way of the lords of light.

There followed a time of the catastrophic destruction in upheaval and fire that destroyed the motherland of man, and lay waste the earth. Those who harkened to warnings of what was to come fled to other lands and colonies were made. The chief among these were the islands of the Atlantides of the Seven Sisters. And these prospered in the affluence of their sweet influences, until a time when it fell subject to illusion that to dominate the whole world was to restore the earth to the world of the First Time, and a paradise lost.

Was it her fault men perverted the way? It was sorrow to see the gifts of life squandered in the earth; to see her influence shape visions in the minds of men warped into illusions; the good she sought turned wickedness. But how was that her fault? She pondered now that failure, and thought on those who had gone before. She was one of seven sisters given to fulfill her mandate in creation. It was said once there were nine, though some said twelve and more before her time; gone and seen no more in Whiter Morn. Who could understand it? No, it was not her fault, but she was judged, and all her works were now in peril.

Maia sat in her fading garden pondering what she must do. It troubled her, what had become of Morgon Kara; that she had lost her challenge to Innkeeper. She would not shame herself by answering his summons. She felt no humility in it, only humiliation. She determined instead after rest to visit her Sister Irkala; she who came no more to Whiter Morn but dwelled in the Shades of the Archaeus, to keep the seal on the powers of the fallen Watchers.

"You dwelled in Abydos, a villa near the House of a Million Years." It was what Flegetanis had said, probing his memory, when Siduri found him half-conscious on the Nile bank and brought him home: old Jakob no longer but again the youth, Caron.

His mind worked back against the undercurrent urging him forward.

He was once servant to Flegetanis, an old man arguing with him over a hoary manuscript. "These are instructions for the living." He read over Flegetanis' shoulder in the dusky light of the subterranean scriptorium, translating as he was taught to do: "'*Who reborn come forth from death, white with fire...*' these people did not die," he insisted, "but ever reborn in the flesh."

"Everyone dies, Jakob."

"Not everyone; not you," Caron whispered, "not now." To utter desolation he had never been closer; the pit of his stomach a yawning void that not food or drink or companionship could fill.

And so he journeyed to Abydos. He had no incentive of his own to sail, so he took passage on a merchant vessel. He paid handsomely to be apart from the crew that worked by measure upstream to Abydos, where once the soul of Egypt, Osiris in Ra, dwelled in the House of a Million Years.

The sailors paid little heed to the man seated with the baggage; they were busy handling winds and the currents to advantage. They heard him talking to himself but he had paid good money and that was enough for them. Mad he may be, but what he said to himself was Allah's business.

"Not everyone dies," Caron whispered: "not the master Flegetanis, not now; not when I survived; not when so much is at stake. To be left alone - it is not enough - it is not the way."

Caron let his gaze drift out over the river, the banks moving slowly by, flocks of white birds rising from the sedge, voices from a distant shore. This time his flight was neither swift nor sure, but the falcon-winged felucca slowly made its way against the current of the river to Abydos driven of the notion planted by Flegetanis that he must first return to the place he once dwelled.

"Betake yourself to the Waterway, fare upstream, travel about Abydos in this spirit-form of yours which the gods command to belong to you... and may a stairway to the Heavens be set up for you to the place where Osiris Is."

"Osiris is Orion," Flegetanis explained, as they poured over the manuscript. "In the heavens is written the divine design of man. The creation of the earth springs from the union of Orion's rays and the sweet influence of the Pleiades. And on these lines of force written in the flesh of man is the resurrection of the earth."

"Then it is forever beyond us," Caron protested, "for who can bind the influences of the stars of the heavens?"

"No, not beyond us, and everything without is likewise within us, or we should never know it. When we awaken to the wonderful one within, we may begin to understand the fields and forces that inform this flesh temple of the living God; we may begin to master what is given us to master."

And in the King's Chamber, it was again as in the night of his renewing; the night he entered the pyramid and come forth a shining presence, white with fire, reborn. So much forgotten he now remembered. But Flegetanis gone, he must pick up the burden the sage carried in life for the regeneration of the world.

"I have walked the path of the shining ones, whether on water or on land and these are the paths of Orion; they are in the limit of the sky."

"Who dwells in the First Time is a shining one, a timeless traveler in the earth - a traveler in time," Caron whispered, "and in the wisdom of Thoth may go down to any sky he wishes to go down to. Now it must be done for an age to come and a world yet to be born."

Caron came to his old villa at dusk and found it occupied. Time passed him by like a riffle in the stream, hardly noticed, but for others a lifetime had come and gone; and what he'd come for was no longer his. Subdued in twilight at first sight the villa appeared dignified as he remembered it; then raucous laughter from the walled court and the curses of a thwarted will drifted on the cool, evening air. Weary, he had no intention of making an issue of it and sought out an inn.

"It once was the dwelling of a merchant prince," his innkeeper reminisced, "pleasant old man as I remember him, generous to a fault." He eyed Caron carefully. Here was a man of real power and authority he bore lightly; solemn he was, one might say even a little sad. But such men can be generous, and hospitality was his business, so he indulged his questions.

"Kept merchant fleets in el-Suwes and Alexandria; traded in deep waters, I am told, as far off as the western isles and east to Hindustan. He has come here not for the past ten years. Last year the district elders judged him dead, his property confiscated and sold to a local merchant who dwells there now in promiscuous excess. Not a pleasant man; no, he isn't this new one. Equal of him he replaced, he thinks, for possessing his property. But you asked after another. Did you know old Jakob?"

Caron dismissed the conversation. "Not for many years," he said, "but had he still dwelled here I should have stayed with him." It was an effort to speak further, but it must be said. "I'll journey to Arabet Abydos and beyond when I'm rested. Will you sell me a camel and provisions for a sojourn in the desert?"

"I will arrange it. Is it a haj; something you seek?"

"I am seeking my soul."

"Are you expecting to find it in the desert?"

"Jesus did."

"Ah, you are a Christian. No matter, here you are among friends, all children of Abraham. But I shall never understand why anyone would seek solace in desert places, when he can dwell comfortably by the river."

"I am already in the desert. I am seeking the everlasting wellspring of a life."

The innkeeper shook his head as Caron went wearily to rest. The man was drained of life, everything robust gone out of him, and he pitied him for it. "Was there such thing as an everlasting spring in the desert, I am sure I would have heard of it. Poor fellow," he whispered after. "What drives these men to seek truth in the desert? Life thrives where there is water." Even so he went straight way to the merchant's villa to bargain over a camel and provisions for his eccentric guest. There was profit in it; who was he to argue with that?

Caron took camel and provisions the innkeeper made, and picked his way from the riverside village the few miles west into the desert to the ruined temple complex at Abydos.

"Betake yourself to the Waterway," the over-voice commanded…*"fare upstream, travel about Abydos in this spirit-form of yours which the gods command to belong to you… and may a stairway to the Heavens be set up for you to the place where Osiris Is."*

And so he came as he was bidden. Something once had happened here and he then party to it; now but a dry husk and ruin of what had been. What could compare to witnessing Flegetanis' ascension; to his experience of flight in the journey of sounding fire, where the hours are suns: compare with coming face to face in the single undying moment that is life, with the Lord of Resurrection?

Anything he might do, anywhere he might go in the wasteland of the world, was desolation to what he had known. He was wretched, poor, blind, and naked before the wonder of the one who dwelled in the light, before whom all the world was dust and ashes. Here among the ruins of Abydos there was nothing but the feeling of loss and desolation to the corrosion of time. And perhaps that was the point in coming. He faced an abyss of nothingness, drank deep of his soul's weariness, but knew he must return to a world he no longer wished to dwell in. And in this wise with none to disturb his reflections, Caron spent his day wandering the melancholy ruins; passing like the shadow of the sun over the leavings of time.

At sunset Caron wandered beyond the funeral temple of Seti to the ruin of the Osirium; what remained above the shifting sands. Long before the temple of Seti, when the land was fertile and Nile bank closer, other temples were raised, but none like the ancient Osirium. Built with cyclopean blocks it was a work more suited to a race of giants than of men. And as he came to it, so came the memories; he'd had his part in this, and forever it was written within him. In a time that followed the great transgression, the Na-Akhu-El Sages opened here a gateway of the worlds; not for the dead as men believed, but for the living: a threshold of life for those who sought the way of resurrection in life. Here among these ruined stones the way of the crossing of the worlds was brought to remembrance.

Other gateways there were, thresholds shaped by the sages of the Na-Akhu-El in places where the veil is thin and the realms without and within touch intimately. To these places, where the sweet influences gather to a focus of light, they journeyed and raised altars to mark the crossing of the worlds. And there walking into the light one might awaken in his true flesh, loosing the regenerative powers of the otherworld in this.

Now in the setting sun the giant stones were no more than long shadows on the sands; for neither here among these old stones, nor on any other threshold of the worlds set for an altar in the earth was it ever just the place itself. Always the power to awaken the substance of the crossing was sustained by the masters who abide to keep the pattern true, and alive in the one who sought the way, or it would not be found.

The realization of it gathered in him as waters mingle and come together. He drank deep of it, until for the first time since he had begun his journey up the river toward its source, he felt himself returning. The world he'd known was passed away, but purpose never. "The fashion of the times puts on a face but nothing has changed," he whispered to the ancient stones. "And so will it be until the day of restoration to the divine design." And then as though pierced of cold steel he thought: "or man by his own hand shall cease to exist."

The beast moaned in the distance calling after him, breaking his reverie. As much as a camel will his obstreperous mount missed him as darkness fell. It didn't care to be hobbled and left alone, but it could wait a little while. Nevertheless, he started back and against the night kindled a small fire and made camp before the temple of Seti, watered the beast and ate a meager meal.

With nightfall sparks spiraling upward into the starry sky, came firefly thoughts. With Flegetanis passing the world he had known had passed, and a vast unknown opened before him. But an empty house is soon possessed, and with the unformed came the hungry ghosts. They tugged at him, seeking response, longing to attach. In the shadowed void he felt the disembodied forms of ancient ills insinuate. Flitting about in the darkness, stirring among the cold stones of the temple, rising from the dark ruins of the past, they drew to the scent of life blood, looking for a host to give them body anew, as if they had some right yet among men to exist.

And with them came the dark wind, gliding forth from the labyrinth of the dead, intent to subvert the way of the sun in his night journey toward the light, and draw the world down again into chaos and old night. Caron felt it all about him, circling, closing in upon, held off by his small fire the whisperings of the serpent of chaos that he yield himself to its possession.

And then it took form. Amidst the pillars of the temple of Seti six figures advanced out of the darkness and stood shadows in the moonlight. Each in pale, reflected light was framed within the faint aura in the shape of what appeared to once have been the upward sweep of radiant, angelic wings - but no more. Instead, the six dark cloaked figures stood barely able to move, trembling on the brink of existence. He watched and waited wondering if these were apparition of the sense or real. For long anxious minutes he stared at them gazing out over the desert wasteland, as if pondering what had become of the world. Held by invisible restraints they could not leave the precincts of the temple to come to him, and so in ragged unison they beckoned Caron to come to them.

And so he came until he stood at the stair to the inner court of the temple and held his ground, for seeing him come they edged back across a margin as if to cause him to enter deeper into the funerary temple, to come closer to them. It was close enough. He could see their drawn faces, each edged with sorrow and defiance. And it was at once plain to him they could not see him clearly and struggled to comprehend what he was that they could not command him.

"How have you overcome him?"

"Overcome whom?" He was answered by silence. At last the response came, again a single, stony voice.

"He whose force once great in the earth now dwells among us in the Shades." The voice was dull, like a deadened echo of stone upon stone.

"Morgon Kara?"

"Who are you to possess the *Uru An-Na*, light of heaven?"

"How is it you do not know?" Again, the long pause, as they sought something in him to attach.

"Why have you cast us out to banish us here when we sought only to serve the greater good?" This time there was sorrow in the voice.

"You must ask that of one greater than I."

"Free us and we who empowered Morgon Kara shall empower you all the more."

"I have no need of you."

"In the way of all kings who seek sovereignty in the earth you will need us. You will need to draw upon our strength to master the ungovernable beast."

In a moment, like a shadow over the moon, their pale light was gone and the temple filled again with darkness. Caron turned away and looked to the river of stars crossing the heavens. The great celestial Nile flowed on toward the dawn when in an epiphany of light risen in Ra, Osiris would vanquish the shadows of the world and shine again triumphant, in the dawn of another day of creation.

He felt it and understood what sought to possess the empty places in him. How had the master of masters, the wonderful one, said it? *"When an unclean spirit comes out of a man, it roams through waterless places looking for rest but finds none....*" He would not again be the dwelling for unclean and restless spirits. Flegetanis had taken him to the mountain top, led into a vision of the First Time and the cleansing of the world. How should he now invite seven devils worse than the first to fill the void of being shriven of that ancient evil? Rather he would ever let a new heaven bring forth a new earth, sunrise upon sunrise, until the natural creative darkness of enfolding night was cleansed of all that hid in the shadows fearing the light.

Only now did he begin to understand his years with Flegetanis. The old sage revealed only what was needful to bring him into a place where the revelation was authentic and his own. He led beyond the dead leavings of darkened minds to pristine truth, revealed in a consciousness attuned to the greater life. That was Flegetanis' gift to him. He could not leave Siduri in darkness. He must find a way to lift her out of despair, so nothing but the light possesses her.

The sun blinded him in its rising. He was at once awake, peered into it and it peered back - a contest he would not win - and so if for no other reason than he was done with Abydos and the heat of the day would soon be upon him, it was time to go. He knew a small oasis, off the well-traveled road the caravans took. It was seldom visited and he might be left alone so long as he wished. He had come to this place in himself before in his descent from Himavat into the hill country of India. In a meadow of blue poppies he'd released his mount to graze. He sat for days by a mountain spring, emptied of himself; until, pausing to drink, a company of pilgrims bade him come down with them from the roof of the world, into their hearts and homes, and so gave him reason to continue.

In the journey of a life there are spots of time when everything is reduced to the utter simplicity of the single thing that comes next. "Thus it is," Caron thought: "No matter how long we journey, no matter how far we have come, these moments return upon us. Times they are that demand we be willing to let go of all we have known to let life move forward with what it will."

And in that spirit he turned to the desert, knowing it was not an oasis he sought but the source of his eternal spring.

5

Sun Temple

Maia awoke to sounds of wind chimes and fragrant air. The soft illumination deepened to morning light and apprehension; she knew at once she was not in her own chambers but a temple in the midst of a garden. Only someone intimately aware of her pattern, attuned to her tone, could so master her principle as to bring her here without her knowledge: only the lord of the crossing.

She rose shyly and crossing the threshold into the courtyard found herself in Temple of the Sun on the heights of Whiter Morn. Other than a whisper of wind and rustle of leaves nothing moved; she was alone in the heights with the sounds of water and shimmering light. From where she stood the temple courts rose in three planes to a high point on the third; small stepped pyramid topped with a dolmen arch framed by an intense blue sky. On each level was a small garden grove with waters in the midst: the first a fountain, the second a pleasant-sounding fall; the third a reflecting pool hedged by a single curved bench facing the high altar that marked the crossing of the worlds.

A narrowing stair led upward but she could not move forward. She must wait alone, feeling the silence of the heights. How long she did not know, a wink in the timelessness of time, but time to realize she had come to the zenith of the worlds. It all came to focus here, where the realms of form cross over into the realms of light, and she was overcome with the realization of the power that brought her. Hardened, her heart yielded and with it came permission to ascend the stair that led to the upper terrace into the air and light of her epiphany.

She knew not what to expect. In times of ceremony, when great cycles consummate; in light body cloaked, the Aton-Re manifest, but so far as she knew only the Elders ever came before him, and would not speak of it. Splendid in his manifestation, she feared him more austere than Innkeeper. But when she reached the height the one who greeted her at the sun-gate arch appeared a man forever in his prime, untouched by the processes of time. Anxious, she challenged, "Who are you?" Her question was impertinent; she knew full well not to expect an answer, for power is essence in Name, given only to those with right to know. Only his title spoke to it: Aton-Re, lord of the crossing.

"*Tai Hoi Ra,* Maia. His word filled her with memory and longing. He spoke in the manner of the lords of light, their modest greeting, in simplest terms: "Let the sun light your path." In the true tongue, words are bearers of the light, subtle bond of radiance and response informing the meaning of the moment. Her heart flooded with warmth, and light broke behind her eyes. But then afraid, feeling exposed, she hedged herself from him. She feared he knew her better than she herself, as he came close she first stepped away. Seeing her discomfort he tempered his radiance so she might see in light favorable. His robes turned azure like the sky, his countenance a soft glow of acceptance, and when he held out his hand to her she took it, elated with his touch. He led her to the reflecting pool where they sat together on the curved bench facing the tiered altar.

"Do you remember me?" he asked, his words now the idiom of the Archaeus. She still felt unaccustomed embarrassment to look too closely on him. When she dared she saw a vigorous man in prime of life, aglow as a fire burned within. And when her eyes settle at last on his features, she thought him not unlike Innkeeper as she remembered him from his time of renewing. He was not the austere presence she feared but so mild she quickly lost her fear of him. Was not the Aton-Re ultimately the source of her complaints?

Fear gave way to petulance. She withdrew her hand. "Why have you brought me here to where it all begins and ends?"

"You think this the limit of the worlds? Could it be you have laboured so long in the dust of the earth, you have forgotten the better part?"

"You have brought me here to show me there is more?"

"You have fallen out with Innkeeper; your light obscured."

The simple directness of his response was disarming. "In his eyes, perhaps," she thought. And though there was no condemnation in his voice she felt shame and thrust it off. "I have engaged in a great matter and he thwarted my will in this."

The Aton-Re waited for Maia to resolve her feelings. Unlike the aggravation she felt toward Innkeeper, here there was no confrontation; no question for a question or absorption in a game of chess, playing out the currents of the world. Here in sun temple was one who appeared to be exactly where he belonged: above it all and content to let what was to come unfold in confidence to some consummation already known. She envied him.

"Here it is different. You are above it all, never suffering the effects of the great transgression. But the world is a working sea of cross-currents, and one can never know the consequences of one's actions," she said. "I have sought to stir men's hearts, given my influences to fire their imaginations with incandescent visions of what they might be," she insisted.

"And they have disappointed you."

"I offer vision and the heart answers with fevered dreams, corrupted minds spawning schemes which lay waste the earth."

"And so the wheat and tares must grow together until the time of harvest. I understand your discouragement, Maia, but that spirit opens the door to the spoiling of all your works."

She did not answer. "I wonder, Maia, if you might see fit to relinquish your sphere of influence in the earth to another. Is it time to let go and return to the realms of light from whence you came? Many have felt that in the fullness of time their cycle was done. Do you desire that union and release? I can give it you."

"There is nothing in the light." How often she had said it. She did not now say it aloud but she could not mask what she felt from him. She believed only in blind force: no divine design for the worlds, no wonderful one - nothing at all. She felt sure the Aton-Re was deluded to believe anything other than the light of the void existed beyond his own artifice and all he imposed here. If anything existed hereafter, anything other than the present gifts of Whiter Morn, she thought it more like a hell than any heaven of the heart's desire.

"Does it not all begin and end in you," she asked, gentling her tone. "And if there is more, walking into the light may I choose what comes hereafter?" If everything began and ended with him, by what right did he judge from on high over all that unfolded beneath him in the realms of time? Most of all, she wanted to know if that power was mutable.

"Is it not true in Whiter Morn: *the greatest among you is the servant of all?* I do what I am given to do. So long as the wonderful one will have it so, I abide in the heights of Whiter Morn, where the realms of light inform the patterns of the Archaeus. But you may cross over. I will guide: Take my hand and come to him."

The nerve of him asking her to cease to be: it stunned her to think it and she balked. "I would see what I have begun to fulfillment," she said, simply, "and so not yet, perhaps."

He paused a moment and moved on. "It is not as it was, is it Maia, these forms we shape to give us presence in the realms of earth? They have fallen into material man. Driven by will and heedless of our presence, all their works are dust and ashes."

She knew this well enough, so what was his point? "I am closer to it than you," Maia said. "The earth is filled with corruption and all caught up in its turbulence. Death, destruction and the battle for survival are man's daily bread. They strive to make of it what they can, but this world they have inherited is exceeding difficult for them; I am full of compassion for their lot."

"And so striving thickens the veil between us."

"How does deepening the darkness in which they labor increase chances they will ever see the light?"

"Hiding in the dark they complain about the dark. And when we send those who bear the light to bring them home again, they destroy our gifts preferring darkness to light."

"Well, it is so," she said, "I have seen it."

"And you and I, Maia, how are we in this matter."

In that moment she felt he could assimilate her, read her every thought and feeling, touch every vibrating tone of her life that left her, permeate her with light so that no shadow remained and nothing could be hidden from him.

He had entered into her substance and she filled with pleasure at the contact, but part of her was dismayed that he had done so readily, and she had no defense against him. She at once thrilled to and resented it, but he did not press the matter and in a moment it was again as it had been, at ease in in his presence but known.

"Come with me." He offered his hand. It seemed now so familiar that she took it, and followed to a casement opening on a view of all that lay below them in a great arc from the summit. From below the swaddling cloud was a dark mirror concealing the summit, but from above a clear glass through which she could see all that lay below. And what she saw was the Archaeus with its varied kingdoms a matrix of patterns informing the world in which she dwelled, until such a time as man was restored to the divine design.

There was a time it was said, more than an hundred thousand years of a golden age, before the time of the great transgression; the world surviving but ash and embers of what once was. And in the world of the First Time, when the worlds were one, two suns there were in the heavens, the greater light to rule the day, the lesser to rule the night; the earth radiant in response, glorious in the light of life.

Not at first came the cataclysms, but earth suffered the fall of man: there came a time when the mother of all living no longer blithely responded to man's voice or answered to his touch but distanced herself barely tolerating him. Not until man grew bold, deaf to all entreaties, and arrogantly determined to wrest the creation from the Makers, did all come to crisis. She saw it all in an instant, as if entering her consciousness he had planted the seed of realization in her. And there it kindled, grew, budded and flowered spontaneous in her memory, her mind on fire with vision.

In the time of reckoning came the rider of the storm, and in its passage comet-like through the kingdoms of the sun, earth was changed utterly. Then were the mountains raised, the seas spilled from their basins and the continents moved out of their places. Not all flesh perished but bore the mark of what it endured. No more the seven dimensional world of the First

Time, the outer planes once radiant in the light of the divine design were fallen into the material earth, and but a measure of the creative power that once was remaining to fallen man.

One by one the remnant of the seven sacred cities of the Motherland, where the powers of creation came to focus, vanished from the earth, but for a remnant of one in the realms of the Archaeus, touching upon the earth and the realms of light. Its presence on the threshold of the worlds is upheld by the lords of light, who dwell in Whiter Morn for the spiritual regeneration of the human race, and the sunrise of the world. And to this end the Na Akhu-El Sages are ever in the earth.

Still, in those days man abused those powers yet remaining to him. Then was a world of giants and men, of machines and machinations, of esoteric technologies and an age of black magic. Its kingdoms were Kemet, Bhārata, Uighur, Hyperborea, Ambertia, Antarktos and many more. But the greatest of these was the Atlantides, a colony of the Motherland lost, shaped in the influences of the seven sisters, and then a beacon of light in a dark world.

And under its guidance again man began to prosper, but not free from the bonds of his traumatic past. In time these defilements of the heart began again to assert themselves, and the healing crisis came. At once proud and vulnerable; proud of all that he had accomplished, fearful it might again all be lost, man willed his own ignorance, began to believe himself sufficient unto himself, preferred darkness to light, hardened his heart. And as disaster is foreshadowed by failure of consciousness; heedless of all warnings, when the rider of the storm again returned, he was unprepared.

Yes, she knew well enough the problem, but was what was to be done? How might she hasten the day? "How often I have struggled with these memories," she thought: "How often I have intended one thing only to bring forth another. How often my influence is misshapen into patterns never intended; bedeviled by transgressions and illusions of men." And as she thought it she felt pity for herself, for she had tried so hard after her heart's desire to have things come out right.

If she saw with his eyes he also had her thoughts. "What is now is not what was made when the seven realms were one," the Aton-Re said. "We must temper our arts to these matters of the earth impinging upon the Archaeus that we may wisely deal with them. Not the Archaeus as a whole but this realm of Whiter Morn alone at its core comes closest true to the tone the Makers wrought for the kingdoms of the world."

Was he asking for sympathy that he had so much to bear? He was such a mild man she knew not what to make of him. "You do not go down to them but dwell here in Whiter Morn where all serve your purpose," she said. "You do not like us bear the cross currents of the world or suffer to see your works distorted at the hands of man. But if indeed at last everything must come to you, I would so bear my own burden that yours is diminished."

She at once regretted for she felt the sting she intended come back upon her. He reacted not at all, but led her away from the vision of the Archaeus below, and walked her back at his arm to the Garden Grove and reflecting pool. And there they sat looking toward the stepped pyramid and the twin columns of the high altar that marked the crossing of the worlds. They sat a long while in silence. It seemed to her he was more interested in the movement of the air and the riffles on the surface of the pool and the melody they made, than her presence and, indeed, it seemed almost that he might melt away in light and air before he spoke again, leaving her alone.

And so she dared, for she knew at the heart of this matter was Morgon Kara, and he was waiting for some admission. "It was not my will the shaman entered into this realm," she said.

"No one crosses over except it is given of one who dwells here. You enabled him. He came through influences opening the way for him, or could not."

"I rebuked him for it. Such influence as I yielded him in my interests he used despite me. In time he grew fiercely strong and I could not prevent him."

"You see how it is, Maia. You look on the suffering of men and taking on their need determine to change the world to better suit you. You are possessed of your own illusions to shape a world after your heart's desire, enter into a contest with me over what shall be, and cannot win."

"I entered into no contest with you."

"There are natural limits to your vision, Maia. You see only the pieces played. What Innkeeper sees as he watches over his board, is the essence of all the forces that inform them. And what Innkeeper sees I see, and yet more from this place where light breaks upon the world.

"I grant you were unaware, but you empowered Morgon Kara with your influences in the earth, and after his nature he used you."

"I chose him to serve me."

"You contested with the Sisters over whose influence was greatest in the earth; you schemed to yield their influence to him." She was stunned. Was that her intention? "You cannot give a man what does not belong to him. The sun-stone is given for purposes beyond your ken."

"I meant no harm."

"You were beguiled by longings, fell into the pattern you wove, and betrayed your influence, and your purpose in creation. Good intentions became conspiracy to slay a man and defeat what life intends in him.

"This is greater than you and I, Maia, or any other incarnate in these realms. These patterns shaped under the hand of the wonderful one in the realms of light are made to unfold in the light and only in the light does the shaping take true form."

"There is nothing in the light." She wanted to say it again. For if there was nothing in the light then despite his beliefs the Aton-Re served nothing but his own good intentions, and was she then not free to do so? She was sure all there was to this was what the Aton-Re wanted, but could not say so in his presence. And again he read her intent.

"He was a great shaman," Maia insisted. "How many, even guided, ever find their way to Whiter Morn?"

"This one shall come never more."

"And who is Caron, his life so precious?"

"He did not fail the wonderful one."

"And for him you slew Morgon Kara."

"Contending with the light, the blow Morgon Kara struck returned in measure upon him."

Now the anger she suppressed surfaced and as her eyes burned with it the temple of the sun blurred and receded from her, as if an illusion passing before her very eyes. But the Lord of the crossing did not fade. Instead the light intensified, concentrating about him, until she could scarce bear any more to look on him.

"What can it matter anymore," she demanded, "that you now bring me here?"

"The sisters were sent into the world to grace the thoughts of men's hearts with sweet influences, to preserve some flesh from the gross distortions imposed upon it, making men of beasts and beasts of men; to heal and rid the earth of those abominations the fallen watchers wrought. You seven graces were given to inspire again in men a passion for truth in beauty, for beauty in truth.

"For the mark of the beast these rebellious spirits left on human flesh lingers. Unresolved, these broken patterns haunt men like ghosts consuming their life force to propagate in heart and mind their depravities. So bond he recreates again and again the very wickedness he would flee."

"I know it," she said, "I have seen evil imagination spoil all I have inspired and turn their works to corruption. And my heart aches for it."

"This one, *Sham-she-el,* who calls himself Morgon Kara, he is one of those, the fallen Watchers, who conspired against us; to possess the flesh of mankind and through it impose their will upon the earth. In the time before they were bound, these fallen watchers took of the sons and daughters of men all they desired, imposed great burdens upon them, spawning atrocities in the earth.

"These despised the limits set upon them, stole from life the power to create what they willed, made beasts that were never to be in the earth; warped human flesh to combine it with that of animals, merged beasts and men in atrocities such as were never seen or ever shall be again for the line was drawn.

"Those among men yet true to the light cried out in distress, for the fallen watchers contesting for power violated the very fabric and weave of life to make war to realize the evil imaginations of their corrupted hearts that the beast has one head only. And so we brought an end to it. But a few must remain for they were so woven into the fabric of fallen man that to have cut them off utterly would have meant the destruction of all flesh. And so for now we must, as the wonderful one has said, let the wheat and tares grow together until the time of harvest.

"*Sham-she-el,* who once knew the ways of Mazzaroth in the seasons of the sun, was one of these left behind when his brethren were banished to the Shades. But that power to take over the life of another, to make himself a parasite on life, was never intended. The influence he stole from the powers of the First Time was of attunement and communion with another being. The gift to enter with tender care, with guidance and blessing into the life of another to lead into the light, he turned to possession and personal need.

"You should never have entered into communion with him, had there not been need for him within the limits proscribed. But rather than serve he has given himself to destruction, even perhaps with intent of trying to hasten the hour of the time of harvest; trespassing on the way of the wonderful one who appoints all things in his season.

"If he now dwells in the Shades, can he be redeemed?"

There was silence a long while between them, for Maia knew whereof he spoke and of the purpose of the seven sisters to inspire the heart and uplift the soul of man.

"He dwells in the Shades among the fallen watchers under your sister, Irkala's, hand. I have confined him not in the vault of the deep as I did the others, but in the Wood of Erebus, where the roots of the tree of life descend into the Unformed. He is not without merit or you would have seen nothing in him, but there he will serve the purpose I proscribe."

She took her subtle flesh in her teeth to say it, but could not let it pass. She was after all not without power, not without authority. She had her own right and these matters concerned her more than anyone. "And is there no way for me to restore him to life in the flesh?"

The Aton-Re blazed up a moment then the light softened about him kindly. "Would you again have him steal the flesh body of another to justify his existence?"

"The earth is full of pointless lives: people drifting to and fro, going up and down, looking for they know not what; there will be many willing to give themselves to the purposes of such an one."

"You think it is his intent to serve?"

"I do."

"I would not have you do so."

"In binding him you have bound something of me in the depths, so that I cannot serve as once I did. In him I found one to center my arts. I entered into his imagination; I inspired him with visions of what might be, and to everything I offered he rose to meet it.

"Now you have taken away an instrument of creation I had prepared for the betterment of humankind. Is that not what you wish of us? We cannot forever see humankind in this degraded state of brutal existence, and still speak of the regeneration of the human race."

"It is not to him you should yield your influence."

"He reaches out for me."

"Let go or lose yourself in him."

"I am bond to him," she said, fiercely.

"And to that measure I must reduce your influence to magnify his will, lest he ever be the spoiler of our works."

"Weaken my influence?"

"If you persist you will draw a veil between us in the Aeon of Whiter Morn and your realm of Eleleth."

That frightened her. "What must I do to set this to rights?"

"Seek out those awakening in the earth. To those who serve to restore the world to the realms of light pour out from the chalice of your heart your gift of influence. Serve the Na-Akhu-El sages and uplift their way."

"And what have they accomplished?"

"It begins, Maia, the third and final call to respond to the realms of light."

"And if man fails to rise to the gift?"

"The very earth will repudiate him. He will destroy himself and we shall look to a new creation in the earth. Even as we speak the light of a rising sun casts its shadow before, and in the fullness of time will bring all things to consummation."

"With Innkeeper it is all a game, how this shall turn out or that; this or that pattern succeed or fail, while I must touch upon and know the suffering of men."

"It is a play of forces greater than any of us, that all things work together to perfection, in the spiritual regeneration of the human race."

"Yes, but what does *he* play for," she insisted.

"Time, Maia, he plays for time. He plays to keep the balance of forces that would otherwise overwhelm and destroy. He plays to keep the cycle open for man, to give him time to turn his heart back again, or it would have been over long ago."

"So you have brought me here to remind me of my part in this, and to speak of what is yet to come," she said, with just a hint of repentance in her voice.

"To remind you of what you already know."

"I am at a loss to know my way forward."

"It is simple enough. Bless and uplift those who bear the light in the way," he said, gently but firmly. "If you cannot another must bear what you have borne.

"I have other matters to attend," he said, rising: "You much to ponder. Let this communion continue between us to resolution, in the substance of what is yet to unfold."

It was as he supposed. Maia had fallen subject to her own gift to engender vision. It was his to engage each who served in the Archaeus: to help give shape, to correct if need be the vibratory patterns that came to point in them. It was rare, for he much preferred to keep true the tone and leave each to his own to see through what was needful. But when Maia would not respond to Innkeeper's invitation, the Aton-Re knew he must intervene. She had not the substance to come to him, so he caused a great sleep to fall upon her, and entering in upon her vibration communed with her in her own chambers. It was real enough, as real as anything her consciousness could sustain in the range to which she had fallen. When she awakened it would not be a half-remembered dream, but full and vivid realization of communion with him.

In the heights of Whiter Morn the sun shimmered like white gold, and today even from without one could see in the radiance of the realms of light the cool blue of the flame, the dwelling of the wonderful one. It was the same sun in all seven worlds, here more serene; a softer radiance than the fiery face that illumined the realms of earth to keep the way of the tree of life. Here the solar ray was fit to the purpose of Whiter Morn, and so it was throughout the realms even to the seventh ray in the realm of the wonderful one.

He was about to rise when a woman came to him in the garden. Where he sat in meditation before the reflecting pool she gathered to him like the glow that surrounds a flame and took her place beside him. And he let her come near for she was a priestess of the temple and engendered the pattern and means for him to enter into Maia's consciousness.

"She would magnify *Sham-she-el* in the earth, and despite what you have said means to do so," she offered.

"I have told her I have restrained him in the Shades among the fallen Watchers."

"That will not be the end of it."

The Aton-Re shook his head. "She has hardened her heart."

"Life in the flesh is brief and brutal, and for many, death a welcome release. It is not easy for those who engage those realms to go untouched by their suffering."

"I must be able to depend upon the sweet influences of the seven sisters," the Aton-Re said. "They engender vision, aspiration, longing for the ineffable in those awakening. Men call them muses, graces, soul mates, inner genius and spirit guides, birthing radiant consciousness leading into the light. They are essential to man's awakening.

"They are the warmth of life's radiance that keeps the cold of the world at bay, which kindles fire upon the hearth of the imagination, which inspires creation and shapes consciousness anew. Their influence thins the veil, bridges the worlds and looses power in creation.

"And because of this closeness to what unfolds in the thoughts of the imaginations of men's hearts, I must know where their hearts are."

"You think she will seek power to impose her own designs," the priestess said.

"The way back must resolve those matters that led astray. We shall see what is in her; let her come to the end of herself and choose."

He understood how taking on soul substance and with it the cross currents of the world, how easily one lost consciousness in the flesh, how few awakened and found their way home. It had happened to many, who coming into the world to reveal the way, fell into self-indulgence; entangled in sense, appetite and response to the things of the world, they dissipated the fine substance of connection to the realms of light. There came a time for these when they could no more cross over to Whiter Morn. And now Maia perhaps other of her sisters trembled on the brink.

One long lost to him was Irkala who was given to keep watch over the Shades, where the patterns of the under-earth touch on the unformed. She, too, was bond to a fallen Watcher and followed him into captivity. She endured in the shadow of the sun, in the realm of the hungry ghosts, and came no more to Whiter Morn. The Aton-Re knew, in search of Morgon Kara, Maia would go to her fallen sister. In fact he was counting on it. But first she would seek out the Fates.

6

Desert Solitaire

Al-Lubbān was a handful of date palms and acacia scattered along the margin of a sheer cliff. Named for the prized, milky white resin of the frankincense, the few remaining hoary trees clung precariously to the cliff face, their swollen roots set in rock, sustained by the morning mist that rose off the oasis. Once worth the visit, the takers came until what remained was worth too little in trade to merit the effort. Otherwise, the oasis was a marshy pool surrounded mostly by reeds and grasses, useful only to the lost that chanced to pass this way.

In the cliff face above the oasis was a shallow cave, refuge from the sun by day, and by night for a sheltering fire. There was some dead wood, a precious commodity in the desert, and if it came to it camel dung for a fire. Caron released his mount to the pleasures of the oasis – the beast would go nowhere so long as it had food and water - and withdrew into the cave. And there he sat, cross legged; the little white stone, given to remind him of who he was, held in the hollow of his hands. And in this wise he gazed out on the desert waste beyond his little oasis, awaiting he knew not what; knowing only it would come.

Three days he sat silent watching the shadows cross the harsh land. He took a little water, but desired nothing more. He lit no fire by night against the cold, but drew a blanket about his shoulders, sat crouched in the cavern mouth, easing in and out of sleep. Asleep, he dreamed not at all. Awake, he forced no thought, no wish, no want to stir feelings, or desire anything should be. Willing nothing he let go of all he had known to step into the unknown, open to what was greater than him to inform his way.

He rested in the unspoken question of what had become of him. There was no way his sensuous mind could rationalize or explain it to himself. His mind could not comprehend the way the master Flegetanis was taken by the light, crossed over, and was no more. Nor could it comprehend, come down to earth, his release from the burden of years; his flight on swift wings above the flow of time into the First Time. Transfigured in radiant light all his senses were transformed, illumined from within: sight and scent, sound, taste, and touch no longer reflective only but radiant, dissolving the veil of material illusion. All he thought real was shadow to what was unveiled. And if he did not understand how could he explain it to Siduri?

And so he came to this desert place, where existence was reduced to utter simplicity, to let go and discover what if anything remained to inform his way forward. Letting go what remained and would not be denied was assurance that beyond the mind made world bedeviling the sense, was not all dust and ashes. There was the truth of a realm lost to man to be revealed and restored. There was reason and purpose, an open heart, and a fallow field for a seed yet to be sown.

On the evening of the fourth day something stirred in him. It came with the last rays of the setting sun lighting the terraced land; its rough red rim rock plateaus disappearing into the desert like a golden staircase opening on the vault of the night. And when the sun was passed through the gate of the days of all our tomorrows, the treasures of the night unveiled the heavens ablaze with kindred fire to proclaim the journey of the hidden sun. The world without was one in the world within, and he in the midst of the wonder, they met in him.

He sat for hours gazing out into the stars until they were alive in him. And in the darkest hour he could sit no more he rose from his vigil, picked his way down the rugged trail and walked off in the cool night air into the desert. And there he lay on his back in the sand, gazed off into the heavens, remembering the stories written in the stars: legends not to be forgotten but patterns given in nightly remembrance of the ordinances of heaven for the heat of the day. Among the stars somewhere, his own story was written: the way of his coming, his purpose, his destiny. He must read and understand the ark of his own life: his flesh a husk about a seed to bear his essence across the flood of time; a seed preserved for the springtime of the world. He thought it and the stars came close to whisper their stories that he might find his own among them.

His heart stirred with memories of friends, they who come to us to remind us of who and what we are. And first, for their loss, he thought of Siduri and Shirazi, half brother and sister of Flegetanis, to him as kindred. These he loved and they doubted him, believing he failed their father Flegetanis. And there was Perrin, whose search for truth in the labyrinth of the poet's heart turned away from him for love of the Cailleach's ward, the Lady Gwendolyn. He had not sought Gwendolyn's love, but it made one more defining triangle in the heavens, which caught him up. Above all was Flegetanis whose life was light, taken by the light and gone, yet evermore in the world. It was then he remembered he was to seek out Origen at the Monastery of Alba on the Red Sea Shore, a third perhaps in the bond he shared with the old sage.

He thought again of old Kalpa, who descending Himavat took him for the god Shiva come to wed his daughter Padma; to free the waters and bring an end to the world drought. In the spirit of the goddess Parvati, she awaited the descent of her Lord Shiva from Mount Kailas; that in their union love's body might be restored to the world. Perhaps it was all a play of seeming, but she would wait for him to return through a life time for an age to come.

Then there were the six who journeyed with him from Waldheim, whose hearts were bound to him; their story, too, was written in the pattern of the stars: the petulant Don Perando who loved Thalia from his youth but loved the youth Delwyn of Wales, who saved her on the road to Paris from the madness of Edouard's crone and the spell-bound Pastoureaux.

And so far as his memory of those times went back there was Branwyn of Wales to whom in youth it seemed he was once betrothed. Of that he remembered little, until the time the aging crone Branwyn stood for him in Green Chapel acknowledging him Grail King. And with the memory of Branwyn came the memory of Esclarmonde the fair, for whom he came in those fateful hours to Montségur in the burning time. She for the telling of her tale would not flee with him but burn a martyr, declaring a life's work is greater than a lifetime.

And of those times of old, came the undying memory of his friend Nautonnier, the great navigator, who found his way through the chaos of the world to serve. If still he lived, now ancient of days, he came to remembrance and Caron knew he must seek out once more the one who kept faith with him against his return.

All the stories came together now in a rush like a mighty wind among the stars, scattering star shine across the dark of his mind; friends of another life, surging memories of distilled essences long past and past on yet never absent, he'd known over how many ages, the generations surging in him, looking for fulfillment of all they had done and came to do in what he must now do. And what was he to do? It was too much to contemplate but he felt their substance gather to him, and with it the stars grew brighter at the thought of them. And there was more; he felt them far and wide, friends known and unknown or not yet known, drawn in anticipation of fulfillment; other lights that shone and lit the path of the heavens to this hour gathering a heavenly host of star folk to witness.

And then there were the others, the spoilers with voracious appetite to consume the lives of others not their own, believing in their own musts. But God is not mocked with impunity. They, too, would be used to advantage. He dismissed them. In that wise he must now gather influence, they could have no place in him. And so he let his thoughts dwell, whatever their limitations, on those who came to serve in the light of life. And they came, enfolding him in a luminous cloak of star shine; some named - most unnamed - but known for what they are, as the vivid air took the imprint of their lives. Distance and time dissolved and they drew closer, whispering blessings in the starry night.

There is a texture of sackcloth and a texture of roses. If his body was coarse as sackcloth, now it was something more; transformed by a fine substance permeating and transmuting the flesh, until it bore the touch and scent of roses. It was substance of the light body he touched among the shining ones in Flegetanis' presence, and now it manifested in him. His body evanesced like the essence of a pure candle flame, transforming the rosy flesh into a fine, shimmering substance. And with it his consciousness in the light returned.

Some say the stars are distant but only to those who grasp at them as fireflies, never knowing them within. But in spirit the stars are nearer than breathing, for in them the essence of the worlds meet, cross over, and enter into substance of the soul. In that fine substance, Caron found interlaced within him an ecstatic harmony of radiant meaning, woven into his soul. One star in particular, a blue-white solitaire, shining in the darkness on the deep, intrigued him. Its meaning just beyond reach, he could not by any effort of his own come closer but must wait on invitation. Still he gazed upon it, until his eyes wearied and he fell asleep in the cold sands under the heavens.

Come dawn Caron arose, washed, drank some cave cool water and continued his fast. Through the heat of the day he sat in the cavern mouth watching the sun's progress across the desert, anxious that night should fall. He watched the play of light casting shadows, illumining dark places, and drawing everything before it in its unrelenting radiance. For a man there was no hiding from the sun in the earth. He might dwell a while in a cave, but necessity demanded he labor in the light, and that must be as must be.

Every day under the sun there is another journey to be made, a trial won. Men and women contrive, bargain, exchange, challenge and are challenged, overcome and are overcome, rise up, stand their ground, enter into agreements, betray and are betrayed, are dishonorable or honorable, loyal or false, true or subject to lies. And though men strive night and day to hide in the shadows, at the last every hidden thing is brought again into the full light of day in the making or breaking of a man on the path of life, and in the distillation of a life all is revealed.

And when the heat of the day is broken, in the cool of the day when troubled heart and busy mind give way to wise serenity, it is all there plain to see, as in a glass reflected back upon him: what work is done or undone, what patterns shaped or spoiled at his hand; what fundamental truth distorted by those who would wrest the world into a shape, neither given man nor ever intended to be, mirrored in the mind made world under the all-seeing sun. The cycle of life is unrelenting but one may choose: to scuttle like a scorpion across the scorched sands of the world, or take flight on eagle's wings.

The night before, he had gone as far as he might. In that name written within that he alone knew, the white stone brought him to the threshold of himself. Now it needed an invitation, for by no might he possessed could he do without. The hours passed as he pondered this until at last, but half conscious of what he did or why, he took three flat stones: two he set upright and the third he laid upon them, making a rough altar at the cavern mouth.

"A jewel must have a setting," he said. "It needs more than to be concealed within the folds of my cloak." Caron took the blue stone Flegetanis called the Aton, held the jewel in the cupped palms of his hands, and his body began to glow warmed by a sun within. His mind stilled in the tranquility that enveloped him; his heart soothed with a healing balm. A pearly essence of fine substance rose out of the earth of his form, and again his body filled with light. In that substance his soul opened as softly as a flower in halcyon clime; with it the inner mind.

It was like holding a book in one's hand and apprehending in a moment the whole of what was written within. A mind caught up in time must parse in time. But the mind he thought he was, he was not. Open to life the mind is fallow earth to sown seed that in time reveals itself: root, stem, leaf, flower and fruit of its informing essence. And out of what was sown, and from whatever depth of understanding the Aton stirred in him, the revelation came and he was drawn inexorably into realization of what had befallen the earth in the day of the journey of sounding fire.

He understood that an age after the great transgression; in a time when all attempts to return man to the divine state were rejected, the earth could no longer endure what fallen man had wrought. For in those days there was yet power under his hand to shape and inform his creations; and by reason of man's corruption the earth was filled with violence and unspeakable abominations. And to that remnant of divine man yet in the earth, it was understood that man would destroy himself except those powers be restrained. It was hoped that faced with loss of power and the consequences of what was wrought he might yet turn his heart from wickedness to walk into the light. For this cause and the hope that faced with consequences man might yet turn his heart back again, they who kept the pattern in form withdrew. The Aton-Re and all who gathered to him ascended in Shekinah fire into the Archaeus within the hedge of the realms of light.

This Caron apprehended in a moment. He sat at the mouth of his cave watching the sun sink beneath the horizon, and all passed vividly before his eyes. It was as if chronicled by a scribe and told by a poet, layer upon layer of meaning revealed in its telling. And though his outer mind could only grasp the sense of it in fragments, it was in this wise it unfolded before him.

... The Aton-Re felt the pattern shift. The balance was broken and destruction was on the wind. The life currents receded in the earth and with them the dominion of powers gifted ...

... The usurper would appear to inherit the earth; he would claim it his own to do with as he willed, until they should even reach out and seek as well to possess the realms of light.

... Even so, where those who had gone before him, and where he now went, they could not follow after. He would seal the way of ascension, confining them to the realms of earth.

... A different fire would burn in the flesh passions enflamed, obscuring all. Drawn to the fire at the center of the earth; the way of undying life closed to them; all turned to dust and ashes.

...In that day the children of the sun walked in the Flame and were no more in the earth. In his heart he blessed the few who remained for a time when those now departed might come again to restore the earth to the patterns of the First Time. And the angry ones came for him.

...Like a wounded creature earth shuddered beneath his feet. He felt her sorrow in what had become of her children, for this was in the heart of the priestess, who stood with him in the altar flame; the one who remained with him to shape the seed of a new heaven and new earth when all shall be restored to the patterns of the First Time.

...There was no help for it. They were warned, told it would come to this, who contrived to steal and warp the forces of creation into patterns of their own devising. They took no heed but turned to destruction, stealing the life blood, enslaving the souls of others to serve themselves.

...Even so fallen man would not be destroyed utterly, but given time to walk again in the way. It was for this the lords of light, the Na Akhu-El must

abide, and to this end he would distill an essence of the First Time to call forth remembrance of the divine design.

…Suspended between the world without, and the world within, the Aton-Re felt the currents of destruction rise, troubling the waters. Warped and twisted forms of light spun and wove deceit in the senses. Wrath rose upon those of clouded sense in whom life diminished and the doors of power closed, leaving them desolate.

…Wonderful the gateways of the senses radiant, illumined in the fire of life; he breathed once more the fragrant, flowered air of earth and she who stood with him drew into him and together they gave themselves to the Flame.

…Anguished voices echoed through the temple courts demanding he appear and render himself accountable to them. Finding the temple empty they ventured into the very sanctuary in search of him, filled with ire he should deprive them anything they demanded of him.

…Within the Holy of Holies the ascending flame was a sun upon the altar. Unable to approach, scarce able to look upon its shining, they felt their death. No more would flesh cross over; no more would they be taken by the Flame, and they wondered at what would become of them when the flesh was no more.

…In a moment it was done, their forms concentrated in light, and as they crossed over. And if only for an instant the angry ones peered into the heart of light touching they had lost before the way closed upon them. Like a setting sun the fire of transmutation burned low and lower, until in a flash of blue in an instant it concentrated in upon itself and was gone. And in place of the Flame a blue jewel remained, illuming the dark with a light from within.

…At first none dare touch it, and then men grew bold and the brash among them reached out to possess the jewel. "We shall not surely perish," they argued. "In this stone is the power of the Flame, and we shall learn how to unlock its power to our purpose." Hiding away their fears, they surrendered their lives and followed those who believed they understood what had befallen them, and the way they must go.

…One generation more… a single dawn… and the earth heaved in her depths and kingdoms torn asunder in a world of water and fire … and when it was done only scattered remnants of peoples in desolate lands remained.

Caron slept, and how long he slept - an instant, a thousand years, a night and a day - it little mattered for when he awakened it was to the sun rising like thunder on the horizon of the world. *"Hor-em-akhet,"* he whispered: "Always you return to us splendid in your rising." Here was the faith of the world taken for granted, for the day the sun did not rise was its doom.

Caught up in the timelessness of time he had no sense of when he was; only that he had awakened in the light of the one who dwells in the midst of the flame. He lifted his head and looked again to his makeshift altar casting long shadows in the morning light, eyes fixed on the jewel. "You are come down the generations through the fall and rise of empires, to come again into the hands of the shining ones who have never forgotten who and what they are. But a jewel needs a setting," he said, again: "it needs a setting in the world, in the flesh." A gust of wind rose scurried across the desert bending the pond grasses, troubling its murky surface.

"And how is it to be done?" They who knew the ordinances of heaven and the way of the First Time, who did not yield to the ways of fallen man but kept faith with the wonderful one: these transcendent ones were returning. Not all at once would their powers be loosed in the earth, but measure by measure binding in love the sweet influences they would transform the darkness with vision anew; and in time restore those lost powers touched only in dreams, remembered in myths.

He saw it all in an instant, but the outcome hung by a slender thread. But what had this to do with him? Others sought to possess the Aton, and he desired neither sovereignty nor power over men. It was enough to cultivate in peace his own rough plot of earth. Even so, he could not dismiss the fact it had come to him, and he had begun to awaken to its power. Surely it was given to him only for safe keeping, until in competent, confident hands.

Two more nights and days Caron sat in the cavern's mouth before his rough-hewn altar, the blue stone refracting the rays of the journeying sun. He waited and watched the stars rise and fall in the soft darkness of his fallow soul, open to receive the shining ordinances of heaven, and nothing more revealed. Nevertheless, on the eve of the seventh day a shadow passed over his eyes; darkening the sun within and without so he could not see.

"Man is a breath of wind; his days a passing shadow. By what right do I ask anything? I am no more than dust and ashes."

"Were you no more than dust and ashes it were true," came the answer. "But love thou art and unto love shalt thou return."

And at his word, the one Caron knew himself in truth to be, still and at peace in the midst of the play of creation, the shadow passed. He watched the sun again set in the terraced west, its last light filling him with gratitude for life. He gazed into the desert vastness; touched the world of sorrow that turned earth into a wasteland. Overflowing with compassion he blessed all living, known and unknown to him, who kept the way of life.

And in blessing he was released. He gazed into the Aton. The blue star rose, igniting the substance of his soul, dissolving everything in his sight in the ray it kindled. He shut his eyes but that changed nothing. He was in the midst of an apocalypse of light; in a moment become what he had sought, and in a moment gone.

Death's kingdom the sages say is but an instant, for in truth there is only life. And if for a moment there was nothing it was but an interval of suspended time; the necessary silence between two notes in which another is shaped, defined, and sounded anew in the music of life.

No more sat down among the ashes Caron opened his eyes in the soft blue twilight; in a place undefined because he had not yet given shape to it in consciousness. Beyond the dissonance of the world, a heaven of starshine enveloped him in a weave of shimmering harmonies; the fire-folk gathered in a radiant masterwork, the song of earth's creation. He breathed an air rich with essence, found it sweet with influences, his senses brilliant, and never so alive.

Encompassing his heaven of perfect peace was a matrix of force and vibrational form: intersecting planes of light, helices, spires, curves, and patterns for which he knew no name. One moment felt, another moment seen his mind's eye filled with images of complex geometrics: some contained within a plane, others whirling through other planes crossing over into unseen dimensions: planes of light at every apex, linked and defined by the radiance of stars in a complex, vibratory field.

He was looking at the world from within out through the planes of a scintillating jewel, a shining blue sun that centered this creation that somehow added up to all the world he knew. It was a world very different than the one he'd come to know in the labyrinth of the human heart and mind. These were patterns through which no human mind might find its way, but for another consciousness he could not yet articulate.

And so centered in the blue star, he rested in silence and understanding came. This matrix of patterns was the weave and design of forces through which he incarnated. His mind was imposing patterns and forms, but in truth it was the score by which he sang himself into existence in the earth; into a fallen world where those who came on angel's wings sat down among the ashes.

Caron had seen wonders but never thought to see this, though Flegetanis had spoken of it. "Between the stars flow streams of subtle force," the old sage said. "These vibratory forces engender a glowing weave of influence; the finer informing the coarser through the seven planes of this world.

"Splendid it is when the forms of this world are filled with the radiant light of the wonderful one; when the one who dwells incarnates into his creation through the flesh body of the earth.

"But we have marred this created world, entangling ourselves in the dark and devious ways of fallen consciousness. And rather than live in our subtle body of light we have chosen the sackcloth and ashes of ignorance, and a world we cannot comprehend."

It had seemed so far off in the telling, and yet now he realized how simple the resolution of it all must be, for everything was in place but man. The greater life was present; the radiance of the wonderful one shone through dust and ashes. All would be resolved at last by the coming forth of angelic being in the flesh of the world, a world that would either respond to the intensification of the radiance of life or perish. "I have set before you life and death," he whispered, remembering: "wherefore, choose life."

When he looked again his eyes opened on first light of dawn on the desert. He watched the shadows retreat along the rim of hills, until the sun shimmered in the facets of the blue stone he'd set upon the makeshift altar. In an instant he realized what was written within: the patterns of the First Time, the way of the crossing, the essence of what was written in the Aton-Re in the day of his ascension into the inner planes of this world. And it was the way of the shining ones. Like a spring of cool water in a dry land, the knowledge of it rose in him overflowing in bliss. He had found the spirit of truth.

Or, rather, it had found him. But even as he thought it a cloud like an inkblot rose covering the low sun in the eastern sky. Moaning like a tired dog, his camel rose from its ruminations on paradise, water and fresh vegetation. Standing on trembling legs, gaze fixed on the eastern rim of hills, the beast shrieked and bellowed like an anxious sheep.

Dust devils that rose a hundred feet off the desert floor, suffocating anything in their path, were a hazard of the desert; but this one, a spiral column of dust and cloud that moaned like a typhoon as it came was unlike anything he'd seen. "Ghost wind," Caron whispered. He stumbled down the trail of broken stone, unhobbled the nervous beast, and led it up and back into the depths of the cavern. Like a load of discarded baggage it groaned beneath its weight, sank in an inconsolable heap and waited, Caron with it.

He saw it coming afar off targeting the small oasis. Above the sky was a pink pearl haze and in the distance still a stunning blue morning sky; but the ghost wind no longer a spire rising gracefully into the pearly haze had become a dark cauldron of churning forces, cauliflower shape, rising on a stem of dense energy feeding upon the earth it ravaged. And within its dark cloak, as if by intent, a ragged web of lightning before and behind drove the mass toward him. Ahead of the storm a hot grit filled wind scorched the cavern face and drove Caron back into its depths.

The mouth of the cave erupted in fiery discharge sending out fingers of fire as if reaching out to draw him into its grasp. The earth quaked beneath his feet shaking fragments from the cavern wall. The camel bellowed with fear, and in the midst of the howling typhoon winds Caron heard the rumble of shifting rock.

The ghost wind struck swallowing up the sun, obliterating everything in its path; and but for the cavern in which he and one lone camel hid from the rage of elements, the whole life of the oasis. The energy of the storm contrived to overwhelm his mind, tugged at every nerve and sinew in his body; strove to turn his emotions into a working sea. It would blot out the light and leave him in darkness. Instead he went deep, calmed his heart, stilled his mind, and let the tone of his home among the stars fill him and his cavern sanctuary with peace.

And as quickly as it had come the fire-wind abated. And still it was not done for in that instant even as the fire-wind passed a great flood of water borne upon the wind surged in the cavern mouth, to overwhelm and wash him out. The force of the wash along the floor swept his feet from under, driving him into the rugged wall before draining off through fissures in the earth. The bedraggled beast moaned, struggled to its feet, shook off like a dog grit and water, and walked painfully toward the light.

Caron followed to a scene of utter desolation. The oasis was gone, all the vegetation root and branch broken and buried under desert sands as if it had never been. Still the spring among the rocks he found returned with a slow trickle. It seeped down among the stones. He cleared the wet sand in its path until the water pooled, and began the work anew of restoring a lost oasis. There would be more spring water from below and in time life would return.

Caron sat to dry in the sun. The camel drank water where it pooled and anxious to go, if ever a camel could show affection, nudged him lovingly. But Caron was not ready to leave. There were questions. Had he mastered that rage of elements come against him, because he first mastered himself? Were the worlds within and without alike one world? And when the heart was pure and the senses cleansed was each known indivisible, part of the other and infinite?

Was dominion over oneself, over one's own body, mind and heart, likewise dominion over those elements of earth given to master? Was this the true heavenly magic, the art of the lords of light, that in mastering the elements in themselves they commanded the elements in creation?

He had seen wonders form in a moment of truth. They who came out of the desert to stand with Flegetanis in his time of need wielded extraordinary powers, and yet in the ordinary course of events seemed reluctant to use them. What was the law of it? Morgon Kara, too, had power. If there was white magic, there was black, and if any of these powers were alike his own he must understand the use of them.

And so Caron fell deep into thought as the day unfolded over that desolate scene, until at last an answer came, as if from the heart of creation itself, a familiar voice.

"Still in the wilderness, Caron: your idyll is done, the work begun. Seek out the Master Origen in the Monastery of Alba. He will set you in the way."

7

The Fates

Ananke was mother to the daughters of necessity who, under the ordinances of heaven, set the measure of life in the realms of earth. "Greater are these, my sisters, than even the lord of the crossing," Maia thought: "for he, too, is apportioned his lot and must serve within the limits imposed upon him. She will know what I must do."

Stung from her encounter with the Aton-Re, the moment Maia left his presence she returned to her own realm of Eleleth and the holy place of the temple. There she stood and gazed into the light that ever shone forth from Whiter Morn, the cloud of glory that illumined its inner court, and pondered what it might mean thwarting his will to never enter in again. So it was she came face to face with her sister Ananke, who came forth through the shining until she stood, neither stern nor condemning, but eyes fixed upon her, curious.

Known by many names to those who sift shadows in search of the meaning of their lives, it is the Moirai who keep the way of creation wrought in the light, who set bounds to patterns shaped in the earth. They are thus far and no further: the daughters of Ananke who preside over the realm of beginnings and endings, and of just limits. It was not unknown for the sisters to seek them out over the timing of matters of birth and death. Issues of justice, retribution, order and peace were matters of necessity, and must from time to time be visited. Even so they were solitary in their watch over what was wrought and inclined to say little, for it was not their lot to intervene but to keep the way of the one law and uphold the pattern of the Holy Norm. Some said their work informed or was reflected in Innkeeper's chess board, but she did not know that of a certainty.

"Night-born, thrice-born," Maia said, "you who keep vigil over the paths of light and shadow, why have you come?"

"Beautiful Maia, whose influence graces our strict art, I am come because I must."

"Had you not, I would have come to you. My affairs now touch upon the measure of a great matter."

"I speak for the Moirai: they in me."

"You have seen what I will do."

"We have seen the frame of it."

"And you do not approve."

"It is not for us to approve or disapprove but to keep the balance in the way of the Holy Norm."

"Will you allow what I shape in the light?"

"Of necessity you are free to create in the substance of the heart. Nevertheless, a measure is given to all things wrought in the Archaeus. Are you prepared to accept the consequences of what is shaped, for in that wise none are exempt?"

"Would you prevent me?"

"Not to prevent but to warn of Irkala, whose portion is the Shades."

"Our fallen sister."

"You will go to her in search of your shaman. She will release him but at a price too dear to pay."

"You know of him."

"Once he came to our isle, totally unaware of us. He is not worthy, Maia, what you are about to do."

"Tell me of Irkala; it has been long since we have seen her."

"She presides over the fallen Watchers; over titanic forces, sealed from the time of the great transgression, as life decrees, and they are utterly dependent upon her. And there in Erebus your shaman is confined."

"If she has the power to release him: at what price?"

"She would have what you have and too little value. If you give it her you and she may yet trade places."

"You are impertinent."

"Of necessity. Beware, Maia: through the things we want, we fall subject to things we do not want."

Ananke was gone and Maia stood alone in the fading light of Whiter Morn upon the altar. It was rare for Ananke to intervene. And still she was not forbidden; only warned not to exceed her measure of influence. But in this preemptive warning she saw evidence of the impact of what she intended and reveled in it. She would enlist the aid of the sisters that all agree together to walk the way she led. Her realm of the Archaeus was closest to the material realms of earth; who knew better than she its needs? She would not of course oppose the lord of the crossing, but he had not her experience of the real world with which she must contend.

And she felt for Irkala. She knew what had become of her, but what of those sisters now vanished from the earth, their realms with them? It was said the world was once more alive with influences now lost to man, and distinctions far more subtle; that they had returned to the realms of light when man fell into darkness. Innkeeper assured them there were those who came and went as needed, and all was well. But the more she pondered the fate of the lost sisters, the burden placed on those remaining, the more keenly she felt tyranny in the Aton-Re's presumptuous summons. She had no idea where her animus came from, but the well was deep, pooled, and overflowed with resentment to be so abused of him.

What she now intended might seem defiant, but she resented giving influence to purpose over the ages, only to see it rejected and twisted into things that ought not to be. And she resented rejection of Morgan Kara's heroic efforts, century after grim century, fighting to exist and out of the raw courage create a world after the heart's desire. In that he typified humankind, and it irked her that all his works should be rejected. Most of all she resented the dismissal of her sympathy for humanity, suffering the yoke of blind force imposed over some ancient transgression.

And so Maia summoned her sisters to agree and join with her

determination to do what she must to restore Morgon Kara. But when she came to the gathering place on the slope of Whiter Morn they did not come. Still she waited, staring down into the dark waters of the well the Sisters call Anguish. Rising up through the strata of time from the deep of the first waters of the unformed, it passes through all the realms of creation, touching the record of all that has been, until it brims in the sanctuary of the sisters where one may read what is wrought in the imaginations of the heart.

And as she gazed within, a whorl on the top of the waters drew her magnetically into its depths, following the swirl down. "I have the power to lay down my life," she said.

"But do you have power to take it up again?"

Maia turned to her sister Anwyn who came to her out of the shadows where she stood by the well. Only she had come when bidden, though Maia was the Elder, the others knowing her willfulness, reluctant, and so Anwyn had come for them.

"Fate goes ever as she will."

"Wisdom is the mistress of us all," Anwyn said, "and Wisdom's well we call Anguish only to remind us we have forsaken our first love and draw up the influences of the world rather than the wellsprings of truth."

"It is how I am made; I can only be what I am."

"Perhaps you have forgotten more than you remember," Anwyn said. "Do you think there is no more to this than your ambition to prevail? You summoned me here to acknowledge your shaman; to dispute with me over the power of your influence in the earth.

"You tasked your shaman to acquire the Aton, the sun stone of the world, to heighten your influence in the earth. Have you forgotten you gathered us here to challenge; that you should be acknowledged the greatest among us?"

"I would see a world restored," she countered: "this well no more anguish at what has been, or omen of what is to come: no more foreboding in the night, but joy in the morning."

"Your shaman would have slain the one to whom the sun stone was given, to possess it to your purpose."

"I did not will Caron's death."

"Your shaman was very skilled and would have slain to possess him.

Not since the time of the fallen Watchers have we seen the like; they who took mortal women and made themselves gods in the earth."

"Morgon Kara is a force needful to our purpose in the earth, and for this cause I magnified him."

"And now you will give him your life?"

"I sought the good and rejected am faced with a great evil," Maia replied. "I will free him from the Wood of Erebus."

"At what cost?"

"I shall, perhaps, come no more to Whiter Morn."

"It is the fate of other sisters who turned away from the Aton-Re," Anwyn said. "This needs not be your choice; let go, abide here and let the way be revealed."

"I am bond to Morgon Kara. I will seek him in the Shades, in the Wood of Erebus, at the roots of the tree of the world, and if I can return him to the land of the living."

"Ananke has told me what you will do, and that I would be unable to convince you otherwise. So, I am come to prepare your descent. To enter into the kingdom of the Shades you must divest yourself of your robe of radiance; lest the powers of these realms be stripped from you, corrupted, and abused by what lies beneath."

"Must I shed the royal diadem?"

"And with it all the influence and virtues that inform the unformed," Anwyn said.

"Say not so," Maia answered, "but take this anklet instead." She stooped and loosed the sliver clasp. Immediately her feet felt heavy and her heart rebelled at the thought of what she must do.

"It is not enough."

Maia loosed the shield and broach that clasped the girdled sash about her loins and let it fall. A great weariness tugged on and drew her to her knees; she struggled under the weight to regain her footing.

"I am filled with longing that knows no answer."

"Your soul sinks earthward," Anwyn said, "and yet if you would you could relent now and retain that power which is yours."

"I cannot."

Anwyn held out her hand. "The Claddagh ring upon your finger, the torque upon your wrist, the shield broach at your breast that binds the shawl." One by one Maia surrendered her powers in the virtues focused on her person. She began to fade before Anwyn's eyes. As the light that shone within her paled, she took on the shade and complexion of what was wrought in the deep below.

"It is enough," Maia whispered. "I shall cease to be."

"Immortal sister," Anwyn said. "That which is not shall never be; that which is shall never cease to be. Yet where you go the powers are different and draw gravely to the realm of the unmaking of things.

"Turn back now. Restore those powers given you to shed your sweet influences in the earth: that the winds blow sweet, the flowers blossom, and green and living things flourish in the light."

"It cannot be," Maia whispered, feeling the cold magnetic draw of the deep bear her down.

"If you will descend into the shades and come to the wood of Erebus, you must," Anwyn said.

"I know why I am doing this, sister," she said impatiently, for with the fading of the light came unbidden the influences of the world, rising upon her until, a shadow of what she was, she stood at the well of anguish, her substance in the place of shaping diminished.

"The shield broach at your breast that holds the shawl in place, the necklace of lapis beads about your throat, the pearl at your eyes and the diadem; all these you must yet yield."

And yield them one by one she did but stopped short of yielding the diadem. "Having surrendered all my powers, how shall I return?"

"What is written in the innermost parts of your being, or ever you were formed in the flesh of these realms, can never be taken from you. You will find the power you seek within." Anwyn said.

"Never forget, the way is through the waters. They who dwell in the Shades cannot cross over, but the waters shall be your refuge, salvation and return: stay close to the waters for they will receive you should you fall into harm's way."

Maia struggled with the thought. It was her last vestige of consciousness of what and where she was, her last moment of awareness in Whiter Morn. Did she indeed know?

"The robe of radiance and the diadem," Anwyn said.

The three shields loosed, Maia stepped out of her gown and stood naked at pool's edge gazing down into the swirling waters, unable to act.

"The diadem," Anwyn said.

"Thine eyes did see my substance, yet being unperfect," Maia whispered, remembering: "and in thy book all my members were written… or ever they were." Weighted with the weariness of the world she removed the shining coronal from her dark hair, and with a final affirmation in life stepped into the pool, and vanished in the depths.

Anwyn knelt and carefully folding gown, shawl and girdle together, placed the precious emblems of Maia's virtues within and whispered after her sister. "These I shall keep, however long, against your return." She would not turn away but lingering light broke a moment on the summit of Whiter Morn; a ray of the sun temple touched into shadowed sanctuary, and she knew at once what she must do. From among the talismans that signified the measure of Maia's virtues she chose the silver torque. Holding it in her hands she dipped her arms in the water and whispered, "Go, seek your mistress out; bring her home to us."

It uncurled a silver serpent that slipped away into the waters to do Anwyn's bidding. She watched the little flash of lightning vanish into the depths, and only when it was long gone did she reluctantly turn away.

After noon prayer the true believers seeped out of Iban Tulua Mosque into the prickly heat. Desert winds harried Cairo, whirling dust clouds down El Saliba Street from the mosque at its foot to the fortress walls of Saladin's citadel on Mokotam hill, where the usurper held sway. Cloaked and hidden behind veils and keffiyeh the city labored on, merchants taking their goods indoors when they could; street stalls raising screens against the dust where they could not. But the heat prickled, the dust crept into everything, and every frustration a dry stick to fuel the fires of repressed rage.

Fury at the usurpation of the youthful Sultan al-Nassir Muhammad and the accession of Baibars al-Jashnakir, the incompetent; fueled by the fears and frustrations of a dying economy and threatening Mongols, smoldered. All it need was the live flame. It came in the person of one of Baibar's lieutenants, arguing over the price of a piece of silk he wanted for a woman. When he could not get it he took the silk and walked away.

The merchant complained loudly and ran into steel. A crowd gathered; the soldiers drew on them slaying the merchant. The throng took up rocks and stoned them to death. Then everyone was enraged; a mob moving as one, rampaging through the streets toward the citadel chanting the Sultan's name: *Rukn...Rukn...Rukn* - demanding Baibars appear.

Into the midst Caron came in pursuit of the Berber slavers who sacked Flegetanis' villa in search of the stone. Finding nothing they took Siduri, for he coveted her and this was Sultan Baibars' price. Was he not *Rukn*, pillar of the Mamluk dynasty? Who was anyone to refuse him? The servants had resisted and there was bloodshed.

Shirazi come home from Alexandria; Caron from his desert vigils, but half an hour late, returned to urgent pleas of a shattered household. Caron at once took horse, following swiftly until he overtook the slavers on *El Saliba* Street. Caught up in the mass and unhorsed he struggled on foot toward them before they made the citadel, but could not advance against the mass.

"Listen to the wind," the wind whispered. He could hear it soughing in the roof tops: out of the desert, dry, dust laden, it surged through the streets. And as there was nothing to be done, Caron flowed with it, searching its way through the dust and debris of protest. And still he fixed his eye on the slavers who held Siduri and found his way into the flow that enveloped the horsemen as they struggled with her toward the Citadel.

"Listen to the wind," he whispered. It moves freely, and living things bend and bow and move, or break. If he could not fight the crowd perhaps he could shape it. First he must find the center of its force. It swayed in the mass like ripening wheat on a storm wind, but there was always a center; somewhere in someone the urge erupted, took flame, and fired the fuel of volatile passions.

"*Rukn...Rukn*," he chanted feeling his way into the heart of their discontent, venting their anger at the Sultan Baibars. The words were the simple pivot of the force that drove them, and as a little rudder can change the direction of a great ship, so the tongue a mob. In the stillness on the wind he found her, a woman altogether unconscious of her part on whom it turned, and he shouldered his way through the mass toward her.

"Listen to the wind."

"*Rukn...Rukn*," she shouted when he came to her.

"*Rakin…Rakin…* useless," he shouted over her. Their eyes locked and lit with passion and a fire blazed between them.

"*Rakin…Rakin,*" she took up the cry, well pleased at the turn on words to loose what she really felt, what he had given her permission to feel.

"*Rakin…Rakin,*" her cronies took up at once. In a minute the turn of phrase swelled through the mob and loosed its anger at the Mamluk lord who usurped the young sultan, devastated the economy, and fought a feckless war.

"*Mawla…Mawla…* protector," he shouted, holding her with his eyes and slapping the flat of his hand on his chest. He pointed to Siduri flung across the saddle. "*Sariqa…Sariqa…* thieves," he shouted, shaking his fist at them.

"*Sariqa…Sariqa,*" she took up the call, and the call swept through the mob like a fiery wind through the desert. In moments the wind swept over the thieving Berbers, pulled from their horses and trampled by the crowd. But helping hands uplifted Siduri, and borne on the crest of the wave toward the warbling ululation of the women gathered at Caron's side, she was returned to him.

Cairo burned through the night, a dull red glow lighting the horizon. Attention was on the riots. Shirazi and Siduri at his side, Caron sailed Nephthys quietly by Rawdah Island where the Bahti Mamluks fortressed, then drew ashore to take his leave.

"And shall we not come back again?" Siduri asked.

"I have given means to those who will keep the estate until we do," Caron said. "But we cannot risk it now. When the mob is stilled Baibars will come again for you. You will be safe with Shirazi."

"There is more to it," Siduri said. "It's that woman, isn't it, the Lady Madelon with whom you dallied; she covets you and the jewel my father sought. They thought it hidden in the villa but could not find it. And now to that end will use me against you."

"It is well hidden."

"They took me in ransom, Hugues, and would keep me in the Citadel until you submitted or sell me to Baibars for their trouble. What is this jewel they seek?"

"It has many names but in the old tongue, *Uru An-Na*, light of heaven.

Your father called it Aton, the sun stone, believing it once the apex stone to the Benben of the Great Pyramid."

"We shall have no peace until this lady Madelon has the stone of us. Give it to her and be done. We can settle this now in Alexandria."

Caron shook his head. "That is not the way of it."

"I heard once my father say the shining ones could bring an end any time they chose," she said deliberately. "An end to what, I asked? He said only that all power was given them to fulfill their purpose in the earth."

"I believe it is true."

"Then if you have power why do you not use it? Why not destroy them who persecute you and bring an end to this?"

"Destroy them?"

"I know what you are, you, my father, both lords of light; the deathless ones, sent into the earth to keep watch over man as he struggles back toward the light.

"But if after all these thousands of years man remains defiant, adding to the bitter brew of the ages, you know as well as I it will only get worse, and with untold suffering to come.

"Why do you not act? Why not at least in this little thing use that power granted you to bring an end to this persecution and leave us in peace."

"And you believe I have such power?"

"I have seen you reborn, and more than once my father transfigured in the light; if at the last he gave his life for you, he must of you expect great things."

"We shall settle this but not in Alexandria," Caron said. "You and Shirazi will sail with the Ariadne for Crete and stay there, until this insurrection is done and the young sultan is brought home and it is settled in Egypt."

"Not without you."

"Yet a little while."

"Very well," she demurred. "I have learned not to wait on your return. I will see something of the world while you are gone."

"And well you should."

"I have heard Demetrius speak of it: I shall have Shirazi take me to this carnival in Venice." She gave him the look. "Perhaps, instead of you I shall marry a rich merchant and sail the seas with him."

"Why trouble yourself?" he countered. "You're already rich beyond telling. Take, instead, a lover."

"I know when a woman is fair lovers are plentiful." She turned away abruptly. "What I want for is a husband I can trust to the years."

Caron took the pouch from about his neck and put it about Siduri's. She felt at once a glow of its warmth at her breast. "Here is the jewel your father sent me to find. Keep it safe in memory of him. And when I come again we shall speak further of this. Or, if you will not, do as you see fit to make an end of sorrows."

She shivered, her whole body shook, as he gave her the stone but she took it, and immediately she felt it bond and her troubled heart shift to the shape of something different than she supposed, for which as yet she had no words.

"Will it change me?"

"It will."

"Seven years you went in search of this, and I waited. Yet another year came and went as you tarried among the women of the Blood Royal, and still I waited for you. You renew your youth like the eagle, but for me the years pass. I fear I shall never have you so long as you are possessed by this."

"I do not think I shall keep this for you, Hugues," she said. "I shall keep it but a little while and if you do not soon return then I will barter with the Lady Madelon who covets our lives and be done with it."

"Ask only whom it serves," Caron said. "And in the answer given, do with it what your heart allows."

"Oh, come with me now and be done with this."

"Your father, my friend, bade me first go into the desert in search of the master Origen. I must honour that."

"I fear you will never stay with me."

He held her a moment and she trembled in his arms. "When I come again, it shall be as you wish."

Rakastaa had not yet made peace with herself over Morgon Kara's seduction of her soul. He was more skilled than she in the arts of shaping, and she thought to learn from him; that mistake nearly cost her life, for he used her mercilessly to work his will in a realm she knew nothing of.

Because thou lovest the burning ground I have made a burning ground of my heart. That Thou, Dark One, haunter of the burning ground, mayest dance the eternal dance.

Lines from a poem one of her drovers sang, as they descend out of the Himalayas into the foothills of northern India, and appropriate, she thought. Her heart was a burning ground, parched as any desert, and she sought in herself the cool clarity of waters to extinguish the fires, but it had not come easy. She was scarred once more by a man and swore nevermore. Still, the spell her father wrought upon her held true; taken against her will the man who would force her perished; as had Morgon Kara, who like a parasite sought to steal her life to feed his own.

"Purusha, I do not know what will become of this journey." They paused in their descent by a late summer meadow refreshed by a mountain stream. "It may be I shall go on myself in search of what I must. In the meantime I have spoken with those who know our affairs well; they will answer to you on my behalf."

"I will go with you."

"Not this time. I will come again, but this is something I must do alone. And the women need you. When you have met Patel we will make a bond with him. No longer will the caravans take the overland trail but descend into India; our goods borne by sea.

"You will watch closely events in Khotan. For now all is stable, and Bator our protector. Much of our wealth is portable property and I have reserves in many places of jade and jewels, silks and gold, along the trade routes. Taqsim is a good man; you may trust him. If it becomes too dangerous for you to remain in Khotan, send word by him. Cross the mountains with the women and take refuge in your valley until I come for you. When you have met Patel you will find we have an ally and through him we will conduct our business affairs in the west.

"You search for Caron," Purusha said.

"I must. I fear in slaying Morgon Kara we have loosed a dragon, and by my soul I believe Caron alone the one to name and master him. As a youth you knew him, when he dwelled a season in your valley under the tutelage of Morgon Kara. Have I read this well?"

"If anyone then him, yes," Purusha said. "But do you say you trust me with the women in your absence?"

"And they in turn will put their trust in you, Purusha. Do not think them foolish because they are women; there is much wisdom among them. Listen to them, treat them with dignity and honour and they will hedge you and our affairs from harm. I will send for you and them together when I am ready, but for now you must do this for me."

Purusha brooded on this change of anticipations as they journeyed down the mountain, but at length the magnitude of the trust she placed in him won over, and his manhood triumphed over childish disappointment.

"In those days it was said a maiden – dare I say one as fair as you – displaying a nugget of gold on her head could wander safely throughout the Mongol realms."

Patel stared to distraction at the beautiful woman sat in his garden; the veil of modesty she had drawn about her face and hair made her the more alluring to him. He had met her only twice before, both times when she was wed to her old husband, now deceased, but this time she had come of her own with train of goods and entourage.

Rakastaa accepted with pleasure the cup of minted tea and chose a honey almond pastry from the silver dish the serving girl placed before her. "But the Pax Mongolica is not what it used to be," she said. "The empire is breaking up into khanates, quarreling among themselves, and commerce along the Silk Road has paid the price. I myself was so taxed in one that there was no profit in the venture; they might as well have stolen my goods for ransom. Others less fortunate still have been pillaged by brigands: men murdered, women and children enslaved."

"We are not without issues of our own," Patel lamented, "and yet you have come through the mountains safely to us."

"Thanks to my protégé Purusha, who led the caravan through passes known only to him, I come not empty handed but bearing jade, spices, medicines, porcelains, perfumes, and many curious artifacts – much more in kind in stores in Khotan. He will tend to these and keep trade with you."

"Always we will find a ready market. But you did not come here of your own to tell me this; something you wish to ask in person of me, I think."

"I know you have done business with Egypt by sea. In these times that route west I think, swiftest and safest. I've come for your advice. I want a ship and crew to trade in deep waters."

"Are you looking for advice or a partner?"

"I would think of you as partner in trade."

"And I am more than willing to enter into profitable relationship with you in this."

"You already have contacts in the west."

"Flegetanis of Alexandria: for many years I have done business with him and old Jakob he said, reminiscing. "Flegetanis still lives – I have not heard otherwise - but Jakob is dead, his son taken up where the father left off.

"And in truth your timing is excellent. Captain Jahleel, one of Flegetanis' trusted captains, awaits my caravan in Daybul to sail for Suways." Patel roused with the thought of partnership in trade with this beautiful woman. Perhaps Parvati had sent her; even Kali.

"Have you heard of the Serene Republic of Venice?" Rakastaa asked. "Years ago a citizen of Venice came to Khotan and dwelled a time in my husband's home. He spoke of an ocean beyond even the Mediterranean Sea; of holy isles at the end of the world, beyond which there is nothing but endless sea."

"Flegetanis will know of this; he has ships as well in the Mediterranean Sea," Patel replied, curious where she was going, and then it dawned on him: "you want to make the journey yourself."

"I want to trade with Venice, and it makes sense to know the kind of people we're trading with."

Patel had been sizing up people for years, and there was something personal in this beyond line of trade. "It has something to do with who she is," he thought. The green eyes and fair hair were not of his world. It seemed to him she wondered how she had come here; she was looking to go home. And as his wealth was likewise involved in the venture he dared ask: "What is it you are really looking for?"

"Who I am looking for," she said. "I will not let it interfere with our business, but for reasons I cannot speak to I must find a man who once came this way."

"The way you go," Patel said, smiling with his eyes: "dangerous no doubt for a man, let alone a woman alone." Dangerous, too, to his affairs were they in trade together.

"With his captain's help I shall seek out Flegetanis," she said, "make arrangements concerning our business, and only then turn my attention to this personal matter. And while I am abroad Purusha will see there is no interruption in trade."

"May I know him?" Patel said: "the man who once came this way."

"I have only a name: Caron, Hugues Caron."

Patel slapped the palms of his hands together. "By my word," he burst out, "we are well met."

"I don't understand."

"No, not yet, but you will. When Shiva weds Parvati, he will give love's body back to his soul. Shiva dances and Parvati seeks her lord."

"You think I look to wed Caron?"

"Have you met the man?"

"Not exactly," she hedged.

"Then you are guided by the passion of Parvati. Why else would a woman seek a man she has never met; willing to journey to the ends of the earth to find him?"

"He needs me," Rakastaa said, and smiled coyly. How else to explain it? Put that way it was best left alone.

"We shall make arrangements for you with our captain Jahleel. You are already half way there, my dear," he said, excited at the prospect of lovers meeting; excited at the prospect of a celestial event incarnating into his otherwise mundane life.

And then it dawned on Rakastaa. "You know him."

"Come this way but two years ago. Hugues Caron, the man you seek, is the son of my old friend Jakob, partner in business with Flegetanis of Alexandria. Find one and you will find the other."

Rakastaa was astonished.

"And when you have met Caron tell me I am wrong. You will find in him, the passion and austerity of Shiva and something more. The lord of light is in this measure, and compels you irresistibly to him."

8

The Shades

It was cruel captivity. Deprived of all he'd imagined exile in the Shades might be: the indomitable will of a fallen angel, a thwarted titan, striving against his oppressors to rise up in glory yet to come. Instead, deprived of his core, mostly he just didn't care: appetites, lusts, desires, passion to possess, to seek, to strive, to achieve, all stripped from him. Only a brooding pride remained to aggravate a futile existence; reminding him he had lost everything yet continued to exist. And there was ire: he clung to that as his sole hedge against nothingness.

He had almost won, but vanquished in an apocalypse of light that rent nerve from sinew, until he pleaded for Purusha's dagger thrust to bring an end. He had not expected this: like a great banyan tree, branch and trunk and roots of the iron dark wood of Erebus spread out as far as eye could see. And in the gloom, shadows of what once they were, listless figures drifted through the wood, for no particular purpose, to no particular end.

He was on the edge of existence. The dark earth beneath him gave way to the waters of the unformed. Even so, high above the wood, here and there the stars still shone; turning in their appointed courses though ancient night, if radiant with cold indifference to his plight.

"It all comes to nothing," he whispered. It was why men took up cause against others, he thought; desperate for the illusion of meaning in their lives. They craved, strove, envied, swaggered, bullied, slain and were slain; all to avoid the horrible silence of insensible nature. He should like to have thought what had become of him was punishment, for punishments have purpose and an end. But this was consigned indifference; it gave him nothing to press for, against, or anything to conjure with. He could do nothing but let things be.

But he was not alone among the fallen Watchers. One of these came to him in his soulless confinement. "You have gone as far as you can go alone," he said. "This nothingness will pass, and you will remember how this came to be. "I am *She-me-haza*. And when you have remembered, *Sham-she-el*," he said, "for your works in the realms of earth, we shall enlarge our kingdom in you." Then he was gone, leaving Morgon Kara alone in the cold with the tinder of a hope.

The woods were beset with phantoms. Fleeting forms of hungry ghosts looking to attach: parasites here as they had been in life, they clung to existence on the margin of the world. In and out of the woods of Erebus they flitted. He paid them little heed as a stray moth blown on the wind; so long as they found nothing in him to feed upon, they were off. And yet he wondered after them. There were moments he felt pangs when they hovered by and with empty faces stared into his own in search of something that meant anything to them.

He quickly learned to feel not even the little they clung to in the petty residue of their lives. Yet there were times he thought he saw in those phantom forms the faces of those whose lives he'd taken to feed his own, contriving to exist beyond his allotted span. He saw mockery in their famished eyes and wondered if he came to dwell a time; to let all he had been dissolve into the residue of creation, until the shape of his soul should dissolve, leaving only a crazed phantom on the edge of existence.

But after *She-me-haza* came to him his ire intensified into surges of welcome anger. Mistakes had been made, but always he had sought to serve the greater good by striving to refashion the world that was. Had he not these many generations contrived to remain in form; not for his own sake but because it is the doom of men that they forget, and ignorant labor in the ashes of what once was. He would create a new age and kingdom of man, but rendered dust and ashes by the shining ones, who loosed upon him an apocalypse of light, condemned him to the Shades.

He languished but did not forget *She-me-haza* came to him. And then there was the *Ishta-deva*, an insubstantial phantom, fluttering on the verge of his consciousness. "*Sham-she-el*," she ever whispered, "Do not fret over this imprisonment. Remember me and I will come for you." And when she came in vision he would stare after her into the abyss of stars above and her image in starshine. Nothing he saw but heard and would reply only, "I am Morgon Kara," and she would reply: "*Sham-she-el* you cannot die. You are elemental, your existence spun into the weave of creation. A hundred forms you have taken but always *Sham-she-el*."

In her presence there was anger, and then again indifference like dark waters arose upon him. Always Maia was illusion, and like illusion caprice and he wondered now if she came to him in this way to taunt him for his failure. He did not trust her. She had more than once abandoned him over her displeasure in him and in his moment of need, nothing.

"You are *Sham-she-el*, he who once taught men the songs of the sun, testifying to what is in the light. You are he who forgot what is in the light is beyond the mind, and took what you could grasp to yourself. Do I name you right?"

This was not Maia. He thought the tone wrong, but unsure he answered: "Do not taunt me *Ishta-deva*. I have left no will of my own and am in your hands."

"Caught up in the realms of earth, so much you have forgotten. I brought you to me to inspire your awakening. Long before you knew I guided your path; I showed you things that were no more and might yet be.

"You are not Maia."

"Maia is illusion. I am Irkala of the Shades, and from everlasting you belong to me."

"You waste your mockery on me. I am empty of ambition, and will venture forth no more."

"Nevermore," Irkala said: "until the power of the Aton is attained; the light of heaven ours again." And she was gone.

"Does it not trouble you to languish in this place and come no more to Whiter Morn?" Morgan Kara lifted his head and it was Maia stood before him. Full form she was to him now, as tangible as the Shades allow, firmer in presence than the one who called himself *She-me-haza*. And still he asked. "Lady of illusions, is it you or one of your deceptions?"

She sat beside him and laid her head in his lap, and feeling the warmth of her in him. "I am come for you," she said.

"There is no escaping this place. Stay long here with me and you, too, will care for nothing."

"Some say beyond the Archaeus above and the waters below, the great void of the unformed is all there is," she answered. "If that is so, is it not ours to shape as we will?"

"Have you come to taunt me?"

"Come to take you from this place."

"To wander in the void: I will have none of it; let it end here."

"To walk again in the earth, where ambition lies," she said. She took his hand and bade him rise with her. "When we possess the Aton all will gather to you. And they, who languish here, their powers locked in the vault of the deep, shall rise up to empower you."

He followed meekly, like a pet feeding at the master's hand. As she led him through the wood, the hungry ghosts flitting about like moths to a flame in Maia but daring not come close; instead, looking for something to attach reflected in Morgon Kara.

In the distance a beam penetrated the iron dark wood and there was sound of falling water. She made toward this, for it was through the waters she had come, and through these she must return. He winced at the half light as they came out of dark wood to the margin of a once great city; buildings fallen into ruin, stubs of a forgotten time, lit by russet glow emanating in the midst.

The broken city sprawled to the horizon crumbling into a shadowed plain of red rock and cracked earth. A vast expanse of great buildings some an hundred feet high, were worn by time and weathers into a surreal landscape of hoodoos: rough-hewn, standing stones rising like giant worn stalactites out of the red earth. Arches, some whole, some broken, suspended on the brink of destruction, linked the hoodoos as passage ways between the crooked towers. And through gaping windows like hollow eyes in solid rock, fire lit sullen shapes moved in the shadows. But from one quarter of the city there was the sound of industry; the noise of broken creatures, gnarled and bent double, some half-men some half-beast, struggling to shore up its crumbling structures and build anew what the dead weight of leaden earth would take from them.

Even so, there was a rugged beauty to the city, like the badlands of a torn wilderness on the edge of existence. But where they came there was water. Among the dust and debris of the city, you could smell the sweet scent of it on the air, and here and there where it pooled among the ruins trees still grew, as if life had not entirely given up on what had become of man, even in the Shades.

"What is it called?"

"Ruin, the city of destruction: the end to which all human striving comes. Once it had another name but I have forgotten it."

"And there is nothing beyond this place."

"Only the Deep: the uncreated wilderness between the stars."

"And what of Whiter Morn?"

"On the highest peak of Whiter Morn the sun temple opens on the realms of light. Of those supposed realms I know nothing but for the light given us to shape chaos to our purpose."

"And those bound in servitude, for nothing more than being of opinion different than those who were victorious over them: what of them?"

"These would impose their designs. It is our duty in the Archaeus to restore all to what was intended in the First Time."

Morgon Kara turned his gaze upon the city. "It is abandoned to us," he said. Come out of Iron-wood, he was feeling strength and interests both returning even among the ruins, which in their own right he thought magnificent.

"Some still come from Erebus to walk the streets of Ruin," she said. "But they who in their time were worshipped as deathless gods brood and crave solitude to company; iron dark wood to light of day."

"And these deathless gods, what do you know of them?"

"Only that many thousands of years ago, those given to guide the fallen home to the divine design dwelled amongst and watched over them," Maia said. "In time, tired of a watch in a night that never ended, and believing they had right and power to do so they began to contrive ways of their own to set things to rights.

"Among these, two of the Watchers, *Yaqum* and *Gadreel*, conceived of combining divine seed of the Watchers with the fallen flesh of men. So doing they hoped to lift up degenerate man, and if not restore him to the way of the First Time, enrich his lot. They took counsel over this and their leader *She-me-haza* agreed, so long as they made a pact they would stand together in principle, for he did not wish alone to be held responsible for the decision after the fact."

"It was an audacious plan" Morgon Kara said. "It should have been approved by the Elders of Whiter Morn."

"Sometimes they are slow to awaken to new measures; sometimes they discuss things an age before change is wrought," Maia said. "Truth be told, they who dwelled in Whiter Morn had reason to be wary, for in the time of the great transgression man fell prey to the seduction of his senses. With the measure of powers under his hand he made a simulacrum of the substance of the earth, to enter into his creation. He was warned to eat only of the tree of life but disobeying, ensnared in the flesh of creation, he fell into the tribulations of the flesh he made, and would not repent.

"No, the Elders must reject what the Watchers intended; the divine plan for fallen man is not manipulation of the flesh, but resurrection and transmutation in the body of light.

"Nevertheless, a pact was made among the Watchers, male and female both, to mingle the patterns of their divine flesh and life force with human flesh in its fallen state."

"With good intent," Morgon Kara insisted.

"Yes, but what was wrought was beyond their understanding: It wreaked havoc upon humankind, whose very existence was threatened by this fiery adulteration of the flesh burned into nerve and sinew and memory of the race.

"In those days were giants born in the earth, offspring of the sons and daughters of God and fallen men. Of normal size at birth these swiftly amassed substance, influence, and forceful stature among men. And these were the Nephilim."

Morgon Kara felt excitement at her words. This is how he had come into the earth. This was how he had the power to sustain himself over the generations. He was remembering, but he must know. "More," he urged her on.

"In those days the way between the worlds was yet open, and the revelation of Whiter Morn and the radiance of the realms of light yet visible in the earth. There came the inevitable rebuke, they knew must come, but assured they knew better they turned obdurate, until at last these challenged the nature of the divine design, even to the threshold of Whiter Morn."

"They had cause."

"They believed they had found a way to restore man to a better place, out of the dust and ashes into which he had fallen. And, indeed, children were born to the sons and daughters of men exalted in their time. And to these the Watchers taught secrets of the Archaeus hidden from the time of the great transgression."

"What teachings?"

"What was needful for an exalted life on earth: how to subjugate the rays of the suns to human need; how to exploit the forces of the cycles of creation in the governance of waters and the life of living things; how to capture the virtues of the stars to imprint their patterns upon the soul; how to structure all that they made to exploit the forces and resources of the earth, so that there should never be want."

"Noble cause," Morgon Kara said.

"Weary with bearing the weight of the fallen state, the goal of these Watchers was to shape creation anew, a universe of living forms centering in earth forces, to supplant the creation centered in the realms of light."

"And now they are imprisoned in the Shades, despite seeking only to improve the lot of men," Morgon Kara lamented.

"That came of their confrontation to possess the Archaeus," Maia said. "There came a time when the Watchers, who remained true to the divine design, restrained the titanic forces loosed in the earth. These prevailed over their fallen brethren and prepared this place where their elemental powers are used to advantage, their transgressions, nevertheless, restrained.

"But not before they had corrupted the way of all flesh. The balances broken much of the world that was, was swept away in the great purifying flood; and a pattern established anew for the spiritual regeneration of the human race to the way of the First Time.

"Not all flesh perished in the deluge. The world around the residuum of the antediluvian world remained, and there are patterns yet in the flesh of the earth and man that haunts him still, tares sown among the wheat.

"And until that hour when the divine design of the seven worlds is again revealed in man restored, those here imprisoned may no more dwell in the earth in any flesh but in the Shades.

"It is why I have done what I have done," Morgon Kara said, eagerly. "For thousands of years men languished. What does it mean to have power and not use it? Having the power to bring change, the Watchers were not wrong to try."

"They challenged the light of the divine design and failing are captive in the Shades."

"And my fate is as theirs."

"No, I have come for you. We will dwell in my realm of the Archaeus."

"You can do this?"

"You underestimate my power. Even this realm, a shadow of what once it was, is a fountain head of force in the world. And where there is force I can weave pattern. We shall draw on its power to shape our world anew."

She took Morgon Kara's hand and they walked the streets of Ruin. And as they walked into the heart of the city they felt the streets of the city pulse with invisible force; a great stream of power pervading the ruins, rising here in intensity, there diminishing, shaping invisible patterns as it surged. It was altogether unlike the iron dark wood of Erebus; Morgon Kara wondered why those who dwelled therein did not come here for renewal, to ponder and contrive the way of their release into the world. In iron dark wood all the forces were at rest, but here the under-currents filled him with zeal.

She led until they came to the precincts of the temple. Four white arches defined the temple grounds, each leading from the city without into a great court where the ruins gave way with sudden surprise to an enduring garden, a shadow perhaps of what once it was, but still of a pale, sunny aspect, the earth moist to the touch; a pleasant relief from the dry, desolation of the city. By whatever gate you entered all paths led through the garden like a maze through the stands of trees, flowering bush and ground cover to a single gateway into a walled inner court and raised terrace where again the light intensified.

The terrace was a circle of white marble, inlaid with twelve black rays, emanating like lightning bolts from a dark obsidian core and fire pit in which burned no flame. It had the appearance of a many pointed star, but Maia knew it was a lock to take a key. From the gateway the path parted left and right and made an arc, hedged by twenty-six seats, raised above the terrace overlooking the dark sun wheel.

The paths met again within the precincts at a small domed rotunda; two erect marble columns defining a gateway within to the holy place. The path to the left led to a cauldron of radiant, blue fire; to the right a basin of waters. Maia led Morgon Kara by his hand through the archway toward the fountain.

"What temple is this?"

"Once we called it Dayspring, but it is now the Temple of Seals. Here in the city of Ruin seals are set upon those powers once gifted men, lest by his own hand he destroy himself."

She pointed to the small rotunda and the pillars that glowed. "Once a gateway to the realms of the Archaeus through which all might pass freely; now hedged by powerful forces that none but the pure of heart may enter in."

"Then how shall we leave?"

"There is another way known to the Sisters. I came through the waters and through the waters we shall return."

He followed her along another path that led past the temple and down to a sunken garden and a pulsating fountain. But as they descended, as if he strove against himself, a force intensified in Morgon Kara that thrust him back. What he felt he now saw. The force took shape shimmering and crackling around them, enveloping the terrace above in great serpentine coils: now white, now green, now red, shifting through the colours of the spectrum then returning in a near blinding blaze of white light that undulated in waves into the sunken garden.

"I can go no farther."

"We have roused the serpent power, yet but a shadow of those forces that were in the hands of those who dwell here. It thrives on the edge of chaos, where things are made and unmade, craving an opening to insinuate itself into the world." She led away from the force of it into the sunken garden toward the edge of the pool and fountain of waters. And there Maia bade Morgon Kara approach the fountain.

She sat on the ledge where it pooled and dipped her hand in the cool waters. The little silver serpent waiting found its mistress, coiled about her arm and firmed into a torque. She felt its power come upon her and knew she could command the serpent power of this realm, and leave at will. Morgon Kara was another matter; she felt the force of the waters repel him as it did the fallen Watchers, and his fear at coming near; she had not anticipated this.

"I cannot leave. I have no body in the earth and like those confined here I fear the waters will wash the last vestige of consciousness from me."

She must guide him slowly through the forces that hedged him out, one step at a time. "We shall find a way," she promised. "No more the flesh body of Morgon Kara, but in the flesh none-the-less, shall you return."

"It cannot be."

"Esquin de Flexian, consort of the Lady Madelon de Faucon, whom you sought to possess as you did Caron, bears the imprint of your soul."

"I did not then think him worthy, his sensual mind unfit; but now to be alive in the flesh… that is another matter." She stood in the sunlight with Morgon Kara on her arm, watching the water fall over a rainbow ledge into a clean pool among the rock. "He is a man of few arts," Morgon Kara said.

"Shrewd, and handsome after a fashion," she said: "ruthless in pursuit of power, he will make a willing subject until you gather your strength and find a better." She bade him step into the pool and toward the falling water.

"When my power was upon me I failed."

"You had not my influence full upon you, nor the influences of this realm, but as you wax strong you shall and together we will possess the stone men call sovereignty."

"It has cost me dearly to learn it can be possessed only by him to whom it is given."

"It is some spell the lord of the crossing has cast upon it," Maia said. "A spell made can be a spell broken."

Maia took Morgon Kara in her arms, and he yielded to her embrace; she would lead him through the gate of dark waters to surface in the light of her own realm.

Again she took his arm and stepped toward the pool and again was thrust back by a force neither could resist. Maia, too, was unable to step forward or enter into the depths of the pool, while she held to him. Morgon Kara was frozen as if in stone by the waters, unable to move, unconscious, on the brink of oblivion; and she feared to let go lest she lose him to the forces that drew him under. She saw his eyes glaze as the last light went out. He could not die but this was as good as death; the fate of any of the fallen Watchers who sought to return through the gate of the waters, a descent into oblivion.

"There is a way," she insisted, "I am promised there is a way, and shall have it."

"Maia." The voice was like dry, crumpled parchment. An old crone stood on the stairs of the dome temple, supporting herself with an iron dark staff. In her outstretched hand she held, as if scooped from the cauldron, a handful of blue flame. "Sister why have you come here?" she asked. "Is it to steal from me, or to learn the virtues of my realm?"

Maia turned to face Irkala of the Shades. Black as obsidian, but for her pale face peering out from beneath her hood, she stared at Maia. For all that she had heard of her, broken and roughhewn as native rock, and altogether unlovely, Maia saw her stature straight and her features aged and in a melancholy sort of way handsome still. But it was her cold magnetism that imposed itself upon the senses. Like ice so frigid it burns to the touch, Irkala burned with an isolate flame so intense it drew everything into itself, and but for Maia's own adamant presence impossible to resist.

9

Irkala

Irkala was the fallen sister, rarely spoken of in Whiter Morn but as wormwood; the distillation of bitterness brought upon herself. But when Maia thought on it, did she not have cause? For Irkala must reign in the Shades over the confinement of the fallen Watchers, and over the spindrift phantoms of those who would not let go to the waters of life. Her lot was inconceivable to the sisters, and she entered into the imaginings of their hearts with somewhat of an alienated majesty, and as an implicit reminder that no focus of influence was beyond the scrutiny of the Makers. And then there was a kind of prevalent fear that one day she might be released and another of their number must take up her part.

Maia did not fear this negation of all that she was. Indeed, she welcomed this encounter, if only to feel better about her lot. She was discouraged: seeing all her good intentions, incandescent visions of what might be, come to naught, corrupted by the bitterness of human hearts. Still she was startled, for Irkala came stealthily upon her, and she had not sensed her leaden presence.

And she came not alone, but with three fallen Watchers: *She-me-haza,*

Bez-ali-el, and *Armaros*. And these glowed with fire, drawing on her obsidian darkness that measure of force meted out to them in their captivity. Fearing for her shaman, Maia raised her hand to prevent Irkala whose touch was lethal from coming closer. And there was force in her still that took even Irkala by surprise. The crone took a step back, dipped her fiery hand in the fountain extinguishing the flame. Taking up water in her palm, giggling like a girl, she splashed a little on Morgon Kara where it turned to ice. Maia felt him slip away from her, held in Irkala's grasp.

"You cannot have him, sister; you cannot lead him forth through the waters against my will." She spoke in a voice of winter, cold and brittle, and then gentled, for this was her sister, and as she did her appearance changed. Irkala brightened, became more youthful, even handsome, but Maia felt a chill pass through her and suddenly old; the life blood of her influence drawn to Irkala, as if they might exchange places. Maia summoned up her strength and held Irkala at bay, though still she did not let go.

"He is elemental and cannot die," Irkala said. "I have but frozen the life force within him that we may talk according to our station." They stood silently together, letting their thoughts gather. Irkala would exact a price. Where to begin?

"Even those I've known an age in Whiter Morn are sometimes here and of a morrow gone."

Irkala suddenly roused, drew back assuming her old shape, loosing Maia from her withering grip. "Do you not think them taken in the light of the wonderful one?" She was anxious to know.

"Is there anything in the light?" Maia asked.

"You who weave water into knots; light into the ten thousand things, do you now say that there is no more to existence than your illusions? Perhaps I am one of these? Tell me dream weaver, if it is all illusion is this realm of mine nothing more than a dream from which I shall presently awaken… to nothing? If so, what is the point of it all?"

Maia shook her head. "Why do you serve?" she asked.

"You come to me here as if there was something meaningful to be done. What have I to offer you whose being is wrought in the light of the creator? The misshapen things of the earth that yet endure; the hungry ghosts that strive to attach themselves to the undying; all things that steal from life to feed like parasites upon the living: what are these to you?"

"It is not for them I have come: it is enough that you suffer them."

"You are discouraged, girl, but I must endure those who in life stole life from life; until they let go, dissolve, and swept away on the river of creation are no more. And it is never done. Legion upon legion they are who come to us, driven with such life as remains to them to rebuild the city of Ruin."

"And the elementals you watch over?"

"You know we must here endure until the last of days, in hope it shall be again as once it was in the First Time. But what shall become of us in that day is known only to the wonderful one."

"Where are those whose powers you restrain? Only three attend you and yet a host defied the wonderful one."

Again Irkala stepped toward Morgon Kara, whose frozen eye was fixed upon her, and again Maia reacted and stepped between. Like the scent of blood to a predator her vibration on the air drew bat like ghostly fleeting forms, the residue of disintegrating souls, seeking as they had in life something to attach, to feed upon and assuage their unrelenting hunger.

Irkala raised her hand, dismissing the drove with a flick of the wrist. "React and these will attach themselves. You have brought with you fear and desire, and on you the scent the world they crave; it has excited them with anticipation. Blind, they know not what you are for appetite alone drives them."

"How do they yet live?"

"On the margin of life they exist; in hope of finding release through another into the world. Sometimes they succeed and are drawn up from the Shades, parasites driving their hosts mad with their hunger."

"Loosed again into the world of men?"

"Those discouraged in life accept all manner of things into their hearts, sacrificing their life blood to the hungry ghosts of ancient ills that brood in the depths; oft times becoming that to which they respond."

"Is there no hope for them?"

"See how they flit about the fountain of waters, at once drawn and repelled, like moths before a flame. These are not immortal souls, but fragments of existence; the residue of lives ill lived. To enter again into the tree of creation, whose roots this world spring nurtures, they must dissolve in the waters of truth, but flee in fear their release."

"I begin to fear where I walk."

"You are one of the deathless, who abide to set to rights the patterns of the Archaeus for the regeneration of the world. It is that business we are about is it not?"

"For that cause," Maia said cautiously. She knew it well enough but Irkala?

"We have long anticipated your coming."

"Anticipated me?"

"Not by chance did you meet with Morgon Kara. We sent him to you. Not by chance are you come here now. All must act boldly to come free at last from this deadly cycle into which the world has fallen."

"Fallen, by reason of those now chained here in the Shades," Maia said.

"Choices made ignorant of consequences," Irkala said, "and the times are not now what the times were, for an age is passing and the light of the central sun of suns shall shine again in its radiance piercing clouds of ignorance that long ago marred our works."

"You speak as if the lord of the crossing spoke in your ear," Maia said, "for I have heard him say we are on the cusp of change."

"Have you?" There was envy in her voice. "Did he speak of me? Sometimes he comes in dreams intensifying my longing to be free."

But for shadows and fleeting lights among the ruins, and the three who stood afar off, Maia saw nothing that spoke to the fallen Watchers who brought man to the edge of destruction corrupting the flesh of the world with their own. And reading her thoughts Irkala replied: "The presence and powers of the fallen Watchers are locked in the vault of the Deep, and the Aton-Re's seal upon it," she said turning to the sun-wheel. "I have no power of my own to loose the seals; and so this realm is but a shadow of what once it was." She beckoned and the three shades approached more closely until they stood behind her. "Do not provoke them; they have power still."

"And I power to bind them in my service, if need be to compel you to release Morgon Kara."

"You have put off the talisman and seals of your power. Your illusions have no influence here; I am the slayer of illusion."

"Not entirely have I put off my powers." Irkala stepped back for she could feel the force of it in her words.

"The lord of the crossing has prescribed each our limits," Irkala said, "determined the nature of our powers and the exercise of dominion in the earth. So, I ask again, what power and purpose bring you to the edge of oblivion, for beyond the city of Ruin is only the deep of the unformed between the stars."

Maia sat on the edge of the fountain pool; dipped her hand in the waters and the little silver serpent stirred, wrapping itself about her arm in a new torque, firming with a shimmer. She felt her virtue rise, her influence wax stronger, and knew in a moment she might leave but for Morgon Kara. "We all have our roles, and were we permitted might play many parts."

"Do not patronize me; I know your writ is greater than mine but in your own realm. And would appear you have come to free one of the subjects of mine own to your purposes."

"It is the lord of the crossing who has appointed our parts in the divine design; yet under the heavens life is so brutal men break beneath the burden of eking out a meager existence."

As she spoke the three shades moved yet closer, intent to hear every word Maia spoke to Irkala, until so close she saw through the spectral glow that enveloped them, the rugged pain in their features.

"And so you wonder what it would mean for man to possess again those powers given him in the First Time."

"Would he not now struggle mightily to lift himself out of the darkness into which he has fallen?"

"Those powers are locked in the vault of the Ages, and sealed with seven seals," Irkala said.

"And if I had the means to loose those seals."

"Then you would possess the *Uru An-Na*, light of heaven," Irkala said: "the key to the Vault of the Ages, the promise that all that was lost might be restored."

"Do your powers extend to that or are these but words, Maia of Eleleth?" His was hollow as death, but no mistaking the edge of cynicism embittered by the ages, for it was he who led the fallen Watchers engendering in the women of the earth, flesh of the Nephilim.

"Be at peace, *She-me-haza*," Irkala said. "We shall hear my sister out."

"It has appeared again, Irkala; its return marks the beginning of a new age." She weighed every word. "It is come under my influence: I need only your assistance to secure it."

All sense and sounds and sights were drawn into her and Irkala a whirlpool of silence. Maia stood and waited; Morgon Kara frozen in time beside her; the three shades inscrutable, lurid-lit doorways opening on darkness.

Maia knew what she was thinking. She need not explain it. Irkala had already seen the implications. She would look to loose fire from the center of the earth to empower the fallen Watchers. And it was the loosing of fire from the center of the earth that brought the world that was to ruin.

"And you seek my help in this."

"My realm of influence is a world where men and women perish for basic needs, where death takes children in infancy, where existence a few brutal decades and life so cheap a man may be slain for the theft of a bread loaf to feed a starving family.

"I have sought through sweet influences to inspire men to rise above all this, but so burdened with eking out a living men dare not live. It is time those who labour in darkness are given means to lift up their heads."

"No mother of mankind could think otherwise," Irkala agreed. But we are as dry wells. Here in the Shades no influence flows, no fire shed its radiance to light our way. And look at me, an elemental withered by time into an aged crone, unable to die; these shades of masters who were, my attendants, likewise bound by stark necessity. I fear we have nothing to offer you."

"And without us what are they?" She had Irkala's attention.

"Without us they accomplish nothing," Irkala agreed. "Sealing the vault of the deep, keeping from man his birthright to possess his powers, we are in the valley of dry bones without power to change, or consciousness to comprehend."

"Then let us take to ourselves the power they have taken from us to shape a way forward, to a world restored," Maia argued.

"And who in the earth will focus these forces to your purpose and take the shape of your hand?"

"I would give Morgon Kara again flesh and presence in the earth that the stone of sovereignty come into his hands. And for this cause I ask you release him from the restrains of your realm." She glanced at the three Shades who attended Irkala. "Release him and I will magnify the powers of those who stand with me in this." It was a boast and she was by no means sure of it, but it was no time to show faint heart.

"What say you *She-me-haza?*" Irkala asked. And you *Bez-ali-el*, and *Armaros*: if Maia of Eleleth can free you into the earth, will you serve under her hand to do her will as you have mine?"

"If she can loose the pattern that binds us," *Armaros* said; his voice rose and fell like a rough gust of wind, "and it is your will that she do so." It was *Armaros* whose gift it was to resolve enchantments. Skilled in the making and unmaking of patterns he had labored long to break the seals on the vault of the Ages but to no avail. Well he knew the *Uru An-Na* stone was the key and the thought of possessing its influence enflamed his elemental soul.

"What of your sisters," *Bez-ali-el* rasped. He was the shadow of all that was made and would not yield to the light; ash of creation he strove to rise up and if sisters could be turned so might this captivity.

"They will rouse from their sleep of ages, throw off their lethargy, and create anew as do I out of the fire of heart's desire."

"And the stone of the Makers; truly, this is come into your hands?"

"Release Morgon Kara and we shall have it."

Irkala's withered breast swelled with emotion at the thought of being free again in the flesh, free to wander in springtime earth, free to indulge in the realm of the ten thousand things. If Maia could fulfill her promise, this was much to be desired. She knew Maia had much discretionary power in the earth; still she was cautious, even a little anxious, but felt the longing of those with whom she shared her bondage that an end might be made.

Maia felt her hesitation and pressed her case. "Our hopes, our fears, our aspirations, center in the clear light of the void. There is nothing written for this world by any wondrous being but that we ourselves write into the substance of it, and I am prepared to break these unnatural bonds that bind us and use my arts to shape a paradise of the heart, beyond the illusion of necessity."

"I confess," Irkala said, "you have thought far beyond my poor dreams in this, but I would be free of all restraints upon us, free to live as we desire."

"Return Morgon Kara to me sister, and he will deliver the stone into our hands."

"There is a way," Irkala said, "but you know there must always be an exchange in substance; one thing cannot be taken without another given."

"Ask what of me what you will; I will give it."

"In the time before the flood the Watchers took of the chosen women of the earth those who were fair and able to bear the seed of the immortals. They desired only to uplift the fallen state of man but failed for the hearts of men were corrupt and the world that was, was lost in a great flood."

"It is well known," Maia said, patiently for she knew Irkala moved toward the heart of the matter that would bind them in purpose.

"In those days there was wrought of the House of Enoch a plan for the restoration of the flesh that the Holy Norm might again be established in the earth."

"It was and is so to this hour."

"And those essences, the design of all things living, were sealed in the stone of sovereignty and entrusted to Noah as a seed of the Ages that first, a window might be kept open in the heavens, and second to bring forth life anew from the waters of creation."

"I have told you," Maia said, a little impatient, "the stone is within our grasp."

"Yes, but you have not spoken of the Blood Royal. It was an order conceived, was it not, of the Na Akhu-El sages, the lords of light, to preserve the untainted essences of the race?"

"It was."

"And create in the flesh anew a setting for the revelation of the sun stone."

"Well, it is so, and to this hour the stone is the lost hallow of the order, though they have but little understanding of what was put in their care."

"It is the duty of the sisters," Irkala said, "to enter betimes into the flesh of the Blood Royal to guide its ways. Now it is your time and it is by that means you will restore the stone."

"Morgon Kara has told you this?"

"How perfect to our purpose," Irkala replied. "For the spiritual regeneration of the human race, the stone must have a setting. If no flesh responds to the virtues of the stone the worlds cannot in man again be made one, and failing that humankind has no further purpose in the earth."

Maia was silent a moment. Was the price of her dreams to yield the order of the Blood Royal to Irkala? From the time of the flood Maia helped shape the destiny of the order, that some flesh true to the divine design might be saved. Irkala had not, but for her transgressions in that time served in the Shades.

"I say only to loose power in the earth we must have an altar in the earth, a threshold imbued with influence connecting the substance of our realms. The Blood Royal would serve admirably. You see, you must yield a measure of your influence to me, if I am to you."

"Yield a measure of my influence to you?"

"We are one in purpose are we not, Sister? To loose those powers bound here I must have influence in your realm as you in mine, a line of agreement drawn between us: you with your gift for shaping incandescent visions; I for mine to inform with fire those creations in the earth. And as this will intensify the influence and substance of the Blood Royal in the earth, you will have lost nothing and gained everything."

"And you will release Morgon Kara to me," Maia said.

"If we agree and these terms are met, he shall return to you to dispose of him as you see fit."

"Then it is well between us," Maia said. If the price was merely a line of agreement she had nothing to lose for their shared agreement was to restore man to the virtues and powers of the First Time. "And Morgon Kara shall again be incarnate in the earth."

Irkala shrugged. "A warning," she said. "Though he has had many names, do not forget your Morgon Kara is *Sham-she-el*, who taught the Nephilim to exploit the rays of the sun, by which they created abominations in the earth.

"Those powers diminished, he and other of the fallen Watchers, were not bound in the Shades but continue to dwell in the earth."

"To what end?"

She did not answer, but said only: "It was needful. So, you shall have *Sham-she-el* to your purpose."

Maia turned to leave but thought better of it. They had made a pact of power and influence, and yet she saw no sign but the shades of three whose force locked up promised little.

"I see only ruins and a wasteland," Maia said. "Show me how you restrain the life force of the fallen Watchers, and how this shall be loosed to our purpose."

"I am but keeper of the seals."

"Show me."

"Very well," Irkala said climbing the stair: "Follow me." Maia let go Morgon Kara's hand where he stood still as stone before the fountain, and followed Irkala onto the terrace of white marble inlaid with black obsidian. Irkala struck her staff in the fire pit at the center of the sun-wheel and it became a well of fire, rising in a serpentine spire upon the staff but not consuming it. The obsidian rays kindled in the flame to the periphery of the arc of the sun-wheel until the terrace glowed, a dark red star radiating influence into the unformed. But Maia felt restraint in it.

"In what is loosed there is great power, but I can go and no further," Irkala said. "I have influence here, but the Aton-Re has set his seal upon the forces of creation, and what here rises from the center of the earth is measured in response to the light focused in him."

And, indeed, there was a sun-wheel in the court of the Sun Temple. Maia remembered seeing it when the lord of the crossing took her hand and led her to view the kingdoms of the Archaeus from the summit of Whiter Morn. "Then there is no way to draw fire from the center of the earth to inform our endeavors beyond that measure given us of him?"

"That is the secret I now confide in you. The earth is full yet with residual force of generations past, locked up, awaiting him who knows the spell of it. The record of all that has been is locked up in the substance of the Archaeus, those patterns accessible by reason of the rift between the worlds."

As she spoke the terrace glowing beneath their feet gave way and they stood upon a dark mirror plane of glass mingled with fire and Irkala bade her gaze into the deep below. At first she saw nothing for she could not shift her attention from the surface of the terrace itself but when she looked into the darkness the fire that glowed vanished and what seemed firmament was a void, a rift in the worlds, descending like a dark well into the unformed.

"Let your eye rest where it will – the upper layers are most visible - then focus where you would see, for only then will the void reveal what is in it, and what of it is within you."

Maia gazed into darkness and gradually, as if some great multi-stratified canyon walls laid down by the sediment of centuries, the outline of the deep began to come into focus, layer after layer, each stacked upon the other.

"I see ruins," Maia said, "ruin upon ruin, kingdoms layered upon kingdoms; age upon age, each an earth under its own sky, vision upon vision come to… What am I looking at?"

"The depths of the civilization called Ruin, imbued with the residual substance of human lives sacrificed to shape it. These are the layers of sediment interposed between the Shades and the clear light of Whiter Morn.

"In the chaos of the world that is, any residual pattern shaped of force in time past can be loosed to purpose from the depths of the human heart. That is the power I hold in my hand, for I know the spell of it and may go down to any sky I choose."

"And how are we to use this?"

"By mining the residuum of resentments and grievances men bear in their hearts to empower and justify their deeds now. And you and I, without ill intent shall mine the residuum of the past to shape the future anew."

"And what is the spell of it?"

"Men are driven by fear and desire. The secret of the left hand path is the spell of it," Irkala said. "Master the fire that transmutes the substance of men's hearts, and you may impose upon those residual patterns that shape him, any design you choose. Indeed, there is no triumph, no tragedy, and no crisis that cannot be used to advantage."

"The left hand path is forbidden," Maia said. "It is black magic."

"So say those who have never mastered the path. Man is driven by concrete passions not by abstract truths. How then shall anything ever change, if we ignore what may be readily used to advantage?"

"But think not ill of it. Is it not the desire and longing of the human heart for a paradise restored?"

"It is an ancient longing of the heart," Maia agreed.

"And that shall be our altar of the heart in the Blood Royal," Irkala said, "the motive for their existence. To that end I will yield up the residual powers of the earth, riches and power to shape our way; you will inspire wealth to industry, means to beauty. And together we shall bring comfort in a harsh world filling the imaginations of men's minds with incandescent visions of what desire can achieve, bringing an end to the bonds of the past and ancient sorrows."

"And you know the spell of it; the way of loosing this force to our purpose," Maia said, trying to adjust to having stood one moment on white marble, another in the midst of dark fire, and now over a yawning void the strata of the world of Ruin exposed beneath her.

"Did I not say you had come here to learn of me?" Irkala said. "And I would also learn of you the powers of your realm, of inspiring men to visions of what might be. Look deep into the void until you can see no deeper and tell me what you see."

Maia pulled herself away from the distraction of the ruins of the deep and let her eyes rest in the darkness where the canyon walls disappeared in the void and as she did one by one the pale stars appeared and in their midst directly in her line of vision a blue star. And when Maia saw it Irkala saw it, too, for the first time in an age.

"It is Whiter Morn," Irkala said, huskily: "Eden's gate that opens on our home. For long before the world was turned to ruin and far longer than man has piled ruin upon ruin, there was the world of the First Time for which the earth was created.

"This realm we call the Shades is but the ash of creation on the periphery of the kingdom of the sun. It will in its own time pass into nothingness and with it this realm of ruin which I keep against that hour.

"Let us hasten that hour, for it was said among the Watchers there will come a time when the gate of the heavens shall open. Then shall the light of the wonderful one so intensify in the seven realms that the ruins of the fallen world shall dissolve leaving God alone revealed in man restored.

"I assure you, sister, my purpose is entirely pure," Maia said. "And to my mind it must be by whatsoever means comes to hand to bring about the restoration of the human race."

"And what is the Aton-Re's will in this?" Irkala asked, a quaver in her voice, for it must be asked.

"I have come here from walking with him in Sun Temple," Maia confided. "He knows my mind and purpose, and asked did not forbid the release of Morgon Kara. Indeed, he told me where he would be found."

"Perhaps, even in his isolation, he now understands the impasse we face," Maia said. "He may well agree that what we do by taking initiative is the very thing he desires of us. It is certain those who have gone before have not succeeded, and perhaps as you say because they have ignored what it is that motivates man."

"Long and hard I have thought on this, sister," Irkala said. "I have had much time to do so, and have concluded there is a way. I have seen those who wealth and power most desire are willing vessels to the hungry ghosts and those forces bound in the canyons of Ruin. By and large these seek only their own, but we shall use them to advantage.

"True, they will be like wolves among the sheep, but one tires of the bleating of sheep. I will fire such fierceness of appetite in those who turn to me for power that all shall burn with ambition to shape a world anew. In the world they will deem it evil what we do, but we shall turn it at the last to perfect end."

10

Desert Fathers

Caron set out on the dark of a new moon. Fourteen days he journeyed away from the riots in al-Qāhira into the silent south-eastern Egyptian desert, until the weary beast that bore him came at last to the pass that opened to the Red Sea shore. By day and night he'd traveled, resting when he must and when he could. By day he advanced under a flawless blue sky into the heart of light penetrating the darkness in him. And by night under the stars, so close you could hear them whisper, he marked Orion's passage in the great procession of time: mighty hunter before the Lord; petty scorpion at his heel ever poised to inject its venom. And the seven sisters who ever flee before him - shall they never yield, or is there yet another story the heavens shall tell?

"Seek him," Caron whispered to the starry night: *"Seek him that maketh the seven stars and Orion, and turneth the shadow of death into the morning, and maketh the day dark with night: that calleth for the waters of the sea, and poureth them out upon the face of the earth. The Lord is His Name."*

The fashions of an age changed but the tales were always the same: of creation, the truth of love, and a paradise lost. And always back of it, always the same sad story of meddling: pride, rebellion, betrayal and loss; the seed of wickedness sown to destroy a soul. And when there is virtue, the tale turns to the task of the redemptive journey: to the turning back of the heart, through whatever trials may come, to radiant life; transforming fallen flesh into heavenly substance and star shine.

"Fire folk of the heavens," he whispered: "These shining ones will not let us forget what we have done, or what must be done to return to them; that we may see through radiant eyes anew the coming of a new earth."

In the course of his journey the moon came to the full and shadowed the stars. It rose slow but steady on the rim of hills, illumining the desert with soft light. And through the pass that opened to the Red Sea shore on a wisp of a wind came the smell of the sea and scent of distant vegetation. And the desert and the moon, and the smell of the sea opened him up like the ocean vast, filling him with the mystery of the night and inexplicable longing.

Larger it grew until it loomed on the horizon filling his sense; a vast, close moon, every detail of its leprous surface assailing his eye until he saw mountains and cliffs and abyssal valleys like the floor of some ancient sea shore, how a waterless realm, its nooks, crannies hills, and caverns now exposed to view.

And in sleep he dreamed again of how it was in a time before the moon was, when the dread one wreaked havoc on the earth. In that day the rider of the storm came on the dark wind of madness; black rain and hot, flocculent ash laying waste God's green earth, slaughtering the children of men.

Glowering by day and ablaze at night, its serpent coils filling the third part of the heavens, a writhing seven-headed dragon: it was looking for him. A man in deep waters, lungs seared and agonizing for breath, Caron thrust himself toward the surface. He broke free, heaving with fear and panic, staring out on a pitiless desert under a white moon. It was a world dead to the past, an old heaven and an old earth, pockmarked with scars and the distilled legacy of madness in the human soul.

He spotted them mid-morning, three Bedouin marauders in pursuit; a *razzia*. Caron altered course and they changed to flank him. He knew their creed: "*I against my brother, my brothers and I against my cousins, my cousins and I against the stranger."* And he was the stranger. These were infamous for their tactics of raiding and looting without direct confrontation, even one's own brother, in blood feuds that fell short of all-out war. Hit and run, deception, false information, feints and counter feints were all part of their strategy; the best of them rose to power in settled communities where their skills of deceit were seen as marks of honour.

But here in the open desert it was pursuit and the knowledge of the terrain to their advantage. They had little to fear in a solitary traveler, and so gradually they herded him toward the last ridge of hills that separated the rough from the sea. They were used to this scouting the desert for those seeking the pass, and he realized there would be those waiting to confront him as others closed in from behind. There was no avoiding it and he would not resist. He had little of worth they wanted, and they were unlikely to take a life to no purpose. There was no profit in blood feuds.

After weeks in the eastern desert his journey narrowed to a focus in a mountain pass to the coast guarded by two waiting Bedouin. He could see them clearly now, swords drawn across their saddles, waiting for the net the *razzia* cast on his flanks to close upon him. He might charge them but the beast was weary and it was not in him. Instead, he halted, sat still in the saddle and did nothing. Carefully they closed on him, but still he did nothing, until at last they encircled him a dozen yards off, held at bay by feelings they failed to comprehend. Was this a holy man?

Five minutes passed and Caron bade the beast kneel and dismounted. "Will you share my water and eat with me?" he asked, shifting the saddle bags. Cause to kill him they might find before the night was done, but an offer of hospitality was sacred and an offense to Allah to abuse. Still they were cautious, and it was customary to refuse the first offer.

"I have enough and some to spare," he said. "I am Jakob," taking the name Flegetanis had given him.

"I am Hamdan al-Bilawi." He dismounted. "You are many days in the desert." That was the second refusal.

"From al-Qāhira, but my needs are small and it is a day to the sea. Eat with me."

Caron gave the man a water skin. The others dismounted.

"Where are you going?"

"Across the Red Sea - to the Hejaz."

"It is not the season of the Hajj," Hamdan said.

"It is an *Umrah*," Caron said. "I have lost a father and walk the path of our father Ibrahim."

"Then we shall eat with you."

Caron rose at first light to continue on his way to the sea. The Bedouin deprived him of camel, saddle bags and reserve water before continuing on their own way to whatever doom awaited them. He relinquished what he had without complaint and they left him the half-full skin Caron offered to drink from to see him as far as it might on foot to the sea. He thanked them as they left and wished them the same kindness they had shown him, when it pleased God to reward them as they had rewarded him. They left bewildered not sure what they should think. Business is business but Allah does not look kindly on taking the life of one on a hajj.

Another day through the mountain pass and a day along the coast, and Caron came early on the third to the white limestone monastery on the sea. It was a sanctuary of white limestone buildings on several acres about a pool and spring with a stand of palms and other vegetation protected within walls from sea winds. A number of general buildings with shallow domed roofs, numerous manshobias as individual residences, and a Coptic chapel completed the settlement. Taken as a whole it reminded him of a small Greek village in shining white and azure blue on the Mediterranean, only here on a remote rocky prominence over the Red Sea.

He was greeted at the gate, presented himself as one sent of the sage Flegetanis to seek out the master Origen, and at once led to chambers and rest. His refuge was a quiet, cool room, a bath in a marble basin, and when he was done a fresh white cotton thawb and woollen besht laid out on his bed. But for those who attended to him he saw no one; asking they bade him wait until another came for him. When he was refreshed and attempted to walk about found he was locked in his room with a view through barred windows of the turquoise sea. He watched and rested and thought on the journey that began when he awakened to Flegetanis: a quest across plains and deserts and mountains, a passage through the wiles of men and the kingdoms of the world until at last this uneasy peace. He slept deeply and awoke only at sunset when a servant came for him.

"There was a time they murdered those who came out of the desert to us," Brother Enos said. He flashed a smile down the table to Brother Origen at its head. "It seems we've made some progress with them."

"Theft, the government tolerates among the Bedouin," Origen explained: "so long as it doesn't compete with their own. Murder it takes more seriously. These can lead to blood feuds and who knows then who will be drawn in."

"You have lost only your goods," Brother Lazarus said, "though they endangered you to leave so little water."

"I wonder they left him anything at all," Enos said. "What did you say to them?"

"I offered the hospitality of my water and food when they closed on me," Caron said. "And parting I wished them the kindness they wished on me."

The half dozen brothers gathered in Origen's chambers laughed heartily. Two he recognized, Enos and Lazarus, as they were those who came out of the desert for Flegetanis in the shadow of the Sphinx, when Rasheed sent Sadar to take Siduri and Flegetanis' life. He knew what they were. He had seen them uncloak and kindle in radiance too intense for human flesh alone to bear. These were Malachim, but he sat and took dinner with Coptic monks. He wondered if the like was true of brothers Minas, Cyril, Macarius, and Antony.

It must also be so of Father Origen. He was a man of late middle years and middle height, round Mediterranean face with deep brown eyes, angular cheek bones and pepper and salt beard: altogether affable. In bidding him come here, again Flegetanis had wished him only well, for already he felt he might comfortably dwell amongst them and go forth no more.

"You were hospitable and have put the fear of God into them," Origen said. "Likely, within a day or two it will dawn upon them what you said, what they have done, and they will come here seeking water and forgiveness, and incidentally return your goods."

"It was little enough and they are welcome to them. But it is Flegetanis bade me come here and I would know why."

"In good time," Lazarus said. "First, we would hear of your journeying; your life with our dear friend."

"Then you don't know," Caron said.

"Oh, we know full well what has become of him," Brother Demetrius said, "but of his colorful life we know little and hope you will share that with us."

And so long into the night Caron told the story of his life as Jakob with Flegetanis of Alexandria, until full of years he was renewed like the eagle, remembering who he had been, where he had gone and what he had done in meeting the shaman Morgon Kara. Of his journey to the west to recover the stone of sovereignty he spoke, and of Morgon Kara's effort to possess him to his purpose until Flegetanis intervened.

"Was it illusion what he showed me when I journeyed with him," Caron asked. "I fear that it was."

"He was skilled to cloak those patterns of life-force he found working in you in familiar forms; manipulating fear and desire to his advantage.

"It is what black magicians do in the minds of those who cleave to them in need. There is always something real attached, even elements of the truth, but caught up in the unresolved issues of the heart we are ensnared, and of this bondage to illusion comes the mirage world that beguiles human sense and soul."

Caron pondered this, and then with great care in the dark hours before dawn he spoke for the first time of the contest over his soul: his vigil with Flegetanis in the King's Chamber, the fire of ascension that took the old sage, and the falcon flight of his free soul into the presence of the lord of resurrection in the First Time.

They listened intently. And as he spoke he was drawn into a peaceful presence that reconciled all he had experienced: a presence that kept watch over eternity and saw in all he endured but a passing show; a masquerade which must at last give way to true identity. It was then he realized they knew him better than he, himself. For when he was done there was silence and he began to wonder if he had but made a fool of himself in the telling, until he realized they all waited for Father Origen to reply. "Have you yet discerned the underlying pattern in your journey; what life would have and where it is taking you?"

"At first it was me who journeyed." Caron answered cautiously. "Then I came to a place in myself when I realized it was no longer I who journeyed but life bringing the world to me. Yes, it was I who moved; but not driven,

I was drawn to where I was needed and for purpose greater than my own satisfaction."

He watched a smile light Origen's eyes. "Drawn to what purpose?"

"To do the right thing simply for the sake of doing the right thing, and to do so in the circumstance just as it was - right action for right action's sake."

A whisper of approval swept round the table. "And yet there is more, is there not?" Origen asked.

"The degenerate heart is a bottomless pit," Caron said. "To treat with it you had might as well pour out water in the desert sands for all the good it does; it takes and gives nothing and precious little changes."

"As you say," Origen replied, "precious little."

"If there is another way to deal with it I would learn of it."

"Corruption goes to corruption, but always we must begin with what remains that is true. And when dealing with human nature it is unwise to judge by appearances, but learn to look upon the heart for what is real.

"What breaks surface is but passing show; the troubled surface of the life-stream. You must learn to work with it where things are wrought in essence. Your journeys served a purpose, but mostly one need go nowhere in this world to accomplish what is needful but simply be where you are.

"We have learned to sow patterns like seed in the fertile deep of the heart and rest until their time is come. Your coming now is the fruit of one of those patterns wrought in the heaven of this world; a pattern shaped to set to rights what was marred in the heart, mind and flesh of the earth by man's fall into time.

"It is a great work that is undertaken with care and diligence; when the hour is come what is wrought in truth shall be irresistible, and the spiritual regeneration of the human race accomplished."

"If irresistible might it not be done now?"

"You saw what became of those unable to bear the light. In the four quarters of the earth, in the deep that lies below, and in the Archaeus where all is wrought, the world must respond to the intensification of what is in the light, or perish in resistance.

"And God is not willing that any should perish. Even so to every measure there is a season, and in the cycles of creation all will come to fulfillment.

"Our work is largely in the heavens, the hidden realms of this world; a place of shaping where what is yet to be, is wrought. Dwelling here in communion we keep watch over what is sown as these essences unfold in the earth.

"Teach me."

"The Master Flegetanis has instructed you in patience. Let this be sufficient to the day."

In the morning Origen and Caron walked the sands of the Red Sea shore below the monastery. They spoke of what he had seen when Brothers Lazarus and Enos stood with Flegetanis in the shadow of the Sphinx, in the day Rasheed sent Sadar and his men to take Siduri, and the old man's life. How had they known to come at that time?

"It was written on the air, in the pulsations of spirit," Origen said. "We call it vibrational perception – it's rather like hearing music no ears hear. And as it happened we had business with him in any case in another matter."

"You are Malachim, yet monks of holy orders."

"And Flegetanis is apothecary, merchant and sage," Origen said. "He always liked to be out among the people. Yet all together we are few and must take care. Here our love of the wonderful one is understood in Christian orders, and in this sanctuary we are free to be about the business of restoring the Holy Norm."

"The Great Work."

"Flegetanis always enjoyed the alchemic metaphor," Origen said. "Indeed, the work is to transmute base mettle into purest gold; earth into soul substance.

"In the time of the great transgression it was understood, because of the hardness of men's hearts, it would take time to bring the restoration of man. And so a staged process of ascension into awareness of divine identity was conceived beginning with an agreement between Melchizedek, lord of the Malachim, and the patriarch Abram. And this was the initiation of three sacred schools for the spiritual regeneration of the human race.

"The first was to address the purification of the carnal nature, the heart's obsession with fertility cults, by turning the heart again to transcendent God and life to His law. And so began the restoration of the divine design in the flesh. There were abominations in the earth in those days, and it was a long and demanding process watched over by the sages, until there came a time when those responsible gave into the obsessions of the flesh, spoiled the pattern of life and loosed destruction.

"Our Master warned, when the house is garnered and cleansed never to again to invite in what was cast out, or it shall come seven devils worse than the first, and these shall usurp and occupy consciousness in His stead.

"We now are in the time of second sacred school, a pattern conceived for the restoration of the mind to the mind that is in the Christ. Much easier this would have been but for the failure of the first sacred school; for the mind that centers in itself is driven by the unresolved appetites of the flesh, rationalizing its existence.

"And yet, as promised, a third sacred school is to under guidance and governance of the Holy Spirit is to come. And to receive this, a level of consciousness transcends the mind of man must awaken."

"Vibrational perception?"

"The Wind blows where it listeth..." Origen said: "Harmonization with the movement of Spirit."

"When the wonderful one walked among us, man betrayed, denied, would slay and so failed him," Origen said. "And yet something was accomplished; something of the second sacred school abides, and we remain to correct, clarify and guide all that has been that these cycles may yet come to fulfillment."

"And is that what you mean when you say set seed patterns and abide their season?"

"Changes may be wrought in substance before ever they enter the world. We must teach you how to work in this realm, while in the earth to let the wheat and tares grow together if need be until the time of harvest."

"And in the time of the third sacred school, how shall that be?"

"In those days the veil between the realms will dissolve, so what is wrought in the Archaeus shall readily take shape in the earth of this world. In that day the vibratory patterns of the heavens of this world will lift up the consciousness of those who respond, to a level where they may begin to participate again in the way of shaping, in the spirit of truth, the informing patterns of the world.

"It is a time yet afar off, perhaps, but already the way of it is with us.

And in that day there will be a legion of Malachim in the earth for the end times of the fallen world; when the tares are gathered up and burned in the fire, and the good grain of the earth given to the kingdom of God.

"And to that end we abide in a kingdom of little things, knowing all we do, wrought in the light, has great implications for all that is to be. Right thoughts, right feelings, right action for right action's sake…are these really little things? Or, are they as the Master taught, the seed of creation. Never underestimate the power of spiritual expression."

That same day Bedouin came out of the desert through the mountain pass seeking water. They approached the monastery delicately, asking to return camel and baggage to one who went this way; to seek forgiveness for interfering with the journey of a holy man on a hajj. Caron gave thanks and bade them keep the camel, for he would have no further need of the beast.

Caron and Origen did not speak again together for more than a week. Caron busied himself with the brothers in the monastery garden and for several days grazed the goats along the coast in the mountain scrub. Likewise none spoke with him but every man went quietly about his business, and though silent at table, there was singing in the garden at dawn and evensong.

But he was full of thought and by the time they came together again must know after what he had seen how this deviation from the way of the First Time had come to pass. After a subdued evening meal, when the longing in the air was palpable, the silence pregnant, and all turned to him expectant, Caron knew he must and so he asked. "I believe I know what I am," he said, "but not who. I do not expect you to tell me, for being told and pretending to what I do not know comes to nothing. To know I must awaken to myself; the self I have been no more.

"But tell me if you will how it came to this, for I have glimpsed a time when everything is as intended to be, and yet it is not: and instead we dwell in a world one vast stain of blood."

"A heavy veil shrouds with fear and shame man's vision and knowledge of the realms of light," Origen said: "and so he dwells in shadow. And yet the kingdom of Heaven is at hand, and once realizing that the question is how to let the kingdom come."

"But how did it come to this?"

Origen folded his hands in front of him and studied the young man while the others waited on his answer. "It is best I think to delay and answer this as we journey together."

Caron was not sure whether he meant in the realm of shaping; the Archaeus or a physical journey, Origen intended no such distinction. To travel with the Malachim was at once a journey within and without, for these would not separate but master the worlds.

"I know you are a skilled seaman," Origen continued, "and this will demand little enough of you. We have a vessel moored in the village up the coast. Tomorrow you and I shall cross over the sea to Midian, the land where Moses in exile dwelled.

"In Holy Mount is a sanctuary of the Na Akhu-El sages. I must compare the copy of a book with its original. I understand you have some art in that. While I am engaged, you may browse freely among our records of how it was, how it came to this, and the way of the redemptive journey."

"It may be a journey I took long ago, now half forgotten." And yet now Caron remembered his flight to the holy mountain when the rider of the storm wreaked havoc upon the earth.

"It will be a journey home, to stir your memory of the time when the ordinances of heaven were known, the foundations of the earth laid, and all the morning stars sang together...

"For in a time before the earth was, when we journeyed to create this home among the stars, we came forth from the realms of light to shape this place of habitation.

"In those days our bodies were not as they now are but given to dwell in the realms of light in our true flesh. And for many hundreds of thousands of years, before this sad interlude, we dwelled in this earth in our true flesh. And it was so, until the time of the great transgression, when in self-wilfulness and despite the warnings; some among us took to themselves the powers of creation. Dwell on that, for therein is the seed of understanding how it came to this fallen state, in which we now dwell, sat down among the ashes of creation."

11

Left Hand Path

Joseph of Arimathea traded in metals, with holdings in tin, silver, and Welsh gold. And it was here in Malta, pausing in their long journey to Albion, that his daughter Mary, great with child, communed by night with the guardian angel who kept watch over her and so the ways of the Blood Royal. That was the legend come down the generations, and so it was in preparation for her investiture every Domina of the Blood Royal must come to this place to seek guidance in the trials that lay before her.

To fulfill that custom, en route for the serene Republic of Venice, the Lady Madelon de Faucon lay over in Malta. Barbary pirates were the scourge of the sea, and no traveler was safe from them until he made harbor. The times dictated prudence, and in company of the Knights Hospitaller they sailed close to Europe's desolate southern shores. Even there, raids were common and hundreds of thousands of European Christians had been enslaved to the caliphates of North Africa.

And so the Masters of Hallows set a hedge about the fleet that no unfriendly sail should be seen. Nor did any inky blot rise upon the horizon swift sailing to intercept. What was more, Gisors assured Magda it was well within their powers to conjure up a storm to confound the enemy.

Yet the journey was without incident, and at length she found herself keeping vigil in precisely the same spot where long ago Mary found guidance, among the great standing stone of a temple ruin, ancient thousands of years before the lord of heaven and earth walked in the earth. Sweet with the scent of the day spent, cool with night longings, Magda was left alone under the stars. Well, almost alone for a guardian circle of knights a hundred yards off secured the perimeter; assuring none should come to disturb her vigil. Unafraid of what might come to pass, still she found it strange to be left alone among temple ruins. Some thought them haunted. Some felt the old stones cloaked in an aura of ancient memories, infused with the distillation of unfulfilled yearnings, and something lost. And it was true: once among the ruins she felt keenly the sorrow of those who came as if in exile, built this place of worship and then abandoned it along with the dreams that raised it up.

This temple was on a bluff facing east over the darkening sea. Turning away toward last light in the west she stared down a long passageway into the darkened temple and was afraid. Her vision ended but for the inky blot of the portal gateway carved of a single great stone. Beyond that was utter darkness, a dark mirror reflecting her fears. The more she feared it, the more it unnerved her, and yet there she must pass the night. But come the dawn, the rising sun would drive shafts of light through the portal gateway, down the central passage into the depths of the temple, to light the most holy place, and illumine a simple, stone altar.

As temples go this seemed peculiar to her, for though one it was three taken together in the shape of a clover leaf with a single path leading up to then diverging into three precincts. The tryptic pattern was repeated in the inner designs of each temple: within each clover petal an oval inner court, then a holy place and a final threshold leading into the holy of holies, where the three again became one.

The Master Gisors believed the temple honoured the powers of the triple goddess as maiden, mother, and crone. But the island priests saw in it the trinity though the stones were thousands of years older than their faith, and marked as were many stones of the Holy Isles with triskelion and spires.

It was Blaise who gave her the meaning she must follow, counseling as she entered in the temple precincts to enter all the more deeply into herself. The outer court, he said, was to be understood as evoking the sensuous life of her body, the inner court her conscious mind, the holy place the setting of her soul for the jewel of divine in the living God. And in all these dimensions of being she was to seek purity of heart.

Magda was not fond of Blaise, but in matters such as this she took him at his word. As the sun set, the temple in shadows, and one by one the stars came out to crown these ancient monoliths, she could feel power in the old stones and knew he was right: the deeper she entered in the more would be demanded of her. What must be must be, and so she it must be, and so she tempered herself to the prospect of passing the night in meditation, moving with the measure of hours from without within, toward the most holy place where the sun would rise to consummate her vigil.

She began, she thought, tranquil with the prospect, and yet crossing the threshold into the outer precincts of the central of the three courts her ire was roused toward Blaise. Old man telling her what to do; the memory rankled her still, how the masters insisted for the Domina of the Blood Royal the sun-wheel offered but one path, and she must walk it.

That was the way of all men; always telling you what to do and expecting obedience. And of course with that prohibition upon her she disobeyed. What woman of spirit would not? Well, then, there had been occasion when she kissed the fire, so to speak; flirted with the left hand path, if little more than to try her power. It had awakened passions she dared not dream exist. It made her feel mature to do so, all others unawakened: worse, now they seemed to her arbitrary and restrictive, confining and repressive, demanding all walk in the same way. She came to believe such stern prohibition contrived by those who had gone before to impose their past on her present; to limit and control the passions of the Domina to their purpose.

There would be changes when she was confirmed Domina; for this surely was that power, the gift of woman to loose fire from the center of the earth, her genius incarnate in the flesh of the world. Was she not the mother of all living, the informing influence that gave life to all that was birthed in the world of the eternal feminine?

It was this knowledge of what was in the deep that men resisted in women. Instead, they sought to repress a flame of fire so intense they feared it would consume and overwhelm their fragile egos and designs they imposed upon the world. The way of the left hand path - the cycle of forces: fire, earth, air and water - yes, she courted it as much as she'd dared under the ever vigilant eyes. Never committing, always retreating lest it overwhelm, for she had no instruction in this. She wondered why not take up that power rather than shunning it; transform the small, enduring order of the Blood Royal into a force to fearlessly shape a world after the heart's desire?

Without passionate purpose nothing changed, but under the Cailleach's hand she kept the path she was given to walk, longing for the day when one of the Masters would give instruction in the left hand but after twenty years the instruction she was given as a youth never changed: she was told she could not, indeed must not walk the left hand path to invoke fire before water, power before truth.

Flegetanis knew the way of it; now, but for the one who watched over her youth, there was only Blaise to consult. And as she entered the temple the memory of it returned. Maia, who first came to her as an imaginary play friend to a child; she must know the way of it. Over time she became as a part of herself, her true but secret name spoken only when she was alone and looking for guidance, until Madelon became but a use name only so her true name would not be discovered, her secret powers taken from her.

She had spoken only once of her imaginary friend to Branwyn of Wales, Domina of the Blood Royal. She called her perhaps, the image of her guardian angel in the days of her youth; and warned that only in purity of her heart would she ever come to know the one who dwelled in the light, the true voice to lead beyond all illusions.

In time Maia grew stronger in her and Magda came to believe, as it was said, the Domina of the Blood Royal was attended by a guardian spirit who oversaw her acts and whispered insight in the way. And as she believed it was her destiny to become Domina, she did not think it strange whenever she stepped into the circle of the sun-wheel that Maia came to guide her path; grew strong and dwelled with her as bosom friends.

And so it was in the temple ruin she turned to Maia. "My hour is come," she whispered: "Teach me the way of the left hand path."

Never before had she seen the one with whom she communed in the secret places of her heart. But staring into the dark of the temple, she felt her life magnified, the virtue go out of her, and Maia the very image of herself appear in a spectral arc of moonlight. And with her came another. With her came all her hopes and fears, and like a dark mirror reflecting back upon all her cares, trials and tribulations, Irkala came also with Maia.

"Who are you?" Her breast tightened, voice faltered, and she fought against panic to run but could not move.

"Do not fear us," Maia replied. "I have been with you from your youth. Trust me now." She cast her hand over Irkala's face and subtly she changed. Still the withered crone, dark as obsidian, pale face white with moonlight, it now seemed to Magda she saw in Irkala the image of the Cailleach Branwyn come to guide through her trials.

"You would learn the way of the left hand path?" Irkala asked. "If you did but know it, despite the restrictions imposed on you by your masters of hallows, you have scarcely walked any other way."

"What you seek is the mastery of it." Maia said.

That Maia was so accepting of Irkala made it easy for her to feel both had come on her behalf. "All my life I have touched fire rising from the well of the deep, from the center of the earth," she replied, "but always constrained never to walk the left hand path and enter into the flame.

"I did not make a wasteland of the world. I have watched the order strive with the ways of the world, the patterns that bedevil us, and done my best with what is given me, but cannot find the way forward.

"And if this is what it means to walk the right hand path, to entrench myself deeper in these ways; believing in what has been without hope of change for what might be, then I am prepared to seek another way."

"The past is dust and ashes," Irkala said. "Together we shall create the future."

"Look into your heart for the way you must go," Maia said. "Let your passions be your guide, for without passion how ever shall you empower your creations?"

"If you fear to loose fire from the center of the earth, stillborn shall all your creations be," Irkala said: "your future a succession of dismal, unrelenting days."

"My lips are touched with fire; I have tasted of the power of the fire, and what I have touched kindled passion in my will. But I am warned the left hand path is the way of destruction."

"To those alone who do not master it," Maia said. "Do you treasure what is in your heart?

"Above all else," Magda said.

"Full of suffering, men have made the earth," Irkala said: "And who knows better than woman that at their hands has suffered most?"

"Who knows better than woman what longings hide in the depths of the heart?" Maia said. "Men are ruthless in plundering the heart's treasure; taking what they can of woman in spoil and leaving her desolate."

"And you, with means at hand to change what men have wrought," Irkala said: "Who better than you to redress all grievances?"

"Walk the path that you must go. I will uphold you in it," Maia said. "Under your hand bring again warmth, pleasure and riches, vitality and vision to an impoverished race; bring an end to this sad interlude of fallen man."

"Let Maia shape what you would do," Irkala said: "And I will empower all that is wrought in her arts with fire from the center of the earth."

And still Maia hesitated for there was the inkling of a doubt. In walking the right hand path she knew to let the waters cleanse the psyche and renew the soul; to let old patterns dissolve and the atmosphere of heaven clear in her that she might see anew what life would shape, and so let wonders form. She understood in principle the way of it, but so often when she tried she could not find the stillness of the sages she sought. So many duties consumed her substance, so many responsibilities burdened her life, and so many cross currents distracted her from the goal.

It was a rough, demanding world she inherited. She had not the patience to endure her burdens without remorse, or with the tender care needful to let the delicate skeins of fine woven designs naturally emerge over an eternity she knew she did not have. No, of necessity she must act and often swiftly. Time passed her by and, like the Cailleach whose image now appeared before her, if she did not act boldly she would accomplish nothing but preside over the diminishing of her realm.

She had no desire to inherit a kingdom challenged by temporal lords who would but keep her as token and govern her will. Indeed, she had long since begun to wonder if this whole contrivance of walking the right hand path was nothing more than a device of the Masters of Hallows, to restrain and temper her will to their own, and subject her to the designs of the temporal lords.

From the shadows Blaise watched as Magda paced back and forth in the inner court of the temple precinct. She was completely preoccupied, inattentive to the process, and yet he could feel the forces working in her, informing her thoughts, shaping her next step; as always with her through issues of her heart and the pattern never pure. Whatever was the Cailleach thinking to let the mantle pass to Magda? She had known what she was, and now she would be the death of the order. Blaise understood for Flegetanis warned: among those sweet influences that infuse the earth, illusion bedeviled the impure heart of these daughters of the Blood Royal. This one was rich with influence and a would-be shaper of the world but not pure in heart to see with clearest vision the way of the wonderful one.

"What shall I do, Maia?"

"You have come a distance, but you must do more to consolidate and rebuild your realm."

Yes she must. That much was clear. She would journey to bind her nobles to her, and inspire vision of the way she would open before them. First, she would gather the women who had suffered Caron's black arts. She would refresh their will and bind their hearts to her, for it was the way of the Blood Royal to place the high born in the great houses of Europe, and through them magnify their influence.

The convent of St. Odile would serve to begin this work. Among the women who sought sanctuary there were the brightest and best. For these she had chosen the life of a deaconess, rather than subject them to fruitless marriage; until such a time as they might be given into marriage to benefit the Order. Her mind was aflame with possibilities and quick to realize that in the nature of man, though weaker of body, she had immense advantage of will and subtle influence; for men were easily shaped in their innermost parts to service, when the guardian mind is beguiled.

It was dawn. "Milady Madelon." Magda started at her name. In first light Blaise stepped out from the shadows of the standing stones. She feared for a moment he saw what she was about but how could he? And he said nothing.

"You interfere," she rebuked him.

"You have a great trial ahead of you," he said, kindly. "It is fitting you came here to prove the substance of your heart before you fall under the scrutiny of the temporal lords."

"We shall have the stone of sovereignty and bring it with us to Caer Myrddin. I know it. And against that hour I will gather up the response of those lords who will stand with me in this great consummation."

"The right hand path," Blaise said. "Only the right hand path is permitted us." He was prescient. Now sure of it, she was certain he knew what transpired between her, Maia and the image of the Cailleach, the one called Irkala. But her power was upon her and she was not to be restrained.

"Perhaps that's why over all the centuries so little has been accomplished."

"Perhaps that's why after all the centuries we still exist," he replied.

"Blaise, you may withdraw. It is a little while I yet need here alone."

"Old man, you do not tell me what to do," she whispered when he was gone. Still, she must be careful. She must bind the hearts of her subjects if she was to prevail. She could not mar the custom of the right hand path and expect them to follow. Her temporal lords must feel passionately about her and the way she led, but at what price this deceit? And then Maia stepped in.

"The esoteric ways of the Order are too much for the temporal lords to understand. And they need not: If you would garner their response touch them where most they respond."

"And where is that, Maia?"

"Wealth and power men most desire, for it subjects to them the pleasures of your sex," Irkala answered for her. "Give them what they want and they will yield substance and sovereignty of their hearts to you as if they worshipped a goddess at an altar of gold.

"This commerce of men, the buying and the selling of souls in the earth," Irkala continued: "it possesses the hearts of men with such great intensity that if he could he would gather the stars of the heavens to serve his industry; bind them to serve that beast, and the image it has wrought in the earth."

"As a bull is led to good purpose but by slipping a ring through its nose, snare this beast of commerce through its tender parts and shape a mighty kingdom that will fill the earth."

It pleased Magda well to hear it of Irkala, for it was after her own heart, but what of Maia who paled at Irkala's urgings, but said at last: "It is our time, Magda," she said. "We will inspire, uplift, and work magic in the earth: bring pleasure, passion, vision, warmth, and affluence to all who yield to our kingdom. We shall create a world new."

And as the three agreed in one, her mingling with Maia and Irkala come full upon her, Magda began to feel complete. She warmed to the vision, until she burned with anticipation of what she intended.

"I will journey throughout my realms," she whispered in the morning light. I shall gather strength and bind the lords to me with vision anew, until the time of the Troth at Caer Myrddin.

"And I will sojourn awhile in *La Dominante*, the most serene republic of Venice, where wealth and gaiety exceed imagination; where commerce has made powerful masters of men who trade in deep waters.

"There for the sake of the order will I enlarge my influence. I will bring my arts to the court of the Doge; fasten a ring in his tender parts, bind him and a thousand like him to our influence and service."

12

Oasis

The waters were welcome and no small relief, though but a pool and cluster of palms surrounded by sandy outcrops of rock; the land bone dry but for morning dew. The high, thin wisps of cloud that veiled their departure across the Red Sea turned sheer sheets and an easy wind on the water as they sailed, and Caron saw Origen took careful note of it as change in the weather.

"We make this journey to return a book?"

Origen reached into his pack. "You helped Flegetanis preserve old manuscripts."

"He knew where the books were taken when the great library burned. We would copy and translate them. Many he hid in desert vaults for a time to come."

"And some were taken to sanctuary in Midian," Origen said. "It is a work we have undertaken to preserve the writings of the Na Akhu-El Sages."

"What need have Malachim of books? In you the Word is inborn."

"You have seen the destruction of men. We keep the library for those who are awakening; to bring them to remembrance of what has always been present with them. Books have their place to remind us of what is in the light. But, yes, better by far even than holy texts is to dwell in the light."

"What book is this?" Caron asked, seeing the manuscript Origen held on his lap before the fire.

"It is the Triune Ray."

The fire was embers and little enough to read by, but Origen gave Caron the book and watched as carefully he settled it on his lap and with the reverence of a priest tenderly opened the vellum pages to read. Flegetanis had taught him well.

"From the shining citadels of Ra-i-ra's Eternal Sphere where we had lived and served through countless ages…"

Caron read straining to see: "*'…we journeyed forth into the deep of space unlighted, that in the vast void of nothingness, the desert places of the cosmos, the unused wilderness between the suns; we might build a place of habitation, a mansion in the boundless heavens, and a home among the stars.'* Whose words are these?"

"In the time before the great transgression he was *Tri-en-Ra*, lord of the sacred three. Always his spirit is in the world, for he must abide until the wonderful one shall come again."

"And does he dwell among you?" Origen said nothing. "And what is *Ra-i-ra*?"

"It is the kingdom of the sun," Origin said, taking the manuscript from Caron. "You may read it when we are in sanctuary. Tomorrow we shall be among the Nibiru; they will keep and shelter us while we are in the way."

Reluctantly, Caron surrendered the manuscript, lay back and stared up into the starlight sky. "You can hear the stars in the heavens of our earth. I have heard them sing," he said, wistfully.

Caron had heard it before in the stillness of the Himalayan heights. But there as here in the desert, where he now lay at water's edge under the night sky, he had first to pass beyond the noise of human nature and yield to the silence.

"I had not thought them shining citadels," he said. "But if what the lord *Tri-en-Ra* says is so, we were born of the sun and traveled a distance from the sun to shape this world."

"And in season we return."

And after days of brooding on what he'd seen as Morgon Kara sought to possess him; and what he'd become when Flegetanis gave his life to lift him up, letting go to the starlit silence was at first painful. So much it had taken to prevail, it seemed like death now to let go of all the world; to find himself now alone and at ease in an oasis in Midian with one he knew to be Malachim.

"And yet it is inconceivable we journeyed from the sun to create this world," Caron said, "I cannot get my mind around it."

"Can you not conceive of a vibratory realm higher than this in which we now dwell; one from which this should take its pattern but is now but a shadow of what once it was?

"You and I have journeyed through this wilderness; and if we were now to say, this place is good, here by this source of water and these few trees, let us build a place of habitation: is that so strange?"

"But this is real."

"Real to the flesh you inhabit; a cloak to the being you are of lower vibration to one whose body is light and ways perfection. It is our desires confused with material things that gives substance to what is mostly space and immaterial and bedevils the mind into thinking only that is real what we can see. In the confusion of our senses we have made a wilderness of what was once a paradise, no more reflecting here below to perfection what is wrought above."

"Then Whiter Morn is real; not illusion."

"Some of what you saw was illusion. Obscured by the veil of your yet impure heart, it was what you could realize in the light given. But, yes, the essence and realm itself are real and not illusion; though cloaked in forms age and custom understand.

We are given to abide an age, and still we come and go and when need be come again for the restoration of this world to its divine estate. And in a time to come, doubtless, you and I will commune again and in an age, perhaps, when knowledge is greatly increased in the earth.

"In those days, beguiled by their myth of progress, men will rush to and fro and up and down in the earth increasing riches in honor of the gods of forces they have wrenched from the earth. And a world whose myth is material progress will be cloaked with different customs and in whatever language will speak of it, a tongue that betrays poverty of consciousness, for the change is superficial and does not speak to the heart of human ills.

And yet beguiled of what they believe they have accomplished, will they not think us primitive in our views and caught up in illusion for it is not the way they calculate their world. And yet the truth is the truth and abides birthless, deathless, changeless, and remains the truth despite the shifting illusions of the impure human heart. They may have little use for a man such as me in those days but though this age passes away the Shekinah of God, the Word, the Tone of the Creator and His creation abide forever. And the truth is as with each successive tone in a musical scale is of a higher vibrational intensity than the one below we live in a seven dimensional world of which this material realm is the lowest level of vibration. Just so are the material realms of body, mind and heart created to be informed by what is greater. The fallen mind is quick to force it to act out its desires, but inclined to believe itself all there is to and unwilling to be governed by the higher dimensions of life. And yet the body, mind and heart were created to reveal the way of life, truth, and love and so divine identity in the flesh.

Yes, the world is full of illusions. Now we see as through a glass darkly, at best in the half-light before dawn the shadows of things that are. And to speak of them we must draw on familiar forms, but never suppose that sufficient. With the mind's eye we discern the forms of the world, but when the soul are truly open we shall see all things as they are and the vibratory realms of which this poor world is but a distorted image. But to see things for what they are the heart must be purified.

Whiter Morn is a vibrational realm within this world established for the restoration of man to his divine estate. It is a place of habitation wrought in a wilderness of illusion. Like this grove and place of waters in the midst of the desert, it is an oasis. It is not yet Eden restored in the earth, but stands at the crossing between the realms of light and the darkness of this world. Call it what you will. Whiter Morn is a name we have given the place of shaping, because it is first light to a world cloaked in unnatural darkness; a world longing for the sunrise and full light of day.

As he spoke Origen uncloaked and light broke through the material frame of his body until he was entirely aglow, intensifying until Caron could no longer bear to look. He covered his eyes and turned away. And still the light shone through and illumined the desert places around them.

It searched him out, permeated his body, sought out resistances to its shining; until as one weary with the heat of the day drinks deep and baths with cool water, Caron felt shriven and his body yielded in response to the light. When at last he was able again to look, he, too, shone as the sun, the desert about them sparkling like waters on a starry night.

"In this wise from the realms of light we journeyed forth from the sun, crossing the yet unformed wilderness between the stars more readily than you and I now cross this desert of sand."

"And what was made is not now what it has become," Caron answered, "but a paradise."

"We are still what we are and dwell where we have always dwelled in Eden. When this matter has been set to rights, a new heaven for this world shaped in the substance of the Archaeus, we shall come forth as the sun with clear shining after rain, and the desert places blossom as the rose." The light glowed and faded like the last of day, until they were alone again in the desert night under the stars.

In the morning Caron was aroused from deep sleep by the bleating of sheep and goats. He awakened to Origen speaking with shepherds come in search of forage and water for their flocks, and they were clearly in awe.

"They are Nibiru come to meet us," Origen said, rousing him up. "We will travel with them to the holy mountain."

"They know what you are."

"Centers of human power are centers of human corruption; from the time of the great transgression we have distrusted them, and chose instead to live apart and simply.

"Long before Abraham left the city of destruction and Lot fled the destruction of the cities of the plains, we dwelt among the Nibiru. It was to us Abram came, in the time when the lord Melchizedek was in the earth. And it was that deathless one who gave Abraham his commission to become a people whose inheritance was the Lord.

"The Nibiru are known among the wandering tribes for their fidelity to the law; to give good judgment, and honest ruling in all affairs, for how shall one ever know the spirit of truth if not first honest?"

"And do they judge by the Law of Moses?"

"The law of the Creator is radiance and in the world response to that radiance. It is the law of light and union with what is in the light. In union with the light comes wisdom and so righteous judgment.

In the radiance of the light of the spirit of the wonderful one, all works are brought to perfection in the revelation of the Holy Norm. For, it is truly written, 'except the Lord build the House they labour in vain who build it.'"

"How in this world can there be perfection, for the world is not what it was created to be, and like a working sea fraught with cross currents."

"True enough, but all thoughts, words and deeds can be perfect to the need of the present moment, and we may find perfection in what can now be done.

"Of course the Nibiru do not always sense the finer nuances of the spirit in these matters, but their leader, Abba Reuel, is a prince among men, and we shall meet with him tonight. It is yet a few days' journey and with these we will travel to the foot of the Holy Mountain.

"It is traditional when I come to bring rain." He said it almost an afterthought.

"I have watched you study the sky. A sailor can tell you the kind of cloud we saw in crossing - these high thin sheets, blowing in the wind like thread bare sails, often promise within days a change of weather."

"It was begun before we left," Origen replied. "We gathered in the place where all things are shaped, and if when we come we shall find open hearts they shall be blessed, as the dry earth to the latter rain. We shall come into agreement concerning this; you might say I have a way with the weathers of the heart; a useful gift for a desert dweller."

The camp of the Nibiru was some forty tents sheltered beneath a ridge of mountains. The camp was set along an old water course: a well, a cracked mud basin and a drying pond in the midst of a grove of scrawny date palms. There was scant vegetation on the hillsides, but enough for browsing flocks, and still it suffered for want of rain.

Abba Reuel was resting at the mouth of his tent when he saw his returning flocks led by the first shepherd his son, and as his vision was true in the company of Malachim. He rose and ran to meet them, and after the custom of his house invited them to dine and dwell with him.

When they were seated in the gate of his tent the ritual began. Abba Reuel's daughters knelt to loose the sandals of their guests, and washed the feet of the weary travelers with cool well water. And when they were done they poured a cup of cool water over the heads of each as carefully as if a precious ointment.

"The springs dry up and the wells go deep," Abba Reuel remarked.

"And yet you drink from the well of living waters," Origen answered.

"We must range far for the flocks to feed; soon we must move closer to what water remains."

"I know it."

"We live by law and keep the order of things, but this way you offer is something more." It was ever the ritual beginning to their meeting with the Malachim. "Muslims tell us God is great and unapproachable; that we must obey through submission to the rule of the Holy Koran."

"But we know you are the lords of light and taught us that we are the temples of the living God; to know that God's spirit dwells within us. Teach us, Master Origen, to know this indwelling one."

They sat in the door of his tent as the sun set behind the ridge of mountains; the evening fires were lit and men and women busied preparing the feast Abba Reuel ordered of his own to be given sustenance for all. Those who were not otherwise engaged but returned tired from the work of the day gathered in a circle about the fire to see and hear.

"The one you seek is within each one only shrouded by steel by rust, like fire by smoke, the impure heart." Origen did but remind them of things they knew, for they had spoken many times before, but this was a ritual of centering.

"And truly this spirit of truth is with us always?"

"If you seek him he dwells with you and shall be in you," Origen said. And he will reprove your world of sin, of righteousness and of judgment,"

"Of sin I understand," Reuel said. "It comes of turning one's heart away from God."

"Of righteousness because the spirit of truth shall lead you into all truth, and all things shall be brought to your remembrance," Origen said.

"I must often render judgment," Reuel said, "and often the books of laws and customs are arbitrary and do not speak to the justice or injustice of the matter, only to the form imposed upon it."

"Let the spirit of truth guide you; for in the spirit of truth is both compassion and righteousness.

"Caron can tell you of this."

Reuel turned to the man who walked with Malachim, until now silent, opening himself to the younger man.

"Embrace the weightier matters of the law: justice, mercy, and faith in life," Caron said. "Offer a thankful heart to God and wait upon his answer, for the prince of this world is judged and gentle or stern, as God will have it, love always finds the way."

Caron felt Origen in his every word, and every word like precious rain in the desert. Abba Reuel was well pleased that two Malachim accepted the hospitality of his tents and as he judged the moment propitious, he pressed his case.

"The ground is cracked because there is no rain in the land," he said. "The farmers are dismayed and cover their heads. There is drought on the fields and the mountains, on the grain, the new wine, the oil and whatever the ground produces, on men and cattle, and on the labor of our hands."

"I know it," Origen said. "Near and far it is the same."

"Do the worthless idols of the nations bring rain?" Abba Reuel asked. "Do the skies themselves send down showers?"

"The wonderful one bestows rain on the earth; He sends water upon the countryside. If He holds back the waters, there is drought; if He lets them loose, they devastate the land, and so all things are given in measure of response," Origen said.

"Truly it is so," Abba Reuel agreed.

"It is written of old that the Almighty made a decree for the rain and a path for the thunderstorm," Origen said. "He draws up the drops of water, which distill as rain to the streams. He says to the snow, 'fall on the earth,' and to the rain shower, 'be a mighty downpour.' He cuts a channel for the torrents of rain, and a path for the thunderstorm."

"I know it," Abba Reuel confessed. "The heavens are shut up and there is no rain because my people have sinned against the Lord of Heaven and earth. Teach us the right way to live, and send rain on the land He gives his people for an inheritance."

Abba Reuel rose to his feet, raised his hands over those who had gathered to his tents. "It is time," he said. "Let us make an altar of thanksgiving and pour out a blessing unto all nations." And he was answered with a shout of promise and joy.

A rough stone altar was raised by the central fire and at sun's setting six women with water jars poured out a slow stream of life giving water on mountain stone. It was an extravagance but a gift of assurance in life. You have to give before you're worthy to receive. And when it was done Origen rose and stood by the altar.

"If your heart be true the Lord will know your response and hear your voice. He also will send you rain for the seed you sow, and like the harvest of the heart, the fruit of the land will be rich and plentiful, and peace be among you."

When he had spoken a ram's horn was given; Abba Reuel blew a shevarim on the shofar, and the feast and dancing began. They ate and drank and danced to the sound of tabor and pipes, whirling about the altars of water and fire like a gathering storm; until exhausted, others took their places.

When the meal was done, the music and the dance faded into the night and the fires burned low, Origen rose and Caron with him. "Let your youngest daughter Lital attend us," Origen said. "The way of this is written in her; I would show her the place where these things are wrought, that she might be a woman of wisdom among you."

Lital came quickly leading the two Malachim into the darkness to a quiet place apart from the encampment. And there sat silently on cool stone under the whispering stars, she said nothing but waited on Origen.

"Ritual of itself is nothing but to focus response," Origen began: "to gather all who will together into one place, so that what is done may be done together in agreement."

"To shape the pattern and loose the power of what is wrought in essence," Caron said.

"Just so," Origen said. "Before we began this journey it was wrought in the Archaeus of this world; a weave of elements shaped to the need, and manifest in perfection so far as the earth answers in response." Caron glanced at Lital and remembered how it was when he came down from Himavat, when Padma took him for Shiva and came as Parvati to him that there might be rain upon the earth. They had wanted him to lay with her to break the drought and summon the rains. Surely Origen did not intend the same.

Origen read his mind. "What is to be done must be done in purity of heart or the pattern spoiled." Lital sat still as stone, eyes fixed on Origen as he spoke.

"I do not wish to take this woman."

"You would consent, would you not, Lital?" Origen said, looking to her. She nodded assent. "It was deemed necessary of old among those who worshiped gods of fertility; and whatever truth there was to that there is no need to shape this pattern," Origen said, anticipating him.

"The foundation of the worlds was established long ago; all the seed patterns necessary to sustaining the life of the earth are present here and now. I would have them understand all that is needful is written within each one of us, to bring to remembrance, and brought forth in agreement."

Caron glanced at the young woman sat across from him. "And the seed of this gift is in Lital?"

"Especially in women are the differentiated essences of the earth. Man is the initiator; woman the sustainer, the field of life in which creation unfolds the child of their communion. Each of us embodies in substance of our souls the essences of creation; a seed sown that in the span of a life may unfold to perfection.

"In truth her father was inspired when he named her, for Lital means, the dew, the rain, are mine. And we shall kindle that gift in her to the blessing of her people."

"He is master of both worlds who can magnify the life of another," Caron said. "Now I understand what Flegetanis meant…'the greatest art is to cultivate the patterns of the Otherworld in this."

"And to do you must bind the sweet influences of response to what is in the light. Lital has brought the response of her people to this purpose."

"And what must we do?" Caron's heart troubled him, for a luster grew about Lital as they spoke; it was rich and compelling and for a moment he dared think despite his words Origen intended union with her to secure the pattern.

"Too quickly we misread the current of the spirit," Origen said. "It springs from an impure heart, a compulsion rooted in flesh that knows only instinct and not the fine essences in the communion of the soul."

Caron drew back, embarrassed by what he felt and the current diminished in him. Origen at once raised a hand. "Do not fear it; open your heart and let the current flow purely between you.

"I do not say these matters never lead to consummation, but you must master these forces, let life so inform you with the sense of the fitness of things that you would never violate what is in the light; never fail to love the spirit of truth, and be true to the spirit of love."

Origen turned to Lital. "Fear nothing, daughter," he said. "If your heart be true God shall know your response and hear your voice."

Caron saw a whorl of energy focus in Origen, light concentrate about his body, and Lital across from him begin to shine with a golden glow. Caron felt his own surrender to contented harmony: the rough edge of the day's heat pass from him; the weariness of his soul with the journey released. Along the tense nerves and sinews of his body a cool stream of waters flowed. His breathing stilled and he felt a glowing presence gather to the crown of his head, then warmth like a rising sun on a cool morning enveloped him, until he was aglow from head to tingling feet with the deep pleasure of a peace born of a place beyond understanding.

Lital yielded, too, with the pleasure of it; her head bowed to her lap, completely enveloped in Origen's radiance.

"He will also send you rain for the seed you sow in the ground, and the food that comes from the land will be rich and plentiful," Origen said. "In the day of your strength, your cattle will graze in broad meadows, and there shall be peace among you."

Late into the night when Lital had retired to her dreams, they sat alone with their host in his tent and Abba Reuel asked the question that troubled Caron.

"If the spirit of truth is in us and we may know God," he said, "how is it that Malachim are in the earth unknown and without honor of men? You have power to rebuke the wicked but do not enter into the affairs of men."

"We keep the way open, but it must be man's choice to walk the path of redemption. Even so, was it not for our presence in the earth, long before now he would have destroyed himself."

Still, Abba Reuel was confused. "Is it you who are within us guiding in the way?"

"It is the spirit of truth reveals the way."

"I live among these broken hills among flocks and herds and a people whose life is already written; each day survival depends on a little grass and rain, while great cities thrive in abundant rich soils, trade in deep waters, and bring luxuries of foreign lands home. And yet we live an honest life. I am not complaining, but what I see in you I cannot see in myself."

"There will come a time when man shall no more steal from God, but tend and keep the Garden, as it was in the First Time."

"Above all I desire heavenly understanding to judge wisely of my people and guide their path. Teach me the way to go that I find in me the part that gives light that I may see the spirit of truth you bring."

"You would see me as I am?"

Reuel bowed his head between his knees where he sat and whispered. "Forgive me Lord, an impulsive and rash man, I should never have asked it." He dared not look up and a long minute of silence passed like an eternity between them. Caron watched his body quiver; shaken with fear he had offended, but Origen put out a hand and touched his shoulder.

"Abba Reuel, do not fear it; lift up your eyes." And as he did so Reuel began to shimmer with light, as Origen lifting the veil enveloped him in radiance. Trembling, Reuel gathered himself to look on Origen; stilled his heart and was at peace with it. Origen burned the brighter, until the tent was filled with a cloud of glory that enveloped the men, transfiguring them with light.

It was not what Caron had seen in the desert when the Malachim came to stand with Flegetanis, nor what he witnessed in the King's Chamber, but it was enough, and no more could Abba Reuel bear. He put his hands before his eyes and hid his face between his knees so that Origen drew back and resumed his outer self, if yet touched with lustre such as things are in the evening hour, in the last light of day with the setting of the sun.

"It is all about the union of the worlds, Abba Reuel," Origen said, "and the union of the worlds is all about the purification of the heart."

"What has become of us?" Abba Reuel asked. "Are there worlds like this, right here with this one but beyond our sight?"

"These realms of heart and mind and body are but a pale reflection of what is. Eden did not cease to be because man fell. But when man fell a veil covered the heart and what was lost was man's consciousness of the realms from which he fell into his obsession with the earth."

"And you have shown me the light of Eden."

"Blessed are the pure in heart."

"Did we not then always have the earthly bodies we now have, but what you have shown me a body of light?"

"Our body in Eden, our true body, is a body of spiritual substance wrought in the light."

"Then at death we do not die?"

"There is no end. Like a ragged cloak we wear against the weathers of the world, we put aside the coarse flesh of earth and find death's kingdom but an instant. When we cross over we do but awaken in our true flesh to that being of light we are and whose body this is.

"Even so, one need not wait for death to know that awakening, for when the heart is pure and we are in our right mind, we know the oneness of heaven and earth here and now, for always the kingdom of Heaven is at hand."

"Truly, lord, even I may know this?"

"And though worms destroy this body, yet in my flesh shall I see God," Caron said.

Origen smiled and Caron felt his great warmth surge through him. "He quotes the Master teacher, Job," Origen said, "an incarnation of the wonderful one. Sat down among the ashes of the fallen creation, he found his way home into the presence of the Almighty, and left his testament of the way to the Ancients."

"And is it permitted to ask what it is they did that brought this all upon us?" Reuel asked, "So we will not make the same mistake again," he added, tentatively.

Origen laughed. When they departed he knew Abu Reuel would embellish and regale his people with stories, but it would be a step along the way.

"Adam and Eve was a people that contrived to delve more deeply into the sensuous realm of the creation: the touch, the taste, the smell, the feel, the sight and sound and other senses we have since lost. To do so they made bodies like unto the flesh of animals, coats of skins as it is written; even so a material form not gross as that which now veils the true body.

"It was the genius of woman that led the way in this, and like a woman putting on a dress to admire herself clothed in bright array, gave it this shape, once far more beautiful than now it appears, breathed life to it and found what she had made good.

"But the timing was wrong, the pattern imperfect, and these bodies of flesh obscured the light of the shining ones. When they were inclined to put down these forms to return to themselves they could not free themselves from what they had made.

"And as that body could not endure in Eden, of their own doing they were thrust out into the realms of earth to a vibratory level where they could survive in that form, and there dwelled among the animals fit to that world.

"It is a law of creation that the creator is responsible for his creation so long as it shall continue to exist. Caught up in time the body became subject to time, and so in season death came as blessing.

"And yet another way was offered to those who would walk in it: the transmutation of the flesh into spiritual substance through the radiance of the wonderful one. And that is the way of the Na Akhu-El sages; the way of the shining ones of the First Time for the redemption of the earth."

And truly, this is how all this has come to pass?" Abu Reuel asked. "And the end of ancient sorrows is in the radiance of the wonderful one and the purification of the heart?"

"Just so," Origen replied. "And now I must walk a little in the evening air before retiring," he said, rising. "The story of what became of the earth thereafter – for it is not now as it was in the First time – must await another evening."

Abba Reuel was silent in thought then turned to Caron. "Before now I had but once seen the transfiguration of the Malachim, and that with the Master Flegetanis, when he took one of my daughters to wife. He must be now full of years. How is the good, old man?"

"Crossed over; his passing like a setting sun."

Abba Reuel nodded knowingly. "It would be so. God willing, we shall meet again in paradise." He paused full of the thought. "And my daughter's son, Shirazi, he has given good service; he is at ease in his city life?"

"Shirazi is your nephew?"

"And Lital his sister," Abu Reuel said.

Was this why Flegetanis sent him to Origen? He could feel the shape of a pattern they conceived forming up within, and wondered what design they would shape in him.

"Shirazi is a fine man," Caron said, "and on more than one occasion has saved my life. He is well established in Flegetanis' world; no harm will come to him."

"Protected of Malachim, I have no doubt in that. And now rest; tomorrow we begin the trek to the holy mountain."

In the morning there was rain.

13

Sanctuary

Origen led and Caron followed. Carefully, they picked their way among the boulders and brush along an ancient trail from the encampment of the Nibiru below toward the summit of holy mount. The ascent brought vision of a world spread out below and memory; the higher they went the deeper the memory that opened to him. At last it became so overpowering he must stop and speak. He was anticipated. Origen stopped, sat upon a stone, and watched until Caron come up the trail behind and sat beside him. "You've been this way before," he said.

"I had a vision of this place." Caron told him of the guile of Morgon Kara, and his flight in the time when the Rider of the Storm lay waste the earth.

Origin let Caron tell his story and when he was done said, simply, "I was there. We gathered in our several places to keep the pattern true, and receive the seed of what is yet to come."

"I thought it my own illusion through which I must pass."

"Some of it shadow, and ever so, until there is no impediment to the light."

"Then I have walked this way before."

"You saw some good in in the shaman."

"Though I feared his intentions toward me, it was not all ill but seemed contrived to serve a greater purpose. He showed me things from the time of the great transgression; I thought what drove him was passion to restore what was lost."

"The longing for paradise is a powerful compulsion; in some a narcotic," Origen said. "Desire to walk the path can lift the soul, or lead one down the path of destruction."

"How could he see and know these things?"

"It is written in the vibratory records of the Archaeus. He drew upon your substance to read what was written in you, and used that knowledge to betray you to his need. There are some black mages very skilled in this.

"But they can only go so far, and in this he failed because the master Flegetanis scattered his force. Yet, so long as there are those who steal from the light, the dark wind gathers again to focus in another.

"They are legion these black magicians, varying only in degree of skill and willfulness. Many are deceived but you may know them, for they know not the essence and spirit of selfless service. They care nothing for what God has wrought, but think only to steal from life to fulfill their own desires."

"I think the whole of mankind guilty of that."

Origen laughed. "Well, where there is ignorance there may yet be light. But there are those who embrace wickedness eating heartily of the forbidden fruit. These have no excuse for they know exactly what they do devouring the lives of others."

They walked another hour and in the upper reaches of the mountain came at last to a cleft in the rock that opened on a clearing where myrtle grew, roots thrust deep into the fissures in the rock in search of water. "Here is the entrance," Origen said, seeking out with his fingertips a keystone inlaid in the rock.

"Do you not fear others will find this place?"

"Not at all. It is hedged from the world, and none shall come here but drawn. And even then it takes more than force of will for rock to yield." He pressed hand to stone. His body brightened. He drew back, pressed the palms of his hands together, and bowed his head. The door opened silently in a whoosh of cool air from within.

Caron took one look back and following after entered into a small antechamber in the cool silence of hewn rock and pale marble. The narrow gateway closed silently behind sealing the way. Origen found the light stone that keyed the temple to him and the walls began to glow in response to his vibratory tone. Carved in live rock the small temple complex comprised a refectory, rest and meditation chambers for a small number: quarters for keepers and visitors, library, scriptorium, and a sanctuary.

"It is as I remembered it."

"We have kept this sanctuary many thousands of years," Origen said. "A Na Akhu-El temple, shaped in the time of the great transgression, it has survived flood, fire and internecine war. And there is yet more: it descends deep into the mountain, a refuge in time of trouble. Below is shelter, fresh water and stores aplenty.

Origen set Caron to work copying manuscripts in the scriptorium working silently beside him. His first task was to translate from Greek into Latin, the lingua franca of Europe, a small manuscript titled: *Steps to the Temple of Light*. It took half a day and earned Origen's praise.

"Flegetanis said you had the poet in you; it takes that to bridge the worlds: to work with symbols in this and know the other. Well done, Caron. You will take this with you when you go."

"Go where?"

"I will send you to Meister Eckhart, a priest of the Dominican Order, and Flegetanis' acquaintance."

"I did not know I was going to Europe."

"Rest now, and when you awaken I will have another manuscript for you."

"Also, for Meister Eckhart?"

"Yes, if you wish you may make two copies."

When he returned Origen was already at work and at Caron's scriptorium laid out a thin vellum volume at his desk, the manuscript Origen showed him in the desert. *The Triune Ray*, Caron read aloud, pleased to have it in hand again.

"It is very old," Origen said, never lifting his head from his work, "a rendering of an excerpt from the *Book of the Na Akhu-el*, the very book you carried here long ago in the time of the Dread One."

Caron read again *The Shining Citadels,* and hands trembling with anticipation thumbed through the seven brief chapters called Radiations: meditations on the present moment, God, creation, fall, the mystery of love and redemptive journey. He wrote slowly, letting the words sink in.

"Creation is eternal. It never ends. It never began. It is and was, and will be eternally… The radiance of god being goes forth and creates, and that which is created is drawn to and absorbed into the radiance so that it may take part in further creative action. Radiation, response, attraction, union, unified expression, which is radiation – thus is the creative cycle fulfilled in yet another unfolding cycle of creation."

"Why have I come here?" Caron asked abruptly. "Why did Flegetanis send me to you?"

Origen raised his head from his work. "I will teach you the mastery of the creative cycle; how to cloak and uncloak and dwell in the light of the wonderful one to accomplish your works. We will begin by mastering patience, the first step to the temple of light."

"Cloak and uncloak?"

"How do you suppose we have survived these many thousands of years in a degenerate world? Outside of divine identity are only argument and the shedding of blood."

"Shape shifting?"

"Water may take the shape of anything into which it is poured, yet remain water. It is the first of the forces you must master in yourself, not to stand arbitrarily apart and demand the world take the shape we would give it. You must know how to blend in and use whatever reality the forms present to the shining of the light, and in the light as the psalmist wrote, to let the Lord build the House."

"I have taken disguise, played parts that none could penetrate," Caron said. "I do not think I stand arbitrarily apart; even so they seek my life to slay me."

"As have they all of us from the time of the great transgression, and so we learn to cloak ourselves in the light of common day.

"It is an art, though oft abused, the remnant of the greater art of shape shifting. Once we could enter in for a time other forms, sharing the life of another, to experience the fullness of creation. And the abuse of that led to this body we now have.

"We are not as able as once we were, but to some degree the art of the metamorph yet remains, to shape our appearance to the end we intend."

"From what I have seen, we have the art to instill in others what we would have them see in us," Caron said.

"If you mean - as they say of players - to con a part; something like that but far more subtle, and never to possess; only to fulfill," Origen said firmly.

"Never to possess," Caron repeated solemnly, remembering what Morgon Kara intended for him.

"In the King's Chamber you saw what we are capable of; I will teach you how to intensify, temper and shape the radiance of your presence in the earth."

"To what end?"

"For the coming forth of the Archangel," Origen said, returning to his work: "that in season the earth may become a splendid sun in the heavens," he added almost as an afterthought.

It seemed almost frivolous at first the way Origen said it, a blithe off handed comment meant perhaps to dismiss a silly question. But this was Origen, a sage of Flegetanis' stature, and he saw in him a revelation of the shining ones of the First Time. He realized it was his own earth bound failing flesh and plodding mental labors that objected. There was that part in him that thrilled to the thought of an earth whose destiny was to become like the sun; a realm of shining citadels, obscured now only by the clouds that obscure human consciousness from the light of God.

Huddled over his desk in the cavern of a mountain it was almost too much to contemplate. He knew not whether it was night or day. He wanted to be out under the night sky staring out into the stars; by day to feel the radiant light of the sun electrifying the flesh. But at length Caron returned to his transcription. He was translating *Radiation Four*, an introduction to a greater work on the fall of man.

Divine man was in perfect harmony with God Being, and when his work of directing the activity of transformation in the earth should be completed the divine plan was that he should be drawn into God Being, that he might be absorbed into eternal being.

Origen had already explained how Elohim created a body off spiritualized substance, the image and likeness of divine being; whereby, the outer soul revealing the inner, earth and the realms of light were one. And this was divine man before the fall.

Had divine man remained in attunement with the positive expression of divine being toward the earth and all physical manifestations, he would never have suffered any limitation and would never have passed through death, for death would not have been known. Complete ascension would have been the lot of all vegetation, all animals, and finally divine man himself.

Then how had he lost his attunement with God that it had come to this; the whole earth fallen into disintegration?

Divine man allowed himself to become negative and responsive to that over which he had control, and thereby he became subject to that over which he was the rightful master, and thereby repelled himself from the Lord God was attracted and fell into subjection to physical substance.

But it was what came next that startled him.

After man began to follow the dictates of his own outer mind he brought about a further fall by blending himself with a species of animal which had been created in the form much like a man of today. These animals did not have an individualized divine being within them and they were controlled from the external, just as all other animals are controlled.

These animals had been created as the servants of divine man, to do whatever physical work might be required in the earth. The fallen being that had been divine man saw these animals that 'they were fair, and they took them wives of all which they chose.' This second step of the fall was that which brought man down into the fleshly, animal body which he is today.

Caron knew he could go no further without Origen. "We have animal bodies," he said aloud.

Origen carefully put down his quill, stretched and smiled at Caron. "'And though worms destroy this body, yet in my flesh shall I see God,'" he said. "Is that news to you? Job knew it eons ago."

Caron let the thought sink in. He remembered what Padma had read him from the *Bhagavad Gita* when he sojourned in India. He spoke it softly to himself:

... But as when one layeth
His worn-out robes away,

> *And taking new ones, sayeth,*
>   *"These will I wear today!"*
> *So putteth by the Spirit*
>   *Lightly its garb of flesh,*
> *And passeth to inherit*
>   *A residence afresh.*

You will find the original text of that here among these works," Origen said. "*The Song Celestial* they called it. Think, Caron, your knights of Christendom put on heavy armor to do battle in the world, and when they are done put armor aside and live as men again. So also is your flesh but a cloak for divine man, who is one with divine being, ever present in this world though unseen, for beyond this outer pattern of things we dwell yet in dimensions veiled to the dulled sense and carnal vision of the forms wherein we are cloaked.

"Now, then," he said, "consider should these knights no longer realize the armor they have put on as other than themselves and so beguiled never take it off, would we not deem them mad? And yet this is exactly what fallen man did to shroud himself from divine being.

"Speaking to which, we have been about our labours within this sanctuary more than a week. There's a passage that leads to the surface in the mountain heights. I should rather like to take the night air and see the stars."

"Is it night?" Night or day he needed no persuasion and rose almost too eagerly, fetching a smile from Origen.

The stairs led up to a sealed passage that yielded, as had the entrance to the sanctuary, to Origen's touch; though it seemed unnecessary for it opened onto a small plateau completely inaccessible from below. Without were benches cut into the mountain rock looking out over the wilderness of earth and air under a vivid heaven of stars. And there they sat silently an hour, gazing out into the vastness, released from the duty of stone into an empyrean of earth, air and star shine in the shining citadels of the night sky.

Three more months Caron worked diligently in the scriptorium copying works Origen set before him with scarce a word, until they gathered to rest in the evening of the new day. And when he was not at work or rest he wandered through the library. Some of the works he recognized among those Flegetanis recovered and preserved from the burning of the great library of Alexandria, and was astonished to find some in both Flegetanis and his own hand. Among them were manuscripts that spoke of a world unimaginably advanced and lost: Egyptian records of Atlantis and Atlantean records of Lemuria, the Motherland, in a kind of archaic Greek; and as well works in languages utterly foreign to him.

"Here is the story of the flood, the last days of Atlantis," Origen said, coming alongside. "And this *Book of the Na Akhu-el*, which you carried here ages past. It speaks of a civilization that existed for more than 100,000 years before the time of the fall; tells of the loss of Eden in the earth, a land that once was in the midst of what is now the world ocean. This," he said, touching another, "is the record of the seven sacred cities of the Motherland; here the *Gospel of the Kingdom of Light*; this a work on the Sacred Four, detailing the cosmic forces the ancients embodied and utilized in creating all things in the earth. And yet these are but reminders," he added, "reminders of what can never be lost, written in the vibratory records of the Archaeus, and ultimately in the enduring heavens of this world."

Caron was overwhelmed. All he could think to say was an impatient: "Why did Flegetanis send me to you; what do you expect of me?"

"When all are ready we shall gather together and intercede for you," Origen said. "We shall enter the Archaeus and bring you to the hall of records. There we shall begin to rekindle the light of memory."

"As for him who knows the spell for going down into them, he himself is a god in the wise of Thoth, and will go down to any sky he wishes to go down to." The thrill of it turned to a chill and then fear in Caron. Origen felt it in him.

"You have spoken to it as the sage Thoth wrote for a reminder. It is true. In the Archaeus we can access any pattern written in the substance of creation. But it is not so much what has been that is of concern to us but how to manage what is now emerging in vibration. We speak to the record of what has been that the patterns that bedevil man now may be cleansed, corrected, and made new.

"True memory is a lost gift," Origen said, "once the gateway, now the bar to experience of what is in the deep, and mostly just as well until we learn to let the light of heaven shine upon it.

"And yet that is what I shall teach you. All true knowledge is revelation; the rest is picking among the ashes of creation in search of a glowing coal. But in truth all things are written in the light and one need only awaken and remember to read what is written."

"We are distracted by shadows and cannot find the focus of light in ourselves," Caron said.

"The way to true memory is twofold: thanksgiving and forgiveness," Origen said. These attitudes of divine being free the spirit of truth to bring all things to remembrance, revealing what is fit in its season. The unforgiving weave a veil of grievance and resentment, accusation and blame, between themselves and the light; these dwell in the shallows of consciousness and never drink deep of life."

"What have I not forgiven? And more, what am I not thankful for?"

"Thanksgiving is forgiving," Origen replied. "Every moment of thanksgiving for life is a moment of living it to the full."

"And so Jesus forgave those who crucified him."

"He would not let them take from him the wonder of knowing the Father; thanksgiving for the blessings of the Holy Spirit."

"He was one of the shining ones?"

"He is the master of masters, the wonderful one who is light of the world; the very sun, its radiance, and our response to it all in one beautiful being. There was so much more to be said in the few brief years he had with us in form, but so little time before the darkness sought to extinguish his light. And for our sake he kept the teaching simple to keep each one in the way, provided the example of the life in himself, and established the pattern new."

"And Morgon Kara?"

"A focus of anti-spirit: once like us a Watcher given to lead but fallen back again; he fell into imposing his will on human flesh, and of course with the best intentions."

"He would see a world restored."

"And instead fell deeper into it. I understand you have seen something remarkable, but it is no more than theft and distortion of the way. Fallen man strives to shape in the earth what he imagines in the heavens, imitate the divine design and superimpose his own.

"So was it in the land of Egypt, where Morgan Kara then the Prince Setana learned his arts. Ancient Egypt retained some knowledge of Atlantis and the world that was, and contrived to conjure up what was in the deep, and draw down the powers of the heavens into the earth. In those days all manner of ritual and spells were devised to manipulate such residual spiritual substance as remained, for crossing to the periphery of the Otherworld."

"And yet there is a true way," Caron said.

"Strait is the gate, and narrow is the way, which leadeth unto life," Origen replied. "It is in the shining of the light and the dissolution of all that stands in the way of the radiance of spirit.

"Intensified radiation of the spirit lifts consciousness into the light; into awareness of the higher realms. Our commission is the clarification of the patterns that stand between the heavens and the earth that the light may shine without hindrance in this world."

Origen brightened as he spoke and the sanctuary began to glow and fill with a tangible substance like a spring air filling him with rest and longing. Caron could not help himself but stretched and yawned as his body relaxed and all cares shed from him, until he was almost giddy with delight in the childlike simplicity that replaced the world weary burdens he shed.

"The others are gathering. It is begun."

"I do not see them."

"And yet they are here. Do we have your permission to intensify our presence in you?"

"I was unable to bear your revelation in the desert."

"Which is why I have called the others," Origen said. "You have begun to break surface from the mass consciousness of fallen man, but you are not yet accomplished in bearing the burden of light, your body, mind and heart not yet toned to it. Without us you could not yet go where we would take you. Will you abide in us as we in you until it is accomplished?"

"You will not possess me as the shaman sought to do?"

Origen felt the sting of fear of being hurt in Caron; he understood what he had gone through. "As loving parent to a child, until you come into your own; we would give you your life, not take it from you."

Caron was silent as he pondered the sense of it. Flegetanis had been there for him. He had not asked him to do it, but when the moment came Flegetanis gave his life to thwart Morgon Kara. And these knew it for they were kin and some present at that moment, doubtless Origen from the start.

"It is not for us to impose upon you, but for you to remember and come into full knowledge of what is inborn in you. We would show you the way; open to you now a place to which you may return when you seek understanding."

It needed no more. Origen uncloaked and Caron was taken into the force of those who gathered to him into the light. One moment he was gazing into it; the next he was standing on a portico before a high narrow gate that opened between two pillars of a temple. At his side was Origen in familiar form but freed of all sense of stress or strain in a body like autumn sunlight. He felt himself utterly real but released from the burden of flesh, and hardly dared speak to spoil the moment but managed a whisper, "where are we?"

"In a place where the flesh of man cannot go," Origen said. "I have brought you to the gate of the temple of memory, the hall of records. I thought you would prefer a garden. Once within it is as you have said, 'who knows the spell can go down to any sky he wishes to go down to'. That is the outer view, for the Watchers abide always in the light and draw up for examination those patterns under any heaven we choose to bring to focus."

A woman appeared in the narrow gate. She was a wonder and Caron must avert his eyes. "Do not shy from her, Caron." He felt Origen's hand firm on his arm. "The second sight; look again." And when he raised his eyes she was radiant still, but he could see into the light. Like the full moon she glowed about her breasts; clothed in the old Grecian style her first white, now golden, then pale blue gown off the shoulder, and gird about the waist with a silver band. It was a thing of beauty, her robe more part than apart from her, a cloak of radiance that shifted as she shifted with the temper of light, as did the veil that fell about her shoulders. Brooches tied in a Celtic knot she had in her sunny hair, and a long tress draped over one half bared shoulder and breast; about her neck a necklace of pearl, and on each arm she wore a silver torque.

"Who is she?"

"Anwyn of the In-World," Origen said. "She who when you came remained behind to guide you. Always she stands at the threshold of your awareness of the Otherworld; she is your memory of all that has been; your realization of all that is, and guide to all that is to be so long as you are incarnate."

"Her beauty is too much for me." Caron felt undone. "In her presence I am corrupt."

"It is natural to feel it because in the flesh we are corrupted, and must manage it. But we are here because permitted. And here we have power to lay down our burdens, until we must take them up again."

"What must I do?"

"If you would enter in you must acknowledge that one who has been with you every step in the way."

"They have all been dreams of her."

"And every woman dreams of the man who abides to guide her. Yet in the world we must find something of each in the other."

"What shall I say?"

"Tell her you love her. She will know if you are true."

"How could I not?" And yet he hesitated.

"Caron, this is not imposed upon you. In agreement we are lifted up. If you wish to go no further, we shall return."

It was unthinkable, but he felt like a child dazzled by beauty he could not catch his breath or dare to speak to, and yet his heart hurt for her. Nevertheless, he approached cautiously, Origen at his side. She softened as he came, the light upon her more like streams of sunlight in a shaded grove, and the air filled with the scent of flowers and splash of falling waters from beyond the threshold where she stood.

And when he stood before her, Origen at his side, looking for words he still found none. She waited, a curious tilt of the head so her tress fell over her bare arm, and his eyes blurred.

"Anwyn," he whispered. It was all he could say. How does one come with words, empty vessels to the wellspring of one's soul?

He was too long in the world, and of his own weary with the weight of it. Yet here he was, and she seemed to understand, for with a benign smile and knowing in her eyes she looked on his heart and released him from the burden of speech. Instead, radiant like sunlight shimmering on waters, she came to him. At arm's length she held out her hand and placed a little white stone in the palm of his opened to receive it. "I love you," she whispered, and on a flutter of air heady with springtime was gone, leaving Caron ashamed he could not speak what he felt.

"You missed an opportunity," Origen said. "But she has received you. Ask and it shall be given."

"Will she not come with us?"

"Memory is a garden: paths, terraces and views; here open, there confined, so vision is concentrated: now on detail; now on a greater vista." Beyond the narrow gate the path curved between banks in the shadow of great overarching trees, until it opened on a terrace with a view so far as a hill of quaking aspen in the distance.

"But will she not come with us?"

"She is everywhere before us, and will illumine what we seek. Watch for her in what is revealed."

"And what shall we seek."

"Illumination: Like ashes from a fire, knowledge of the world is but a residue of what is known within. All true knowledge is revealed; it rises within like remembering; a true use of memory is the revelation of what we already know, and what is written in the current of the spirit. In this place you may ask, and the answer you can bear will be given."

And still from where they stood Caron could not see the extent of the terraced garden that was his to know, but from where he stood every nook and cranny, terrace, hollow, berm and bed was cultivated with all manner of herb, leaf and flower in its place.

"Life in the desert of the world," Caron said. "Had we not come here, I would not have believed it."

"And every plant of the field before it was in the earth, and every herb of the field before it grew…" Origen said. "It all begins in the heavens, in the place of shaping, before ever it is in the earth."

Caron stood on the threshold. It was all curiously familiar to him, like a half remembered melody. In the distance sunlight glinted off pooling waters in glistening, rainbow mists. He heard the enchanting sounds of brooks, splashing fountains and whispering falls: everywhere the sound of waters gushing, plashing, tumbling, made melodies; soft subdued sounds blending the perfume of the garden with air, earth and colour. And upon the air, bright spritely forms of birds flitted to and fro, full of the melody of life.

He had crossed seas of grass green and sere with summer, picked his way through soaring forests along great cataracts, rested in perfumed gardens in castle courts: but to this the world was but a desert. The clarity and warmth of light, the misted perfumed air and mystical melodies, the many shapes and living forms of herb, tree and flower all conspired to drain him of himself and any motive to do anything but be here and now. And so he let go, breathed deep its essence, and went slack with longing for all the garden promised.

"How are we come here for remembrance?"

"As a butterfly seeks nectar," Origen said. "Let us walk a little."

"There are many paths."

"And many perspectives through light and air and hours, but ever one garden," Origen said. "So, what now takes your attention? Ask that it reveal itself, and it will unfold its heart of light to you."

"That distant grove of green and gold aspen takes my eye."

Origen led the way. The garden changed with each step revealing something previously unseen and Caron marveled at the detail. "Everything is a differentiation of essence; everything made is rooted in the sun that shines at the center of these realms.

"It begins with the sun?"

"And ends there," Origen said.

Caron took a long look into the sun. Here he did not need to shade his eyes from the clear shining and the hint of blue he saw in the midst. "It is in some wise a different sun."

"It is the same sun at a higher vibratory level; stepped down in the outer realms that the earth may bear it. Here you can begin to see the cool blue core at the heart of the flame: the heaven of this world at the center of creation; the secret place of the most high.

"In the Archaeus everything is in essence, its seed within itself; and as conditions permit, root and flower in the earth, lifting up its virtue into the sun.

"Born of the sun, all things return to the sun; its cycle of life transmuting the earth in ascension, though man has marred the cycle and brought death and delay into the earth.

"And still the virtue of all things is to uplift the substance of the earth for the healing of the world; everything a path to what is rooted in the deep awaiting transformation. We may ask of all things here and they will speak to us of the remembering of the garden world and what it is we seek in healing.

"Have you never thought of your memory as a garden, seeded by life and experience, unfolding under the sun in the cycles of creation, sustained by the forces of water, air, earth and fire; each part finding a natural relationship with every other part. And in the midst of all of that your own tree of life, your own abiding identity that both nurtures and receives and gives understanding to all that gathers to you?"

"Things come and go and I more or less remember them. I can connect what happened yesterday with what is happening now, and the path that opens before me makes some kind of sense."

"Did you ever consider in the deep, there are experiences long gone from your surface memory that influence all that rises up in you? Under the impulse of life those things which break surface in the sunlight are not only dealing with the here and now, but things marred and things established from the foundation of the world."

They walked a short distance along the path and the sounds of waters to a fall rushing into a pool, overflowed its basin into brook banked with flowering bushes. There was a bench and there they sat, listening to the falls, feeling the mist on their faces and watching the sunlight glint and sparkle on the surface of the stream.

"May I pick a flower?"

"This is your garden. Ask of her and see what it is Anwyn would show you now. She knows full well what must awaken in you."

Caron picked a small white flower from a bunch that grew among the rocks. It reminded him of edelweiss but had the scent of lily of the valley. "And what must I awaken to?"

"What flowers in you now distills an essence opening to the light. Ask true and you will be led to what needs uplifting in the sunlight of your being."

And, indeed, in the perfume of the flower, the prayer of its being,

Caron felt the upward longing of the subtle substance of this garden of essence rising to meet the sun. He felt its shimmering life within him, listened to the rustling of the wind through the tree tops, felt the magnetic influence of water drawing him in. Drawn into the healing currents of the garden of life, his eyes grew heavy and on the bosom of sleep in a moment he was gone.

14

Garden Grove

"You slept." Caron felt Origen's hand upon his arm. He opened his hand and found not the flower but the little white stone pressed in his palm.

"It seems we came to one of those places in you in need of healing. We could not sustain the pattern and move forward until it was attended.

"Time is different here than in the outer world; the higher essence, the shorter interval," Origen said. "One may conceive in a moment what is to be, but the playing out of that in pattern and time appointed is the art of tending and keeping the garden in the cycle of creation."

"The aspen grove," Caron said. The sound of falling waters filled his mind as they walked the path to the berm of white stemmed, green and golden trees at the turning of a season. He felt the scorched places within himself cool, the evening air fill with the prayer of the garden; gratitude for the day deepening into longing in him to touch deeper into the presence that informed this place. And Origen felt it in him.

"Anwyn, the guardian at the gate," Caron said. "She fills the garden with longing."

"She is your threshold to the Archaeus, but consent is given in the light.

Ask truly and she will show what you can now bear; stir to remembrance the essences of the garden of life she keeps, awaiting your return."

"As a child I would walk in the woods. There was a little hollow, a glade or a spring so alive it seemed there was a presence there watching... and a grove of aspen."

"The whole earth is alive," Origen said. "She has her own spirit, everywhere her own beauties, but here and there a special spirit of place, sacred ground where the nymphs still gather with telling influences."

"This grove is like that: I would sit for hours watching the sunlight in the leaves. If I were to build an altar to the glory of God and the spirit of life, I'd raise it up under the sun open to the winds and rain on a mountainside in a green and golden grove of shimmering aspen."

"Anwyn has brought you here for remembrance," Origen said, "she shows you a time when man imbued our earth with love, and as a man with a woman of his heart formed a partnership in living with her."

Origen watched as enchanted Caron walked deeper into the grove among the trees, here gently touching, there standing with a quiet rapture taking him amid the shimmering leaves until caught up in the golden glow his mind misted. Caron closed his eyes to focus and when he opened them again it was on a mountain vista of meadows, with a thatching of pine forest, vanishing afar off into a distant blue valley. Caron turned to see Origin looking off into the distance. "What has happened?"

"It is the time we have come for." They stood still in the grove but where the grove stood the garden was gone, and Origen pointing to the citadels of a city afar off. It was above the shores of sea on a well-watered plain between two low ranges of undulating hills, green and gold with aspen where the waters came down. "It is this you must remember."

Even as they looked the sun vanished, the sky blackened and dark shadows gathered to the city walls as its own light began to fade. In a stream of sunlight Caron saw a fleet, a thousand boats in flotillas, sail out from the city, driven off shore by swift wind surging over the land. And, wonder, there were ships that flew in the air. But even as he watched them rise up in flight, and as Origen pointed to them, they began to fall into the sea. "The pattern degrades and will no longer sustain their flight... but by sea."

"Who are they?"

"It is the city of Noah. Like driftwood they who came after clung to fragments of a memory on the sea of time, but his story began far away from what became the holy land and the land of Kemet to which they sail."

"It is the flood they flee?"

"The end of the world is upon them. But this fleet sails within the ark of God's influence; and, in diverse places, where righteousness yet dwells, others will survive to begin anew and tell their cautionary tale."

"But this is Noah?"

"The patriarch of a people true to the divine design, he saw and warned what would come, and those who have heeded, wherever they dwell, will journey with him in spirit.

"Noah was a prince of the House of Enoch in Atlantis," Origen said, "and remained when Enoch ascended that a remnant of flesh might be saved. And it has come to this; the eve of the destruction of the Atlantides. In a single night the land perished and for many generations to come the sea was impassible for the bars and shoals and detritus of destruction carried on the flood."

"Then this flotilla of ships is the Ark?"

"Bound within the ark of his influence, he did not fail them."

"And how did it come to this."

"So long as man prefers his will to God's revelation in him supplanting the divine design with his own, all he makes comes to destruction."

"And shall we go back again?" Caron expected no answer for he saw no way past the shame and willfulness of man to prove how without God he could be as God.

"Those who ascended, those in whom the pattern is inborn, even now return. And their return shall be the moment of truth for the world and the parting of the ways: those who respond; those who reject the way open before them. In that day there shall be time no more for the fallen world; and this sad interlude brought to an end.

"And for our part now, we must return to the life that kindles the sun and shines through the planets. And, yes, as you have seen even pulses in these old human hides when given half a chance to come through."

Caron listened and let his eyes wander among the shimmering leaves of the aspen in his line of vision, and caught himself drifting. Its form became an indistinct golden haze, and the past came again before his eyes. He tried to focus but could not separate out light from gold, gold from light. Origen rose and walked slowly toward the tree; he stopped and seemed to gaze off into infinity through it.

"What is it?" Caron asked, coming beside him. "What's happening?" The leaves of the tree were like little heart shaped flames bright against the sunlight. The tree was incandescent but there was no acrid smoke, no crackling, no heat, and no fire burning the boughs.

"Touch it," Origen said as Caron stepped forward and cautiously moved his hand through the leaves of the tree. His fingers passed among the leaves as if they were not there but left a scintillating glow at his fingertips. They watched as the leaves silently sublimated into light, melting away like dew and the grove passed from expectation to passion to profound peace.

There was no fear of harm, no sense of threat. They stood not wanting to move in the midst of the grove and watched in awe as the leaves of the trees around them, one after the other the glory of entire trees dissolved in light as if the entire grove was on fire. The leaves of the tree had simply begun to evanesce, not falling to the earth to rot but shift to a substance so fine it was as if they burned a moment incandescent into light and were gone.

"As the sparks fly upward," Origen said. "Now we see again how it was in the day Enoch ascended." He pointed to the city on the sea afar off. Great whorls of light streamed up from within its walls, filled with the forms of angels, lighting the heavens above the city in a golden glow, until like the leaves of the aspen the tangible forms in air dissolved in a glory of light and were gone.

"And Enoch walked with God and was not," Caron said, "for God took him."

"All these withdrew into the realms of light leaving fallen man sat down among the ashes; near driven to madness with the realization of what he had done. Some repented; some hardened their hearts blaming God for what had befallen them.

"And still we few remain among them: serving, teaching, offering a way of resurrection into divine identity: for without is only contention over dust and ashes.

"We serve that the way of the ascending cycle might be restored, and this entanglement in the flesh of the world come to an end by reason of the transmutation of the flesh into our true flesh in the body of light."

"And age to age this is the work of the Na Akhu-El Sages," Caron said.

"By that or any other name, they who serve the restoration of man to his divine estate are the shining ones of the First Time. And to return we must retrace and cleanse from the heart of man those patterns that led to his fall.

We are now on the verge of times the sage Daniel foresaw; an age in which knowledge will be increased, when men shall again go to and fro and up and down in the earth; a time when the masses of men will be driven to madness over coveting the whole earth.

"In that day centering in the light shall be lost and in darkness, obsessed with appetite, the angry ones shall cry grievance over every issue of existence, play the victim of life, and blame God for all their woes. And they shall worship gods of force of which they will demand comfort, and but for the few that keep the way of the redemptive journey the holy place of the covenant shall be left desolate."

"And shall any keep the covenant?"

"It is these we shall seek to come out of the masses of the world, to keep the flame for the purification of the heart on the altar of life; a vibrational hedge of radiance against the conflagration of the world in the time of tribulation. And to this end we shall set you a task."

"What task?" He scarce dared ask, for now he felt he was being taken where he had not thought to go. But having come this far, how does one turn back?

"You are bound in the way to the loosing of the power of the Aton, the stone the Blood Royal calls sovereignty. Every detail of life that comes to you shall serve this end. Live to magnify the life of the wonderful one."

"I no longer have the stone."

"You've given it into the keeping of Siduri's heart." Caron nodded. "Well then you've initiated a cycle of consequence. And the responsibility of preparing you for what comes of it falls to me.

"Look around," he continued. "Take a good look at what remains of the place of shaping for this world, for it may be some time before you see it again."

Caron did and felt it impress itself upon his soul. Here beauty and truth met; here every lovely thing despite time and chance and the weathers of the world, imbedded in enduring essence.

"Now take up a handful of soil."

Caron pressed the soil lightly in his palm and let it run through his fingers. It was earthy and sensual, yet never coarse; a soil grounded yet lustrous with a higher life.

"You feel the earth as it is in this realm," Origen said, "the life force surge within it. It is how the earth should be." Origen reached out with his fingertips and touched Caron on the forehead. "Now see this."

The garden vanished. They were on a darkling plain, amongst heaps of broken red rock and on the horizon glowering clouds and dry thunder. He had been here before. Caron felt the dread of his dismemberment in the Chod under the hand of Maia to subject him to Morgon Kara's will.

"Once, four great rivers flowed out of Eden to water the whole garden. Eden was our earth and the garden all the realms of earth throughout the kingdom of the sun; brought to ruin by what fallen man has wrought.

"Maia brought you here to convince you the earth no more than dust and ashes, except you yield to her designs upon you."

"Why have we come here?"

"Throughout the kingdom of the sun, adjustments were made to allow man to survive in the fallen state. Terrible they were the upheavals in those days." Origen welled up, touching for a moment the immensity of it. "His powers stripped from him and all that was wrought diminished, a bound was set to his life to curtail his destructiveness. Thus far and no farther," he murmured, gathering himself. "Should man in the fallen state contrive to cross that bound, the powers he contrives to release shall destroy him.

"We have hedged this realm of troubled substance in the heart of man. And more than he deserves we have given him beauty for ashes, and the promise of undying life an inheritance that he might begin with his journey of redemption. Had we not done so, for the desolation of the human heart, the earth had perished long ago.

"And we have let this place in the heart on the margin of the Shades where we have set before men life and death and the power to choose. To those who stray too far from the living center it is a wasteland of the soul, an abyss of nothingness to which they come; a reminder of the consequences of separating himself from God."

"Thrust into this realm I was stripped of everything."

"And come to that part which cannot die; for here you are, awake and alive."

"And there is more."

"Yes, that was the beginning. Now we are come here to learn the way of creation. Again, pick up a handful of ash of creation."

It was dry and slipped like dust through his fingers, and gone on an idle gust of wind. Unlike the earth of the garden there seemed no force in it. "And how shall we give it life," Origen asked. "What is your will for it?"

"I would see the wilderness blossom as the rose," Caron said, and added cautiously, for he had seen too much not to check his will, "not wrought of mind, but of what is in the light."

"Then you must master the four forces, for all things are wrought of these in the current of life. These architects of creation are four: water, air, earth and fire. And in any cycle of creation initiated in the earth, the first of these forces dominant is water. Men have known of these forces – the manifest evidence of them is inescapable for they shape the world - but he has not known how to center in the light of life to dwell within them and let unfold the cycles of what is wrought therein. Learning to harmonize the four forces in the light of life and to keep one's balance in creation is the difference between wasteland and garden.

"The seed of this world was established long ago, and these may be evoked in creation as you saw me among the Nibiru shape a pattern of influences and loose the blessing of rain."

The sound of dry thunder reverberated among the rocks and canyon walls; the wind picked up and blew a scurry of dust before it, and Caron tasted dry dirt on his lips and thirsted.

"How did you do it?" Caron asked, "how did you make it rain?"

"It was a little thing," Origen said, "a work of composition that begins with centering in the divine ground given us of God where all things meet, for it is in the vibratory realm of essence where all that is made is made before ever it is in the earth.

"These bodies that cloak our being are shaped there as well in perfection. And when we come we bring with us those seeds of life natural to our being and fitting now to be brought forth into the world in our cycle of creation. But we come into a fallen world and much is blighted from the start except we learn to walk in the light.

"Even so, these essences must unfold in all the days of our tomorrows, just as surely as worthy seed planted in good earth must go through its cycle, however long to come to harvest, despite the tares among the wheat."

"You speak in allegory."

"I speak the simple truth of a realm hidden from sense by the noise and distractions of the world. And yet we have many practical gifts, as you might say, to reveal that realm in living. And whatever they might be whether it be the making of a pudding or a chair, or what have you, they are useful to the extent life is increased in the earth by reason of them.

"Further, in the world there are those skilled in the arts: artisans who carve, weave and shape the materials of the earth into items of use and beauty; poets who conjure with words, musicians with tones wrought cunningly out of instruments contrived to sustain vibratory patterns that enchant the soul; architects and artists who shape in colour and stone; makers of stories and actors of parts taking on the colour of imagination to reveal hidden realms of the heart and mind, and much more.

"And yet there is another level to all of this for if the art is true it is generative and touches into a realm of life that informs and quickens it with luster and radiance that makes glad the heart."

"But how did you make it rain; and here, how do we create water in a barren wilderness?"

"It begins with love for the creative source in the divine ground." Origen said. "Whether or not you can yet give a name to what you touch in the heart's core, it begins with response to the one who dwells in the light. And in that response one begins to realize in the light is the divine design for this world.

"Even so, I did not create water. A garden is a dynamic balance of forces under the hand of life to bring forth life. So far as I was able I let an imbalance in the forces be redressed. I did not make it rain, I asked by reason of my being there to let some healing come to the garden, a harmony in purpose of the four forces.

"Within are the higher arts, and as artists in the world vary in their gifts and perceptions, so in the vibrational realms to which you must awaken there are varied manifestations of the gift of shaping: thoughts, musical patterns and tones, colours, images, concord of thought and form, all before they inform the substance of the earth: all harmonious in the radiance of the light, all responsive to the shaping influences of the spirit.

"One may become an artist in the weaving of patterns in the current of the spirit, but never without reference to what is in the light or we shall surely fail, because all things created must resolve at last in the wonderful one to make a harmony, and if they are aberrant they shall surely fail.

"And that is why we ask and not demand. That is why we learn to let what can now be unfold to perfection. And so you must ask when you enter your garden of pattern and memory what may be revealed, what may be fulfilled. For as I was aware of the need for rain in these desert places, together at the Monastery of Alba we shaped a pattern in the sacred four in the response of the Nibiru to that effect; not willing that it be, but willing to let it be."

"How does it begin, this work?"

"We must love what we wish to bring forth into manifestation, and if our love for the wonderful one is true, it will be in that love we bring forth what is in our heart. So, then, we must concentrate the force of our life on the manifestation of what is to be."

"And that was the reason for Abu Reuel's ceremony."

"It is what they understand. It is a way to let the people bring their hearts to focus," Origen said. "Not the ceremony itself you understand, but the substance generated and lifted up into the light was needful, for it was in them the response of the earth to the need for rain was manifest. If they could have done that without the ritual it would not have been needful, but in the fallen state the human mind and heart are easily distracted by the play of sense and so we must give them allegory, as you put it, to focus the heart and mind."

"And the ritual pouring of water?"

"Fulfilled the next step: visualizing what they would see brought into manifestation. Again, if the mind and heart are centered in the wonderful one, concentrated on the act of creation, able to clearly visualize what it would manifest, the ritual reminders would be unnecessary. But the visualization must be clear in every detail or what is manifest will be flawed, and to that extent distort its manifestation in the earth."

"Given such powers it is a wonder man has survived,"

"He very nearly did not. These powers that remain are but a remnant of the arts of creation granted him in the First Time."

"It is how the Master healed, turned water into wine, raised up Lazarus, walked upon the sea," Caron said.

"Every miracle a specific act of creation to open a door of consciousness; to restore the way of life," Origen said: "A reminder to man of what man in spiritual expression should be. That was his sole purpose in coming, to rend the veil and heal the rift between the worlds."

"And if the visualization be true?"

"You imbue your creations with life; you incarnate into your creation so that you become the very thing you would create; as the musician enters in to give life to his music, the poet his poem, the lover his beloved. And so doing you reveal and bring forth yourself.

"In the very act of doing so, in your heart of hearts you speak the word that is your name revealed, the focus of your power, and let what you have shaped be imbued with your life and identity. Thereafter, you are responsible for your creation so long as it shall continue to exist."

"And is that not what man did when he fell into the flesh?"

"He did, but the process failed long before that when warned not to do what he did, he disobeyed the voice of the wonderful one."

"And having so disobeyed when it came to the final step in the cycle of creation he was unable to free himself from what he had made and so found himself snared in the sensuous flesh form he had created to dwell among the living things of the created world."

"Shame binds us to its object," Origen said, tersely. "When we attach ourselves to our works we fall into them, separating ourselves from the divine ground. The true creator is free in his work. He lets go, offering in thanksgiving for what is wrought in the wonder of life and light and the power of creation.

"And thanksgiving frees us, for the final stage of creation in anything is the regaining of one's own consciousness apart from what is made, by yielding all into the light to the wonderful one."

"This is yet beyond me."

"In the fullest sense beyond all of us for there is always more, but we may know the principle and art of it and our consciousness transformed grows in understanding. In time you will learn to perceive the forces at work, observe the patterns unfold, and see them for what they are. You will discover what can be done, perceive what must be done, and learn to shape a pattern to that end.

"And these very steps toward attainment of mastery of both worlds are present in every act of your life in the world; the source of your love for what you do, the concentration of your consciousness in thought, word and deed, your vision of what is unfolding, your bringing yourself forth through your works, the clarity of your consciousness in the act, your thanksgiving for the gift of life and creation when you fulfill your labours.

"None of these things are a mystery to us, only the extent to which all our acts are imbued with the power of creation and our failure to understand the implications of our acts. If we would deepen our understanding of what is at our hand, we must deepen our centering in life."

Origen took Caron's hand and passed it over a dry creek bed. Caron felt a stream of power flow through his body and especially the arm Origen held, and in a moment the dry ground bubbled up and began to flow with water, dirty at first but then clearing into a crystalline stream.

He felt his heart fill with thanksgiving. Origen released his hand and the water continued to flow, and Caron felt the flow of the force of water in him and it awakened the force from which it sprang. Caron knew better than to ask how he'd done it; of course he'd evoked an essence. Intellectually, he knew that, but the act was so much greater than his mind could comprehend. If he asked he knew Origen would say the force of water already existed and he had merely brought its essence to focus in him and let it take the outer form of the inner force. But already Origen had moved on.

"Dip your fingers first, then your whole hand in it. You cannot set your mind on it, but feel the water flow within you. Feel the force and nature of it until in form, or formless, you are familiar with its essence. As with all the forces, it is that essence in yourself you must master to be free in them. For to the awakened soul these manifest unseen virtues, and through them the light of creation shines."

Caron dipped his whole arm in the flowing stream; it was like the flow of life in him, cooling nerve and sinew, refreshing and renewing something yet deeper.

"You are an order made of time, a masterful blend of the sacred four, and yet you are more than this, for you are the life that through the four forces has created the world of your soul in body, mind and heart. You have made these to manifest yourself in the world, and in you the greater life has seeded all those patterns needful to the mastering of your world."

"I feel it," Caron said.

"In time you will come into your mastery by mastering each of the forces in all of its forms. You must comprehend the force of water within you as it flows as a river, surges as an ocean, springs as a fountain, falls as rain, rises as a mist or dew upon the earth, and in the deep silence of wells; even ice and snow and hail must be known to you for their essence within.

"And so also with air, elemental earth essence, and fire," he said. "You do not have to drown in water to know it, or burn with fire, but know each of the elements in their manifestations for this will speak to you of the virtues and powers of the forces.

"The whole world is essence, and word of the wonderful one. Everything manifest is the gateway of a pattern of force; a revelation without of what is within, as the dancer is revealed in the dance, the poet in the poem, and yet ever more.

"These essences come to focus in unique ways in both male and female, and together in the creation of the world."

"As in Lital you drew forth essence gifted to bring rain?"

"Among her gifts, it was her gift to do so. It needed only someone to recognize and bring it forth. But first and last," he warned, "you must always yield what you create in the light of the wonderful one, so all may be one in the weave of life."

Origen raised a hand and the grumbling of thunder gave birth to a flash of lightning searing across the horizon, lighting a moment the rugged hills. Then the wind picked up, and with the fragrance of rain fresh on the air great drops began to fall kicking up dust, and loosing the scent of gratitude from the earth.

"You may return here as you will to practice," Origen said, "and though you must take responsibility for what you have made even in this place, no harm will come of it if you remember what I have said.

"Even so, day by day, the real gift is to let the magic of life return to realms of earth in which we dwell, living so that all things that come to your hand may be blessed and all that is set in motion caused to work together to perfection."

"And the shaping, the shape shifting, is it of this wise?" Caron asked.

"Precisely, and though it may take some practice to master the art, it begins with love for what we wish to bring forth into manifestation. And as I have said, if our love for the wonderful one is true, it will be the love of the wonderful one with which we love to bring forth what is in our heart.

"So, then we concentrate the force of our life on the manifestation of what is to be, and entering into the realm where things are shaped, we seek to visualize perfectly the essences of what would take shape and asking if it might be, let it unfold."

"If I am so able to enter into the vibration of another, then I am also able to influence the consciousness of another," Caron said cautiously. "This could be much abused."

"Spiritual wickedness in high places," Origen said. "Its abuse is the root of black magic, and may go so far as the possession of another, which is how Morgon Kara remained incarnate and what he intended for you."

"And the lords of light prevented him."

"He could not penetrate the hedge of radiance we set about you, nor ever anyone who dwells in the light of the wonderful one except he agree."

"Agree?"

"The gift may be used to touch into the soul of another for the purpose of healing and in the time of their communion the two are as one. There is much to master and for that mastery the heart must be purified.

"But if you have heard what I have said, you will understand that in all his life a man may travel not a mile from his home and still be a master of hallows. In the kingdom of little things - in the patterns of daily life - all that is needful is present, to establish the pattern anew, and restore the jewel of the earth to the realms of light."

15

Carnival

Magda roused from uneasy sleep to feelings of strangeness and beauty. She'd dreamed of a forgotten realm, curiously familiar and compelling, awakening to the firelight glow of her bed chamber and to a man she knew not seated before the fire. "Who are you?" she demanded. "Where are we?"

"Go back to sleep, Magda."

"Maia," she said, petulant. She sat up drawing the covers to her breast. "I am Maia of Whiter Morn, and your thinking is keeping me awake."

"Go back to sleep, Magda."

Hearing her name again grounded her. It was true. She was Madelon de Faucon, Domina of the Blood Royal. But something still in her was Maia, and somehow that mattered more. And the man in her chamber was he not her sycophantic lover, Esquin de Flexian? In Maia something more was much desired but Squin was available: "Come make love to me, Esquin," she said.

"No."

That was his duty and she would rebuke him but took pleasure in a strength she had not known in him before. "What are you thinking, Squin, tell me."

"We are not safe and never shall be until we have an end to this matter with Caron."

"Does he still live?" She put on a night gown and drew close to the fire with Squin.

"Flegetanis is dead. Caron yet lives."

"Your Berber spies have told you this?"

"I have word from Ulcinj and my Berbers confirm it. Flegetanis is dead these six months. His daughter Siduri has assumed his business interests, which will bring her into our sphere."

"And you are sure Caron still lives?"

"I contrived to have Siduri taken hostage to the jewel, but Caron intervened. He saved her from abduction and she is escaped to Crete. Again Caron prevails."

"It is the stone, you see," Magda said. "It hedges him who possesses it."

Squin stared into the fire feeling strange movements within, almost the presence of another person he'd always known was there but half unawares. The fire coals mesmerized him; the part he had known was burning away and the fiery core of something else emerging. The fire crackled, hissed and settled in a shower of sparks. For a moment he felt he might walk into the flame and become that other one.

"You believe Caron would be willing to trade the stone for Siduri?"

"He would trade his soul for her."

It hurt Magda to hear it. "We must try again. I have seduced and enchanted the Doge. In matters of passion and profit he is easily entreated, and we shall use this to our advantage. Crete is under his sway, and Siduri must come to settle her affairs in Venice. This time shall we not contrive something a little subtler?"

Their eyes met in the firelight. Half aware, Morgon Kara glowing in Squin's eyes met Maia's distant gaze in the eyes of the Lady Madelon. And Magda knew at once these intuitions would strengthen, until she became what she dreamed.

"You shall play a part in this my handsome confidant, and to that end we will draw in the Masters of Hallows to weave a pattern for us to beguile the sense and snare Siduri's soul."

Magda took Squin's arm and stood upon the balcony to watch the procession in the square. "The Doge must parade with the rabble, but we shall watch the triumph from above." She drew her cloak about her. "Attend us, Gisors." The old Master of Hallows followed dutifully. "What news of Caron," she asked. "You have told me he lives; what are we to expect of him?"

It was cloudy bright in the February air, a chill wind off the Adriatic, but it didn't dampen the spirits of the Venetians gathered in Piazza San Marco; strutting about recklessly, masked and liberated in the rites of Carnival.

"Vanished into the desert," Gisors said.

"He troubles my soul. I would have the stone and an end of him."

"You have put a generous bounty on Caron, and all of Europe hopes to profit. Patience, milady, if he leaves his desert sanctuary he will fall into our hands.

"As for Siduri," Gisors continued, "I am told she will come to Venice with, Demetrius, Captain of the Ariadne, to secure her father's enterprise. Flegetanis was in business with the family of Polo and she will be a guest in San Giovanni Crisostomo."

Magda laughed out of pure delight. "How do you know this?"

"For a price anyone will spy on anyone in Venice, and we have a spy in the household."

With the cadence of oncoming music all eyes turned to the high archway of Merceria. From there the procession would emerge from the Rialto, with its markets and merchants, into the great square of the Doge's palace and Basilica of San Marco.

"Do you have a plan?" Magda asked.

"Siduri has Caron's heart; not as lover but sister," Gisors said. "For her and the old master's sake, he will follow after."

The sun broke through and a band of colourful acrobats, jugglers and players, accompanied by musicians on: pipes, psaltery, recorders, crumhorn, rebec, shawn, tambors, cymbals and hurdy-gurdy; all spilled into the piazza. Like the spectators all were masked and in motley depicted the life of Venice: Arlecchino, the amorous acrobat with cat like mask, Brighella his crony, roguish, sophisticated villain who would do anything for money; Il Capitano the soldier, Ill Dottore, the pompous, fraudulent doctor, Pantalone, a caricature of the Venetian merchant, lovers, gossips, maids and rogues, all lampooned to a merry saltarello: the procession of fools in their humors. For today it was Carnival. Autocratic Venice had put on its masks, and to purge the commune of anxiety every hidden thing was possible.

"She must be taken."

"Patience, milady, Polo is well connected and will not take kindly to interference with his guests."

"True, my good Gisors, I would increase our power with the Doge and not alienate him by meddling in his commerce with the east."

"If I might suggest another course, milady; there is more than one way to take a woman captive," Gisors said, looking to Squin. "Hold sense hostage. Body, mind and heart will follow."

"And you think Esquin is the man for that?"

"If you will grant me your influence, and the use of the black mirror, we will snare her soul in the reflections of her heart."

"We have advantage of her," Squin said. "She will wonder after Flegetanis service as Master of Hallows. And if she were first approached over her father's business interests in Venice, and offered the prospect of expanding her affairs into Europe, it might easily lead on to other matters."

"And in the way of men who follow their hearts, Caron will follow after. Are you able to win her, Squin?"

Squin shrugged. "Is it not obvious?"

"Who knows what a woman sees in a man," Magda countered.

"When we are done," Gisors said, "Siduri will see in Squin only what she wants to see."

"It is a procession of fools, this display," Squin said, turning to the pageant unfolding below, but Magda held him with her eye and he relented.

"What you see is a triumph," she said, "a reminder to all where duty lies, where prosperity comes from, and what it takes to hold together human society. It is done that everyone might understand full well what would become of them if they broke from station, for this is the beginning of Carnival, and Carnival is the world turned upside down."

"It begins with the fools who work the streets," Gisors explained, "leading from the least to the greatest, when the merchant princes and

Doge shall appear. Mark it well for it is the currency of this world we must look to for alliance to bring wealth and power to our purpose."

Following the Buskers came eighteen masked performers with quarter staves who began a mock battle. Seven of the staves were beribboned with the seven colours of the rainbow; their counterparts with plain quarter staves were masked as the seven deadly sins: pride, envy, sloth, avarice, wrath, lechery and gluttony; and each costume chosen to exemplify the manner of corruption and the virtue it contrived to overmatch and defeat.

On the heels of buskers, led by their tune came: the merchants, workers and craftsmen, grocers, furriers, hatters, butchers, tanners, glaziers, bakers, brewers, drapers, goldsmiths, haberdashers, makers of durable goods and military equipment, metal wares, ship wrights and chandlers; skills and services, clerks, teamsters and entertainers: mercers, apprentices, paid assistants, and companions all.

And, finally, through the great gate came the guild masters into the piazza: the parable begun, filling the senses with all the colour and display of things the soul needs and lusts after. All was revealed in the morning light, throbbing with vitality the life and purpose of Venice, under the colourful banners of each trade and merchant, flags snapping in the gusts off the sea. And the meaning of it clear: one and all were held in place by a powerful oligarchy.

"Why is everyone masked?" Rakastaa asked.

"Because they are not who they seem," Polo said. "And especially in Carnival everyone wears a mask."

"Is this square named after you, Polo?"

Polo laughed. "After Saint Mark, a disciple of Jesus: I am named for him."

"And the rest of the time?" she asked. Polo glanced to his beautiful guest unmasked but in a caped robe, every eye near torn between gazing on her and watching the Triumph. He must talk with her; she drew too much attention and must not go about like this. And she would need another name.

"When they are about their affairs," Polo explained, "many wear the bauta mask, cloaked and tricorn hat. It is a kind of business dress by which we may conduct dealings with anonymity, out of sight of envious eyes."

The mock battles between virtues and vices continued their beribboned, quarter stave antics. As the merchants passed, Sloth battled Fortitude. Having spent most of his energy in avoiding his industrious opponent, Sloth at last in comic retreat ran and hid among the crowd, who with good humor, enjoying a day of indolence absorbed him willingly in their midst, until rejuvenated he returned and gave Fortitude a mighty wack that knocked him to the ground.

The battle between Avarice and Charity was pitched and long, and even as the merchants passed by and soldiers entered the square remained inconclusive. As the soldiers came on this conflict was thrust to the sidelines by Wrath hard pressing Patience. But Patience, enduring many heavy blows, skilfully turned wrath aside, and though undefeated prevailed not against his fierce opponent.

Despite the logic of the procession, most eyes were on Lechery and Chastity for it included a shapely young woman, masked and very competent in the acrobatics of the dance. Assault and defense ebbed and flowed in a sometimes brusque exchange, giving way to skillful stratagems as each comically took the measure of the other calculating how to proceed.

To the drum beat following the merchants came the watchers over the public weal; the keepers of law and order, defenders of the republic and merchant fleet on land and sea. Leather tunic, leggings, light armor armed with sword and spear, colourful scarves and banners aflutter, they came led by captains and followed by lesser men at arms, until the company of noble bowmen formed from the young aristocrats of the city, roused the blood in every feminine heart. Then came unmasked Admiral Pisani, master of the Venetian fleet; in ox-blood red leather tunic and shining greaves, on a black horse. Sword drawn, tucked to his shoulder in salute, he was accompanied with much applause by armored spearmen, for after the death of Admiral Dondolo at the disastrous battle with Genoa at Curzola, it was his family who forged the navy into shape and reestablished Venetian preeminence on the seas.

"And why must they hide their affairs?"

"When you have lived here a season you will understand," Polo said. "Venice is powerful but very small. Everyone seeks his own advantage and there are spies everywhere."

Rakastaa listened intently. "Then you would suppose in Carnival they would be delighted to take off their masks and celebrate."

Immediately after came a mockery of the great families of the oligarchy, hereditary rulers of Venice. All were masked, the younger patrician women in Colombina to allow a hint of beauty, the elders in Moreta and veil, all exotic gowns conspicuously displaying the wealth of the family; the men masked with the square chinned Bauta with red fur trimmed cape and tricorn that guaranteed their anonymity. But it was easy enough to guess, for the great families were few in number and the shape and force of each one well studied.

Meanwhile the mock battle between Pride and Humility, Envy and Kindness intensified, whirling around them as they entered the piazza from Basilica San Marco. It was inconclusive, though Humility was taking a beating and Envy had gotten the upper hand just when the sound of drum, flute and psaltery gave way to the litany of the clergy.

"Venice is a republic, a very structured society with everything in its place," Polo explained. "For the ten days of the world is turned upside down, and all are loosed from their restraints."

"And is it hidden from God?"

"Even priests and nuns join in."

"But why would you want to hide your identity?"

"My dear Constanza," Polo said, "many find it liberating to be someone other than who they are."

"Rakastaa," she corrected.

"No, we have spoken of this; in these realms it must be Constanza," Polo said. "You are partner in trade but our advantage is in revealing nothing. You have the look of the far northern people, and that is what we shall say you are."

"Very well," she agreed, "henceforth it shall be Constanza."

"You see how useful the mask? Venice is a conspiracy of wealth and opportunism, an unforgiving oligarchy of power with spies everywhere seeking advantage. Here you must consider every encounter, however casual, an intrigue."

"I shall wear a mask and walk about and see this for myself."

"With great care, Constanza, and we will speak further of this. I've arranged for you and guests from Crete to join in the festivities." Polo took a quick look at the sun shadow across the square. "One day we shall have a clock tower," he said, "but I am a good judge of time. The Ariadne will soon arrive and never seen in Venice, a cargo of fire flowers to consummate our carnival. Stay close to me." He led through the mass in San Marco square. Every eye followed Constanza, wondering after the fair haired beauty; the women wondering how to emulate her; the men how she might be had.

Chastity was taking a beating by Lechery as the priests, the Doge's primicerio, entered the piazza from Basilica San Marco, and the fray was taken up by Gluttony and Temperance as they emerged from St. Mark's Basilica to join the Triumph. The procession was led by neophytes chanting psalms, as ungainly Gluttony stumbled and struggled to avoid the blows of Temperance - who was anything but temperate in laying on. All the more enthused by the presence of such exalted company, these fell in the way and bumped unceremoniously into the priest carrying the banner of St. Marks.

Humbly, the clergy walked bare headed and unmasked. Two by two they came by lowest rank to highest, and lastly bishop with miter, morse and cope, and all with grave solemnity; banners depicting child and virgin and holy martyrs slapping in the wind. By the time the high clergy had joined the Triumph all battles were done: vices beaten back into the crowd in the wake of the passing show, leaving only garland staves, attire and pennants proclaiming the triumph of life's high virtues. And these arraigned themselves at the entrance to the Piazzetta and Doge's palace, their banners lifted high to greet the Doge.

With a flourish of trumpets, His Serenity, Giovanni Soranzo, ecclesiastical, civil and military leader of Venice, without masquerade emerged from the palace and entered the square. A discreet distance behind the primicerio followed the high council members, noble magistrates, and for no apparent reason each accompanied by boys struggling with parasols in the gusts that blew in from the sea.

The Doge, dressed in ceremonial robes and como ducale set firmly on his head, was flanked by players gathered to him proclaiming the triumph of temperance, wisdom, justice and courage in the archetype of the state. And in this wise the Doge entered Piazza San Marco to cheering crowds, affirming bonds of community and service, and anticipation of Carnival.

It should have ended with Soranzo's processional, but it was not done. Coming up from behind the last of the magistrates was one more figure, in flowing black tabarro and white Bauta mask. He followed grim as death, and like death carried a scythe for the reaping of the world. A moment there, a moment gone: the moment not lost on the celebrants as all wondered who had the cheek to upstage the Doge in the Triumph.

"Perrin," Magda whispered, watching from the balcony. "Only you would dare that." She first recoiled then wondered at it. She needed Perrin. "I do not think that intended," she said, drawing back from the balcony, "but it completes the cycle; a reminder how little time we have in this world. We shall not waste a moment of it in regrets."

"Gisors you shall beguile Siduri's sense; Squin you will possess her, discreetly mind you. Caron shall know of her seduction, and we will retire to Château de Blâmont to await her ransom and redemption. There we shall gather in the Masters of Hallows each to his art, and all together we will weave a binding spell to defeat Caron and possess the stone of sovereignty."

Polo and Shirazi offered a half pound measure each of pepper, nutmeg, cinnamon, cardamom, ginger, and cloves to the Doge's pleasure. Constanza and Siduri stood by watching the face of the old man try to mask his astonishment.

"Consider this a gift," Constanza said. "With my sources, routes and alignments, I can arrange to deliver as much of this as you desire by caravan in trade with Siduri, by sea and thence to Polo through Alexandria and Crete."

"And silk?" the Doge said, a quaver in his voice, "is it possible? I have never seen finer quality." He rose and came to Constanza. "May I?" His hand lingered on her arm feeling the sensuous quality of the silk robe that cloaked her.

"I have never felt the like. Pure Oriental silk is hard to come by, and though the monks have learned and there is some production of our own, not so here in Venice and not the same quality."

"It is my own silk," she said, "the heart of my fortune in Hotan."

"It was in Hotan I met Constanza," Polo said, "her husband was a good friend. God rest his soul."

"Then you are a widow." The Doge was intrigued. "How did you break China's hold on silk?"

"I am just told this story," Siduri said, laughing. "She smuggled the silk worm out of China in her servant's hair."

"In truth long before my time my husband smuggled the eggs of the silk moth in hollow bamboo," she said, "and in my time taught me the craft."

"But you are not Asian." The Dodge admired her blue eyes and fair hair.

"A story of loss and redemption for another time," Constanza said.

"And you Siduri," the Doge said, turning to the young woman. "I am sorry for your loss. I knew your father well; an excellent man who indulged my weakness for books by sending something new with each voyage.

"You will have inherited his wealth. I trust you have good advice to guide you. Are you up to this? Do you commit your fortunes to this venture with Polo and Constanza?"

"We have only met this past week but are fast friends," Siduri said. "My father was partner in business with his old friend Jakob." She looked for words that did not require her to explain what had happened: "Now his protégé Hugues, Comte de Caron. He, my allies in trade, Shirazi, Demetrius, captain of the Ariadne and master of my father's ships; these men shall guide me in all matters. And Constanza," she added, affectionately.

"This Caron, is it he who has a price upon his head?"

"He was my father's protégé," she insisted.

"I know nothing of Caron personally, but the Hapsburgs would have him for abetting the Swiss rebellion. I have heard he knows the whereabouts of the missing Templar treasure, and that he is funding the Swiss rebellion by this means. And there are many other charges."

"He seems a resourceful man; one well suited to the trials of trade," Constanza said.

"It is a hateful and deceitful conspiracy, more telling of those who shaped it than the man himself. You do not know the man," Siduri said, fiercely, "but I know him. He has had his bellyful of these machinations and will not venture again into Europe, until these cursed accusations are void.

"You will excuse my anger at these injustices, but by me you will see him through other eyes, and I will give you every reason to discredit those who discredit him."

"Innocent Caron may be, but trouble seems to follow wherever he goes. It is a matter of risk and rewards, you understand."

"He is a force of nature," Siduri said. "He loved my father Flegetanis as his own, and would do nothing to hurt my affairs."

"There will be no issue," Polo said, mildly. "Caron respects Siduri's wishes in her father's fortunes, and defers business decisions in Europe to others."

"Well, then, we shall draft a contract." The Doge glanced at the bounty of spices. "We shall take your advice and withhold judgment. In time I trust we may find a place for Caron's signature and seal on our document, but for now a silent partner. But I am curious, if not in Europe, where is this rogue all Europe seeks?"

"Last I know in Egypt," Siduri said. "He was much concerned about the fate of the young caliph in exile."

"We have had word Sultan al-Nassir Muhammad is returned to power, and the usurper, Baibars al-Jashnakir, is fled."

"That bodes well," Siduri said. "Al-Nassir respected Flegetanis, and our trade with him has been profitable. All, I am sure, will be well, but until matters are fully settled we can ship out of Ashkelon."

"And when may we expect the first delivery?"

"Already cached in Crete," Constanza said: "and another caravan presently in the way to Ashkelon."

"Then, as you see no difficulty I see none." The Dodge's hands shook with anticipation, "I see no reason why we cannot proceed at once to procure as many shiploads as possible of silks and spices. Venice is the gateway to Europe, and the demand boundless. We need only discuss what you will accept in return."

"For now silver and gold, and we would have residence here in Venice."

"You will brighten our age, and engender a legion of suitors," the Doge said. "I will give you a villa of my own, nearby and particularly suitable to you."

"One thing more," the Dodge said. "I have a particularly wealthy friend in the Lady Madelon de Faucon, a very wealthy guest who would do business in the east with us. On my recommendation would you consider her in this alliance?"

Constanza saw Siduri cautious. "I will think on it and discuss with my partners," she said, discreetly, and smiled at Siduri. "But let us first meet the Lady Madelon."

"I'll arrange you meet face to face during the ball. And Polo," the Dodge said as they rose to leave. "Since you brought flash powder from Cathay, in use the art of this has continued to grow. There are those among the German princelings who are experimenting with perfecting cannone to hurl projectiles that could reputedly smash castle walls or sink a ship. Have you seen this in your travels? Or you Constanza?"

"In Cathay used in battle to little effect other than to frighten with fire and thunder," Polo said.

"Hugues has spoken of it," Siduri said, "iron rods and lethal they are, carried by men, but their power spent as lightning in a single flash."

"Will you ask after this for me?" the Dodge said. "If there is a new weapon here we must defend our ships. Since learning of this I have pondered how to put this invention of black powder to use in defense of the realm."

"I will show you something," Polo said. "This year we shall light the night sky with fire flowers. It is beauty to behold and a power by which one day we shall ride the air in chariots of fire."

"Always the dreamer, Polo," the Doge said. "I suppose you must attend to this display but will find time, I trust, to attend the ducal ball in our Hall of Mirrors." The Dodge cast an admiring glance at Constanza and Siduri. "It will be a shame to mask your beauty but expedient, for none must learn of our business until it is accomplished.

"Will you wear these for me," he said giving each of the women an emerald pendant. "Then I will know you for who you are. In these affairs we must be prepared for anything. You are visitors and new to our ways, so you may count on me to intervene in your honour."

"You are most generous," Siduri said, fondling the stone. Constanza said nothing but acknowledged with a nod. Full well she knew men who gave gifts had expectations.

"And something more," the Doge said, "a sample of our art from the Isle of Murano. A glass unlike any in the world is fashioned there, by alchemical lore that begs nothing of those who would turn base metal into gold. This is a gift of the Lady Madelon," he said, "to each of you with hopes you may find pleasure in it." He gave them each a gold compact within which two mirrors, one framed in silver, the other in black obsidian. When the compacts were open Siduri gave a little gasp of delight; never had she seen her reflection with such perfection; even Constanza betrayed amazement, for no mirrors such as these had she ever seen, brilliant as the life that animated them.

"The one will show you as the world sees by light of day; the other what you alone may see: yourself, not as others see you but as you are," the Doge said. "And some say looking long and intently into the dark mirror one may see the future. It is a novelty, but I cannot account for the truth of that."

Siduri gazed deep into the dark, obsidian set mirror. Her image was not as brilliant but drew her in, stirring her deeply. It attracted her beyond the surface light, summoning the deep of her soul. And what she saw fascinated her.

"Thank you," Constanza said, snapping her compact shut. She reached out to Siduri and closed hands around the gift, closing off the compact. "These are thoughtful gifts and if any measure of your skill in the art of glass making, you are assured much profit. I cannot think of a single woman in the world who is not enthralled by reflecting on her own image in a glass."

"I sense your caution," the Doge said. "Wisely, for the dark mirror is rare and unsettling for some, what it draws out in the viewer. But as for trade, we will arrange a tour and you will see for yourself how accomplished the artisans of Murano when you are come to the Hall of Mirrors."

16

Cross Currents

An Arcadian fantasy was called for; the final night of Carnival at the Palazzo Ducale, the center of *La Serenissima,* serene republic of Venice. And the elite shall attend.

The poet Perrin came, too; he and his fellow musicians dressed simply in shapeless white Ionic chiton garment with purple trim, wearing a half, sunny mask of Apollo. They were the Troppus Amphion, commissioned by the Doge from the Gild of Musicians to uplift, uphold, and fulfill the evening. For after the legend, it is said when Amphion played the very stones gathered in from the wilderness to build a wall and hedge the city of Thebes. Perrin wondered if no less a task was before him.

He watched the gondola ceremonially arrive by sea, landing and passing through the pillars of Saints Mark and Theodore to disembark at the Piazzetta di San Marco. Crowds of revelers pressed the armed guard to catch a glimpse of the masked celebrities guessing who they might be, as one by one they shed their dark cloaks against the night air, to make their entrance in character into the ducal palace.

Shepherds and shepherdesses dressed in peplos and chlmyas, himataion and chiton, each with its typical Venetian flair of colored silk, the crowd supposed the lesser nobles. The bolder came as gods and goddesses, such as one might encounter in the fields, woods and sea shore of Arcady. There were even satyrs and nymphs, and never doubting his identity the Doge himself appeared as great Zeus to oversee the revelry; his wife, Hera, on his arm. All the rest, masked as they were and so garbed were tacitly anonymous, but at this level of society Venice was a very small community; every voice, inflection, nuance, line of form and motion duly studied, noted and known. But tonight the pretense was everything for husband and wife, damsel or gallant. To court another tonight was to court the elemental mystery of force, freed from form and function, to let nature take its course.

A cacophony of musical instruments tuning - there were four and twenty in the ensemble - reminded Perrin of his duty to the troupe. Apart from these there could be no other reason for his being here, and forewarned of Polo it must be for Siduri's sake. She and the fair Constanza entered a world of predators ill prepared for their stratagems.

A year Perrin waited the return of Hugues Caron, for they had pledged to meet again at the Champs Sacree, but he did not come. Determined to learn what had become of him Perrin made his way to Venice where he sought out the merchant, Marco Polo, who was in business with the Master Flegetanis. It was there the Lady Constanza came also in search of Caron, though it was unclear how she had come to know of him. Did Perrin know the Master Flegetanis was dead? He was at sixes and sevens, unsure of his next move, for he was reluctant on his own to strike out for Egypt, and so he abode in Venice brooding on the way forward.

To his relief the Ariadne with Captain Demetrius arrived and with him Siduri, come on her father's business. Yes, Caron was alive; gone off into the desert for some purpose known only to him. It was curious to observe the Lady Constanza in this. It was a mere glance, but seemed to Perrin she was more relieved even than he. What was Caron to her that she should cross the wilderness of the world in search of him? And, hearing of him Constanza sought Siduri's friendship, and though as different as first light and twilight, the two seemed as one.

Back to the task at hand: Perrin preferred the harp and song, but in an orchestra of viols, lutes, rebecs, horns, pipes, tabors and an assortment of flutes, he was obliged as master musician to adjust on request. He was late come to Venice, but proving an accomplished trouvère was readily accepted into the guild with prominence. Indeed, he had made a significant contribution to the procession, and here he was now amidst a profusion of candlelight, flowers, perfume scented air, richly spiced foods, music, song and dance and dress such as he dearly loved: beauty full of grace in an otherwise harsh world.

And the mirrors – the mirrors were a mirage, a mind-altering brilliance, and a fantasy of light such as was never seen. The grand ballroom shimmered with light reflected upon light, their full lengths ablaze with a holocaust of candles; image reflecting upon image compelling the guests to pause, to admire themselves and reflect on a kaleidoscope of images of that special one reflected there.

Each longed for the moment given at the grand entry to lift the mask and reflect, as if for the first time on their image of perfection. But it was not to be: tonight was entirely masquerade, and each must play the part fortune assigned. It was a wonderful revelation, a lustrous display of humanity glorying in itself, and Perrin realized how he had decidedly come to adore Venice and would gladly stay.

And then she entered, the Lady Madelon de Faucon, Domina of the Blood Royal. She came as a special guest of the Doge, who hovered about her as one might royalty. Perrin felt her presence the moment she entered, concealing his own among the musicians. Though half-masked in Columbino, the line and manners of Lady Madelon were unmistakable. And with her came - arrogant bearing, tell-tale limp and jeweled cane betraying him - Squin de Flexian. She was Artemis, one breast half-bared, goddess of the hunt; Squin, half-masked with the face of sun. But no Apollo, god of the golden mean was he, his every gesture wrought in self-reflecting love.

Known to be a great beauty, the Lady Madelon brought an enchanting air of bewitching delight that wove and knit the two hundred or so gathered in one conspiracy. All knew her guest of the Doge. All women envied her and all men wondered if on this night of nights she might be attainable. That air set the tone for the evening's intrigues of wine, food, music, dance and spirited seduction. But Perrin forgot himself and the refinement of the Lady Madelon's gift, like so many beautiful women the gift to know when she is being intensely watched. Unwittingly, he'd reached out and touched her across the threshold. She turned a moment toward the musician's gallery and their eyes met. If but for a moment she held his gaze. He knew that he was read and despite the mask known. It was her art and Perrin must play the evening out wondering what would become of it, for they had not parted amicably.

"Squin, the author of this Carnival's pageant was none other than our own Perrin," Magda said. "On the morrow I shall ask the Doge after these players. You will seek out Perrin and bring him to me, unharmed, mind you, for the Doge takes pleasure in him."

In the midst of a measure Siduri and Constanza arrived, and a moment of silence swept over the company. Each half masked but not their beauty came dressed in white and rare indigo blue silks: the one dark haired, bejeweled with sapphires, speaking of incalculable wealth and the mystery of the Nile; the other fair with the first full light of dawn, hair bejeweled with diamonds and emeralds, radiant with cool, clarity. They were two and yet one: sisters, nymphs of the Pleiades, lustrous with influence.

They crossed the threshold in the company of old Polo, for all the world to see a Socrates indifferent to rank, to praise or blame, yet sure for all the world of an audience. At once attention turned from the Lady Madelon. Perrin felt the force of her command tremble on the air and knew well enough she would have none of that. With the Doge in tow she at once advanced on them, and Squin came also.

First oeuvre was a basse in a combination of 6/4 and 3/2 time, and Perrin must pay attention to the art of his fellows. But he saw at once the Doge assert right to Constanza whom he strategically attached to his nephew, Lothario Vitale, captain of the cavalry, clearly entranced by the sight of her lovely, tight-laced bosom. Doubtless, he was wondering what it would take to get a glimpse of that, and unmask as well a stunning beauty. Urged by Magda, Squin, who really preferred no woman at all, quickly claimed Siduri's hand. This she gave willingly, entranced with the strangeness and beauty of her surrounds.

Pressed by suitors abandoning their wives, the Lady Madelon gave into a tall, well-built gallant of younger years and the evening began in a procession of partner trading partner, moved quietly and elegantly in a slow gliding motion of the dance that gave grace to acquaintance each with the other. The basse led on to a lively saltarello and so the evening unfolded: dance, wine, flirtations, breaks for sweet meats and whispered invitations, a flurry of partners, more wine and assignations. Perrin watched as Squin and Magda drew Siduri and Constanza aside, and led by the Doge disappeared along a passage that led upstairs to his apartments. They were not seen again even when Polo's fire flowers lit the sky and despite the chill hour all were drawn into the Piazzetti del Marco to watch in awe the aerial display. Out of concern for Siduri and Constanza, Perrin took little pleasure in it.

What followed in the night was anyone's guess as the ritual bacchanalia turning this rigid, hierarchical state inside out came to fiery consummation. Few left with those with whom they came, for the last night of carnival turned by day into Lenten repentance, led by those who even tonight allowed themselves unquestionable liberties. Indeed, the higher clergy numbered among the Doge's guests, and it was not uncommon on the last night of Carnival for priests and young gallants alike to scale the walls of the nunneries: *Via intemperantiae ad turrem sapientiae ducit…* as the saying goes: the road of excess leads… etc.

Well before the evening was done it was clear no one would accomplish Siduri or Constanza. None took offense. They were after all visitors, guests of the Doge, and unaccustomed. Or, they supposed, he had taken a proprietorial interest. So, the would be suitors calculated early and left off trying, intent on assuring themselves of an assignation before the night was done.

As for Siduri and Constanza, the talk was entirely of trade. Having concluded their business, they turned to watch the fire flowers from the Doge's rooftop garden; for the lateness of the night he invited the women to stay over but they demurred, and politic he waived the custom realizing they were unapproachable. He instructed his personal servant to accompany Polo and the women home, but Squin zealous for Magda's will, intervened begging the privilege.

They were not alone leaving the Canale di San Marco, but entered into the Grand Canal in the midst of a little fleet of burning lanterns, floating like fire flies in the night surrounding the Doge's batela, wending their ways home from the Piazzetta de San Marco. The sounds of revelry still sounded on the embankments. Behind candlelit windows and in torch lit streets, cloaked figures made assignations in the shadows, all determined to savor the last few hours of Carnival.

Polo dwelled in the central quarter, contrada San Giovanni Giustiniani. One by one the batelas disappeared before and behind along canals branching from the main, until they were alone on the water with few following after. And still they were not alone. There were cries from the streets: some merriment, some sounds of desperation, sometimes music, and then afar off a scream of despair. Then only the sluice of the oar in the water and a single boat remained with them as they turned off the Grand Canal into the capillary that fed into the central quarter.

Siduri was full of the evening, an intoxication of the senses, and much drawn to Esquin though Constanza had exactly the opposite reaction. Something in Squin reminded her of Morgan Kara, and being near left her with the feeling of having the life blood sucked out of her. She was much concerned Siduri seemed so readily taken in by one Constanza so deeply distrusted. She could not hear clearly but Squin spoke low, intimating closeness between intended to exclude all others. But she heard and Squin spoke perfect Arabic: too perfect.

"And what impressed you most?"

"The Mirrors, full of motion, color, brilliance, they made a hundred seem a thousand, a movement of the dance a moment in eternity?" Siduri turned to Constanza. "What of you, Constanza? What most impressed you?"

"The vanity," Constanza said.

"Oh, but it was all quite wonderful," Siduri objected. "Squin has been telling me about snow," she added with a little laugh. "Truly, is there such a thing? He speaks of the sky whitening with shining falling stars in light, great billows blowing in the wind. Is he teasing, Constanza? Have you ever seen such a thing?"

"I have seen the world turned white with snow," Constanza said. "And many months turn desperate cold follow in its wake, until sweet spring returned."

"I should dearly love to see this."

"Then you shall. The Lady Madelon has invited you. Come with us to Waldheim," Squin said, "a land where the mountains are covered with it. You come, too, Constanza." He drew closer to Siduri to speak over her. "We shall have wonders to show you as well."

"I have business to attend in Crete."

"Is it not wise to know more of those with whom you would do business?"

"There will be time enough when I return."

"And I have business here," Siduri said, reluctantly.

"I have not told you I knew your father," Squin pressed. "We were, after a fashion, in business together. I visited him once with the Lord Roland of Waldheim in Alexandria. There was an old one, name of Jakob allied with him. Do you remember? What is become of him?"

"My half-brother Shirazi now manages much of my father's affairs on my behalf, and my father's protégée, Hugues Caron, has taken up Jakob's part."

"And this Hugues Caron," Squin said: "are you close to him; I mean, is your alliance one that you trust?"

"Like the desert fathers he prefers his liberties to affairs of trade. But he is entirely trustworthy."

"Cares not for business?"

"It is what I feel." She shook her head.

"The Lady Madelon knew your father as well," Squin said. "Indeed, he was of some importance to her."

"How is that?" Constanza asked.

"While he lived he was one of four who wielded great power in her service."

"What kind of power?"

"Some say knowledge of things invisible: esoteric powers. He bore the title, Master of Hallows. I know nothing of these things, but perhaps, you have inherited his gifts, Siduri?"

"I am about my father's business, which is why I have come to Venice."

"Perhaps that knowledge is yet to come. In any case you should know the Lady Madelon holds you in great esteem and for his sake has great confidence in our liaison - in trade."

His words were punctuated by a grappling hook that clattered aboard, gripped the batela and at once began to draw the two boats together. Before the guard could react, he was shot through with a crossbow bolt. Squin was at once on his feet. A dark cloak leaped into the batela, stiletto in hand. Another followed with sword. Squin drew his sword but could manage only a quick thrust to the shoulder. It was enough. He dropped his steel and plunged over the side to avoid a second.

The boat heaved and emptied out Siduri into the dark canal waters. The second assailant came on and fell clumsily between the boats. Constanza reached for the stiletto in the hull. The heavy weight of water soaked clothing and the receding tide drew Siduri down. Squin dived into the water after her. The third assailant came and Constanza plunged the stiletto of steel into his heart. It was over in an instant. The boatman watched it all flash by so quickly he'd not had time to react. Instead he made quickly toward Squin struggling with Siduri in the water, and together with Constanza brought them aboard.

Siduri huddled up to Squin for warmth. She clung to him in the dark and he whispered soft encouragements, until the boatman made the landing of Polo's villa. There he scooped her up and despite the limp carried her into the portico and home. Constanza watched and followed in disbelief how easily Siduri had fallen under Squin's spell, but again there was that feeling of something of Morgon Kara in him, and she wondered at it for in Khotan it had beguiled her. She knew Siduri was being caught up in a weave of illusion, and must speak with her on the morrow. Siduri was altogether unprepared for the web they wove to snare her. If she could be convinced, Constanza determined they would leave Venice together, and seek out Caron. For the moment she said nothing but hedged herself and put on as all good Venetians had learned to do, a social mask.

At home with Polo they paused to say goodnight, Siduri took Constanza by the hand and looked earnestly into her eyes. "The black mirror," she said, "when I came to thank the Lady Madelon for her gift, she said when I am at rest to gaze within and see looking back at me the face of him whom I will wed."

"Do not look into the black mirror," Constanza urged. "I have seen these before though none so sophisticated. Scrying is an ancient art, the like of this is used in divination, to draw out and reflect back upon us what we and others have hidden within."

"Then it is true I may see my heart's desire, for in his study I have seen my father gaze into a vessel of still water in contemplation. And he was a man of great wisdom."

"What may be rightly can be wrongly used. I once heard a shaman say these can even be gateways to another world, drawing us into their influences."

"Do you say the black mirror is bewitched? I do not think Magda means me harm."

Siduri laughed nervously. Constanza drew Siduri into her arms and gave her a sisterly embrace. "Your father's heart was pure. I would not trust the Lady Madelon or her creature Squin in that wise." She felt Siduri go cold in her arms. "Remember," Constanza said, "your father took himself apart from these to live in Egypt."

Alone in her room Siduri took out her prize, beautifully wrought in gold compact, and within the two mirrors, light and dark. She studied her reflection first in the bright glass by candlelight. The ball in hall of mirrors had been so dazzling. She had longed to take off her mask and see herself for the first time. Now was her moment. She gazed at the bright reflection smiling back at her and made mouths at it, lips parted in a smile, now pursed, now a tad petulant, and then open in wonder. "I am beautiful," she whispered to the image of herself, "other women scarce compare; other than Constanza, of course," she added as afterthought, "of her there is none so fair, but if she is the sun I am the moon, full of mystery and romance to her sunny frankness."

With that she turned to the dark mirror, inlaid in black obsidian, its image seductive, inviting her in to discover more than the distracting light of pure reflection. It haunted her like the full moon moving among billows of clouds, now seen, now unseen, casting shadows on the earth, filling the heart with longing, inviting her to look deeper into the dark mirror, loosing what she had so long kept hidden in her soul. And if her father, Flegetanis, looked into dark waters to see what would be, was she not her father's daughter? "Will it be Hugues?" she asked, gazing into deep waters. "If so, let him come to me and show himself now."

Her heart brimmed to flood, a mix of love longing, resentment and desire that drew her into a vortex of dark apprehension. Did he love her, or was it respect for her father that bound him in duty? Would he come again as he had in her moment of need, only to vanish into the desert on another incomprehensible journey once he felt her in secure hands?

He would never be a husband, would he? Such men were wed beyond women, not subject to the bonds that tie lives together. Her feelings drew her deeper and deeper into the black mirror; she saw darkly her reflection, and though she was beautiful still for a moment she saw the apprehension of age flit across her face, and with it a vision of empty, dark years ahead without the human warmth she craved now that her father was gone.

"Let a door open. Let me see the end of this. Show me what I must do to fulfill my father's life and win Caron to bridal bed."

And, indeed, a door did open. Constanza was beside Siduri in a moment, her arms on her shoulders. She reached over and closed the compact, jolting Siduri back to awareness. "Patience, dear one, lest you come to a place without power to return: when the moment is right, I will show you the use of it."

If the Doge's palace was the head of the beast, the Arsenal of Venice was its labyrinthine lair. Squin had never seen the like. On 110 acres, surrounded by a two mile defended rampart hiding the arsenal from public view, the instruments of the republic's power were conceived and birthed. Squin choked at the smell of it: brackish sea; milled lumber from the hills of Veneto, debarked, bucked, ripped and planed; coking and smoke of iron smelting, all mingled with the smell of boiling tar for the seasonal caulking of old hulls; and the screech and unearthly din of the great beast like a dragon in labour.

But it was the scale of the enterprise that overwhelmed. More than fifty galleons in various stages of development; from framing through planking to final assembly and all to pattern, all parts interchangeable, lay line astern along a narrow canal. Each vessel moved along in turn in timetable to match the skills of specialists at each stage of construction; hastening to finish one but to move on to another. Behind these walls 12,000 souls laboured to produce all the serene republic needed to maintain its supremacy on the seas: from smelting through blacksmithing to weapon making; carpentry and ship chandlery, to rope walking and sail making. All the crafts were wrought to the securing of trade, projection of power and defense of this beast of commerce arisen out of the sea.

And the bureaucrats came also among them, housed in an enclave set apart within the gates of the fortress; affording overview and quick access to both the elite of the city and operations of the arsenal. One of these was Fidelio Lo Giudice, a solicitor in acquisitions for the arsenal; a stout man with a round face, short dark, cropped hair and shoulders arched forward like a bulldog. His bearing said it all: one way or another he'd have you, and not let go his grip until you relented. But his outer manner was in fact solicitous.

"It did not go well," Lo Giudice said. "My men were overzealous and now one dead, one wounded and the other like to catch his death of cold."

"I had no way of knowing real or feigned," Squin said. "They slew one of the Doge's men. I thought we were to meet upon the pavement."

"That was my instruction, and you paid me well," Lo Giudice said. "They overstepped. How shall I make it up to you?"

"The Ariadne is in the arsenal for recaulking," Squin said: "How long?"

"A week and she can sail."

"I want you to take passage on the Ariadne to Agios Nikolas."

"As it fits I have business with the arsenal in Crete."

"Attend as well to my business and I will pay you handsomely," Squin said. "Do we understand each other?" Lo Giudice shrugged. He was a blunt man and did not like reading between the lines.

"I know you have connections with the St. Vitus conspirators, who fled with Tiepolo; I know you are known there; I know you've had, shall we say, dealings with that animal, Barbas, before."

Lo Giudice hunched forward challenging, thought better of it and sat back squat on his haunches. "You want the Ariadne to fall to the Beast of Ulcinj?"

"I will pay you well and alike Barbas. You will carry word of the tragedy to her owners in Crete. Tell them you have been approached; that the vessel is being held for ransom, and for a price you can arrange its release."

"Barbas is ruthless in these matters," Lo Giudice said. "The price will be high not to take ship, ransom and cargo, and still sell its crew into slavery."

"I care not what becomes of passengers and crew, only that you deliver my letter to Barbas. He will be paid well to let you carry his ransom demands to Crete."

"I have seen many delivered into his hands; many lost souls sold back again into slavery in Venice. I think I might persuade him to put me aboard another ship, if the price is right."

"When you arrive in Agios Nikolas, ask after the Ariadne and you will be directed to Shirazi, in trade with the late Flegetanis of Alexandria.

"To him only will you deliver Barbas' terms." Squin reached beneath his doublet, "which I have outlined in my letter. These turn on this letter being delivered to one Hugues Caron, who must himself come to Ulcinj to pay the ransom."

"The same who has the blood price upon his head?" Squin nodded. "What is to become of the Ariadne; her passengers and crew?"

"So long as Caron is taken, it matters not a wit."

Simple truth was Caron didn't want to return. Origen's serene presence, a millennial library, the simplicity of wilderness under the night sky, the haunting garden, its mystic guardian, and the sense of the presence of the one who dwelled in the midst - all contrived to engender a sense of the timelessness of time, and reluctance to return into its grinding processes. He would stay under Origen's hand, master the ways of the lords of light who kept the way of the tree of life, and not go back to a world determined to hew it into cord wood to feed a dying fire.

But it was not to be, and so reluctantly Caron took leave of Origen and sought his way north into the Levant in search of passage to Crete. In White Village, the Nabataean seaport Mas'udu on the Red Sea, Caron joined an Arabian caravan on the old incense road bound for Petra; and after many days, incessant wind and dust at his back, he came to Ashkelon.

There he waited to take passage for Crete on the Aletheia, an 80-foot cog, 180 tons, with a complement of captain and 16 crew; her cargo spice and incense resins to warehouse in Crete. The cog was originally one of Jakob's designs for Flegetanis' ships, unique in the harbors of the Mediterranean. He studied the Nile feluccas, took the basic cog design, deepened its keel, and added a second mast. Now lateen rigged with triangular sails, she was able to beat into the eye of the wind, when others must hug the shores. She was a vessel well and true, and Flegetanis christened her Aletheia.

Caron had but once met Captain Macarius but Flegetanis spoke well of him, and was good as his word. Seeing Caron road weary, Macarius made him as comfortable as possible until Aletheia should sail in a caravanserai off the waterfront. It was as neutral a ground as one might find in the Muslim world where, in the name of the uninterrupted flow of commerce, travelers from across the known earth found sanctuary. The caravanserai of Ashkelon at the end of the Silk Road was two acres of walled grounds with a single gate, just wide enough for heavily laden beasts to enter. It lay open under the sky, but within were stalls and chambers for merchants, servants, animals and merchandise; an inn for food, refreshment and sundry diversions. This one was well appointed with water and fodder for animals. There were also baths and shops for travelers, where they could barter and resupply for the long journey home. Indeed, the Arabian caravan Caron joined in White Village settled here, too, in the dust of a sultry afternoon, seeking the blessings of water and the safety within these royally sanctioned walls. And but for the true believers, here also was the solace of wine.

Caron settled with Macarius within a palm grove, a place of peace amidst the bustle of a caravan disburdening itself of the trials and tribulations of the open road.

"Baibars, the incompetent, has fled," Macarius said. "It is safe to trade again with Egypt."

"And the Sultan al-Nassir Muhammad?"

"Returned from exile in Al-Karak to the throne in Cairo."

"The young sultan admired Flegetanis, and oft took his counsel, but not entirely in the matter of his handlers."

"It is difficult for an old let alone a young man to throw off the yoke of courtiers and creatures," Macarius said.

"He was wise to leave them to their devices until the people had enough of them. Now he is welcomed and his rule will be long and prosperous. It was Flegetanis who counseled him in that wise, was it not?"

Caron nodded, remembering with a smile how guileless but shrewd his old mentor in dealing with human nature. He did not resist but instead deflected the force of will that would impose, until it fell of the burden of its own works. He took another cup of water, more precious than wine, and was about to propose they rest deeply before sailing on the tide when there was a ruckus at the gate. Two figures stumbled into the sanctuary of walls, followed by a volley of spoiled vegetables and an angry crowd crying infidel, but none dared enter after. Caron watched the refugees make way to the well, one a Mathurian friar upholding his ransomed brother, wounded in the way.

"What order is he?"

"Dirty white robe, red and blue cross - a Trinitarian friar," Caron said.

"A mendicant?"

"The Mathurian collect alms to ransom enslaved Christians."

The friar had a sense of opportunity, and he saw it now in the men sat under the palm. He knew his own when he saw them, and drawing the younger man after half-stumbled across the sun baked courtyard toward their table.

"The friar does not look well."

"He will seek passage."

"We have little enough room this voyage and they will not be fit to work."

Caron thought of his own journey over the sea of grass to the roof of the world, across the seas to a land yet unknown, and the odyssey through time that brought him to this cool glass of water under a merciful palm. He knew at once what he would do. "We will not leave men come thus far to perish for want of charity."

"I take you for good Christian men," the friar said, arms outstretched, bracing himself at table. "I fear I am not well."

Caron poured him a cup of cold water. He offered first the cup to his companion, and drank thankfully of another. "Johannes of Oxford," the friar said: "Trinitarian Ministry to Christian Captives. My companion is Robert Hode. I came to ransom but it is he has saved my life and brought us thus far home. The man was faint. Caron yielded his own place in the shade, where the friar laid his head upon the table.

"It is against the law of hospitality and nations not to honor the terms of ransom," Caron said.

"This good man came for me, paid the ransom and released me. They have not killed but harassed us in the way," Hode said. We have been deprived of hospitality, of food and rest, of succor in the wilderness. And when we were most in need, they made sport of us in the way. Only in the caravanserai have they left us alone."

"You are bound for England."

"We beg passage."

"Friar Johannes, do you know the Sandford Preceptory?" Caron asked.

"Templar Grange at the river crossing," Johannes said wistfully. "There is an inn at the ford: The King's Arms."

"Indeed there is. Rest here until we come for you," Caron said rising. "We sail first for Venice, but I will see you home and shall raise a cup together at the King's Arms."

Johannes lifted his head to Caron's eye. "Praise the Lord." Caron felt the pain in him and feared the man was dying. "We are well met, sir," Johannes said. "May the time come that I shall serve your need as well as you have mine."

"As you have served God's need; so do I serve yours."

Caron was as listless as the sea and Macarius moody; neither one willing to sail, until the brooding heat broke, and a light wind came on to fill their sails. Then the dust rolled in and with it electricity in the air; both sensed what was to come. There was a sirocco in the making, but on the leading edge they might make good time and so they sailed.

Caron brightened with the sea, but wondered at how to follow through on what he'd come to know? How do you explain the ineffable to those who struggle to merely survive: plotting and plodding on from day to day, knowing little more than getting and spending trying to wrest some gratification out of life. The irony was he was aboard a merchant ship with cargo of everything human hearts desired. His voyage home was a journey into the belly of the beast that digested everything it could consume, and he owned it. Origen kept watch over eternity, but Flegetanis had used every act of every moment in the mundane world to translate his inherent knowledge of the Otherworld in this. And now he must master the art of living.

Two days on the open sea the world weathers caught up with them. Macarius was a good captain. Caron would stay out of his way and let him do his duty. It began under a clouded, sun-split sky spilling pools of light on the water, filling the air with sheet- lightning and dry thunder. It was what he felt brooding, coming out of the wilderness: a hot, abrasive wind from the Arabian Desert, clashing at sea with cold northern moisture in a great cyclone that swept the shores of the Mediterranean.

For the moment the winds allowed a broad reach, and like a gull on the wind, and for a day and a half they rode the crest of the storm, until afar off they sighted Crete. Then the wind shifted and everything changed. A sudden gale, an unseasonable nor'easter, beat down from the mountaintops of Crete with such ferocity they were forced to turn away and run before the wind, driven inexorably toward the African coast. Macarius set a sea anchor to stabilize the ship's motion on the great waves and went below for Caron.

"I was raised a coastal captain."

"You've set a drogue and reefed the sails?"

"I've stabilized us in the swells, but we are driven off Crete to the African coast." Caron sat on the edge of his bunk and wondered at his detachment; a complete paralysis of will, devoid of care whether he lived or died. This, returning, he had not expected. But there were others.

"You designed this ship for deep waters. Well, we are in deep waters now, and can you also sail her?"

"She's your vessel, captain."

"Then come topside," he ordered. Caron gathered up his cloak and followed the beleaguered captain above, but there was no fire in the belly.

The sky was hardened in a dark barrier ridge from horizon to horizon, drawing a line north and south between continents, above and below the heavens and the sea. As he came up from below Caron saw the dark mass pulse and congeal, a sudden shaft of light create a rainbow at his right hand, and a long white filament of swirling energy descend from the clouds above into the sea and raise a spire of water to the heavens above.

Then a second filament appeared, a third, and a fourth, as if the beast Briareos of the hundred hands and fifty heads, who guarded the gates of the storm pit of Tartarus, was loosed again on the earth. Yes, he was come to drink up the wilderness of sea and sky, making them one vast chaos of uncreated earth. Caron watched as a rage of waterspouts threatened the Aletheia sweeping her decks with ocean, but she held steady in her sea anchor as the twisters crossed over, and the masts held firm.

Macarius came face to face with Caron. "My crew is terrified." Robes drenched with salt water Caron saw them clung to the sheets the decks awash, awaiting the next wave of twisters to wash over them. "If I lose any number the ship is lost."

In the midst of the spume that washed over the ship leaving its spindrift traces, Johannes of Oxford, sick to the death, came above deck into the elements, and knelt before the mast praying for the safety of the ship and her crew. Robert Hode lashed him to the mast, and held the mendicant friar upright his arms raised in supplication to God who dwelled beyond the storm.

Caron felt the friar's virtue fill his prayer; his influence streaming out of him through an open heart transcending failing flesh. He was reaching beyond his power to sustain the force he sought, heart and soul given, all it had left to give, until there was nothing left to sustain his own existence. Caron came swiftly to him. "You must let go Johannes." He held the man's face between his hands, shouting against the storm.

"The Lord on high is mightier than the noise of many waters," Johannes said: "Yea, than the mighty waves of the sea."

"It is in God's hands the resolution of this mortal storm."

"I know it, but the Lord has spoken to me. And I know you have also need of me.

"The flesh fails but if you will bear me in your heart and so my charge home again, I will be a prayer to the Almighty in the way with you."

On the very margin of life looking into the heart of light in the soul of a man, Caron knew what he must do; knew what he could do. "Let go in me," he said, "and I shall bring you home again to your brethren."

"Hode to his home and home to my heart in Holy Isle of Lindisfarne," Johannes asked. "Can you do that?"

"I can and will if you will let it be."

"So be it," Johannes said. "There comes a time when death comes as compassion, bringing us home again to life."

And giving up the ghost Caron took Johannes in. He let go the cloak of flesh that had borne him across the world to ransom a soul and rested in Caron.

"Greater love hath no man," Caron whispered. And as he felt it in himself, where there had been nothing but darkness on the face of the deep, the greater life began to stir. It urged first with shame for his indolence in a world wracked with need, and with it came a flood of compassion for those who struggled to see their way through the storms of their lives to harbor peace.

And when it was in him, as in the poor, mendicant who prayed for mercy and redemption and gave his life for his friends in Christ, his power came upon him; then the frame of things began to shift. It was enough to begin. He saw the friar slump before the mast, held up only by Robert of Hode whom he had freed, and as he passed for a moment at least the wind abated and a way opened and Caron turned to the storm. "The Lord has set a bound on the sea," he whispered. "Here shall your proud waves be stayed."

"Demetrius claims the Ariadne can sail into the eye of the wind," Macarius shouted. "I have tried her in fair weather but not in foul."

"Do you give me the ship, captain?"

"Christ, man, it's yours anyway."

"And yours to command."

"Then I am your mate."

Caron saw the crew sensed the moment; all looked toward their captain.

"Half-reef the sails. When I say, hold on for the ship will heel. When I say cut the drogue, without hesitation take an ax to the line."

Caron took the helm watching the rise and fall of the swell, as the crew reefed the sails; Macarius ready with his ax to release the sea anchor.

"Prepare to come about," Caron shouted on the wind: "Now, Macarius do it now."

The drogue cut free, the little vessel leaped forward on the crest of a wave. To not lose the wind and stall the ship, or risk falling back upon the rudder and losing the Aletheia in the trough, Caron found the groove between a close haul and close reach and took the wave close on 20 degrees and sailed the channel. And in this wise Aletheia turned back to Crete, Caron threading the needle's eye of wind and wave, until storm-weary they came into the lee of an island off Crete, reset a sea anchor, hove to and waited out the tempest.

Macarius and his crew were ecstatic with the sea worthiness of Aletheia. Pride of the Mediterranean they called it, and praised Caron for his seamanship. It did their hearts good to know that their master of ships was himself a master seaman. Caron felt again his affirmation of life; the wisdom of waiting for the right moment to act, of doing the right thing on the crest of the need. In right action for right action's sake was the key to living that unlocked the oneness of the worlds.

In Crete, his feet firm again upon the earth, Caron gave Christian burial, cleaned and folded the friar's habit, and spoke to Hode of his duty to return it to his heart's home and give account of his life.

"And mine to speak to his sacrifice," Hode answered.

"We shall speak further. If you will first heal here in Crete then bide your time a while with us in Venice, I will see you also home again."

Hode clasped Caron's arm in friendship. "The serene republic, how shall I bear the luxury of it?"

"We shall both as he who gave his life for us. And if you will bear with me, we will continue his work to bring us all home."

17

Beast of Ulcinj

"Have a care," Lo Giudice warned. They were under escort to council chambers. "With good reason Barbas is called the beast."

Caron stood with his advocate and took in the situation. Barbas, master of the citadel at Ulcinj, was a coarse, stocky man, muscular, about forty, with sea worn face of pirate days, and shock of black curly hair. You would not call him handsome but he didn't have to be: he had presence and power, was physically intimidating, and with personality to match. Now he was predator eyeing Caron, calculating to what extent he might be prey.

"Milord Barbas, at my word I have returned in good faith with the owner of the Ariadne and its crew. I present Hugues, le Comte de Caron."

"Nobility," Barbas said, with a gruff nod: "good, very good." In a moment he was all condescension. Caron's nobility meant nothing but strategy in how to broker the situation.

He'd sailed from Crete with Lo Giudice. Come ashore he ordered Aletheia up coast to Korčula to await the release of the Ariadne, then continued on foot to the Ulcinj. Letters of transit opened the gates of the walled city and earned them escort to the citadel on the rock. What

Caron learned in the way was that his advocate was not only familiar with the process, but known to the guards and functionaries alike. This was a business of ransoming vessels and captives, no doubt profitable to Barbas and Lo Giudice alike. Conducted without rancor it should all soon be settled and the Ariadne on its way. Payback would have to wait another day.

What concerned him more was the other missive Lo Giudice bore to Crete: Squin de Flexian demanded the stone of sovereignty in ransom for Siduri. If Lo Giudice knew the content of the letter, this negotiation could be more complex than anticipated, but Lo Giudice was all business and was bought for a price. It was Barbas who was more curious about Caron than he should be.

"So, you will pay the ransom without protest?" Barbas asked.

"Would it help if I objected?"

"Not at all, though most do."

"Then let us conclude our business."

"I've been lenient in my demands; you know I must answer to Despotes Zoran who governs this region of the Nemanjić realms." There was disdain in his voice; Caron marked him ambitious. "He keeps an immense estate and profits from me while I Prometheus like am chained to this rock on the edge of the world." He paused a moment indulging in feelings of regret.

"Here you are your own master," Caron said.

The suggestion pleased Barbas. Despite himself he was beginning to like Caron. "Yes, it is for me to decide how to go about our business in Ulcinj. I understand the trade."

"The trade of dealing in the souls of men," Caron said.

"And women, Caron. Our business is more than slaves of course. We take only what others have to excess. We are open to receive whatever goods and services the winds of trade blow to this God forsaken rock. Yes, I capture the occasional Venetian vessel that strays into our waters. The serene republic can afford it. In return I sell slaves to wealthy Venetians, and deal in other matters for them where they would rather keep their hands clean. We strike something of a balance overall. Lo Giudice here has become quite adept at negotiating terms in matters such as these.

"But I'm very democratic. I trade with the Byzantines and Arabs as far off as Morocco. I hold no prejudice, and for a fair price I will broker slaves with anyone. Who comes here in good faith to buy or sell need fear nothing."

"Then I would complete our business and be on our way." Caron took a pouch of gold coin from beneath his cloak.

"You have the gold with you? Most expect some protocol of exchange. They think I'm a thief. In good faith, perhaps you will join me for dinner before we conclude our business."

"We can talk," Caron said, "when you have released the Ariadne and its crew,"

Barbas' *kaznac* took the money at once, and as keeper of the treasury eagerly retired to his counting house.

"You have given in too easily, Count Caron. "Does gold mean so little to you that you part with it without protest?" Barbas bade them to sit. "What am I missing? Why do I feel I should further profit from this venture? What do you say to that?"

"This day is yours," Caron said. "But do not take my mildness as compliance." Caron was not intimidated and Barbas desired it.

"You are a man of great property. Shall I ransom you?"

"Milord," Lo Giudice intervened, "Caron is Christian and of noble blood."

"How should that prevent me?"

"He will have connections, perhaps even blood relatives in the Nemanjić realms.

"That would be inconvenient. Do you have such relations, Caron?"

"None that I know."

"Then what is to prevent me ransoming one, even of noble blood? I am speculating only, mind you."

"The politics of piracy."

Barbas challenged, thrust his heavy shoulders forward and glaring at Caron through glowing eyes. He did not like to feel restraints on him. "What politics."

"Break you word, and even among thieves you will not be trusted."

"You have a point," Barbas said. "I have always been an honest broker, but politics?"

"You exist at the pleasure of Venice," Caron said. "In return for the nuisance of an occasional hijacked vessel, held for ransom, Venice profits from your trade in slaves. It has calculated that you are useful, at this point not worth a war to dislodge you."

"That would not sit well with the Nemanjić princes."

"Do you think they want war with Venice over your business affairs?" Caron asked. "King Stefan would replace you rather than welcome a war with Venice over your excesses."

Barbas coloured and hunched up under his robes. Caron was right. It would not do to provoke the Venetians or unsettle his own. Still, he didn't like being told as much by one at his mercy.

"And why should one ship and one noble make any difference to them."

"Because you infringe on the Doge's own interests in the Ariadne," Caron said.

"You are in trade with him?"

"I am."

"He is as much a pirate as I am; only conducted under the cloak of legality."

"It was the Ariadne's first voyage commissioned by Doge Giovanni Soranzo," Caron said. "This loss will prove costly to him; if you interfere further, it will not go well."

"Is this true Lo Giudice?"

"I have heard as much."

"Are you threatening me to leave your ships alone? Beware, for another time I may not be so politic and have you in one of my cells." He was angry but he'd heard and would not press the issue further. How far you could push the Doge without inviting war was a constant question among his superiors.

"I am saying there is a balance in all affairs. That balance once broken, change is inevitable. We will pass this way again. Hereafter, expect my ships to be armed with the Doge's men."

Barbas frowned then his face lit up suddenly, like the sun breaking from behind a dark cloud. "You intrigue me, Caron. See to your ship, and crew. All your men are in the slave's quarter. Take your advocate, Lo Giudice, with you. Here is your authority," he said, handing Lo Giudice the paper. "It instructs they be clothed, fed and returned to their ship before dawn.

"And when you are done you shall both return to me for a night of pleasure. I never send anyone away without showing appreciation for business brought to my door. It pays to be acquainted, as I expect we shall do business together again."

Lo Giudice led a familiar path through the fortress along a rocky corridor between stone buildings, scarce wide enough for two men side by side to pass, until they came to a great wrought iron gate separating the slave square and vaulted cells. There were nine cells, each opened on one side to a cobbled square, and on the other to a walled in open space on the sheer cliff's edge for exercise and ablutions. Here the slaves were exposed, and sold to ready buyers. It didn't do to pamper but neither was it profitable to degrade the goods. The Ariadne's crew gathered in two cells; for the moment the others were empty, an auction recently concluded shipping these lost souls to masters among the Albanians, Turks and Byzantines.

"But for word you were on your way, he near sold us." Demetrius said.

Lo Giudice shrugged it off. "I'm a businessman; I protect my investments." He presented Barbas' orders. The leather clad jailer, a muscular man with a look of hopelessness in his eyes, shrugged and turned to Demetrius. "Fortune favours you, friend. The Beast has set you free, and I your jailer, as much a slave as ever you were, must endure."

"Come with us," Demetrius replied.

"With or without me, sail at dawn," Caron said. "Macarius is with the Aletheia in Korčula. I've given him instructions for modification of the two vessels. I wanted them fitted with canon."

"What will you do?"

"Dine with the Beast."

"He will not go back on his word," Lo Giudice assured. "You hit the mark when you warned it would be bad for business. And the Beast of Ulcinj is all about trade."

"We are missing one," Demetrius said. "The Lady Constanza was taken from us, and not seen her since."

"She is in the citadel," Lo Giudice said. "You must forget her. She is a great prize intended for a pasha. Already the bidding is begun."

"A passenger, Demetrius; Venetian is she?"

"No, she is come out of the east; rich in goods and mistress of many things the heart desires. She is fast friends with Siduri, and sailed with us hoping to find you in Crete."

Caron's mind lingered on his journey to the east, but all he could remember was his descent from the high Himalaya into India and his sojourn with Padma in the valley of the immortals. "Is she Hindi?"

"No," Demetrius said, "as fair as the women of the northern reaches. She says that having met you will know her."

"I will find a way to free her, but you must be ready to sail as soon as she is aboard - no matter the hour."

"We will not leave you to the Beast."

"If I do not come you will sail without me; tell the others I am dead freeing her so they will go with you. Tell only Shirazi the truth when you meet with him; tell him to await me in Venice."

"Will you be my advocate in this, Signor Lo Giudice," Caron asked. "Whatever it costs I will make it worth your while."

The two returned, bathed and refreshed, were ushered into Barbas' chambers to take dinner by the fire.

"Would you have me say she was a passenger and you would ransom her as well?"

"He will toy with me, and I must pay dearly for this."

"But why not seek a bargain?"

"The amount of ransom doesn't matter. He already believes there is a fortune in her. No amount of gold will persuade him, unless he gains some other satisfaction from the transaction."

"I don't understand."

"He would master me. He must believe I suffer some humiliation to find satisfaction in his generosity."

"What would you have me do?"

"She is a heathen woman, a visitor from the east. I shall not say it, but you must confide in him. Tell him I already own this woman; purchased as a slave, yet unbroken to my will, she was being brought to me. Tell him I was smitten with her on an eastern journey and am desperate to recover her."

"He will charge you all the more for her."

"I shall pretend she is of little interest to me until this plays out. And then you shall confide in him my passion for her."

"Then you do know her."

"She has watched over me, as her I do now."

After the fish course of fire-grilled grouper came the meat dish, a slow turned lamb, redolent with oregano. The Beast's appetite was prodigious but methodical, his table arts practiced to impress. And it appeared that's exactly what he wanted to do; overwhelm Caron with style and generosity. Used to depriving himself, Caron could not keep up and found himself picking at his food and drinking sparingly to keep faith with the feast and his own wit.

Lo Giudice, and the half dozen or so captains, Tepčija, and clerics invited to dine were engrossed in eating, taking in the modest entertainment of a few jugglers, tumblers, and forced merriment of a handful of musicians, anticipating the moment the women would be brought in. The Beast was known for his generosity in such matters. For his part Caron felt Barbas' eyes constantly on him, calculating what advantage might yet be had.

"There was a woman taken in passage with the Ariadne," Barbas said, a Signorina Constanza. "Lo Giudice tells me you have an interest in her."

"You are misinformed. I knew nothing of her until my captain mentioned her to me. Barbas caught a tremor in Caron's voice that betrayed weakness.

"Just as well you have no interest in her," he said, dipping his hands in the finger bowl and wiping them carefully. "She's worth a king's ransom."

"I would have supposed her released with the others."

"I have two emirs bidding to add to their harems."

"You would give a Christian woman into a harem?"

"I'm at a loss to say what she is. She says she comes from the far off Himalaya, but is as fair as the women of the north."

Caron held out his cup for wine: "daughter of Alexander, perhaps."

"An interesting thought, Caron," Barbas said. "It seems to me you are at least a little bit curious."

"She was aboard the Ariadne. I ransomed ship and crew. I owe her some consideration."

"I do not think you can afford her. I have emptied your purse, but let us visit her. Looking will cost you nothing but envy. I would have her myself but for that." Barbas led down a labyrinth of corridors into the heart of the fortress, past his own lodgings into the slave and servant quarters. "I must contend with jealous masters, you understand. They would not long tolerate my having one more beautiful than any they possess. So, I will take profit of her and taste for myself before serving her up. Follow," he said, looking over his shoulder, "the dungeons are not far."

"I wonder you do not better care for your property."

"Bondage and a little suffering bring out the best in a woman. They are treacherous creatures, Caron. If you are kind to them they seduce you; if you indulge them they betray you; if you teach them their hearts grow hard, and you spoil the bloom of lust. Free and independent they are arrogant and do only what is right in their own eyes.

"The one who taught me told me to think of them as you would a horse to be broken; trained to the halter and ridden to obedience.

"No, Caron, holding them in thrall absolutely subservient to your will is the only course. Persist in that and in time she may become serviceable; as your own body to you, quick to command, trembling to obey, as familiar and responsive as your own flesh.

"This one, however," he said, putting his shoulder to a great iron and oak door, "is not yet broken to the saddle, and by rights should be put to the whip. I think I am too kind but I do not wish to mar that magnificent flesh."

They entered a stone chamber lit by two torches, with a single barred window through which Caron caught a whiff of the sea. With it came longing to be under sail and gone from this place. In the middle of the room in shadows, strung from the beams of the wooden ceiling was a woman full extended; arms strung over her head so she could but touch the flagstone floor only on the balls of her feet.

"I had her prepared for inspection," Barbas said: "This way we see the best of her. "Constanza," Barbas said, kindly, "I have brought a friend to see you." He took a torch from the rack, lit it, and led Caron up to her so she could see his face and a flicker of recognition in her still fierce eyes.

"She is not yet humbled, M. le Comte," he said. "The emirs devalue a forward woman, so she must be trained. When I am done with her she will be worth more. What do you think, a real beauty isn't she? What wouldn't you give for her?"

She was clothed in a white cotton shift that broke above the knee, open at the neck to reveal her leather slave collar. It was shapeless but draped over the mounds and shadowed hollows of her body, emphasizing hips and breasts and concealed little. He could see her wrists were raw from struggling with the ropes, and she was cold.

Barbas followed his eyes in torchlight, and in Caron he saw passion. "You can see why I'd keep her," he said. "She does look a little ragged doesn't she, but not to worry. It is all part of her training to serve; her sole purpose to yield to a sultan's pleasure, nothing more. When she learns that everything will change for her. What she suffers now will be made up by the one she serves: silks and jewels, the finest of everything, no doubt, for this one, provided she learns her lessons well."

"I have found many women wise," Caron said.

"It may be, but not in my experience. This one is a vain, froward creature, too beautiful to be taken seriously."

"What do you want for her?" Despite himself he wanted her, or was it just for her to be free and on her way again.

"You are in the market for a slave," Barbas said, enjoying his discomfort. He paid Lo Giudice well for his services, had always found his information about shipping invaluable, and again the Venetian advocate had come through for him. This was, indeed, the woman Caron purchased as his slave but would not now own up to it hoping for a reasonable price, doubtless. "Very well, I shall find one for you, one you can afford Caron."

At Caron's name Constanza brightened. She raised her head and glowered at Barbas, but managed a faint smile for Caron. She said nothing, but the moment was not lost on him.

"Does he interest you Constanza: Nothing to say, not a word for le Comte de Caron?"

"Sell me to whom you will, but I am hedged with power. The man who takes me against my will shall die as will you Barbas for this dishonour. The darkness already gathers to you."

Caron felt the surge of influence between them, a power he felt in Origen's presence. Their eyes met and there was knowing between them. Even the Beast felt the force of it before she drew back and hid herself. Barbas took it as attraction. "She likes you, Caron, but she is altogether undisciplined. I cannot sell her until she is bridled, broken to the saddle and ridden."

"You do not break a horse."

"Are you a master horseman, Caron?"

"Enough to know a broken spirit is useless."

"With horseflesh you have a point," Barbas said, enjoying the exchange of with, but interested in playing Caron to submission. "Perhaps her arrogance lessens her value. The sheiks have no tolerance for that and it would be a shame to see her beauty marred. You, however, I think are taken by her and would spoil her with simpering love longings, as you Europeans do your women.

"Well, perhaps, we can find a price. But as a good merchant you should have a chance to see what I'm selling before we discuss the details. Let's see what we have here, hidden by custom. You may change your mind; perhaps I will change mine.

"As I've told you," he said, reaching for the bucket of water, "Constanza has become the center of a bidding war, but I will entertain your entering into that." He drenched Constanza with the full bucket of water, so she was soaked head to foot and the wet, thin shift now sheer clung to her body.

"Check her teeth," he said: "they speak to her health. Be careful, she may bite you." Caron turned away. "Come. Come, you don't buy a hare in a sack," he said, leading the way. Constanza endured as Barbas coming behind to avoid her kick spread her lips to reveal her teeth. "Perfect," he said, "come close, Caron, take a look." Caron laid his hand gently on Constanza's cheek and she opened her mouth for him, and he saw hurt and hope in her eyes.

"She's learning. Just weeks ago when we brought her here she'd kick, scream and thrash out at anyone dared touch her. She was like a chained wolf, but I think she likes you Caron."

"I've seen enough to bid on her." The seed he'd sown through Lo Giudice had taken root. Humiliated by his betters, Barbas would humiliate him; not gold but humbling was the price for Constanza. It was his way of dominating Caron, a man whose station was above his own, but who like all men great or small he'd learned could be mastered by manipulating what most they desired.

"No, no," Barbas objected, "her price is greater than rubies – isn't that how the passage goes – I insist you understand what you're bidding on."

He grasped the shift at the collar and with one fierce tug tore the thin dress from her.

"Shape shifters they all are," he said. "They paint their faces; shape their bodies, contrive their clothing and practice their ways all to deceive a man. This much at least is real for as many years as she may hold up and you still desire her.

"Feel the breasts, Caron," he said, coming again from behind and taking each in the palm of a hand. She struggled a moment then went still. "Her flesh is magnificent. Feel her belly," Barbas said. Caron put his hand on her waist. "Thrust your hand between her thighs. What, have you never taken a slave before? Must I show you how this is done? You have to handle them Caron; like a snarly bitch of a dog you have to handle them, until they let go and fawn after your touch.

"She's quite remarkable isn't she this one, but you knew that didn't you? You've already had her."

"I've never met this woman before," Caron said, catching her eyes on him, as close to pleading as she'd ever come.

"You're lying to me, Caron," Barbas said. "I have my sources, and this woman was once your property – now mine - on her way to you in Crete."

"I don't take slaves, but this woman doesn't belong in your world and I will make an offer."

"I don't know," Barbas said. He was roused by the bargain he was driving. He ran his hands over Constanza's loins and reached between her legs. "I don't know; she's special this one, a thoroughbred. I'm inclined to keep her myself."

"And you might well keep her," Caron said, playing back into the snare the Beast set for him, "until your overlords have her from you. Word of a woman of this beauty will reach them, and most likely there are already whispers."

"Curious, isn't it Caron," Barbas replied, coming away from Constanza, "in our own way we're all slaves; we all belong to another who has his mastery over us. I possess this woman for a moment; if another has the power to take her from me. How then is anyone free?

"Even the king is a servant. He fears those who would take from him what is his, and lives his whole life trying to shore himself up and secure," Caron said.

"We are mastered by what we want, are we not?" Barbas replied. "You want this woman and I possess what you want and so I master you."

"Slave, beggar or king, the sinner is the servant of sin," Caron said. "In God only are we free, yet mastered by the love of God."

"But you do want her, don't you."

"I do," Caron admitted.

Barbas sighed deeply. "You call me pirate but I am a businessman and must show profit. In the eyes of princes their acts are legal though they dictate them; my own they tolerate but judge illegal except to their advantage. You understand the perilous life I live. Wealth only gives security.

"Well, you shall have her, but I shall have great profit in this, such that I wonder you are able to pay."

Barbas let the feeling of victory sink in. Again he had humiliated a man over his own property: first his ship and crew; now this woman he once possessed. It was the supreme satisfaction of his work; taking from others what was their own; returning it to them at a price. Domination and trade in souls was his business. And today he had broken a noble over a whore.

But he could also be magnanimous. "You shall pay again what it cost to free the Ariadne and her crew. Seeing the disposition of your heart toward her, I shall not ask more though well I might, but I am merciful. Perhaps, however, I have already taken from you all you possess."

"You have cost me much in time and trade, but if you will leave my ships free to pass for a season I will recover my loss before we meet again. Caron drew his knife and cut the seam of his cloak. Three rubies like great drops of blood fell into the palm of his hand. "Taken in trade with India," he said.

The Beast's eyes narrowed on the three grape size rubies in Caron's palm, ablaze in torchlight. "As for this woman, she is partner in trade with the Doge and came seeking accommodations with me." Caron felt the breath drain out of Barbas. "You've plucked a fruit too high from the tree, yet I will intercede for you.

"If you will accept these stones and a pact between us that you will give my ships free passage for a season, have your women clothe and bring her to Demetrius, who waits upon the morning tide. Further, I will compensate the Doge for his loss of cargo aboard the Ariadne, and blunt the edge of his anger."

Barbas revealed nothing but Caron felt the arrogance give way to anxiety; his own masters wanted no conflict, not yet at least with Venice, and the Doge was Venice. Still, it would not do to reveal weakness. "I will give you the woman for these," the Beast agreed, "but no future guarantee on your ships. Nothing personal Caron; it is just business."

"Then my business must be to elude your grasp."

"So, we understand one another," Barbas said amiably. He ran his hand over Constanza's shoulder, down her back and rested on her buttocks. "I will have her clothed and sent with Lo Giudice who will take passage with her to Venice. You and I, meanwhile, shall drink an oath to conclude our business.

"You will speak to me of trade with India in precious stones. Perhaps we can do business together. I believe you understand as I do that the merchants of the earth are truly her mighty men. A time will come when princes seek of them approval for their deeds, and I perceive you as a noble are riding that tide before them."

"You are one fortress on a rocky shore owing allegiance to a greater kingdom over which you have no control."

"Yes, but it is a rock in the river of commerce… and upon this rock many a vessel… well you see what I'm suggesting – in time the whole world will come under the rule of commerce and the order of things that now is will be dictated by those who control the wealth that comes from the flow of it. And who controls that will control the hearts and minds of men.

"For now I serve a prince who loves his comforts and depends on me to provide them. Such men are amenable to manipulation. There's a whole world to be gained, Caron."

"At what cost?"

"Hear me out," the Beast said. "I can be most persuasive."

"My ship sails at dawn."

"Your ship, yes, but let me put this thought in your mind. I have bargained with many a captain who came this way, taking my tithe but making them and their masters rich; those who refused came this way but once or twice thereafter, and never more. Over time I have accumulated wealth enough to buy and sell princes."

"And you would put your mark on me."

"In your case there are special circumstances. Your advocate, Lo Giudice, has a powerful client," he said, drawing a paper from beneath his cloak, "who offers payment for proof of your death.

"It asks I search your person for a precious blue stone, for which I am offered literally a king's ransom. Having seen the three rubies I'm inclined to believe it. This request comes from very powerful patrons. I will need a very good reason not to fulfill this to the letter."

"Search me."

"Then you no longer have it."

"You will free the others."

"I am a man of my word. You were given safe passage to ransom your ship and crew, and we negotiated the release of the woman. They are free to go.

"You see, I have beaten you, Caron. Lo Giudice confirmed the Lady Constanza was in alliance with the Doge. Her being here was apparently a mistake, and despite my game with you I should never have detained her.

"You should not have confided in Lo Giudice. He alerted me to your knowledge of her, humbling yourself to secure her release. And so another man falls to another woman over his desires. Tonight you and I shall drink to that, rather too much I suspect, and you will miss your boat. You will be searched and kept in slave quarters a week to ponder my offer. When we meet again it will be to discuss your fate."

"You are the son of your father," Caron said.

"And what do you know of my father?"

"That he is the father of lies."

"You think me the image of the Beast?" He sounded almost hurt.

"I imagine you suppose your actions all very logical; indeed, inevitable."

"My premise is profit; the rest is detail. Your future is with me, Caron. I see immense profit in you alive. What intrigues me, though, is why powerful people want you dead."

"They who destroyed the Templars would destroy me," Caron said. "They have been looking for me all over Europe. Doubtless the letter bears the signature of Lord Roland of Waldheim or the Lady Madelon de Faucon."

Barbas shook his head. "No, Caron," he said, "It bears the seal and signature of the Doge of Venice. You would have returned to your death. You see the mercy of keeping you here, until I decide what is to be done with you."

"So, what do you want of me?"

"Your agreement to serve: There is a world to win, together, an empire."

Caron could hear the weeping of women and the cry of children in a distant cell, but he was confined alone. What made his confinement worse was the smell of spring in the air filling the soul with longing. The front of the cells opened on a stone courtyard where slaves were auctioned, but in back barred windows opened on a small walled garden on a sheer cliff's edge that fell away to the sea. And there he watched the white sails of the Ariadne cross the path of moonlight as she sailed away without him. He could feel Demetrius and crew look back reluctantly. The tow on him was irresistible: he felt the Lady Constanza filled his senses, her thoughts his heart and mind with gratitude. And on the air she whispered assurance she would not abandon him. But what could she do? Still, he felt her warmth for him, and alone in his stony cell she brought him rest.

And there he remained until the week of his interview with water only, but he was used to fasting and found no hardship in it. He quieted himself, rested in the eye of peace, and let the days in the old city and slave square pass by in a cacophony of human sounds: loud and soft, harsh, strained, and strident, cries of concern and complaints and sometimes, though rare, laughter; all mingled and mellowed by sounds of the sea on the rocky shore below. And still he did not feel abandoned but loved if from afar. This buying and selling of the souls of men; it was all in stark contrast to God's gift to live free in the spirit of His love in the world.

Again another wanted to possess him. It was what all those who would force the world to their own desires wanted. These were parasites on the body of life, taking from others what they had no right. Barbas had seriously underestimated his mark. He had suffered worse, but wondered how God should sort this out with man, when men reckon nothing the lives of others but to serve their own. Worst of these were the likes of Morgon Kara. It was the worst kind of slavery; exploiting longing for of a world to believe in, torturing truth to serve his purpose; promising a world for a soul, and consuming that soul to feed the fire of his own desires.

Having overcome Morgon Kara, he would not yield his life to pirate and parasite, or agree to serve the idols of the Beast of Ulcinj to save his life. If he lived he would honor the truth of love in all he met, so that agreeing in life there would be life and more abundantly. He would do what all the princes of the world would not do: let God create His kingdom through the yielded heart, the still mind, and answering spirit. He would live to let the wonderful one shape His world in the spirit of truth.

And then in the night came Maia, mistress of illusions who could weave water into knots, and shape the ten thousand things that beguile the sense. He had opened his heart in thinking upon her and again she entered in. "You surprise me, Caron," she coaxed. "I did not think you had it in you to slay Morgon Kara."

"He who dwells in the light is greater than he who covets the earth."

"There is nothing in the light but power to shape what I will. I chose Morgon Kara because he cherished my influence. And you may have it if you will," she teased, "to make a world after the longings of your heart."

"I will embrace your purpose if you will meet me in the one who dwells in the light."

"There is nothing in the light."

"Then there is nothing between us."

In the twinkling of an eye she was come and gone, though the sense of her lingered a half forgotten memory. And after Maia came a vision of Constanza in the night. She sat before him on his narrow cot, not as he had seen her in distress but splendid with radiance. She looked on him with eyes at once curious, compassionate and touched with love. Whether he dreamed or not he could not say, but full five minutes she sat with him silently and then spoke so her voice within him.

"I have suffered his possession and understand, perhaps, more than you what Morgan Kara is. Two paths there are in the world, Caron. Most walk the path of the son of perdition whose end is death. But the way less traveled is the way of the wonderful one, the path of undying life. When we are well met, we shall make certain the way that leads into the heart of light."

Toward dawn of the fourth day a great mist rose out of the ocean and enveloped the fortress and old town of Ulcinj. So thick it was Caron could not see in torchlight beyond his bars the slave square onto which the cells opened. There was weeping and low moans from the cells about him for animal comforts. Food and a brazier of coals for each cell were brought to keep the value of the Beast's property and preserve his profits.

But Caron received no succor. He was left yet alone in cold and darkness, the mist creeping in upon him until he could scarce see his hand before his face. He had not now eaten in four days, and was frozen to the bone but with the mist came a blessing. A voice whispered at the grate at the back of his cell where the cliff dropped off sheer to the sea below. "Ali, my brother, you did not think I would leave you." Shirazi took keys and opened the door. "Shall I free the others?"

"By all means free them, but I fear these are resigned to seeking masters to care for them. Their bonds are in their souls."

"None will awaken until first light. The Lady Constanza made the village sleep. And she has made this mist to conceal your escape."

"How has she done this?"

"She confessed she once of a year was mistress to Morgon Kara. Arts of her own she has but certain he taught her things."

"The shaman *is* dead. I saw him slain."

"We spoke of this. On that day she saw a dagger thrust into his very heart. But in his essence, among the rulers of the darkness of this world, she says no, he is not dead. And that this focus of iniquity shall dissolve into nothingness, she would stand with you however long to that end."

"I have seen many things, Shirazi, some of this world, some of the other, but I am amazed a woman would search across a wilderness of world and time to stand with me."

"From what I have seen," Shirazi replied, "this one need never have left home to do so."

18

Amour

Two weeks after her ordeal the Doge visited Terra Ferma, his estate in Veneto, where he'd settled Constanza amongst attentive servants and watchful physicians anxious to rehabilitate her. He was deeply chagrined, profusely apologetic, but a May morning conspired to bring out the best in both. Constanza took the old man's arm and walked the rose gardens with him, accounting with some reservation her ordeal in Ulcinj. Old man that he was and jaded in the ways of the world, he nevertheless was most attentive to the tribulations of his beautiful guest.

For her part, Constanza was much aggrieved over Caron. "I have learned there is an edict commanding his capture, stipulating alive or dead. Yet he came to me in my distress, and face to face with wickedness I found him noble. He risked himself to ransom ship and crew from the Beast of Ulcinj, saved me from being sold into slavery; even went into captivity to secure our freedom. I owe him my life but know not whether he is alive or dead."

"It's difficult for a stranger, but he is contrary to our politics and wanted throughout Christendom as reprobate. The price on his head is for the theft of treasure, and conspiring with the Grand Master of the Knights Templar to form alliance with Ismaili assassins."

"I have heard in awe the courage and fortitude of the Templars in the face of overwhelming odds."

"Nevertheless, they made enemies of kings, and the order is no more. Some say they were innocent of charges brought against them, but they grew too powerful for crowned heads to sit in comfort on their thrones."

"So it is the same everywhere," Constanza said. "Men of honour rendered dishonorable by the powerful who fear and envy their virtue."

"To Caron's virtue I cannot speak never having met the man, but the Lady Madelon de Faucon has personal knowledge of his perfidy. She claims he trifled with her heart, seduced her, and stole a great blue jewel, talisman of her ancient royal line."

"And she has put a price on his head?"

"Her influence is deeply infused in the ruling families of Europe. The loss of the stone could affect relations with these states, for it has meaning to them beyond mere material worth."

"Truly?"

The Doge drew Constanza close to him on the path of the rose garden. Especially at his age it was stimulating to feel a warm body pressed to him, and beyond her wealth he coveted her. "Do you know our story of the search for the holy grail?" he asked.

"When he dwelled a season with us in Hotan, Polo told a tale of a mysterious chalice."

"If you would know the whole of it you should speak to the poet Perrin among our players. He will tell you this tale of a cup is a blind for something other."

"Something put for something else?"

"Some account it a tale of loss and quest for a hallowed talisman given of God to awaken man again to the way of creation. It is a poet's tale but the Lady Madelon is sincere in her beliefs, and the mystery of it shared by many a noble house of Europe. For my part I see in this a poet's device, a reminder to think on things of importance we should never cease seeking in our lives."

She pressed his arm close to her and he felt the warmth of her bosom through his silken cloak and a shiver went up his spine. With such response, what more he wondered could he tell her?

"You have not issued a warrant of arrest," Constanza said, amiably.

"I sail between Scylla and Charybdis," the Doge said, bringing a puzzled look in response: "between the devil and the deep blue sea," he added. "The Lady Madelon came here in part to persuade me to her company; in part to expand her sphere and enter into mutually beneficial trade. She is a shrewd one that, and with the right hand upon her passions will build an empire."

They came to the gate of the rose garden and the Doge led Constanza on to small arbor overgrown with leaf and spring roses.

"I would not readily do business with one who is intent on murdering my salvation. Can we not look for a way to appease all parties in a grand bargain? I would have Caron live, and hunted no more."

"You think as I do, but it is complicated. It would greatly ease matters if Caron could be persuaded to return the stone. In return we might enlist the Lady Madelon's aid to turn the force of law aside, leaving us free to concentrate on mutual interests.

"But I must warn you Constanza, we have lost many souls to the Beast of Ulcinj, and most likely Caron. Still, I have in place an advocate who will discover his fate.

"As we are of a mind in this, and you the Lady Siduri's friend, might you not encourage her not to let the politics of the matter interfere with trade? The Lady Madelon is passionate to recover the stone and fears she will recoil over Caron."

"Should she not?"

"I will hear from Ulcinj in a matter of days. So, then, let us hold a festive gathering here within the week; gather all together and court reconciliation."

"I feared for your life. Demetrius told me how Hugues came to pay the ransom: so, he is alive."

"He was."

"Fear nothing, he will make good his escape. "But have you heard, I am invited to journey with the Lady Madelon to France and then Albion? She will show me the world of my father before exile in Egypt."

"Siduri, is this wise?"

"My whole life I have dwelled on Nile bank watching the tide of seasons pass; in my imagination following the river's flow to places where men go down to the sea, crossing over to the ends of the earth. I wish no longer to wait on a river's bank watching life pass me by. You journeyed here from the ends of the earth. Are you not just a little bit curious to go further and come at last to the last of shores… beyond which they say is only sea? Come with us."

"My dear sister, I came from the ends of the earth to find Caron, and I found him. He saved my life and saving his is my purpose now."

"Did you meet him when he journeyed to the east?" For the first time she thought a rival in Constanza, and despite her love for Constanza it troubled her.

"Nothing like that," Constanza said.

"Then how could you know?"

"I came to find him. I cannot now abandon him."

"But how could you know of him?"

"I am given to do so." And Siduri could tell that was an end on it for now. "But would you not have him safe, come back to you?" Constanza added.

"Of course, but my feelings have changed; my heart is inclined toward another."

"You cannot mean Signore de Flexian?"

"And why not: He is noble in bearing, courteous in speech and deed and possesses all the knightly virtues of these realms. And his only desire is to serve me in the way of courtly gentleman."

"It is sickness or pretense in men that makes them craven toward women; either way it comes to no good."

"Of course I am not entirely decided on him, but it is for once mine to choose."

"And what of Caron?"

"What of him. Old Jakob and my father conspired together over abstruse things, and after Jakob, came Caron. Yes, there was affection there once, but seven years he abandoned me in search of some mystical jewel my father set him after, and now all of Europe is up in arms over it."

"Who was old Jakob?"

Siduri cocked her head and looked askance. "He was an old friend of my father and of my youth. It no longer matters."

"I knew one who had known Caron, who said he had the power of the phoenix birth, the gift of resurrection and undying life. Was Caron first Jakob and before him yet another?"

"You and I will perish," Siduri said. "We must live deeply while we may; so I will journey with the Lady Madelon before succumbing to a life of dreary trade in the dust of the earth."

"If he is like unto an angel of God whom the desert fathers call Malachim," Constanza said: "We have found in him the pearl of great price; nothing should deflect us from this."

"I love him for the perfect and virtuous knight he is and one I cannot have. As it was with my father what he loves is forever beyond me. I want someone who above all others will love me."

"And what of those who seek his death?"

"He greatly offended the Lady Madelon abandoning her and fleeing to Egypt with that cursed stone."

"And yet you would journey with them."

"My father was once numbered among their Masters of Hallows, privy to the ways of the Blood Royal. If it was important to him, I would understand that."

"Tell me about the Blood Royal." Their conversation was interrupted by a chambermaid hastening Siduri to the garden gathering where Squin awaited her, she said, and the Doge himself would welcome Constanza to the pageant. Constanza demurred.

"Journey with me and see for yourself," Siduri said, anxious to go: "It is what I must do to understand what sweeps me up and bears me on."

"Will you abandon Caron?"

"I would free him," Siduri said, thoughtfully, "from obligation, from hurt – free him to you if you desire it - what more can one do for another?"

"But fear nothing, Constanza; I suspect the Doge has put you up to this. Assure him business will prosper; the issue of Caron will not harm our relations."

"You misunderstand me, Siduri. I would readily sacrifice my business interests in these waters to see him land on some safe shore."

"Then we are of a mind. Let us both see what we can do to lift his burdens; free him to that higher purpose we mere mortals can scarce comprehend."

Constanza was not sure if it was cynicism or longing that affected Siduri's voice. "It is, I think, a kind of sickness of soul, this romantic love," Constanza said.

"It is a sickness of soul that can only be cured by its agent," Siduri parried.

"Then one must be sure to choose one's beloved wisely."

"I am most impressed with these players. They have excelled of late in Venice and I saw fit to become their patron. And now at our command they will offer an entertainment in your honour, Constanza."

His wife on his arm, the old Doge escorted his guests into the rose garden: Magda on old Gisors' arm; Siduri clinging like life to Squin's. They were followed by an entourage of nobles, all come from Venice to Veneto to greet the May on terra firma, where forests greened and orchards blossomed.

"It is based on the work of Guillaume de Lorris," he continued, "The Romance of the Rose. Do you know it?"

"I do know the poem, a work of chivalry. And you Squinset," she said, looking over her shoulder: "Do you remember?" His attention to the Lady Siduri had begun to irk her. To whom did he actually belong?

"An unfinished work and best left so," Squin said: "Spoiled by Jean de Meun: philosophy is the bane of romance."

"You will find little of that in this rendering," the Doge replied, "but skillfully adapted for players by a trouvère of the company, the poet Perrin von Grünschnabel."

"What good can come of Perrin?" Magda mumbled to Gisors, who simply squeezed her arm. "The Lady Constanza," Magda said, "will she not join us?"

"Still bruised in body and soul by her ordeal," the Doge replied, "I thought it best she watch from the balcony and a servant to attend. She has the lingua franca but this I think too much for her."

The festivities began with music and a chain dance of players as the troupe joined hands and danced a carol to the low beat of a tabor, and a ballade extoling the virtues of chivalry.

"Squin's quite taken by her," Magda said, leaning into Gisors, "one might think rather she was sent to seduce him."

"She is a daughter of the Blood Royal," Gisors reminded her: "And daughter of a great master, God rest his soul, full of virtue and influence."

"This is more than I expected."

"Fear nothing, she is smitten by Squin; see how she hangs on his arm and dotes on his every word."

"You have outdone yourself Gisors. I expected after a life of restraint she would take pleasure in our attention. I thought it would take time to win her but she is most certainly won if not bedded, and I must speak to Squin about this lest it come too soon."

The dance in praise of chivalry done, the troupe turned to its major work. To a soft background of the lute, the players masked to their parts, took their places, and the prolog to the piece spoken.

"Many a man holds dreams to be but lies."

"He shows a nice leg," Magda said to Gisors with a nod to the prolog.

"All fabulous," Perrin continued, encouraged behind his mask by Magda's appreciative glance. *"But there have been some dreams, no whit deceptive, as was later found.*

"One might well cite Macrobius, who dwelled upon the Dream of Scipio, assured that dreams are oft times true."

"Well, now, this is right out of the text," Gisors complained, "can he not parse to please this company? No, Magda," he insisted, "he has not bedded her, and I have spoken to him of this, as to the way of an angler who too soon seeks to land his trout. He must play her until she is utterly his, but with enough spirit to make it interesting at the last. I am assured he understands how serious it is what we undertake in her."

"Well, there is more to it I am sure," Magda said, ill at ease. I know chivalry has given us the upper hand, but like this play it is all too tedious. We have made men into dreamers; dreamers into lovers in search of the ineffable which they cannot attain, and we at the last being mere flesh and blood and not goddesses, after all cannot supply."

Gisors felt the anger rising in the Lady Madelon as her attention was drawn again to the piece. "Do you see what they have done? In this play upon the poem they have taken our garden for the walled garden to which the lover comes in search of his vision. See, he is both intrigued and yet fears to approach, but his dream is powerful. Here he will seek his rose and we the watchers cunningly cast as virtues and vices that assist and impede his quest.

"Oh, this is Perrin's work for sure. At once he entertains comments on, and mocks us. He would shine his light on his betters. He wants what we have, and we are to see in ourselves hostilities to his life preventing him from fulfilling his dream: hate, violence, abuse, greed, misery and covetousness. As if holding a mirror up to us, all these things he would have us see in ourselves, and absorbed in our pleasures we see naught in it but an entertainment."

She was taking her anger out on the play and would break his spell in Siduri did she not comfort herself with kindlier thought. And yet Gisors would not, could not oppose her.

"This spell I wrought in Siduri exceeds the powers I intended over her nature," Gisors said. "I meant only that she sees in Squin those things for which she longed; that in his image she might find the longings of her heart revealed. Yet so intensely has it come upon her that Squin is drawn into her passions."

"Well, we have conditioned men to serve us," she said, mulling on the enigma of Siduri and what she might mean to her. "And again, she is a daughter of the Blood Royal."

"Old Flegetanis was a taskmaster," Gisors said, "had little regard for the life of the senses; she has not known the things you freely give and now she craves. It is like liquor to one who has never tasted drink."

Magda glanced to Siduri, leaned forward rapt with the play: the lover now seeking entrance to the garden by the good graces of its protector, the Lady Leisure, the garden's protector.

"She will let him in," Magda said to Gisors.

"She must not let him enter."

"No, the Lady Oiseuse, the play," she said, "Lady Ease with the mirror will let him in."

"As you have Siduri," Gisors said. "Now watch what shall happen, for the same befalls a woman as much a man who seeks the image of herself in the other."

They watched the pageant unfold as the dreamer admitted to his paradise encountered pleasure, friendship, openness, and reason shaped to the desires of his heart, until he came to a deep pool in the garden's midst, hedged by roses and for a moment gazed into its depths and spoke his lone soliloquy.

"'Whene'er the searching sun lets fall its rays into the fountain and its depths they reach, then the crystal stones there do appear more than a hundred hues; for they become yellow and red and blue. So wonderful are they that by their power is all the place – flowers and trees – whate'er the garden holds – transfigured."

He gazed a moment into the depths on the luminous jewels, until unable to fix his stare his gaze returned again to the image of his love longing reflected back upon the surface of the waters and at his face the reflection of a rose bud.

"So do these crystals undistorted show the garden's each detail to anyone who looks into the waters of the spring. For, from whichever side one chance to look, he sees one half the garden; if he turns and from the other gaze he sees the rest. So there is nothing in the place so small or so enclosed and hid but that it shows as if portrayed upon the crystal stones."

"Is this what you have done to him," Magda asked: "caused Squin to gaze into the depths, so now fallen into the dream you wove to snare Siduri, all Squin can see is her reflection in his soul?"

"Shall I tell you what I think?"

"If it will ease my concern."

"The dark mirror has not alone accomplished this. There is another force at work. Caron has revealed something to her of the power of the stone of sovereignty and unwitting caught up in its sway has drawn Squin into her sphere of influence."

"Taking him from me?"

"It is in the nature of the stone to intensify all within its possessor. I think she has come into contact with the stone. It works its influence in her to the purification of her heart, or failing that the destruction of her soul."

Magda was absorbed by the thought of it. She watched as the lover, the distillation of all lovers, leaning over the pool; smitten with love for the rose he sees in his reflection, and overcome with passion, when there are none to see, plucks the rose. In that moment, for the first time, she feared in Siduri the loss of her office. What had Flegetanis and the Cailleach Branwyn together wrought in secret and now loosed upon her. "Has Flegetanis set a snare and betrayed us into this?"

"I cannot think it."

"We must contain this." The play moved on to a dispute between virtues and vices over the plucking of the rose. "She must not yield to Squin. If Siduri has become the setting for the outpouring of the influences of the stone of sovereignty, we must first bind her to our purpose, for given the chance at power in his own right Squin will take full advantage."

"It shall be resolved in the gathering of the Masters of Hallows at Caer Myrddin when our power is at the full."

"And yet I fear it now." Magda saw the play end and musicians take up the burden of the evening. "I thought I knew what Squin was, but as he masters Siduri, this new power comes upon him, and I am altogether unsure where this will go."

"Fear nothing, Domina. The stone will be returned to your hand; at Caer Myrddin you will bind the temporal lords to you, and the Masters of Hallows will set a pattern for loosing its power to purpose. And when it is accomplished, you shall magnify that power at will through your soul and so your kingdom. We are your bone and your flesh."

"My good and noble Gisors," she said. "In your confidence is my strength."

Siduri sat on her bed, alone in her bed chamber, and gazed into the mirror. She saw still a young woman in her late twenties in black, silk nightgown gazing back at her. But time was passing her by. She was young when Caron came into her life; she had waited first seven years, then another two for him, and now again he was gone. She ran a brush through her long dark hair and her soul filled with longing. Her father used to say she had beauty to rival the goddess Nephthys. "'As beautiful as twilight, you are,' he used to say: "'Milady of the temple; home of the gods.'"

Her hand went to the silk pouch beneath her nightgown where the blue stone nestled between her breasts, and glowed like a blue sun. Aton, the sun-stone, her father called it. More to him and Hugues it meant than her. Of that she was sure, for it had taken both from her leaving only a wilderness of years. She slipped it from her neck and placed it carefully in a drawer of the night table.

"You are approaching an age where men turn away and neither woo nor marry." She spoke aloud. It was silly of course, and she knew it for she was beautiful yet. But she was feeling not only a little sorry for herself but motivated to bring the issue. Master Esquin doted on her and she found him compelling; he had a way about him that drew her in. "And what then shall become of Hugues should I give myself to another?" A flash of anger fired her blood and clouded her mind. "My father would not give me to him. She saw her face contort in the mirror. "He would give me instead to Shirazi, and have Caron breed me."

There was a tap on the door. She stood angry but composed herself and opened to Squin. He stood silent on the threshold, his eyes filled with the lovely woman who answered to him; her eyes questioning his purpose, and guessing the answer she let him in.

"Excuse my presumption." He was nothing if not gallant when it served his purpose. "We have become so caught up in affairs, never alone, I thought we might now have some time together before we leave for the Lorraine." He saw Siduri's eyes moisten; her lips pout as if to protest his leaving, and felt the way open to press his suit. "Will you not come with us?"

"Do you give me good reason, Esquin?" she asked, sitting on the edge of the bed. He came and sat close beside her.

"Are you not curious about your father's life? In a time before Magda became Domina of the Blood Royal, your father was a Master of Hallows to Branwyn of Wales. He was a great and powerful man until he chose exile in Egypt over some disagreement. It was there sent by Branwyn to inquire after the stone of sovereignty, I first met him. There were rumors and its recovery the price of his return."

"It means much to you, doesn't it?"

"I have but once seen it at the Gathering, when Caron courted the Lady Madelon. Seen even from afar it was breathtaking, but not half your radiance."

Siduri flushed a little even in firelight. She believed not a word. It was expected of men to speak so, for it raised the value of the possession sought and tonight that was she.

Squin moved closer, letting his hand rest on her knee. "Were it mine to do so, I would trade it gladly for your favoring my suit; nay, my pursuit of your heart."

Chivalry she found refreshing after the matter of fact purchase and possession of females that was literally stock in trade in Egypt. Twice she had been carried off, as if she was no more than a sheep or goat stolen from a neighbor, to become part of some thief's bordello or sheik's harem: it mattered little which. Here men courted, so she let his hand remain.

He leaned into her, slipping one hand under the silk of her gown, and with the other fingering the nightdress tie at her breasts. She sighed and let it be. And why not: she was tired of waiting. He was handsome, not undesirable and conveniently present. The nightgown fell from her shoulder and finding no resistance Squin advanced, tracing with deft fingers the shape of her breast, until his whole hand closed on her to the nipple.

"I do not think I can go with you to Lorraine," she whispered, face against his. "I have the Doge's business to attend in Crete with Constanza."

"He can be prevailed upon. You should first be about your father's business in Europe." He'd managed to advance his hand until it rested on the inside of her thigh and still she did not protest, and so he pressed her back upon the bed to come upon her.

Magda did not knock. She never did. She had no need to be delicate in such matters. "Leave us, Squin," she said flatly. Squin gathered up his doublet and was gone without a word. But as he left their eyes met with a knowing glance telling her what she had supposed: Siduri could be had and there was power in it.

"I have not yet seen the Lady Constanza," Magda began. "I'm told she suffered indignities."

"She was most cruelly treated. It is barbaric any woman should be treated so."

"You come from a world where buying and selling of women like cattle is common, and never ask the maiden."

"Do you not also trade in women to secure fortunes and make alliances?" Siduri asked.

"You and I, others of our mettle, can turn this all to rights."

"A woman alone in the world has little power," Siduri answered, gathering herself up. "You see how I struggle to secure my father's fortunes. And Constanza, a woman of spirit and means, subject at a tyrant's whim to slavery and servitude."

"Now is as good a time as any to speak of it." Magda sat beside Siduri on the bed, both at once looking at the image of the other in the mirror. "You nearly gave away to Squin tonight what you should give no man except you first master him.

"We have worked long and hard to raise ourselves from subjection to the beast, and if you are to be part of us you must understand the arts of mastering the male. You must train him up as you would a horse or dog to your advantage. If the world is to advance the finer substance must ever master the coarser, and so the feminine, the masculine. Do you understand, Siduri?"

"I do."

"I'm told you were once yourself abducted by men who would use you."

"Twice, and both times Hugues came for me as he did for Constanza."

"And here in Venice very nearly a third, were it not for Squin."

"It may be or, perhaps, theft only."

"No, they would have had their way with you," Magda assured her. "It is the way of men who take to leave nothing precious behind. You love him, don't you, Hugues Caron," Magda said, a tremor in her voice. "And Constanza, there is love in her, too; inevitable, I suppose, when need rules sense."

"I'm told you once did, too, before you set a price upon his head."

"He betrayed me," Magda said, flatly. "Let me tell you about men. Some fall easily to our influences, others it is a long battle for mastery; but diligent, in the end, all succumb."

"I am not so ignorant as you may think," Siduri protested. "It may appear in my world women are repressed and men dominate. But appearances are deceiving for who rules the heart governs, and I have found men's minds, even those who think themselves guided by reason, easily shaped by emotions they do not comprehend, rationalizing what they feel."

Magda smiled and nodded: "Govern his emotions and mind and body follow, just as you would put a small ring through the nose of a great bull. Siduri let me tell you how we play them here to gain the mastery. This capitulation to romance is something new, and will in time free women into their rightful place of authority over the brute male tamed to our purpose.

"I know this well for it was in my own land, after a long dark age of cruelty that the art of loving was reborn under our hand. We learned again the power of yielding in the granting of our favors and through uplifting and inspiring troubadours, poets and singers of love longing to fashion a code of love making gave leave to celebrate this new chivalry. And as the fashion of men of substance followed, so also the men of mud and clay aping their betters took it up, and by this we have reshaped the world."

"I have seen some of this artifice in Squin," Siduri said, "but tonight he was determined to have had me one way or another."

"You must know how to govern what you have awakened. And this is the first rule, as a poet of our order once framed it for us a hundred and fifty years ago: *Love easily obtained is of little value. Difficulty in obtaining makes it precious.* If you had yielded to Squin he would have had his desires, and before long accounted it nothing. Then would opportunity have been lost."

"I have not yet yielded to any man."

"Have you not, dearest? Learn from me and we shall set you to govern one of the greatest households in Europe. For now let us practice on Squin, but within limits. So, this is our second rule: *You have drawn him on and now you must make him wonder if he can possess you.* A man in love is always fearful he may not attain to his beloved. Fill him with fear for your affections and so garner respect of your person."

"But is that genuine?"

"Genuine? The only thing genuine about a man's desires is that he would enter at his will into the friendship of your thighs. Except you coax him out of his bestiality, he will never discover his higher nature. He will never respect the greater beauty in you, and as you age – nay, he will not even see a passage of years before his eyes wander and seek another to please him – he will care less and less for you as an object of his desire, and we shall have nothing of them when most we need it.

"No, dear, the truly genuine here is to have the fortitude and the wit to lift the brute out of himself to dwell in the rarefied atmosphere of your own heart. And to this end, with Squin as your object, we come to the third rule: *You must study to make him jealous, even if you care not in the least for another.* The ardor of love is always increased by true jealousy, the fear of losing what one most desires.

"You may take this as far as you will; even to the point of conflict between your suitors, ready to fight a duel over your love, so long as you do not succumb to the one or the other, for then it is over. You must so play your paramour that he becomes obsessed with you, for the fourth rule is this: *A true lover is emotionally and without interruption obsessed by the image of his beloved.*

"You must drive him to distraction over you. You have the beauty and the wit; you need only practice these time tested rules to realize the power of your influence over the male. You see how by degrees he is made pliant and responsive to you."

"And should I never yield to him?" she asked, thinking how she had sought but not won Hugues, and whether there was advice here that might raise her value in his eyes.

"Never," Magda said. "Even if you give yourself to him you must not yield but keep the mastery. You must be able in an instant, even at the height of passion to withdraw the heart, leaving him confused and dazed, to keep control of him. And if he angers turn it against him, citing his failings as a man and as a lover, if need be cruelly to the point of humiliation, but never quite so that you draw back and offer encouragement to bring more to be worthy and seek more of your sweet attentions."

"Then I must play him like a fish on a hook."

"How apt your analogy: play him until he is exhausted with fighting and yields his affections to you whatever might come. You must be to him the goddess sought but never utterly attainable. Which brings us to the fifth rule: *You must bring him at last to being obedient in all things to the commands of ladies.* Of course most especially to you, and so cultivate him that he studies constantly to be enrolled in the service of woman's praise.

"When you are sure of him, then you may in measure yield yourself to him, but cautiously for accustomed to the sweet harvest of his labours may dull his sense of the rewards. Always study to keep sharp his appetite for you. And that leads us to consider the arts of making love so that you create rather than cloy appetites, but we shall leave that for another time. For now, study occasion to bring your lover with devotion into your service."

"My father spoke none of these things to me. I grew up in a very different world, my father the good master of my life."

"He was a good father," Magda agreed, "but I speak to you of lovers in a world of men who now would use you. Do not let them. Learn of me. Grasp your heritage and fulfill your destiny."

"What destiny?"

"Did he never speak to you of that, dearest? Do you not know who you are?" Magda spoke to her mirror image. "You are a princess of the Blood Royal: daughter of an order hidden from the foundation of the world, from a time before the flood: We are the beginning and the ending, abiding to keep the bloodline pure, until the last of days is come upon us." Her voice filled with reverie, rich with influence, and Siduri could not but help be drawn into the reflecting spell she wove.

"You are of that ancient spring, the blood line that endures through the House of Enoch unto the House of Melchizedek, and through the holy blood of Jesus made flesh again in the womb of his sweetheart Mary who bore to him the daughter of God."

Siduri looked long and hard her eyes penetrating, seeking out the depths of her words and Magda felt her move like a presence within her, unnerving for she had not felt such intensity searching and finding at last confirmation. "I understand," Siduri said simply.

"Do you?" Magda struggled to master her breath.

"You believe you are of the flesh and blood of Jesus of Nazareth. I understand you have prevailed in spite of the Church. And I have been told of the excesses of Rome in persecuting those who differ from them in doctrine."

"It is a delicate balance. If we press the issue hotly, they have the temporal power to overwhelm us. In our own way we are stubborn and tenacious, and by what the Church calls cunning device have held it and kings at bay."

"What device."

"Evidence of who we are; but for now the outcome of conflict between us would be devastating to them as well as us but there will come a time."

"And is that what it means to you, the stone of sovereignty: evidence of who you are?"

"A lost hallow and keystone to our power."

"And Hugues would not yield, so you have set a price upon his head."

"The future of the order hangs upon its return."

"And if it was returned to you, would you relent?"

"He is a fallen Templar and for those who would root out the remnant of that order, I cannot speak."

"You are a woman of great influence," Siduri said, "even to the extent of exacting a measure of obedience from the Church. You could seek his forgiveness."

"I would do my best to see his honor restored."

"If that is all it takes to keep him safe, there may be something I can do for you."

"And what is that, Siduri," Magda said, kindly.

"Give you this." Siduri took the silken purse from beneath the night table drawer and pressed it into Magda's hand.

Magda recoiled as an electric shock riveted her body. She tossed it involuntarily back into Siduri's lap, rubbing her hands together for the sting of it. "In God's name what is it?"

"The stone you seek," Siduri said, picking up and holding in her hands.

"Let me see it," she whispered huskily, still stung by the flash of power that moved through her. The revelation left her speechless, and she struggled for voice. At length she said: "It cannot be given that way, precious. There is a rite."

"Without restraint Hugues gave it to me, bidding me do with it as I will. So now in whatever rite you choose, I will give it to you to lift the price upon his head and clear his name.

"That promised I will enter into trade, journey with you, learn your ways, and under your tutelage claim mastery of my father's house. For mystery that he ever was to me, I believe in him and this path intended."

"We have it." Magda was beside herself with joy. "The stone, Gisors, we have it. Siduri wears it about her neck like a bauble. I held it in my hand, but it scorched to the touch and hurt to the bone to hold it."

"Then it has begun to loose its power," Gisors said. "You hazard your life to take it from her."

"But we have it," Magda said, "and her heart is turned toward us. Must she alone possess it; can she not give it to us?"

"We shall have it, but a great jewel needs a setting to reveal its many facets, what is written within," Gisors said. "It cannot be done until gathering at Caer Myrddin, when pattern and power come to the full.

There we shall make a setting for the jewel and with ceremony deliver it into your hands. Will Siduri come willingly?"

"In return for Caron's life."

"Then you must agree but keep this from her. We have learned that Caron fell to his death attempting to escape. Barbas of Ulcinj will claim the reward."

"It matters nothing."

"Understand, Domina, there is danger in the rites of Caer Myrddin. There you may legitimately be challenged by another daughter of the Blood Royal. Siduri must not understand what lies ahead or yield herself to Squin. So doing she makes him Grail King, and with power come upon him no more your trusted servant."

"I have already spoken to her of the ways of a maid with a man," Magda said. "She will tease but not yield to him. Her heart, I think, is still with Caron."

"And yours?"

"I am mistress of my own."

"And if by chance Caron yet lives he must in no wise survive to challenge us, for in giving her this stone he has chosen, and its power tied to them."

"You do not believe he died at Ulcinj?"

"In truth, I sense his presence like a weight upon us."

"And curiously so do I feel burdened of this Lady Constanza's devotion to him," Magda replied. "I fear she will contend with us over sovereignty of Siduri's heart."

"You can and shall do better Perrin. It was a pretty play to delight the senses, but I will need something more of you, for this art I think may be used to shape souls to our purpose."

"Domina, our poor players gave performance at the Doge's command. He is the patron of our art, and we do but strive to please him."

"And you are mine as you were the Cailleach's before me. In your absence I was reminded of this. 'The poet has a gift,' Lord Roland said to me. 'There is power in his words; he can be useful to us as he was to the Cailleach of old.' And I agree, Perrin."

Perrin cast his eyes to the ground until it was uncomfortable to deny her any longer his reply. "I cannot give you what belongs to the Doge or the troupe that answers to Signor Falconieri."

"Perrin, Perrin, do you think I have not thought of this? As part of my agreement in trade with the Doge I am now patron to the Falconieri Players, and with the Doge we will grant you license throughout our realms of influence.

"And now for some sad news: your friend Hugues Caron is dead. I am sorry, Perrin; I know you thought well of him, as did I until he betrayed me, but still I feel sorrow at his death."

"You are sure of this?"

"The Doge has it from spies in Ulcinj that in trying to escape Caron fell from the cliffs into the sea. Barbas, the beast of Ulcinj, will claim the prize. The affair of the stone is done, Perrin. You are no more in exile but free to pursue your life amongst us again; it is yours, this troupe, and so long as you serve our purpose you shall want for nothing.

"And now to a happier matter," Magda said. "What I want of you is this: you shall create a ceremonial processional that the temporal lords might revel in, all wrapped up in a play of pomp and circumstance. Fill it with such light, colour and music of praise that it shall be worthy to celebrate the return of the stone of sovereignty to the Blood Royal."

"And when shall it please you this play be performed?" Perrin asked, curious where this was going.

"Come the fall at Caer Myrddin. From here you will journey to Sierck les Baines to entertain Duke Frederick of Lorraine, and from there onto Britain to begin preparations for our arrival.

"But mark, Perrin, I would have this play a celebration nothing less than opening the very gates of heaven: a play of redemption and promise of a paradise restored." Her imagination was on fire. "You shall call it Eden's Gate, or the like, the Garden of Life, perhaps. As you will but celebrate a brave new world to come, for working together in the power of the stone we shall surely accomplish this."

"Such visions are beyond my art, but I will make a beginning."

"An inspired poet will accomplish," Magda said. "For our final nights here you shall shape something to entertain, something light and delightful to bind the hearts in pleasure."

Perrin agreed. What else was he to do? But he could not help but feel they all were being written into a play, the authorship of which was beyond him. But the affair of the stone was done? Did this mean Magda possessed it and Caron truly dead, or did she deceive herself? In other wise this eased the burdens on his heart. He did not think himself a man born to endure as Caron had, but one for the tender pleasures of the flesh: noble houses, fine clothes, food, wine and the passions of women to inspire his art. And all this Magda promised.

The unspoken heart of the matter was somehow the Blood Royal had come again into the possession of the stone of sovereignty. Nothing less than this could have enflamed Magda's imagination so; nothing less make her so willing to overlook the bitterness of the past between them. For all the aspirations Caron roused, Magda had just put him in his proper place.

When Perrin was gone from her, musing on the privileges and responsibilities she had generously heaped upon him, the Lady Madelon sent for her two spies, the brothers Timor and Formido. Naming them after Roman gods of fear and panic was her little jest. If pressed she could remember their real names but what does a spy want with a real name? They came cautiously for she had not spoken to them since they botched Siduri's kidnapping.

"You failed us in Egypt," she began, "but the woman has delivered herself into our hands and that in part fulfills what you were sent to do." Formido was about to answer but Timor pressed his brother's arm and silenced him.

"Part of that task remains: I am told Hugues Caron is dead, fallen from the fortress cliffs at Ulcinj."

"We arrived too late to assure that," Timor said.

"Lo Giudice has word from Barbas confirming this, but he is a man who will do anything for money. I want to believe Barbas but also need assurances. If Caron lives he will follow after the Lady Siduri, who journeys with me now."

"We will be watchful," Formido ventured.

"You will do more than that. If he is alive he is alone and vulnerable. He will seek a way to disguise his coming, and in that I assure you he is very cunning.

"He has yet one friend in my poet Perrin who, if I am any reader of men, does not believe him dead. It may be he even knows something we do not.

"Perrin will journey with me, but within the week his troupe will follow to meet with us in Sierck les Baines. It is in Caron's nature to deceive. If he lives I believe he will con a part and join the troupe disguising himself among them.

"You will follow where they go, and using all your arts uncover if he is among them. Above all, prevent him from coming anywhere near Siduri."

"We will Domina."

"Let us understand one another. You will hurt none of the players for I have need of them. But should you find Caron among them, you will separate him out in a way that no suspicion falls upon us, and slay him as you see fit to my pleasure in you."

19

Dark Mirror

Caron was tempted to conceal his identity by donning the traditional bauta mask, black cape and tricorn hat that enabled Venetians to walk abroad incognito, like one among so many crows scavenging in the streets. But nothing ventured is opportunity lost. It was the craft of the consummate actor to con a part and submerge his own persona in the role. And as theater was once ritual shaping of a creative field to purpose, so was acting a remnant of the greater art of shaping patterns to focus life essence. What was more Origen taught him the rudiments of shape shifting; to evoke the archetype influencing perceptions, shaping scene and sense.

There was far more but he knew enough to begin to master the art. So Caron chose the part of the Trinitarian, John of Oxford. From the moment John gave up the ghost into his care, Caron practiced to know the life of the one he had undertaken to bring again to his heart's home. So it was through their soul's bonding Caron wrought his transformation; into such a profound likeness of John of Oxford it rendered Sir Robert Hode breathless with wonder at the change.

Leaving Hode for the moment in Shirazi's care, Caron went abroad in homespun robes in the persona of the itinerant monk, John of Oxford, to prepare his journey home to the Holy Isles. He took the Canal St. Marco from the arsenal to the plaza landing at the Piazzetta between the granite pillars of Theodore and Mark. Here at the gateway of Venice in full view of the Doge's palace were the courts, the prisons and place of public execution; reminding one and all of the head that governed the beast of commerce. Still, it was an ecstatic spring day; sunny, with a fresh wind off the sea, if mingled with a hint of tar from the arsenal, where Ariadne and Aletheia were being refitted. After the confinement of Ulcinj it was pure pleasure to walk freely abroad. What was more there was a pageant in play and a crowd gathered in St. Mark's square. From the pennants snapping in the wind above the makeshift stage, it was a company sanctioned by the Doge himself.

One and all were laughing at the pantomime antics of an old man called Miser bent over with age. Bent over, back and forth across the stage he paced clutching a money bag to his breast. Hips forward, making great strides until he stopped, his forward momentum gone, he was thrown off his balance and fell over backwards like a turtle. Still clutching a large leather bag to his chest, unwilling to let go of it and unable to free his hands to right himself, he lay there ridiculously, his grotesque belly exposed to the sun. Swift after came his pursuer, an obese old doctor staggering along, clutching in one hand a wine bottle and in the other a manuscript, disputing with himself the worth of putting one or the other down to help the old miser.

Quick on the scene came another: Pierrot, a guileless youth in loose white blouse and wide white pantaloons, his head covered by a close fitting crown cap, his face whitened. Caron saw at once through the costume, Perrin; in this guise at sixes and sevens about his master and what was to be done. He was urging Doctor to be true to his profession and act, but the doctor would not relinquish either book or bottle to do so. This sad, moon-faced naïve was joined by a maid, a frisky wench in ragged, patched dress carrying a tambourine. When she appeared the youth doted on her, as if the very flower of innocence. Such is the power of illusion.

True to his feckless nature Pierrot turned away, pacing about disconsolate about the situation, overwhelmed by the presence of the maid. The maid, Patches, pleaded with the doctor to act on behalf of Miser, her master, whose outstretched legs thrashed the air looking to get a grip on some reality or other that capriciously escaped him. But only when she bent to speak to her master, presenting her pretty hind to Doctor, did he act and that swiftly. Down went bottle and book with a crash, and with outstretched hands to peals of laughter from the crowd, he sprang into action grasping her by the hips and thrusting with his loins like a dog in heat. Patches uttered a little yelp, tossed back her head and hair and shook a reproving finger at the old lecher, but for all that gave him a winning smile.

"Shall we consult Alrecchino," she declared in stilted line, breaking but for a moment the pantomime. "Where is his servant Alrecchino. Oh, where can he be? Alrecchino," she called, "Alrecchino appear."

Meanwhile Pierrot was pleading with Doctor - inconsolable over his spilled wine - to work his wonders and right the old man. Instead, the doctor disputed with him over Miser's condition. Arms raised to the high heavens, gestures of lofty insights, the shaking of fingers and admonitions, hands and features distorted into pompous pronouncements and prognostications over Miser's recovery accomplished nothing.

Into the midst of this dispute came Alrecchino with a leap, a bound, and a cartwheel. He was the picture of virility and manhood but vacant. When the whirligig came to a standstill and finally arrived, he took a quick glance at his fallen master and concluded at once there was nothing to be done. Instead, behind his master's back, while the old doctor ruminated, Alrecchino took Patches in his arms and at once began to untie the lacings on her bodice: advances she in no wise resisted, but with a glance about made it clear she was now less concerned for her fallen master than finding a way to let Alrecchino have his way with her.

"I have it," Doctor shouted, again breaking the pantomime silence. "I shall relieve him of his burden." Patches hastily adjusted her dress, and without reproof Perrin cast a longing glance at her, and a suffering smile for Alrecchino who had her in his stead. Meanwhile, a tug of war ensued between the doctor and the old miser, as Doctor struggled to wrest the money bag clutched to his chest.

"It is too great a price to be paid."

"Give it me and you shall walk again."

"You ask too much."

And so it went back and forth until Miser finally yielded, stood again with the help of Pierrot, Patches and Alrecchino, and the doctor left the stage to boos, hisses, and laughter; exchanging knowing glances with Patches who shook her tambourine and followed after him, money bag and book in hand, in search of a new bottle of wine.

The crowd loved the pantomime. It touched the heart of their hurts and loosed them in public spirit. It was a libidinous extravagance, unlikely to win the approval of the self-important. But Caron saw at once its potential and why the Doge allowed it, so long as it kept the decadent and an upstart class in line and didn't touch on the rulers. That he allowed it, spoke to the moral concerns of the elite that human failings be exposed – within reason - and good governance imposed.

Acrobats and street musicians took over from the players. Caron made his way back of the set where they were gathered, and offered a gift of money in appreciation; fittingly to the elderly man who played Miser, master of the players, Signor Falconieri.

"Thank you Brother," Falconieri said, with a courteous nod of acknowledgment, "an unusual generosity for the clergy."

"Friar John of Oxford," Caron said. "You lighten the heart, signor."

"I am Falconieri," the elderly man replied: "after a fashion master of this troupe of upstarts."

"With a stable of stock characters, a dozen or so types caricaturing human nature, you might compass the whole human comedy. I see you are well on your way."

"We do also miracle and mystery plays, and processionals. But this is new and very popular with the people."

"If I may, do not advance too quickly or you will turn to tragedy what should release in laughter. Many know nothing of themselves but the customs they cling to, and easily take offense."

Perrin heard and came at once to the voice, but betrayed no recognition.

"You give good counsel," Falconieri said. He was a cautious man and seemed he would say no more, until he knew to whom he spoke.

"I understand you must be careful, but not too careful. Others have gone this way before you: the Greeks who led from ritual into revealing drama; the Romans who turned the art to crafting social behavior."

"What do I know of such things," Falconieri said with the slightest hint of irony in his voice. "Our work is a poor pantomime of manners; the mere holding up of a mirror for man to gaze upon and find humor in the human condition. Yes, there are times I would raise a lamp that all might see, but no license have we to light the way to man's salvation: that is for betters: yourself, good friar."

All of us, men and women alike, must fall in with our role and spend life in making our play as perfect as possible."

"I am glad to hear it from a friar's lips."

"My lips, Plato's words, and through this craft you might weave a pattern to loose such power as to astonish one and all."

Falconieri was cautious at Caron's enthusiasm, but Perrin ecstatic. "Perrin, I am Perrin," he said, offering his hand: "Finally, Falconieri, a learned man of the Church who understands the rites of the stage. What, Brother, did you see in my artifice?"

"The gentle mockery of one who too readily practices submission to his heart," Caron said. "One beguiled by the influences of women and cannot see through their artifice."

"There you have him, the man turned inside out wearing his heart on a very great sleeve," Perrin said, swishing his own through the air. "That is the callow youth, Pierrot; and my colleague Falconieri has crafted old Miser out of his own experience, for he pays his players but a pittance. Do we have a name yet for your miser, for he shall soon be on everyone's lips?'

"Pantalone, the miserly merchant of Venice."

"Well, that means nothing to me. The audience must have a name to remember, and so a name, not unlike my own, for he reflects some of my own flaws and faults of character."

"I think this Pantalone will be a famous character in the comedy of life."

Falconieri was pleased Caron approved his Pantalone, for Perrin seemed not to see through the trope. In Miser he mocked these merchants of Venice as *pianta leone,* planters of the lion of Venice, in their greed to possess the earth. Falconieri appeared to care less for money than the cultivation of his art.

"This weaving of a pattern to release the power of our art," Perrin said: "Would you speak more to this taking of an affectation to reveal a repressed truth?" Caron was pleased one so close could not penetrate his art, for facing him full on it was clear Perrin saw only John of Oxford.

Then Perrin was gone in a shot, off to a group of admiring masked ladies wanting to make his acquaintance, for he showed verve and a fine leg.

Soberly, Falconieri offered his hand. "I will gladly drink wine with such a man who understands my art, but I must now see to my players."

"Will you perform again in Venice? I am here but a short while but would see more."

"We have a new patron in the Lady Madelon de Faucon. In two days she will leave Veneto for the Lorraine, and the Doge would have us follow after and so we must as far as Paris: the seat of your order is it not?"

"I must bring my charge home again to England. I think by way of Strasbourg and the Rhine."

"It is in the way we go. I would say travel with us, but there is intrigue in the air and your journey is doubtless difficult enough without the troubles that gather to us."

"My coming here was not entirely by chance. In my journey I met a man - this is not the time or place to speak of it, for it may upset other matters - but when you are in the way would you tell your player, Perrin, for me: if he would have news of an old friend, late deceased, he must come to the Stag's Head Inn in Strasbourg in June and wait a week upon Saint John's Eve."

Falconieri looked curiously at Caron. "You are more than you seem. But none would ever suppose you anything other than a servant of God."

"And that is all that I am."

"She's traveled far and endured much, but patience, Lothario. The Lady Madelon tells us to trust in Gisors. He will deliver her body and soul."

"There's a hard edge to Constanza none can soften."

"You show more courage as captain of the cavalry. Any woman can be had by the brave. Much depends on it, so you must rein her in; bring her under your spell. Overcome, young Vitale, surmount these obstacles and ride her hotly."

"Most fervently shall I uncle. She is a great beauty; I would have her were she heathen and pauper."

"If a rival win her, she has beauty, wealth and therein power enough to upset the order of things in Venice. Stay on her until you bed her, wed her or unwed sire a child on her, for we must tie her fortunes to our own."

The Doge smiled wistfully at his nephew, Lothario Vitale. His wife's brother killed in the wars, he had taken Lothario as a son and had great expectations. "Come now, this is a pleasant task is it not? I would have her myself but for age and infirmity. But to you she will cleave as a sheep in rut to a ram.

"We must make full use of this time. In a week the players are come again on their way north. I would have them stay on a week in servants' quarters and ply their art for the notables of Veneto. Take advantage, Lothario. Beguile the lady with feasting and frivolity, for she must not feel prisoner even to good intentions.

"You will give a ball in her honor; invite all the notables from our circle to attend at Terra Firma. You will dote on her the way women love to be admired; entertain her with color, pageant and music until her senses reel; then when she is pliant lead her into the ways of a man with a maid, free in the Venetian way to indulge themselves in each other. So will you accomplish her.

"Spare not your charms, for you have manly virtue to woo and when she has tasted of it she will languish apart from you and ache for your return. Let us consummate this affair to obtain not only a great beauty to our line, but immense fortune to consolidate our sovereignty in Venice and affect alliances throughout Europe."

The Doge's endorsement and hunger for entertainment with promise of three nights of jongleurs, minstrels and pageantry brought out the notables of Veneto in droves to Terra Firma, and the great villa and all its apartments bustled with activity of its weekend guests. Constanza understood Doge Soranzo had left the household in the care of his nephew Lothario, and made it clear in his absence he was responsible for her well-being, putting servants at her disposal and planning a festive week in her honour. She had hoped to avoid it, but Constanza knew at once they'd marked her for conquest and were in some haste.

It began almost at once. Festivities were set on the high terrace overlooking the evening hills. Husbands and wives, courting couples, hopeful maidens and young gallants, all gathered by torchlight eager to indulge every sense. Troubadours, minstrels, and orchestra assembled in the gallery to rain enchantment down on the company of pleasure seekers.

Lothario was determined no expense be avoided; no pleasure denied, no opportunity lost.

Constanza, in blue silk gown, blonde hair twisted up with yellow ribbon and set with a sapphire pin, sat at Lothario's right hand where he dotted on her, conveying exactly the impression to one and all that here was his beloved. Husbands and wives nodded knowingly, courting couples saw promise in wealth and beauty; hopeful maidens despaired and sought solace among the young gallants. And though the manner differed - noble suitor playing the devoted servant of beauty, bringing peers to witness his infatuation with his beloved - Constanza read it all with consummate ease and understood the game of manners, its ultimate prize seduction.

It began with little things over dinner. He acknowledged her beauty and the fineness of silk in her gown; and all agreed, all within the bounds of polite company. Thereafter, it was all conquest mapped out with the precision of a military campaign. He sallied into her personal space, crossed the barrier between them by clasping her hand, assuring her all delighted in her company. He spoke of wonderful days to come, his eyes confessing fire; holding on only long enough to let a hint of possession inform his grasp before withdrawing.

Moments later in conversation with Gisors, Lothario's foot touched her own beneath the table and lingered. Shoulders brushed when he leaned in to speak to her, and did not immediately draw away. And when food was served he took precisely what she took and no more from the sumptuous platters set before them. And when she reached he anticipated and their fingers met, before yielding to accommodate her need.

And so it was by many signs. When she lowered her cup to table to applaud a minstrel's song, he took it up and drinking precisely from where her lips had touched it treated the vessel as if fit for the altar of a temple. This she knew would go on interminably until she consented to play the match with him; by degrees yield and at last let him have his will of her. He was predator; she was prey. The lore of the game was prelude to cultivated rape, and so she determined to invert the reality, take the initiative and master him who would master her.

Truth was Lothario though adept in manners was not very bright, and his feeling he was making no progress troubling to him. Any other woman would have risen like a trout to a fly. He had done everything according to the rules of love for young cavaliers and still she lavished attention on others. What had gone wrong? The fête was in her honor and he master of the feast. She was seen by all as the object of his affections. He was generous to a fault: turned pale in the presence of his beloved, showed jealousy when she took the arm of another, was modest, courteous in all matters, speaking no evil, refrained from idle complaints and asked no favors but to be ever in the sunlight of her life. He had done all a man might do to humble himself before a woman and yet remain a man, and she spurned him. And in this wise it continued several days into the festivities.

True, she was foreign born and perhaps unacquainted with their ways; yet she was a woman of the world and from a land where women yielded as property bought and sold. So, why not him where advantage was to be had? She had given occasional encouragement, whispered appreciation for his dutiful care in his ear, touched from time to time his hand and once almost through pursed lips whispered a kiss, enflaming his passions. Then she was off again on the arm of another; most maddening of all his rivals in love and status, the brothers Filano and Tizio. She would yield to one or another in the dance, or to walk the gardens making conversation in the evening cool under the whispering stars. Gisors counseled him that most like Constanza being foreign born expected him to be more forthcoming. He suggested a direct assault on her defenses was in order. "And I will be with you in this," he promised.

Lothario vowed to take the initiative his uncle insisted upon; to first plead his case to the lady, and if that failed assume instead the manner of a sheik with a property. He was not unfamiliar with the ways of that world. Indeed, was there not more of mastery in conquest than in the craven ways of men to subvert their manhood beseeching the beloved to enter into the friendship of their tender thighs? It was resolved. One way or the other tonight he would have it out and so heart in throat he whispered huskily in her ear: "Tonight, when the night watch is set and the guests are settled, I will come for you."

"Why?" Constanza asked. Her manner said no, but if he was not mistaken her eyes shone.

Orchestrating the grand affair, the Doge removed Constanza from sheltered convalescence into new quarters facing east over the rose garden, to fill with morning light his vision of her future.

The bed chamber was larger than she would have preferred and more ornate, with a huge poster bed its centerpiece. After the bed a conical, sculptured chimney of stone and plaster over a hearth of perpetual fire coals, dominated the room. It was not a place of peace and sanctuary but a room with a story to tell; a story she was supposed to enter into. And so she took it all in: the walls of warm Venetian plaster in golden honey hue; frescos of lush vine, meadow and orchard with scant clad maidens at sport and gathering flowers, where spritely imps peeked out from among leafy greenery. Overhead, fresco images of gods and goddesses, she imagined - or were they angels - looked down on the scene as parents might on children at play in some unspoiled Eden.

There was other furniture: chairs by the fire, a great wardrobe, screen, wash bowl and basin, bench and ornate table of inlaid veneers. The table was set with coloured glass vessels filled with confections, flowers, and a crystal clear glass carafe of wine and two glasses so light you could scarce feel their weight in your hand. Lit by shining candelabra two great full length mirrors met in an inside corner of the room opposite the hearth, each inset within walls bordered with mother of pearl reflecting and diffusing fire and candlelight through the whole chamber.

But still it all came together in the canopy bed, draped with fine, white silk hangings and swags gathered up and carefully tied with bows. Plush, cool white pillows, a plump feather eiderdown and great blue comforter was her nest; a white silk and lace nightgown laid carefully upon it by her chambermaid, invitation to what was to come. It was nothing less than a bridal chamber and clearly Lothario Vitale, the Doge's nephew, her intended.

Well enough, she understood intent and how to play it, but it was the great mirrors that held her eye, drew in and troubled her. Like all the arts of Venice they were perfect, her reflection undiminished returned crystal clear from the very eyes that observed to the eyes that looked back. And in it she was able with motion of the eyes alone to glimpse the profile of herself and herself looking at herself. This was not the dark mirror of the compact that seduced Siduri's soul with hidden desire. Here was something more: influences mingled with the illusions of the glass. There was fascination in it, as if someone looked out at you from the other side, someone to whom this reality was the other. She found herself wondering what was on the other side of the mirror.

Perrin had heard of the chamber and mirrors from Colombina, a maid who had taken a shine to him on his first visit. "The old Doge is very fond of young women," she confided, "but has to get it up," and laughed as servants will at the foibles of their masters. "He has this chamber of love he calls it where his young women stay. And there's a mirror, you see, in that room. Well you can see yourself in its reflection from the lady's side, but straight through as a pane of glass in sunlight from the other. And there he can watch unseen, the old lecher, the preening of his mistresses and make himself wet with anticipation."

"And they know nothing of this?"

"No, I told you, silly, you can only see through from the dark side; on the other the glass is a mirror sure as any other. But if the truth be told," Colombina confided, "I think most of them know, but it gives them a thrill as well to tease their lover into passion. Rather like knowing God is watching, I should think; a delicious combination of desire and sweet sinfulness; though, mind you, I have no personal experience of this, but for the whereabouts of the room."

"Will you show it me?"

"You are a naughty one."

"It's only that I've never seen such a mirror. Great mirrors are rare and of this nature unheard of. I think most likely, and think it only a rumor you've heard."

"It is no such thing." She rose with a swish of skirts. "But we must be wary of Lothario. She has already frustrated him beyond measure; he's a hot blooded one and needs no rousing to get it up."

"A mirror that looks out on you: it is a myth worthy of a tale. But who would believe it?"

"Never, you mind, while our betters are carousing without, I'll show you sure enough how it works."

And so Perrin followed first the maid to the room prepared for Constanza's seduction. There he stood before the full length mirrors in the inside corner of the room and though he peered into them intently saw nothing but Perrin reflected back. When he was sure of the mirror she led him into the hall into the Doge's study, and then through a passage opening behind his desk into a dark recess between the walls that led to the chamber. It was just as she said; just as he had seen it, the chamber revealed as clearly as one might look through a doorway into another room.

"You wait here," she said, loosing his hand, "I'll show you."

Minutes later she appeared again before the mirror, where they had stood, turned, swirling her skirts for him, dressed her hair, and began undoing the lacings on her blouse, playing the great lady under the gaze of the Doge. "You must be very quiet," Colombina said, for you can be heard through the glass." And, indeed, she could. But all Perrin was thinking at that moment was he must breach decorum and warn Constanza of the ruse, when she returned to find her chambermaid before the glass. "Just finishing up milady," she said in a swirl of skirts. "I look quite the mess."

Constanza looked about the room appreciatively. "You've done well. I've no further need; you may retire to your own room for the night."

"Milady," she said, retreating with restrained haste. Retire she would and bring Perrin to her room for the night. But in the hall she encountered Lothario who questioned about her lady's disposition, and seeing she was free at once instructed her not to return but lend a hand to clearing up after the guests to prepare for the morrow, leaving Perrin between walls reflecting on his fate.

He prayed the maid was right and none other knew of the Doge's ways, but there was noise in the study, two men talking, and one standing close by. He waited in darkness expecting the panel to the darkened room to open, but it did not. Instead, the voices fell off and in the darkness he heard a rustle of skirts and felt a hand in his own. "Follow," she whispered, leading him through the darkness, another sliding panel, a narrow passage, a finally a lamp waiting at the head of a descending stair that branched three ways. They took the right and it ended in a large sealed chamber, well provisioned with comfortable bedding, food, water and weapons.

"A safe room," Colombina said, "there are three, all kept at the ready but unused since the late war with Genoa."

"And is there a way out of the villa from here?"

"Oh yes, but here we will be alone," she said, settling herself on a bed, unlacing her waistcoat.

Gisors thought three nights to win Constanza would suffice. If she yielded not at once, by degrees he would come to terms with what informed her responses and weave a pattern fit to bind her to Lothario. For now Gisors watched as Constanza undressed before the mirror, searching her for tell tales he could take hold of to bind her influences and shape her perceptions. Instead, fierce for control over sensual influence, he was aroused, overwhelmed by the luster that gathered to her and shamed at his inability to envelop and subdue her to his art. Like spring she made him feel mortality.

Constanza loosed the clasp on her silver belt, letting it slip listless through her hands to the cool tile floor. It was studied spontaneity, the art of artlessness and utterly erotic. And as she drew him in he could not but wonder if she saw right through the mirror into his heart of hearts. One by one she loosed the lacers on the bodice and clasps of her midnight blue gown, and slipped it from her shoulders over her hips, until it lay in a bundle at her feet.

And Constanza, too, was intrigued by the mirror. Was she not wonderfully made? A few bruises from the beast of Ulcinj, but they were healing. God could not but have taken pleasure in this creation, she thought, for she felt the pleasure in herself of a life in full flower, and understood those who desired her. She was beautiful as men had said of her, but where they wanted only to possess that beauty, she saw now in her own nakedness reflected back upon her with pearl like essence, the perfection of beauty in human form. With a sigh of contentment she unclasped her looped, ribbon bound hair and let it fall loose over her shoulders, honey pale in candlelight.

She was being watched; she was sure of it, the vibration was on the air, and again she wondered what lay beyond the mirror. No more was the curiosity of other worlds looking in upon this; she felt something more immediate and imminent danger. The shaman, her father, knowing men would want to use her had hedged her with spells to the destruction of her abusers, and ever she felt his presence with her. Even Morgon Kara who sought to steal the life from her had not been able at the last to possess her, and the predator righteously slain. It was in the nature of the spell to turn and intensify destruction in those who would defile the life. She would that all women were so hedged.

Gisors knew little of the powers wielded by the masters of sword, spear and grail hallows; only enough to know these consummated in the stone of sovereignty. He was a master of his own gift and come to power early in life had many years' experience shaping its force to the purposes of the Blood Royal.

It was not known if the Paten they possessed was the true Paten he had once seen in a vision of the Grail Procession, but it was a focus to his arts. The one they possessed was brightest silver, kept to a mirror like finish and engraved with a five pointed star, denoting the five senses, virtues and the mastery of them. The relic itself was safe in the company of acolytes; he dared not travel with it but to Caer Myrddin, but they who embodied its powers were with him though afar off, and a simple symbol would suffice to bring its power to focus in his consciousness.

He had chosen the mirror for this purpose, the silver perfectly reflecting the face of reality; the dark revealing what hidden informed it. In its use it had failed never but once, when Caron turned the mirrored surface back upon him and bade him reveal what was in his own soul. Bound in the truth to the Cailleach who set the task, he was compelled to admit reflecting he looked upon a man who had sinned much. He was humiliated, all the more for the old one had stood with Caron in this against one of her own.

In the aftermath he'd remembered the days of innocence, where every new moment was Eden, where nothing within could deflect the power of radiant sight, sense and vision. But how can one be in the world and not, like the dyer's hand, be stained by it? Again and again he'd found guile and sensual corruption in those he must master. He'd learned to shape illusions in the human sense; to entangle schemers in snares of their own making. In so doing he had in some wise lost the tone of life he was given to uphold, succumbed to human nature, and though he convinced himself it was for the greater good, felt shame.

Beguiling sense to shape illusions in the mind begins with a spell of binding. It can be as coarse as exploiting grievances to acquire power at another's expense, to artfully implanting a thought an otherwise unwilling individual will accept as his own, and to which he will surrender his life and will. He had begun by embracing and cultivating the radiant virtues of the senses, and in time turned to mastering the illusions that beset those fallen into the sensuous realm.

And that was now how it always began. With subtle force, invisible and unrecognized, in broadest terms he searched out smoldering fears and desires that darken and obscure the sense. Anxiety, insecurity, discouragement with life, distraction, greed and despair and a host of ill spirits willingly yielded substance to his spell of binding. Bravado, mockery and vanity were surest tell tales among the powerful, for they betrayed fear, shame, and greed to his seeing eye. Even fiery fanaticism masked hidden doubt, and little more was needful to bind any of these to his art other than insinuation of fulfillment, attached to a person, place or event and time, all cloaked in deceitful illusions. What did it matter? Is it not we who betray ourselves, succumb to our wants, project and fall into subjection to what we ourselves have created?

Siduri was blissfully simple. She deceived herself. All her hurt was desire for a man she could not have and fulfillment in one she could. And underlying her vulnerability was a father she had lost and felt she'd never known. Gisors insinuated in her illusion all of this was to be compensated in Squin and her association with the Blood Royal. She would never see Squin for what he was, only what she wished to see: the illusion was everything.

And was there anyone free from the spell of binding? He had found it only in the pure in heart who wanted nothing but to live the radiant life and they were rare; their very life a rebuke to his arts. He had encountered this once when peevishly he tried a spell of binding on the Master Flegetanis. His reward was two weeks' convalescence and a residue like coals of burning enmity for the man who treated his art as child's play.

But here he had no concern; he would search out weakness in Constanza, until she was bound to them. He would magnify feelings of beauty abused and vulnerable, for what woman does not think herself abused, and Constanza had reason. Already he had counseled Lothario – the lady's aspiring knight and champion - to play on those insecurities.

The mirror darkened with Gisors' art, and Constanza standing before it, looking on her own reflected image, grew thoughtful on her tribulations, especially in Morgon Kara. Gazing into the glass she felt her inner life being drawn outward into the mirror image, as if some stream of witchery took what she was to animate what was reflected there.

In her mirror image Constanza felt danger. Would it be possible, she wondered, to make a mirror that reflected back the twin of her who gazed into, but window to one unseen on the other side? The thought returned on her as certainty. There was someone on the other side. The mirrors on the wall opened in another place and there another watched and calculated. She turned away to gather up the nightdress from the bed. Turning again to the mirror, she held it before her and in an act of defiance, with a long, languid gesture slipped it over head and shoulders; its soft folds over her breasts, until it fell over her thighs and she laced it at the bosom with a bow.

It gave her pleasure to do it. In fact Constanza found herself in a particularly susceptible frame of mind, receptive as if nothing was quite like it seemed. Curious it was to her because she was adept at keeping her focus; her heart and mind under control. She found herself hung between willingness and reluctance, and open to see how it evolved with Lothario. It did not seem wise to resist but rather manage his advances, until it proved disadvantageous to do otherwise. She turned to the night fire and sat in its warmth preparing, wondering how long it would be before lusty youth came to claim his prize. She had not long to wait: there was a tap upon the door.

Steeped in Andreas Capellanus' *Art of Courtly Love*, his constant reading to hone his skills to the conquest of beauty, Lothario girded up his proverbial loins and made his first attempt to scale the fortress walls of Constanza's virtue. He paused a moment at her door to cue his line… "I ought to give God great thanks…."

A soft voice bade him and he entered Constanza's chamber, heart heaving, for she was wealth and beauty in an erotic blend to strike a man dumb.

"*What is the power a woman has over a man*," he came musing on the text: "*our will is no match for their influence; they enter unbidden where they will, beguile and have their way with us, and we turn mortal force, mental might and all our will to the death to attain for them what they desire.*

"Curiously," he thought, "they still complain we rule over them when we are but servants to their sweet influences."

Constanza rose from the fire and stood in candlelight, dressed in nightgown laced at the throat, to greet Lothario.

"Milady," he said, advancing boldly, restrained only at the last when he did not know where to rest his outstretched hands, but stopped and fumbled nervously. No woman had ever this effect on him. He'd made many a conquest but for the first time felt outmatched. And he could not play her superior for though he was of one order, she another and no measure. Thank God for Andreas Capellanus, his voice when he had none other.

"I ought to give God greater thanks than any other living man in the whole world," he began - yes, that was the proper text for this occasion - *"'because it is now granted me to see with my eyes what my soul has desired above all else to see."*

"We've met before," Constanza said, demurely: "last, earlier this evening."

"Yes, we have," he said clumsily, "but in solitude and firelight your soul burns brighter than ever and your beauty…"

"Do go on."

"Now I know in truth that human tongue is not able to tell the tale of your beauty."

"But tongue may try," she said sweetly.

"Try I may but to fail." This was going rather well. He took her hand and led her where they sat together on the edge of her bed: she with hands folded in her lap, he frozen awkwardly in position with one hand on her arm, looking on into the fire. He wanted to move his hand but could not; so far only his tongue, after a fashion, continued to function on its own. He had been in battle, but never like this before, unmanned.

"I wish ever to dedicate to your praise all the good deeds that I have done or will do and to serve your honour in every way: for whatever good I may do, you may know that it is done with you in mind."

Constanza felt compulsion rise within, urging her to yield to Lothario. It was at once comforting, insistent and full of promise that all she had sought was brought before her now. The thoughts were not her own but she did not fight them, for still she was mistress of herself and would see this through. So this was courtly love, the drama to which Siduri had succumbed, though under what influence she could not say, for she saw nothing in Squin to suggest he had such powers of persuasion. So, then, how was she to reply but to play the game demurely and discover what lay behind the shimmering façade, for there was more to this than Lothario.

"How can I but thank you for your ambitious praise," she said, "and if I am, indeed, to be the cause of your many good deeds to come, you may be assured you shall have my approval in all matters when you do honorably and well."

To Lothario it seemed a rather correct reply to his ardor, but he persisted. After all *The Art of Courtly Love* taught him a virtuous woman does not readily surrender to every cavalier who whispers sweet nothings in praise of her beauty, or what would be the point? He must go deeper, and at the same time overcome the restraint between them, for well he knew in love touch was by far more eloquent than words.

And so he moved his hand, at first as stone, and placed it on her knee. She did not resist but put her hand atop his own, and there held it firmly down until it melted. And feeling himself suddenly fill with ardor, he pressed her gown back above her knees but could go no further. And there his hand rested while he sought words needful to justify what would come next.

"I have chosen you from among all women to be my lady," he whispered, voice husky with feeling.

Constanza lifted her hand to her breast and sighed. "Oh, I don't really think you should do so. You know nothing of me or I of you, but I venture you have known many a woman eager to hear those words spoken over her."

Lothario advanced along her leg to the softness of her thigh and there he paused. To move too swiftly might well undo all he had accomplished. *"It is you to whom I would ever devote my service and to whose credit I would ascribe all my good deeds in this callous world."*

She took his hand and returned it to her knee where she held it gently in her own. "You did say that," she replied. How could he break that soft embrace, but must to advance firmly on her? Patience, she needed warming to those embraces yet to come.

"I ask you mercy that you look upon me as your special man, just as I shall devote myself to serve you, and that my deeds in your name may obtain from you the reward I desire."

The pressure to surrender to his entreaties was now full upon her. It seemed at first to rise from within but now she felt as if it emanated like dark light from the mirror, and knew some figure etched therein was intent upon engraving itself upon her soul and it sent a shiver up her spine to feel it. The black arts: Lothario felt it, too, and was emboldened by it. One arm about her waist he freed his hand from her own, and finding the bow tied at the bodice of her nightgown pulled gently, until the knot slipped revealing her shoulder and half a breast. She covered her shoulder and drew softly away with a coy smile.

Had Siduri been subjected to this pretense of virtue and manners as a pretext to assault on her person? For all their pretty words and protestations, these were no better than the legion of men who had tried to force her. Only here it was refined evil, but with the same intent to beguile, possess and exploit. She pressed back on the force compelling her like a rape of the soul, and was about to end it there when she decided to learn what was behind this. What was in the dark beyond the shining mirror, for it seemed not unlike the *Seithr* force her father, Koivu, taught the mastery, and this practitioner was skilled. She must know what they were, must understand the Blood Royal, and to do so see this through.

"That I should consider you my special man devoted to my service and that I should give you the reward you hope for puzzles me," she said. "How can I grant seeing it may be to the disadvantage of others who have as much desire or more for me?

"What is more, I am not particularly clear what reward you expect from me," she said, relaxing so her nightgown slipped again away from one shoulder making no attempt to correct it. "You must explain yourself more clearly," she said, as Lothario stumbled trying to decide how to advance.

This was not now going entirely well, but more or less as Capellanus predicted. He had been over this ground before, and at this point it was always best to persist, with a yet more personal appeal to her pity. He leaned over her and rested hand on her bare shoulder but did not press, and felt her fire rise in him. *"The reward I ask you to promise to give me is one which it is unbearable agony to be without."*

She gave a little laugh and he dared believe he was making some progress. "And what is that," she asked, demurely.

"It is that you be pleasant to me," he said softening the appeal a little, *"it is your love that I seek to restore my health, for you have smitten me with heart sickness, and my soul is in agony over you."* He pressed her back gently, until her head rested upon a great down pillow: he felt her yield but not utterly.

"You are in haste to ask for love," she said, struggling to rise, "and I do not think you should be speaking to me in this way." She sat upright but did not remove his hand from her shoulder. "We are separated by too wide and too rough an expanse of worlds to be able to offer each other love's solaces, or hereafter to find proper opportunities for meeting."

"You cannot properly refuse me your love with the excuse of the long and difficult distance between us," he replied, giving thanks for his study and ready lines of Capellanus treatise. *"The world is a dangerous place and we may never meet again; shall we not take pleasure and comfort in each other's arms now, here, while nature and destiny have brought us together? Should we deny the God of love the fruit of his love in us by denying each other?"*

"There is another fact, by no means trivial, which keeps me from loving you," she replied. "I am promised in my heart to one who is greatly distinguished by his nobility, his good character, and his destiny: it would be wicked of me to violate the bed that is rightfully his, or submit to the embraces of any other man while he dwells in my heart."

"And may I know the name of my rival in love?"

"It is Hugues, Comte de Caron," she said, "who came to me in my great need and willingly would give his life to free me from the Beast of Ulcinj."

Lothario was swept by fire wind, like a mountain blaze out of control in a firestorm. Constanza felt it, too. It emanated from the mirror, a dark wrath that intimidated even the fire on the hearth so that it burned lower. Now she must be very careful. Constanza fell silent, playing out the sense of influence insinuating itself in her. It was not by chance Siduri had been seduced, she kidnapped and now confined, and Caron her salvation hunted to the death. And what she felt imposed on Caron's name emanating in the darkness was raw hatred, and she declared his ally.

Flared up and gone as quickly as it had come, Lothario was somewhat chastened. *"I do not think one love should extinguish another, and so I dare think there is hope for me,"* he said, returning to script. *"Every woman of character ought to love, prudently. In me you can, without doing yourself any harm, accept the prayers of a suppliant and endow your suitor with your love. Let me show you it can be done at no cost to your tender affections for one, unknown to me, who before now has possessed your heart."* He pressed her again toward the bed and she yielded with a laugh.

"Do you not," she whispered, as he came down upon her, slipping the nightgown from her breasts. "Well," she said at his lips, "I will ponder these matters in my heart, and tomorrow if you desire you may come again."

"Tomorrow?" he said, pressing her legs apart with his knee. "Come this far I have no intention of turning back. He was heady with her luster and filled with her influences, reaching so deep into the heart he scarce could form a thought.

"Do you not?" she whispered at his lips, "and yet I say it is now time to sleep."

"It is time to sleep?"

"Sleep," she said, and her Seithr arts drew him under, until he vanished in deep waters and with him the passion that emanated from the darkened mirror. Constanza rose from the bed, stood before the dark mirror, shook the skirts of her nightdress in a swirl, and with a toss of her hair declaring she'd won, turned away to the fire. And there she sat in silent thought into the small hours of the night, until rising as if drugged, having no idea who or where he was, Lothario stumbled out of her chamber into the candlelight hall, and she bolted the door behind him.

20

Charade

Gisors awakened wedged between two walls; the mirror between him and Constanza's chamber, dimly lit by the flicker of a fire and hint of daylight at the casement. He hastily drew the black curtain between them, lest someone peering beyond the surface of the mirror should see his shadow within. Despite his art he was bested by a woman, who so shaped the influences he brought to bear through the blind mirror, that on a word he fell into a dark pit of unconsciousness. It bore the mark of the Nordic Seithr arts. He could manage that, but she had dwelled in the east and that was worrying, for he knew nothing of that world.

Chastened and humiliated, Gisors retired to his own chambers and slept until the sun was high and his servants concerned, roused him. He took a scant meal in his chambers, fell into meditation about what was to be done, and feeling danger reached out to the Lady Madelon de Faucon. She was young but the power ran deep in her and Gisors knew only by joining together to overcome Constanza would they prevail; all the more important, for she openly declared to Lothario her allegiance to Magda's bête noir, the Comte de Caron.

It was a small glass of Obsidian shaped in fire from the center of the earth, but crucial to his art of scrying out the heart of darkness informing patterns underlying those matters he must engage. When he looked deep into the black mirror it roused an answer within him, something looked back informing him with insight and power to shape the sense of it. He had neglected this with Constanza believing she would readily take to suggestion, and paid the price of negligence.

"Magda," he whispered, eyes locked on the dark mirror: "We shall fail except you join with me in this." There was a long silence but often it was like that. He held his gaze fixed waiting for the connection he knew must be there. And finally it came; not the Lady Madelon but a power unlike any he had known.

"Who are you," he whispered. Scrying had its dangers. He had known those who lost themselves looking into the darkness and descended into insanity. "Where is Magda?"

"I am Magda and Maia, and more. You called us; we have answered." He found assurance in her voice. This was the Lady Madelon her power come upon her.

"I was outmatched. This one they call Constanza is not what she seems. She caused a deep sleep to overcome, leaving me powerless."

"I had added my power to your own. Do not waiver in this, for she endangers all we desire. Feed smoldering passion in Lothario until it turns to burning. Raise his ardor and urge him vigorously upon her."

Lothario awoke exhausted, believing he had fallen asleep with Constanza close to yielding. He chastised himself for his impotence and insult to the lady. Gisors chose not to disavow his notion but urged he seek respite from the heat of the day and demands of the guests upon him, and to take up again his pursuit of Constanza in the cool of the evening.

Gisors knew in some hearts sensuous lust could come to such intensity its object was indiscriminate. There was lust enough in Lothario, even if he moodily doubted his potency; it was lust in Constanza he wished to rouse. If she did not now desire Lothario, there were other ways of rousing her to readiness. And so all evening long he would bring her into the presence of vigorous young men, who might raise ardor in her to the point she scarcely cared who came to her bed. Of course at the last it must be Lothario.

Occasion came with evening light in the terrace garden, all gathered to indulge in music and verse, a ribald drama late imported from France. It was a play of the green world caricaturing without much finesse the calculated rape of a village girl by a passing knight, who promised her sun, moon and stars if she would abandon her intended and couple with him. The night air was warm and fragrant; troubadours courted guests in the rose garden, serenading their way to the pageant through groves of olive, almond and flowering Judas.

"Do you know this tale?" Constanza leaned into Lothario, so he felt the warmth of her breast on his arm. "You must help me through it." She lingered and did not pull away, as if seeking confidence but loosing a torrent of pent up emotion in him. Lothario's breath caught in his throat, his voice breaking struggling to reply.

She drew away and waited as he sought composure. Why was he so affected? He was elite, exalted in this world. Always he had what he wanted, and never overwhelmed by a mere touch. "It is a tale of the greenwood," he said, chest tightening. "I confess I have never quite understood the dénouement.

"A noble knight passes through a forest and comes to a village. There he encounters a beautiful maiden, Marion, with whom he is smitten. She is in love with a rustic village lad, Robin of the Greenwood, but he can offer her nothing. Though she is common the knight would ennoble her, offers her his love and the security of his rank and family if she will come with him."

"And yet she refuses him?"

"Wealth, position, security, all she gives up for poverty and the love of a poor rival to the knight's generous offer."

"Is it some kind of morality tale to teach young women where advantage lies?" Constanza leaned again into him to speak, for the play had begun. A minstrel with a lute proclaimed the setting and the tale much as Lothario had described it. "Or, is it she realizes he will have his way and then abandon her?"

"If she proved worthy he might well keep her," Lothario said. "If not, she would have returned the more worthy for having been with him.

"No, to my mind, the play lacks only the final act, wherein rejecting his suit she struggles in poverty, dies in childbirth widowing Robin, leaving another child to be raised in penury."

Her lips for a moment touched his ear, a loose lock of hair brushed his neck. She felt his whole frame shake with her influence in him. "How could any poet dare to see life void and life meaningless," she said drawing away. "For my part I must think it full of luster and noble vigor, fronting the sorrows of the world."

There followed a candlelight ball, the gala event of the gathering to honour Constanza, and it was well they moved indoors for a summer storm followed after. Within the setting was perfect comfort from the confining weather, a refined atmosphere of elegant rooms enlightened by candlelight, a feast to sate any sense. And without, the covered terraces were torch lit for any who would take a moment apart to venture out into the rain-fragrant gardens.

An ensemble of troubadours and minstrels, instruments of flute, violas, horns and lutes, and masters of the dance to lead in the dance, the balli, carola estampe, saltarello, farandole and whatever the ladies desired. Lothario knew this would be his night to accomplish Constanza and set out with that intent like a hound after a bitch in heat.

But like Marion of the Greenwood she would not have him. All evening she first drew in then brushed aside his insistent advances; never rejecting, never receiving' but teasing him out. She danced but rarely with him, and much to the dismay of the unattached maidens preferred to mingle and play instead to the attentions of the young gallants. Indeed, she danced and flirted shamelessly with Tizio and Filano, the twin Donato brothers, a family rivaling Doge Soranzo's power.

Perrin joined the troubadours and plied his arts. A passing fair lutist, he played and watched from the orchestra as Constanza, mistress of all weathers, played Lothario to distraction. For a moment she would flower for him like a sunlit garden after rain, then she'd draw back, and with the winds of change watch the dark clouds gather to his brow.

She turned him on and off like a keg spigot at festival, until he was utterly subject to her changing disposition. Poor man, in his exaggerated sense of himself, all bravado and virility, a bull ever ready to mount a cow, he was ringed like a bull through his tender parts and drawn whithersoever she wished. By the time the evening was done Perrin was certain that denied, nothing short of rape would slay the dragon of frustration that devoured Lothario's self-esteem. Curious, Perrin thought, what a woman can do to the soul of a man. Thinking himself master of himself, too easily he surrenders consciousness; too easily woman becomes his emotional master. And with sorrow Perrin realized he had drunk as deep as any of that intoxicating brew.

But he didn't blame Constanza. For what was inflicted on her she responded in kind. She gave as good as she got and more, a woman to be trifled with. He felt in Constanza a force well able to destroy any man who crossed her, and wondered at the inevitable fate of the beast of Ulcinj having defiled such a woman.

Tonight Constanza was ready for the sport. It was a foolish game men and women played for mastery of the other, if a game with life and death consequences. Nevertheless, the sport roused her senses filling her with unaccustomed currents of longing to be known. She would know love as sweet music yielded at the artist's hand, rather than a chain about neck or waist to tug upon.

All she had known of men was their obsession to possess against her will, and the harvest of destruction that followed. In Venice, too, it was a game of power and influence, but in its own way intoxicating. Here men were full of deference and the luster of romance gathered to them. True, the end was the same but not through brutal conquest.

In Venice her wealth and beauty intoxicated her suitors. She delighted in the power: her influence irresistible, her decisions honoured, her intentions obeyed, and her purposes fulfilled. What was more she had resources and skills, the gifts of her father; none could even begin to imagine what she was capable of but for old Gisors, and she mastered him.

All day she felt him seeking influence in her; trying to subliminally set a pattern of his devising, leading to the end he desired, her consummation with Lothario. She watched him work at shaping influences in and around her, and he was skilled. But she read him well and admitting his power in her only so far as it pleased her to manage his pretensions, hedged herself from him. And so tonight to keep Lothario at bay, she would play one of the Donatello brothers - ardent, virile, and smitten – which one hardly mattered.

Between the brothers Filano won the toss, and reluctantly Tizio agreed

Filano would be first to attempt her. "Woo her fervently, openly," Tizio counseled.

"Fetch me a troubadour," Filano urged, "that one, Perrin, he shows and sings well, and she was touched by his song. Bring him to the rose garden. The rain is over and gone and the night scent of roses on the air. Her room overlooks. We shall serenade and so grace our way into her chamber.

"We?"

"From the shadow you and Perrin shall sing for me, but to be fair, if our song does not win her, you shall try your art as poet and accomplish her instead. Who knows, tonight we both may triumph."

"You are a true brother," Tizio affirmed, clasping arms. "I will find Perrin."

"Tell him also to bring a second lute that imitating I might feign to play as well as he."

Constanza prepared herself for the inevitable. It was a May summer night after the rain, an evening of spirited pleasures, of young men and warm women under a full moon. She would not be alone among the fair sex attempted before dawn. And so Constanza chose a nightdress of pale blue satin with lace bodice, let down her long fair hair and combed it out, pensively gazing into the brilliant, candle lit mirror. The poet Perrin warned of the nook on the other side, but she had already sensed it. She could feel Gisors now and recognized in him the will that directed Lothario.

Gisors was skilled but she had no fear of him. Lothario was another matter. He was impulsive and could be violent. She adjusted her gown, set her hair in place, indifferent to the old man who presumed to shape her will to his own. When she was done she turned away, put a screen before the mirror, and deflected the wave of anguish she felt rise over her.

Gisors cursed and turned deep within to find his way again to Magda. Instead he found a cold, magnetic power grip him, a leaden hand upon his shoulder so tangible he turned to see and found nothing but shadow and the heavy voice within insisting: "I know her ways. We will make an altar of her in the earth. Mastering her we shall loose power to shape a world."

"Then if need be, it is to the death." For the very weight of Irkala's presence, no other words served.

Constanza had a plan for dealing with Gisors' calculated rape.

Throughout the day she'd roused the interests of the Donatello brothers to white heat, knowing tonight the courtship would begin. The Donatello twins were not without interest: they were youthful and attractive and she would play it out, banking on the frustration of rivals. She calculated Lothario, restrained by duty and protection of the Doge's financial interests, would not press suit under adverse conditions. She didn't have long to wait to find out. The lesser annoyance came in the form of a serenade beneath her balcony from the rose garden.

"When the fresh grass and the foliage appear and the flowers break out on the bough, the nightingale raises his voice and begins his song, high and clear..." It was the troubadour, Perrin von Grünschnabel. She came to the balcony and below in the rose garden was one of the Donatello twins embracing a lute like a woman, mimicking Perrin. She smiled and leaned on the balustrade to listen.

"You are the true sapphire that can heal all my sufferings, the emerald which brings rejoicing, the ruby to brighten and comfort the heart.

"I would find you, sleeping, or pretending to sleep, so that I could steal a sweet kiss from you, for I am not worthy to request it.

"By God, Lady, how little we are taking advantage of love! Time is passing and we are missing..."

Constanza laughed appealingly and bade her lover come to her. He didn't need to be invited twice. Before Constanza had turned away he was in the branches of the Gethsemane Olive, reaching precariously for the balustrade. It was not elegant but it was an entrance, and the moment he laid eyes on her knew it was worth any effort he had made, might make, to possess her.

"Are you Tizio or Filano?"

"You have both of us in thrall." He took and kissed her hand, "together we are forever in your service. Shall I call him up?"

"Am I to have one in daily use and the other spare?"

He took her hand and led her to her bed. Now come the pretty speeches, she thought, but not so with Filano. He was full of lust. Overcome with ardor he was upon her, tugging at the draw strings of her lace bodice, and before she could respond, hand upon her breasts. Overwrought with passion he would make no good lover and so she gently but firmly removed his hand.

"Patience," she whispered at his lips. "You are all impulse. What should spend a night in consummating must not be squandered in a minute."

"Lady," he began, and was interrupted by a knock upon the door.

"Lady Constanza," the voice muffled by the door, "will you not let me in."

"I must answer," she whispered: "A moment Lothario."

"I was here first."

"Lothario is my host. You must hide."

"Lady Constanza," the voice was stronger now, penetrating the oak.

"I shall not hide my love for you."

"You're in heat," she said. "It is too soon to claim love your guardian in this. But fear nothing." She moved him toward the balcony. "We shall have words, and you will listen from without. I will keep him by the fire to hear his petition, and be done with him for the night."

"He comes to petition you?"

"Go," Constanza pushed him onto the porch.

"Constanza let me in. Do you have someone with you?"

Constanza went to the mirror, removed the screen leaving the room again in full view, and with an impish smile looked right into the glass. In full view of Gisors she plumped her breasts beneath the nightgown, straightened the sleeves and collar, smoothed the silken dress, then turned away to open the door.

It was not the same Lothario who came the night before; this one came not to plead his case but claim his trophy. This one was arrogant, self-righteous and determined, and had she not answered at once was prepared to force his entrance.

"Why do you keep yourself from me?"

She took his hand – it was ice – and led him to the fire.

Yet confined by Irkala's will to the Shades, Maia led Morgon Kara into the inner court of the temple and the threshold of waters she alone could cross. With a fingertip she touched the surface of the well spring and Constanza's chamber appeared. "We see what Gisors sees." The pool stilled again and Morgon Kara watched Constanza come to the mirror, comb out her long fair hair; straightened her nightdress, and with an impish smile turn away.

"She is very fair," Maia said, a hint of jealousy in her voice. "She might almost be as one of us."

"She was once useful to me. She gave of her substance and would have to the death, was it not for Purusha who slew me."

"Lothario Vitale," Maia said, "a man of wealth, influence, prowess and full of stratagems. He would make a worthy host."

"He is no healer as was Morgon Kara, the Bon Po priest I took."

"But here, now might serve our purpose. "Irkala's hand is upon this; she has turned the power of her realms to inform Gisors. In that moment of consummation would you not possess Lothario as he does Constanza, and enter again into that world?"

Morgon Kara stared down into wellspring of the waters whose name is Dayspring but the Sisters called Regret.

"There is much to regret," Maia said: "what might have been done, undone, or shaped the more wisely. And yet these waters remind us of the power we have to shape a world, and the price of consequences."

"With such power, why speak of regret?"

Maia took the silver torque from her arm. It came alive in her hand. "Irkala and I are agreed in this. I may loose you from the Shades into one more suitable to our purpose.

"Seek out Lothario's soul, and I will do the rest," she whispered, loosing the silver serpent into the mirror of the pool. "If you will, follow," she said, turning to Morgon Kara, "I will bind Constanza's life to mine; yield her substance in Lothario and loose our influences into your new world."

Morgon Kara felt himself drawn down into the waters; dissolve and follow the shimmering trail of the little serpent into the deep; searching out and following the current to fulfill its mistress' command.

Lothario was come into his power. It was now or never. He had fussed over this woman, played her game by the rules and she had not responded. Now it didn't matter. It was hard to describe what he felt – indestructible, perhaps - he was possessed with the feeling that for him there were no limits and that anything was possible and wilfully within his rights. Why, he might even become Doge.

This woman was nothing of herself but means to an end. Through her they might extend the trade of Venice and Europe deep into the Moslem lands and beyond to Cathay, harvesting unimaginable wealth to their purpose. Lothario lusted after Constanza, but what was his lust if not to magnify the power of wealth, until everything from the meanest blade of grass to the crowned kingdoms of this world bore the imprint of Venice, la Serenissima.

Lothario took a deep breath and looked again at Constanza. He saw her poised, waiting for his advance, sure in herself in fending him off, he supposed, because though she offered him audience and kindness she showed no disposition to receive him. Was there someone else in the room? The thought insinuated itself. Lothario looked around, his eyes settled on the mirror where Gisors watched. He was riveted a moment on the dark, glassy reflection of the chamber mirrored there as if seeing its reflection in a deep, dark pool, feeling its power surge and rise in him. And when he turned again to Constanza he saw a smile in her eyes, and it filled him with ire. She mocked him, knowing his intentions; knowing already the end of it when she would reject him.

How odd, and he spoke again, a disembodied voice for the words came of no effort of his own, putting an edge on his usually mellow baritone voice. Constanza sat bolt upright.

"Do not pretend you do not remember me." Lothario was swept along on a flood of dark waters. Unconscious of what he did, he loosed his belt and folding his hand about the sheathed dagger, leaned forward to face Constanza.

She eyed him coldly. "Lothario, leave this place now, while you still can." She struggled under the cold magnetic weight that burdened her chest and drew on her, until she could scarce breathe. There was urgency in her voice and on the patio without Filano heard but was frozen in place by unaccustomed fears rising; obliterating the passions he had felt climbing the balcony to her chamber.

Lothario felt the urgency in her voice, part of him struggling to break surface and obey, but fell back again overwhelmed by the presence that took him. "It is too much," he whispered, turning toward the mirror, "I cannot bear this burden. He felt hunted, fled from the predator that sought him, seeking desperately to go to ground. And then he was taken.

Lothario turned to Constanza, again composed, but no more Lothario.

In Gisors' power a cold magnetism that sucked the life from her: she had underestimated the forces she confronted. The illusion was perfect. No more was it Lothario but Morgon Kara, and no more her chamber in Villa Terra Firma but the shaman's mountain cave where Purusha thrust through the heart of the shaman his own Phurba dagger. Now, she sat again across the fire from him its flames frozen in time, and again his dagger only in his own hand, his eyes dark with passion.

"Did you think I was so easily slain? Even then I had already begun to take another, but this one I like well enough."

"He did it for you. Purusha… you pleaded with him." And as she said it she felt Purusha's substance flood into the chamber, and feared at once she had betrayed the lad by mention of his name.

"Thank you," he said, growing more substantial. "And now I shall take back what he took from me."

"You are but a hyena lapping up the life blood of others," she chided. She was appalled at his disdain for life other than his own. She sought to hedge herself from him, had little strength to prevent it and her heart began to search for some firmness in the midst of this madness.

"It is illusion," she told herself.

He was within her now, knowing her thought before she could speak it. "I take back what is mine. Yet willing you may serve to birth this moment." She was in a whirlwind of force without bearings, a whirligig of patterns: Purusha, Squin, Magda, Gisors, and forces she did not comprehend, all converging on Lothario; Morgon Kara taking possession and she the instrument of this tortured dream of achievement.

"You shall not have me," she whispered across the fire.

"This is beyond you," he replied. "You were useful once and now again to consummate my possession in Lothario Vitale."

Filano's passions were a working sea, but something in him told him Constanza was in trouble. He was cavalier in his ways toward women, but he was also a man and this woman meant something to him. He beckoned to his brother Tizio and Perrin who stood below ready to resume their song. With a sweep of the arm he gestured for his sword.

"There is danger," Perrin cautioned, abruptly sobered from the night's fantasies. "There are dark arts in this. Hugues, do you live?" he whispered. "Have we not been here before?"

"I will go to him," Tizio replied, slinging the scabbards over his shoulder and started the climb. And as Tizio climbed Filano peeked around the corner and saw Constanza sat before the fire with Lothario, her gaze frozen with his eyes upon her. It was not the look of love but of prey held in the sight of predator. He could not determine the words but the tone was menacing. It was clear Constanza was in trouble.

"There is one who has and will again defeat you," Constanza said. She felt her life force stream out like heart's blood through a wicked wound. She said it and the fire blazed up. Morgon Kara drew back from the heat of it.

"If you resist I will have your life. Yield and something more than the husk of a woman will remain."

But Constanza would not yield. The fire burned brighter, she within its glow, and for the moment it held him at bay, as Morgon Kara sought to master the force of it. He reached out for Maia and found her and she filled him with herself. She drew deeply upon old Gisors who watched in amazement things he had never seen, a roiling of forces that ignited the air in the chamber, and at its center two before the fire who stared each other down. They would win but Constanza would not go easily.

Perrin began to sing. *"You are the true sapphire that can heal all my sufferings, the emerald which brings rejoicing, the ruby to brighten and comfort the heart..."* The voice troubled and for a moment distracted Morgon Kara.

"Take of me what you can," Constanza said, finding an opening in the grip upon her. "There is that in me endures torture and time, and so it shall until the day of your destruction."

What Filano saw was Lothario disturbed with Constanza. And did he not just hear Lothario threaten Constanza's life if she resisted him?

"Your words, your face, your bearing," Perrin sang, *"make one flee, hate and detest all vice and cherish and desire all that is good, beautiful, and true."*

"It appears you have a lover," Morgon Kara said, "and he lends his force to you. Have you given yourself to a poet who cannot even mend his lines let alone a rift in creation?"

Tizio made the balcony. Perrin put down the lute and followed after. Filano could not believe his ears. Lothario had once disputed Filano over a property. The dispute had ended in a minor skirmish before the Council found in favor of Filano. He knew there was affection in Constanza but was this not a protestation of love for him? Then he was her defender against this intended rape, enough to encourage a bold entry. Fools rush in and Perrin who had climbed the balcony was right behind him.

"Who has power to defeat me? Even the lords of light thought me vanquished, yet here I am."

He pressed back on her, forcing her to retreat deep into herself. There were too many forces marshaled against her, and yet at the very core there was something adamant, unyielding, a bright blue star that should never be extinguished. She vowed he should not have that whatever became of her. And still he pressed her and she was driven back. There were others with him. She felt Gisors' power magnified through the dark mirror. With him came the Lady Madelon and her creature Squin, yielding up their substance to sustain Morgon Kara. And Siduri who might stand with her in this, she was drawn and remote, her heart troubled and caught up in forces she could not comprehend.

And there was dear Purusha, the lad who saved her life from Morgon Kara in the very image of this place where once again in the cavern depths she faced him down across the fire. She felt Purusha in agony as Morgon Kara took back all he claimed was his and so much more. And Maia and Irkala, the names drifted into her mind as she was pressed back, retreating deeper and deeper into herself, until she was enveloped in the cool blue radiance of her star and there she took her stand.

Who was Maia, who Irkala? Irkala she felt keenly, the cold magnetic force that drew the life from her to possess her very self. Maia, a name more familiar, what did she have to do with this? Softly the answer came: "Anwyn who keeps the sweet influences of truth at the crossing of the worlds. It is your sister Maia, for love of Morgon Kara who betrays the life of her sister Anwyn to his purpose.

"It is Maia who drives you back to the crossing of the worlds, where first things are shaped or ever they are in the earth. And it is she who would deprive you of your presence in the earth."

It was then Constanza understood. She was Anwyn who stood at the crossing of the worlds. And then everything changed. Gathering all her remaining substance, she confronted Morgon Kara: "Thus far and no farther," she decreed.

She took Morgon Kara's eyes across the fire and fixed them in Anwyn's radiant gaze. The fire on the hearth froze. The cavern disappeared. They sat again in Constanza's chambers, Lothario across from her, but Morgon Kara yielded not a wit. He stood frozen in his place, Lothario still as stone. Power gathered to Constanza and in the midst of it was Caron's presence enfolding her with a flame of fire. Her words thrust home like a bright blade. Powerless to act of his own, Morgon Kara was frozen in a moment over which he had no power.

But there was a cry of agony from beyond the mirror. Gisors struggled to hold on to a pattern disintegrating and a possession slipping away. Gisors felt the cold force in him turn insistent demand to complete what was begun. Maia rebuked, Morgon Kara restrained, Irkala would not denied. All illusion spent, in the raw force of will remaining Irkala struck out at Constanza who yielded not a whit. Instead she held what Morgon Kara in her eyes and answered: "I rebuke thee."

Obsessed, Lothario drew his dagger from its sheath. If Constanza would not yield he would have her blood. That was Filano's cue. His family was exalted in Venice, and the testimony of his brother and the poet Perrin would stand with him in this. Perrin behind, Filano and Ticino drew their swords on Lothario. "Sheath your dagger, Lothario," Ticino confronted, "the lady is a guest in your house."

Lothario looked up slowly and challenged by two who appeared as one, each the mirror image of the other, and part of him now afar off, not knowing what was real and unreal, utterly confused. He struggled with an unaccustomed world, a woman who defied him, his grasp on sanity slipping away. And now he was thrust aside. He saw himself turn brusquely away to stride from the room leaving the spoils to the three who came for Constanza, like a battlefield shrouded in a haze of spent lives.

And that was the last Lothario saw, for though his mind told him one thing, what his body did was another. He lunged at Constanza with dagger and impaled himself on Filano's sword. Lothario fell like a bag of rags. Ticino went down on one knee and took her hand. "Has he hurt you, lady?"

"We have the right with us," Filano said. "Nevertheless, we must go before the house is raised and let our family speak for us."

Perrin stared straight into the mirror. "It will be well," he said, "or the spiritual wickedness that blackened this night will be exposed. The Doge is a man of power and knows its limits He will not be deprived of Constanza's friendship through depravity in a cousin."

"And most gratefully I will speak for you, Ticino, Filano. Constanza said. "I thought to say nothing of it but this Lothario had dealings with the Beast of Ulcinj. I caught sight of him among those who sought to buy me. What say you, Perrin, will you take me at once to the Doge to let me plead their case?"

"I know a way to safety," Perrin said. "It is through the glass." Perrin took a brass candlestick and smashed the mirror. Amidst the shards Gisors, near to death, was fallen exhausted in the backlash of the forces he unleashed.

Filano and Ticino went before, swords drawn. Constanza took Perrin's hand and followed after, down the passage from her chambers into the safe rooms and tunnels beyond the villa to the stables. Constanza now understood what Siduri faced. She would travel with her to bring the innocent home again.

21

Cockaigne

Roused by clatter above deck, Caron climbed out of the hold to a chill morn and shadowed hills banking the river. Hode was still asleep below. Caron washed, drank a ladle of cold water, and went to the prow of the vessel to take in the river. By degrees they'd made their way, finding willing boatmen over one stretch after another, until it flowed into Lake Constance and Rheinfall.

Below the falls at Basel river traffic swelled into managed commerce, and they took passage on the Lorelei, a barge carrying olive oil and wine, spices, jewellery and textiles from Italy to Amsterdam. Lorelei was fortressed against theft by crossbowmen but an itinerant monk and his charge were no threat and they easily secured passage to Strasbourg.

They were in mid river running north freely with the current, but on either bank in first light Caron made out the dark shapes of dray horses, heard the crack of whips and shouts of men on the air; the animals straining against the current towing the barges upstream.

"I did not see you come aboard." Caron turned to the old man come to his side at the bow. The action was aft and they two stood alone watching the current carry them to Strasbourg. "You are Blaise, Master of Hallows," Caron said. "Your handmaiden presented me with a beautiful sword, broken."

"Do you remember my question?"

"How what cannot be broken can be made whole again."

"You answered, 'in the world there is one steadfast law; ever present, undeviating, absolute, written in us from the foundation of the world; a law to which man is held accountable for every thought, word and deed.'"

"I did."

"No matter how a man chooses the world is whole, for God's sovereignty inevitably prevails. Did you think the test of your virtue ended with the Gathering in Green Chapel? To conceive in the mind's eye that the worlds are one, that the sword of truth is one, is but the beginning; it must be realized in fact."

"I am not accountable to those who gathered in Green Chapel."

"However you account your life, you must live to see it whole," Blaise insisted.

Caron did not reply and there was silence between them but for the sounds of the river passing. "So you have come to test me?"

"No, I have come to warn you. Life is the test, every moment of cursing a moment of dying; every moment of thankfulness a moment of living."

"And yet you serve one who seeks my life. If we are of a company and you know what I must do, why put needless obstacles in my way?"

"What is most exquisite in the earth is not gold and precious stones; neither is it knowledge or any gift of mind, talent or motion of the heart that seeks fulfillment in the abundance of the earth.

"No, what is most precious is the blessing that springs fresh from the spirit of truth in living, a fine substance that links us now that we may commune together.

"The finer the quality of it, the brighter the shining of the light, and the more profound the communion of the worlds, so at last they may be seen as one and indivisible.

"I would have you so live in communion with the wonderful one that your life might be a blessing so full the earth is not room enough to contain it.

"Like your master Flegetanis, I must work with what we have. In the way you go I pray you will prevail; that the fine substance of creation will gather to you, the sweet influences of life uplift you, and those powers bound by the limitations of the world be loosed in you."

Blaise pointed to a dark tower rising like a sooty finger out of the rocky crags at the bend in the river. "My warning," he said. "Here, Telgesinus has set a stumbling block in your way."

"Eingemauert, here we go ashore to deliver goods before passing tolls at the Black Tower of Ransbach, five miles on. Chains across the river and another toll; they are no better than pirates." Not Blaise but Captain von Bayern stood beside, and with him came Hode cloaked against the morning air. He was still not recovered from his ordeals but Caron saw the spirit strengthening in him.

"This stretch is taxed by the Count Manegold von Rheinsfeld, Bishop of Ransbach. His tithes are exacted by Schnabel, the slippery. He commands an island fortress five miles downriver, Schnabel's lair. From there he controls the flow of commerce up and down river: Lothringen to the west, Schwaben to the east. But we must put in here first for cargo."

"I have heard of the Black Tower," Caron said. Hode spoke little German, and to include him Caron translated fragments as they spoke

"Why Schnabel, the slippery?"

"Cunning as a serpent, in no wise harmless, unsatisfied with his fee he is known to take hostages against the return journey." He put his hand on the friar's shoulder. "The price Brother John we have to pay for other people's greed. All the wealth of the world will never satisfy by feeding the need: Schnabel all appetite, Ransbach ambition."

The barge eased into the embankment where officers and pike men waited to board. "And ever parasites on other's lives," Caron said.

Von Bayern laughed. "Ransbach is the worst. Count and bishop both, warrior and confidant of the Hapsburgs; his ambition is to build his own *Schlaraffenland,* and for this he needs our money."

Von Bayern's first standing by the landing overheard. "O Ja, he will have his land of milk and honey; his paradise borne on other's backs. *Schaffe, schaffe, Häusle baue,"* he said proudly, returning to his own work.

"Working, working building a home," Caron asked?

"Rommel is Swabian," von Bayern said: "careful, frugal, hard worker, never wanting something for nothing."

"Tell me about *Schlaraffenland*."

"Land of milk and honey," Hode mused, "does he mean the land of Cockaigne?"

"Do you know of it?"

"The world turned upside down. There is a poem about a community of corrupt monks," Hode said. Von Bayern put a finger to his lips. The boat was docking, soldiers preparing to board, and he must have his own stand down. "Laughter is verboten. So, when we are done here," von Bayern promised merrily.

"Eingemauert is Ransbach's face on the world. We shall take on and unload; it will be several hours. I have business in the town; come along if you wish. Here it is permitted."

"Permitted?"

"To a point," he said, "other villages are closed to outsiders, but the river is the life blood and here they must do commerce."

The land rose sharply from the river; in some places sheer cliff, but along a steep embankment there was a rock-solid system of docks sheltered from the current, allowing three or four barges to enter line astern at the foot of the hill. Ashore was a waterwheel crane, a cunning device driven by sluicing river currents, for unloading barges. Within minutes of arrival it turned without manpower on an axis and positioned to winch up cargo from deck and hold onto a chain of waggons that ran up and down a circuit on wooded rails from dock to headland. These were drawn on a windlass, worked by handsome Schwarzwälder drays, like those that pulled barges against the current up the Rhine.

It was all very efficient and ingenious, but it was the dock workers and their overseers that caught his eye. They were all dressed the same, in dark brown homespun, without distinction. The overseers wore the same but were distinguished by coloured shoulder patches of orange. All were intent on their work, silent and oblivious to the crew of the vessel. If a word was needed, it came only from an overseer. Caron in monk's robe and cowl stood out not at all, though he feared he should be mistaken and indeed an eye or two fell on him as he followed von Bayern up the narrow stair to the headland. Hode was advised to stay aboard.

"Gateway to Ransbach's *Schlaraffenland*," von Bayern said. Here everything is held in common; everything to standard, everything the same. Here everyone owns everything, and no one owns anything, other than Ransbach, of course."

Of itself Eingemauert was a small walled town at the end of a forested road that led to the shore. The old town was a warren of cobbled streets, a deserted village market square and a church yard, all under the shadow of a ramshackle citadel, home now only to bats and birds. But there was still a village life of sorts: a few shops, an inn and offices that processed the business of the port. He'd seen a thousand villages like it but usually bustling with life. What took his attention here were three great warehouses guarded by men in brown with red shoulder patches. And beyond the warehouses outside the village wall a thousand yards off was another village of houses ranked in rows, every one identical in size, shape, and color, white plaster, dark wood, red clay tiles.

"Eingemauert is trade and warehousing," von Bayern said. "Nothing else goes on here unconnected to that, except for the patrols that watch the countryside for intruders. The soldiers are the red patches, overseers orange; the workers in homespun, men in brown; women in gray distinguished with a patch of green. You may see also a few black patches; these keep records and reports.

"There are other villages?"

"Oh, yes, all specialized for efficiency: mostly agricultural, some crafts of weaving, tanning, smithing, horse and cattle breeding and the like. Some can be visited by invitation; others are utterly forbidden even to those who dwell in Ransbach's demesne, and no one knows what goes on there. I'm told some manufacture armaments for the Hapsburgs that are highly prized."

"And are they all like this."

"Allowing for their specializations, theirs is a world of conformity, of watchers and workers."

Von Bayern led into an old inn with dark fire pit, low ceiling and a shaft of futile light from a window that seemed more afterthought than design. It all put Caron in a mood to understand what Ransbach was about.

"Here we will wait for a black patch to review and sign our papers," von Bayern said. "It will ease our passage through customs." Immediately they were seated by a woman in gray homespun, brightened by a patch of daffodil yellow on the shoulder, who brought them beer, bread, cheese and sausage and disappeared in the darkness, while they ate by candle light.

"Try it; it's good," von Bayern said. "Never turn down a free meal. You never know when you'll eat again."

Caron reached for his purse. "They don't use money you know," von Bayern said, over a mouthful of bread.

"How do they keep track?"

"The distribution of goods is watched very closely; everyone has just the needs of their class, but no more. The rest Ransbach holds in trust for them."

"The distribution of these goods and services, how is that done?"

"It is the work of the Allocators to see all things are done in set proportion; they wear the green patches. There are a few here as in every other village for oversight. These work very closely with Ransbach and other than his personal guard among the few who have direct access to him."

"It has a certain monastic appeal," Caron said. "Simplify the needs; devote a life to works and contemplation."

"Then a mockery it is of it, Brother John," von Bayern said. "It is not God they serve but Mammon, and Ransbach is his prophet. Religion is for show only. He has made a secular state to serve his will. This is no spiritual kingdom of God on earth, but a ruthless, mind-made world, corrupt to the core."

The black patch appeared with a sheath of papers and sat across from von Bayern, stared a moment at Caron in the candlelight, then arranged his papers carefully before him on the table. "It is largely in order, but there are some minor discrepancies we must discuss." He snapped his fingers and the serving maid hurried to the table. "See to this gentleman," he said, nodding to Caron. She scurried off into the darkness.

It was clear he wanted to be alone, so von Bayern gave Caron the nod. "It's a fine old village," he said. "Take a moment and visit the church."

"There is nothing there," black patch said, but he did not object. So with some relief Caron let himself out of the sooty den into the afternoon light of an early summer's day. He'd gone only a few paces toward the old church when he felt a hand tug on his sleeve. It was the maid from the inn. She'd taken off her apron, straightened her hair and dashed a little water to wash the soot smudges from her face.

"What is it like, Father, the world beyond the river?" They walked the cobbled path until they came to the church where they sat on a stone bench under a linden. The village streets were virtually deserted. There was no market garden, no private merchant shops, none of the coming and going characteristic of a country town; only the occasional neigh of a horse, the creek of a wagon toward the barge, and voices on the wind from the warehouse yards.

"Have you never journeyed from here to other villages," Caron asked. "Across the river and a half day's journey down is a great, ancient city."

"I have never left this village but to be trained in my duties."

"You are schooled?"

"The Allocators watch each child to see how it might best serve, and at an early age each is assigned a trade and goes to where it may best be learned. When we have learned our duties we are assigned our status," she said, touching the yellow patch on her shoulder. "And we are given a job to deserve our livelihood. I was assigned the Inn at Eingemauert."

"It is a pleasant land." Caron let his eye roam over the green fields that ran to the margin of a great forest. She opened to him and he felt himself curiously drawn. Despite the dowdy gown and somewhat severe cut hair – it was chestnut in the sunlight - she was quite lovely. "I should think you could be happy here," he said, "a quiet village, a simple life, with all your needs provided. One day a young man will come courting, and you'll make a life together."

"Yes," she said, "if they decide I shall marry, when it is time he will come for me. I shall move out of the woman's hall and they will give us a cottage over there," she said, pointing to the row of identical houses.

"Your marriage will be arranged?"

"If it is decided I am to bear children, yes. We shall have a number of years together with the one best chosen for me, and we shall beget children before returning to our duties. Does that sound very strange? Is it not that way everywhere?"

"What of the children?"

"At four they are taken to the children's village. There everything is wonderful for them. I am told in the world abroad they are often abandoned to whatever befalls them. Like a mother bird when it is done nesting; the fledglings must fly or perish. Is that true? Here we prepare our children to their special place."

Caron looked around and still not a soul. He nodded to the church. "You took me for a priest. I am in fact an itinerant monk. Do many still go to church?"

"From time to time a teacher of the professional caste comes to us and we gather to hear him lecture on our duties."

"Are there many of these?"

"The blue patches are few in number, but masters of many fields; they have knowledge of reading and writings, music, medicine, the paths of the stars, and of God. But they rarely travel and so when one comes to us it is a great event. Then we gather in this church to hear his wisdom."

"And what does he saw when he speaks of God?"

"How in God's kingdom none are rich and none are poor. How from earliest times all Christians held everything in common as now we do; how many failed and departed from the way. He tells us it is God's will we should live for our neighbor, envy no one, and be thankful we are provided for and not forced to compete for our livelihood.

"We are also told the world is full of the wicked who seek all things for themselves; that only here in our special kingdom under the watchful eye of Bishop Ransbach, and with the protection of the Holy Emperor von Hapsburg, are we kept safe from these depredations of the world. Is it true? Is the world so very wicked?"

"It can be very wicked," he said. "It is also full of color and beauty, of aspiration and challenge to grow in grace and stature in the path life opens for us."

"Sometimes the older folk speak that way," she said. "It is forbidden, but they are old and rarely punished for it."

"Punished?"

"I must return to the Inn," she said, rising nervously. "I have my duty and if I am not there for him when his conversation is done, black patch will be angry with me. With that she was gone as if by instinct, for von Bayern appeared in the street and beckoned Caron to follow back to the barge.

"All is well?" Caron caught up.

"The black patch insists we shorted their order for spices by a pound, eight ounces of cloves and eight ounces of cinnamon he said were missing, and refuses to sign off until accounted for. He will hold us until we made good, or offers to send word to further tax our cargo when we come to the Black Tower.

"What will you do?"

"The order is accurate, but extortion is the price of doing business on the Rhine. I agreed to give him eight ounces of cloves to overlook the omission. He knows that I know the weight was true, and will not press the matter further in hope of future concessions."

"Even in *Schlaraffenland*."

"Here sheep may safely graze, but neither Ransbach nor any of his overlords are the least bit shy about fleecing the flock.

"And the young woman who served in the inn - the lamb you were speaking with at the church – if she was unable to make money off you, black patch will have her for lunch. The yellow patch is for *Huren*."

Five miles on the river parted and flowed to either side of a ragged island rising in its midst. On the island *die Schwarzen Turm* of Ransbach, a dark towering mass rising up in the middle of the river, blocked the passage of Rhine barges coming and going. Here must all go ashore to pay the tolls. And to make the point abundantly clear, on the evening air was the noise of grinding wheels and clatter as the Rhine guardians lifted their rusting load of chains out of the river to block the way and force ships ashore.

Caron remembered von Bayern's warning: "All the wealth of the world would not satisfy these - Schnabel all appetite, Ransbach all ambition." His curiosity was roused at the chance of meeting Schnabel the Slippery who did his lord's duty on the river. He was not to be disappointed. Schnabel, as if especially alerted to intercept this barge, appeared on the quayside surrounded by his soldiers in military tunic, displaying the red patches of authority that set them apart from all others.

Today Schnabel was rigorous, determined to exact every obligation due in gold or goods; determined to be seen at the point of control and passionate in his lord's service, for the Lord Bishop of Ransbach was expected this day. Schnabel had spent a week in preparations and did not wish in any wise to have his Excellency think him slack in duties.

Normally, he would exact tribute dockside and move the vessels on. But today he disembarked passengers and crew, transferred them to holdings, and feeling generous fed them on sausage, black bread and beer, while a thorough inventory of the barge was made and compared to its documents. Whatever his losses in hospitality he would take out in cargo. And this he would do both sides of the river with every barge that came his way so long as the Bishop was in residence. It was a nuisance, but forewarned is prepared and Schnabel turned his men out en masse to display for all to see him fulfilling his feudal obligation. Never mind it had been done only a few miles upriver. Let the river merchants complain, not one jot or tittle should escape his scrutiny.

And so Caron and Hode found themselves locked and guarded within doors in what amounted to an inn of sorts, with open fire, bench and tables, rough rations and time to talk. They were soon joined by the crew of yet another barge come in half an hour behind Lorelei. Aided by drink, nerves turned to laughter and conversation to Ransbach's *Schlaraffenland*. It began with the captain of the *Brederode*, a wide, red barge half the length again of the Lorelei, at the beginning of her long journey home to Amsterdam. Captain de Beers, a red bearded, gruff, boar-like man who relished his humor as much as his food and pleasures had brought a minstrel along to ease the journey. He was playing his lute solemnly in the background as the crews began to drink and mingle. Rough as it was it pleased Hode, for this was more like home he knew than anything he experienced in many a year and Caron saw he was greatly affected.

"Your promised land of milk and honey, Captain," Caron said, "you promised to tell me about *Schlaraffenland*, or as Hode knows it, Cockaigne."

"Ah, Kockengen we call it, too," de Beers intervened. "Do you not know this story: Houses made of barley sugar and cake, streets paved with pastry, and shops that provide goods for nothing?"

"Skies rain cheeses," someone shouted over the laughter: "Roasted pigs wander the streets, knives in their backs to make carving easy," another.

"Grilled geese fly directly into your mouth," one shouted, merrily.

"My minstrel knows the tale," de Beers said. "Halfgaar," he called across the room. "Sing of Kockengen, the world turned upside down."

And as entertainers are, Halfgaar was only too pleased to be the center of attention, and started reciting the lines he knew to a ballade of the lute. *"…The geese when roasted on the spit fly to the abbey and cry out 'geese, all hot, all hot!'…And drinking there needs no request; you simply take what you like best."*

Two guards broke out in laugher, relaxed and relieved to have a happy throng rather than the usual sullen detainees. "Don't forget," one shouted, "the weather is always mild, wine flows freely, women are hot, ready and more than willing, and all enjoy eternal youth."

Halfgaar was having a time being heard over the raucous din. He was being upstaged by their humor, but determined to go on.

"And the women, minstrel, tell us about the women…'the nuns stripping naked for their play…' I like that part," de Beers said.

Halfgaar cast a quick glance at the friar standing with his captain, who returned a reassuring smile, and at his captain's pleasure pressed on. *"When the Masses have been said, and the service has been read, the crystal turns to glass once more in the state it was before."*

"Boring," someone shouted, and hurled a crust of bread at the minstrel. "Get to the part about a dozen wives for every year."

Halfgaar was in a tizzy; the whole sequence was botched, and his memory suffering with it, and so he began where he could remember. *"The monks, reluctant to obey, in headlong flight swoop far away. When the abbot sees this sight, his monks refusing to alight, he takes a maiden standing near, and upon her snow-white rear beats tattoo with open hand, to make his monks come down to land."*

"That's better half-wit."

"This does not offend you, I trust," de Beers said: "it is pure fancy."

Caron laughed. "Say, rather, utter chaos, but it serves to distract a nervous company."

The guards were all attentive until a shaft of light streamed into the dusky cavern and the captain of the guards stood in the doorway. Nevertheless, Halfgaar persevered. It was a shambles; his sensibilities savaged, but he needed some closure. *"When his young monks see that sight, by the maiden they alight, round about her they career, and each one pats her snow-white rear, and then, with all their labour done, soberly they walk, each one, home for a drink at their collation, in file according to their station."*

Everyone was in a rollicking good mood. "Captains to me," the officer ordered. "Everyone back to your boats - there are others waiting."

"The world turned upside down," Caron said.

"A peasant's dream," von Bayern said, "some of it pure fancy; some of it wish fulfillment; some resentment. Ransbach exploits such fantasies, and we are taxed for it."

"Are you saying such a land exists within his realms?"

"No, never, they starve and are fed on assurances; he promises all in common but holds all himself; extracts labor now for ease in time to come. None can advance, all are held in thrall to his will, and yet many are intoxicated by this vision, which is why we are not allowed to wander freely when we come ashore lest we betray those beguiled by his model kingdom for a perfect world."

"Captain von Bayern," the officer said handing him a paper. "You are bound for Strasbourg. We have determined the worth of your cargo and the levy on your vessel is one tenth part of all goods. You can pay now in goods or gold, but as we are familiar with your reputation for honesty, on your return other side of the river."

Von Bayern lowered his head, said nothing as he pondered what was to be done – it was rarely so costly to him. "With that levy I shall have to renegotiate the price in Strasbourg. I must pay in coin on return."

"As you wish: You have two passengers aboard, they will remain here until your return."

"Ransom?"

"It is Schnabel's will for the monk and his companion."

"It will delay their journey."

"Then you had better hasten yours. Meanwhile, we will make them comfortable."

"He is a Mathurian friar."

"Then a cell will be no discomfort to him." The officer was quite pleased with himself, and moved on to Captain de Beers, whose levy was much lower for distance yet to travel and tolls to come. Schnabel knew the Rhine League was disposed to act against robber barons, and he walked a fine line between appearance and reality.

"I am sorry," von Bayern said, clasping Caron's shoulder. "I have seen this before and there is no arguing it. When I return, they will release you. Only beware of Schnabel and give no offense. So long as Ransbach is here he is on his best behavior, but I have heard he has an appetite for monks."

"How is that?"

"Schnabel is but half a man. It rankles for he has an unyielding soul, but he must humble himself before the Bishop. He takes his shame out on vulnerable clergy who do not subscribe to the Bishop's vision. How shall I say, he may try to make a woman of you that he may feel more the man for it. God's speed and bring you home again."

"One of us he will offer amnesty." The voice came out of the gloom. "The Bishop is in residence; it is custom."

As his eyes adjusted Caron made out the form of a man sat bolt upright across the holding cell, staring blankly at him.

"I am not a prisoner but detained a little while," Caron said.

He heard a wisp of laughter, and the man rose wearily, steadied and made for him in the half dark. "You don't know the hell into which you have fallen. Who are you; what is your crime?"

"Friar John of Oxford: I've committed no crime."

"Ah, then Schnabel detains you because you are a monk. As Bishop of Ransbach, Rheinsfeld must defend you, but as Count von Rheinsfeld I would not expect much from him if Schnabel has his eye on you. He controls the beast by distracting and feeding it."

"He would allow a man of the cloth to be defiled?"

"Rheinsfeld lives in his mind; despises inferiors, fears superiors. He will weigh your use. That you are a friar will mean little to him except you offer advantage. Markus Veidt," he said, offering his hand: "Freischütz to Albert von Hapsburg, until his death."

"Marksman?"

"I served him well." Veidt opened his eyes and even in the half-light Caron could see them swollen and scarred. "He rewarded me with an estate bordering on Ransbach lands. The Bishop - Count von Rheinsfeld - coveted my lands, made an offer which I refused. He sent Schnabel to press his suit over an incident of a wounded deer. There was an argument. I was taken. They scorched my eyes. What is the day, friar?"

"Middle June."

"June," he said, wistfully. "There was snow that day. Now the green world is awake and I am in darkness."

"I will speak for you."

"You must speak for yourself, Father. I am sorry for you, but come here you may never again see the light of day."

Veidt put out his hand and touched Caron's shoulder. "You are wearing coarse, homespun."

"For the journey," Caron said, partially uncloaking as Origen had shown him to do. He let the light in him intensify a little, enveloping the flesh in a golden glow.

"I seem to see you," Veidt said. "I sense your shape; the first I have seen since my eyes were savaged."

"There is a way to see within when darkness gathers without. I will teach you this."

"He will account you nothing in homespun. If you have the cloak of your Order put it on with your piety. You may yet shame him into being what he claims to be, a Bishop of the Church."

"I have in my possession a papal prerogative that none in my care can be detained in Christendom. I assure you we shall leave this place together."

"It is enough that you care."

"And to that end I must prepare myself," Caron said, moving off to a corner of their confinement, leaving Hode to low conversation with Veidt.

"I've journeyed with him only a short time but he is like that," Hode said, "contemplative, given to withdrawing, at times very inward, but never lost to reality. Indeed, he emerges from it more adept in dealing with what is at hand."

"The others are gathering." Origen spoke at Caron's ear, nearer than breathing, but he alone heard. "Fear nothing. This is but a stumbling block in the way, and the greater the resolution of all this is begun."

It was the way of the degenerate mind to dominate, and if to its advantage number every blade of grass. There was a way through this but not in struggle against the structures of the mind made world. In anguish nothing, but in stillness there was always found a point of release.

Physically, he was barred by a great oak and wrought iron door, but four walls do not a prison make and Caron felt blessed by the presence that enveloped him. In measure he brightened as gradually he uncloaked and the very cell filled with a tangible substance like a spring air filling him with rest and longing. Even so with it came old memories of the dark siege of Montségur, of sorrows unresolved.

"We chose the power of love over the love of power," Esclarmonde said on the eve of its destruction. Now it came to him in a voice familiar, elusive but known, lustrous with the influence of the shining ones. "We asked nothing of the world but tolerance and the prince of this world denies even that. How then should we fail the truth?"

He knew full well though fashions change and customs veil, patterns persist and this came as warning. Was it this he was walking into again, the slaughter of innocence; the arbitrary and ruthless order of the son of perdition imposed on the tender flesh of life?

"You must answer to this," her voice urged in him: "How shall we fail to live now, knowing our deeds matter, and that we shall come again?"

Then the memory was full upon him: the small procession of men, women and children down the mountainside to the raging fires of the Bishop's self-righteous envy. The effort to save Branwyn as Esclarmonde desired of him, his impulsive charge at Bezu against de Blanchefort's knights, his fall and loss, even what memory remained to him, and awakening to slavery in Egypt. All that followed had it come round again to this? Was he being led to repeat an old ordeal?

"Move on," Origen counseled. "You have broken surface from the mass of the comatose in life to walk the path of the ascending ones. And the rulers of the darkness of this world resist your return."

Hode watched as Caron went deeper into meditation. He had seen it in the friar who had died to bring him out of bondage, but never so deep. It amazed him how Caron had taken on his persona, and now almost in a trance. But that was the way of devout monks. He heard faint whispers like prayer on his lips, as if he was talking to another but never able to discern the words or even the tongue. It must be God, he thought.

"He is aglow," Veidt said. "I can see him, not with my eyes, but see him none the less, and he is aglow."

"You are not yet accomplished in bearing the burden of light." It was

Origen again who spoke: "Be modest in this for your heart and mind are not yet fully toned. Walk wisely and know you are never alone."

Hode could see it too now, faintly perhaps, but it did appear Caron was enveloped in soft luminescence but he put it to a trick of the flickering torchlight and darkness enveloping them and turned again to hear the rest of Veidt's story.

Caron felt himself enter deep into memory, deeper than he desired until he could sustain it no more and was overwhelmed with sleep. He nodded once, caught himself and struggled to open his eyes. Caron awoke, and looked up through the branches of a flowering apple tree into the sun, and before him the eyes of a woman, his head upon her lap in the midst of the garden. She held a twig of apple blossom, and they were in an orchard filled with scent and birdsong.

"Death's kingdom is but an instant."

"Who are you?"

"You went for us and I am given care of you. You've slept, dreamed, and forgotten, but in the timelessness of time there is only life, and we are closer now than you understand."

She shook out her fair hair. It shimmered in the sunlight filtering down through the trees. The light, that's what struck him. It seemed at once to come from everywhere and everything about him its own radiance.

He sat up slowly and looked about him. He was in an orchard of white blowing blossom, his head on the Lady Anwyn's lap. The trees were in all stages of life, from bud to leaf to blossom to fruit and falling leaf. There was an oak, and a fountain, and a waterfall, and a flowing stream that pooled just beyond the grassy bank where they lay. It meandered off to a distant sea where there were islands and small white sails blown like blossom on the air.

"Whiter Morn?" he asked.

"In form you can envision. Now I must tell you, in the garden of the world we would tend and keep there are tares sown among the wheat. You must abide yet a little while, for the blessing of the issue of life that stirs again in the earth."

"Is this then the past that lies before me, to come again and again to the same issues that bedevil men?"

"There is only now and the making and unmaking of things: the illusion of time into which man has fallen, and still we have this eternal moment. Awaken now and the world will awaken with you. And when it is done, we shall be together again in the company of friends."

He would ask but she put a finger to his lips. "You shall not be alone. I am in the world and will come to you." She pointed to the brook and the fall of waters, where they pooled before overflowing and meandering to the sea.

"Beloved, when we meet, remember me." She was gone, and he alone in an orchard of blossom, birdsong and the sound of flowing waters. He awoke entranced to the comforting image of Origen a shining point in an umbra of light that took him in.

"Whatever fair shape she may assume she is always Anwyn, sweet influences she has never betrayed, and abides with you from the beginning."

"What would you have me do? For with the sowing and reaping in time, in which man must choose to rise or fall, I see now the world in such deep denial it can only come to great tribulation."

"He comes forth in us, Caron. The archangel and power of the wonderful one is upon us to do what we came to do. A greater wisdom than mine guides the path of restoration to the First Time. Dwell in the light. The way will open, and in your flesh you shall see God."

22

Black Tower

Caron was first summoned. His escort came in hot haste but faltered at the cell. The homespun friar was transformed, dressed in white cloak, cowl and surplice; the splayed blue and red bar cross of the Order of the Holy Trinity emblazoned on his chest. It was a stunning conversion from what they expected; no more just another eunuch monk to serve their master's appetites.

"We shall all go together." It was not a request.

Cloaked with ineffable light, the friar radiated authority, and certain to be of high interest to the Bishop of Ransbach. Like a high emissary of the pope, John of Oxford communicated power, and fear of offending the Holy See overwhelmed fear of Schnabel. And so the three came together into the great hall, and with swift retreat that none take notice were gracelessly delivered. Even so they came like the sound of rolling thunder that brought everything to silence.

Raucous laughter, the chatter of women, clatter of knives on plates, the dissonance of musicians stumbling to a halt, acrobats falling in a heap, the juggler dropping his balls and cursing, never expecting to be heard: all silence to the sounds of the settling fire on the hearth, the wind and rain in the rafters. Pale faces, dazed eyes, pinned to the soundless moment: all turned to see what cut across their pageant like searing lightning reducing their frivolity to nothing; none knowing how to pick up and continue, all waiting for a cue.

The light in measure still upon him, glorifying and ennobling the robes he wore, Caron as John of Oxford stood silently with his two friends. Unspoken, all knew someone truly noble had come among them. All eyes turned and fixed on Caron. The Bishop of Ransbach, jealous for his own authority, knew he must seize the moment to himself. But it was neither Schnabel nor Ransbach that took Caron's notice, for seated at Ransbach's right hand was the lord Telgesinus, Madelon de Faucon's Master of Spear Hallows. Caron watched him struggle to comprehend the influences that filled the hall. He fixed Caron with his eye, first with the pitiless stare of a reared cobra, then broke off deliberately and returned to his drink as if in fear of what he'd discerned. Ransbach rose and hesitant Schnabel at his side.

"Never a feast begins without welcoming guests. Who have we here Schnabel? Some entertainment you thought to contrive?" It was half apology, half accusation, and all shifting of blame.

"A blind archer, eunuch monk and degenerate Templar he claims to have ransomed. Forgive, my lord, I intended only that the mendicant join our company."

"Mendicant, you say? Charity, charity, he is a Mathurian of the Order of the Holy Trinity. What have you done, Schnabel? These two, the friar and his charge, should never have been interrupted in their journey."

"He was not robed a Mathurian when he came ashore," Schnabel winged.

"Eyes, eyes," Ransbach chided pointing two fingers in Schnabel's face. "As Mother Church has ransomed this soul from the heathen he must be honoured. He carries, I dare say, an ordinance from the Pope exhorting us to uphold and render all assistance to him in the way."

"As you shall see presently," Caron said.

"You have mistaken him, Schnabel," Ransbach chided. "You are on your way to your Order in Paris, I dare say. And this knight, brother, your charge?"

"Sir Robert Hode: I am John of Oxford."

"Whence came you, Friar John?"

"From the ends of the earth."

"Will you say where?

"My journey took me to Bactria and the realms of the Old Man of the Mountain, and by misadventure into the high Himalayas men call roof of the world. I am returned again through India and Egypt."

"Do you hear that Schnabel? We set our nets to fish on either side of the river, and this man has journeyed into the kingdoms of Kublai Khan, perhaps walked in the footsteps of Prester John, all to save a single soul and bring him safely home. He shames us with faith and fortitude, and you detain him here in Christendom? Make a seat for him. Give him yours."

Schnabel nudged his Chamberlain out of the seat next to the Bishop and pointed to the end of the table. The Chamberlain in turn ousted the next in line, and so it went, but the Bishop's interest was only in the Mathurian. Hode and Veidt were seated at the foot of a distant table, and given the Bishop's tone treated courteously. Caron was ceremoniously guided to sit beside the Bishop and, if more subdued, the din began anew, for men are uncomfortable with silence. Telgesinus leaned over and spoke in Ransbach's ear.

"I am remiss," Ransbach apologized: "an introduction is in order. My guest, the Master Telgesinus, a learned man, dare I say the sage of the Languedoc, is anxious to hear of your travels.

"We have this day come from the castle of Duke Frederick, Sierck-les-Baines, where currently dwells his liege, the Lady Madelon de Faucon, to view the progress of our project in the perfection of man. You will, perhaps, have seen a little of that in coming here?"

Telgesinus leaned forward to take in Caron. He was vaguely familiar, but then clergy was clergy. "Where do you come from in coming here?"

"Venice and Konstanz to Schnabel's dungeons," Caron answered: "on our way to Strasbourg."

"Schnabel, when our guest desires you will see him safely on his way to Strasbourg."

"And the Templar," Schnabel protested.

"Schnabel, you cannot build a kingdom on contempt. He is ransomed of the Church, and whatever he may have been he is free to go."

"And yet this priest's charge stripped of his robes fits the description of that reprobate Templar, Hugues Caron." Schnabel insisted. "Shall we not at least determine what he is?"

"Strip any man of his robes, and but for blots and blemishes and ravages of the flesh, hardly a one of us differs in any measure from any other."

"We had word from Ulcinj of Caron's death, attempting to escape the slaver's prison," Telgesinus said. "The one you seek, Herr Schnabel, is dead."

"Let us have no more of this and before the night is done have Friar John's story, if that pleases you?"

Caron told the tale of his journey to the east, so far as it pleased him to tell it, and the tale went on well into the night, until Schnabel their host was besotted. But as the fire burned low the Bishop's ardor burned the brighter, and also Telgesinus absorbed in the account.

"The kingdoms of this world, Brother John, the kingdoms of this world," Ransbach said, speech slurred by wine. "If ever they are to become the kingdoms of our Lord, must be made worthy of Him. We must shape degenerate man into a vassal worthy of a great king.

"If Hashashin will hurl themselves from parapets into cataracts below at the word of the Old Man, it reveals what passion burns in the human souls to yield one's life to one greater. Should not our own kingdoms burn with the same ardor to serve their masters?"

"It is addiction their master feeds," Caron said. "He enslaves the body with potions and beguiles the sense, binding them to his purpose. Passion, yes, but these men are not in possession of their lives."

"It is the passion that fascinates me," Ransbach said. "It is just such passion as drove you across the wilderness of the world; the passion that led our Lord to walk the path of the cross for the ransom of the world."

"There is a line not to be crossed between passion and obsession. Obsession breeds fanatics. In India there are those who befriend to take the lives of travelers. These Thuggee seek in the death throes of their victims' agonies union with the goddess Kali: she whom they call slayer of time, destroyer of the illusions of the world."

"Look at these," Ransbach gestured about the hall. "Sated with food and drunk on wine they sleep and snort like swine; those still awake fall mumbling and morose over their cups at their lot in life. But give them an entertainment and they'll be wide awake, eager to suck the marrow out of it to feed their destitute souls."

"Albertus Magnus taught me to stay the path of reason," Caron said. "Fanaticism masks hidden doubt."

"Magnus is long dead." Something in Telgesinus wanted to diminish this itinerant friar; he was jealous for his experience.

"Magnus had a place for mystery in him and wonder in creation. But always he sought to cultivate consciousness on the firm foundation of reason and practical appliance in the world."

Telgesinus turned to Ransbach. "What you have achieved has come of rational planning and passionate implementation for the greater good."

"I am, likewise, much indebted to Magnus but perhaps even more Aquinas," Ransbach said.

"The common heart needs only be full of desire to serve," Telgesinus insisted. "It is for their betters to keep a cool head, focused mind and careful application of logic and reason to build and manage the state."

"Brother John will have seen only the village of Eingemauert," Ransbach said. "Believe me, it is the least of our accomplishments and in no small measure by Telgesinus' genius, for he has contributed greatly to our thought and practice."

"And what is the price, Lord Bishop?"

"Oh, it is a money maker. Carefully screening of talent, training in the trades, efficiency in living and elimination of all that is superfluous in the under-classes has given us a healthy, productive workforce. And you see how they live, well educated in their duties, suitably and comfortably housed, fed and clothed. True, our Lord said His kingdom was not of this world but until His kingdom comes it is ours, and we must make the best of it."

"One must take thought for the morrow," Telgesinus said. "In this world you cannot just consider the lilies of the fields."

"And what of His kingdom here and now," Caron said.

"Heaven is hereafter," Telgesinus said. "Here and now we must be pragmatic. What better way to prepare for what is to come than our good works?"

"Our Master taught the kingdom of Heaven is at hand. Yet, fallen creatures that we are, if we do not first address the purity of our hearts do we not mar the divine design for man as God would have it?" Caron replied.

"Is it not for us to *let* Heaven shape the kingdom of God in us, and never in its place impose the contrivances of man upon the earth, however well intended?

"I do not mean to say there is no room for logic and reason, and yes, efficiency in our affairs, but are we not reminded of Him that the mind is but the light bearer and not the light," Caron persisted. "Should the mind determine these things, or ought they to come of the unfolding of the spirit of God in us?"

"Have a care, Brother Friar. You will be accused of mysticism. There are those who would put their own conscience before the Church, and that is heresy in these times."

"I do not mean to offend. I thought only that a Bishop of the Church would speak to the mystical body of Christ," Caron said, gently: "that you would naturally agree, 'except the Lord build the House they labor in vain who build it.'"

Telgesinus laughed but the Bishop was more cautious. His enthusiasm blindsided him; he could not afford to distill the impression he was indifferent to the mystical union of the Church and God.

"It is I think a matter of degree, this involvement in improving the world," Ransbach said cautiously. "The Cathar cult, you will recall, was so disdainful of the world they were deemed heretic and war waged against them."

"I remember it well."

"And again there is in this very land. They, who call themselves *Brethren of the Free Spirit*, speak as you have done of mystery and wonder in the impulse of the spirit shaping a world. These claim guidance from higher realms, care little for the order of the Church, and are under scrutiny for deviating from the sanctioned path."

"I cannot imagine the Church would wish another blood bath such as the Cathars," Telgesinus said.

"You are newly returned," Ransbach continued. "Having traveled far, exposed to other beliefs, I would advise caution until you are again accustomed.

"Good advice at any time," Caron agreed. "But what of you Master

Telgesinus, you are a man of intellect. Do you believe the substance of this world was given to be shaped by man's mind alone? Or, is there a higher realm of life to which mind must defer?

"We defer to the will of the Church, of course," Telgesinus said, glancing to the Bishop. "But it is impossible for a man of intellect to believe in illusions.

"Beyond my faith in the wisdom of the Church, in this world I believe only in what I can see, smell, touch, taste and hear. And of these I form my opinions and calculate what can be done."

"Thales, Anaxagoras, Democritus, and Epicurus in some wise thought as you," Caron said. "There is also the Hindu sage, Kanada, who believed matter absolute and indivisible. Democritus' atoms he called *anu*, indivisible. Among my things I have a Persian translation of his manuscript. I would gladly read it to you.

"I think also of the Chinese Xunzi who developed a doctrine of realism and materialism more than 1500 years ago. So, there are those who have gone before opening the way for your thinking, but none I think who would deny the existence of other realms than these material."

Telgesinus paled. He resented this encounter. It was humiliating this Mathurian had read works never heard of, let alone able to translate and read them to him. But he was dumb to say it. His chest tightened, his emotions overwhelming the delicate balance of his mind and sense as he sought for breath to answer.

Ransbach rescued him. "Did you visit Cathay in your travels?"

"I learned only of those I met in the high Himalaya on the frontiers of that populous realm, who spoke of a philosopher called Kongzi who shaped their nation."

"And are they reasonable, pragmatic people?"

"By fits and starts, they strive for balance often losing it. But there was a time of great violence, even cannibalism from which emerged Kongzi, a teacher who taught the way of the ancestors to harmonize their lives and learn again to live in peace. For stability they infuse his teachings in their young."

"That human nature is degenerate we agree, Friar John," Telgesinus said, "but I would go further. Only by confining and conforming man's nature within a system of laws can we achieve a single people, create predictable behavior, and mold a society fit to be called civilized. It appears this teacher, Kongzi would agree."

"Laws, Brother John, laws," Ransbach said. "The Ten Commandments were good enough to get Moses struggling with a rag tag group of people through the wilderness, but we who aspire to civilization need laws to govern every detail of life from cradle to the grave.

"And so this Cathay must be a very happy realm, indeed, so ordered and governed. If we could modify the way we live together, bring all human passions under rule and regulation, and by careful programming adjust the behaviors of the people to the way of their betters, we could bring an end to sin, greed and war.

"We could contrive the perfect context for life, provide for every want, and so discipline unregenerate man to fit behaviors that one might come as close as possible this side of the veil to recreate that paradise of the soul again on earth."

"Is that what you have begun to do, Lord Bishop?" Caron asked. "Eingemauert opened my eyes to your industry."

"Neat and tidy was it not?"

"Every house the same size, all of a russet and green and of one construction laid out upon a square of intersecting streets: neat and tidy, yes, but the eye wanted for variety."

"Well, the art will come later," Ransbach said. "For now there is variety enough in nature; too much in man is unbecoming. What we have made is by design sufficient and efficient, and fair. Everyone has what he needs to do what is needful, and there is no dissent because there are no distinctions. Everything is the same for everyone. Is it not said of the early Christians, the ideal was to hold all things in common?"

"Not wives." Caron said.

"No, no, of course not, each man has his own wife, and there is some envy and a modicum of strife in that matter as one might suppose," Ransbach answered. "But if I may use the term cautiously, I jealously maintain *droit du seigneur* over everyone's wife – in spirit you understand – that they might all know in essence they belong to me and Holy Church. And that has somewhat dampened the flames of jealousy among them over this or that woman's beauty, knowing they can never entirely own her.

"The children, however, are another matter. I determine weddings and family planning," Ransbach continued. "Children are raised by a common hand and commonly schooled to fit to their service, and each is looked out for by each and every one. All educated as one there are no aberrant patterns, no discrimination based on abilities – for each will serve his purpose – and absolute tolerance, for all raised in the best traditions of the land think the same. It produces a remarkable homogeneity and agreement in kind. All I ask is that each gives according to his ability. In return I assure they receive exactly what they need."

"There is no hunger, no theft, no hoarding of goods," Telgesinus said. "Whatever the crop or yield, all is gathered into the communal barns; when the Lord Bishop has taken his portion of the harvest to administer it wisely, all that remains is divided equally according to family and their numbers. And those who work in trades receive likewise in type and in proportion to their needs for the contribution of their own labors."

"And all are favorably disposed to this?" Caron asked.

"There is no dissent because there are no distinctions but those dictated by natural need and ability," Ransbach said. "These are my lands and these vassals. Even so, if one or another of them chooses not to live in this wise, he is free to go and make his way in the world as he will. Only doing so, it is understood he leaves all behind and shall not return."

"And are all your villages the same?"

"But for the natural variations in their purpose identical; though for efficiency sake each is given its part to perform in the whole: some weavers, some smiths, some farmers and shepherds, you understand. But taken together sufficient, efficient and fair."

"And no other distinctions," Caron dared to press him, for Ransbach was fanatic about his vision. He seemed not to hear.

"In time when by rule of law I have overcome degenerate human nature, there will be changes. As my lands increase and villages grow in number, I will delegate my responsibilities to others, giving them authority over workers to see to the administration of these matters for me. I have already begun this; you will have met a black patch in Eingemauert. Then there are the greens, fewer in number.

"Scholars, also, will I support who will come to study how to implement strategies to increase yields, livestock health, farms management, and as well contrive tools and means to make our workers yet more efficient.

These I shall mark in blue. Others I have in mind for practical artisans, weavers, potters, smiths and the like all true to their colours and devoted to making our enterprise sufficient, efficient and fair: a glorious spectrum of light.

"That is my dream Brother John. And no doubt you have heard the scoffers mock and the bawdy jokes - my kingdom of Cockaigne they call it – I have heard of the songs the sailors sing - when all I do is seek to shape my realm to the greatest good of the greatest number, and as a model kingdom for kingdoms to come."

Caron glanced at a weary Schnabel. "They are most concerned about your gargoyles, fortress chains across the river, and taxes imposed for right to pass in pursuit of their commercial ventures."

"Gargoyles, yes, very good, even a church has gargoyles to unnerve the wicked, and right to tithes and a kingdom is built on taxes. I ask only that those who pass our way render unto Caesar what is Caesar's, so we may render in kind to our superiors. In my case that is von Hapsburg, my feudal lord and master in these matters."

Schnabel was feeling left out. Ransbach was passing through with Telgesinus and must leave on the morrow. There were matters to discuss but instead with such wit as he had he was stuck on the mendicant who exercised a peculiar hold over his liege. With his discontent came feelings of jealousy. When Ransbach was gone he would teach this monkish character his place in the new order.

"Give me a moment," Caron said, "I would speak to your vision and the matter of a philosopher king to rule such a kingdom; it strikes me the linchpin of your thinking to explore the justice of such realm."

"To hear a mendicant friar speak of Plato should be entertaining," Telgesinus said.

"My charge, Sir Robert Hode, was long imprisoned in Islam. I must assure him that what seems long night, at your Grace's pleasure will yet have its dawn." The Bishop nodded graciously, intrigued at the thought of contrasting his realistic application with Plato's idealism, withal seeing the need for an impartial king to whom all deferred. But for the freedom from ambition and the poverty of goods Plato said must attend the part, it was rather an attractive role.

Caron excused himself for a moment and went to the low end of the table where Hode and Veidt were seated. Telgesinus leaned in toward his host and spoke his mind. "This is a most extraordinary friar. He is a different man but something familiar in his manner; was I not assured the man was dead I might suppose this the fugitive, Caron."

Schnabel seized the moment and came to the head of the table. "I do not trust the mendicant," he urged, "and that fellow Hode; he, too, is a Templar, your Grace. I see it in his manner."

"I believe you are mistaken in this John of Oxford and Sir Robert Hode." Ransbach shook his head. "This friar who graced our table with conversation and tales of travel is who he says he is, and shall be seen safely on his way."

"If you are wrong Hapsburg's ire may fall upon us," Schnabel said.

"Restrain yourself, Schnabel. These Mathurins have powerful protectors among the nobility. It is no small thing to have those who will go to the ends of the earth to ransom a Christian soul, and it is those with wealth and prestige who most need their services."

"Then let us try him but subtly," Schnabel said.

"Oh must you, Schnabel, very well but discreetly. If, indeed, they are Templars they are warriors of the highest caste, and you had best first rouse your men from their stupor to contain what might come. Propose an entertainment to rouse them up," Ransbach said.

"I have kept Veidt alive for just such a moment: With your leave, Lord Bishop, a trial to keep or set him free?"

"Do with the Freischütz as you will. None there are to speak for him, and were an issue made Hapsburg will find for us."

"This should be amusing, Friar John," Ransbach said as Caron returned. "Schnabel tells me concerning Veidt, that he has a little entertainment illustrating the nature of justice."

"With the loss of his eyes this man has suffered enough," Caron said. "Will you not show him mercy?"

"Laws, Friar John, laws," Ransbach said. "Veidt owned lands adjacent to mine. He gave succor to this apostate cult that believes God incarnate in man. They flaunt every law and institution, asserting these must pass away in favor of God alone revealed in man.

"Can you imagine these creatures," Ransbach said with a sweep of his hand, "unfettered by laws and institutions, following only the impulse of whatever moves in them?"

Caron looked at the drunken guests and soldiery sprawled like a great, ragged creature snoring at the foot of its master. "He is not now what God made him in the beginning, and still he must find his way back," he said.

"Some of these brethren dared enter my lands to stir up dissent. I repeatedly warned Veidt of this. I offered to put a price on their heads; even offered a fair price for his land but he refused. And when pressed in the name of Hapsburg, he challenged me.

"Schnabel was my champion and as Veidt challenged, the choice of weapons was Schnabel's. He is an excellent swordsman and Veidt lost."

"He was a Freischütz not a swordsman, and you blinded him," Caron said.

Ransbach shrugged. "Tonight he will have opportunity to earn his freedom. We shall have a show of justice and mercy to whet our appetite for Plato."

Schnabel roused the great hall from its stupor with the blast of a trumpet to awaken the dead. The awake clasped their ears, drooping heads snapped up, dogs moaned, a falcon screeched, and still some too deep in their cups even to hear; most roused like a great beast from its stupor to groans, guffaws and idiot grins of anticipation at what was next to come.

Veidt was dragged to his feet by Schnabel's soldiery and forced into the square between the tables. Having so long survived by his wits Hode realized it was all coming to a head. With one eye on Caron he rose quietly when all attention was on Veidt. He moved to the back of the hall and cast eyes about for a carelessly placed weapon.

"You all know me for a just man," Schnabel began. "This Freischütz challenged and was defeated in battle, my hand more skilled than his. His life was mine to take and yet I spared him."

A banging of cups on the table seemed fit to the occasion; so also the raucous laughter, for though they feared their master like an abused hound, together one and all they clung to him for advantage, taking their pleasure as they might and frustrations out when they could. It was a hard world and Schnabel was their patron.

"And what was the cause of our quarrel with him? He harbored enemies of the Church who believe they have no need for her ordinances or the laws of kings; blind to the dictates of their betters to follow alone the impulse of the spirit.

"Herr Veidt, blind to the world you hate, have you found an inner light half so useful as once your eyes?" Schnabel thought this a splendid joke and could not help but laugh himself; the soldiery banged their cups on the soiled tables and a roar of approval swelled through the hall. "Tonight you can show us what you have learned, test your vision of the inner light."

He was feeling very clever; perhaps the company, he thought, brought out the best in him. "What say you?" Schnabel asked. "Shall we have a test of skill to prove your faith? Nothing to say, Herr Veidt; overwhelmed by the generosity of my offer?"

"What do you wish of me?"

Schnabel took a cup from the table and beckoned a guard. "Give him your crossbow."

"On my word I shall throw this cup in the air and, Freischütz, if you strike it you shall earn your freedom. What say you?"

"The being and the nature of God are mine; Jesus enters into the castle of the soul; even here he is present and I must be in Him for Him, and not in me for me."

Ransbach laughed. "Who taught you that?"

"One wiser than you," Veidt replied.

"Let us have our entertainment. On with it, Schnabel," he said, disgusted.

Flanked by two soldiers Veidt was given the cross bow. "On my word, then," Schnabel said and retired from the floor back of the table where Bishop Ransbach sat amused at the farce unfolding before him and stood behind his master, cup held in hand. "So, then, now," Schnabel shouted and hand outstretched threw the cup into the air.

The bolt flew true, passed directly over the Lord Bishop's head, pierced the hollow of the cup as Schnabel lifted to release it, smashed on through open mouth and slammed through the back of Schnabel's head, killing him instantly. He fell with cup and clatter, into a grotesque heap at Ransbach's chair.

None moved but Hode. Across the hall he drew the long bow, loosed one arrow swishing past Caron pinning Telgesinus' cloak to the back of his chair, and in a breath drew another aimed at Ransbach's heart, and held.

Stunned, drunken soldiery, the Bishop's entourage and guests alike fell in a silent abyss. But the bishop took in the scene, saw the long bowman's sight fixed on him, and acceded. Telgesinus was ashen, caught up in the sublime moment, stunned to silence, yet feeling the justice of it, his own life hung on an arrow's point. He searched desperately about the room for his attendants, the two assassins who yet accompanied him, and with a glance warned them to do nothing that would endanger either himself or the bishop.

To Caron's surprise the bishop raised not a hand against them "Veidt's shot was true," Ransbach said softly. "Veidt is free to go." He dismissed the few sober guards and bade the shocked guests leave the banquet room quietly. "Leave this place," he said, a quaver in his voice, "go now to your quarters; soldiers to your barracks; leave me with these guests." Stunned and drunken revelers stumbled from the hall. Veidt stood silently, head bowed, fallow to whatever came next, and Caron spoke for him.

"Schnabel invited his own fate. You cannot blame a blind Freischütz for a killing shot."

"You coveted my lands," Veidt said, raising his head staring blindly at Ransbach, a soft light enveloped him with the peace of the resigned. "When I would not yield you set your creature on me."

"You subverted my designs."

"Now your gargoyle is dead," Veidt said. "Who now will guard the threshold to your worker's paradise?"

"Aptly put," Ransbach said, glancing at the disheveled heap on the floor at his feet. "A useful beast, but blinded by devotion he exceeded his writ. I should merely have waited you out. My own methods so far superior, my rewards generous, your own tenants would in time have seen the sense of it."

Ransbach glanced across the banquet hall; Hode had drawn closer now, arrow still drawn aimed at the Bishop's chest. "You may call your bowman off lest his fingers tire," he said to Caron. "I am a man of my word.

"Veidt was ill-used, but not of my doing. Let this be a just and lasting end to it. I will not raise my hand against you but I would know who you are."

"I am a servant of God with a commission to return my charge to his home in England. You have shown less than a hospitable spirit for one who serves as I do the same God of mercy. And as you are a man of the Church I charge you to do none harm to those who come this way in his name."

"Heaven forbid." Ransbach was now more concerned for what might subsequently be said of him, for interfering in the work of a Mathurian, than any second guessing on Telgesinus' part.

"We are all overwrought on this business concerning the Templars and that recreant knight, Caron. Aggravated by the edict of death and rich reward for his corpse, every stranger is suspect. Schnabel was sure you were he and so detained you. It is most unchristian but the secular lords will have their way."

"I told you, Caron is dead," Telgesinus insisted, coldly.

"With your leave we shall be on our way." Hode took Veidt's arm and drew near. "Shall we go in peace, or will there be bloodshed?" They backed toward the portal that led down to dungeons and river.

"Go in peace."

Telgesinus extracted the arrow from his cloak, and glanced at Ransbach. They were alone in an empty, smoky hall, smelling of stale dinners, sour liquor and the rancorous bled out creature at their feet. It was disgusting. The world was so coarse and all either desired they told themselves, was that it be beautiful.

Alone in her quarters Magda gazed into the small dark mirror wrought for her of Venetian glass. She let the mask she wore for others slip away, and gazed into the darkness of her soul. "What next, Maia?" she whispered in the glass, paused and waited for her thoughts to form. "You must bind the women to you," the answer came. "For where fair women go, men's hearts will surely follow; and through our influence in them magnify our will."

Magda turned away and opened the curtains to the early morning light. Her view from the castle heights was summer meadows to the deep flowing Moselle and the village of Sierck-les-Bains. It was a splendid morning with the promise of a day of gentle labors and fulfillment to come.

It was impossible to say exactly when it happened, but she awoke one morning and found herself imbued with Maia. All the memory of her life was intact and she was Magda still but more; this communion she entered into she kept to herself. Her past seemed shadow cast in the light, and she dared think the power of the Domina of the Blood Royal had come upon her. She knew things she had not known before, saw things she had not seen before; indeed, her senses filled with new revelations, and she found herself capable of things she had only sensed as latent power.

Not the least of those abilities enhanced was her power to enter into the hidden life of another, to engender visions, to influence and shape wills to her own. Caught up in her influence one could not but believe he acted out of his own will in fulfilling hers. Of course it was not so with everyone; some were not as susceptible as others. Even so her powers increased and she luxuriated in it promising herself to test it to the full.

Springtide brought occasion; desire like gathered blossoms filling the arms with longing, making anxious the heart to break through and flower in the sun. The orchards had come into blossom and her young host, Duke Frederick of Lorraine, and his wife Elizabeth, ordered a picnic under the flowering trees for Madelon de Faucon, her entourage, and guests of the Court of Lorraine at Château Fort du Sierck-les-Bains. They gathered in the gardens above the Moselle River, everyone as merry as the season glorying in the day.

It was opportunity to be used to advantage. Magda need hardly influence Siduri. Rumors of Caron's death at the hands of the Beast of Ulcinj had intensified Siduri's passion to be about her father's business. She was fascinated with Europe and the mystery of her father's life before he came to dwell in Egypt. Now the season had taken her, too, buoying her along. Intoxicated with new life she wandered on Squin's arm under the flowering trees, half in a daze what changes a few swift months had wrought. She seemed to Magda very much in love and Magda envied her for it.

So Siduri should have Squin and that was well, for as her empire grew she would need such as Siduri at her side, one among the sisters, if not the true blood line, who had a head on her shoulders. Already she was important to Magda. Siduri brought with her to Venice the wealth of eastern trade. What's more she helped Magda broker a deal with the Doge of Venice, encompassed the Lady Constanza whose reach extended so far as Cathay; and opened up prospects almost unimaginable for deepening her influence, enriching her realms, and drawing kingdoms into the palm of her hand.

For all that Magda was at a loss what to offer Constanza; she seemed to desire and need nothing she did not already have. Even Gisors' arts of sensuous seduction had been to no avail, and she had broken pattern and rebuffed Lothario to the death. In her world, Siduri confided, Constanza was so hedged with spells it was death to possess against her will. These spells were wrought by a powerful wizard in some distant land, for when Constanza and Siduri had spoken of it they were rapt to find each had a master of shamanic arts for a father. And when Magda had taken to her mirror to seek the truth of it Maia normally forthright hedged her reply. Yes, she acknowledged, there was a guiding hand upon Constanza, and it would take some occasion yet unknown to artfully bind her to their purpose.

Again the key to this was Siduri. Constanza first refused to accompany Siduri on her journey into Europe, and after the fiasco with Lothario one might suppose all was lost. But, unwilling to give up access to a vast mercantile empire over the clumsy efforts of a nephew, the Doge was reconciled. He was appalled at his nephew's behavior; solicitous of continuing alliances and future cordial relations. The business of Venice was business.

And then with a stroke of unanticipated good fortune, Constanza had appeared with Perrin at Sierck-les-Bains. Having come this far from the ends of the earth, she might as well travel to the ends of the earth, and return having seen it all. Siduri was delighted. Their fathers' gifts they held in common, they spoke a common language, shared a great adventure, and like sisters bonded to know each other's mind with scarce a word.

She pondered what to do with Perrin. He so readily had the hearts of her ladies, and where the hearts are held so is power. When she came to the orchard Perrin was already in song in the midst of a group of young women, each one of whom was sure he sang to her alone.

> *...you rose up like rays of dawn*
> *That separate day from darkest night.*
> *From you springs up a glimmer new,*
> *That all this world be filled with light.*
> *There is no maiden of such a hue*
> *So fair, so lovely, so rosy, so bright,*
> *O my sweet lady have mercy true*
> *Take pity on me your poor knight.*

She knew this ballad. In the court in Languedoc the ladies swooned over it; though written in praise of the Virgin Mary not one but saw herself in it. And Perrin had a gift the Cailleach had seen and cultivated in him. He was not meant for the road but the court where she would need the power of his words to serve; for silly creatures that they are, it took a gift like Perrin's to bind them, and in turn that meant her own firm grip on him.

When Perrin was done she drew him aside and together they walked the path among the flowering apple. "We have had our differences, Perrin," she began, "but I think these now more the trauma of the loss of your late mistress, the Lady Branwyn, Domina of the Blood Royal, to whom I know your heart was given."

"It was milady." Perrin wondered at the reason and direction of this encounter. "Times of change are never easy for anyone, and yet life goes on."

"Indeed it does," Magda agreed. "Have you heard of late from the Lady Gwyn?"

"That she is well - returned to Caer Myrddin - and she said something about being reconciled with you," he added, cautiously.

"We have, indeed, reconciled our differences. I dare say there was fault on both sides; I see now Squin was no match for her, and she has repented her resistance to my accession to power."

"Branwyn left no doubt it should pass to you," Perrin said, "and you are given to deal with your own as you must."

"Thank you," Magda said. "I see now you were trying only to protect the daughters of the Blood Royal from that time of madness. I swear an evil spirit possessed Squin, which is now exorcised, for he is quite in love. And what greater healing can God offer than to let a hardened heart love again.

"You, I believe, were drawn into this somewhat against your will. To protect the honor and defend the virtue of the ladies is your natural instinct. A knightly virtue is it not, and you so gifted in the ways of moving a woman's heart?"

"I seek only to continue in your grace."

"I have spoken with the Duke of Lorraine, and before we leave this place you shall be made a knight of the realms of Lorraine and Languedoc, and shall hereafter journey with me when I go abroad." Perrin fell stone silent. "What ho, little bird, no sweet song?"

"I do not know what to say milady, except of my heart's honour I seek virtue in all my art, but why a knight of the realm?"

"The world is all about honours, Perrin, for these ennoble men in the eyes of others and bestow power whether they deserve it or not. You deserve it, and what is more it must be if you are to wed the Lady Gwyn."

"Lady Gwyn? But she will not agree to this."

"She has agreed already," Magda said. "All now know Caron, whose name you dared not speak, lives no more and his debt paid in return of the stone at the hand of the Lady Siduri.

"And in time, dear Perrin, if I find in you that trust the Cailleach found - and with study to prepare you for the task of course - there is another matter I think you well fit to."

"Milady?"

"With Flegetanis' death I need a Master of Grail Hallows. I have pondered this and wonder who knows more the mysteries of the heart? Who has greater gift to shape incandescent visions to words, inspiring duty and devotion, than you my Perrin, immortal bard? It is what the Cailleach saw in you. It is what I now see."

23

Rose Window

"What side of the river?" Hode secured the skiff as Caron helped Veidt ashore. There was a narrow path along which the horses pulled barges against the current, and a trail that led up through the wooded hillside to the road above. But there was nothing on the path or the road; the night was silent and the drovers still abed.

"West bank, Markus," Caron said. "We're a dozen or so miles south of Strasbourg."

"I am a burden to you."

"No burden."

"I am, but if I could ask one more thing; then you are done with me." Caron helped him climb the embankment to the roadway.

"Ask it," he said, "and if it is in my power."

Hode caught up and grasped Veidt's other arm. "Lead me to the monastery of Mount Saint Odile."

"In the Vosges Mountains," Caron said.

"About a day's journey from Strasbourg," Veidt confirmed. Hode broke through the brush to the roadway. They were alone with an hour before dawn. "The brethren dwell nearby."

"You have family?" Hode asked.

"Yes, family," Veidt brightened: "not in the abbey but in the forest nearby, the Brethren of the Free Spirit gather."

"Until tonight I had not heard of these," Hode said.

"We herald the dawning Age of the Holy Spirit," Veidt said. "And Ransbach used this against me as excuse to take my lands."

"I have a meeting I must keep in Strasbourg. Thereafter, gladly," Caron said.

They made their way north to the old Roman city along a dark road until at hint of first light they came to an intersect. One road led north away from the river into forest and mountains, the other on to Strasbourg. At the junction was a small shrine to Saint Odilia, the image of a youthful woman holding under one arm a book, and in an outstretched hand a cup with a pair of eyes peaking over the brim. There were stone benches, a font of running water, and a stand of purple larkspur about the shrine. On the lintel were the words: *Sancta Odilia precibus suis liberate purgatorio animam patris sui*. "It is a prayer for liberation of the soul from purgatory," Caron translated.

"Liberation from a purgatory of darkness into the light: she is patron saint of the blind," Veidt said. "This is the road I must walk. I have yet a little light; perhaps, she will make it full."

They drank from the font and sat silently for ten minutes until at last Caron rose. "I have a set time to meet, but I have promised and will take you to Mount Saint Odilia."

"Let me take him," Hode said. "He has the tongue, and I have the eyes. We can make this journey together." Hode's old wound was troubling and he had lost his staff in the way. So Caron gave his own, the one shaped to uphold him in his way across the wilderness of the world. Letting go was like letting go of a familiar friend. But so they parted: Caron to deliver Origen's manuscript to Meister Eckhart in Strasbourg and perchance to meet with Perrin; Hode to lead Veidt to his brethren, in search of a miracle of intercession by the tender mercies of Saint Odilia.

Strasbourg Cathedral was a work in progress; it had been for an hundred and thirty-eight years, and might well be for another hundred to completion. What is time when you are building for eternity? It was a stunning achievement wrought in rose sandstone, and Caron could not help but stop to admire the workmanship of successive generations of masons. Even from the time of the Roman Argentoratum there was a sanctuary on the site: first a temple to Diana; followed by a church dedicated to the Virgin and in turn, plagued by a succession of disasters, a cathedral that led on to laying the foundations of Notre Dame de Strasbourg. Yet another great, medieval cathedral dedicated to *Maria Theotokos*.

Through his influence, St. Bernard de Clairvaux had elevated Mary in Christendom to Queen of Heaven, claiming her free of original sin, intercessor for humankind, Bride of Christ, and cultivated her worship throughout Christendom. Caron went through the list in his mind of the host of cathedrals all dedicated to the cult of the ever redeeming virgin, mediatrix, queen of heaven and mother of God. But by what impulse, and to what end?

He stood gazing into the exquisite architecture of the west front and main entrance of the cathedral approaching completion, with the great rose window surmounting. What were they thinking that Christ was unapproachable? For in their veneration of the Virgin they kept him juvenile; held Him off, and lost the immanent presence of the Christ Spirit.

"Whom do you seek Brother?"

Caron turned to a man of some seventy years, a little bent but firm in shoulder and stance. Grey hair, high cheek bones on a rugged face, strong chin and aquiline nose, altogether put him in mind of Albertus Magnus. But this was architect and master builder. For his appearance on the scene brought at once to focus a half dozen pressing matters to which he replied each in turn patiently and presently.

"Is it you who have built this?" Caron asked.

"Erwin Von Steinbach," he said holding out his hands. They were worn but not leathered. "Others have labored and I have entered into their labours, some thirty years."

"And you are the architect."

"Others came before me; others will follow after, but this" he said, pointing to the west front entrance, towers, and rose window, "is my design, though I freely admit the iconography of the tympanum and archivolts were inspired by Albertus Magnus."

"He died more than thirty years ago."

"Thirty-four, but many have contributed to this work."

"I'm told he was far more deeply into alchemy than the church will allow. I knew a man, Flegetanis of Alexandria, who had known and provided him with books of alchemy from the east."

Von Steinbach took Caron's arm and led him toward western façade into the nave. "Who are you?"

"A weary traveler late returned to Christendom," Caron said.

"I, too, was once a weary traveler, until I found my commission here. From whence do you journey?"

"Out of the east," Caron said.

"And where do you journey?"

"The wind blows where it will, but bears me home at last to the Holy Isles."

"And fares a weary traveler to my door," von Steinbach said with a sweep of the hand. Caron stood within the vaginal arch to the sanctum that lay deep within. In India it was made explicit and he had come to understand, but in Christendom it was locked in symbol and not to be spoken only experienced. And experience it was entering between the towers, the tympanum arch, face to face with the statue of mother and child, and so into the vestibule. "What do you make of our work?"

"I was standing here pondering what motivation built these cathedrals."

"I am curious you should wonder at it."

"Like you I celebrate our love of God, but I wonder at our confinement of Him," Caron said. Von Steinbach put a finger to his lips. As Caron supposed he must take care. The wilderness changes a man in ways those who huddle together in cities never understand.

"It overwhelms the sense," Caron said. "You witness in stone God's enduring orders of creation in the materia of the world: vesica piscis, Platonic solids, Pythagorean numbers, divine proportion – more than that, perhaps, if I could see it right - all beautifully wrought in uplifting stone as if it were light and air, but truthfully…" he hesitated and fell still. It was dangerous to go there.

But von Steinbach was roused. An itinerant friar emerges out of nowhere and understands his work to the letter; and more than praise what is done to enchant the eye craves understanding of his invisible art the brother so appropriately describes as uplifting stone as if it were light and air. "Say on," von Steinbach urged.

"I have been abroad these many years; traveled where no churches are to ransom souls for Christian charity. I wonder now returning if I am fit to speak to this, or simply admire what you have accomplished." As he said it Caron's mind began to blur and he felt a heat come upon him, his head swim. Was it the mass of stone before him, or the desert wilderness of time behind him? He could not say, only he felt sudden fatigue that drained strength and loosed irrepressible weariness in his soul, and still he must endure.

"Have you seen the St. Sophia?" von Steinbach asked, eagerly.

"I have, and the Dome of the Rock where Solomon's Temple once stood; the pyramids and temples of the Nile raised thousands of years before Christ in tribute to Isis and Osiris, and the sun god Ra. In India I have seen vast temples, mountains of stone striving for the heavens; others cavernous, carved out of the rock in the depths of the earth: monuments to gods who themselves are said to dissolve at last into the infinite."

"Then you will appreciate this." Von Steinbach led into the nave of the cathedral. It was a stunning achievement. Again, light and air; great pillars rose to support a lofty canopy and light through windows of many coloured glass filtered down into the dusky light, catching here and there a column of dust, to the tap, tap of a mason's hammer working off in the soft gloom.

"A forest grove, half-light that filters through the midst of ancient trees: your cathedral is a wide spreading tree of life," Caron said. He wanted to rest beneath that tree of life.

"Just so, just so," von Steinbach said, much pleased. "Our forebears worshipped in the deep woods and in high places, raising altars to pagan gods, who were but embers of remembrance of the glory they sought of our Lord then lost to them. And here," he said, pointing to a place on the floor where the light of the Rose Window fell, "here I am considering a complement to the window in a maze inlaid in the paving stone such as is found at Chartres to depict the journey of the soul in light to God."

"Like Noah you have built an ark." Caron turned to the great rose window over the western gate, rich deep saturated reds and yellows, greens and blues. "You have opened a window in heaven."

"To bear within the essences of the divine design across the winter waters of the world," von Steinbach said, "until the day of judgment when all things shall come in remembrance before Him."

"I have seen that day written in the Cathedral Rose at Chartres."

"Then you have seen with the eye of the soul. The rose window of each cathedral is a glimpse into the heart of creation. Here you are within the divine design; a revelation written in the living stone of the earth for those who will read it."

"And each cathedral rose is a sun wheel," Caron said, gazing into it: "each colour, each character shapes and tones the white radiance of eternity."

"We live under the sun," von Steinbach said.

"Since the fathers fell asleep." His weariness drew upon him unbearable as he spoke.

"I don't understand." He was impressed with Caron's knowledge, curious where this was going.

"Each cathedral is dedicated to Mary," Caron said, "especially here in France but elsewhere, too: Notre Dame de Chartres, Paris, Burges, Reims, Cologne - others in other lands – Lincoln Cathedral, Santa Maria del Fiore - and now here Strasbourg. This wealth of cathedrals is an immense accomplishment, but why all dedicated to Mary?"

"Mary is Queen of Heaven, Mother of God," von Steinbach said. "In the church you are within her even as Jesus was within the womb of his mother."

He could see Caron was in a fever. Von Steinbach crossed himself and looked nervously about him. "You had better come home with me." He took Caron's arm and led out again into the bustle of the city center. "You have been too long abroad," he said softly. "Your ignorance of the times endangers you." They stood a moment in the cathedral square; a light, feathery rain began to fall.

"There are marvels here written in stone I would discuss with you." Caron heard himself speaking almost as if another spoke in spite of him. He was concerned he had overstepped the mark of wisdom in this.

"And we shall have that discussion." Von Steinbach urged him along. Caron was not well and taken with a fever. Von Steinbach saw it, too, and helped the man to the Mason's Hall adjacent Temple Square. There were guest quarters adjacent his own. He made Caron comfortable and sent for a broth of beef to give him strength. "You need rest," he said, settling him in.

"But what is it we are seeking?" Caron pressed. "Long before us the Egyptians sought permanence and built monuments to defy time; but time has taken them and in the desert winds their monuments turn to dust.

"And the Hindu who knows there is no permanence in the world is still driven to live in it, clinging to his gods in mountains of striving stone. And yet the best of them walk away from the rite and rituals that order their day, and in stillness seek the indwelling one they call Atman."

"Do they truly believe God is within them?"

"Where else would he be? *'Know ye not that ye are the temple* of *God, and that the Spirit of God dwelleth in you?'* For the desert fathers, shelter from the elements and shifting sands in caves, in tents, in desert oasis under the stars was enough to come to know His presence. Now even these confine him in stony rule and monuments of stone for fear in the twinkling of an eye they shall lose Him. What they fear comes upon them, and God is lost in the maze and willfulness of the mind."

"All that you say is true," von Steinbach agreed, "but we are dealing with forward children who must be brought along and disciplined to truth. They need parables; even parables in stone if need be to feel secure and make a beginning."

"You will excuse me," Caron said, "I am abusing your hospitality. You must understand I have traveled through the emptiness of the world and found God or he me as surely there as any place of worship; he is not confined within those beautiful structures we have made to bind him to us. And so I ask, as wonderful as this cathedral is, is it to worship God or to seek a mother and so a state to protect us from Him?"

"We do but honour her as His mother," von Steinbach said, warily.

"Woman, what have I to do with thee?" Caron snapped back, on the verge of delirium.

"For God's sake man, have a care. Mary is Mother of God; Mother of the Church," von Steinbach said again, looking about cautiously. "And so we have raised these monuments in praise of Her as Queen of Heaven."

"That which is born of flesh is flesh; that which is born of Spirit is spirit. And yet at the last the worlds must be one. Your work is pure genius,

Erwin," Caron said, grasping his arm. "I have abused your gifts, your hospitality over my own anguish with the world."

"It cannot be easy to return a long journey," von Steinbach said. "There are always adjustments to be made."

"Do you know the Stag's Head?" Caron asked. "Someone there I must meet today, or tomorrow perhaps he will come. Can you leave a message for him to come to me here?"

"I will."

"Something more I must impose, a matter you will appreciate," Caron said. "I am late come from the Coptic Monastery of Alba on the Red Sea shore."

"You have made your own crossing, I think," von Steinbach said bringing a smile.

"I have a precious manuscript from the Master Origen of Alba for the Meister Eckhart. Can you find or bring him to me?"

If von Steinbach had any doubts in Caron, he relaxed visibly at the mention of Eckhart. "He is at the Hohenburg Abbey at Mount Saint Odile, about a day's journey from here, instructing the nuns," von Steinbach said. "A few days' rest with me and you shall come to him yourself."

In three days the fever broke and Caron was more himself again, grateful where before he had been, perhaps, a little petulant when tact was called for. Still, it didn't seem to trouble von Steinbach. Caron waited two more days before venturing himself to the Stag's Head Inn in search of Perrin or word of him. But there was no sign of him or any member of Falconieri's troupe of players he supposed would travel with. But there were two who came and lodging there for two days scrutinized all who came and went from the inn, and put Caron in mind of the black cloaks who served Squin. Someone supposed he lived and that Perrin would come to his aid. And what better way to traverse Europe undetected than with a troupe of players, road gypsies in search of an audience, hidden in plain sight.

Once or twice venturing into the inn was passable, but for a monk to loiter in such a place would be suspicious, and so Caron set out alone on foot at dawn for Mount St. Odile in search of Meister Eckhart at Hohenburg Abbey, one eye all the while to his back, wondering after Perrin.

He had always wondered if the bard might be had for a price; he was much subject to his feelings, and Magda mistress of the longings of the heart. His price would be honours and the hand of the Lady Gwendolyn. In that moment he was sure of it, and felt the loss of a friend to the seductions of the world. But he had promises to keep and so he took his leave of von Steinbach and began his journey to Mount Saint Odile to do what Origen had asked and deliver a manuscript into the hands of Meister Eckhart.

The road to St. Odile led through Alsatian farmlands into the forests of the Vosges. In the heat of the day Caron stopped by a small mountain fall and there he sat and rested in the cool spray and scent of woodlands. For a spell he nodded off but was awakened by the sound of horses scenting water, voices calling and the creaking wheels of a caravan.

"Is the water sweet, Brother?"

Caron roused himself up rising slowly to meet the lead wagon. It was Signor Falconieri. Delighted to encounter this traveling company, Caron greeted him cheerfully: "As sweet as applause to an actor."

Falconieri laughed. "You're alert for one just roused from sleep. I am sorry to disturb your rest, but I must water the horses and reach Mount St. Odile by nightfall."

"And that is my destination."

"Then ride with us inscrutable friar, and I will permit you seek to save my soul while I try to plumb the depths of yours."

Caron enjoyed Falconieri from meeting in Venice. All the more pleased because who better than an actor to see through the artifice of another. And yet even here as Origen taught, his power to shape the sense of others held. He thought it pleasant to journey with him, until the two dark cloaks he'd avoided at Stag's Head Inn wedged in alongside; bringing their horses to water before Falconieri had time to unhitch his wagon.

Falconieri ignored them. "Unhitch the horses, one wagon at a time," Falconieri shouted. "Pull forward when you are done."

"We had little time in Venice; what is your Order, Brother John?"

"Mathurian," Caron said.

"Ah, Trinitarian; the red friars," Falconieri said. "Your order is well spoken of; your ransom of captives, a noble work."

"The Saracens have made a Muslim lake of the Mediterranean," Caron said, "pirates and thieves one and all. They plunder ashore and at sea and take everything: all manner of provisions, metals, jewels, money, fabrics, whatever they can carry away; especially men, women and children to be sold in slave markets."

"I have late heard a story of a beautiful Venetian woman taken captive on a voyage to Crete," Falconieri said. "The Doge of Venice is so incensed he will now lay siege to the slave colony of Ulcinj. The one who told this to me – you remember Perrin, one of our company - was distraught over the loss of his friend who freed her at cost of his life."

Caron wanted to ask what had become of Perrin but thought better of it. "They harass Christendom wherever they can where gain seems easy and profit assured, and some day they will come again in force. Those who fall prey to Islam must submit to the absolute domination of their masters; or to whomever they choose to sell them. And when we resist their demands they contend it is us who disrespect and afflict them, for all they do is in the name of Allah. And so we raise the money and send emissaries like myself to pay the blood price."

"You are returning from such a journey unaccompanied?"

"My ransom, Sir Robert Hode, has gone on before to St. Odile, and from there we will complete our journey home to England."

As Falconieri spoke one of the two black cloaks rode up alongside and interrupted. "Monk, did you journey from the east?"

"From Sidon," Caron said.

"Mind your manners, Timor," Falconieri chided. "This is a holy man and even were he not, he is our guest."

Timor said nothing but reined off his horse and fell back to join his companion. "Timor and Formido," Falconieri said. "They followed us out of Venice. We became aware of them after several days. When we learned their destination is the same as ours, the castle Sierck-les-Baines, we invited them to join us. Better to keep them close. They tell us they were sent by the Lady Madelon de Faucon to escort us, but in fact they appear to be looking for someone. You're just the latest they've cast suspicious eyes on."

"Well named," Caron said.

Falconieri thought a moment, checking his memory. "Timor and Formido were the children of Venus and Mars.

"To the Greeks, Phobos and Deimos, fear and panic," Caron said.

"Do you think they are Greek?" Falconieri asked. "They are dark; I thought maybe Sicilian. They work for a creature of the Lady Madelon so what can I say?"

"These are slavers and assassins," Caron said, "Berbers. I'd recognize them anywhere."

"They seem inordinately interested in you, too," Falconieri said, after a long, thoughtful silence. "Nevertheless, we will see you safely to Hohenburg Abbey. If it comes to it, I believe together we are well able to take on the likes of these."

The afternoon passed with ease as Caron told stories of his travels to Egypt and the Holy Land, and Falconieri eager to encourage, responding with stories of his own. "I've been this way before," Falconieri confessed. "At the foot of Mount Odile is Niedermunster Abbey, a convent and hospital. She was inspired to build it – the good Saint Odile – in a vision of John the Baptist. Coincidentally, tomorrow night is Saint John's Eve. I imagine they'll be in quite a celebratory mood… as nuns go."

"A chance to rehearse your arts," Caron said.

"I've a tale or two for the telling; in trade, perhaps, for provisions. But the story I'd really like to tell is of Odile herself; make a play of it."

"I don't know the legend."

"Truly, perhaps you have simply forgotten it, your life so full of affairs," Falconieri replied. "Well, I had best tell you, the nuns and deaconesses will expect you to know. This is what I know.

"Odile was born to Bethswinda and Aldaric, Duke of Alsace, a child blind at birth. So handicapped her father saw no occasion in her for advancing his realm; unwanted he sent her off to be raised by peasants. Not until the age of twelve was she baptized, by an itinerant bishop. And that is the first miracle: she not only regained her sight but saw the light of God, and was christened Odile, lady of light."

"Ah, I do now recall," Caron said. But the muse had taken Falconieri and his heart was into the telling. "She had a brother name of Hughes who went to her and brought her home. This so enraged the father, being faced with what he had done, he impulsively killed his son.

"And this was the second miracle, for Odile miraculously revived him. Not repenting, her father all the more enraged Odile was forced to flee.

Obsessed with guilt and passionate to destroy this divine revelation, the duke pursued his daughter with intent to kill. She took refuge in a cavern in the Alps, the valley of Musbach near Freiburg some say, and there the mountains protected her by felling rock on any who approached with ill intent. There is a shrine to mark the spot of her refuge, for this was the third miracle.

"And the fourth miracle was her father's repentance to bring the cycle full. He made a gift of Hohenburg castle for an abbey; there Odile founded a monastic community after the Augustine order, herself its abbess. Here she spent her life aiding the deaf and blind. It's even said at her own death the sisters' prayers brought her back showing the power of their Order. Thereafter by her own decision, with grace in her heart and her lord waiting, Odile took communion, let go to him, and passed from these realms into eternal bliss. It would make a good drama don't you think?"

"It is their legend. If you mar it in the telling, you will pay dearly."

"Always the problem isn't it; even with good intentions, except you flatter, there are those who take offense. Niedermunster Abbey," Falconieri said, rounding the bend. "Above us is Hohenburg, the Abbey of St. Odile." Caron followed his gaze to the mountain top, the abbey perched on a ridge above a great megalithic wall that ran along the mountain side.

"Those who dwell within believe the world no place for a woman. There are few nuns, numerous deaconesses engaged in learning, teaching and healing. Many are daughters of noble families come for education; each held in waiting for her family's decision as to what is to become of her.

"For this reason there are many guards about the mountain. The roads are patrolled, and all under the watchful eye of the Bergers of Birkenfells Castle, vassals of the Bishop of Strasbourg."

"Rather like a prison."

"To the likes of you and me who love the open road," Falconieri said, forgetting himself. "But no, it is a place most powerful, most holy that they protect. And this is Sainte Odile," he said, the caravan rounding the bend. Her statue stood before the gate to Niedermunster hospital: a young woman in one hand holding a book; in the other a chalice over the rim of which gazed a pair of eyes. And, likewise, looking out from within the depths of the book there were eyes on the cover beseeching the reader to enter in.

"Hohenburg Abbey above, Niedermunster hospital below; above a place of contemplation, and here below the works are done in hospital by a convent of nuns to shelter and give succor and shelter to travelers.

"Nearby there is a fountain of waters issuing from a rock said to have remarkable healing powers, for it is said here as a child baptized in those waters Odile gained her sight. From here there is a path leading up to the summit of the mountain, but none go that way uninvited.

"A sanctuary for canonesses regular and secular," Caron said.

"No woman wishes to be chattel," Falconieri said. "There are many noble born women who desire solitude to marriage against their will; many who desire a contemplative life, without the taking of vows that may yet interfere with what they seek when they have found it."

The caravan pulled up to a halt by the abbey gates and Caron stood down. "If they will not have you Brother, find us in the river camp," Falconieri said. "Unless they engage a performance or two here or in nearby Ottrott, two days only we shall stay before going on to Nancy and Sierck-les-Baines to meet with our patrons. Hereafter, journey with us if you will wherever it is you go."

Falconieri urged the horses on. The two dark cloaks rode up to watch Caron turn aside, eyeing him once more with the watchfulness of ravens for road-kill, but concluded he was no more than what he seemed. Departing from them now and of no further interest, they rode on.

"If they will not have you pilgrim," Falconieri called back, "find us at the river."

24

The Play's the Thing

"I'm come for Meister Eckhart."

A Trinitarian returning from the Holy Land was of immense interest to the two monks at the gate. But it did not change their rule; he must be admitted decently and in order. The nunnery itself was closed within four walls, its cloisters separated by a great courtyard from hospital and lodgings for travelers come to bring loved ones for healing. Many came with sick family, weary with travels, awaiting what attention the hospital and guesthouse could offer, and always the sentinel monks escorted them to the warming room. And so they did Brother John of Oxford, where already half a dozen travelers arrived before awaited evaluation.

Monks they were but as Templar Caron was trained to an order of warrior monks, and in these he recognized the craft. Each carried a quarter stave and though pleasant enough, each had in his eyes the look of one who always knew what lay ahead, to left or right, and what was at his back.

After the warming room Caron was taken to the guesthouse for travelers where he rested briefly, washed away the dust of the day, and somewhat unwillingly let one of the monks in a pious act of humility wash his feet. From there he was led onto the refectory and fed a simple meal, all the while pleasantly if closely watched. When done Caron was escorted to the outer parlour where business without the cloisters was conducted, and there met by the abbess of Niedermunster, Sister Albertus Magnus, who had been told of this traveler from the Holy Land. For an hour she fed on his tales of travels; accounts of sacred sites he knew in Jerusalem and of the land the Master walked.

"Your archer is well," she said, once sure of Caron. "The sisters in hospital sent him to the village of Ottrott, but half an hour's brisk walk from here, committing him to the skilled ministrations of our apothecary. They believe with care he will regain at least some sight. Sir Robert Hode has taken him."

"But to the purpose of my coming," Caron said, "I must meet with Meister Eckhart."

"That good man is up at Hohenburg. It is his duty to visit the abbeys and instruct the nuns. He will be here another week. But even for a Brother, one must have the permission of our Abbess, Mother Aletheia, to ascend the mount to the abbey."

"I have documents from Bishop Origen in Egypt for Meister Eckhart. I have carried them a thousand miles."

"I am unwilling to send a sister up the mountain at this hour when I know they are in vigil, and will not grant permission until morning. Meanwhile, we will find you quarters for the night."

"Many are in need of what you would give me," Caron said. "I journeyed here with a caravan now camped by the river, in need of what I can give them. I will return again in the morning for Meister Eckhart."

"It's late, a steep trail by dark, and would disturb the sisters in vespers," Caron explained. "May I sit by your fire tonight?"

"We shall do better. When we have eaten we will perform a new play – a legend of Elijah the prophet - written by that upstart Perrin von Grünschnabel. Still, I think it a decent play but as you are a man of the cloth, learned in such things, you shall tell us what rings true and what offends." It was after dark when the sparks from the campfire flew upward among the stars, the Falconieri Players gathered to perform their play of Elijah and the Prophets of Baal.

Falconieri handed Caron, Perrin's manuscript. He sat a space before the fire reading the script Perrin penned; Falconieri drinking wine, chatting with his players and watching, curious for any reaction he could discern from the Mathurian monk. He was not illiterate Caron thought, but appeared to have little Latin and must know the stories only from the telling. It was true the Church was touchy about unsolicited interpretation of scripture by clergy, let alone the laity. Still, such plays in bare outline of the biblical text were increasingly popular and more or less acceptable to the Church, for they fired imagination and gave context for living.

"It is well written," Caron said at length. "He is close to the text; weak in understanding what Elijah faced, but well-acted that can be overcome. Yet, I believe your play needs a more provocative title than Elijah and the Prophets of Baal."

"We are of a mind in this; shall we call it our play of the miracle or mystery on Mount Carmel."

"A good title, but bring it yet closer to earth where the contest for possession of heart, mind and soul is center stage."

"So let us call it the Contest on Mount Carmel," Falconieri said. "You may judge by our performance that we fall not short but rebuke the princes of this world reminding them of their duty to God." With that the impresario gathered his troupe.

"And Ahab the son of Omri did evil in the sight of the Lord above all that were before him." Falconieri turned narrator.

"And he took to wife Jezebel the daughter of the king of the Zidonians, and went and served Baal and worshiped him.

"And he reared up an altar for Baal in the house of Baal, which he had built in Samaria.

"And Ahab did more to provoke the Lord God of Israel to anger than all the kings of Israel that were before him."

As he spoke actors of his troupe emerged out of the shadows into the light of the campfire, assuming the roles of Ahab and Jezebel and their attendants. Jezebel, a managing and contentious woman, her royal husband less than kingly under her withering glance, shaped the drama.

The art was stilted but at once raised a knowing nod from those gathered to the pageant, for they knew well enough the characters lived on.

Falconieri spoke the prologue well: experienced and full of years and with high seriousness, for well he knew the Church would not abide a frivolous presentation of the mystery of the prophet Elijah. Meanwhile, at the edge of the circle of firelight, Elijah, played by the same player who played Alrecchino the faithless servant, stood awaiting his entrance. Caron knew this was the moment of truth; whether the play would move forward or descend into caricature.

"As the Lord God of Israel liveth, before whom I stand, there shall not be dew nor rain these years but according to my word," Alrecchino said, entering; not like he meant it or had any inkling of the impact, and certainly not how it might be accomplished. Nevertheless, both Jezebel and her subservient husband were greatly enraged, and drove him off stage with sweeping pantomime gestures.

And so Elijah fled from Ahab appearing, if it was possible, even more the henpecked husband than Ahab before the fury of his wife. It was theater with each trying to upstage the other in reaction to Jezebel - hell hath no fury - herself. Too readily the players gave up the tension of the play to cop a response; too easily they crossed the line into jape, ridicule and mockery. They knew only the surface and not the substance of what they were about.

Falconieri knew it, too, and with a quick glance at Caron tried to pick up after. "And the word of the Lord came unto him, saying, "Get thee hence, Elijah, and turn thee eastward, and hide thyself by the brook Cherith that is before Jordan.

"And it shall be that thou shalt drink of the brook; and I have commanded the ravens to feed thee there."

The play unfolded in kind: the brook in time dried up, the parched land cracked, life withdrew to the germ, and the crops withered as season after season passed without rain. In time the Lord appeared again to Elijah and sent him to a widow and her son. She hid him from the wrath of Jezebel, and fed him from a handful of meal and a little oil that in his presence never failed them.

The players got into stride and Caron brightened to see it as the widow's child revived of Elijah was brought back from the brink of death.

She who played the widow – Caron took to be Falconieri's mistress, Anna for his attentiveness to her – performed as if she had some secret sorrow of her own; teared but never lost control of her part as she dwelled upon and entered into her lines: "Now by this I know that thou art a man of God, and that the word of the Lord in thy mouth is true."

Falconieri himself found a greater voice, and delivered his commentary with the power of a prophet: "And it came to pass after many days that the word of the Lord came to Elijah in the third year, saying, Go, shew thyself unto Ahab and I will send rain upon the earth."

Thereafter the drama was weak, the contest with the prophets of Baal void because Elijah never showed up. Utterly out of his depth Alrecchino played Alrecchino, as faithless a servant in his part to the tone of the Lord, as he had been faithless to his master the miser, instead taking up with the old man's maid in his time of need. Well versed in what he aped, in that he had been brilliant, bringing laughter in abundance from the Venetian throng. Elijah, however, was not in his repertoire.

"We will work on it." Falconieri apologized as he drew close again to the fire. "It is unfamiliar yet." It had begun to rain lightly in the forest, but the canopy of trees broke the fall and by the campfire it was but a light mist shining in firelight. "You don't need to tell me about the actors," Falconieri said, "I have already noted their weaknesses and changes will be made."

Others drew into the fire; mostly the players but including Timor and Formido - Phobos and Deimos - and like water wine flowed freely to celebrate the first performance. Falconieri was restrained in his praise but wanted Caron's response to the play; if circumspect, for players could be temperamental. Caron must give it but said nothing.

"Off with you all, off to your own fires," Falconieri ordered his troupe. "We'll talk later. First, I need to speak with our friar. You, too," he said to the brothers Timor and Formido. They balked but withdrew to the nearest fire. Caron was sure they had again marked him and would not willingly let him out of their sight. Falconieri saw it, too, and it troubled him but for the moment the play was more to issue: "Out with it then. I will hear the worst of it before mollifying my troupe."

"There is a simple remedy," Caron said. "Take away their wine and have your players go without water through the heat of a single day before they play the part again."

"Then they shall have no voice for the part."

"They will touch the spirit of the piece," Caron said. "The setting is a wasteland. For months at a time in the Holy Land there is no rain; but three years without rain when the streams run no more, the wells dry up, the crops fail, and livestock perishes for want of grass: that is the scene. And it is God who has withheld His blessing for the wickedness of Israel, and spoken his judgment through his prophet Elijah, that they might turn their hearts back again."

"Baal is a god of fertility," Falconieri said. "And the prophets of Baal call upon him to bring rain."

"For these fertility and prosperity are the heart and soul of the contest. But God gives or withholds his blessings according to the righteousness of his people. Those who today flourish acknowledging Him, tomorrow perish for turning from Him. God is not mocked of those chosen to serve Him."

"Then this play is a parable for our times," Falconieri said. "Today Venice flourishes…."

"And in self-indulgent corruption, tomorrow withers the vine," Caron said. "Certainly, if there is no more to it than the worship of Mammon, wealth and fertility, that is the inevitable end."

"In the world is great disparity of wealth."

"Better a cup where kindness is than a banquet of envy. You have played the miser to a knowing crowd and drawn laughter at what you do not see going on behind your back. So though the people envy the miser they ask what profit is there in it? You have felt that in the playing of the part have you not?"

"I have felt also the keen edge of poverty."

"That, too, but if you're looking for justice in the fallen world, trouble yourself no more: seek, first, justice in your relations with God. Then let come what may, it will not find you wanting."

"I forget I speak to a friar, but it is true we have become very self-satisfied," Falconieri agreed, "but to the play. What is to be done?"

"I have told you. I have walked in the footsteps of the desert fathers, thirsting for a cup of cool water. Now, I am returned to a land of wetlands and grasses, forests and rivers, and rain," he said, holding out his hand to catch the droplets. "We live amidst many blessings in a land flowing with milk and honey and find complaint, when others overflow with thankfulness for a cup of cold water."

"But to the actors."

"Your lead, Anna, is a fine actress. And he who played Alrecchino in Venice is a rake; unreliable, filled with the lusts of the flesh. He cannot begin to comprehend the intensity of purpose in God who for three years will withhold rain to turn the hearts of his chosen from corruption."

"Well, it is hopeless then," Falconieri said, "for it appears this troupe can play only at japes and jibes and mockery."

Caron wanted to use the language of Origen to reply. To take a part was to discover the vibrational essence of that part; to become one with that very essence and embody it as one's own, playing it through until time should come to put it down again.

"What greater play was there ever than our Master's coming into this fallen world? He took up his part on the stage come what may, and as men and women responded or reacted to his presence nevertheless played the part given Him through to perfection.

"Your actors must know in their souls the part they play. Their art must serve a greater purpose than mimicry. They cannot alone hold up a mirror to human foibles. However clever that may for the moment seem, it is all a reflection of surface. No, rather they must shine with light that illumines the eye, kindles the imagination. They must see with radiant eyes and loose the very essences of the part they would play, for the moment becoming that very thing. They must play the part to perfection to set to rights in essence what man has marred. Your Elijah must be Elijah.

"You are asking too much of my poor players," Falconieri said. 'These are sometimes rough, uncouth; used to live the life of a gypsy player or busking on the streets. They are not high born or educated; they have cultivated such talent as they have to survive."

"I know, and it was for just such as these that Jesus came, for God knows what is in the hearts of all men. The sophisticated in the ways of this world are wise in their own eyes, but have no idea how ignorant they are of the way things truly are, or what treasure is held in store for those who yield their hearts and minds to the Lord of heaven and earth."

"I confess you are a true friar well versed in your art, and with insights worthy of consideration for my own. Well, I will think on it, speak to them, and practice to embody the essences of the drama as you say, though I do not expect my troupe will easily change let alone understand what you ask."

"Anna's portrayal of the widow and her son; that was made true in her, and yet when it was done she put the part down readily and moved on. The others can learn from her."

"You are right about her," Falconieri said: "She is gifted, and I have sought to protect and nurture that gift."

"She has a heart pure to find her way to the center of a life," Caron said. "That is her true gift."

"One request I'd make of you," Falconieri said, as others began to return to his fire: "If you would recommend us to the sisters, we might here attempt our play of Elijah for their pleasure. There is some risk, perhaps, but having a true audience will bring out the best in my troupe. Perrin, I know, would much appreciate our having attempted it before we arrive at Sierck-les-Baines.

"Has he then gone before you?" He had been looking for occasion to press the matter of the meeting that never was.

"The Lady Madelon has bound him to her side," Falconieri said. "I believe he will be knighted for duty to her. And so we have another patron and work fit for the clergy, if with your help we can take the measure of it once performed."

"Deprive them of water for a day as they practice, and I will speak for you," Caron said.

Every new day begins with nightfall, the harvest of the last, and darkness on the face of the deep of what yet shall be. And in the deep of night, long before first light, Caron roused from sleep his body aglow, lustrous in the dark, enveloped in starshine. He felt no fear, no sense of danger; only he was suddenly vividly alert, drawn to the sound of falling water. He could not be seen like this lest someone awake and panic at the sight of a man aglow. He drew back as Origen taught to cloak himself but to little effect. What possessed him was greater than he and would not be denied. So gathering up his mantle, hoping it would conceal what he could not, Caron quietly left camp and followed the pilgrim's path along into the dark wood toward the waters.

But in the solitude of the woodland what had been a rushing in his ears hushed. His path led to a road at the forest edge below the mountaintop abbey, dark against a moonless sky, with only a few flickering torches to mark its place in a wilderness of stars.

The silhouette of the castle, starlit sky, dark wood and path, and again a splash of falling water and whisper of a stream: all conspired to dissolve his sense of time. If any had come he would have seemed an apparition, aglow in the dead of night on the forest path; a spirit out of the timelessness of time, loosed to wander a little space in earth in the world of things. Indeed, that is exactly what he felt.

The path led to a great rock and a paved stair that led up to a mountain grotto, overhung with vegetation. From within the natural shrine a light that glowed illumined a font of waters. Bubbling up from within the rock the well-spring gathered in a basin, overflowed and trickled down a stone conduit into the valley below. Caron splashed water on his face washing the sleep from his eyes, turned to the stair and the light within, intensifying as he came to its source.

Within, glorified in the same light that transfigured him three awaited his coming. Two, as his sense allowed, he saw in familiar form as Origen and Blaise, but for the one in their midst he found no name. And it was he who greeted him: *"Tai Hoi, Na-Akhu-El,"* but without words, for the voice spoke from within a communion of souls and not alone a greeting.

"It is the lord Aton-Re, the speaker who speaks and keeps the way of the crossing," Origen said. He would commune with you; Blaise and I have come to keep pattern with him in you, that you might bear his presence. Will you hear him?"

"I will, so far as my gifts allow."

"It is a good answer," the Aton-Re said. "Lost to yourself and now returning your instincts were true. You did well to thwart him who would possess your soul."

"And would have but for that good old man, Flegetanis, who gave his life that I might live."

"It was his gift and he regrets it not," the Aton-Re replied. "Flegetanis lives the life undying. But it is to this matter I must speak for the time is fast upon us. I must ask of you something you are not yet entirely prepared to bear."

"I have left no life or interest in this world other than the purpose and company of the lords of light."

"Well enough, but I would take this yet to another level." The Aton-Re turned first to Blaise and then Origen. "Will you permit; can you accommodate me in this?"

A moment of deepening silence swelled between them so it seemed each took a deep breath, then Origen nodded and Blaise agreed, but asked, "Is Caron able?"

"If given an adequate creative field that what is loosed shall not destroy where it should create. We must seek out and bind such sweet influences of response given to focus and sustain that field, loosing the bands of power proportionate to the need."

"It shall be done," Blaise said.

"Then I will ask of you something that may mean journey's end of this your incarnate life, Caron. Are you willing to go so far with me in this as you are able?"

"So far as you see fit," Caron agreed.

He stepped forward. Caron felt his radiance intensify and permeate his flesh. "On my own ray I shall bear and uplift until you are able to sustain the pattern of your own." The Aton-Re touched him on the forehead, and Caron was taken by the light.

Magda was driven, literally possessed to speak with Blaise, her master of Sword Hallows. Perhaps it was the uneasiness she felt about Caron. Was he really dead? If alive what are his intentions? She could no longer count on Gisors and wondered if Perrin was the one to succeed him. Who better than a poet to weave illusions in the sense? And yet, she rather fancied him for his ability to charm the heart, as Master of Grail Hallows as well. Who now was worthy; indeed, who even understood how to come again into possession of those powers? The Cailleach never revealed to her or any other the source of Flegetanis' power and the whereabouts of the Grail vessel and she realized how little she knew of the surviving masters.

The thoughts possessed her in the night so she could not sleep; the voices of those who had gone before her, all were singularly silent on how to proceed. She must sort this out before Caer Myrddin. She wondered if

Squin's bond to Siduri might serve the purpose. Was she not the daughter of the Grail Master? And she knew she could secure Perrin to her purpose by marriage to the Lady Gwen whom he adored, surrounding him with all the gifts of grace and admiration for his art within her power, but in what role? She was anxious to have that done to strengthen her hand among the women.

In short she was unsure of the way ahead, yet Blaise who journeyed with her seemed singularly indifferent to her discontent offering little of substance to allay her concerns. He was supposed to be her mainstay in these times and must rise to her need. In the dead of night she gathered her cloak to her, and like a thing possessed raged out of her chambers, rousing chambermaids fluttering like storm petrels blown on gusts of the sea before her.

She came to Blaise's chambers, and though he must sleep did not pause to knock but thrust open wide the door. In a tempest of robes she collided like a squall on an ocean crag into the unyielding wall of Blaise's handmaiden, who sat serenely in a great chair in Magda's path, hands still upon the sword hallows laid across her lap. Part of her mind took in but through her anger could not then reconcile what she saw: the fractured sword of truth in pieces two was now whole and shone. Try as she could, Magda could advance no further against the force that hedged her way.

"I will speak with Blaise." It was not a request.

"Milady, you cannot. This night he communes with the powers that inform the Sword Hallows. He will know you have come and when he is done, whatever the hour, will come to you."

"Blaise owes me fealty and none other. He may commune at his leisure but not at mine."

"If he did not first serve that which empowers his gift, he would have no power to serve you."

"Insolent whelp," Magda shrieked, and stepped forward. The maiden rose turning the sword once in an arc then held it upright before her. And now it burned, for with the same force she thrust upon the sword maiden that force thrust back upon her double, and she was repelled to the open door.

"These forces are beyond us mistress. They inform our purpose when our purpose is just, but never are they our possession. I have been all my life given to this duty and I tell you now I do only what is wrought in me, and cannot otherwise."

Again Magda tried but could not advance a step. What had been aggravation and impulse in her now turned cold fury at being told by the whore of a Master of Hallows that his power was hers to command only at his pleasure and convenience.

"I will have your life for this."

"My life belongs to the Master of Hallows. If you will you must ask him for it."

Magda slammed the chamber door behind in a final petulant gesture of rage. Her influence dissipated she drifted aimlessly, a flurry of rebuffed wind blowing dust before it, down the hall to her chambers. There, huffing and puffing with contempt, she collapsed at last like a spent draft before the fire and wept. And then her defeat turned to steely resolve. The one she called Maia rose in her and also came Irkala.

"I have power these know nothing of," Maia whispered, "power to draw fire from the center of the earth that all things shall take the shape my will dictates."

"These old masters are passing for a new order to come," Magda answered. "Telgesinus I will keep for he is purposed to my hand. Soon I shall have no further need for Blaise. I will give Roland of Waldheim to be Master of Sword Hallows, and that bitch of a handmaiden who defied me," she said aloud to the fire, "I will give to the guards to do with as they will, and when they have had enough of her… to the dogs the same."

At length Blaise came to her chambers, and found her composed. "I would have you journey with Squin, Perrin, Siduri and Constanza to Hohenburg, the Monastery of St. Odile, "about a day's journey," she said, ignoring what had gone before.

"Many of the daughters of the Blood Royal who suffered Caron's sorcery took refuge there under the hand of the Abbess Aletheia Lotharing. I am told some of those who dwell there still blame Squin, though guiltless he was, and project their wrath on me that it should happen at his hand. They need to get past this."

Blaise would speak but she raised her hand to silence him. "Often on his visits to Europe the Master Flegetanis would stay over at the abbey, bringing manuscripts desired of him, offering instruction in the ways of our Order.

"And by reason of this, from the time of Esclarmonde and the destruction of Montségur, none know better than the deaconesses of St. Odile the nature of the Grail Hallows. It is even said their eyes once opened by the sage's instruction, they have from time to time borne witness of the Grail."

"I have heard Flegetanis speak of it." Blaise said.

"Well then, mistaken as they are about me, I need to win back the hearts of these women; not just because they are of the Blood Royal, but because the yielding of their substance to their Domina is essential to my trial in walking the pattern at Caer Myrddin."

"What would you have me do?"

"Abbess Lotharing knows you almost as well as she did Flegetanis," Magda said. " She will have heard of his death and will take comfort in your presence. Introduce her to Siduri as Flegetanis' daughter. Constanza is exotic, of distant lands and yet fair as the northern folk. Together she and Siduri will charm the maidens with tales of far off places, reminding them that they were not brought into this world to seek refuge in a nunnery, but to engage in the purposes of the Blood Royal."

"And Perrin?"

"None who serves me is so adept at winning the hearts of women than our poet Perrin. They fairly dote over him, and by all reports it was he who led them to safety through the holocaust borne on the evil wind."

"They will be ecstatic to see him; all the more when you tell them in Flegetanis stead I believe Perrin fit to be Master of Grail Hallows."

"He has not the art," Blaise said.

"You who are masters will teach him the way of mastery, and he will come into it of his own as time goes by. What is more, he already has the hearts and so the response of the maidens of the Blood Royal; and does that not touch on the essence of the mystery of the Grail?"

"And Blaise," Magda said, the old Master turning to go, "Telgesinus will meet you there on his return from the Rhineland. Two masters and a third in the making will make my case as nothing could."

"Except, of course, banishing Squin," Blaise said brusquely, "for you know as well as I do Caron had nothing to do with it." It was like a sword point at the throat, and gone before she could even struggle to make reply, his words lingered in the open doorway as a direct challenge to her.

"Insolent!" she shouted after him. But the worst of it was he was right and she knew it. However she might have it otherwise, she knew the truth of it. The daughters of the Blood Royal knew, the temporal lords knew, and all who dwelled in Waldheim knew what was in Squin. He could never be Grail King and she must choose another. What was more, she must grudgingly admit Blaise was right. Squin must go.

"For now I need you, old man," she cursed. "But after Caer Myrddin I will study to turn your own sword upon you."

25

Heaven and Earth

Caron was in a high place, the paved court of a mountain top temple with a view of a vast panorama of shimmering hills, verdant plains, lakes, valleys, streams and falls. From this prospect he could see a patchwork of villages and afar off a shining sea; all within a hedge of radiance that veiled whatever was beyond.

It was in the images of the earth he knew but pristine, untainted by the hand of man. Here looking out was seeing within and he felt its revelation keenly. The wonderful detail of rocks and trees, of waters, brooks and falls and seas, of cold and warmth and texture of earth; every bird, beast and flower: all aligned with life in its essence, serving some great purpose,

And all consummated here in this temple of light at the zenith of the realm. He turned to look to the high point of the temple mount, a small pyramid etched against the blue of the sky. Seven stairs, each measured to a man's step, led to the upper tier, converging on a core of blue flame burning within a dolmen arch that crowned the altar and gateway of the worlds.

Where he stood, below the stepped altar, was a reflecting pool edged with blue lapis. At the center through a fissure in a great white stone, water brimmed from a hidden spring, and in a light air set patterns on the water's face rippling in the sunlight. A white marble bench curved about the pool, and there Caron sat waiting, watching over the face of the waters, until he began to discern unfolding patterns like melody in riffles that glimmered on its surface.

"Images in familiar forms; images informed with forces seeking resolution in simple acts: that is how a shaman journeys," Caron said. But this was different: he was transported to a place of utter simplicity above the clouded realms of the world below, in which the shaman worked his arts; a place unsullied by the storm and stress of consciousness caught up in the cross currents of the earth. As he reckoned time, it took perhaps half an hour before his thoughts stilled from wondering after what he first thought in coming here, illusion. Now it firmed into assurance that this was real and the world of the ten thousand things, imperfect shadow.

The rule here was silence before thought; thought before words and deeds. And when the words came to him they came like a whisper of wind: "Let all the earth keep silence before Him." Part of him said he should be awed by all that was unfolding; another assured him he was where he belonged. And then the voice hauntingly familiar, "what do you see in the waters?"

"I have lost all track of time."

"At the crossing of the worlds we dwell in the timelessness of time," the Aton-Re said. "And still we must enter into time for the sake of a world fallen and caught up in it."

"This is the place of shaping."

"In some matters, yes, and a place of reflection on what is shaped in essence in the realms of light, for here all comes to focus in the light."

"All shaped here in essence before ever it is seeded in the cycles of time in the earth."

"Origen has spoken to you of this."

"And in some measure the shaman Morgon Kara," Caron confessed, ashamed to mention his name but sensing he was meant to.

"He it was who taught the Nephilim to devise means to manipulate the twelve rays of the sun; to loose fire from the center of the earth and inform the misbegotten of their arts."

"You may not wish me here, for I know not what trace of him remains in me."

"We are hedged by radiance so intense that none may enter in except it is given him."

"Then my journey with him was illusion."

"Yes, though cloaked in hints of what you are, and matters of the heart then unresolved."

"And this is illusion."

"No, this is real. You see what you are able; the very truth cloaked in familiar forms. And still the world is not what it was made to be. Were it not for the shining ones who ever abide for the regeneration of the earth, deviant man would by now have destroyed himself laying waste the earth.

"Yet life ever new, like a fountain springing forth keeps giving. The truth that never fails abides, and the wonderful one holds all in his love."

"Morgon Kara: is he dead?"

"One of many names he has taken, he is *Sham-she-el*, a prince of the fallen world so cloaked in façade of good intentions he might seduce even an angel to his prospects. And yet the wise know him for always he comes, the liar mining grievances, manipulating lives, and spoiling the divine design of the wonderful one."

"And Maia enabled him."

"In fallen man it is a fine line between inspiration and illusion."

The Aton-Re led to the hedge of the mountain terrace and turned to face the distant sea. "You do not ask how all this came to be."

"I have seen the time when the Lord *Ka Ra Na* fled under a molten sky; in the day when the Dread One lay waste the earth. It was then the human race was overwhelmed with madness."

"The disruption of the patterns in the houses of heaven, what men call war in heaven, was an effect of the great transgression. It was a time when by reason of man the divine design could no longer be sustained, and the forces of creation must be mitigated or an end made. In that day it was understood the only way to bring him home was to give him his head and let him reap the consequences of his sowing."

The Aton-Re pointed out toward the distant sea. "In Whiter Morn this sea with its shining islands is an essence of a great ocean that now covers half the earth with its waters; here and there a mountaintop breaking surface as a reminder of what once was. In the First Time there was a land in the midst of that wilderness of water that was the Motherland of man.

"What remains in the earth is but a withered simulacrum of what one was; man's very body of a substance much finer than the coarse one he now inhabits. He dwelled there in a pristine paradise for many tens of thousands of years before this sad interlude into which he has fallen. And though his heart and mind are troubled by what has become of him, when the veil parts light breaks through and the deeper self remembers.

"Over the generations divine man gradually colonized the earth in harmony with the realms of light, under the hand of the lord of truth. Chief among those colonies were the realm of Atlantis, Kemet, Bhārata, Ambertia, Zealandia, Hyperborea, others; so that seed of the kingdom of the sun was sown in all the earth.

"But it was in the Motherland, in the northern realm of the three lands that made up the kingdom, the great transgression occurred; in a time when the creation was in the midst of a cycle of transmuting fire that would have blended the realms of earth with the realms of light in the unified radiance of the Creator."

Caron let the thought fill him. He did not know how to think of it then, so he let it be and simply asked: "How long ago?"

"Some twenty thousand years is the time of fallen man. It is but a fraction of the time man dwelled in harmony with the divine design. Thereafter man was given every opportunity to return to the Holy Norm, but shame wove a veil in the heart and the pattern deteriorated until what was in the earth could no longer be sustained. The foundations of the world were corrupted, the Motherland was consumed in fire and water leaving hardly a trace of what had been but memories and visions of a paradise lost.

"Those who survived fled to other lands. Confusion overwhelmed the consciousness of man, for the heavens and the earth were greatly changed. But some found their way to Kemet, Bhārata and Atlantis, most advanced of the colonies, and it was there the work of restoration was begun anew.

"But I dwell on it. All these things are written in the vibrational records of the Archaeus. Origen has shown you how to enter into your garden of memory, and at your leisure you may seek the detail of these matters as they are written, as they touch especially upon you: what faces you have worn, what names taken, deeds done, patterns resolved, matters left unresolved, to bring you to this hour."

"I have heard your words," Caron said, "but words are one thing, an understanding heart, another; I feel keenly that burden of ignorance."

"The regeneration of the earth begins with the cleansing of the human heart. In time Atlantis failed and descended into darkness, and like the Motherland what was once the light of the world vanished in the Deep. That was in the time of Noah, who under the hand of Melchizedek opened the way to what was to come for the spiritual regeneration of the human race."

"So long departed from the way, it seems an impossible task."

"What becomes of the human race remains to be seen, but in all generations there are those among the children of men who have never failed, never parted from the way."

"I do not understand," Caron said. "If, for tens of thousands of years, man dwelled in harmony in the knowledge that the worlds were one - well, perhaps I am not capable of understanding."

"You do not understand his transgression. In the First Time those powers in the hands of man were much more like those given to they who now dwell in the place of shaping.

The art of creation given man can be compared in part to the coming together of the gifts of a core of musicians under the hand of a master of the art. Each one, accomplished in his own instrument, gives his gift in time with the gifts of others, harmonized by the master in an exquisite field of vibratory essences. More than an entertainment, the shaping of vibrational essences was the foundation of creation in the earth, informing it with life."

Caron's own pure memory rose upon him. "And the morning stars sang together," he said, "and all the sons of God shouted for joy."

The Aton-Re nodded assent. "And do not think these gifts lost, for the arts are the embers of the way of creation and those powers once vested in man.

"In the world that was these forces were finely focused, and though each was able to mature into full awareness of his gifts, there were those whose gift it was to bring together these factors in harmony with life, as a conductor might bring together an ensemble of accomplished musicians in the creation of something more than any one of them alone might accomplish.

"In that sense the master plays the orchestra, for under his hand it is his instrument and his mastery the coordination, timing, emphasis and interpretation of the complex of vibrational factors coming to focus in the moment.

"Of course beyond him is the source of the music itself, and what might seem intangible but very real response of the listeners, for it is in their substance that the vibration he creates must find a setting."

"And something went wrong," Caron said.

"Man was warned in a particular matter and did not heed the warning. To put it simply, his heart was in his work and off tone, off key. And rather than accept the correction he insisted on what he had made, and persisting marred the divine design."

"To have had such great impact those who led astray must have been high placed," Caron said.

"In so far as the immediate realms of earth, yes: spiritual wickedness in high places," the Aton-Re agreed. "Adam and Eve as the story goes were not just two hapless souls but a people. And even then they are symbols of the human capacity of heart and mind for creation.

"In this wise the heart led the way in the fall and the mind followed after. And so it is to this day: the heart proposes, the mind disposes; rationalizing its actions, while playing to the heart."

"You fell to this at Bezu when you challenged de Blanchefort's knights over the honor of Branwyn of Wales. It seemed to you most necessary. It was heroic, noble, and impulsive but ill-timed and unnecessary; for there were patterns at work you knew nothing of and might have waited another day. But this led on to a road of trials and needless sorrows."

"It is what Flegetanis said. I acted impulsively. I did not know it could be done another way."

"No human mind is adequate to see and know all that shall come of its choices, and so rather than trusting life to find the way it judges what it believes good or evil, follows the heart's desires to optimize its gratification, and rationalizes its choices."

"What choice did man make that day the story tells the serpent beguiled Eve."

"In those days the body of man was very different than now it is," the Aton-Re said. "Eve was beguiled with the thought she might enter into the life of those living things they had made. She contrived to use the life force that informed the materia of the world to make a body of the coarser substance of the earth, imbuing it with her life, believing it would heighten her pleasure in the creation.

"Adam entered into her purpose. Without reference to the realms of light they were caught up in an imperfect creation and responsible for its existence. They put on for themselves coats of skins, exalted yet like unto the animals of the earth, and were snared in the flesh."

"And now he thinks he is the animal he made," Caron said.

"There remains a sense that he is something more; that he is in possession of an immortal soul. He is rather like a player who falls so readily into a part he has chosen to play he forgets who he is. He becomes the part, and when the play is done cannot get out of it.

"It is a common failing. So many there are in the world who think themselves: soldier, farmer, priest or lord, poet, musician, tradesman, husband, wife, or what have you, who cling to one or another false identity. How few realize it is all a part they play a moment on this little stage and when at last it shall pass away awaken to the one who never awakened in the world to his divine identity."

"After these many thousands of years I do not see man awakening again to what he is."

"With the Lord a thousand years is as a day. But soon there shall be time no more, for the fallen state cannot accommodate what is to come. The universe of light unfolds and man must enter in again into attunement with the divine design to dwell in the tree of life or perish. This is the dawning of a new day, Caron, and the last call for humankind to the spiritual regeneration of the human race. Whatever his choice, it is the beginning of the end of this sad interlude."

Two women, priestesses of the Aton-Re, ascended the stair from the courts below and stood a discreet distance off and waited. Caron knew his time was short so he stilled his thought and waited for the revelation of the purpose for his coming; to understand why the three had agreed together to bring him here.

"Man may fail love, but love never fails," the Aton-Re said. "In Sidon you met a man, John of Oxford, who came to you on death's door, desiring only to complete his mission of mercy to return his charge again to home and family."

"He perished in the way."

"Yet you had the art to take him in."

"Origen taught me how to assume the vibration of another; to shift one's shape in the eyes of others that they see only the pattern you have taken."

"And yet you did more, for John of Oxford lives in you. You gave place in yourself to bear his soul substance, and as you promised him he lives on in you to fulfill his journey."

It was true. He had not thought of it entirely in that way; compassionate he had made a promise, but the vibratory essence of John did live on in him and through that he masked himself and shaped the image others saw alone in him, no more Caron but John of Oxford.

"It is an art to take up the vibrational pattern of another into oneself in service; an art Morgon Kara turned to possess the life blood, bone and flesh of others to sustain his existence.

"The Soul is the spirit bride, the vessel overflowing that sustains body, mind and heart, but you are that spirit, born of the life undying, a being of radiant light, birthless, deathless and changeless.

"And I know at the last you will free the soul of John of Oxford that he may fulfill his journey of sounding fire and ascend into the realms of light."

"How could I stand in the way of his fulfillment in God?"

"In the carnal world these matters are mistranslated and come to destruction, but it is in the power of love to so enter into another's life that we are of one mind, one heart, and one spirit."

He was being invited to walk in the way of the shining ones. Of course he already assumed this was where his path led, but there was more to it than he understood and still in the answering love that flowered in his heart he leaped to acknowledge it. "Ask of me, and so far as it is my gift to give it I shall do so."

"Having known the burden of darkness upon you," the Aton-Re said, carefully: "do you think you might now bear my burden of light?"

"I will."

"I do not think you entirely understand. If you agree, there will come a time when I shall ask that you lose yourself in me and bear the burden of my presence upon you."

A pang of fear rose in Caron and the question, though he dared not ask it: "How is this not what Morgon Kara wanted of me?"

"In that time the veil of the worlds between us will dissolve, my voice shall be in you, my power upon you, and you will know yourself as you are in me and for that time you will become as John of Oxford now is to you."

And should he then, as Morgon Kara contrived, disappear, be absorbed into the being of another so that he was taken by another who usurped his opportunity for life? He fell still and let the forces settle in him. This was different. The master beckoned, and he was called home to him. And so he took his flesh in his teeth. "Say what I must do."

"Fulfill your promise to John of Oxford but go first to Lindisfarne, for there the cycle of his life began. You shall not go to Caer Myrddin but rest and await me in Lindisfarne. When the moment comes upon you, you will know what is needful."

Caron bowed his head in assent, and when he lifted it again the Aton-Re was gone. In his stead Caron found himself standing before the stepped stair to the pyramid altar and its flame, his hands at the level of his heart, a priestess upholding each arm with her hand at his elbow, and together they began to climb the stair.

"Lord, to whom do you speak?" the one to his right asked.

He glanced to her and she bore resemblance to the Lady Constanza. But how had this come to be; what did she see; what was he seeing?

"Rest in me," the voice comforted, reminding him of the bond that was made. "All will be made clear."

"You stood a long while alone, looking out over the sea," the other replied. He turned to her and she bore resemblance to the Lady Siduri.

To neither did he reply but they climbed together the stair to the dolmen arch and high altar of the world. This will within him now, a light hand upon him, was very like his own; in the sanctum of his heart burned an undying flame. It was all beyond words, and with the silence of the heavens upon him he paused on the threshold of the worlds.

Come before the high altar a cloud of glory encompassed them, and a light shone round about that cast no shadow. Within the radiance emanating from the dolmen arch a fire burned, and in the midst of the flame a blue sun.

At either hand, like two great wings of white radiance folded about him, the women transfigured in the fire, light and cloud of glory of the triune ray. As one being they crossed the threshold of the worlds, entering in through the blue of the flame into the realms of light.

26

Brethren of the Free Spirit

It was a summer morn but still dew dripped from wagon wheels and carts, and the grass was wet with it. Caron awoke to find himself without his calotte, bare headed, and went in search of his cap. He retraced his steps of the night before as he remembered them in his dream, along the trail back to the grotto. There on the stone seat where he sat across from Origen and Blaise was his cap. It was no dream. He stayed awhile to dwell on it, washed, drank some cool water and made his way back to the encampment.

When he returned the fires were lit and Falconieri gave him a cup of hot broth of boiled beef bone steeped with onion. "There was a priest looking for you. High orders. Remember, you promised to speak for us - our play for Midsummer's eve?"

"When I see Meister Eckhart," Caron agreed. Falconieri pointed to the man coming up from behind the wagons.

"I am Eckhart," he said, with fraternal embrace. "Your friends are well. There is a hermitage in the woods on the road to Ottrott, and an herbalist much skilled in these matters. The sisters realize healing is a matter of both worlds; spirit and the responsive substance of this made one in blessing.

Today, I must minister in the village of Ottrott. Shall we go together and talk in the way?" And that was the last word spoken between them for the best part of half an hour, as they walked the country road from Mount Ste. Odile into the valley of Ottrott.

Eckhart was a man in his mid-fifties, lean, somewhat severe of features with hollow eyes that seemed to look more inward than out upon the world. But he was spry and with assurance in his step they covered the ground rapidly. Caron was unsure how to interpret Eckhart's silence, distracted by thought or so deeply at peace words were unnecessary. Even as he thought it Eckhart spoke. "Here is a thought to ponder. God is at home. It is we who have gone out for a walk in the world." Then, as if a burden was lifted, he chuckled aloud at the thought of it. "Are you uncomfortable with silence?"

"I have walked a thousand miles with no one to speak to, and still God nearer than breathing."

They sat on a grassy bank of a creek and Eckhart closed his eyes, breathed deep and let the sun penetrate his uplifted face. Caron undid his satchel. "Father Origen has sent a book for you."

"How long were you with him in Egypt?"

"Almost a year," Caron said, handing him the manuscript.

"And did you meet Flegetanis of Alexandria?"

"Indeed."

"Curious how one meeting can change a life," Eckhart said. "Flegetanis often came to St. Odile when he journeyed this way. The deaconesses will be much impressed to meet one late come from him." Caron handed him the bundled manuscript and cautiously, hand trembling, Eckhart unlaced the covering. "*The Triune Ray*," he read, voice breaking, "and yet another: *Seven Steps to the Temple of Light*. Oh wonderful," he whispered and opened it at once. "*Love is the power of the wonderful one, and in it is the creative essence*," he read. "*Love is the fire of fusion whereby the outer self is uplifted into oneness with the master within.*"

"You understand its meaning, do you?" Eckhart asked. Reverently, he retied the bundle and concealed it in his own satchel. "I am very pleased to meet you, whoever you are, for I am in some doubt you are entirely what you seem."

"We play the parts given us."

"Amen," Eckhart said, rising. "And whoever knows God in his being, in him the light of God shines through whatever part he is given to play. Fellow traveler, I need to be silent for a while. Worlds are forming in my heart." And so it was for the best part of half an hour, until Eckhart returned to Caron. "Have you considered that all disorders of the heart and mind, from insanity through sin to spiritual wickedness in high places, all spring from denial of *God, as He Is*?

"Some who account themselves righteous have greater blame than the lunatic in this, for they have made a graven image of the Almighty in their minds, and suffer no man to enter in and know *God, as He Is*. We must not suffer the mind to make a barrier between us and the experience of the kingdom of God is within us."

Caron stopped up short in the middle of the road. "I confess I had not thought of it that way, but I know when a man loses his centering in God, however attractive the way seems to be open before him, it is a path of death he is set upon."

"Yes, yes," he said. "It is the whole duty of man to anchor in divine identity." Eckhart knelt and touched a flower by the roadside. "And as a plant is rooted in the earth, so is man rooted in the divine meant to flower in the light and air of this world. Heart, mind and body like stem, leaf and flower are to bear the fruit of the soul. But if man takes not root in that divine ground...."

As he spoke three coaches blocked the narrow road. They lumbered toward them with escort and team of four; pulling waggons festooned with red and white banners, the colors of the Birkenfells, snapping in the breeze. Four horsemen made up the escort: two in black, Timor and Formido, and another two in Birkenfells livery. The two in livery pressed Caron and Eckhart aside into the ditch so the carriages could pass, and there was a fuss with the horses as the village dogs followed nipping at the heels and wheels of the extraordinary display.

Curtains tied up for fair weather, the passengers were clearly visible. Chief among them was Berger, Seigneur of Birkenfells and vassal to the Bishop of Strasbourg, with his wife, Isabel. Across from the Bergers, dressed the country squire for a journey, came Perrin von Grünschnabel. Beside him sat the Lady Constanza. Seeing Eckhart, Berger ordered the procession stopped, and without the slightest hint of deference at forcing the clergy from the roadway, lay in at once. "Eckhart, I trust you're in Ottrott to discipline those heretics. I shall want a full accounting; if I don't get it I shall speak to the Bishop of Strasbourg concerning you."

"In three days the Duke of Lorraine, his young wife, along with the Lady Madelon de Faucon of Languedoc, shall be my guests. I will have no incidents with this Brethren of the Free Spirit; no interference with the life of my vassals. You will either bring these heretics in line with the order of the Church, or I will expel them from hostel lands."

In the second coach Squin and Siduri sat across from each other exchanging pleasantries, and beside Siduri was Master of Hallows, Blaise, who took it all in with a quick glance. Siduri was distracted by Squin, but even as Berger spoke the Lady Constanza turned to Caron. Her pale blue eyes met with his, full with curiosity. "I hope we have not inconvenienced you," she said, searching him. He felt her influence stir in him, and a surge of passion cross over between them. He lowered his head in humility to avoid her scrutiny. And sensing the others moved by what flowed between them, Constanza drew back concealing herself.

"You are his vassal seigneur, and if these are the Bishop's wishes, it is your duty to fulfill them," Eckhart said. "And as God's vassal, you may be sure I shall fulfill mine."

"They are come in from all about to hear you preach," Berger said. "See that you keep them orderly, and from lodging in the *Hôtel-Dieu*. It is a hostel of God for the physically ill; not lodgings for the spiritually depraved."

"You will need to speak to the sisters about that. I am here for their spiritual enlightenment, not their material comforts."

"And when you are done report to Bailiff Beadle," Berger ordered. "Move on!"

But Perrin leaned forward and spoke to the monks. "This is the road to Odile?" he asked, seeming to feel the last word should be his, and somewhat kinder in tone. It was but a moment but Caron saw something changed in him. He was petulant, preening but touched with remorse.

"If that's where you're going, "Caron said, "You're well on the road."

It fell on deaf ears. Perrin heard nothing and settled back in his upholstered seat. But Constanza, her pale sun streaked hair blown in the breeze, gave Caron her fairest smile as they moved on. After them came

Timor and Formido's dark and ruthless scrutiny as they passed by. But it was Perrin, Caron pondered; what would become of him, privileged poet and knight in the Order of the Blood Royal. Magda had shrewdly estimated Perrin's price, made accommodations, and brought him home again into her sphere.

"So we are to report to Bailiff Beadle of Beadledom. How rare," Caron said.

Eckhart laughed as the procession passed on. "When we are filled with ourselves, we are empty of God." And with a glance back at the coach.

"Berger's companion in the coach is Perrin von Grünschnabel, poet to the Lady Madelon de Faucon; now, at the Duke of Lorraine's pleasure, resident in Nancy. The abbess told me of his coming ahead to prepare the way before her. Many of the deaconesses, especially the ladies secular at St Odile were of her company.

"There had been some falling out, conflict between her and the great families whose daughters these are. She sends this one now to affect the beginnings of some reconciliation. I don't know the details but those who speak of Perrin do so with some affection." Again Eckhart fell silent, as if again he had said rather more than he intended, and settled again into the stillness.

"And the Brethren of the Free Spirit," Caron said.

"They gather in small numbers along the Rhine valley. The notion of free men in a feudal kingdom offends him, and Berger would subject everything and everyone to his control. But wherever and whenever I can, I minister to them."

Images of Montségur, the Cathar wars, and the burning time crowded Caron's mind. He remembered the words of the Bishop of Carcassonne: *"burn them all and let God sort out his own."* It was typical of those in whom the letter kills, where spirit would give life.

"Are you not concerned what Berger might say to the Bishop?"

"He will say what he will, and I will speak as I must. Berger is ever full of complaints and Bailiff Beadle many more. There is little I can do about that, but the Bishop knows my mind in this and he is a good man. Most of this nonsense stops with him. If you are concerned you need not attend me."

Caron laughed. "Ministering to a free spirit, I wouldn't miss it for the world."

They walked a little distance on in a vibrant silence deepening between them. "You are a blithe spirit, Brother John, but who is it dwells within you?"

"I dwell in my soul's joy, in the one who sees through my eyes what has become of His world," Caron said. He counsels wisdom and peace, to be still and let it be, until the time of harvest."

"We are very well met," Eckhart said, satisfied.

A half mile on, at the margin of the wood before the village of Ottrott, they came to an Apothecary, on a path just off the road in the margin of the woods. In a clearing behind the cottage were herb gardens and a hospice.

"We shall find your friends here. I'm told the Freischütz, Marcus Veidt, has greatly improved. They burned his eyes with a torch, but with rest and remedies the sisters believe he will regain at least partial sight. They seem quite fond of him: his healing validates their mission."

The fragrant gloom of the apothecary brought back thoughts of Flegetanis' own in Alexandria: memories of the old man compounding his concoctions above; delving betimes into his books in the scriptorium below. It was there this cycle of coming again to himself began, and in a curious way it was come round again. Here the apothecary was a monk of middle years, who immediately Caron entered the shop caught and for a moment held his eyes.

"Meister Eckhart," the apothecary said, folding his hands before him. "You honour our endeavors by coming here to teach."

"Brother Girard," Eckhart said, warmly, "I have brought a friend whose friends are in your care."

"Then you are the Trinitarian who ransomed Hode and brings him home," Girard said. A sister of St. Odile assigned to the hospice bustled into the shop, looking for a fresh tincture of Valerian root for a sedative. When she was gone Girard turned to Caron. "Have we met before? I am almost sure of it."

"Kindred spirits recognize each other. I too share a passion for healing."

"That must be it," Girard said, folding his hands and bowing in acknowledgment, "those who meet in spirit are never parted and ever meet again." He turned to Eckhart. "Come; let me take you to the hospice. Many are anxious for your arrival.

"I have recently been visited by Bailiff Beadle," Girard confined to Eckhart. "Berger sent him to give account of our activities here. He demands an inventory of all our medicines, an accounting of all our practices, and lists of patients in our care, updated regularly and weekly available to him in writing copied thrice. Berger, he says, demands it so he may know our person, our affairs, and our readiness to support his realm to assist his officials in time of trouble, of famine, plague or war.

"He spoke, too, of putting a price on our use of the wild herbs I collect for medicines taken from his lord's lands - so that whatever we pick may be taxed to support his estates. Beadle is a man who understands nothing but ledgers.

"I swear he is the most officious man I have ever had the displeasure to meet," Girard said. "He comes here at his whim, takes tally of every item of value, every person who serves, every patient in hospital, seeks out every trait, attitude, circumstance or transgression great or small both here and in the villages so he can use such information to advantage to control the serfdom. And for this and his fawning upon him, the lord dotes on him."

"I have seen the type too often before," Eckhart said. "He will serve his lord's whims until Berger cannot do without him, and Berger becomes Beadle's vassal in all but name."

"Is there nothing to be done?"

"There is much to be done and we have begun the work. The Beadles of the world think it will disintegrate without their hand upon it. They do not think the earth is the Lord's, paying no more than lip service to the ways of God's kingdom. Beadles do not trust life and so all the more we must."

Girard sighed. "I fear this compulsion to catalog God's creation to serve man's designs upon it will obsess the world. Then shall neither nook nor cranny be but to be recorded, organized, and owned."

"The so the coming of the kingdom of Beadledom," Caron said.

They laughed heartily over that, but in the sinking feeling that followed: "They will have their Babylon," Eckhart said. "They will strive to set their seal on everything that is God's to make it their own, and then shall the end come. In those days the Lord shall have run out of patience with man, and no more abide this den of thieves in the Father's House."

It must have been like this ages past when his disciples and the multitude gathered about him where there was water. Caron could not but think on the Sermon on the Mount, when the Master offered his timeless words on the attitudes of being. And now true to the tone sounded in the timelessness of time, Meister Eckhart sat on a knoll by a brook shimmering under the June sun. Seventy and more brethren of the free spirit with patients from the hostel, settled about Eckhart in the warm, meadow grass; among them Hode, keeping close watch over his companion, Veidt, who sat silently facing into the sun.

They were in a mood, restless with anticipation for what Eckhart would say; troubled, too, by the persecutions that had taken some of their number, remembering the stories of the burning time. But Eckhart did not preach; instead he listened. And only when his silence endured longer than most could bear, he raised his head to the host. "I am looking for a way to explain to you the experience of transcendence in God. It is an experience that dissolves the mind-made world. It is an experience that frees Him in you, from what man has wrought to keep Him out."

One called Tomas, one of three to whom the group looked for its voice, took that as invitation to speak. "There are those who say in His Holy Spirit we enter into union with God, and can sin no more. There are those who aspire to our company who say this permits them any woman, wed or unwed be she willing, whom he would possess, for in him it is God who would possess her."

Another, whose name was Godefroi, added: "These things are said of us, and for rumors of these sayings many revile us. The Church teaches that Christ has taught adultery a sin; that even to look upon a woman, and lust after her in one's heart, is as if it were the very act. What say you?" Eckhart's Sermon on the Mount was beginning to look more like a challenge of scribes and Pharisees, but he took it in his stride.

"In the first instance you present me with the most difficult case, because it most troubles your hearts. This matter touches on one of the remaining, great creative powers entrusted to man. From the time of the fall it is a power he but little understands. In right use is spiritual regeneration in the magic of creation. Abused it is degradation and the very essence of spiritual wickedness."

"They say we mar the message; that Christ revealed all that is necessary to the salvation of man; that the Church is the repository of his teachings, the provenance of their authority."

"Brother Kellner," Eckhart said, "did not our Master say, "I have many things to tell you but you cannot bear them yet? Do you not think that after nearly fourteen hundred years we might bear a little more?

"And did he not say that in leaving to prepare a place for us, a Comforter would come; even the Spirit of Truth who should be with us and in us, and lead us into all truth? So let me first address that.

"From the time of Noah, twice has God reached out his hand to save us from drowning in our sins. In Abraham we had the beginning of an age in which the desert fathers set us in the way of the redemptive journey. In those days through these He gave us the laws of life. He schooled us that we might orient our hearts to Him again; that through our centering in Him, Heaven might begin to manifest in the earth.

"And you know the story of how in the time of Solomon this might have consummated but for that sad king's backsliding, perverting the way through his love of many strange women.

"A dark age ensued, and yet a second time He reached out his hand to reveal the way, the truth and the life, manifesting Himself to us as the Son of God in the son of man. Amidst the ruins of an opportunity lost, he showed us how to be in this world and not of it; how to let the spirit of the Son of God manifest in us even as it did in the Master.

"And for his righteousness they crucified him who came in God's Name," Eckhart said softly. "And so do we crucify the way, the truth, and the life in us when in self-righteousness we turn our hearts away from God to lust after the things of the earth. In this age of the Son we yet labour, for men have not yet learned to let God's spirit be God's spirit in every moment of living, but hide ourselves from him in the thickets of the mind.

"Blessed ones, like the first hint of light on a springtide morn, we are in the early dawn of a third and final day for the spiritual regeneration of the human race: the day of the coming of the comforter, even the spirit of truth, who shall be with us and in us. And we brethren are the heralds of that age.

"Not in our time, perhaps, shall it be made plain as day to all But as surely as the sun rises it is begun, and you are the first light of the great day of the coming of the Lord. What then is required of you that this day may be, 'as the light of the morning, when the sun riseth, even a morning without clouds; as the tender grass springing out of the earth by clear shining after rain.'"

Caron felt it coming. From several directions a dozen soldiers under the direction of Bailiff Beadle had roughly encircled the perimeter of the meadow and now advanced slowly toward the gathered host, Beadle leading the way. There was no immediate danger in it but Beadle was arbitrary. Caron would warn Eckhart when with a glance he saw him already perfectly aware.

"And so what kind of life should we live to this end that the Holy Spirit emerge full and free in us. Shall we be proud and petulant as the great of this world, magnifying ourselves before men? Or shall we find our greatness in humility and tenderness as exemplified by our Lord. When we welcome that spirit into our hearts we will find ourselves at peace in the power and humility of Christ. There is no need to do battle with a world that will pass away as readily as darkness in the sunrise of the world. Let it be in quietness and in confidence that is our strength.

"This is not to say we shall never need to take a stand, but however forceful, let it ever be right action for right action's sake. We act but do not react to what would destroy and will surely pass away, for reacting we steal from God and give life to corruption anew."

Fifty yards off they were now and closing so the gathering itself had become aware of them, and there was some shuffling but most remained riveted on Eckhart's words.

"So then to your question, Tomas," Eckhart said. "When after the word of the first great commandment your heart is wholly given to God, you cannot commit adultery because your heart belongs to God, and God will not commit adultery with the fallen world.

"Adultery is of the heart, the mingling of things that ought not to be mingled. If you lust after another rather than God you commit adultery.

"But there follows another commandment from the first: you shall love your neighbor as yourself. In this commandment is the basis of our love for one another in God's love. For, if the heart is wholly given to God, self and soul are transformed in Him, and all that remains is God revealed in man restored. So, then, the love of the neighbor is God's love, and no craven human need masquerading as love." Some appeared confused.

"Do I not speak plainly enough?" Eckhart said. "If you cannot hear me you may be sure you have not yet fulfilled the great commandment. For when you have fulfilled the great commandment and know oneness with God, there is only God's love. The issue of adultery is no more, for after God's own heart you will do only what God will do.

"Those of you who take to wife do not fear your passions. Rather, let those passions center in God and you will find magnified in your life powers of creation you never imagined. God has given His great spirit of love into creation through male and female, and when they find their hearts in Him, God makes his home with them."

"But you are not wed," Tomas objected.

"For the kingdom of Heaven's sake," Eckhart replied. "Nor is it needful for all to wed who serve God.

"But man, male and female, were made to be one with God in letting wonders form. Love the Lord your God with all your heart, mind, soul and strength; and through you in your several ways, let God's will be done in earth even as it is in heaven to let His kingdom come."

"Eckhart," Beadle interrupted. "My master instructed you were to clear this field and not preach to this rabble."

"As you are a vassal to Berger," Eckhart answered, mildly. "I am God's vassal. You work the work of your master, I mine of God. Which would you say, Beadle, is the greater work?"

Beadle would not answer. "Some of my master's vassals attend these meetings. He wants to know who and why. Stand up so I may see you," Beadle ordered. But no one moved.

Caron felt his power rise within, contemplating what he might do, for Beadle thwarted was capable of mean spirited violence against his authority. "I understand the Duke of Lorraine will soon visit Birkenfells," Caron said. "If he would address your serfs and freemen alike who came to hear him, would you object?"

"Never," Beadle replied, dismissively. "But I do not take your case, monk. Why would an exalted person speak to rabble?"

"All these come to hear Meister Eckhart. He comes in the Name of the Master of us all; as well Birkenfells and the Duke of Lorraine. And though that one is Lord of Lords and King of Kings, he taught us to minister to all whatever their station in life whose hearts are open to Him."

They were all now on their feet and their numbers caused the soldiers instinctively to draw back seeing the odds. Beadle saw it, too, and it took a little of the petulance out of his bearing. Eckhart said nothing but looked on, watching Caron with wry interest.

"Whom do you serve Beadle?" Caron asked, softly

"I am the Bailiff of Birkenfells."

"That I know, but whom do you serve?"

"The Seigneur," he replied, half reluctantly.

"You are his vassal," Caron agreed. "And whose vassal is your master?"

"My master?" Beadle winced at the word.

"A simple question, who does your master serve?"

"He is the vassal of the Bishop of Strasbourg," Beadle replied, reluctantly.

"Whose lands these are: Church lands. You are out of your jurisdiction, Bailiff. If you have issue with the Church then under Salic law you must have your lord take it up with the Bishop of Strasbourg, for you have no authority here with God or men."

Beadle nodded to his lieutenant and gestured to the gathering. The lieutenant drew his sword. Eckhart came between him and the brethren. The lieutenant threatened. "Will you impale your soul upon that sword," Eckhart asked. The lieutenant drew back confused, looking to Beadle for guidance.

"The seigneur is given authority to defend the roads for the pilgrims and see to the wellbeing of the deaconesses of St. Odile. Would you keep us from our duty?" Beadle asked

"Well then you had best see to it, for there are no issues here that cannot be resolved by the one whom these serve."

Beadle took him to mean the church, but he was not entirely sure and so asked. "And who is that?"

"God," Eckhart said. "Such issues as are raised here can be resolved only by God."

Now Beadle was thoroughly confused. "I shall take this up with the seigneur whom I serve," he said, at once rallying and retreating for shelter into the system that sustained him.

"Do, and if he has any concerns about my ministrations, let him take it up with his liege the Bishop of Strasbourg.

"It is the old question, isn't it," Eckhart said when Beadle was gone: "Whom do we serve? Some insist it is the state, that here and now the earth belongs to man; hereafter heaven to God. It appears man would possess the earth and keep God out of his affairs. And the Church succumbs and at times couples with secular powers to survive in a world where it is only things and possessions that matter."

"Today you have taken a stand," Tomas said. "There will be repercussions."

"It was the right thing at the right moment," Eckhart said. "And in this you see, too, how sometimes the institution of the Church is useful. Fear of excommunication runs deep; enough to keep the wolves at bay when fear is all they understand.

"No, the Church is useful; a provision made until such a time as man himself is again the temple of the living God.

"Beadle is the worst of men," Kellner said.

"No, but caught up in illusion Beadle thinks he must impose order on the world, altogether unaware of what governs and shapes him. In the dawning of the Age of the Holy Spirit we must come to understand what it is we face," Eckhart said. "For, as was said long ago, we wrestle not with flesh and blood, but the rulers of the darkness of this world.

"From the time of the fall we are possessed of ill spirits. Only the manifestation of the Holy Spirit can cast them out. And so it must be until the heavens of this earth are cleansed and in divine identity a new heaven brings forth a new earth.

"And as it begins with us here now, we must ask ourselves how in this day shall man be restored?" And as none gave reply, Eckhart continued: "It shall be, if we let it be, by the Word of God. Let it be by His kingdom, by His power, to His glory. Let no human desire remain. Let no human doctrine be kept, or belief sustained. Let all religions and temporal systems pass from the earth, leaving only God revealed in man restored.

"This is the Word of God spoken this day by His angels in agreement on earth: Glory to God in the highest!"

When he was done and the silence that followed gave way to the sounds of running water and birdsong, Girard, the apothecary, went up to Eckhart who stood in the afternoon sunshine enveloped in its warmth letting the moment dissolve into what was to come. Brother Girard took his hand and whispered so only Eckhart and Caron could hear: "Take care old wisdom. The world will not take this kindly, and we have much to lose in losing you."

27

Castle of Women

"Art thou he that troubleth Israel?" Falconieri played the part of Ahab to perfection.

He stood before the prophet Elijah, shoulders drooped with burdens: Ahab, king of a perishing kingdom, cowardly husband of a tempestuous queen, intent on the ruin of the prophet of the Lord. And Caron come out of the desert, bearing the mien and burden of the prophet, was come to challenge the insane king, and bring an end to the drought that savaged the land.

The dress rehearsal in the court of Niedermunster Abbey had gone remarkably well, considering it was Alrecchino who played the prophet. Following Caron's advice, taking no drink for a day he discovered the agony of drought and the trials of the desert. He played to an adoring crowd so well that pantomime, eloquence and unrealized passion for his art combined in an alchemy that lifted him out of his banal life into a performance of pure gold.

Only after the few desultory fireworks were lit to the astonishment of all depicting the fire of God falling from heaven, did Alrecchino himself descend to earth again and realize he was terribly thirsty. Carried on the hubris of his success he promptly took to excessive drink interrupted only by solicitation of praise.

"And did I truly touch the character of the prophet?" Yes, yes, came the replies, you were wonderful. "And was I truly wonderful?" he asked swiftly dissolving in alcohol. "And did you believe I was none other than he I played, as if it were his very own self?" Yes, yes, again the replies as the bottles were passed around. "You are too kind, too gracious." And so it went, until he fell into a stupor and slept his catharsis.

Falconieri went in search of Caron. They were to present the play that evening on the mountain top, followed by a great display of fireworks at Hohenburg Castle to consummate the drama, and mark the solstice eve. What was more, beside the women of the abbey, guests had arrived including the Seigneur of Birkenfells, vassal of the Bishop of Strasbourg.

Caron resisted. He played the monk and not the monk a player and was concerned he might reveal himself. But among the guests were Siduri and Perrin. Things had gone so far from the course they'd known together under Flegetanis' hand; he would have the measure of them. With Origen's tutelage he had advanced in the art of shape shifting; even so it would be a great challenge. He must keep the part of John of Oxford playing the part of the prophet Elijah, with the passion of a desert father, before those who had known him, without betraying himself to their prior and intimate knowledge of him.

Caron looked up from under his weatherworn hood to the finery of the gathered host of Saint Odile. The maidens fair of the Blood Royal who took refuge here after the calamities of Waldheim, gathered tonight in procession with such serene beauty the heart ached for their loveliness. He saw the Abbess Lotharing - Aletheia they called her - and with her Perrin and Squin, Siduri and Constanza, all gathered to hear the voice of one they thought dead.

"Art thou he that troubleth Israel." Falconieri spoke again with greater force. He was concerned his new Elijah was suffering stage fright.

Caron heard but still he held back, his eyes passing over the Seigneur of Birkenfells and his entourage falling at last on the Meister Eckhart, who alone of all gathered knew who played Elijah. And then he saw Blaise, whose eyes rested upon him in a way that gave Caron pause, for they seemed to see through the layers of cloaking to the very man. Finally, there was Telgesinus, late arrived in the company of the Bishop of Strasburg, who by his look of wary anticipation appeared to assume it was in his honor this play was contrived, and was yet to take the measure of it. Telgesinus shared the same critical eye.

He took them all in, and when the words came they were as uncompromising as a sharp two edged sword: adamant as diamond, weighted with the substance of stars, perfect to the moment as the first flash of lightning drawn.

"It is not I who trouble Israel; but thou, and thy father's house, for you have forsaken the commandments of the Lord, and thou hast followed Baalim."

Wealth that brings power; prosperity that brings security; fertility that brings plenty; sensuality that brings lavish pleasures and self-indulgences: these were the gods of the House of Baalim of old. Though the names change, Caron knew it was those man worshipped yet and all his means to these ends.

And this was Israel before him scattered abroad in the earth. It was the same alike, whatever colour, creed, or nation; the question put to those who believe the sole reason for their existence is their own fulfillment. It was the question put to those who cannot get past the material demands of their lives to hear what life is asking of them.

"Now gather to me all Israel upon this mount, and the prophets of Baal four hundred and fifty, and the prophets of the groves four hundred, which eat at Jezebel's table."

So Ahab in the person of Falconieri mimed with grand gestures the gathering to Mount Carmel. In shuffled the spares of his troupe to play the parts assigned to the prophets of Baal. And then another two, led to the sacrifice, enter the pantomime bullocks, kicking up heels and jostling one another to delight the audience.

Caron watched from within his cowl, letting his eyes drift across the audience who took the part of the Israel. They looked on smiling on the common chaos of the world, not realizing the role they played. This was drama wrought in the timelessness of time. Roughhewn as may be, this little mystery play served to loose the power of the realms of light in a world of sensual darkness.

Baal's prophets gathered to Ahab oozing contempt and fear of Elijah; for if by their arts they were unable to loose the waters, their cult of fertility was dust and ashes. Caron ignored them and took in his audience, the sons and daughters of Israel gathered to the mount. His eyes lighted on Siduri and held her in his gaze. "How long halt you between two opinions?" he asked. "If the Lord be God serve him, but if Baal, serve him."

She shivered at the contact for the word came in the same uncompromising tone she'd known in Flegetanis; a voice obscured in the cacophony of Venice. It reminded her of Caron. She whispered something nervously and Perrin heard her but could not tell what she said; only he saw her moved, troubled in her soul, and he put his arm about to comfort her. She touched his vanity, and Perrin dared think the script he crafted was the cause.

"I, even I only remain a prophet of the Lord," Elijah said. "But you are many. Wherefore choose one bullock and cut it in pieces, and lay it on wood and put no fire under, and I will dress the other and put no fire under.

"And call upon the name of your gods, and I will call on the name of the Lord: and the God that answers with fire let him be God."

The abbess of St. Odile and all the deaconesses of the abbey, for well they knew the text, and now the part given them, answered with once voice: "It is well spoken."

The host with them, the troupe was in its element. Falconieri recast himself as one of the prophets of Baal and led the farce in leaping upon the altar, where the hapless heifer lay as still as still he could, hoping none of the flashing of knives would come any closer than a ritual gesture. The priests shouted to their gods of thunder and rain, the fertility goddesses of seed and crop and harvest, and by all the names of the cults of Baalim known to them.

"Upon the earth Baal, rain," they shouted, "upon the fields rain down upon us. Sweet rain to the earth is Baal: water to bring life to the fields, laughter to the child and light in the virgin's eyes. Upon the earth Baal rain…" And so it went, the whole litany of the gods of fertility and prosperity summoned and unresponsive, until as in that time of old the night began to fall, and the time of the evening sacrifice.

The prophets of Baal weary with leaping sat upon the altar and watched as meticulously Elijah paced out a circle four and twenty feet in diameter; and with ritual restraint set twelve large stones each in its place to mark the arc of the altar of life. And when he was done he turned to the prophets of Baal exhausted with futile frenzy over the altar of sacrifice.

"Where is he now your rider of the storm?" Elijah raised his hands toward the prophets of Baal. "Has he gone a journey? Do you interrupt his wooing and he will not be disturbed? Or, perhaps he sleeps and will not be awakened?"

The second pantomime bullock was frisking to the side; drawing attention to itself for it was to be his moment on stage. But off script Elijah began a second time to walk about the circle of stones he placed. Falconieri taken up in Caron's performance, and wise enough not to interfere, nudged the bullock out of sight. The fireworks would be spectacular to override any small deviations from text.

"It is not exactly as I have written it," Perrin whispered to Siduri, "but he is convincing. The twelve stones are for the twelve tribes of Israel."

With ritual care Elijah walked the arc of his circular altar a second time, and when he was done paused, reached into the doe-skin pouch that hung about his neck and took out a small white stone. In closed hand he held it a moment to come to center, and placed the white stone in the midst of the circle of twelve.

"The stone the builders rejected," Caron whispered.

"Was it not to have been a bullock, Perrin? What is the white stone?" Siduri asked. Perrin shook his head.

Blaise turned to Meister Eckhart who was riveted on Caron. "Who takes Elijah's part is no mere player. Has he not so entered into the part that he has become Elijah?"

"It is the Trinitarian friar, John of Oxford, who takes the part of Elijah," Eckhart said. "He rebuilds the altar of life that was broken down. But I think true to character he will offer no bullock in sacrifice, for the John I know has overcome obstinacy of heart and mind, and in its stead will offer himself."

"Then it is the white stone of divine identity he offers," Blaise said. "And within a Name given that only he knows, offered to the glory of God."

Water was poured over stones and pavement, as of old proof no fire or fuel was set under. And for Israel faith in the mercy of the Lord, for after years of drought water was gold.

Elijah walked a third time the arc of the altar until he came again to the threshold where he began. There he felt the sheaths of the existence he affected fall away. John of Oxford was no more, nor the part of Elijah he played. Even Caron veiled in the persona of his masquerade dissolved into pure essence. What his audience saw he could not say – he supposed what they were able, and likely Elijah, but it no longer mattered, for there was only the moment. Everything was suspended enveloped in the power of an overarching presence, as if an Archangelic being spread wings of life and light over the abbey of St. Odile, manifest in the gathered host and finding heart and voice in him.

"Come near unto me."

Caron raised open arms to the gathered host to receive them into God's great heart of love. And then he waited.

He waited for those gathered to rise up in themselves and break the oppressive grip of mad king and insane queen upon their souls to offer God their hearts.

Entertainment was one thing; being asked to give something was another. There was tension. The audience grew restless with the need for completion. What was expected of them? And still Caron waited, searching the hearts for what each might bring into the circle of life. The answer gathered to the Abbess of St. Odile. It was her realm and with her came the response of those gathered to her and it was she who understood and opened to him.

And so the stage was set for the fire to fall from heaven, but out of the corner of his eye Caron caught Signor Falconieri's desperate gestures to intervene. "There are no fire flowers," Falconieri mimed: "Thieves. There are no fireworks."

"You'll like this part if ever we get to it," Perrin said to Siduri. "God will not answer with fire of course. So, here we substitute a little human ingenuity with Venetian fire-flowers."

"Why will not God answer for Himself?" Constanza asked and Perrin laughed at her. "He never does that anymore."

In the way of the earth about the sun, again Elijah walked the arc of the altar of life, until he came to the half-way point in the fourth cycle, feeling the anticipation gather to him, for all who knew the legend knew what should come next. And there the over-arching brooding presence grew even more intense. And so it was on the threshold of the fire he turned to the abbess, Aletheia, and spoke to her alone.

"Let the God who answers with Fire be God."

"It is well spoken," Aletheia answered. "Let God be God, for there is none other."

Caron could only follow through and ritually finish what was begun, letting the imagination of the host play it out, for Falconieri could bring no fireworks to the climax. And still in the sense of the presence that enveloped the abbey there was assurance that in what he did all would come to the full in him. And Elijah declared it.

"Let it be known this day that thou art God in Israel; that I am thy servant, and have done all these things at thy Word, that this people may know thou art the Lord God, and has turned their heart back again."

Into the unknown Caron stepped; into the fourth quadrant of the altar of the sun-wheel and the floodgates opened. The forces gathered loosing fire from above, and fire from the center of the earth, filling heart and mind and body and overflowing until he was utterly possessed of a flame that enveloped and burned, and consumed him not.

Caron fell upon his knees, for in the blaze he saw the windows of heaven open so there was no distinguishing within or without, above or below, but one in the fires of fusion in the flame of creation.

Everything burned, pinwheels and fountains of light, all the earth ablaze in one glorious combustion; rising in a great spiraling conflagration of fire and light and shining glorious in the night sky.

In his eyes each of the gathered host kindled in the flame. Some few burned clean and bright like crystal in firelight, some translucent like amber, others in colours of blue and red and green across the spectrum, but all in the ascending flame. Most smoked and smoldered in the blaze, as if more they could not bear but turn flocculent ash blown on the fire-wind that swept them.

When it was done and Caron could see again by the evening light and torches lit about the court, in the dazed silence that had fallen over the host, Caron took the little stone from the center of the ark of stones that he had made as an altar, and turned away.

Some fainted, others heads bowed low upon their laps; a few lifted their eyes to see. A voice of adoration in the midst brought again the security of the familiar, touched with new reverence. The abbess Aletheia, in the afterglow of the ascending flame, fulfilled the cycle. "The Lord, he is the God," she affirmed. "The Lord, he is the God."

Telgesinus was outraged. "It is illusion. This charlatan pretends to knowledge of our arts."

"It is very clear he knows exactly what he is doing," Blaise answered. "This is no fire wrought of men. He has drawn together the forces and taken us up into himself. Of rough stone he has shaped an altar of life to let the invisible be made visible. And in response to the fire filled word, he has wrought wonders in the light. Only one other I have known is capable of this."

"Flegetanis is dead."

"Then tonight you have seen another master at work."

But Telgesinus couldn't hear. Obsessed, his mind heard only what it wished to hear. "We must expose this black mage."

Blaise shook his head. "It would be worth your life to challenge him. His art far outstrips your own."

With that Telgesinus was much offended and parted from the master. Blaise watched him go and saw Telgesinus make his way across the court to where the players basked in the afterglow of their performance. There he took up with two men in black and Squin came also to join them. Cautious words were spoken and the two vanished from the court into the shadows as Telgesinus went in search of the Abbess of Saint Odile.

"These fireworks, Perrin," Siduri said. "It was not like Venice. You must find another way to conclude your play. They are dangerous, overwhelming. Many of the maidens swooned for fear of them and unaccustomed they rouse passions and in the afterglow, and I fear…" There she caught herself for it was improper for a lady to say more.

"I will ask Falconieri to subdue his performance. But it was wonderful. I saw fire fall within the altar of stones, the same it kindled within me in response, and I am like you roused and shriven beyond telling to speak of it."

Abbess Lotharing came to Meister Eckhart. "Is it your Trinitarian, John of Oxford, who took the part of Elijah?"

"He was taken into the part, but, yes, it was him."

"I would have him join us at table tonight," Aletheia said. "And as he is itinerant Mathurian he deserves of us the best we may offer. Meister Eckhart, have him stay with us in guest quarters at the abbey, until those he came for are again ready to travel."

"This night at least," Eckhart said.

Dusk fell on the abbey and the company in procession by torchlight wended its way toward the great hall. Against the dark indigo of the night sky bursts of flame ignited into cascading reds and blues and greens, flowers of fire from the valley below, soaring high about the forests and beyond the peak of Saint Odile kindling the night sky.

"Brother John," Falconieri asked. "How did you do it?"

"Did you not do it?"

"The fireworks were stolen. This display now," he said, with a sweep of the hand, "is not my doing but the work of thieves and we shall find them out. Tonight I was afraid for my reputation, nay for my life to have failed before such an illustrious company.

"How did you do it? Was it some illusion learned in your journeying, for I am told that world is filled with fakirs and mages skilled in the arts of illusion?"

"I did only as Elijah did, and let it be what it would be."

"And what is that?"

"I yielded my heart to God, and under His hand rebuilt the altar of the Lord, waiting on His Word."

"Who taught you this?" Falconieri asked.

"My master Flegetanis," Caron said, fondly: "one who took great pains to teach a froward soul, to let the lord build the house, lest they labour in vain who build it."

Caron's quarters were small but comfortable; more than he expected, with a fire lit and a basin of water hot for washing before the dinner gathering. There he shed the robes of the prophet and became again the Mathurian monk, white surplice with red and blue cross emblazoned; a weary man returning from the holy land on the long journey home. And in this wise Caron made his way across the cobbled court toward the great hall where the guests of Saint Odile gathered, hoping to make as little impression as possible upon them.

The abbess kept a fine but modest table befitting an abbey, whose object was normally a reflective sanctuary of learning and meditation for the well born. But this night in honor of her guests Aletheia gathered to Hohenburg Castle her nuns, deaconesses, lay clergy, guests, and all those freed from duties from Niedermünster convent and hospital below, to High Table for the midsummer feast of St. John's Eve. Birkenfells, anxious to please his liege the Bishop of Strasburg, insisted he bear the burden in provisions, service and cost to the abbey and spared nothing.

The Bishop was given place of honor, and about him emissaries of the Duke of Lorraine in the persons of Telgesinus, Squin and Blaise, Siduri and Perrin. The tables arranged in a great open square filled with a procession of nuns and noble ladies pleased for the occasion to shed their homespun. Instead, they came in the fine silks of their station, arrayed in colourful pageant of dazzling feminine beauty, doing justice to the great houses that sired them. Abbess Aletheia sat to the foot of the table with Caron at her right hand. To her left she sat the Lady Constanza, and as she beckoned explained her purpose.

"The Lady Constanza has some Greek and Latin, but with you she may converse freely. Do translate for us, for I should so like to hear of her life and journey from the east. And you, too, if you are willing, for Meister Eckhart tells us you have met with the Master Flegetanis and bring us a manuscript from the Bishop Origen of Egypt. The Lady Siduri, whom I gather you know, though she says you two have never met, is his daughter."

"Flegetanis gave me passage on one of his ships to the Holy Land," Caron said. "We met only for a few days in Alexandria. There is no reason why she should remember me."

"Flegetanis was a great patron of our Abbey," Aletheia said. "We shall miss him so."

Abbess Aletheia was turned aside to answer a question and give instructions. Caron took the moment to survey the great hall. Siduri was caught up in conversation and showed no curiosity toward him. He was a player who had played a part and otherwise an itinerant of little interest to her. Perrin was another matter. Caron found him looking and when their eyes met Perrin smiled and nodded; more a nod of appreciation Caron thought for the performance than any recognition. The Bishop of

Strasbourg was in conversation with Birkenfells; the latter no doubt filling his ear about Eckhart and the Brethren of the Free Spirit. Evidently the Bishop was hearing none of it, for he appeared warmly disposed toward Eckhart.

Of all gathered it was Telgesinus who fixed upon him. This was their second meeting within a short span and the last had made an indelible impression. And here John of Oxford was come again, he must be thinking, the role he played as curious as any he had seen. But Telgesinus was in conversation with the Master Blaise and Blaise with several glances Caron's way and one toward the Bishop of Strasbourg who was ecstatic with the evening, told him in no uncertain terms Telgesinus' speculations were unacceptable, and to be dismissed. And as he thought it Telgesinus rose from table and crossed the hall to Caron.

"It appears we are on the same path to meet again so readily."

"I am still bound for England, and this detour for the sake of Marcus Veidt."

"Ah, yes, the Abbey of St. Odile, where by faith the blind are made to see. Were it only true."

"By faith, compassion and tender ministering, he has made some improvement."

"Well, I came not to argue theology, but in my own way to apologize for my doubts at Ransbach. The Meister Eckhart and my colleague the Master Blaise speak well of you, in terms that assure me your soul and experiences speak exactly to what you are."

He was probing but Caron nodded graciously; finding nothing to attach to Telgesinus turned aside with a perfunctory, "be at peace Brother John." Apology given, if insincere, Telgesinus returned to his cups and conversation with Blaise and the Meister Eckhart. As Caron's eyes followed he met with Blaise who nodded with an enigmatic smile and turned away. Aletheia noticed.

"Have you had some issue with this Telgesinus who serves the Lady Madelon Faucon?"

"He has put me and my brethren in the way to some distress."

"His nature is contention," Aletheia said, "and will take exception to anything that does not square with his obsessions. But Brother John, she seems a most agreeable companion, so will you not now ask the Lady

Constanza to tell us of her journey; translate if you will those parts difficult for her."

So the Lady Constanza spoke of her life in Khotan in the great Tarim under the shadow of the Himalayas. And though she spoke of the shaman Morgon Kara who saved the people from the plague she revealed little. At the same time she seemed to be watching for knowledge in Caron of what she spoke.

Aletheia was intrigued. "What brought you to journey west?" Caron felt eyes upon him, and Telgesinus on the periphery of his vision. He was fixated but seemed also to be trying to catch the Abbess Lotharing's eye.

"The shaman Morgon Kara told me he knew of a man in the west who could not die, a man who when he reached fullness of years renewed his youth like the eagle. It was that secret of undying life he sought. He named him and I have come in search of him."

"My goodness," said Aletheia, "and you think, indeed, there might be such an one?"

"Indeed, he is Hugues Caron. I owe him my life and liberty, and now I am told he was taken captive in my stead, and died attempting to escape, but I do not believe it."

"I am most distressed to hear it. Caron was beloved of the sage Flegetanis, a light to our way," Aletheia said. At last Telgesinus caught Aletheia's eye and it was clear he wished to speak and for a moment occupied her attention, but she delayed him.

"And so it was on the word of this shaman you came in search of Hugues Caron?" Brother John said.

Their eyes met as if she was looking into his heart to discern what he was. "Never," she said, softly, "but he did bring something to remembrance. My own father was a shaman of a northern race. He acquainted me as a child with the Anwyn, the inner one who guides my path in this world. She it was who sent me in search of Hugues Caron. She it is who watches over my way."

Aletheia sighed deeply and turned back to Brother John who patiently and transparently translated their words to each other. And Constanza turned again to making such conversation as she could with Dendrane. "They all want my attention," Aletheia said. "Some of these men are like children, and what have they done to stake a claim to manhood? They have lived luxuriously and that prepares them for what, only more luxury.

"We must give you every consideration while you are with us," Aletheia said. "This commission to ransom the Lord Herne -was this the first journey you have undertaken to the east? How can we assist you in this/"

"By no means the first, nor will it be the last."

"And all of them dangerous?" she said, laying her hand on his arm.

"There are those who would take ransom and life as well," he said. "All that prevents them is concern future ransom will not be paid."

"You have powerful patrons among the wealthy," she observed.

"The order is useful to the powerful; its emissaries expendable."

Aletheia fell silent, full of thought and then replied. "And yet the spiritual power in this is yours, not given you of another. You risk your life for the ransom of the souls and have chosen the better part of power, for 'greater love hath no man than this; that a man lay down his life for his friends.'"

Caron felt Brother John's compassion in him well up at the simple wisdom of the Abbess Aletheia. And though he relished her company, even so he felt deathly tired. "It is the great work," Caron said, wearily. "It seems unending and so much to be done to the hour of redemption.

Caron looked away to the colour and swirl of the assembled host, each caught up in his own world of cares; never the ultimate, profound stillness from which all things rise, and to which at last they must return. Unaccountably, Caron was gripped with the desire to be away from the noise, alone in the night air, utterly silent under the stars. And even as he thought it, a momentary stillness fell over the host, that unaccountable lull when everyone at the same time comes to a point of not knowing what next to say, and for a brief instant all wait on the Word.

And in that stillness Aletheia her hand upon his arm came close, and in the midst of the crowd spoke to him alone. "Sometimes a life work, takes more than a life's time. We have chosen the power of love over the love of power. How shall we fail our truth?"

The abbey hall dissolved about him. Caron's mind filled with memories of the burning time, when in Montségur Esclarmonde had spoken like words to him. She returned to now, an age suddenly contracted into a moment, and the long intervening years played out over deserts of vast eternity compressed into a single timeless moment.

Telgesinus had risen from his place to come and speak with Aletheia.

Caron must leave table. He desired neither courtly intrigue, nor posturing and positioning, or to be caught up in the machinations of the powerful as they positioned for influence, and with a glance Aletheia knew it, too.

"It has been a strenuous day," Brother John said to the Abbess. "I beg your leave for a space to take some air. I will return."

"An ancient wall hedges Hohenburg," she said, "built long before the castle itself, some say by Druids to hedge a sacred space. A path through the forests more than six miles in length encircles it.

"I would advise you not to stray too far but a short distance along brings marvelous views under moonlight of the plain of Alsace. Rest and return to us, if you will, for in honour of the day, those who stand with me, shall this night keep vigil in the Chapel of Angels."

"Where is he going?" Telgesinus leaned hard over the abbess so that she could smell wine upon his breath.

She pressed her fingers against his breast and pushed him away to arm's length. "I beg your pardon," she said correctly, "to whom are you referring?"

He sat beside her in the empty chair, and suddenly aware of Constanza turned abruptly to her. "Who are you?" he asked admiration in his voice. Constanza tipped her head quizzically.

"The Lady Constanza is of the Lady Madelon's party, come before her with the poet Perrin and Lady Siduri," Aletheia said. "She is a guest from afar, and does not speak your tongue."

Telgesinus allowed himself an approving glance. "Very well then, listen," he said, turning back to Aletheia. "This Mathurian is not who he seems; I have reason to believe him none other than the recreant, Hugues Caron." He waited for the accusation to register, but Aletheia stared at him blankly. "Your mistress, the Lady Madelon – how can I put this delicately – has put a bounty on him."

"She would John of Oxford, dead?"

"I have seen through him. He is Caron, a dangerous necromancer, known to have raised the spectral hunt of the dead, and threatened the lives and virtue of any number of maidens gathered here this night."

"They have spoken to me of it, and all of the opinion what happened that night falls to Squin." She nodded a little way off toward Madelon's creature, who appeared upset at Perrin's attentions to Siduri.

"The Lady Madelon says it was Caron," Telgesinus bit back, as if that was the end of it.

"Have a care that you do not accuse before the Bishop of Strasbourg a Mathurian of black magic," Aletheia countered. "The Trinitarians are under the protection of every great lord in Christendom, and whoever fears one day he may need its services. So doing you will open yourself to scrutiny of powers uncommon and expose us all."

"You are right, of course," Telgesinus said, moderating. He had come on too strong but was, none-the-less, determined. "Is there a place I can go to be apart" He glanced again toward Constanza in conversation with the Lady Dendrane. "I must needs quiet myself and take the measure of my passion in this. It has been an unusual day, and I fear I am overwrought."

"On the terrace are two small chapels. The Chapel of Tears on the very spot where Sainte Odile's sight was restored would, I suspect, suit your purpose."

"Where is the friar gone?"

"A walk along the Pagan Wall; he will return presently. And Telgesinus," she said, as he turned to go, "if what you say is true, and this one at our table is who you say he is, you had better be very careful. For all I have heard and seen this day suggest his powers far outmatch your own."

Telgesinus abhorred being diminished, especially in the eyes of women. He frowned disapproval at her words and went brusquely, with a snap of the fingers summoning the handmaiden who attended him; then went in search of the Chapel of Tears. Aletheia shook her head, allowed a hint of a smile as she watched him go, and then turned her attention to Constanza who chilled visibly at Telgesinus' presence.

"He is of the Lady Madelon's inner circle."

"I've known the like, and not liked what I've known."

"Then we shall be sure to keep you out of his way."

28

Shadow and Substance

Caron walked briskly the first half hour, following a moon bright track along the inside perimeter of the guardian wall. He was expecting trouble, it was in the air. And it was time to move on, if for now the path led inevitably back to the Abbey. Knowing he was followed, he stopped at a prospect point looking east. Under a haunting moon the landscape opened below, mile after mile toward the shining Rhine and spires of Strasbourg Cathedral. He watched shadows rise and fall fleeing across the silent land, stilling himself for what must come. Then he heard the cracking of fallen branches on the trail behind him; they were moving quickly now unafraid of being heard.

Caron took the little white stone from the beneath his cloak, seed of memory of who and what he was, borne across an eternity of wilderness and time to this moment. Here he must face the last of what was hidden in the darkness, and rise to all that he was and ever would be.

There were three of them and Telgesinus. He felt the spear master's pointed probe for weakness in him. He felt him seek to take possession of any reaction he could provoke. And gathering such strength as he might from his rationalizations, he'd sent his agents of fear to impale and thrust home his will.

It was not that which concerned him but the aftermath when he returned, as he must, to the abbey. He had defeated the likes of these before, and those who came now but shadows of all that bedeviled him. Caron closed his hand firmly about the little white stone and let its cool certainty pervade him.

Unarmed, Caron was cornered at prospect point. There he stood and watched his assassins come out of the dark wood into the uncertain moonlight, the two dark cloaks that plagued Falconieri's caravan, and then a third. Squin, shrouded with intent, came for Telgesinus who conjured in some place apart to shape Caron's death. Gusts of wind rocked the trees, the sky darkened with broken clouds across the moon, and the forest floor crawled serpents among the roots with undulating shadows. But the dark cloaks hesitated as if unsure of what they were about, restrained for the moment by Squin who must have his say.

Even in the midst of a whirlwind of knives there is a place apart; a place from whence every detail is apprehended in a moment. A ship in storm at sea, a hundred things that must be done, the master seaman is at rest to oversee every act fit to every other in the poise and perfection of the moment. And riding that storm of fear and hate that gathered to him, Squin advanced within two spear lengths and held, for Caron wavered not at all.

"I will teach you how to die," Squin said. Morgon Kara blazed up in the creature's eyes, for but in body Squin was no more. "Did you think I was done with you, Caron," Morgon Kara pressed.

"Go back to your realm of shadows shaman, and lady of illusions," Caron said. "We are well beyond this."

With a feint of his spear Squin took one step more forward and froze in place. Caron did not move. "Still the fool Caron," Morgon Kara said: "forever blind to weakness, fault and failure." The glow intensified about Caron and thrust Squin back a step. "What you think you are - that is illusion." Caron felt the tendrils of Telgesinus art mingling with Morgon Kara's power seeking him out; looking for a hold in the shadows of the hidden self. And as he did one of the dark cloaks, now more assured of their part, came closer, daggers drawn to assault the hedge of light, and Caron felt the prick of the spear probing to penetrate:

"Is the world better for your life?"

"Have you not failed those closest to you?"

"Might you not pass in a moment forgotten?"

"Think you by what you do you serve man?"

"There is no redeeming the human race," Morgon Kara thrust. "Drag them from their trough, give them occasion to rise up, turn your back and like pigs they return to their filth, indulging all the more.

"You believe you have done nobly, overcome wickedness, and vested your life in a greater world to come. But here you are, diminished and alone, conning the part of an itinerant monk on the road to nowhere.

"Tell me there is no truth in what I have said," Morgon Kara demanded.

"You see through a glass darkly," Caron said.

The first shadow drew close and stood at his side, and the second standing just off came forward to join him. Mingled with Telgesinus the shaman's power intensified in Squin. Now the spear tip glowed and again Caron felt the prick of it but it could not yet penetrate.

"And for all your service, Caron, for your very life's blood, has the earth in any wise risen to meet you? No, every step is but another stumbling block to defeat your way.

"And what of those you loved? Flegetanis is dead and you to blame for his death. It was to save your worthless life he gave his own. Savor the irony of that in him you thought defeated returned, and that they who as you once loved your master turn against you. It is too delicious.

"And the woman to stand at your side, share your burdens and open a world to you; though you have crossed the miles and it may be the centuries, where is she?

"No, they flee from you, Caron. They yield nothing of their influence and instead gather to me; yes, even Siduri whom once you loved yields to my purpose and has delivered the stone of sovereignty into my hand."

The second shadow stood now aside Squin and in the force of Morgon Kara and together they advanced, the spear penetrating the hedge until it came close upon Caron's heart. And still he stood and said nothing.

"What, no reply? No fear of body's hurt, Caron. I know you have the gift to renew yourself like the eagle, but flesh is not indestructible, and your body can be slain. You know in the way I might have slain you long ago, but kept your life under my hand to greater use. Together we might have accomplished wonders. It should not have come to this moment where I care nothing for you and all that remains is death."

And still Caron answered Morgon Kara not a word. The effort to subvert the man and play to the fear of nothingness touched him not at all. But Caron felt the body's natural fear and assured his heart that in the one who dwells nothing is left out of the kingdom of care, and would not be left comfortless.

"Nothing to say Caron?"

At the point of Telgesinus' spear Caron glimpsed the fate of hapless master, fallen to Morgon Kara's arts. Squin was expendable. It was the Master Telgesinus the shaman had chosen. He saw where the force of the hidden thrust would come, where spear and dagger would attempt to breech the hedge of life about him. And as Morgon Kara's power peaked the moment came to pass.

Caron took the little stone and raised it between his fingertips. "I will not strive with shadows, or play mirror to your soul." Morgon Kara drew back but did not retreat.

"Let all that you have said resolve in the light of the wonderful one.

"Let all those burdens you would impose on the lives of others return upon you.

"And where you have hidden in darkness, let there be light."

For an instant the little stone kindled like a sun. Any watching from the battlements of Hohenburg Abbey would have seen in darkest night a sun break through the firmament of heaven, and in a moment gone.

It was enough and all that was needed. In the place where Sainte Odile had regained her sight, Telgesinus grasped hands to eyes and screamed like an animal pierced. As a man awakened by night terrors, shadows breaking into mind and filling the body with pain and fear, Telgesinus fell to the floor, knees pressed to his chest and cowered in the corner of the Chapel of Tears, sobbing. For days thereafter he was kept in hospital, passing in and out of consciousness, beset by fears, blind, and fearful of sleep, until exhaustion overcame him. After many days he returned to a semblance of himself, to the concerns of Lady Madelon, who arriving in the aftermath awaited his account.

For on that night on the prospect point of Mount St. Odile, Squin and the two black cloaks went mad. Driven by illusion, blindly they charged at Caron, slashing, thrusting, plunging aimlessly where they thought him to have been; by slaying him, thinking to overcome what possessed them. Two of the number slew the third before turning on each other. In the ensuing battle at cliff's edge, where he thought to have backed Caron, the last black cloak fell to his death.

That left Squin, thrusting wildly with his spear, striking out at imagined enemies. Blind to the direction from which the threat might come, yet driven by some instinct beyond him, Squin centered on and charged Caron. A spear length off his target, the rush of an arrow crossed Caron's shoulder and pierced Squin above the heart. Yet upheld by force beyond his life, like a dying animal on reflex alone, he rushed the wood toward the archer; stumbling over a fallen tree, impaling him upon the spear point of a broken branch.

Bow in hand a cloaked woman came out of the wood, and stood over Squin. "Did you think I was done with you?" Constanza asked. Beyond any mortal aid Squin writhed in agony but a moment, and with a final roar of rage at being again denied, Morgon Kara fierce in his eyes, Squin mercifully died.

Under the tender ministrations of the sisters of Sainte Odile Telgesinus returned to himself, diligent and obsessed about what he must do. When she arrived, he confessed to Magda in strictest confidence what had befallen him. He confessed he underestimated Caron, who had greatly grown in power. They must at once master the irresistible powers of the stone of sovereignty or be overcome.

Of Aletheia Magda could learn nothing. She confessed ignorance of the events that troubled Telgesinus and gratitude only that the Abbey of Sainte-Odile with its many blessings was soon able to return him to health. As for the monk, whose performance as Elijah and presence at the banquet had so disturbed Telgesinus, he was gone a journey home to Holy Isle with his charge, Robert Herne. Questioned, neither Perrin nor Siduri showed the slightest inclination to believe that the monk in question was Caron; indeed, the suggestion was ridiculous.

In the end Magda concluded Telgesinus was involved in the shaping of some pattern that collapsed upon him and with it came consequences. She could learn little more than that of the two handmaidens who attended Telgesinus, for they were barely conscious of his art and were little more than a supportive presence. These were unhurt, but swooned and spoke of being overwhelmed, as if upon the shore of a sea overtaken by a wave and dashed upon the sands.

As for the dead Berbers, Telgesinus argued these were commissioned only to follow and report. He had not ordered these, he said, under Squin's direction, to set upon Caron. Squin had overstepped his mark. Even so, in the matter of Squin's death Magda was inconsolable. She swore the friar, whoever he was, should be tracked down and pay with his life.

The situation was altogether embarrassing; and it was convenient for the Bishop of Strasbourg to believe these same Berbers had fallen upon one another. It was, after all, the nature of the desert tribes to put oneself before one's brothers, one's brothers before one's cousins, one's cousins before one's clan, one's clan before one's tribe and the tribe against all strangers, but always first to seek one's own. Who knows what dispute may have arisen between them? The only explanation given the wounds was that they had fallen on each other and come to no good end. Still, fevered as it was, she heeded Telgesinus' warning.

But on that fateful night, Caron returned from his walk about the precincts of Sainte Odile, in the company of the Lady Constanza. And at peace with all that transpired together they attended Compline. The Bishop of Strasbourg and guests secular, for the labour of their journey, quantity of drink, and lateness of the hour, opted for the celebration of their beds. Nevertheless, the Abbess Aletheia chose to fulfill the midsummer's eve with a simple gathering, a half hour of antiphonal plain song, a meditation on psalm 90… *a thousand years in thy sight are but as yesterday when it is past, and as a watch in the night…* followed by a simple hymn *Ut queant laxis…* to John the Baptist, a brief lesson on the perfection of the present moment in the life of a day, leading into a time of silent meditation. The *Kyrie elision*, benediction, and dismissal concluded the small compline: *In manus tuas, Domine…* into thy hands, O lord… and with that the beginning of the great silence.

When it was done Caron took leave of the Lady Constanza, said farewell to Meister Eckhart, and returned to his chamber where he slept soundly, until he felt Abbess Aletheia's cool hand upon his forehead. "Peace," she whispered, "will you not rise and come with me?" She took his hand and led across the terrace toward the two small chapels in the dark, away from any torchlight or human view but in starlight so bright they cast shadows. She stopped on the balustrade before the round Chapel of Angels and turned to him.

"Flegetanis was our Master of Grail Hallows. Now that he is dead… I know who you are," she said, "if not entirely what you are. You know the Lady Madelon de Faucon is Domina of the Blood Royal. In two days she will be here to put to us the matter of our duty to her.

"To prepare her way she has sent us the poet Perrin von Grünschnabel. Once knighted, she will set him over us as Master of Grail Hallows. He is a decent man. The women delight in his fantasies and foibles but, other than a wonderful mystery to him he knows nothing of Grail hallows.

"He has told tales of your demise in defense of the Lady Constanza, and Siduri has spoken how you and her father entered into the mysteries of life and death in the Great Pyramid. It was there, she says, her father perished and only you survived, for which she still blames you.

"So, I must ask you plainly, Hugues, does Flegetanis of Alexandria yet live? For after our arts of attunement and spiritual discernment at a distance, I have searched him out and can find no trace of him."

"I believe he lives and has cloaked himself from us," Caron said. "That he has done so is his affair and what it might now mean to your order I cannot say."

She flowered to his answer and went very still. "I knew it," she whispered. The night air was moist and mystical shimmering with the intensity of stars. He could feel the feeling intensify in her; not ragged feelings but like a deep pool of pure water reflecting the radiant heavens; the kind of passion those given to torrents of emotion can never bear.

"He was your lover wasn't he?"

She nodded. "He used to say that you could see the Grail among the stars, and on the cusp of its arc the shining of the light of the central sun of suns in the universe of universes, the very Godhead. Do you think that is true?"

"He never spoke of things without but in the same breath spoke of things within," Caron said. "The stars without reveal the stars within, and in that wise I have seen... have begun to know whereof he speaks."

"I thought as much." She came closer until he could feel her warmth through the night chill. "I have tried to put my mind around it but cannot. When I look upon the night sky, sometimes it is in wonder; on others so strange to me that anything should exist at all. Where does it exist and why? And God who made it all, where does He exist and why that all this should spring from Him?

"When I think it I am like a puppy chasing its tail," she continued. "Inside out, my mind turns outside in and tells me it would be even stranger if nothing existed. Just because I cannot see past beginnings and endings, I tell myself, why should there be anything other than existence?"

"Perhaps, we must simply let it be. We might as well put that puppy in your Abbey library and expect of him to understand what is written there. The closer it gets to the tail it chases the more it slips away for trying."

"Then we cannot know."

"What you are feeling is the limits of the mind; the finite nature of thought. Yet in life we can be taken by God and become that which we have sought, and in being, know."

"Now I think I know not only who but what you are." She led him by the hand into the Chapel of the Angels. "And I must now reveal to you what we are."

The chamber was lit from floor to domed ceiling by candlelight. Caron's eye followed the blue and gold mosaic of an angelic host, apocalyptic images of angels carrying palms, burning like flames of fire; angels on horseback rising over the carnage of the earth, and transcending death and destruction. Three lancet windows in triangle shed light by day in the nave onto images of the nativity, and a centerpiece depicting Christ rising toward a roof of stars - a galaxy of whirling suns shedding radiant grace. All this came to focus at the apex of the rotunda in a window built foursquare of a balanced cross of four panels of indigo blue stained glass opening on the heavens above. No words need be spoken. It was the visual story of man in the moment of epiphany, when all the forces of creation come together at once in seed, cycle and harvest of the incarnation of the divine in the flesh.

She led him deep into the little chapel, across the circular nave until they stood in the midst the inlaid pattern of a sun-wheel. "It is for meditation," she said, "a path we must learn to walk." Nine chairs were set in an arc about a low altar at the center on which stood two lit candlesticks upon an altar cloth and nothing more. And there they sat silently waiting, facing the door through which they had come enveloped in an atmosphere of peace and quiet anticipation.

"You came to us as John of Oxford," Aletheia said. "If it pleases you to continue so, it pleases me. But in the year of the Cailleach I was present at Green Chapel. I saw you victorious return with the stone of sovereignty, and the master Flegetanis' delight in you. I saw you rise to the challenge of the Masters of Hallows, and your refusal to yield the stone to the Lady Madelon who would make herself above you, for the stone was already yielded you of the goddess of sovereignty.

"Thereafter, my Lord Flegetanis revealed to me the significance of that moment, for that very stone once in your possession long ago was yielded in just such a ceremony, and you were betrayed. And for that violation in time the stone lost to the Blood Royal. What then became of you I cannot say, but the master Flegetanis led me to believe that led to your long sojourn in the wilderness until it could be set to rights."

"You are speaking of things of another time, and those you speak of no longer live."

"What is time but the sensation of an unfolding cycle? Returning as you did to the ceremony of Green Chapel, though Flegetanis thought it untimely; you took back what was yours. But now you have given the stone to Flegetanis' daughter Siduri, and I do not understand why you have done so.

"I must tell you since you confronted the Lady Madelon she has grown powerful in her intrigues and drawn much influence to herself. When she is come to the gathering at Caer Myrddin to confirm her authority as Domina of the Blood Royal, Siduri is prepared to yield this stone to the Lady Madelon. What then will have become of your journey?"

"To come into her strength, I would have her see through Magda's intrigues."

"Intrigue is Magda's stock in trade," Aletheia said. "In the mirage world there are powerful forces at work to beguile mind and heart."

"And for that cause I gave Siduri the stone."

"I understand I do not see you wholly as you are," Aletheia said, "but I see something, as does the Master Blaise, who must yet stand in your way except you give him reason to yield. He knows you have overcome the trials set before you by the masters before him. Gisors is much diminished. Telgesinus languishes blind in the monastery below. And those that are set against your life, including Magda's favorite, Squin de Flexian, perish.

"Blaise knows you did but return upon them what they willed upon you, and yet he fears for himself. He knows you are protégé of Flegetanis whom he much admired, but unless your purpose in the truth of this exceeds his own, his duty is to the Blood Royal. As Gisors shifts shadows of sense with his mirror of the soul, Telgesinus probes and pierces with his mind-spear, Blaise will turn his sword of truth upon you to prove your righteousness."

"I expect nothing less of him."

"I do not know how much Flegetanis has revealed, or what you may have forgotten you once knew, but I will speak to you as he did to me of the purpose of the Blood Royal."

"Anything you can tell me is pure gold. For all Flegetanis has said to me of this, is that in a time of tribulation it was a contrivance of the House of Mérovée to unite in them a kingdom of secular and spiritual authority."

"In that time, yes, so far as it goes," Aletheia said, "but the Blood Royal is older by far. The way of it springs from the time of Enoch, before the great flood upon the earth. Its purpose then as now to redress the destruction of the fallen Watchers wrought upon the children of men, and set the seed for the salvation for humankind. And it was that quintessential seed Noah bore across the winter waters of the world in the husk of the ark, for the time of the spiritual regeneration of the human race."

"I know Noah was a people that fled the destruction of Atlantis," Caron said.

"There were many the world around who survived the destruction of the world that was," Aletheia said. "So vast was the devastation most thought they were sole survivors. The tale is told far and wide lest memory of the world that was be lost, but it was to Noah God entrusted the seed of salvation.

"And of that seed are the women of the blood royal, daughters of House of Atlantis. Among those chosen were priestesses in the temple of the most High God, the wonderful one who made the heavens and the earth," she said with reverent awe.

"And you are of that order that carry the seed of salvation, yet an abbess of the Church."

"The wheat and the tares grow together, lest uprooting all we spoil the harvest."

"'I am the immortal bard; I defend the true lineage until the end of time.'" A line from one of Perrin's poems," Caron said. "Does he know whereof he speaks or is it rhetoric?"

"Of Perrin I will say this: little enough he knows, and perpetual adolescent he may be, but his heart is good, which offsets his lack of wisdom."

"So this begins with the fallen Watchers that brought man to the brink of extinction."

"It is common knowledge to the daughters of the Blood Royal. It bears on their heritage and what they are given to uphold. They are told it was given the Watchers to lead man back again to the divine design and the way of the First Time. In those days they dwelled in Atlantis, for then it was a city set upon a hill, a light to the world,

"They are told among the Watchers there were those who grew impatient with progress toward the goal. It had been many thousands of years since the time of the fall, and they came to believe that without direct intervention the world would never be restored; that man would continue to seek to shape his own kingdom apart from the Kingdom of God. And it began as always with good intentions.

"Among the Watchers there were those who took counsel together concerning this, but knowing others would not agree undertook on their own a plan they devised. They determined to manipulate the patterns of the flesh of fallen man as one might select and breed cattle for a more productive breed. And to this end they determined to mingle their seed and substance with fallen man.

"Is it not written, the sons of God saw the daughters of men that they were fair and took of them all they chose? So was it also with the daughters of God and the sons of men, and of these unions came the mighty men of old but also magnifying distortions," she said, crossing herself.

"The pattern broken, all manner of atrocities followed; the flesh was twisted and transformed into creatures that should never have been. Degenerate man through perverted consciousness, shaped the abominations of the earth, and loosed these on their enemies: manticore, Minotaur, harpies, gorgons; Cerberus, Charybdis, and chimera: the mingling of birds, beasts, serpents, limbs and the body parts and broken minds of men.

"Believing the power of creation had returned, man in his wickedness magnified and the imaginations of his heart only evil continually, turned life in the flesh to madness. He tore the pages from the Book of Life, scattered them on an ill wind, and the earth suffered offenses such as never seen, for they determined they might make of life whatsoever they desired.

"On the eve of its destruction, many fled Atlantis and found sanctuary there in Egypt and Greece which bear witness and record of these chimeras. But I dare guess the record of these abominations is found throughout the earth.

"Enoch as a people remained true to the truth, kept the holy norm and the way of the Book of Life," Aletheia said. "And under his hand the sages of the *Na-Akhu-El* who did not follow their brethren into destruction, but stayed true to the wonderful one.

"And Enoch walked with God and was not, for God took him," Caron said.

"Just so," Aletheia said, gratified he understood.

"I have seen this with mine own eyes," Caron said. "It was determined Enoch should withdraw from the earth; that a remnant of the *Na-Akhu-El* should remain in the aftermath of what followed, to keep open the way of restoration."

"On the day of destruction the heavens rained flint and fire, ash and burning stone upon the earth," Aletheia said. "The fountains of the deep were loosed, and the heavens rained sweet waters upon a scarred earth. The mass of men surviving those times were become at first little more than degenerate beasts hiding in caves, venturing forth into the wasteland of the world."

"So, an end was made and a new beginning." Caron spoke gently, for she was deeply moved by the memory. "And that those seed patterns in the word of the flesh might be transferred true from generation to generation, the way of the Blood Royal was ordained to keep the way of the Tree of Life."

"And have done so to this very hour." She paused and looked to Caron in the candlelight to read if she might his response, and found only stillness in him.

"The *Na-Akhu-El* watch over you," Caron said.

"In the persons of Flegetanis and Blaise, both Masters of Hallows," she said.

Caron she thought had grown very pensive, and knew not what now to expect of this protégé of the sage Flegetanis, if not up to what she supposed.

"*Thine eyes did see my substance, yet being unperfect*," Caron said softly, remembering the psalm. "*And in thy book all my members were written, which in continuance were fashioned, when as yet there was none of them.* There is more to this than what is written in the flesh, Aletheia."

"Of course there is," she said. "*Before I formed thee in the womb I knew thee, and before thou camest forth out of the womb I sanctified thee, and I ordained thee as a prophet unto the nations.*

"I know what is written in the flesh of itself profits nothing; but what is written in the flesh that is the tabernacle of God, the vessel for the outpouring of the Holy Spirit, and in the purification of that is the salvation of the world."

"And yet you are celibate."

"I serve an Abbess to these women, but the daughters of the Blood Royal who now take sanctuary under my roof are deaconesses. We will in time find those for them in whom they may fulfill the pattern they have carried across the ages to all corners of the earth. It is with great care we seek unions that will not mar what is written in the book of life."

"And yet you among all the women I have met under your care come closest to full knowledge of what you are and exemplify that in fullness of your heart and the beauty of your being," he said. "Surely this should be passed on."

"Thank you Hugues. But you do not yet fully understand. The Lady Siduri - though she knows it not - is my daughter, fathered of the sage Flegetanis. So, now, you may more fully understand my concerns."

If Caron was dumbfounded he did not show it; something in him already knew and this but confirmation. Instead he asked, "Does the Lady Madelon know this?"

"No, and it would confound her if she did and create schism in the Blood Royal, for my daughter would take precedence over her. And so we hid her away for a time to come, when matters of greater importance yet to come shall be set to rights.

"You do understand what the stone means to the Blood Royal as well the *Na-Akhu-El*? Yes, there are essences of the First Time written therein, but also within are the seed essences of the book of life; the patterns written in the flesh of the women of the Blood Royal for the tabernacle of man and the restoration of the world.

"It was perhaps with purest instinct you entrusted it to Siduri. Now we must see what she will do. My daughter is still not free from the influences of the world, and now she will deliver the stone of sovereignty into the hands of the Lady Madelon, a woman not fit to rule. If at Caer Myrddin all hallows are yielded to her, she will have the setting to possess the stone of sovereignty, magnifying her will in the earth.

"Within the week she will come to Sainte-Odile to claim the response of the daughters of the Blood Royal who took refuge here. She blames you, of course, and I am expected to accept her explanation that you are a necromancer who raised the winds of chaos to ravish the maidens and destroy the Order.

"She knows I do not believe a word of it, but insists I must accept it. And she will require that gathering for the *Troth* at Caer Myrddin I yield to her substance and influence of the Grail Hallow, and agree to her investiture as Domina of the Blood Royal.

"When she is come to Caer Myrddin she must walk the path of the Sonnenrad to demonstrate her mastery of the forces. There she will have Siduri place the stone of sovereignty at the center of the sun-wheel to draw all the forces and influences to her focus. Thereafter she will magnify them in a way no Domina of the order has had occasion so long as memory serves.

"As others have failed her, she will place the burden on me to guarantee I will give her everything she asks and more in her support. And yet it is my obligation to uphold the integrity of the Order; it is upon me to know to whom I should yield our response."

"I did not come seeking the response of the Blood Royal," Caron said, "but for the healing of a friend."

"You need the response of the Hallows Maidens," Aletheia said. "But for me to yield it you, I must know your intentions toward us; I must know you are who I think you are."

29

Chapel of Angels

Out of the night across the threshold of the nave came the procession of maidens. One by one Caron watched them enter out of the darkness of centuries into the soft light of the Chapel of Angels. Each maiden, modest in bearing, wore a coronal of flowers in her hair: an alluring image of feminine beauty, in this moment turned away from the cares of the world, to an inward grace infusing them with light and sweet influence.

Each in one hand carried a small lantern to light the way, and in the other a budded rose; but for the last who entered the Chapel of Angels bearing in folded hands a chalice. As the others filled out the arc about the central dais she came forward, knelt and placed the chalice filled with rose petals upon the altar. And when the image of the Grail was set, each maiden came forward with her rose - white through all the shades of pink and red, from pale yellow to orange and yellow gold - and one by one placed them on the altar. So doing the vessel began to glow until its light filled the Chapel of Angels with a lustrous cloud of glory.

"These are of they in whom the words of the Book of Life are written,"

Aletheia said. "In them are the essences of the spiritual flesh, which did not yield to corruption, come down from the First Time."

Caron felt a kind of shyness at being so enveloped with refined, feminine substance, a stark contrast to how he had been greeted in the way. In their presence he felt the anguish of the miles and brittleness of the flesh yield; his body lustrous evanesce like incense. They released him. It was all together alluring, compelling heart's ease, but he'd come to engage their purpose here, and so one by one he took the eyes of each in the arc about the altar. Some he knew: the ladies Yvonne, Brigit, Elaine, Dendrane, Igerna; others he recognized from the gathering in Green Chapel and his ministrations at Waldheim. None he supposed would know him, but curiosity was in the air and resolve had taken Aletheia. If what was to be done was to be done it was here and now, tonight.

"Brother John is likewise the old healer who came to you at Waldheim," she said, slowly with ritual in her voice. "Many of you have reason to be grateful to him. Skilled as he is in the healing arts, is he in the art of shape shifting, and comes to us now a Mathurian monk. Why, he may be Flegetanis himself might he not?" she said, to a hint of pleasant laughter in the winsome air that filled the Chapel of Angels.

"Is there one among you in purity of heart, blessed with that gift to look beyond appearances, to look upon the heart, to say who it is that has come to us."

There was silence as all eyes turned shyly upon him. He could see guesses on their lips, and still no one spoke until Dendrane ventured. "It is Hugues Caron," she said, hesitating, feeling that wasn't enough, "more than a name, more than he was."

"Yes, for those names we give do but touch the surface of what is, as the vessel you see before you on the altar but bears witness to the light."

Aletheia looked reverently about the chapel before her eyes lighted and dwelled on the company of maidens. "Can this hallow now bear his presence in the world," Aletheia asked. Shall we ask him to show us who he truly is? If you are who I think you are, you will understand this," she said, turning to Caron.

"What you ask is not mine to give," Caron replied. "Love commands. Not commanded, its transforming grace is the gift of the wonderful one." She lowered her head at his words, acknowledging but also wondering.

"Such as I have to give, I shall." Caron took the little pouch from his breast and the white stone that was his to focus in heart and mind and body, the light of divine identity that was his to give. "This vessel set upon the altar serves to bear witness to the one true Grail," Caron said. He came to the altar, all eyes upon him; small white stone in the palm of his hand. "Answer this true, and I will give what I am given to give. Whom does the one true Grail serve?"

"That the tabernacle of God should be with men," Aletheia said, "flesh is given to bear witness to the light.

"And the heart, which is the grail on the altar of life, is given to serve the wonderful one, Lord of Heaven and Earth."

"Then the Lord is in His holy temple." Caron placed the little stone on the bed of rose petals within the vessel. "Let all the earth keep silence before Him."

At once the glow about the vessel intensified and Caron felt magnified in the current of power that emanated from him. It was evident at once in the arc of maidens, enfolded in effulgence that melded all distinctions in one golden glow. The light intensified in a lustrous bloom of radiance that beguiled sight then focused before the altar in shape of a cloven flame, as if a gateway through which one might pass if drawn. But no one moved for the force that radiated from it, until gradually it tempered intensity and finally faded away leaving a still, silent chapel in candlelight.

"Do you now understand what we are," Aletheia said: "the sweet influences given for the union of the worlds?

"These gathered to me in the light bear witness to the Book of Life, the divine design incarnate in the flesh of the world.

"Do you understand why you have need of us, to let the Word be made flesh?"

"All this was written in a world on the brink of destruction, in the day in which Enoch ascended," Caron said. "The way of the First Time is even now ingrained in the stone of sovereignty.

"You know then what the stone, whose setting is the Gail Hallows, means to us."

"A window opened in heaven, a gateway of the worlds; yes I understand, but there is more to it."

"Then you know what you must do. Those who master the stone of sovereignty may let wonders form. Open the way that the king of Glory might come in unto us, for we have come thus far before but can go no further."

Caron looked into Aletheia's eyes and saw a soul, trembling on the brink, filled with anticipation but afraid that it might not be so. "Show us you understand," she insisted. "Open the door of the worlds."

Caron rose lightly. "It is not yours to command," he said, in a voice above a whisper. "I will not, Aletheia, perform at your will."

"Then how shall we know you are who you say you are? How shall we let go and yield to you?"

"Do as you will. I make no claim of who I am."

"At Caer Myrddin I must choose between you and the Lady Madelon. I must understand the choice I am making."

"How can you know before? When the moment is come, you will know what is to be done."

Aletheia would protest the more but could find no words. Caron took his leave passing slowly but surely through the circle of maidens toward the chapel door then at the last, standing framed a moment in the light of the opening he looked back toward the altar and Aletheia.

"You must understand," she said, "that if you are not what I think you are, I must give all this to upholding the Lady Madelon come into her power. And she will surely give it to whomever she will."

"I understand you will do what you must do."

Aletheia let go. She picked a long stemmed budded rose from the altar, and came to Caron on the threshold of the soft chapel light and the night without. All the daughters of the Blood Royal turned to Aletheia as she gave Caron a white budded rose.

Taking it he was pricked by a thorn, and a drop of blood fell on the white petals. Even so, he folded his hand gently over the bud, and it blossomed. Petal upon petal it unfolded, until the whole bloom filled his hand. And with its flowering, the vessel upon the altar glowed once more, filling the chapel with glorious effulgence and the heady scent of roses and light dissolving dusk and candlelight.

Caron returned the rose to Aletheia and the chapel filled with an air of spring, like a field of flowers in sunlight. They who were in the midst of the effulgence fell to their knees, bowed their heads and covered their faces in their laps, scarce able to look upon it. Where they had stood, to Caron and Aletheia's eyes now appeared beings of light in their place, and in the midst a man cloaked in blue flame, who spoke in a voice pleasant as summer rain.

"*Who receives me, receives Him who sent me. And in him will I loose the spirit of the wonderful one.*"

The figure vanished in the flame, the light upon the altar abated, and Aletheia turned to look to Caron but he was gone. She would after him but the maidens all had swooned, and hours of the night passed before she was able to gather all up and settle in chambers. Thereafter, she determined on the morrow to speak with Caron but in her watch in the night she began to wonder after it. Had not Magda called Caron a black mage? Had he not, perhaps, woven illusion in the sense to appear not as he is, but as he would have her see him? And so fear entered in and she knew not which way to turn, or any in whom she might seek confidence.

The time was come to travel on alone. But it was too late of a night and too early of the day to come, so Caron returned to his chamber, surrendered to the unaccustomed luxury of a feather bed, and let go to sleep. She came to him in the darkest hour of the night. He awakened to the rustle of a falling gown, and the gathering warmth of her body drawing to him beneath the eiderdown. He could taste her breath of mint and rosemary. She said nothing but traced her fingertips down the small of his back, and again along his arm to the curve of his shoulder to the nape of his neck where she paused, breathing heavily, as if waiting for words.

"Why, Constanza?" Caron asked.

"I have never lain with you and yet you know my body," she answered.

"By your presence alone I would know you. You came once to me in the burning time when there was war in the heavens, when fire rained death and white ash like snow upon the earth until the rains came."

"In such a time I came to you?"

"You led across a wasteland toward the light, and kept from me the black mage who would possess my soul."

"I was subject of a time to him," she confided, "until I knew him determined to use me to have your life, and in my heart of hearts I would have none of it."

"How is it you found me out?"

"As you know the shape and line of my body, I know the pattern of your soul."

"Then you are very skilled."

"Having but once walked in the Otherworld, I saw my arts but remnants of a greater life, lost to us. I would live to see that world restored." She felt Caron withdraw, but still his hand rested warmly upon her and then he was back.

"So also would Morgon Kara, but to a very different end."

"I saw him slain but live again to take another. Tonight I slew one possessed of him. I fear he will try again, but know not how to bring an end to it."

"He is diminished but full of intent. As you journey with the Lady Madelon de Faucon, beware the master Telgesinus, for Morgon Kara has set his mark upon him."

She drew closer and firmed her arms about him. "You delivered me from the Beast of Ulcinj, when he would have sold me into slavery."

"There is no obligation."

"Then understand I come also for Anwyn of the In-world, who watches over you. In the hour I was freed from the grasp of Morgon Kara, she touched my soul and bade me come in her name to stand with you. Willingly I do so."

"Then do this for me," Caron said. "Journey and keep faith with Siduri, for she is not herself."

"I have suffered it, this allure of the unreal; this bondage to a mirage world of dazzling reflections that never resolve but in more illusion. Despite this we have become fast friends and I have found my way past Magda's influences to make a place for myself in Siduri's heart. It irks her but there is little Magda can do. She sees me tributary to her dream of an empire of commerce that bestrides the world.

"It is not for this alone Anwyn sends me to you." Constanza matched her rhythm to his, their breath one long, slow undulating pulse. "In me you shall have what you need to restore love's body to his soul: sweet influences at love's command, to loose the bonds that bind you and free you in this world."

"I am told you cannot be taken against your will, without harm come upon him who would do you harm."

"Who told you this?"

"Few realize what they bring upon themselves who force what should be given," Caron said, "for fate comes upon them according to the deed."

"Don't play the celibate monk with me," she whispered. "For I would have you master me." She rolled over upon him propping herself with her hands atop him, bending to touch his lips, her breasts pendulant, hair cascading over his chest and shoulders. He felt the press of her thighs at his own, smoldering.

"There is no offense," she whispered at his lips. "It is the way of a man with a maid. Everything beautiful in the world comes of God."

Caron took her into his arms and turned over upon her. "And everything wicked of the forcing of things that ought not to be," he said.

"So, then, shall we leave the field to the wicked that pervert the way of life, or in those God given powers let wonders form, restore love's body to His soul?"

Caron could not answer for both were taken, lifted up and in one passion blended, like a rose to the sun, flowering in the white flame of life.

After Matins the sisters of Niedermunster Abbey made their rounds. Brother John of Oxford came down from Saint Odile to inquire after the health of the patient Telgesinus. In the abbey was a healing font of waters known in the faithful to cure defects of the eyes. It was for the proving of this, and to the glory of God, the nuns supposed, that Telgesinus affliction came to pass on Saint John's Eve, and that a miraculous healing was at hand.

"Telgesinus is at rest," the sister told him. "Soon he will begin his daily ritual of herbal remedies from the apothecary of Ottrott; the changing of dressings and a sacred washing of his eyes in the well waters of St. Odile. If you would assure the Abbess Aletheia, I see no harm in visiting to ask after him."

The nursing-sister led Caron through a warren of passages to a scrupulously clean but darkened cell, where Telgesinus was abed but in light slumber only. Caron watched until Telgesinus roused to his presence. He said nothing at first, but after an enduring minute Telgesinus rolled over, and trying to pierce the dark within and without stared toward where Caron stood. He saw nothing but struggled to take measure of his presence.

"Caron, it is you, isn't it? I knew it."

"I regret your affliction."

"You might well rejoice in it."

"I take no pleasure in the ills of others, even though you sought to slay me."

"It was to keep you from destroying so much good to the world."

"Except the Lord build the house, they labour in vain who build it."

"Spoken like a monk. You are very skilled, but trespass on Caer Myrddin, and all our forces shall be ranged against you and you alone."

"Sow the wind; reap the whirlwind."

"Full of comfortable homilies, aren't we: sometimes the monk, sometimes the prophet. You do not really know what you are or what you contend with, do you Caron?"

"I know you are taken and become *Sham-she-el*; the fallen watcher who knew the ways of the sun, until blinded by his own vain glory defiled the way of the lords of light to serve himself."

"Who told you this?" Telgesinus darkened; an inky blot in the gloom of the cell, and the darkness burned with ire but could not touch him. In a moment it abated, and Telgesinus, his breathing laboured, stared blindly at Caron through a veil of despair. "Who are you really?" he demanded: "Why have you come?"

"To offer a blessing."

"Your blessings are a curse on humankind. I will have none of it."

"Then for prophecy: You, *Sham-she-el,* thief of life, are judged and the judgment shall stand against the hour when you shall have influence no more.

"And you, Telgesinus, who are given to the deceits of the wicked, will live but pay a price in sorrows.

"You will regain your sight but not your vision. You will think you see, but what you see will ever be limited by what you do not see.

"Thinking you see, you will exalt yourself over the blind leaders of the blind, and those who follow after you, despite their good intentions, shall surely fall into the ditch.

"And so it will be until you turn again from seeking to pry, penetrate and manipulate the earth into the shapes of your obsessions.

"Ignorant of what you do, your sorrows will multiply until at last the hour is come when you yield all that in self-will you have imposed upon life, to flow freely again in the current of the river of life.

"Only when you turn to seek again the one who dwells in the light, shall these burdens be lifted from you."

"When you are come to Caer Myrddin, we shall see who is blind and who sees; who falls and who is left standing," Telgesinus countered. "We have Siduri's heart and so the stone of sovereignty, Caron, and you shall not stand against it."

"If not held by right, it will destroy the one who takes by force to possess it. As for the rest, I do not know it is worth my time to come to Caer Myrddin, for when destruction comes it shall be not of mine but your own doing."

"You shall not lift a hand against us?"

"I shall never do more than stand my ground, and let the law of creation work to perfection."

Telgesinus coiled up his wiry frame as if ready to strike Caron, then the spirit went out of him and he sat heavily on the side of his cot, grasping for breath. "You could have had everything, Caron. Now you have nothing remaining, but to die stranded lonely on some strange shore, your life meaningless.

"Cursed be the ground upon which you stand. Curse you, Caron, for the damage you have done our cause. Curse you for it is the likes of you would condemn the world for its failings, when you should serve to shape it to prosperity and peace."

"It is what you do not see that thwarts your best intentions," Caron said. "I leave you to your darkness."

Falconieri sat alone by his morning fire drinking a hot, black liquid from an earthen cup, when Caron came to the caravan. "Qahwah," Caron said, accepting a cup. "I had not thought to find it here."

"The Turks call it kahve. I developed a taste for it in…I do not remember, but it is rare here," Falconieri caught himself, "apparently not unfamiliar to you."

"I was long in Egypt, and an old friend," he paused as memories of Flegetanis flooded his senses, "with an old friend, I used to share this drink. He traded for it in Ethiopia."

"A man might do well for himself to import this beverage to Venice and serve it with some confection." Falconieri said. "Perhaps, when this journey is done, I'll look up your old friend."

There was no stirring in the camp; a traveling troupe was under no obligation to attend Matins and most preferred to linger in each other's arms, but Falconieri did not appear to have slept at all that night.

"I'm leaving this morning," Caron said. "Perhaps we shall meet again."

"I am commanded to collaborate with Perrin to write a pageant of investiture for a noble patron, to be presented in ceremony some months hence in England," Falconieri said, with a flourish of his cup. "Shall we see you there, for you seem woven into this human comedy?"

"I am bound for England, and for the sake of one who has journeyed with me in the way, the Holy Isle of Lindisfarne."

"And when that is accomplished, Brother John you shall be no more," Falconieri said. "No, you need not deny it, for though you are as fine a master of the art as I have seen, another poor player like myself may glimpse through the veil you draw about yourself.

"You have enemies as well as friends among those gathered here. Last night you near gave yourself away, and would have had I not at the last released those fire flowers into the night sky."

"For which I am most grateful Signor Falconieri," Caron said, "but it was you cast me in your drama, which was as favor to you."

"You endangered yourself because of me. I shall make it up to you. Why not travel with us to England? Beyond this place we have, I think, much to share and now alone without those black cloaks croaking over us."

"I would not come too close to the poet Perrin."

"He has a gift, untutored, undisciplined, adolescent and often self-serving, but a gift, none-the-less," Falconieri said. "Where he thinks he leads we shall bring him on by degrees. Even so, I do not think we shall see much of him. The Lady Madelon de Faucon has ambitions for him."

"There is something of the hurt child yet; deal kindly with him."

"If you will not journey with us, what shall we do to ease you on your way?"

"With two I came to Sainte Odile; the one blinded by the Bishop of Ransbach's creature, the other returning from captivity in Islam. Let them journey with you, for I would turn aside and take the Rhine to the sea."

Caron reached beneath his cloak and palmed three small rubies. "It is too much," Falconieri said, turning his hand away. "I will do it for friendship."

"You do, but shall also have these," Caron said. "These will fetch a price, one for yourself; the others to keep your charges in the way until Sir Robert Hode can come again home to England.

"You must tell them for me that what I must do, I must do alone; that when I am done I will seek them out and make amends for abandoning them so."

"They shall do well with me," Falconieri said. "With a light heart, we shall make our way merry together."

"I would myself look forward to that." Caron took up his staff and made ready.

"And in England," Falconieri said, "shall I ever meet Brother John again?"

"As you say you have yet to meet me."

"So, then, when this masquerade of souls is done, I know we shall be well met, you and I."

As Caron took to the road he chanced once more to meet with Meister Eckhart on his way again to the village apothecary and congregation of the Free Spirit. They talked a few moments, Eckhart embracing one of kindred spirit. And when they parted it was with these words.

"Brother John, a word of advice, my friend, if I may be so bold to quote scripture: *It is not flesh and blood with which we wrestle, but the rulers of the darkness of this world… with spiritual wickedness in high places.*

"Believe me, I know whereof I speak. Be you ever so alone; never forget one with God is a majority."

30

Chapel of Tears

"You let him slip away?"

The Lady Madelon assembled her acolytes in the Chapel of Tears. Her Masters of Hallows Blaise along with Gisors and Telgesinus - both still convalescing - and the Abbess Aletheia of Lotharinga gathered to her. Over Telgesinus' injuries and Squin's death she would not be consoled. But knowing she must at once fulfill the pattern of the four powers she would command, she determined to make the poet Perrin von Grünschnabel her master of Grail Hallows. And so he, too, totally out of his depth, came among them. She was in a rage but dare not show it lest it betray weakness. Of all things now they needed to feel she was in control, but in her heart of hearts she knew she was challenged and overmatched.

"You could not prevent him."

"All three we sent to detain him slain," Telgesinus said. "And me he blinded by deflecting the pattern I wrought and turning it full force upon me."

"And you are sure it was Caron?"

"I have known only one other, Flegetanis of Alexandria, to possess such powers."

Magda turned to the pensive poet. "What think you Perrin, does Hugues Caron live?"

"This friar has been in the east many years; perhaps he has acquired skills of his own for use when threatened."

"And did you threaten him, Telgesinus?"

"It is possible he felt threatened. What Perrin says may be the truth of it." He did not then feel it prudent to reveal his final moments with Caron in the infirmary. There is power in knowledge and that warning was for Magda's ear alone.

"To have stood up to a Master of Hallows, reflecting and magnifying his own powers back upon him, is not the work of a dilettante but a master shaper in the use of the vibratory forces. Such an one foiled you as well Gisors."

"And near cost my life."

"We will not forget that when these matters come to reckoning. Whoever he is, he intrudes upon our business and the pattern we are shaping. Should he dare do so again, together we shall overcome him, by force of agreement within the arc of the Sonnenrad.

"And you, Master Blaise, where were you when Telgesinus was in need of you?"

"Unaware of his need, for he spoke nothing of this matter to me."

"I felt I must keep my speculations to myself… until I could confirm them," Telgesinus whinged. "I did speak with the Abbess Aletheia who doubted my word in this."

"Would you have me harass and attempt to slay a Mathurian monk, guest of our abbey, in the presence of the Meister Eckhart and the Lord Bishop of Strasbourg?"

"I do protest."

"Your arts are your business," Aletheia said, "but the three corpses you left in your wake became mine, and I must persuade Birkenfells these three fell in a drunken brawl and put upon each other to the death."

"Quite rightly and well done," Magda said. "We shall need your cool head and loyal heart in the days to come. I would have you tutor our servant Perrin in our ways," she said with a nod to the poet. "He shall mature under your guidance into an understanding of what it means to keep the force and way of the Grail Hallows. And I will expect you to accompany us in the remainder of our journey, until we are come to Caer Myrddin where your arts will be needed in what we shall do."

With Maia come full upon her, the Lady Madelon was taking charge and she very much liked the feel of it, for the one who guided was accustomed to command and very much mistress of those influences she wielded. Magda prided herself she was become increasingly a powerful, an attractive woman before whom men trembled with desire; she who must be obeyed in return for whatever favors she might bestow, be it no more than her smile of pleasure in them.

"But tell me of this pageant," she said, lightening the mood, with deference to Perrin.

"A pageant for the longest day of the year," Perrin said, more in his element, "a celebration of Saint John's Eve, scripted by myself and Andreas Falconieri to the occasion."

"And this was the eve when you were smitten with blindness, mine own Telgesinus," Magda said, tenderly.

"It was a most extraordinary event. This same Mathurian played the part of the prophet Elijah challenging the priesthood of Baal. And I swear even as Elijah did, this one loosed fire from the heavens."

"Fire flowers," Perrin said. "You have seen them in Venice, milady, imported from the east. Falconieri had some in his possession to dramatize the moment."

"It was more was it not Blaise?"

"A skilled illusion, to have so beguiled us he must have entered into the minds of all present, mine own included.

"Why did you choose for Saint John's Eve a play of the Contest on Mount Carmel? What relevance to this abbey; what relevance to us?"

"Falconieri believes we must have material relevant to our faith, and I agreed," Perrin said.

"They who dwell here are models of continence and modesty in their needs," Magda said with a nod to Aletheia. "Do you not think it rather maligns us, that those upon this mount are by insinuation prophets of Baal, a pagan god of wealth and fertility? I think you, Master Telgesinus, were shocked in the portrayal? You thought it inappropriate for this time and place." He nodded assent. "And you, Master Blaise, what of you?"

Blaise shrugged it off. "A play is a play, but this a revelation I would not have missed."

"Abbess Aletheia?"

"I took it those gathered to the prophet were like unto the Children of Israel, drawn to turn their hearts back again. I saw it as an assertion of faith in the power of the Almighty, when his prophet appears but one against many."

"It might have been done in many ways, and that point made. Do you see a deeper meaning in this choice of drama, Perrin?"

"Falconieri would not have thought thus deeply," Perrin said. "We joked only that the play seemed appropriate to Saint John's Eve as a reminder in difficult circumstance to keep one's head on one's shoulders."

Aletheia laughed in spite of herself.

"What I am asking is whether this Mathurian monk had anything to do with the selection of the theme," Magda pressed, "and if so what he intended?" None dare say she was obsessed with the subject, but clearly the presentation troubled her, and she would root it out.

"Falconieri told me they journeyed together some days and that he had a hand in coaching his actors in the ways of the desert fathers," Perrin said. "Taking the part of Elijah was late necessity; his principal took to drink earlier in the day, and he persuaded this reluctant monk to take the part."

"I must speak with Falconieri."

"He has gone a week before us. He has business in Paris but will cross over and join us at Caer Myrddin."

"I will have no more of this." She flared up suddenly and Perrin shrank from contact with the red heat that radiated from her wrath, for she was a moment full of it and the next again calm, but all took note. "I have had enough of this subversion of our purpose," she said, calmly. "Too much these artists think themselves a lamp to light our way; nay, a force to shape our paths. We shall have them rather mirror *our* ways, celebrate *our* victories; make display of *our* glories to shape the public weal to *our* purpose.

"Their minds are too much a tangle. Too much are we caught up in those narratives they contrive to shape our lives, as if the fashion of the day to clothe us in their whims. Falconieri has done this to us from the beginning, with his lampooning of the offices of Venice, his manipulation of the ways of love, and now insinuating my servant Squin the weak king Ahab and me his corrupt queen Jezebel for the entertainment of the abbey."

"It was not intended."

"My dear Perrin, the poet of true lineage is not yet awake in you to see beyond these fictions contrived to define and confine our lives."

"Milady," Aletheia said, looking to still the waters, "this play of wonders was framed precisely to the biblical testament to a matter that occurred long ago."

"And has what relevance to us now," Magda snapped.

"A timely reminder, that the Lord, He is God."

But Magda didn't hear. As a dog scents a trail, she was after the fox of a thought that troubled her. "Why must we interpret everything in our lives by the dictates of the Bible? Is it not time for us to make our own way forward. Must we be constrained by visions engrained in us by events thousands of years past, by desert shepherds who know nothing of the world we live in now?

"What do we leave out by letting these stories guide us? Rather, let us take up matters fresh and bring to bear the resources of our own hearts and minds upon them."

She paused feeling she had gone too far then defiant looked about her to see what agreement she had. Telgesinus was all smiles. These were his thoughts. He would hold the world at spear point, until it gave up its secrets. Gisors smiled wanly caught up in his age, knowing this was a world he would never live in. Blaise was impassive. She could never read him. Perrin was bemused, wondering what abandoning the frame of the world might mean to him, seeking metaphors for poetry, and she took his bemusement for agreement. Perrin was working out. He would make a talented and compliant master of Hallows. All this was rather as she expected. Only the Abbess Aletheia when Magda turned to register her response took her by surprise.

"There are few stories worth telling. Those that are speak to the kind of things that happen, again and again; each retelling to whatever fashion of the time, an incarnation of enduring patterns and values. Must we not merely read deeper and take the meaning we have missed or determined not to acknowledge?

"From most ancient times these are the story of man. The best of them hold up a mirror and then a lamp to guide us through the dark and devious ways of men to identity in God. And that is why we read the Bible," she said firmly, brooking no resistance even from the Lady Madelon.

"Because within that story from first to last of days," she continued, "every permutation of creation, of human nature, and its resolution is found. If I did not know it was so, I should not be Abbess of Sainte Odile but follow mammon to seek wealth and power to build a kingdom of influence for however long the Lord God suffered it to endure."

It was an utter rebuke but Magda could not refute without undermining the very foundations of her own order as Domina of the Blood Royal, whose own story was intimately entwined with the destiny of man on his redemptive journey.

"I take your point," Magda demurred, "but I have had my fill of these dramas contrived by poets and peasants to ensnare their betters. You, Perrin, be sure that whatever Falconieri plots for the *Troth* at Caer Myrddin in no wise is critical or instructive in our power. I want a pageant of music and poetry, and if he resorts to spectacle let it celebrate who and what we are."

When they were gone into the night Magda remained alone in the flickering candlelight in the Chapel of Tears to chase down that fox of a thought that so disturbed her. She was sure the drama of Elijah and the priests of Baal were meant to depict her efforts to draw together a kingdom of influence; that she was cast as the wicked queen Jezebel. Who was setting her up for a fall? Who were they mocking her? She was sure they were playing her out, believing she was not wise to their sedition, and their chosen moment to challenge her authority would be the gathering at Caer Myrddin. Were the temporal lords behind this, perhaps even Blaise? But Telgesinus was loyal and worked with her. He confided to her alone his assurance it was Caron who came in the part of Elijah to challenge the corrupt queen and the insane king who troubled Israel.

But they were greatly mistaken in her. She was more than they understood. Beyond the façade of days, she was Maia who would guide her in the way. And she who stood with Maia, Irkala of the Shades, who better understood the ways of those who wrought secrets in darkness, and could give her power over those who conspired against her?

On the pavement of both chapels some ancient art wrought the seal of the House of Mérovée, the Sonnenrad, though she doubted here it had ever been used for the cause she was about to put it. On her path to the *Troth*, in the trefoil temple of Malta, she crossed a threshold into a realm of influence much desired to empower her designs. And so Magda made no protest when Maia came conjoined with the presence of Irkala.

Under Maia's hand she turned to the black sun in the midst of the Sonnenrad and set there a glowing candle. Undulating like a silk veil in a whisper of wind, its flame glorified until the chapel filled with its glow. Knowing what she must do, she walked purposefully to the periphery of the arc of the sun-wheel, and junction of the forces of fire and water. Hesitating not a moment, her eyes fixed upon the flame of the dark sun, taking the left hand path she stepped into the arc of fire.

Irkala awaited her coming. She was no more Magda but Maia, and no more in the Chapel of Tears but the Temple of Irkala, within the circle of the great seal that shut up the powers of the Deep. And Irkala did not stand on ceremony. "If you are prepared to walk our path we have in you an altar in the earth to magnify our powers," she said. "Through you we may open the Vault of the Ages, to loose those powers so long constrained, binding hearts and minds together in our cause."

"The Aton-Re is jealous for his power," Maia said. "What is wrought must meet his expectations."

"Vast powers at my hand answer to me, for I am given to bind and loose what is wrought in this realm."

"Those powers here confined are bound by forces neither you nor I command."

"And the key to unlock their confinement is the stone of sovereignty come into Magda's hands. When it shall come into Magda's hands, it is in our hands. When she possesses it wholly, in us she possesses the world."

In gesture Maia opened her hands aglow with light, for even now its influence was felt as presence.

"If you would change the world, resolve the issues that beguile man, we must have an altar in the earth. No power is loosed but through focus in the realm where it is needful. If we would loose those powers to inform your kingdom, we must raise an altar at threshold of the worlds.

"And you, my dear, are that altar," she said, speaking through Maia so the sense of it rose from the deep of Magda's heart, and found in her affirmation.

"You shall speak to me, not past me," Maia demurred.

"Very well," Irkala agreed. "Do not fear it. We are elemental, and cannot take what is another's. I have no power to take your influences to myself except you yield to me; nor you to draw upon my powers except I yield them you. My interests are one with your own. I would release what is bound in the Vault of the Ages into the world, but we must have a presence at the threshold of the worlds to loose the power of the stone."

"And when this altar is raised in Magda?"

"Those confined shall be loosed to seek out those who will accommodate them, choosing from among them as they will. The Lord *Sham-she-el* shall lead in this: possessed of more liberty than those bound here an age, he has found one in the Master Telgesinus, willing to serve the purposes of the Lady Madelon, your purposes. And he will come into the fullness of his power as she does her own.

"And I have likewise found one worth to accommodate me. Together we shall be free from this cruel bondage, loosing the force and majesty of our realms in creativity, prosperity and power in the earth. Oh fear nothing," Irkala insisted, "you will lose nothing of your influence in the way of it. I am sure when you have tasted the delights of the fires of creation here confined; you will wonder that you were ever troubled over this."

"Then we agree," Maia said. She held out her hand and, as if pouring from a cup of fire, the contents into Irkala's hands; these she closed firmly about the flame that glowed filling her hair, her face, her breast until her whole body shone with the influence of it. And before Maia's eyes Irkala took on again the appearance of a woman in the prime of her youth. But Maia was drained, her appearance suffered and she felt diminished.

At the same time, she was filled with unaccustomed passions that would overwhelm should she permit them. She wondered how long in taking the cloak of the Shades about her she could endure it, and for a moment fear in the mingling of influence and power that was not hers to define. And she could see Irkala, though delighted by the transformation in her presence, unsure the same but determined to persevere in it. And so while there was strain between them, they parted amicably, each determined to master the changes wrought in them.

In the Chapel of Tears, as if from a trance, the Lady Madelon awoke with a start. The candles burned low and a hint of light coloured the stained glass window in the east. She arose to it determined to overcome whatever conspired against her right to rule, and magnify her kingdom in the earth. And she vowed in the time remaining her, until the Troth of Caer Myrddin, to use every opportunity, long denied her, to master the way of the left hand path. She would isolate herself seven nights, and in that attitude walk the pattern of the sun-wheel in the Chapel of Tears.

31

Thresholds

Storm clouds loomed over the Northumbria coast threatening a deluge. Caron took shelter in Maiden's Veil, a coastal inn on the road to Lindisfarne. His Rhine journey from Strasburg to Rotterdam and the wait for passage on a Flemish merchant to Berwick, like an eclipse of the sun had eaten up the day. Summer turned to the changing season, he was unresolved whether to bide his time and let things be, or make haste for Caer Myrddin.

Settled at the Maiden's Veil, Caron first took a mug of mulled wine by the fire. Then out of doors, in the shelter of the gables he watched the clouds billow over a furrowed sea, afire with lightnings, until sky and sea were awash in thunder.

What came next was clear enough. He must keep faith with Brother John, borne with him across the miles. John's excitement at coming home welled up within. "I know this place. Here I played as a child: these fields, this stream, yon sea shore." Though Caron's eyes these were the last sights John would see of a realm in which love and devotion shaped his path into a gift of life for others. His memories filled Caron's mind with half-forgotten dreams of youth, seen again in the golden light of fulfillment.

It was the least Caron could give to one so much deserving, to let his wonder at being home again carry him to the verge of another birth. At rest in this world, he would awaken to act in another unobscured by a veil of illusion. There was no hiatus, only the adventure of life.

On the morrow come calm and slack tide, Caron crossed the pilgrim's path over the bar to Lindisfarne, bringing John home to Holy Isle. The isle was flat and though meadowland near desolate but for the abbey and its buildings, some fisher's huts and a rocky outcrop that formed the headland. "Why here: why not Oxford where you took orders?" Caron whispered the thought.

"Here my soul was shaped," the answer came. "Here my child's eyes were opened. Here the world was still bright with splendor, before the weight of the world a burden to be borne."

"A burden of light in the world," Caron said. "I know because these many miles you have uplifted me in the way."

"We are born into a world in darkness. Here I was taken up into the light. The intellectuals of Oxford are complicated. It is the simple, cloistered monks who dwell here I would honour, letting go… to what, Caron?"

"Love thou art, and unto love shalt thou return."

Caron sought out the Abbot of Lindisfarne and told the story of his meeting in Ashkelon with Brother John of Oxford, and his desire to return to Lindisfarne. He gave account of the perils of journeying in the east and what Brother John suffered; how their lives crossed and John's death on the journey home with his charge.

Brother John desired his cross, rosaries, and garments - his meager portable property - brought to the Abbey, where there were those who might yet remember him. And, indeed, there were yet those among the brothers, including the Abbot, who recalled him as a youth. Seeing potential they had taken him in, educated, and in time sent him to Oxford to take holy orders.

"He became a Mathurian." The Abbot took the clothing. "It was a perfect commission for one not easily given to cloisters, but loved to roam the hills."

Caron gave the Abbot two small rubies and received in return a look of disbelief. "It is for remembrance. I will continue on from here to Oxford to complete our journey that they might know what became of him and his charge."

"You will stay, I trust, a few days so we can keep vigil and conduct a requiem."

"I would have you think him an exemplary soul."

"Greater love hath no man…" the Abbot replied.

"Yes," Caron answered, wearily. "Your Worship, I am in need of deep rest and utter solitude for a time… if you could accommodate me, for a week or two before continuing on."

"There's a small cottage we keep for vigils at the headland of the isle over the sea. It shall be set apart for you so long as you will stay with us. I will instruct that no one trouble you there."

Brother John attended his own mass and was much affected. And when it was done Caron, with his companion in the way, walked the seashore to the headland of Lindisfarne. There on the beach they searched the tidal pools for minnows, scared up tiny crabs scuttling across the rocks for cover, picked up empty sea shells to listen for the ocean within, and at last climbed the rocky headland and sat looking out over the darkling sea. It was the season. Again afar off clouds gathered, and there was a single stroke of lightning in the dark mass. It would storm again tonight, but for the moment all was silent and still with the last lingering light of an autumn day.

"It is time to go, isn't it?"

"I have things I must attend; things borne of those greater than I to which I must give myself."

"I have seen wonders I never thought to see. Now it is time to part, you to yours and me to mine; though where I go now, it must be I think to some purgatory of the soul, for I am not perfect in all my ways."

"It is of the moment, perfection," Caron said. "You enter in the substance of love into this world to redeem it in your living. You choose to come. You have power to lay down your life, and power to take it up again."

"I have longed to know Him as He is."

"God is Love - all that is solid at the core of you. You know His presence in heart. You soar with him in your thoughts. You find him shining in your every act of living. All that and more is who you are and shall never pass away."

"But what will happen?"

"Even as a child enters the world to loving parents, you will be greeted in love unconditional. They know you coming forth into the heart of light, and with truest eyes you will see what is given to see, filling you with the bliss of the greatest love you have ever known.

"And there may be one," Caron added with a laugh, "who will offer you a game of chess, and a question for a question. Give him my greetings for he is my friend and once my mentor in the way."

"I am anxious for leaving. I have seen the path you walk and the power under your hand. Yet I am concerned and had I my way I would see this through with you."

"There is nothing for anyone to fear," Caron said. "Only a veil of clouded consciousness obscures what is ever present. Once lifted, we see all things as they truly are."

Caron felt a familiar presence gather and intensify about him. He was at rest in the earth and awakening to the radiance of another realm whose influence informed and uplifted his soul. And there was another voice.

"The landscape of our lives unfolds the inscape of our souls," Caron heard himself say. "And though we rest here in Lindisfarne, we may journey to a place and time dear to your heart, and in the company of friends."

John let go with him and the view of the sea and headlands of Lindisfarne dissolved to a path under a canopy of trees. John again stood at his side, not as he had been road weary in Ashkelon, but cloaked with the freshness of a dewy sunlight morn, and a presence about him all together familiar. It seemed only natural that they should walk this way together.

Familiar, too, was the setting though it took the air of what came forth in John's soul, mingled with something of his own. Their path led between meadow and stream. On the far bank was a Templar Grange he knew. In the distance the arches of Balliol and Merton rose above the trees and low rolling hills. It was John's Oxford. Here he took orders to risk life to ransom souls in far off lands.

They were green and golden days for him. He felt John fill with wonder to come again. It was a perfect English evening: the sound of a rising lark from the meadow, the smell of the long grass after the warmth of the day, the moist evening scent of the river. And there was that air mysterious with a slant of light that roused longings of the heart for something lost and promised, so close you could hardly bear to feel but hope, and yet not know how to come to it.

"I was never good at cloisters. I tramped these woods and meadows; gained a reputation for a blithe, some said feckless, spirit. There's an inn nearby, I know it well," he said, "before I took orders."

"Many a monk has drained many a flagon."

"Well, it is true," John confessed. "A lovely little inn it is."

They crossed a stile onto a trail edged with hedgerows, filled with evening birdsong, and followed it to a parting of the ways. One path led on through the valley toward Oxford, the other into the courtyard of a tavern where small boats hove to for the comforts of the inn.

John was beside himself. Caron took his arm and steadied him. The setting was different but not unfamiliar, and not unlike the Inn at the Parting of the Ways. He understood now how each one cloaked experience in the familiar forms; how within each one, as shadows dissolve and the heart is cleansed, the senses radiant with light see the essence of everything as it is, infinite.

John was quite animated, drawn yet holding back, daring not to move until Caron opened the door. "What shall I find within?" he asked clasping Caron's arm.

"Some gone before, some still in the world, some you have met in the way: Who would you have meet you?"

"There were teachers, friends, I remember."

"I would not be surprised, if all the faculty and students of Oxford turned out to welcome you home from your travels. Shall we see?"

Caron leaned across the threshold and looked into the firelight haven within. There in the corner by the hearth was an old man about his game of chess. He raised his head from his game and met Caron's eyes with the slightest smile then returned to his board. Inside the inn was full and a heady conversation under way fueled by tankards of hearty ale, pretty much Caron thought the comradery John would most have missed in his desert solitudes among those who called him infidel. "It's not for me to enter here," Caron said, standing at the threshold. "So, for now, it is God be with you."

"Why, what is within?"

"Friends, absent friends, those you love and loved you and are gathered to welcome you home."

"It is you who have brought me home."

"When you understand what lies ahead of you, I ask only that you watch over me in the way."

"With all that is given me, I will." Caron stepped aside so John could enter. "And shall we ever meet again, for it seems to me now this is all but a dream that will melt away in the light of day to come."

"We were well met," Caron said, "and having once met, how shall we not meet again?" They clasped hands a moment and John stepped cautiously into the rosy dusk. The inn fell silent a moment with his presence; Caron softly closed the door behind and turned away.

"A little time among accustomed friends and he'll awaken to the larger life."

Caron turned to the voice but the evening sun was in his eyes. It streamed through the autumn leaf of a great maple, and set up a rosy hue about the tree, half in light, half in shadow and in the midst of that the silhouette of a tall, slender man whose face he could not clearly see.

He knew only a moment full of the peace of an accomplished day, and would say nothing but listen to the rustle of a breeze in the leaves. After the heat of the day the evening air was fragrant with the smell of fresh water pooling in a red rock cistern without the inn and Caron breathed it all in deeply. The man took a step forward out of shadow into the light so Caron could see his face clearly. It was the voice of the Aton-Re that spoke but transparent with light, and of a flesh subtler than his own, it was his own image looked back at him, but something of John of Oxford in the mix.

"It was always you," Caron said, "even in Ashkelon."

"John would have perished in the wilderness, but his heart was pure; I took him to myself to uphold him in the way, and brought him to you and a beginning was made."

"I wondered at St. Odile," Caron said. "When the lords of light gathered and I came into your presence, what had become of John?"

"In what he offered you, it was always me."

"You have seen all that I have seen."

"Through your eyes; through the hearts and minds of multitudes," he answered.

"The ways of men are dark and devious. Men with hooks in their faces are dragged this and that way by the tows of the world. They are caught up in obsessions with the flesh, the machinations of minds, and the mire of their hearts. They are subject to passions, suffer anguish, and are led by appetite rather than wisdom."

"He has chosen the beast over the man," the Aton-Re said. "It has been so many thousands of years, and yet always the righteous among them, good wheat among the tares.

"Yet there shall come a time when all is gathered in, and there shall be time no more, and what fallen man has wrought shall be transformed in the light or pass from the earth."

The man was so mild that Caron was emboldened to press the matter. But before he could speak the answer came.

"It will take a new race of men to come forth through all the races of men, a race born not of the flesh but of the way of love and the waters of truth in the spirit of life.

"In that day shall the light within intensify, transmuting the flesh into the flesh of spirit, and every realm of the seven-fold world be given true flesh. All that responds shall be restored to the way of the wonderful one."

"And all that does not?"

"Death comes as compassion, purging the earth of unresponsive forms, to bring man home to life everlasting."

"When?"

"Be it a thousand years or a day, we are moving into the fire toward the consummation of this cycle of creation for the spiritual regeneration of the human race."

Caron sat silently on the stone wall under a scarlet maple in the last light of day, with the one who now seemed to him his very double, for what could he see that was not in him? There seemed little more to say. He knew why he had come and was content.

"You bore John across many miles to bring him home. And I uplifted you in the way. I do not think you found him or me a burden."

"I would call him friend who made light my way."

"There is something to be done and we must do it. Will you now call me friend and bear the burden I put upon you?"

"It is you, isn't it, who ascending imprinted the divine design in the sun stone?"

"So a bound might be set on human depravity, and the way of resurrection written in the substance of man. And now there are those who would use the stone to loose powers unfit for men."

"To what end?"

"They would restore to man those powers lost to him in the time of the great transgression. Do you think men now wiser than then they were in the use of power? How well do they use such power as is still granted them? What they contrive will but intensify corruption of the fallen heart and mind, obscuring the way."

"The Lady Madelon Is not easily turned aside. She will have what she will have," Caron said.

"And she is caught up in influences that would give it her," the Aton-Re said. "To that end we will attend the gathering at Caer Myrddin."

"If there were time…"

"You shall not leave the sanctuary of this isle, and yet come to them. And they shall see what I shall have them see, reflecting in the mirror of their souls what is within them.

"And as Brother John has journeyed with us across the miles shall we not include him to make a whole, for in his heart he would see this journey through."

"Let it be." Caron answered and in a moment it was done. He felt John gather to him, full of interest in what lay ahead. And no longer sat beside him in the evening air, the Aton-Re was a tangible presence filling his consciousness with light, and Caron waited silently upon him.

Until well after dark he sat on the headland of Holy Isle looking out over a still, moonlit ocean, as the fire of fusion in love came to the full in him. He thought of Enoch long ago who walked with God and was not for God took him. He was in the earth but not of it, and in that wise no longer Caron, for the spirit of the lord of the crossing was upon him. And still within, like the surface of the waters that give birth to light, the worlds in him were one, as ever they are in the First Time.

32

Facade

It began in the small of her back, a sensation like a bud of flame urging upwards along her spine, until she glowed with warmth that blossomed a rosy flame in her breast. It took total possession of her; filling her senses and overflowing in a kaleidoscope of colours, sounds and scents; all resolving at last into haunting strains of music utterly enchanting. To have fought against it would have thrust her down into darkness. Her flesh, hardened against the world yielded, tender as rose petals, fragrant as spring. Magda was known and she knew it. "The threshold of Caer Myrddin," she ventured.

"We are crossed over and within the hedge," Blaise confirmed.

"I had heard of it but never thought it so compelling. It is unlike our own."

"Other thresholds there are, the tone of each unique. But this on the verge of the Otherworld is shaped to our purpose. Here we are free from intrusion."

"And should any come unbidden?"

"What is hidden in the heart shall turn them aside."

"I felt nothing but pleasure; sights and sounds and wondrous music never minstrel contrived, and it turned us not aside."

"We are expected; attuned to the pattern that comes to focus here," Blaise said, "as are all who come to join us in this purpose."

"You speak as if Caer Myrddin was another realm."

"Here more readily the worlds cross over," Blaise said.

"How is that?" Magda asked. "All seems as it appeared from the sea. The headland is unchanged, the castle ruin upon it, and that far ridge... between them they make a calm sea. And now I see a stair in the distance where we shall make landfall, rising to the plain above."

"Bran deems it a marvelous beauty, in his coracle across the clear sea. While to me in my chariot from afar, it is a flowery plain on which he rides...."

"Poetry Master Blaise? I see nothing but sea. Still, it is a pleasant fancy."

"No fancy, milady, you see what your soul permits, but use the second sight. The worlds coexist as tones on a musical scale, each level above as spirit to a level of form below.

"We dwell in worlds within worlds, and when the heart is pure and the senses radiant we see all things as they really are in the one whole and holy creation of this earth."

"You tell me you see a plain where I see only sea?"

"I say only there is more to be seen."

"You have no idea what I have seen," she countered.

"I say only we see not things as they are but the features of a fallen world, life strained through a fallen soul."

"Well, I see what I see. Caer Myrddin, is it far?"

"Beyond the castle ruin on that foreshore a path across the meadowland leads on to Caer Myrddin. It has a pleasant seat, wooded upon a hill. There you shall find your comforts, for all is in preparation for your coming."

Magda glanced to a castle ruin on the foreshore. There was a man standing on the rugged cliff. He was a distance off but she saw clearly he steadied himself with a staff, his broad brimmed hat shading his eyes as he watched the approaching boat; his cloak blowing in the breeze. And riding on a wimple of wind a windhover falcon attached to him it seemed by invisible cords, for when he turned aside wind and bird both turned with him. It was more than curious and she grew anxious at the sight of him. "Do you see that man?"

Blaise glanced where she pointed. "I see nothing. Perhaps, what you saw was meant for you alone. It is the nature of this place."

"He was very real."

"Then I would guess Bran, Gwen's guardian and lord of Caer Myrddin."

"Branwyn's brother?"

"He will take little interest in our proceedings. He is old and prefers his books and daily walk to the sea in search of what the tide has brought to his shores, and to collect a modicum of shellfish for his meals. I have heard with years he has become quite eccentric, preferring the company of peasants to courtiers, and gathers with them in the tavern. But don't let that fool you. He entirely understands what we are about, and somehow manages to stay above it."

"Above it: what is above it?

"Worlds within worlds," Blaise said. "Do not mistake his powers. We are guests in his home, and it is he who has drawn this hedge about us."

"Not the Masters?"

"Lady, this level is well beyond our art. It is Bran who has shaped this music, taken us in, and lifted us to the threshold of the Otherworld. Other than that I cannot say; you will see little of him for this is your time and your rite of passage."

"Who is it shall set the test of sovereignty?"

"I know only that none shall enter here who is not attuned to what we do."

"Then Caron cannot."

"I do not know that, though I see no reason to suppose he will come upon us."

"You talk of vision but do you not see he will come for the stone and the lady Siduri?"

"He may have moved beyond all this; it may be he no longer cares. But if so it will be because Bran allows. In that case we must stay true to the tone that allows us, and let it unfold as it will."

"We shall talk further of this," she insisted. The little vessel glided gracefully into landfall at the foot of the stair.

It revolted her to have to do so, but she must sit and hear Blaise instruct her in the way of the Troth. She knew his part in it, but it was not easy to be under the hand of one whose loyalties transcended those due her as Domina. Well, if she must: tradition dictated that the Master who oversaw the Troth must be master of Grail or Sword Hallows. Still, she didn't have to like it and shutting Blaise out she turned inward and sought Maia's presence. "It matters nothing," Maia assured. "We have power to amaze, and magic at our hand to reveal before this is done." Would Blaise never cease talking?

"You understand this is a genuine challenge to your arts and right to sovereignty. Though I know of none there may also come a challenger from among the daughters of the Blood Royal. More likely you will be challenged by the temporal lords over your competence to fulfill your purpose, and duties to them."

"I have taken care of that in gold and opportunity. But what if I am challenged by one of my sisters?"

"Then even as you, she must fulfill everything in full measure to prevail."

"They owe it to me."

"They owe it to the Order, and she who would be Domina must earn respect and devotion."

She was raised with a notion of her right to rule; it unnerved her to realize she might be rejected for another. "And if they are not convinced?"

"None, including the temporal lords, will pledge their troth, until you have satisfied their concerns."

"Arrogance," she shot back.

"The lords have grown both strong and restless, and did at first impose limitations upon the rule of Branwyn of Wales. For in the burning time Gaston de Blanchefort plucked the maiden Branwyn from the Inquisition's fires, bedded and against her will took her to wife.

"Even so for her friendship with the Cathar princess, Esclarmonde de Péreille, and their cause, they did not trust her, and for many years she suffered his hand in her affairs, until at last she won the hearts of the Temporal Lords and skewered de Blanchefort."

"Spare me the history lesson, Blaise. I know full well how the Masters of Hallows labored to free Branwyn from de Blanchefort's oppression; how they sought to save the Cathars, and the Templar Order that resisted their slaughter. But I am more interested in those issues that face me now, and would know of any threat to my sovereignty."

"I know of none," Blaise said, patiently, "though you might consider Roland of Waldheim was wed to the daughter de Blanchefort sired upon Branwyn. The temporal lords look to him for leadership in matters concerning the Blood Royal."

"I have considered this, and though Roland is a bull of a man, I have devised a way to put a ring through his nose. I will deny Perrin and promise the Lady Gwendolyn's hand in return for his loyalty."

"And wed to Roland you don't suppose the Lady Gwendolyn might challenge you?"

"We were raised in the arts together. She is brilliant but not my equal. But to my greatest concern, the Masters of Hallows: I know the minds of Gisors and Telgesinus; Perrin has scarcely a mind at all and fawns on women. But where do you stand in this?"

"I am Master of Sword Hallows," Blaise said with ritual clarity, "not because it is a title conferred by preference upon me, but because *I am* Master of Sword Hallows. My duty is to the truth, and if we meet there you may be confident in me."

"And if Caron should appear and challenge for Siduri and the stone she is to yield to me in solemn ceremony?"

"I have power in earth; I have power in the heavens, and yet the sword of my power is broken until heaven and earth are known as one."

"Is that an answer to my question?"

"Then let me be plain. If Caron should appear and stand in the truth of the oneness of the worlds, he will find no enemy in me. For then were it so, an offense against him would be an offense against the truth the Blood Royal was created to serve."

"You will not defend me against him?"

"I will defend the truth. But do you no longer believe he died at Ulcinj."

"What was inflicted upon Gisors near cost his life. I can only believe Caron behind that. And at Sainte Odile - well you were there and saw what this Brother John did to the Master Telgesinus."

"If he lives he has learned much of the vibratory arts since last you encountered him. I do not think for a moment you could bind him to you.

"If you are right he has the gift of the shape-shifter, and the power to work in the realms of the invisible patterns that inform this world. Yes, I do think it was he who appeared at Sainte Odile, in appearance an itinerant monk, but more the empowered sage than a man of the cloth - and something more.

"I could not lay my hand upon him for wrong doing, for he it was who was wronged. Had he been left alone no harm would have come of it. He came without ill intent, was assaulted by Telgesinus' arts, and did no more than reflect back what Telgesinus would inflict upon him. And not without mercy, for he might then have slain Telgesinus as he did Squin who would take his life."

"What Telgesinus did was in my defense, and I will empower him the more. But you, Blaise, what will you do to defend your Mistress should he come to subvert the Troth?"

"You do not entirely understand, Magda, where you have come. You are on the margin of the Otherworld where all unfolds in essence. Here every thought, word and deed is intensified, and every soul infused with light.

"Here the sword of truth upholds the truth. If he comes here against the truth, he comes against the one sovereign power no king on earth can long resist, or ever prevail. All you must do is to abide in the truth, and all is well."

"Very well, I will grant this place peculiar, and we shall let it be what it shall be."

Even so, in that moment she resolved in her heart Caron should be slain on sight. He had shadowed their path across Europe and even though he had not revealed himself to her or taken the stone from Siduri, he would be the challenge of her Troth and must steel herself to face him. What's more, Blaise knew it, too.

"The Troth is in the nature of a wedding," Blaise continued. "More than about you, it is about the community and Order of the Blood Royal. It is a confirmation of powers and principalities wed to you, even as you are wed to the truth that informs your purpose.

"The ceremony unfolds over seven days, beginning with *Declarations* on the first day through *Departures* on the seventh. We will go into greater detail on this when we meet again, but on the first day you will declare yourself, your right to rule, and your claim for tenure as Domina. The second day is *Manifestations*; bearing witness to the enduring truths of the Blood Royal. This will include various performances of a dramatic nature - music and ritual observances in tribute to those principles and forces which inform our authority and creative endeavors - consummating with the showing of the Hallows.

"The third day is *Visualizations*. This will be your opportunity to shape a vision of the future for those you seek to govern. Here your full arts may come into play and you may draw upon the resources of the Masters of Hallows to make vivid your intent. On the fourth day we have *Consummations*. If there are unions to be made concerning your consolidation of your powers within the Order, here those matters are brought before the assembled lords. I understand you have made some matches. I pray you have chosen wisely and that each deepens the communion of the Order in your purposes, for people can be most particular about these things.

"Each day leading to the night of *Consummations* constitutes a cycle of preparation, bringing to focus in those gathered to you that substance needful to uplift and bear witness on the fourth day to your transit of the sun-wheel. It is a given you have come this far that a transit of the sun-wheel is not needful the first three days, that all cycles will consolidate in you and come up for clarification on the fourth. On that day you must take the right hand path beginning with the water of truth and the air of spirit, informing material things offered up and purified in consummating fire. You know the way and how to harmonize the powers inherent in the passage.

"If on the first night, the night of *Declarations*, you are challenged, she must likewise present her case. If it is accepted, on the fourth day she, like you, must walk the pattern to prove worthy. One of you must prevail to complete the circuit to bind and seal your destiny to the Blood Royal's own. And of course there will be feasting, entertainment and merry making to celebrate the growing bonds of this core of the new emerging Order as it unfolds."

"The fourth night is the crisis?"

"On the night of *Consummations* the veil thins, and the presence of the Otherworld is most keenly felt. And, yes, that will be the night of your final challenge."

"Speak to it."

"I cannot say, for it bears on the purification of your heart and the virtue or corruption of the Order. I do not know how that challenge will present itself to you. I know only that in the three days leading to it, things will present themselves to you for consideration. If you are wise you will see and understand what is needful, for the consummation of that union of the worlds in you. But the promise is this. When this cycle is fulfilled, it will come with the gifts and powers needful to govern wisely and well as Domina of the Blood Royal."

"And what follows after?"

"Do not take this transit of the sun-wheel for granted," Blaise urged. "If you fail it will not leave you unscathed."

"You have said it," Magda countered, "I will be held in suspicion and the temporal lords will refuse to affix their testimony to my right of rule, until such a time as they are satisfied in me."

"Or, you may perish in the attempt."

"Perish?" It had never occurred her life was on the line.

"But as to what follows, if you succeed it is for you to bond in purpose; to receive wisely and graciously tribute of response.

"The fifth day is the *Resolutions* of the gathered lords. They shall present opportunities they see, envision designs that may be implemented on your behalf, lodge corrections and clarifications to present patterns, and offer all for your consideration. It is a day of lively business, but neither overlook any detail of it, nor fail to read the many cross-currents at work beneath the surface. It is a day of essences, and if you have come this far you will be able to read in each one their strengths and weaknesses, and detect any hidden agendas that might weaken the Order.

"On the sixth day we shall have *Confirmations* consisting of pledges, the giving of gifts of responsive love, offerings of substance to uplift the purposes of the Order, and a celebration of communion to seal the bonds of the future that shall release the powers you have become heir to in the realms of this world.

"And on the seventh day we shall not try to do what God did not but rest from our labors before initiating another cycle of creation. It is a day of *Reconciliations*. Final words shall be spoken; tribute made; there shall be leave taking and promise of a gathering to come as each makes ready to return to his own realm, imbued anew in the love they bear for you."

"We shall speak then in greater detail of each part of this," Magda said, "but for now it is enough for I have matters to ponder and must consult with others."

"In pondering these matters weigh carefully what you intend for Siduri who possesses the stone of sovereignty, for the outcome of your trials may well depend on this."

"Is that all? Well, I am content. My Masters of Hallows shall judge my passage of the sun-wheel."

"Not entirely," Blaise answered. "You will be judged of the Watchers. It will be their decision as to whether or not you become Domina of the Blood Royal."

"Those gathered?"

"You will be judged of the lords of light, the shining ones of the First Time. One or more of these will attend your Troth to oversee your trial of investiture."

Magda objected. She felt Maia's confidence wane in her. "But this is a myth. We heard tales of this as children, of powers chained in the deeps for their transgressions, and since no one has ever seen… this cannot be."

"It is no myth. There were those among the Watchers who fell, but it is those who abide always, without beginning of days or end of life, who shaped the Blood Royal to their purpose. One of these appears at every investiture to confirm the Domina in her office. And it is these to whom we all must ultimately answer."

"But I am Domina and you my Masters of Hallows," she objected.

"Did you think there were none greater in the earth? From the time of the great transgression the Watchers abide among us, and it is to these all answer. It is the test of your investiture how you rise to this. If you have mastered the pattern and cycle of the sun-wheel, you will find no difficulty in this."

"And shall these interfere in the matter of the stone of sovereignty now returned?"

"By right all Hallows are theirs and they have remained among us to shape a pattern fit to the powers of creation. It was for that cause the Domina Branwyn had Flegetanis journey to the east to seek out and recover the stone. That his daughter Siduri now returns it to us is not by chance. If the shining ones find your heart true, they will uplift you to offer a true setting for the jewel of sovereignty within our Order."

"How will I know them?"

"Look upon the heart and take heed, lest you entertain angels unawares."

"Then no one has sight of him," Magda said.

"The patrols report nothing extraordinary," Telgesinus replied. "The village is about its business as usual; there are drovers in the fields but all keeping their distance from us. There was one old man sighted from the cliff gathering shellfish on the shore below, but commanded he moved on."

"He will come."

"You have read this in the weave of things?"

"No, and that is what troubles me. I should have sensed something, but it is as if Caron no longer exists."

"Perhaps he did perish in the way; all the rest coincidence."

"When he comes you will have him slain."

"I no longer think that wise," Telgesinus demurred. "Blaise is right in this matter. If Caron comes it will be because whatever forces shape this place welcomes him. So then, what we inflict upon him will return upon us."

"Have someone who matters not in the least do it."

"I have already experienced what happens if the intent rises in us. We are beyond that. Declarations have been made, the day of Challenges is done; none came forward."

It is very good," she agreed. "But now we must give some attention to this matter of the stone. I would begin to draw upon its power. However, Blaise has warned we must weigh our decision concerning Siduri with great care, for the stone cannot be taken with impunity from the one to whom it is given."

"I have consulted all records I can find of it," Telgesinus said. "It is clear great power is vested in the stone of sovereignty. Some speak to it as the distillation in essence of a world that was and shall be in the hands of one who knows to loose the seals that bind it.

"But with this warning: The stone must be given true setting or its power once loosed will destroy all who violate its divine design in essence."

Magda pondered Telgesinus' words. She was sure it would not have come this close at this time were it not for her to unveil its mysteries. What was more Maia confirmed it was given her to do so. "I am sure we shall find the masters and women of the Blood Royal equal to the task," she said, confidently. "Just as I am sure Siduri has brought it to yield to us.

"I have considered these matters and we shall include her and the greenhorn Perrin in our night of Consummation. I am of a mind to couple these two, for even before Squin's demise I saw the beginnings of love looking and longing between them."

"What does the poet know but fantasy? This matter is beyond his art. I do not advise it."

"It is your time to lead, and what you have said I will consider, but also what is to come only I can fulfill, and fantasy as you call it can be very useful in shaping men's minds and women's hearts.

"But Master Telgesinus," she said, drawing close to him, "do you not already feel the bounty of our labour increase its substance in us; do you not feel, as I do, there is that growing in you, deepening your soul, that is not only up to the task of governing the Masters of Hallows but of standing with me?

"And it may be in our prevailing in this" she said, brushing her lips with his own, so he tasted her breath, "you may prove my worthy consort.

"I have seen something of the future and a mind as yours is needful to pierce the night of gross darkness that envelops human understanding. You and I together, Master Telgesinus, might shape a new dawn for our Order and humankind."

If she took Telgesinus by surprise he didn't show it, for what rose up in him confirmed at once what he had in his own heart come to believe, that this woman was his by art and right. And so he did not resist when she pressed against him, but drew her down to her couch and let his hands speak for him. Even so, having roused the fire in him she pressed him off gently, but not too far, and continued. "What is your advice?"

"Take command," he said, searching for breath. "Walk the pattern successfully with intent to return the jewel to its true setting, and none shall challenge but rest content in you."

"Oh, I shall, I shall, and still Caron troubles my soul."

"What can one man do against the powers at your hand, the powers of Caer Myrddin hedging you?"

"And yet I fear - but that is for the morrow - tonight I will amaze."

"What is it you intend, Lady?"

"I shall evoke my arts of visualization, show how much I have grown in the vibratory arts of shaping and spontaneous manifestation; power to shape in the mind's eye things yet unseen and yet to come. In vision I have seen wonders, and some of this I shall reveal in this company, lighting the mirror of their souls with radiant sights and sounds, scent and taste and touch, and a shadow play of the world that shall be."

"Inspire us Magda." Telgesinus drew back from his intimacy, for she was now passionately self-obsessed and had nothing for any other. "Inspire greatness in us. Create in us the patterns of the way you would go. Establish them in our hearts and minds, and we who labor in the forces of the world will take inspiration of you to give shape and form in the substance of this world, to fulfill your very heart's desire."

The great banquet hall was artfully prepared for the evening to come, its secrets hidden behind colourful veils of muslin depicting scenes from classic mythologies. The day of Visualizations was to begin with what Magda first judged a rather ill-conceived presentation of a new play, a work of the poet Perrin performed by Falconieri's troupe. Still, the more she thought upon it the more she saw Perrin's play useful to her purpose, and so at last permitted. It was a work to be taken as depicting the degraded life they now lived, and to which, come into her power, she would put an end.

The allegory began with a man receiving a summons to journey and meet with Death. In a world in which famine, war, pestilence, and the shocks of the flesh were all too familiar it struck a nerve, for what does man more desire than health, wealth and long life. For most the promise of an afterlife in compensation for the brutal journey with its abrupt and painful end seemed poor recompense to one snared in the flesh of it all. It intrigued her to see the reactions of her lords as they watched the pageant unfold; the very things their souls lusted after abandon them at the last.

Summoned, the poor man sought out from among his friends in this grim world those who might journey with him to meet with Death. One by one they abandoned his fellowship and fell away: Kindred, Cousins,

Fellowship, Beauty, Strength, Discretion, and Five Wits, each somewhat narrowly epitomized in a character. At length only Knowledge, Confession, Good Deeds and Faith in Life remained. And, of course one by one these too were challenged by the prospect of attending him to his summons.

In reviewing the play there was a point of contention between Magda and Perrin left unresolved. She would have Good Deeds attend the man in his meeting with Death, but Perrin insisted at the last only Faith in Life would attend him. Faith in life she maintained could do little – one either had it or one did not - but good deeds she could define as she saw fit to her purpose, which made the drama infinitely more useful to her. And then there was the title. Perrin called the work, *The Summons*, but Magda preferred the grand sweep and opted for, "*Sooner or Later, Herald Comes for Everybody.*"

On this point Perrin demurred. Titles, he argued, must be terse. But he agreed the play needed a good deal of work. Magda suggested perhaps a hundred years or more to get it right, but agreed it had potential and it played to what she intended. At last they came into agreement to settle for Good Works attending Everybody in his journey, though Perrin was not pleased. Still, Falconieri reminded Perrin, she was patron of the piece and for the moment this was about her. Better to avoid an argument, for adjustments could be made later.

Her own art required mood, and when yet in Venice she thought on it she knew creating the mood she wanted in this northern clime would present a challenge. So with the help of the Doge, ever in search of new markets, ships from Venice brought rare and wonderful things. She filled the hall with forced flowers, greenery, rare song birds; candelabra alive with lights in the shape of fruiting trees, all in silver and emerald leaf bearing fruits of gold; and these with silks of many colours and a faint hint of incense, like the scent of a perfect spring day blended all in all. The assembly was in awe as the display was revealed, each item set perfectly in its place to create the impression of dwelling within an exotic walled garden, for it was her intention to create a garden of paradise in their minds before she began in earnest to make that promised world reality.

It was not so difficult to contrive, for the imagination provides what the heart desires to see, man so easily moved by the image of his hopes and fears symbolized in cross or crescent or banner of office and state to live and die under. And was it not true of her Order: cup, sword, paten, and spear taken for the powers they represent; seeing in symbol far more than is present in fact, confusing the evidence of something that might be with the very thing itself?

It was easy for her to devise images to trigger the responses she sought, and tonight she was about to convince even the most affluent of those gathered how little they had; instill in them the belief they could have everything they dreamed of, had they the will to make their will her own. By the time Perrin's play was done the assembly was more than in the mood for something more light hearted.

It began with the wine. When the scene was set kegs of wine from the Doge's cellars were carted in, vented, tapped, and flowed freely. Music, song and dance were ordered, sweet and sensuous as the wine, creating the mood she intended. And when all was merry, when the heart's hurts were numbed, the erotic longings for ease and comfort roused, and the mind lulled into almost believing itself in a state of bliss, she rose to work her magic.

"I have looked into the mirror of your souls," she began. The pages lit the silver branched candelabras. "I know your hurts, your desires, your loves your fears; the longings of your hearts for fulfillment." All the silver branched trees lit with light shone together and the great chamber warmed and glowed in candlelight. "And so welcome, to the Garden of Wish Fulfilling Trees." She gestured to the pages to pull the muslin veils. "Welcome to our Garden of Reflecting Light."

The veils fell, and the chamber walls vanished as the priceless mirrors, gift of the Doge of Venice to the Lady Madelon, caught up the light in maze of reflections. Each mirror was perfectly placed. No more could one sort sense from sensation. Firelight and fellowship, candlelight, flowers, greenery, and a grove of cunningly wrought silver branched trees ablaze, cast reflection upon reflection to beguile the eye. All mingled with the spiced wine and the paradise drug of longing, until the only orientation possible was the image of Magda herself, for she alone was at the center of the field of illusion and held it all under her hand.

"Now I will show you something before which all this pales. I will show you things that shall be hereafter, as we walk in the way I open before you. I will show you things not seen from the foundation of the world, of a time before the great flood swept away the world that was."

Magda set the stage for Maia, for all Maia ever needed were the passions of the flesh, the yearnings of a hurt or hungry heart, and a mind beguiled with dreaming to weave incandescent visions in the souls of men. Under her hand Maia would shape that response into longing, loose the restraints upon the heart that bound up the powers of the Deep, create hunger to give flesh to force, and put into the hands of man the means to restore the world to what she believed it once was.

But even Magda was unprepared for the vivid illusion Maia invoked. Gathering up the forces of the fallen Watchers, Irkala empowered Maia the more, and under her influence the stone cold walls melted away. The illusion of mirrors gave way to the wind and rain, the cold, grey stone in firelight, and these in turn to a paradise of the senses: a vision of a garden city of habitation, strange but familiar in the evening longings of the heart.

No steely, grey overcast suppressed, no torrid sun oppressed; no gathering storm or blood smeared horizon marked end of day or limit of the heavens. Instead, a dome of white radiance infusing an iridescent sky of tints and tones arched from horizon to horizon. And the air was filled with the melody, the sweet influences of a fair folk that came forth to walk its garden paths in the cool of the day.

"I offer a vison of a world that was and again shall be; a world of fulfillment to which I shall show the way."

What more came of that Magda could not say, for she awakened in her own bed with full morning light streaming through the coloured glass at the casement. And there she lay alone, trying to remember what followed the momentary vision Maia contrived in her of the world of her heart's desire.

33

Blue Shaman

Magda sent for Blaise but he did not respond, nor did anyone know the whereabouts of any her Masters of Hallows, and so alone she explored Caer Myrddin in search of the sun-wheel. She found nothing, so early afternoon she walked to the castle ruin she had seen on the promontory over the sea, and sat an hour watching the spindrift waves break upon the shore

There was nothing in the old ruin to suggest the fabled sun-wheel of Caer Myrddin. What she saw, however, was curious; Bran picking his way cautiously along the rocky shore below. The tide was out and toting a bucket he was gathering shellfish, prying them from the rocks with a knife, in work fit for a peasant.

He was careful as old men are in such places; vigilant, until etched against the darkening sky a figure cloaked in monk's robe of blue appeared on the strand, bearing a staff and marking his stride along the beach to the beat of it. Bran stood tall, studied a moment the apparition of light, then abandoning his bucket of shellfish ran to meet him. And when he was come, Magda watched amazed as Bran, lord of Caer Myrddin, knelt at the man's feet.

That was all she saw before the squall overtook them obliterating all and dissolving the moment into passions she could not comprehend. "It is the blue shaman," she whispered with certainty, wondering at her words, "the one who has come to judge me." She turned aside and returned hastily to Caer Myrddin. Wet, chilled and shriven, she bundled and cheered herself before her fire through the remains of the day.

It was not until late supper was taken in the great hall she saw the man again, for Bran sat his guest beside him at table. And a more curious guest she had never seen. He remained cloaked, his face but partially visible in the dusky light of the hall, so she was unable to settle on his features or firm him in her mind as tangible presence. She began to wonder if any other saw him. He reminded her first of this and then that one she had known; it seemed he was every man of a moment remembered in the reflection of an eye. She began to worry there was truth in Perrin's play, that death had come to the great hall unseen of all but her and this now her summons.

"Maia, what is this, who is he?" Maia, too, was perplexed. Despite her mastery of the arts of illusion, she found Bran's guest cloaked from any intrusion by the power that enveloped him. Magda worried it was Caron come to her discomfort. Not that he had the appearance entire but the build was right, and there was enough of him there to make her believe she saw through the façade. She asked of Blaise and he added to her perplexity, for it seemed to him Bran's guest had the likeness of the monk who came to St. Odile. Telgesinus concurred. The more they pondered it the more they were unsure.

"It is in Bran's hand, and we are not yet given to see the guest for whom he is," Blaise said. "For now it is important only to be still, to realize that *he is,* and trust all will be revealed."

But Magda would not let go. "It must be Caron to hide himself so. He cannot be allowed to interfere. He must be taken."

"You are courting hysteria, on the verge of losing all if you persist." Blaise rebuked her soundly. "You are not mistress of these conditions. Embrace the unknown with grace and confidence in your being."

She stung at his word, and felt the ire of Irkala upon her, incensed at the suggestion she was not mistress but mastered of those who set her trial. "Let me strip this veil from him," Irkala raged. The surge of feeling at once reflected back upon her filling Magda with dread. And still she felt Irkala's impulse to act and confront the stranger whom she feared the spoiler of her plans. Then she felt Maia's firm hand upon her, and as had Blaise she urged caution. "Far more to this there is than we understand," she whispered within. "If the evening is to be ours we must bide our time for our moment."

But there he was apparition in a robe of midnight blue, transparent yet corporeal, and unwilling to relent she must ask others near at hand what they saw. Variously, Siduri, Constanza, and Perrin said what they discerned, first this way and then upon reflection another, revealing more of themselves than the intruder. At last the whole image wavered in their minds and they must all agree to disagree, and Magda all the more convinced it was Caron beguiling sense.

To Bran, however, the man appeared to offer no contradictions but welcome companionship. There was animated conversation between them and often quiet laughter. Indeed, he fit in so easily at table with their host that Magda's imagination on fire with what she would that night accomplish, at length forgot him.

After the raw weather of her day, the meal was warm and wholesome, if nothing compared to the delicacies of Venice; and the fire was bright on the hearth warming body and mind as well as heart. But by some order her mirrors were gone from the walls, and the silver wish fulfilling trees, as if to say we shall have no illusions here. All that remained were the tapestries and a curtain drawn behind Bran. When it was withdrawn, inlaid in stone and set as a seal upon the wall was an image of the sun-wheel, engraved with the very markings she knew from the Sonnenrad in Green Chapel. But how was she to walk a pattern sealed in stone upon a wall; the whole affair seemed suddenly to her, ridiculous.

And so it was, the chamber mellow with fire and candlelight; drowsy with food and drink she began to dismiss the whole affair as farce, musing on the pleasures of an early night to bed, until Blaise catching her mood pressed her arm in warning. It was then she remembered this night the matter of her investiture as Domina of the Blood Royal was upon her, and she would have the matter settled. But this delay was intolerable.

She decided to take the initiative, and after sweetmeats rose before the company to address Bran as host of the feast.

"Last night I brought too much of another world into this," she began, almost confession, "I would ask your patience in my unfamiliarity with your simpler ways.

"So, lest we further misunderstand one another, let us move swiftly to the consummation of this event in the manner known to all of us." She concluded with homilies and gestures of appreciation for her hosts, and sat satisfied she had put matters back in perspective.

"It is well said." Bran rose and lifted his cup to the Lady Madelon. "And so to the purpose of our gathering this evening. Take it away, the remnants of our feast, and those of you who would follow after into the outer chambers do so, leaving us to conclude our affairs." There was some shuffling and noise of clearing until all fell silent and Bran spoke again.

"To complete the investiture of the Lady Madelon into the power of her Order, as rite of passage she must demonstrate her mastery of the cycle of forces focused in the sun-wheel of Caer Myrddin. And, milady, it must be done in the spirit of the task the Guardian sets when you entered into the way to come to us. Are you prepared to do this?"

"And to show you things that shall be hereafter," she replied.

Bram nodded turning to the man at his side. "The Guardian will oversee the trial. "With your permission, my lord, we shall now address the consummation of this trial of sovereignty."

The one at Bran's side suddenly took on stature none supposed, "Let the Troth begin," he answered, and all Magda could think was that Bran, lord of Caer Myrddin, addressed the stranger sat at his side as his lord. These few words hung like fate in the air; she burned with animus at the thought she had a master.

"The trial of sovereignty is a time of clarification, a time for setting to rights any issues that come to focus in initiating a new cycle," Bran began. "As it is for the Domina so is this a trial of the Masters of Hallows ability to uphold the cycle of her tenure, bearing true witness to those forces given into their hands."

It could not be Caron with Bran, and yet she could not be sure. It was all high seriousness and Bran, seashore scavenger and gatherer of shellfish, was gone. His tone was absolute and she knew what lay before her was no passive ceremony but life and death.

"So, then," she said, gathering up her dignity like a bundle of rags from a basket of laundry. After a long painful moment, she whispered, hoarsely: "If you will but lead me to the Sonnenrad, I will show you how it shall be under my hand."

"Where would you have us lead you?" Bran asked.

"I cannot walk upon a wall," she snapped.

Those who journeyed with Magda to Caer Myrddin sat petrified, unaware how to assist, until Blaise spoke. "If I may offer some assistance, Lady Madelon," he said, approaching her in confidence. "The way of the sun-wheel is the ascension of consciousness and the incarnation of force in creation. It is the seal upon this world. The seal upon the wall is to be seen not as the thing itself but remembrance of what is written within.

"Visualize in your mind's eye what you have accomplished at Green Chapel. Nothing has changed but what was without must now be found within. Go beyond the beguiling illusions of the world to the threshold of the worlds within yourself. There shall you walk the pattern that opens before you. You can only lead by your own passage through that state of consciousness you bring to focus.

"Transcending the illusions that bedevil human consciousness, mastering of the forces of creation, and walking the path of life established in the Holy Norm: This is what is expected of you as Domina of the Blood Royal.

"As you do so those gathered here will bear witness to your experience. They will see through your eyes, hear with your ears, feel what you feel, and so have the measure of what you offer them."

"Am I to let them into my world within, my thoughts, my feelings, my aspirations?"

"Those with the purity of heart to journey with you will; those who cannot will sleep their sensual sleep and awaken none the wiser. But deal generously with those who enter into the cycle with you, for these are your kingdom."

"I have right of blood to rule and yet you behave as if you have the power to deny me that. Who are these people to put such demands upon me?"

"All they ask of you is proof you have mastered the way within yourself so you may be trusted in it. You are here to show them mastery, Magda. Do so."

"Very well, you shall have what you ask and more." They had no idea of what she was capable. Maia and Irkala would see to that in ways they could not begin to comprehend.

"We ask of you only that you be a revelation of that pattern you would magnify in the earth."

Despite the distance between them the others had apparently heard all, but only then did the Guardian speak. "You have come here, Magda, believing the Troth is entirely about you." His voice was like falling rain on parched, dusty earth to her, and roused longings. "It is not about you, but the oneness of creation and Creator. It is affirmation of the great cycle for the spiritual regeneration of the human race. Do we understand one another?"

Not about her? Of course it was about her, but she nodded assent. Bran continued. "In anticipation of the Troth, the Master Flegetanis saw that his daughter, Siduri, bearing the lost Hallow we know as the stone of sovereignty to this gathering. In her he has fulfilled his commission to return it to the place where the jewel has its true setting."

A gift of Flegetanis through his daughter, Siduri; it stung her. That was not how it had come about. But Bran was not done. It appeared he was about to lecture her on its meaning.

"The Blood Royal is one of seven patterns shaped in the time of the great transgression, for the spiritual regeneration of the human race. I will not speak to that now for this work is before us. Giving the stone its setting at the core of the sun-wheel is the focus of this timeless rite of passage and its consummation, is of no small consequence and, indeed, a matter of life and death.

"Lady Madelon, if you feel this responsibility beyond your present powers there is no shame in it, and you may wish to continue in your rite of confirmation and leave the fulfillment of this challenge to another yet to come."

Was he offering her an easier way on and out? His words cut to the quick and she answered swiftly. "If you allude to past failures, they are none fault of my own, for I was betrayed by that false knight, Hugues

Caron, and occasion lost. I am well able, so let us wait no longer what humankind has so long awaited, but address the issue now."

"Very well," Bran replied. "Gather up into to your heart and bind to you the sweet influences of those who would stand with you that together you may serve to loose those wonders written in the substance of the stone of sovereignty."

He was barely seated when she challenged. "Shall you not bid Siduri yield me the stone to bear with me in my trial?"

"The Ladies Siduri and Constanza will bear it in their bosom, until all these things are accomplished. When your consultations with the Master Blaise are done you may begin."

Bear it in their bosom? That made no sense. It was tangible, real in its powers and she needed it, but dared say nothing more.

"What you will see in the way of trials is all within you, milady," Blaise began. "This present order of things was framed in a time when the true creative field for this world was mitigated lest all flesh come to destruction. You will touch into the core of it and bear witness to the great seal set upon those forces which must in measure and in season be loosed to restore the world to the pattern of the First Time."

"But you my Masters of Hallows govern these forces."

"They are beyond all of us. We have but touched into their powers and among us Flegetanis alone could claim any true level of mastery, and he would not."

Her assurance in what lay ahead was shaken by this admission. "So what is your point?" she asked.

"Humility," he replied. "'Except the Lord builds the House, they labor in vain who build it'. We are here not to master the universe but to learn to let the divine design in every present moment reveal itself in living."

Magda crossed her hands firmly before her, bowed her head in meditation and turned inward, shaping in her mind's eye the sun-wheel at Green Chapel. Maia rose upon her. "Fear nothing. You shall see through my eyes, and though we walk through darkest night, we are one in this. Those gathered here shall see what I will have them see of the world we will shape."

"What of Irkala?" Magda had developed a dependence on her obstreperous nature. She told herself it came naturally. Brutally frank as the crone was, she reminded Magda of the ways of the Cailleach, who as a young woman, too, had walked this path.

Irkala answered from the depths. "To Maia is given to tie water into knots. But if you would have my power upon you, when the moment comes you must choose the left hand path and walk into the fire." Irkala did not need to press her case with Magda. A mix of discouragement and anger turned to petulance already betrayed her, and where the heart fails the shades enter in. She had every intention of doing as Irkala counseled. Nevertheless, Maia guided now and led into her vision of the sun-wheel at Green Chapel. She saw herself again standing in the rain on the threshold of the sanctuary. One step more across the limen and she would stand on her own ground, and well she knew what lay within.

She crossed the threshold but it was neither Green Chapel nor the hall of Caer Myrddin she entered in but in a twilight hour before dawn into a great circle of standing stones, aglow under an indigo sky. She'd heard stories how the sage Myrddin once transported great stones over vast distances shaping a standing monument to his arts and shaped a sun-wheel. But this was unlike anything she'd imagined. It was a place apart, a threshold where a focus of forces of the Otherworld touched upon the earth, and she now in the midst of it.

Unlike the Sonnenrad of Green Chapel there were no marked zones; no lightning rays leading out from the core to the cryptic rune markings on the periphery; no visible path to guide the initiate through the cycle of the forces. There was no eternal flame burning in a fire pit of black obsidian. She was not looking at the body of the sun-wheel but the design of its core. The dark sun was gone, and in its place a circle of five great dolmens, four bracketing an inner space. The fifth at their head, a superior arch rising slightly above the others, defined the arc, and within the arc of gateways a circle of twelve standing stones about the height of a man.

She stood on the threshold of the sanctum. Between her and the fifth gate within the arc of standing stones was a polished altar of white marble. Back of the altar before the fifth gate was a djed pillar about the height of a man, a white obelisk topped with the sun-stone of sovereignty. Its radiance illumined the altar, the arc of gateways, the space within the dolmen arches, and penetrated beyond the periphery of the circle into outer darkness. It was by this light looking out from the core she saw an outer circle of megalithic gateways, and that she was not alone, for through those arches others in twilight gathered to the margin of the rite about to unfold.

To either side of the fifth gate, transfixed into something more than what they were, sat Siduri to left and Constanza to the right of the altar. On low pedestals of stone, palms flat upon their laps, backs upright, eyes fixed sphinxlike, they kept watch for eternity over all who should enter into the inner sanctum of the five gates. She wondered if they were at all conscious or merely present, for they betrayed nothing.

Her Masters of Hallows stood each at his gate, and at each one's side the handmaiden who bore the Hallows of his order. The fifth gate beyond the altar bearing the stone of sovereignty was unattended, but for the silent witness of Siduri and Constanza to something yet to be.

"It is the divine design of man to which these stones bear witness," Blaise said, coming near. "Here the worlds meet in man: the sword of spirit, the chalice of the heart, the spear of intellect, the paten of sense: each in his turn will place these upon the altar of the golden bowl, the soul and setting for the jewel of divine identity.

"I can offer you no more, but must now take my place in this circle of life. What unfolds now is a revelation of what is within you, and you must rise up and prevail to offer a true setting for the jewel of sovereignty. The Guardian of the Way will attend you. Abide in him and you will come through."

Gathered about to the periphery of the circle was the host of Caer Myrddin: servant to lords, all who dwelled, all who came to bear witness, all shadows on the margin of her consciousness. She panicked a moment at the thought they should all look upon her innermost heart in the moment of her vulnerability. Then her thoughts turned again to Maia and Irkala and the matter of her passage. She would implant vision in these feeble minds of the way the world would go, exercising her power over the imaginations of their hearts.

With that thought in mind she stepped across the threshold of the sanctum and entered into the forces at the heart of the Sonnenrad. She walked confidently to where Siduri and Constanza sat with cool, ceremonial countenance until she stood in the midst of the five gates before the altar and stone pillar before the fifth gate. Impassive, the two women faced her: dark haired Siduri and fair Constanza, like night and day, twilight and light gathered in a single being that showed as two yet one and inseparable. She knew now she should never have accepted Constanza into her sphere, but for the wealth she promised. She wondered what these two united might mean to her, impartial witnesses as still a stone to watch over her way.

A long silent minute she stood and nothing happened; then a voice behind her firm as dawn called her by name: "Magda is it for the purposes of the Blood Royal, or for Maia and Irkala of the Shades you come to us?"

Magda turned, behind her now in the way she had come, to the voice. In the core of the inner sanctum stood the Guardian cloaked in indigo blue, staff in hand. He waited that she should rest in him, and still Magda was troubled, unable to discern his face.

"You are not the first and until the heart is turned back again, not the last to turn for purpose and power to those who steal from life. It is for this cause we must clarify what the impure heart obscures to establish pattern, purpose and power anew.

"At each of these four gates are your Masters of Hallows. Each according to his response and so ability will open the gateway to his power to mastery of what is within.

"What you do here wrought in essence will establish patterns in the substance of your soul, to inform the seed of all you would tend in the earth as Domina of the Blood Royal."

His words were precise but their tone so mild and encouraging that somewhat of her earlier defensiveness let go and she felt emboldened. Determined to show only confidence, she answered, "I would reveal the world that was before the time of the great transgression."

"To what end?"

"So that was lost be restored and come again." It was ritually correct. She knew the litany.

"Very well, Lady Madelon, let us see what is written within you." His voice was like the latter rain penetrating her dry earth to a depth where she felt even Maia moved and roused to answer. But Irkala was hidden. "What does he want of me, Maia?"

And Maia answered. "This is a remnant of the work of the *Na-Akhu-El* sages, entirely to our advantage, for it is wrought in the place of shaping where I have advantage. This sun-wheel of Caer Myrddin is a seed of the seven worlds. Do but confirm the purpose of the masters in their gates and through them we will shape vision to substance and force to purpose.

"We shall enter in through the gate of the earth force; show them things that have been and the image of the world we shall together forge. Gisors is full of days but skilled and he will reflect the mirror of your mind that they may see what you see and what shall be hereafter."

And so Magda passed by and confirmed her Masters of Hallows in their powers: Gisors at the gate of earth and sense; Telgesinus at the gate of fire and intellect. Blaise must serve the gate of air and spirit, and Flegetanis no more her master of living waters, she assigned Perrin the task. He had no art but was simple and bound to her for promises made. And did not the daughters of the Blood Royal trust him with the delicate affections of their hearts? So then if not for wisdom then his sweetness of soul would bind the daughters to uplift him in his task.

When she was done confirming her Masters of Hallows in their places, the seal of Caer Myrddin was loosed. In the twilight before dawn flickering rays of dark fire rose filling the core. A soft answering pearly, white nebula enveloped the standing stones, and a field of forces with the power to shape creation came to focus in the sun-wheel of Caer Myrddin.

Irkala roused now eager to fill with force and fire whatever Maia shaped, but the impact of loosing the seal of the Makers at Caer Myrddin troubled Maia. The imaginations of her heart were one thing, but she underestimated the reality. She thought with Irkala to mine the deeps; to break down and release the residual force of old forms to new purpose, and fulfill her vision of a world restored. She believed the stone of sovereignty would intensify their will for change in this. She had never understood why the Aton-Re was content to let things be; why he was slow to bring change to a world suffering the bonds of the past.

The great seal of the sun-wheel of Caer Myrddin was more than she bargained for, perhaps even beyond her powers. She wondered if unawares she was caught up again in some game of chess with Innkeeper, a mere pawn upon his board. She saw him smiling over her ignorance and the implications of her acts. It angered her to think she was betrayed to a fate already seen and sealed.

This place to which she had come, this field of force within which she now stood, was no charade but a zone of intense power, a dimension of Archaeus she knew nothing of. It was an image of the vibrational seal wrought in the soul of man, to keep him from loosing power beyond him to destruction. And those who kept this place were none other than the lords of light she thought no more. Yet here they were the remnant of the Watchers, not fallen to the paradise drug of self-indulgence but true to the one law of creation; never entering into the exploitation of the flesh contriving to improve upon what is wrought in the wonderful one.

Maia panicked. Magda filled with fear. Irkala loosed a fiery tirade of resentment at all the suffering and sorrows visited upon man for his transgressions, though wrought of good intentions.

"I cannot cross over water," Irkala urged. "Come to me through earth and fire, and I will prevail."

"Silence sister," Maia countered. "We shall begin where last we left off, with the revelation of what has been in the earth and what might again be."

"Then receive my gifts," Irkala said. "Behold, your Masters of Hallows."

Magda turned to Gisors the oldest and feeblest of her masters. Were these men up to what she intended, or by her efforts might she well destroy them? But as she looked upon him she saw at once Gisors began to glow with such force as she had never seen in him.

"Now he is become *Arakiel*," Irkala said: "*Arakiel* who divines the signs of the earth, as readily as you might read words in a book, and by this power mates substance and light giving form to vision."

Magda turned to Perrin and saw shadow like a hand pass across his face and the man was gone. "*Armaros*, master and resolver of enchantments," Irkala whispered. "He will inform this feckless creature with power to gather up the hearts of the daughters of the Blood Royal to our use. Whatsoever they have hidden from you shall be as light of day to him. He will deliver them to you as vassals to be filled with your will.

"*Bezaliel* will influence Blaise in the way," Irkala continued. "His gift is to enter into the shadowed places of the human soul to inform and influence what will take shape. But Blaise is strong in his own right, and though in time he will succumb, it is no time for conflict. Even so, *Bezaliel* will seek out all that is hidden in Blaise and turn it to our purpose.

"As for Telgesinus, he is no more but the vessel of *Sham-she-el*, who so long endured against all odds to bring us to this hour. He it is who knows the ways of the sun to illumine the mind. In time he will awaken man again to the power of the intellect.

"He will become the most accomplished among the Masters of Hallows to lead where now we must go. All these principalities I give into your hand to inform with power the incandescent visions Maia kindles in your soul, Magda. And to you, Maia, in this I give you back your shaman Morgan Kara, and so much more."

"It is well," Maia whispered, ecstatic with Irkala's gifts. And Magda possessed of her and aflame with Irkala's craving stood again poised, hands flat upon the altar touched with fire in anticipation of what was to come. Irkala was exultant. This had gone very well. Already she accomplished more than she had dared hope; already she had positioned the vibration of those long repressed in the Shades in a place where their influence would once again be in the world to forge their pattern anew.

Magda composed her heart, and returned to the center of the great seal of Caer Myrddin. Her masters were in place but the stone of sovereignty and the fifth gate in which no one stood remained a mystery to her. Handmaidens to something yet to come, Siduri and Constanza betrayed nothing. Silent as eternity they offered no clue what was to come through the fifth gate, or how to enter into the power of the stone they guarded; by right, she supposed, the possession of the Domina of the Blood Royal.

Even Maia and Irkala were silent before the mystery of the stone of sovereignty. Its radiance encompassed the precincts of the sanctum and temple, but what was the key to shaping that radiance? Must she act in some fashion? Was it thought or feeling that would kindle vision, shape purpose and give dominion? And still she could find no way forward. She closed her eyes pondering the mystery, and when she opened again the Guardian in blue indigo stood before her.

"Are you now ready?"

"Who are you?"

He said nothing but stepped forward to within an arm's length. She resisted and would hold him back, but yielded in his presence. Still she could not see his face with any clarity beneath the cowl, but must. "How shall we begin?" Her voice faltered. He touched her in the forehead with three centered fingers, dissolving her world.

"It is begun."

34

Elysium

She was in a dewdrop, a bead of light falling in slow motion toward an ocean of still waters, and she was not alone. Her fall was not unpleasant, rather in the way one sinks gratefully into down-feathered rest at end of day. Still it unsettled her, for there was nothing to which she could attach meaning. The stones of Caer Myrddin had vanished, and she was in the midst of a heaven of firefly stars, descending toward a great sphere enveloped in luminous waters.

The little vessel penetrated the waters above the earth, inducing a kaleidoscope of colours about the vessel. In a moment it was done, and they fell into halcyon twilight. Yet even in twilight, earth answering to the call of the sun, spires of radiance rose from the deep to illumine the waters above and cast a soft glow over all the land. And by that light she watched a pastoral land rise up to meet them.

And there were other lights below, crisscrossing the land in a woven web of radiance, as if to mirror on the surface of the earth below the order of the starry heavens above. She could not measure the extent of the land, but by the arc of dawn on the Eastern horizon she saw it bounded by sea and appeared an island kingdom, for in a moment the land was gone and the waters below them sea.

Sensing the others to whom she must give answer to this flight of the soul, she dared at last look to the Guardian at her side. "You journey in the vessel of my soul to a world that was and is and is to come. Rest in me and all will be well."

What was she to do but watch and pray? Like the morning star they flew before the sun across a great wrinkled sea flushing rose in the first light of a new day, until at last again there was land. There the little dewdrop of starlight bearing Magda's soul descended slowly toward a great city that shimmered on the edge of dawn like a brilliant jewel dazzling the air. It seemed to her at once she was come to the core of the web of radiance crisscrossing the earth with filaments of light. Somehow it all began and gathered to this city.

"This weave of light is a vestige of what once it was," the Guardian said. "There was a time when the fire, the light, and the cloud of glory rising from within in answer to the sun, transfigured the earth."

"How vast the world," she answered, overcome.

"And yet a grain of sand on the shores of eternity," he said. "Upon this earth other realms long before our own have come and gone. And here where I have brought you now are the Atlantean, Bhāratan and Uighur empires; the kingdoms of Kemet, Ambertia, Thule, Hyperborea, Hellas, Elyria and more. All these once colonies of the Motherland and the Seven Sacred Cities are now passed from the earth."

"The Cailleach spoke of this, but I never thought…" She was overwhelmed.

There was no moon but two suns - a greater and a lesser - in the arc of the heavens to light night and day. The lesser sun was a pale blue star, its light as serene twilight. It was setting in the west as the greater light arose, and the city answered with an effulgence of light of its own. Radiant, it emanated from the center of the city, as if from the hub of a wheel, filling its avenues and lochs with a golden glow. And wheel it was for she saw at once the city was wrought in the likeness of the sun-wheel built on the island's shore. Three concentric circles of land, divided each from the other by an inlet of sea, were united by channels and bridges leading in from the ocean to the central harbors and city core.

At the core of the sun-wheel, where the eternal flame burned, in its stead rose a great white obelisk, hexagonal in design, and in height, she estimated, upwards of five hundred feet, topped with a shining pyramidion. At the base of the tower was a pyramid, about a third the height of the obelisk. It was the first of seven, evenly spaced along the arc of an expanding spiral that began at the point of the obelisk, encircling it three and one half times to the seventh pyramid on the shore of the central isle. From above the spiral put Magda in mind of the cutaway of a Nautilus seashell.

"Is it the Kingdom of the Atlantides?" she asked.

"From the time of the destruction of the Motherland, for two thousand years Atlantis bore the virtues and burdens of the world until it, too, fell into corruption.

"It was never Eden, but when man's first estate was lost it endured for the hour of his awakening again to divine identity. To that end, to restore what was lost, man must retrace his path and set to rights what then he failed in."

"And what was that?"

"He forgot whom he served."

"And for that all this was lost?"

"Now the legacy is ours, and the task the same."

Vast by any measure she knew, the inner circle of the city she thought more than 10,000 acres. Beyond that two more circles enveloped the core populated with homes, estates and parks. Only out beyond the order of the inner circles toward the periphery were signs of agriculture; a green and pleasant land of carefully patterned fields, nothing within sight haphazard.

Ships sailed the canals from the outer sea, tiny dots on the surface of the waters, and other airships like hers rose from the depths of the city into the morning skies. Like some geometric puzzle solved, everything was set to work in pattern. It was efficient, well ordered, controlled compared to the messy world of human affairs she had to deal with.

She longed to walk among and learn of them, for it was exactly that she wanted, utter clarity of purpose in her right and response to her rule. But no matter how hard she tried to engage and understand she was forbidden. It was beyond her mind, for a hedge was set against her and what lay beneath that would not yield or take the shape of her demands. Frustrated, she summoned up Maia.

"Hold." The voice shook her to the core and she could not resist. His word froze her revelation in the midst of its unfolding. When she was still again spoke. "What do you know of Maia?" he asked kindly. "Is it through her eyes you would see what I unfold in you?"

Her emotions flared but she yielded. "Is it not she who guides the path of every Domina of the Blood Royal?"

"She guides you in this to what purpose?"

"An end of sorrows," Magda said.

"She can inspire visions, but can she show you, does she understand what lies beneath?"

"I am taught of the masters that who knows the spell of it can go down to any sky he wishes."

"And to this end you seek not only the guidance of Maia, but Irkala of the Shades?"

"I wonder that man once had powers to shape a world like this, but now ekes out his meager existence pillaging the earth. Is it wrong to wish to see again man restored to what once he was?"

"In that end you must ask how it came to this, and hearing answer true."

"I shall ask of Maia and she will answer true." She said it fearing he might deny her soul's guide in this, but when she looked to him he seemed indifferent.

"It is your path. You will make your choices and in time to come live with the consequences. I am the Watcher who watches that no harm come to you in your trial."

Magda chose. Maia led and she followed. The Guardian was nowhere to be seen. Instead she found herself in the gardens of a temple precinct on the shore of a freshwater sea. The temple complex itself was bounded by four dolmen arches marking the four quarters and threshold of its expanse. Beyond the nearest gate so far as she could see the land was vast and uncultivated, green hills and flowering meadow. The temple city itself was mostly parklands, interspersed with water courses, fountains and falls, rambling pathways, groves of trees and two main boulevards intersecting toward the center. In the midst of the city was a small crystalline pyramid shimmering like cut jewel in the sunlight.

Among the parklands were homes, small estates surrounded by trees, open and ample greens and flowering gardens. Nowhere was there sign of farmland or commerce for this was a city of the Na Akhu-El priesthood. They who dwelled in the populous city of the Atlantides were busy about many things; here the numbers were few and those seen went their purpose along the treed ways that crisscrossed the city, as if the day was light as air.

No horses, no form of carriage or conveyance was evident, until a shimmering dew-drop shaped vessel passed noiselessly over them, casting its shadow a moment upon the ground and vanishing in a trail of colour, like the flash of plumage of a bright bird seen in an instant.

"Not a dragon," Magda assured herself, remembering her fall through the waters above.

"Vimana," Maia answered. "They journey wheresoever they will, and not by this means alone compass the earth. They have many arts. Come, I will show you."

In a parkland a party of joyful children played by a fountain. The air was sweet with the scent of misted waters, flowers, and springtide sun; with green grass and the fresh air off the sea. The children were like sunshine; they seemed less an element of earth and more light and air. It was into Maia's garden of memory she had come and she now their teacher appeared, a woman of about thirty years, watching over the children at play.

Maia was dressed in ancient Grecian style, off shoulder gown leaving her other bare, in plain white fell to the ankles and gathered at the waist with a golden tie. The children, boys and girls in tunic and short kirtle, hemmed with bands of bright colour, gathered together to the fountain for their lesson. Each held a silver flute like instrument, eager to play.

"Maia." Magda was amazed. They were so like unto each other, she could scarce think her apart. But Maia was no more the guide within, rather the companion at her side.

"This is the first instrument for the children to master. "Each has visited the *Mu-aulos*, maker of instruments, and the *Enarmon* to attune their first *Tau-re*," Maia said. "Each instrument contains a small crystal harmonizing it to the vibration of the one to whom it belongs. None other may play it but those authorized in need to enter in upon their vibration. From the day they receive their first *Tau-re* they are regarded as *Anomon,* neophytes in the ascending way. And so they are until they achieve mastery, or are content to go no farther. What is possible to them is not imposed, and only according to readiness and response is it given.

"For most of these it is beginning of a lifelong path of mastery. As their specific gifts emerge they will be given instruments fit to their purpose, until they come into their own. Through a succession of *Tau-re*, they learn the vibratory arts of shaping; their relationship one to another in the unfolding patterns of creation."

Magda did not need to ask for Maia at once discerned. "These few are drawn to class from throughout the realms, noted from earliest years for their gifts, or they would not have come here to the masters of vibration for their training. Among these are those to whom we will in time entrust our future. But today they are children, and I have brought them here to play."

There were some two dozen or more boys and girls, disciplined to wait, but in the way of youth eager to get on with trying their first *Tau-re*. Eager, yes, but held in the invisible embrace of a loving, guiding force that gathered about the parkland, and tempered by their teacher until at length with a smile she raised her open hands, clapped once, and loosed them in play.

And play they did; each on his own vibration, each seeking his own inspiration. Maia watched in wonder as from the *Tau-re* of one little girl of about six years a cluster of blue and golden butterflies took form, engendered from the vibration of sound and soul substance focused through her instrument. They fluttered a moment on the wind and dissolved in the light. Another cluster emerged in pinks and orange as she changed key and these, too, dissolved in the wind. Butterflies there were in profusion from the children's *Tau-re,* drifting like blown soap bubbles glistening in the light a moment, and always in a moment gone.

But there were also flowers of many hues, blossom and petal fall from the current of sound like windblown apple before the leaf when their season is done. And flowers out of the earth, as if time for them was reduced to a brief moment of existence, rose up, leafed, flowered, petals blown on the wind and gone with haste to stun even the most stoic in the brevity of life. Fish leaped in the pond, silver and orange and reds and luminescent blues and greens, flashed a moment in the shining spray and dissolved. And birds, a feathered glory of little wren like creatures, flitted off into the bright air as the ray of their creation was touched, evoked a moment, and released in a stream of melody in light and air.

"We are in a haven," Maia explained. "All things here are shaped but a moment. Students of vibratory creation must first learn how all things wrought in vibration are brought into harmony, each with the other, before loosed in the earth. The masters who sustain this field so that no harm may come as they learn, have set the pattern of control today for the children to learn the vibratory patterns that inform the shaping of flowers, fish and birds. And, of course, the children's perennial favorite, butterflies.

"They will learn that all this springs from the current of life within; to understand that every thought, word and deed wrought in the current of life contains vibration and power to shape. They will likewise be taught that not everything man conceives need be given form. Indeed, nothing should take form until harmonized in the divine ground of life, with *That Which Is*. And so their elementary education is not only in vibratory creation, but how to let go, dissolve those things that are of a moment, and move on."

"Wonderful."

It was all Magda could say, but Maia countered. "Once it was so, but the age is fallen and we are entered upon a degraded time. Most here gathered will not go the distance, and many are like to defile their arts and fall into chicanery. Some few we trust will prevail to lead home again."

And as she said it one small boy entranced with the power of the *Tau-re* piped up a falcon-like clawed bird with mottled feathers. It hovered a moment in the vibration of its creator's instrument, uttered a piercing cry, and rose up on the wind. At that cry of life everyone fell silent, watching the bird circle lazily on the wind, expecting every moment it would dissolve but did not. Instead, it circled effortlessly until it found a rising current and never faltering rose high above them in sunlight and air until it was but a speck and gone vanished into the sun. The children all gathered round wanting to know how he had done it.

"He is a child of five years," Maia said. "If he continues in this wise, he may well be the master of all our arts, and we look to him for the way we must go. But if we fail him now we may yet learn to dread his life."

They left the children in the care of another who came to watch over them. They walked the path along a watercourse, flowing through gardens of flowers the likes of which she had never seen, each filling the air with the prayer of its being, and it seemed to her a perfume of longing. Some began to blossom as the greater sun rose higher on the horizon.

"The greater light to rule the day; the lesser light to rule the night," Maia said. "So was it in the First Time, in a time before the moon was. Between them they modulate the pulse of time and keep the rhythms of creation. Between them they differentiate in the earth the vibrational essences of solar rays across a vast spectrum. And the earth answers with radiation of her own far more subtle than anything the world now knows."

They passed a tight grove of olive trees, and from behind a flowering bush peered a satyr. And the creature with a man's torso, horsey human face, goat tail, legs and phallus full erect, was decidedly leering at them.

"Satyros," Maia said. "Ignore him, for this forbidden work is the abomination of those who have perverted the vibratory arts."

As they passed the satyr put his pipes to his lips and began to play, a haunting melody to seduce the vulnerable soul, and for a moment Magda was drawn.

"Be gone," Maia said. With the heft of her hand upon the air she thrust the satyr back, and he dissolved in the shadows of the wood. "I show you this to warn you of the thorn in the flesh."

It was not something Magda wished to remember, for her response left her with a feeling of disgust. In a moment it had taken on a life beyond her powers and she wondered at it. Still, it served nothing for her to seem naïve. Did it not ennoble Magda's cause to be aware, and with the courage to face and overcome those things that must be overcome on the redemptive journey home?

"This time emerged again after a long dark age. And in that time through powers now lost to us all manner of abominations were wrought in the flesh of this world. The creature you saw was once a man, warped by abusing vibrational arts to shape something life never intended. 'What is to prevent us', the erring argued. 'How shall we learn what can be, if we do exploit all possibilities come before us'?

"Some have even done these things to themselves, thinking they may impose upon their own flesh whatsoever they will. They think to tarry as they will in these deviant forms of creation for the sating of lusts, as sport for the ladies, or the mere challenge of it, and return at will to their exalted places. Perhaps, this poor satyr is one such wizard trapped in flesh of his own making, come here seeking redemption from the masters of vibration.

"And there are those who perversely distort the flesh mingling man and beast for revenge or murderous intent. These have no regard for those laws of creation we seek here to instill in the young, as we grant them the gifts of their heritage as sons and daughters of God. Yet it is the law of life that unstable in creation most of these aberrant forms pass swiftly, though some linger longer and would wreak havoc among us except we are hedged from them."

"A satyr among the children?"

"Here his power is diminished," Maia said. "Did you not feel it when I dismissed him? Here any child could easily overcome his song, and he must obey."

"Beasts such as these reflect distortions of an earth force warped to a mood or temper. It may be through someone here, caught up in self-indulgent humors, he found his way through a breach in the hedge into our garden. More likely something human in him yet has come for healing. He will be dealt with humanely, and if he can be found in that distorted flesh will be restored to what once he was. Failing that he will be given to live out his time in the wilds of this world."

"The masters have means to restore him?"

"If life's design is yet wrought in him and a control pattern fit to the need can be established and held until the work is done, yes. It all depends on his willingness, his response."

"If this is your memory, Maia, what became of the world that was?"

"Some things I remember, and some things I have been told: it is hard to say which is which anymore. Six thousand years after the fall, the world that was could sustain no more what was wrought upon it. And this came to climax in the destruction of the Motherland in a region of the earth you know nothing of.

It is remembered as the expulsion from paradise, from the Eden of the soul, and the way kept by cherubim and a flaming sword. It was for the sake of man that some life might be preserved, for in that day the powers men then possessed brought the very earth to the brink of destruction. Thereafter, the mantle of power passed to Atlantis, and though the powers of old were greatly diminished, for a thousand years the kingdom of Atlantis served to light the way. What you see now are its last days."

"Then Plato's story is not myth?"

"What is myth but memory obscured by an impure heart?"

"And now Atlantis is come to destruction."

"From the time of the great transgression there are those who have never forgotten their first estate. These are the Watchers, the sons and daughters of God in the earth who live and serve to restore man to divine identity.

"Some thought the way hard, the course too slow," she said, hedging her thoughts. For a moment speech failed her. Maia felt Irkala resisting lest saying too much she undermine their agreement. But it was beyond Maia's craft not to answer truly. She was moved by what had come upon her, and began to doubt the way she was set upon. "There was division among the Watchers," she said, cautiously, "and a conspiracy.

"Knowing the power they had to shape the flesh, some among the Watchers contrived to blend their god-like substance with the patterns wrought in human flesh that mankind might more readily be restored. Of this they said nothing to those who would not agree, for they believed in the righteousness of their intent.

"Taking of all the fair they chose, the fallen Watchers bred of them god-like offspring, but also mutilated giants, beasts, and abominations of the flesh to make this satyr we saw appear almost human. A dark age ensued, and I show you now a time in the last days of the world that was, a place apart where the sages of old yet dwell. Here the best of our generations have come to learn the vibratory arts of the Holy Norm, taught in harmony with the divine design of God, free from the perverse impulses of the impure heart.

"Here that some flesh true to the divine design might be saved, the lords of light shape the seed of the Blood Royal for a world to come. You were made to bear the seed of light that the kingdom of God shall be again, and such things as ought never to have been shall be nevermore."

"We are then in the time of Noah," Magda said, "when the seed of salvation was sown in the husk of the ark upon the waters of the world."

"In the time of Enoch," Maia replied, "when the work was done, and the wonderful one took that people into Himself to empower the seed of restoration. And it was given Noah to prevail and preserve that seed in the time of the great flood that overwhelmed Atlantis and the kingdoms of this world."

They walked silently toward the temple gardens, Maia troubled realizing this was beyond her, not what she shaped but alike given to see. She knew the Aton-Re must have a hand in this revelation, and she hung between exaltation and fear, not knowing where the path led, only that she must walk it. If only she was attentive to Innkeeper, it should not have come to this.

They stopped at a great gateway to the central precincts of the city. Beyond the threshold was more parkland, a triune temple of outer and inner courtyards leading to its inner sanctuary – and, at its core, a polished blue quartzite pyramid. And there they stood because they could go no further. If they pressed forward they were thrust back in proportion, and to press on despite the repulsion raised a fire within that burned to warn and repel the offender.

And though they could not enter they could see in the distance those who dwelled within the fiery hedge, and to see it struck holy dread in Magda's heart. Even Irkala whom she sensed urging her forward in their purpose, drew back in fear unwilling to be revealed in this company.

They were about four times the height of a full grown man of stature, about 24 feet Magda judged; and of that shape of men and women, as if by long and careful cultivation, come to perfection in them. From afar off she watched them come and go, so graceful in their ways they seemed to glide along the pathways, for though of great stature refined and infused with light. It was as if the form of human flesh a quarter their size was measured out to cloak a being of great stature, shining through gossamer weave of substance. And that shining, enveloping each in a cloud of glory, rose above them as a flame rises to a point, wings of radiance furled in arcs of glowing light.

"Incarnate angels?" Magda asked.

"*Malachim* uncloaked," Maia whispered, with a pang of fear. "We cannot go further. This place is hedged against all but these one hundred and forty and four Watchers who abide to keep the way of the tree of life. Except invited, even I cannot enter here.

"All I can give you is a glimpse of man as once he was and truth be told may be again, angels incarnate. Soon even these will depart," she said sadly. "And when these have ascended the way between the inner and outer realms will diminish to barest necessity to sustain this fallen world."

"It is cruel to inflict sorrows upon man."

"He refuses to acknowledge the source of his life. In every imagination of the thoughts of his heart he defiles the holy place of his being, contriving to impose his will upon creation. If he continues in this wise he will destroy himself utterly." Maia surprised herself for though she argued as Magda did, she saw now with the eyes of necessity.

"Enoch is the focus of those higher powers given man. Ascended, those powers shall be no more, and man will be faced with the consequences of what he has wrought. If there is any wisdom left in him, he will again seek the light."

In the current of the moment Maia felt keenly her discouragement with the obstinacy of man. Thousands of years had passed from this moment revisited, and still man resisted, insisting that earth was his own, and for him there was no divine design. They stood at the gate Magda watching the lesser sun, not yet visible but a light touching the eastern horizon with twilight blue, begin to rise. The greater sun settled in the western sky.

"It is not the firmament of heaven I know," Magda said, wistful and lost.

"When these powers are withdrawn, man cannot bear the complex patterns or survive the spectrum of forces loosed in the earth by reason of these two suns. One will go a journey, and instead of the blue star, the lesser light of a moon that waxes and wanes will remind him to reflect on the cycles of existence, and measure with care the journey of his days."

In the heavens the radiance of the gold and blue suns mingled; the gold gradually diminishing, the blue promising a contemplative mood of evening. Their blended radiance drew longing from the earth, gathering up essence like a petaled flower closing in upon itself in rest, distilling the perfume of the day in an offering to the day to come. In the cool of the evening, gazing into the temple gardens a great peace come upon them, and one of the *Malachim* turned toward them.

As he came he drew in his substance and his form concentrated, until standing before them in the gateway he had the appearance of a man of normal stature. Even so there was a presence about him that spoke of hidden dimensions of light and force, of informing power, and so much more before them than met the eye. He glanced a moment at Magda with a smile, but his attention was fixed on Maia.

"Maia," he asked, "when do you come from that you are here now?"

It was a strange question to Magda seeing they walked here from the park where children practiced with their *Tau-re*, but it seemed normal enough to Maia. "From the time for which you now prepare," she said: "from a time when what you now take from man shall in measure be given again, and he must rise to it or an end made."

"In the time of the coming forth of the Archangel," he said. "And are you now here because you would fulfill the purpose for which the Blood Royal was wrought in the patterns of the flesh?" he asked with a glance to Maia. "Are you come through this one?"

"And the Guardian of the Order," she replied, for she knew she had not come to this of her own.

"Then I will tell you what I have seen of the times to come. In the last of days, despite the many blessings of the open way set before him, men will abandon reason and yield to impulse, acting in hot haste, despite the consequences.

"Do you not do so to succumb to emotion, for then shall all things be in such delicate balance that in the midst of the fury you must awaken and inspire those who will to dwell in the eye of the storm.

"And for that day mar nothing given you to uphold. And when abomination of desolation is seen in all the earth, never forget there are many in diverse places that have never forsaken the way. And as you live to inspire vision in the hearts and minds of men, rising above the tide of the times, these shall come to abide in the secret place of the Most High.

"Man will survive but this perversion of life shall cease to be. The heart of man is defiled, his mind in its service a wily beast, and this shall be no more. These things will pass from the earth and those who cling thereto, with them. Only the body of life, the temple of the living God, shall remain. From inception to fulfillment this inexorable cycle we have wrought will run true to course that divine man shall dwell again in the living earth."

She envisioned only offering glimpses of the past she knew from the records of the Archaeus to inspire Magda to act. This went well beyond what she knew. The lords of light she once thought passed from the earth in some number did yet abide, and she feared now she trespassed on their works.

For her part Magda was dumbfounded. She had thought this was all about her, and now must stand silent by for the *Malakh* was intent only on bonding with Maia. A medley of colourful patterns of light filled the silence between them as they fused in a current of life that illumined the flesh, and burned a steady flame between them. Nothing was said but Magda knew Maia was changed.

The Watcher said nothing more but when it was done raised his hand in blessing and was gone. But the connection made across the hedge with those who kept the sanctum of the garden city. And the sense of it lingered, a current of longing in the liquid blue evening light of a star, which was soon to go cold for the hardness of the human heart.

"Were it not for the fallen Watchers it would not have come to this," Maia said. "But wise in their own eyes and desiring change, they sought to improve on what was wrought in the unfolding cycle of creation.

"And now those who yet dwell within the hedge will bring an end to the abominations they have wrought in the earth that the way of restoration remains open to man. And to that end they have seeded in essence in the flesh of the Blood Royal the patterns of the Holy Norm, and initiated a cycle by which all this may come to fulfillment.

"They have gathered up the essence patterns of all things in the vibrational ark of life, and recorded the memory of this in the Archaeus of these worlds, that so long as man lives there will be those who do not forget. All these things are written within, and sealed in the stone of sovereignty, that in the hour appointed they may be restored in the consciousness of man and in all the earth.

"This they have accomplished. Hereafter, the powers of the fallen Watchers shall be confined a shadow of what they were, and an end brought to the corruption of the flesh of this world.

"I had not thought to show you these things, Magda," Maia confessed. She wondered herself at the spirit that had compelled her. "Nevertheless, as Domina of the Order of the Blood Royal, you must understand what you are."

Magda felt Irkala's passions rising in her, full of ire at the injustice.

"But for those who were banished, what of them," she said, curtly. And the question struck a chord with Maia. What of Morgon Kara? What of her own passion for change. "It is unfair they should languish in a world of shadows," Magda said. "Were not their intentions good? Did they not act to benefit man? How will anything change for the better if all efforts are punished?"

It was clear to Maia that Magda failed to grasp the magnitude of this corruption of the heart, and defilement of the flesh. So serious was it that the end of all things living had come before the Lord. The more she thought, the more the turn this had taken from what she intended troubled her. What was written in the Archaeus, revealed in the garden of her memory, challenged her understanding of the powers at her hand to shape what was in the light. Had she forgotten something? Had she been a part of the transgression of the Watchers, and spared the memory? The *Malakh* had known her, and the revelation had taken on a life of its own. Keenly now she felt the warning of the Moirai that for anything Irkala promised, she would exact a terrible price. She feared she was being drawn into a cycle of ancient evil come round again.

The moment passed. Magda stood alone within the circle of light at Caer Myrddin. As if they had never parted company, the Guardian stood still at her side, but the Master Gisors no longer kept his gate. One she did not know had taken the place of the Master Gisors, and through him she had entered in.

"Gisors was old, compromised, and unable to bear what was asked of him," the Guardian said. "His place is taken by the Master Origen of the monastery of Alba. He has shown you what you have seen, but cannot abide long for other duties await him. When this passage is fulfilled you will need to seek another in Gisors' stead, for he is full of years and his day is done."

35

What Lies Beneath

Where once there was sea, there were mountains; everything green and fresh, colourful and wonderful vanished in a lifeless wasteland of weathered rock and drifting sand. Where once a sacred city stood scant ruins - the residue of centuries of human folly - alone remained. And still she recognized something of the outline of what she'd seen. The lintels of four gates were visible above the sands, the upper tiers of the temple in the midst of the city, an obelisk, the apex of a pyramid: all these threatened by looming dunes, driven by relentless winds under a fierce sun. And there was no water. She despaired that after all man's efforts to shape the world of his heart's desire, it should come to this.

"Can Maia show you what lies beneath?" The Guardian's words came back to haunt her, now more important than ever to understand what lay beneath that all man's works came to ruin.

She was utterly alone. Magda no longer felt the presence of the multitude that gathered to her rite of passage. She reached out for Maia seeking guidance and no longer felt her presence. She went deep into herself in search of search of Irkala's fiery obstinacy and found nothing. No one answered. She was utterly alone in a wasteland under an unrelenting sun, with the wind driving sharp little grains of sand into her hands and face. There was no way forward, or any way back and nowhere to go. An abyss of nothingness opened before her, and she was on the edge of despair.

She turned slowly in a circle away from the sun and there was nothing to see but the stumps of time and the last standing stones of a city where once children played the games of shaping in the parks, while their elders kept watch over the ways of the world. Only when she returned again face to face and peered into the now blinding light did she begin to see. In the sun there was a speck and then a spot; the spot became a quaver in the shimmering shape of a cloaked man coming toward her. And though she feared him she quickened at his coming; relieved not to be left alone she ran to meet the Guardian who came for her to Caer Myrddin.

"You have chosen a fine place," he said. "Could we not have met in a well-watered garden in the cool of the day?"

"Where are we?"

"At the end of willfulness," he said. "Always it comes to this. But I have told you no harm shall come to you and those who gather to Caer Myrddin to serve the purpose of the wonderful one."

"And out of the desert, where do you now come from?"

"From measuring the city of man," he said, holding up his staff.

"What shall become of us?"

"Ruin to all those who enslave the souls of men and lay waste the earth. With the coming forth of the Archangel shall an end shall be made. And it shall be in this wise, through the intensification of the radiance of life in the flesh." She did not grasp his meaning; but the tone, the spirit in which he spoke the words, were filled with the white heat of purifying fire. "And to the end that some flesh might be saved, I have taken the measure of the holy place; and of the holy of holies given for the indwelling of those who find union in the wonderful one."

"And the earth, what of her," she protested.

"She bears but a semblance of the beauty that once was hers. She shall return to us, our home among the stars in the kingdom of the sun."

She was afraid of him. "What are you that you have this authority?"

"I am the Watcher who watches. What I see in the darkness of the world, the wonderful one also sees, and answers in light." He drew back his hood and Magda stumbled backwards, as if she'd seen a serpent.

"Caron," she gasped.

"A greater than Caron is here."

She looked again and saw herself mistaken. "You have something of his semblance but more…like unto the *Malachim*."

"You have seen us."

"But a moment and through Maia's eyes," she said.

"Your heart is yet more a mirror of the earth than a window of heaven," he answered. "The man you saw in me disturbs you?"

"The man betrayed me."

"Betrayal and redemption turn on what is in the heart."

"He left me with child."

"You sought to slay him."

"Where is Maia?" She was anxious now, her throat rough with heat, and the wind blew grit in her face. And what in isolation was fallow now filled with animus, anger at being here and so treated, vexed that she was judged by one who reminded her of Caron.

"Shall we continue, or shall the *Troth* end here?"

"I am Domina of the Blood Royal," she whispered, hoarsely. The purpose of generations drives me on."

"None gathered to Caer Myrddin are awake to this: neither Maia nor Irkala can penetrate the hedge I have drawn about us, except I permit," the Guardian said. "Even so where we go you must keep governance of your heart, lest the hungry ghosts possess you. For it is by these in what lies beneath that all man's works come to naught."

It troubled her the Guardian bore some semblance of Caron, but when he offered her an open hand she took it, feeling again the pang of love she once felt and how mercurial the heart. And as she did they stood in the midst of the city of Ruin in the Archaeus of the Shades, where Maia came in search of power to create the world of her heart's desire.

She knew now this was all beyond her. A wasteland is a wasteland. If this is what lay beneath and brought the world to ruin, she would give up her claim to Domina of the Blood Royal if only she might return to the comforts she had known without the responsibilities that attended them. In this desert place she longed for the rains that brought lilacs in the spring, in the summer fields of lavender that left the air heavy with their scent; and with the latter rain the robust fruits and red wines of autumn.

"We are on the margin of the uncreated world." The Guardian raised his staff and pointed toward the horizon. Through the air tainted with yellow haze she saw afar off a ragged backbone of hills which resolved into fractured shapes of broken buildings.

"Shall we go there?" she asked. There would at least be some relief, she thought, from this unrelenting nothingness.

"First I will show you the rift in the world, for in a day of war in the heavens the earth near came undone."

He turned her about to face away from the city and pointed with his staff. Where he pointed the air quickened. Afar off a column of dark cloud arched up against the pale sky, and the air turned electric crackling about them, until they were aglow with the force of it.

"Do not fear its coming." On the horizon, like a tornado canted to the earth, on long serpentine coils the dark column writhed across the wasteland toward them, an umbilical connecting the city of Ruin with what dwelled in the depths of the rift.

The Guardian turned slowly in a circle scribing an arc about them with the point of his staff, and when he was done opened his cloak and drew her into him. The dragon of the wilderness brooded over the land a gathering storm, its influence held at bay by the hedge he'd drawn about them. As it passed over she saw within the vortex of its coils forces discharging lightnings; fire that filled with smoke of burning in the gloom. On the tide of its passing phantom faces stared out of its midst, filled with rage and despair caught up in its coils. And following after came emotions of fear and greed, and the wrath of humanity knowing no way out of the vitriolic essence of all that was anti-life and yet drew them in.

"It is the dark wind, the distillation of all unreal spirits to which mankind is given, and with it comes madness."

It might have broken them where they stood, like great surf a tiny shell upon the reefs of the world, but it passed over with but a moment of darkness, and no more than a whisper of influence, as it coiled its way across the sands to inform the city of Ruin.

"It has not touched us," she whispered.

"There is no need to make it one's own. Come, and I will show you, despite the gift that man should dwell at home among the stars, how in conflict with life he is down among the ashes of existence."

They stood together on the canyon walls overlooking the rift of the world. Looking down into the cavernous depths it was easy to believe there was a time when the earth was near torn asunder. It was a time of worlds in collision, of vast forces thrown out of balance straining the foundations of creation. And the ruin of that was buried deep within the strata of the human heart.

Magda stood with the Guardian over a scene so vast she felt she stood on a firmament of air, the great void beneath them all that was real and the rest a dream. Trembling on the brink, she peered into the chasm that opened beneath her feet into the canyon of a million years. And she saw written there as in the pages of a book, the detritus of ages, the ruins of one civilization stacked upon another, all sapping life from the tree of life. "These are the generations of the old heavens and the old earth," the Guardian said. You see before you the record of all that has been written in the grains of the earth."

She stood upon the substance of seasons past informing civilizations, sustaining them a little time, giving way to a new season in the life of the tree. So long as they lived they were part of the tree of life. Root and branch, past and future, the tree unfolded in time, each age a day in the life of the sun; each sun a twinkle in the eternity of the present moment, all marred with the seed of destruction in them, from the time of the great transgression.

In the depths of the canyon below eagles rising on the spiral currents of time, crossing the strata of worlds. Seeing them in flight she was filled with the urge to cast herself into the depths and soar if she might as they did. Might she not enter into any one of those realms grained in time, and work change? She focused her eyes upon the strata of ages until the general became particular. Here and there vistas of landscape opened up before her: treed, barren, mountainous, meadow lands, and distant beings moving upon them.

"Night and day, season upon season, the sun-seed unfolds itself in the living forms to make a dwelling place in the wilderness between the stars. In the First Time, past, present and future is but one time, illumined in the sun, brought forth in the tree of life."

"Might one enter again into these realms," Magda asked, "unconstrained by time?"

"Here there is no time, only content. And knowing the way of it, one may go down to any sky he wishes to go down to. He swept his staff across the canyon walls and with the tip of it pointed deep into its depths. Far below, down beneath all the layers of sediment piled up over time, in the deepest grains of the earth, through the narrow canyon a shining river flowed. "It is a glimpse of the river of life," the Guardian said. "Let it rise in you."

Her eyes rested on it and the canyon walls dissolved from view. Sight and sound and sensation of the river filled her senses until she trembled with the rush of it. The river flowed in a deep smooth current but the air above it glowed, shimmering with rainbow light. Within the whorls of light forces flared out about it like feathers of flame. It seemed to her like the long body of great rainbow serpent rising up out of the deep, gliding through this ancient canyon and rift between the worlds.

"It is a glimpse of Leviathan," the Guardian said. "Born of the waters under the earth it is the force within all things, rising in the grains of the earth through the essence of all that is, to sustain the tree of life in the garden of earth. Thence it parts into four heads, four great forces flowing onwards to inform the whole garden of creation in the kingdom of the sun."

"What is it if not God?"

"It is the answer to the urge of the Almighty; the waters of the Deep rising in resonant response to the radiance of the wonderful one.

"I have felt its impulse in me in the turning of the year," she said, "and the earth answer with spring."

The Guardian touched her on the forehead. Her mind blazed with light and when her sense cleared she was far above the earth looking down so that it was now a shimmering blue jewel, radiant with its own light, moving silently against the darkness of the Deep trailing clouds of glory.

"In the eyes of the wonderful one the radiance of the river of life informs the whole earth," the Guardian said, "but not earth alone for it fills the created places between the stars, uplifts and informs the whole garden of the kingdom of the sun.

"Though we dwell in the earth and are all but unconscious of it, we are in the midst of titanic forces. No flesh would survive were it not for this place of habitation at the balance point of life."

"Our home among the stars," Magda said.

"A paradise were we but willing to awaken in the light."

In a moment it was done and again the land was barren beneath her and Eden, close as a heartbeat, elusive. "How did it come to this?" she asked.

"When man fell, changes must be made to preserve life in the earth. A planet once a sun was a sun no more. Others were moved in their places. All these things are recorded in the Archaeus, remembered in legends of the gods and war in the heavens."

"I have been told these things, but what of the dark wind?"

The Guardian swept his staff across the radiance of the river and she followed with her eyes where it flowed, a narrow sunlit stream deep in the canyon depths. The canyon walls heavily stratified with civilizations past, as if the detritus of the river had left them there in its passage through time, came again into focus. But now brought closer she saw them crawling with bloated forms like maggots on a corpse, gripping like leeches sucking the life blood from the residue of ages past. It revolted her to see it, as if a bloated tick sucking the life blood of her.

"These are the hungry ghosts," the Guardian said, "full of industry, parasites passionate in their pursuit of wealth."

"What riches are they mining?"

"The ills of generations past, to empower Irkala and the fallen Watchers of the Shades," he said.

"Do they yet live? Is this the end of human life?"

"There is no being here, no divine identity," the Guardian said. "Here only is the residue of those in life lost to life, those who would not let go and make the crossing. Wealth and power only they desire and this reward. Scarcely sentient they to win life from Irkala and possess the flesh of the world, they mine grievances from sorrows of the past, thinking them jewels and precious stones.

"And not these alone who wealth and power desire serve her need, for many are possessed of causes, obsessed with perversions, fanatic to obtain and possess, and driven to impose their ways upon others. All these, too, who survive in the rift, do but mine grievances of the things that have been.

"In life these will not be told otherwise, for the rational part to discern proportion, balance and the fitness of things they gave up long ago rationalizing obsessions."

"But wealth and power…" she started to say, and bit her tongue. She had steeled herself to the pursuit of it for the purposes of the Order.

"In the world these are the arbiters of human will," he finished for her. "It follows that one utterly devoted to the acquisition of wealth values it above all, and when he comes to viewing the world is utterly deluded, believing these alone give shape to the world.

"The hungry ghosts of the rift worlds are but a residue of life essence bound a season by passions, until they dissipate and are no more. They see only what most possess them, but whatever they may believe all they mine are grievances: fear, greed, shame, wrath, resentments, regrets, discouragements, and a host of broken patterns of lives lived in bondage to sorrows by reason of them.

"These precious hurts they extract from layers of substance laid down by the generations of sorrow and suffering of man caught up in the fallen state.

"And Irkala exploits the residual patterns of their obsessions. She sows and reaps and gathers in on the black wind; shapes her seed and sows again, aggravation in the human heart like tares among the wheat. None of this begins or ends with her but she has become mistress of exploiting the darkness of the heart. Her purpose in this realm, when she was given charge over the fallen Watchers to keep the seal on their powers locked in the Deep, was subverted long ago."

"Is there no hope for them?"

"The same for one and all, to let go and enter again into the tree of life and let come what may," the Guardian said. "But fearing oblivion they live in hope of a host among the living, where many are possessed of ill spirits that override their own and give them welcome. This is most like to come about when the human heart sinks into discouragement, for then almost any ill spirit may enter in and take up residence in that one."

"She does this for the fallen Watchers?"

"Irkala, too, is obsessed. She gathers substance to force the seals which confine their powers in the Deep. To end her own bondage and that of the Watchers, she would release those titanic forces once again upon the earth. To that end she conjures the dark wind surging through the hearts of men. And many there are, thinking themselves rational, given cause are driven by what lies beneath, swept along on the dark wind of grievance.

"Of this come wars, which she dearly loves, to harvest yet more substance to her purpose. It is spiritual wickedness and yet she does not see it so. She believes freeing the powers of the fallen Watchers will bring the world swiftly to order, that through suffering and sorrow man will awaken to a new tomorrow."

"How else is it to be done?"

"An altar of the heart on the threshold of the realms of light: kept by the shining ones of the First Time. Those who answer in the light rise up in it. Those who prefer darkness to light shall have it, and it will be as if they never were. That is the truth of it from the beginning, and so is it now and ever shall be."

"And this is the purpose of the Blood Royal," she said, "an altar to the lords of light?"

"The order was made for the time when the white fire of life will purify the heavens and the earth of all corruption, a time when those patterns ingrained in the flesh and in the grains of the earth shall be purged and come never more to remembrance."

"How long," she asked.

"It will be as in the time of Noah, a time of intensification of the fire of life as it were a flood upon the earth. And in that time there will be an ark of truth to sustain those who respond in the light of the wonderful one. And for that cause your order was established, that some flesh might be saved. Come now, I will show you Irkala's realm in dark heart of the city of Ruin."

They came to the gates of the city through which the dark wind flowed, and a force that would possess and consume her. Though it seemed not to affect the Guardian not at all she strove against it, and again he drew her into his cloak to protect her from it. And what she felt she now saw, the city wrapped in serpentine coils of force from which no light radiated, but concentrated darkness in a hunger that would not be assuaged, that gnawed at the pit of her stomach, and left her speechless.

"In the Deep the river of life rises, parting into four heads to sustain the way of the tree of life in creation," the Guardian said. "Of itself the dark wind is nothing, all that comprises it is force stolen from life, without which it would not exist.

"The hungry ghosts mine grievances of ancient ills to feed the dark wind. Here it informs the city of Ruin, enters into the roots of the pattern tree, beguiles with darkness the senses of men, and insinuates into the world of the ten thousand things.

"Let go in me. Do not regard the dark wind, not for a moment," he said, taking her hand. Still, she felt murky sexual currents rise at its presence, and fevered opinion on all she had seen flood in upon her. "Rest in me," he urged. "To live in and by the dark wind is perversion of all life, engendering things in the earth of our worlds that ought not to be."

And so it was she passed through its coils, unsure for a moment whether she lived or died, through the gates of the city of Ruin into the darkness within.

36

Ruin

It was impossible to say at a glance how large the city. Under a leaden sky gloomy with discouragement, one could see little more than a half mile in any direction. And part of the city was no more, fractured by broken intrusions of rock running like a ragged spine across the horizon. On the edge of what remained were roadways, overlaid with rubble of broken columns and fallen buildings, left to time for the futility of building up what would inevitably come down again.

It was a city that had all but given up. Yet some buildings still stood, some hundreds of feet high carved out of weathered rock and worn by time into a surreal landscape of rough-hewn standing spires rising like giant stalactites out of the red earth. Rough arches linked the hoodoos, and here and there a light glimmered through the hollow eyes of passage ways, small shelter from the dark wind that scourged the empty streets.

"What is it you would show me?"

"The end to which all the works of men come," the Guardian said. "So long as he strives for good or ill to impose his own and thwart the will of the wonderful one, everything he contrives comes to ruin in these withered stumps of time. I have brought you here to teach you to let go, to free you from the bondage you unwitting seek."

It was not to her alone he spoke. Immediately before Magda was Maia; again very much her own likeness but without the ravages of the world upon her.

"How did you come here without me?" Maia demanded. She appeared with a shining that sundered the grey gloom of the city and first made Magda turn away. Shaken by the accusation in Maia's voice, Magda drew close to the Guardian and felt his confidence rise in her.

"I had not yet summoned you," the Guardian said, "but as you are here you may now walk with us, or withdraw as you choose."

"The Watcher has shown me the rift in the worlds," Magda said, regaining her composure.

"I cannot go there," Maia said.

"As you slept she walked with me," the Guardian replied.

"Slept?" Maia's attention fixed fiercely on the Watcher. "Few there are in Whiter Morn could have done this." She sought him out, insinuating by every subtle influence she knew to penetrate and know this one who stood before her, but found no way to take hold of him.

Instead, her own force returned upon her and she drew back unaccountably in pain. "Who are you?" she urged.

The Watcher drew back his hood. They stared into the face of the Watcher and he held them with his eyes, until he felt confusion rise in both of them. Maia fought back her ire, and as mildly as she could command she composed herself. "Caron," she said, "is it you? Have you come this far?"

"I do not think it Caron," Magda demurred. "What he has done is well beyond Caron's arts."

"You are deceived," Maia countered. "It must be Caron."

And the Watcher watched. He saw the play of force between them, the scattering of focus, their inability to see through the veil of confusion that clouded their hearts, and said at last, kindly, "how is it you do not know me, Maia? Magda speaks true. What I have done is beyond Caron."

Magda felt for the first time Maia's uncertainty in what they did, but she must trust her who guided over the years, and so she took her part to confront the Guardian. "If it is Maia's will, I shall go no further with you."

"Then let it end here," the Watcher said.

The dark wind moaned in the hollows of the tent rocks, as it wound out of the badlands toward its destination in Ironwood. The women listened, lost a moment rapt in the pervasive emptiness of its passage. Maia was troubled, caught up in the presence of something she did not understand but must. What remained if she failed to grasp this matter for despite herself she felt his power in her? "We will see this through with you."

"Is that your will, also, Magda? You were content to rest in me, until I brought Maia back."

"If Maia wills it," she said.

"This is an unaccustomed place for you Maia," the Watcher said. "I would you had never set foot here. You found your way but do not understand this realm. But as you have now you must choose whom you will serve."

"That is for one greater than you to say," she countered.

"Indeed, it is," the Guardian said. But they followed, none-the-less, and he led away from the hollow wind toward the sound of falling water. "The City of Ruin was once called Day-Spring, and was a holy place giving substance to the things of the earth before ever they took form in the world. Beyond this realm is the uncreated wilderness between the stars."

There were none to be seen coming and going in courtyard plazas among the broken towers. Squares and roads all were empty but for the wind, and flitting shapes of undefined forms clinging to a whisper of life force wherever it could be found. These ephemera took momentary shape dissolving again on the listless wind. They saw nothing but a gathering of cloaked, silent figures watching in the distance; far from indifferent to their presence, for as they moved toward the precincts of the old temple garden, the Watchers followed afar off.

"Who are they who watch our every move?" Magda asked.

Maia had not thought it would come to this. It was unimaginable the power this one held, but she must reassert herself and answered for him. "They are the fallen Watchers who rebelled against the light of the wonderful one.

"Stripped of their powers they languish here, caught up in the City of Ruin, striving to maintain their world, but powerless to prevent its decay."

She could not resist her rebuke. "It is a tragedy, a waste of their powers, when the world languishes in need of those gifts they once possessed."

"Possessed to the destruction of the human race," the Guardian answered.

Maia was infuriated but calmed herself, reconciled to seeing this through until the moment was hers. For now she felt Irkala's presence upon her full of ire that her realm should so readily be penetrated by one uninvited, and her wrath fed upon Maia's influence threatening to overwhelm her.

Magda, too, felt force on the dark wind. A wave of hidden power welled up, fire from the center of the earth surging through the decaying peace of the city. It shimmered and crackled among the ruins, roiling in great serpentine coils: now white, now green, and now red, shifting through the colours of the spectrum, then returning in a near blinding flash of lightning. In a flurry the flitting shapes were drawn to it, blazed up a moment and were gone. And they who followed afar off drew near but were held at bay.

Magda stared into the Guardian's face. Her gaze, Maia's gaze, the force of Irkala's ire; not one alone or together could they take hold. There was nothing to take hold of, nothing to attach. The one who looked back was transparent in the light, untouched by the flux of their influences. He is no plaything of the heart, Magda thought. And unaccountably Maia felt fear as for the first time her heart failed her.

"We must speak to Irkala's part in this," the Guardian said. "You three conspire together, and in that to heal the rift that sunders the worlds or hasten an end. It is you, Maia, who came here seeking agreement with Irkala of the Shades. Lead on."

Full of fears Maia led on, knowing what unfolded now was utterly beyond her. She led until they came to the temple precincts where Irkala kept vigil over the great seal binding the powers of the Deep. Four white arches defined the temple grounds, each leading from the city without into a court of terraced grounds. There the ruins gave way to a small but enduring garden. A shadow of what once it was, still the scent of water and smell of vegetation were pleasant relief from the desolation of the city. And it was here Irkala dwelled on the edge of Ironwood.

By whatever gate you entered all paths led through the garden maze to a narrow winding stair leading up through a rugged outcrop of rock to a smooth plateau, where the temple stood overlooking a quarry where water flowed and Maia first had come. They paused at the stair and looked into the vale.

"It is a gateway of the worlds." Maia said for Magda's sake. "From here none may cross the waters into the realms of earth and the Archaeus, and never Whiter Morn unless given them. And, yes, I have been here before," said defiantly. "I came from the Aton-Re to seek out the soul of one I would save," she said, putting her best face on it.

"One may not cross and yet influences rise out of this place?" Magda asked.

"When they find a willing vassal," the Guardian said.

From their vantage they could see the shape of Ironwood where Morgon Kara languished. Out of the rift of the worlds wound tendrils of dark wind through tangled undergrowth. It coiled among the thicket of roots, a parasite distilling the venom of fear, greed and shame; engendering creepers of grievance, resentment, and blame, burdening the tree of life.

"Once the pattern tree was the true image of the tree of life, given to unfold in the earth what was written in the heavens of this world. But man has so marred the Word of creation in violation of the spirit of life, all he engenders tends at last to destruction."

Down the rugged walls of the streams of water fell through a mist of green life clinging to the nooks and crannies along the escarpments. The water rose from the very rock itself, not from the surface rising but from the deep under the earth. In the vale was a great pool, its surface rippled by the falling waters, and in its midst a fountain of seven heads. As if a window opened in the heavens, a steady, undeviating beam of light fell upon the seven wellsprings of water that rose to meet it stirring immortal longings in the play of waters for the light and life that lay beyond.

The central stream rose straight up into the light, and the streams to either side pulsing first toward and then away from each other in steady, undeviating pattern. Likewise the outer two streams pulsed first toward and then away from each other, rising higher and counterpoint to the inner streams, creating the image of the body of an angel with great wings, wrought in shining waters and rising phoenix-like into the light.

"This image is given in remembrance of how they have fallen," the Guardian said. "And though they cannot approach the waters or in any wise amend its pattern to their liking, through that reminder they are privileged to look upon the light of the wonderful one shining through a rent in the veil that confines them here."

"She is waiting for us. We must attend her." Driven, Maia led the way up the stair toward the temple on the plateau over the vale of waters. The terrace was a circle of white marble, inlaid with twelve black rays emanating like lightning bolts from a dark obsidian core in which burned no flame. From the gateway the path parted left and right and led in a greater circle hedged by twenty-four seats, twelve to a side, evenly spaced around the margin and raised above the terrace to overlook the dark sun-wheel. At the head were three seats behind which Irkala stood, flanked by *Sham-she-el*, who was Morgon Kara, to her right; and to her left *She-me-haza*, who led the fallen Watchers in the day they sowed their seed in human flesh.

In each of the twenty-four seats about the terrace, male and female alike, were chief among those who followed after *She-me-haza*. Whichever path one took to left or right they met again at a small domed rotunda set in a wall of stone. Two erect marble columns defined a gateway within. Irkala stood and bade the three come to her across the obsidian terrace, but the Guardian went only so far as to ascend the stair and stand opposite her across the terrace. In fear of what came next, Maia and Magda both stood also beside him not daring to move.

"Would you have an old woman come to you?" Hunched over, the old crone hobbled to the arc of the sun-wheel across from them. Her court watched in silence. Stripped of their powers of old, most of what remained to them was stolen from the life stream of the living, and none to spare. Their hopes rested on what Irkala might wrest from this rare visit of one who dwelled in the light.

"This city once was Day Spring, the world in which men now dwell but a shadow of what once was. Come here, dear, come here." Irkala beckoned to Magda. "You have nothing to fear in me." Magda went to her without a glance back. "And Maia you came to me because your heart hungered for the paradise that once was; the paradise the likes of this Guardian," she said with a dismissive nod, "have taken from us. Come to me, sister, come to me," she said, her withered form taking on substance as they answered to her. And Maia came as ordered but with a furtive glance back to the Guardian Watcher who stood now alone.

"Here, Magda, long ago," Irkala said, "an unjust seal was set upon the powers of men. Those powers lost, the life force repressed, and man restrained to meager existence: you see what has become of him, sat down among the ashes of what once was. Man mourns his loss and knows not what he mourns. But we know locked up here in the Deep under the ruins of the world, is the power to bring again a world full and fair as once it was."

"And how would you do this?" the Guardian asked.

"The stone of sovereignty," Magda petulant answered for Irkala. "The power to loose in earth what is locked in the Deep."

"I know it is the key used to seal up these forces," Maia said. "Is it not the intent of the lords of light, in time to loose the seals set upon the vault of the ages?"

"It was so promised," Irkala swore. "And for that cause you came to me."

"For that cause," Magda echoed, realizing in her distraction she had forgotten Caer Myrddin. Now she felt the hearts of those gathered to her rite drawn in. Was this not her moment? Through her eyes they saw the ruin of the world and the undoing of all their labours. She must inspire them to bring forth with her a new order of the ages.

Maia and Irkala felt it, too, and with Magda came to the center of the great seal, and there they stood staring into the dark mirror of the Deep. The obsidian black yielded to Magda's eye, catching her up in sinuous patterns of force and form swirling in the depths. She gazed into the dark fire and in her mind emerged an image of mankind laboring generation after generation to destruction. Age upon age, civilization upon civilization, rose and fell, as dreams turn to dust and ashes, all seeking the power of fire from the center of the earth. And when her sense could cope no more it gave way silently to rest, the dark fires of her mind dissolving in a wilderness of stars. "What is in the Deep is beyond knowing," Magda said, turning away.

"And yet who knows the spell of it may go down to any sky she wishes," Irkala answered.

"To what end?" Magda asked.

"To seek out those things hidden in the depths of the heart," Maia said, "to make right what was wronged, to restore those patterns marred."

"And the spell of it is written in the Stone of Sovereignty," Irkala said.

"All that has been, all that is locked in the depths of the soul: patterns, purposes, powers sealed from us reach out for us. We need only come to this altar to remember. We need only loose what is sealed in the Deep to come again into our power and destiny."

"Do you not fear what you loosed will again possess you to your destruction?" the Guardian asked. "Too often what man creates possesses him, and falling subject to his creation he loses himself in its image."

"You cannot hide from me." Now filled with sudden wrath Irkala dared approach him. "I have found you out. It is Caron isn't it? Morgon Kara warned of you, but here it ends." She would draw three together in judgment over him, but Maia could not. Instead, she edged forward toward the Guardian.

"He will have told you, Magda, that I mine human ills to feed the Dark Wind, to influence the flux of the tree of life and mold the will of man to my own," Irkala said. "I have no will but to bring an end to sorrows they have inflicted upon us through their self-righteous judgment. For what have the thousands of years of the so-called lords of light served but the destruction of the world that was in the Flood? Nothing of any substance has been accomplished to compare with that shining city, that beacon of light to the world that was Atlantis.

"Look on your works, Watcher. Ten thousand years have passed, and for all your devotion to the wonderful one it is an abomination of desolation; a world of diseased men and women who endure a few score years in nightmare poverty, amidst violence, rapine will, and war.

"This one will tell you that I mine all these ills of the heart and mind, and shocks of the flesh to my advantage, but look about you; does it appear I have taken any advantage? No, but I am realistic about what is in the world and use those things that are in the world to goad man into action.

"In the earth are those still who bear within them the life germs, the seed of the essences of the Watchers. It is this seed I would empower to rise up as giants in the earth, take hold of this miserable fallen creature that curses his day, believing himself the victim of life.

"Look about you," Irkala said, with a sweep of her hand about the gathered host. "These are the Watchers of old who dared move the heavens and the earth. These are they who will set to rights all that fails for want of a compelling hand.

"Awash in grievances, left to its own devices the human race will destroy itself. But I have found a way to use the bitter harvest of the heart to compel man to follow the will of greater men. The lesser feeding the fires of the greater shall forge through will an order fit to his salvation."

"And when you have imposed the will of the greater upon the lesser to shape the world you envision, what then, Irkala," the Guardian asked?

Caught up in Irkala's passions, Maia and Magda forgot the Guardian. His question cut through the hypnotic haze of words that beguiled them.

"When we have awakened again the seed of greatness in man and brought this slovenly race into order, we shall weed out the tares from among the wheat and sow the seed of an entirely righteous world," Irkala said.

"But it cannot be done until mankind is brought into order, for in the mass he is entirely incapable of cleansing his own heart and mind. That is the great mistake the lords of light have made, believing teaching the way of wisdom and letting the spirit unfold a life, man would awaken and reform himself.

"It hasn't worked in 20,000 years, not from the time of the great transgression. And now there remain but a few of you in the earth, you of the *Na-Akhu-El* brotherhood. Oh, yes," Irkala said, "I know you for what you are, Caron. It was your kind who withdrew from the world that was, betraying the balance of creation.

"It was you who condemned and incarcerated these Watchers in the Shades, judging them fallen when all they sought was the salvation of man. And still the world is filled with violence; still the imaginations of the thoughts of men's hearts are only evil continually."

"Out of the root of bitterness, do you have anything more to say, Irkala?" the Guardian asked.

"I have no more to say. Everyone who grieves, everyone who looks into the depths of the heart for solace and a way through; yea, even the very stones of the earth, everything that crawls or runs, flies or swims and turns to the earth for comfort, speak for me."

"And you Maia, you and Irkala are sisters of old, though different as night and day. Cautioned of the Aton-Re, warned of the Fates, you sought her out and entered into agreement with her concerning these things. Would you still walk in the way she proposes?

"How is what she said not true?" Maia asked. "I have labored with those who dwell in Whiter Morn to turn man's heart back again and make straight his way. I have filled men's minds with incandescent visions of what might be; inspired, encouraged, uplifted and given my substance to their labors. Still, from the time of the great transgression, across a wilderness of years, he will not respond. And when he does it is but a little while before his petty nature drags him back, and he is sat down again among the ashes of his life.

"The sages of the *Na-Akhu-El*, the lords of light, have sought time and time again to illumine the inward path," Maia said. "But who can walk the way they walk, and what has become of them, for it seems all their efforts come to naught. Perhaps Irkala is right. Perhaps it will take loosing giants among men to impose order upon him, discipline him in every detail of his life, until he comes again to his senses."

Maia glanced at *Sham-she-el*, who was Morgon Kara, impassive seated at the head of the arc of fallen watchers looking on. She read more than they revealed. She saw after long captivity these daring to believe their moment had come round again to reside freely in the earth directing the affairs of men. And in that moment she felt unclean and unable to endure the feeling, sought to hide it away.

"These two with whom you have entered into agreement, make clear the choice before you, Magda," the Guardian said.

"A choice," Magda said dazed, for in so many ways Irkala spoke her mind.

"The choice the same from the time of the great transgression; the same the day your Order was ordained by the lords of light. The choice is the answer to a question you must also ask."

Maia sensed it coming and moved closer to the Guardian. She did so and looked again toward the temple where sat both *Sham-she-el* and *She-me-haza*. *Sham-she-el* caught Maia's eye and what she read in him was hope of release from the Shades into the earth, as it was for Morgon Kara. It all depended on Magda's answer, for by her choice alone would Irkala have an altar of flesh in the substance of the Blood Royal.

"What choice?" Magda repeated. The Guardian was silent. "Do you have no more to say; will you not make reply to Maia and Irkala?"

"Nothing more to say to these, but you must answer to all these things to reveal the measure of your sovereignty in the Order of the Blood Royal."

"Let her walk the pattern of the sun-wheel here that we may all understand these powers of the Deep you keep from us," Irkala urged.

"It is a matter for those gathered to Caer Myrddin and not for you, Irkala, to initiate a cycle of the Blood Royal."

"We have as great a stake as any in the restoration of the world of the First Time," Irkala challenged, "given our hurt, even greater. Lift us up. Help us to see. Give us our due."

"Think you we should yield this pattern to you, that you may inform all things with the dark wind; that you might steal the life force from all that yields to its influences?"

"Deny us this and you shall not go from this place, but I will bind you here to suffer with us."

"Could you do that, you would have done so by now. Could I not leave, I would not have come. I have promised no harm shall come to Magda in this rite of passage. But you, Maia, consider what you have hidden away that would bind you to Irkala, for I would rather you follow me."

In herself divided, Magda looked on as the Watcher raised his staff over the obsidian seal of the sun-wheel. The four and twenty seated about the Sonnenrad rose at once to their feet and the two at their head, *She-me-haza* and *Sham-she-el,* reacted, thrust to their feet with the force of it. Irkala fell backward three steps, and supported by Magda regained her precarious balance. But Maia moved closer to the Guardian.

"This is unfair."

"There is one law for all the worlds, Irkala, one undeviating law of radiation and response, action and reaction, sowing and reaping what is sown."

"What of mercy," she whinged.

"Despite your intrigues, you still exist."

37

The Mind on Fire

Again they stood in the midst of the five gates of Caer Myrddin, the stone of sovereignty aglow atop the djed pillar behind the altar, before the fifth gate. And still to either side sat Siduri and Constanza hands rested, open and upright on their laps, as if not a moment had passed, and without wavering they kept watch on that very spot a thousand years.

Even so something was not the same. Magda looked for Gisors remembering he was replaced by the Master Origen of Alba. She quickly turned to the others. Blaise was in place yet, and Telgesinus, too, but Perrin was no more, for at the first gate the player Falconieri was in his place. "But this is unthinkable," she protested. "Falconieri leads a traveling troupe of half-witted buffoons."

"You have mistaken him as you have mistaken me," the Guardian said, "and will accept our judgement in this."

"You all conspire against me," she protested.

"Nothing contrived. Caught up in time the Order suffers the ravages of time. In each Domina we must confirm her focus in the light that her heart be purified and a new beginning made.

"Through three gates we have passed to awaken you to your task. Yet a fourth remains and the force of it is fire." He glanced to Telgesinus. "If the Master of Hallows can bear we shall continue."

She had no intention of refusing, for she was filled with the promise of power to come but she was irate they held power like fate over her destiny. She would object but knew not how to overcome her feeling of being utterly vulnerable.

"Maia is inspiration to me," she appealed. "In her I have seen things I thought never to see, incandescent visions of what has been and what again may be.

"And Irkala, wronged by fate most cruel, yet endures to inform what Maia shapes with fire, to birth the world of my heart's desire."

"I understand," the Guardian said, "but you must answer for their influence in your life. As God gives you light to see the way, you must choose between ascension and the descending path. It is a simple choice and when you have made it we are done here."

"Has any Domina of the Blood Royal failed her trial of sovereignty?"

"Let me show you," he replied, "what became of the world that was."

Irkala, in her realm of Shades, felt the crossing but could not penetrate the presence that cloaked Magda. Nevertheless, the Master Telgesinus had given way to Morgan Kara's presence in him, and soon his possession would be complete. Maia's genius in shaping the light, and Magda, an altar in the world, together assured her own liberation. Others would follow loosing again the powers of the fallen Watchers in the flesh of man. In Magda's heart Irkala provoked sorrow in the memory of what was lost, and longing for what might be. "I cannot cross over water," she whispered. "To come into possession of your powers, you must come to me in the fire."

It stood a lighthouse, a great obelisk at the center of the triple city, an octagonal crystal tower hundreds of yards in height rising straight up out of the earth toward the heavens. It was not opaque but translucent like opalescent pearl, a glassy sea mingled with fire, alive and undulating with energies.

Magda was enraptured by the play of forces ebbing and flowing within the opalescent monolith; enchanted by the pulse of unheard music that set the soul resonating in response. She gazed into the heart of interlacing fields of intricate vibratory patterns; watched whorls of negative life essence rise in colourful spires to the apex of the obelisk, where all gathered to focus and shone as a jewel in the sun.

"It is the Tekhenos," the Guardian said, "the tower at the center of the matrix of power for the world, linking the heavens and the earth.

"Every pyramid, every henge, every megalith, every temple construct in keeping with the design laid out by the lords of light, right down to the dolmen arches, obelisks and every standing stone raised to that purpose the earth around, all these are attuned to the Tekhenos.

"And by reason of the Tekhenos enabled to establish a creative field of energy; focus light from the ambient medium and draw fire from the center of the earth to distribute radiant power to purpose from kingdom to kingdom. Without the Tekhenos the light of the world would go out and a dark age ensure

"It was this tower to heaven to establish anew an identity, refugees from Atlantis sought to rebuild after the Flood on the plains of Shinar in the time of the confusion of tongues."

"And that is what happened? It was lost to the Flood?"

"We are here upon the cusp of it. Those at war with the Atlantides will destroy the Tekhenos, believing there are those among them who have mastered its principle."

"Who will do this?"

"Atlantis is at war: so, also, Uighur, Bhārata, Kemet, Hellas, Ambertia, and lesser nations. The alliances are mixed and changeable. Most focus their wrath on Atlantis, fearing it gone astray from the way it so long upheld."

"And for the cause; in our time there are many?"

"If it were not one thing it would be another. In the end it is always insecurity, always the same sad story of struggle for wealth and power, influence in the earth, and dominion over those we fear. Man has chosen the way of the beast rather than the way of man. When the same old cycle comes round again and might be addressed: fear, greed, and shame obscure the way and man falls to the beast.

"And the beast will have but one head. Men fight among themselves who it shall be. Each fears what shall be taken from him, each fears to be cut off in the earth, each fears to live under the yoke of another. And the fear is real enough so long as man is driven by the appetites of the beast. So has it been from age to age as the cycle comes round again. And so shall it be, until the heart is whole in truth and restored to life, in a new cycle of creation."

"The air is charged," Magda said. She moved her hand through the air before her. It glowed and streamed colors of the rainbow in its traces. It amused her for a moment, for so much to contemplate; then she turned her attention again. "They do not think Atlantis fit to govern?"

"For two thousand years it was a gift to a world struggling back out from a dark age past; from the destruction of the world that was. Much progress was made; then there was division among the Watchers. Corrupt with power, those now confined in the Shades fell to manipulating the forces yet given into their hands, perverting the way of all flesh to shape things that ought not to be. They imposed their will where they had no right to violate the distinctions in the souls of others. And then they fell to quarreling among themselves.

"Other nations were little better. They, too, lost that fixity of soul that keeps the path of spirit true to restore the way of the First Time. Now it is come to climax. And, because the gifts of vision were lavished on Atlantis, so also is hers the greater offense.

"In the warring of the nations there have been many offenses against life. For its part, Atlantis has manipulated the matrix of power that centers here in the Tekhenos. They manipulate life currents in the earth and turn weathers against all living things in the lands of their enemies.

"Animals will not breed but fall to disease. Crops do not grow, and everything living sickens from within. The waters are withheld and peoples perish in torrid heat and cruel winters for want of those blessings nature fully intended for all. The mother of all living is disturbed in her very soul and the face of the land laid waste for want of her answering life."

"It is our myth of a wasteland, transformed only by the freeing of the waters; by a vision of the Grail, and of a question asked and answered truly."

"In this time," the Guardian said, "the Order of the Blood Royal was created that the true seed perish not in the earth. For these in warping the vibrational matrix of creation, have imposed abominations on the flesh of the world, such as was never seen from the destruction of the Motherland to this day.

"Perverting the power of the Tekhenos, the fallen Watchers bred giants among men to rule over them. And out of curiosity, because they could, they mingled animal and human flesh, taking diverse parts and tempering these abominations to serve their will. These they shaped to rapine and to murder, to the fulfillment of all their pleasures in a copulation of forms never intended. So it was that man fell yet further into the bestiality of the world, and we began to fear him lost.

"In varying degree the world around all followed in this path, mingling in a perversion of flesh remnants of the consciousness of man with the instincts of beasts, obscuring the light of divinity in the flesh, and loosing madness in the world.

"And from this abomination of desolation inflicted upon the earth, regeneration of the world was impossible without a new creation. To this end a seed was shaped to bear the essence of the divine design for all living, a seed sown upon the winter waters of the world, to unfold its reality in the springtime of an earth reborn."

"And this seed is the ark of salvation?" she asked, grasping for his meaning.

"All the wonders of creation are coded in the vibrational matrix of the human soul. Noah, a prince of Atlantis, was forewarned of what was to come. Heeding his word they who bore the seed of restoration prepared to leave this land. And so was it also in other lands under the guidance of the lords of light. This is the seed of a new heaven and a new earth given to bring forth in season the divine design of the wonderful one."

"And none dare attack Atlantis for the power of the Tekhenos that sustains their kingdoms?"

"The Bhāratan Alliance has found a way, a new weapon that kindles like the sun. Daring the outcome they will seek to penetrate the hedge drawn about Atlantis to destroy the triple city and Tekhenos, contriving to take up where Atlantis leaves off."

"Empires have come and gone," she said, "but nothing again has risen to this level."

"In the House of the Sun are powers fallen man cannot begin to comprehend. Hereafter, he will find his powers, his consciousness and even his physical stature greatly diminished. His days will be numbered to but a fraction of what once they were.

"And the path is long from this you now see until the age in which you live, many thousands of years. Across this wilderness of time man will journey toward redemption in the last of days for which this provision was made."

"And is that time now?"

"Even at the doors, and yet a little while. In those days to come things shall be again not unlike the time of Atlantis. Then shall all things gather to man's final decision of the way he will go. He will choose between life and death, the way of destruction or the spiritual regeneration of the human race."

"And the seal upon the Deep that binds these ancient powers in the Deep, shall they then be loosed again in the earth under our hand?"

For all he had told her it was an obstinate question, as if despite his care she had not comprehended his intent but craved to come into power of her own. He answered with restraint in his voice. "In that day each man must be able to rise up in response to what is loosed in him," he said, "or perish from the intensity of the revelation in the flesh."

While they spoke the Rider of the Storm returned and the tempest gathered to them. From the four quarters of the earth it began with omens in the weather; the earth in a fever under a dark cloak of troubled atmosphere gathered to her. At the core of the city of Atlan, the air was still and the sun shone through, but laden with foreboding. Afar off at sea, like a great bank of dark cloud blotting out the western sky, a titanic wall of water bore down upon the land. And still two suns shone high in the heavens.

"Come," the Guardian said. "We must view what is to come but from the high place on the mountain of the world." She took his hand and he drew her in, folding her in the mantle of his cloak. When she turned to look again they were upon the ramparts of a great temple high above the earth, so that she looked down on the kingdoms of the world below so far as the eye could see.

"I have brought you to the summit of Whiter Morn where the realms of this world touch on the realms of light. Here everything is in essence, a garden planted eastward in Eden for all the days of our tomorrows.

We have looked into the depths of the Shades, where those who sowed destruction in the earth are confined. But it is here in the heights of Whiter Morn that all the kingdoms of this world come into perspective in the light of the wonderful one.

"Is this Maia's realm?"

The Guardian pointed below and for a moment a realm she had not seen came into focus, vast before her. "This is the Archaeus of the worlds of heaven and earth, the realms of essence from which the world of the ten thousand things springs. They are four and twenty in number and lesser realms within, and one of those is where Maia dwells."

"But how are we come here?"

"The way of the crossing in consciousness is written in the Aton, the sun stone you call sovereignty."

She looked again and the kingdoms of the world stretched out before her in plains and rolling hills and aspiring mountain tops reaching above the clouds all awash in the radiance of two suns, the lesser that illumined the night, the greater the day. They were together now high in the heavens, marking the transitions in the cycles of the heavens and the earth, opening wide the doors of the worlds.

And on every horizon encircling the mountain of the world, great spiraling columns and chasms of cloud rose, dark and threatening, shrouding the land and the seas, shot through with the rays of two suns so they glowed within.

"It is the beginning of the seven days of light." The Watcher pointed toward the lesser sun. But you shall see it all in an instant of time, for now Lord Kronos who ruled the land of Atlan will pass judgment on what has become of the kingdoms of this world."

As he spoke the lesser sun kindled, its light obscuring the greater sun, intensifying until it was brighter than a thousand suns in the heavens, penetrating everything upon the earth with the radiance of a nova stella. Those not blinded in the radiance sought out the dark places within walls and in the caverns of the earth, though its essence penetrated even these.

"Seven days Kronos blazed forth pure virtue," the Guardian said. "Other lights, too, appeared in the heavens, seven in number all taken together, and by this outpouring of radiance the mandates of the realms of light were written anew in the grains of the earth. When it was done the waters above and the waters below were loosed, purging the earth of the world that was. And the earth herself was asked to give answer as to what should become of man, whether he should live or die."

"What choice does the earth have but to bear man?"

"If the earth was made for man so also was man made for the earth. Come a time when he no longer responds to the light of life, then she has no further purpose in him. In that day she will no longer support a life so much at odds with her own, and man will cease to be. The mother of all living, still held in the radiance of the wonderful one, has been most patient with man, but there comes a time when it is, *thus far and no farther*." And the Guardian remembered in silence, but let Magda see as he saw.

On that day Atlantis died the mother of all living wracked in her bones, and pained to be delivered of her burden man. Every volcano erupted, and mountains smoked discharging fire and ash. An incandescent mass of roiling flame seared the air, and in thunder and lightning earth discharged her burden of hurt. A great rift opened in the earth, the land unfurled like a carpet shaken, shattering the kingdoms of man in earthquake and fire. Mountains fell and valleys rose changing places. Seas slipped their bounds. Here withdrawing, there advancing, drowning the broken land. Such commotion there never was in the heavens and the earth, for reverberating through every valley, resounding from every mountain top, she cried: *It is enough.*

After the seven days of the light of a thousand suns the star began to dim. Then it was come round again an ancient nightmare glowered in the heavens. With writhing tentacles like serpents on the head of a Medusa, the Rider of the Storm returned. Its tail stretched from horizon to horizon; the air bristled with its presence. And the head of the comet was like unto a dragon that spewed fire and bitumen upon the earth.

"In the day when all things shall be set to order," the Guardian said, "the one we call the Rider of the Storm will take his rightful place again in the house of the heavens in the kingdom of the sun."

Still, it was not that she feared but the dying sun. Magda watched as writhing streams of incandescent vapors, substance flowing from the stella nova plunged into the mantle of shining waters about the earth. The hedge broken the deluge from above began, first like great drops of dew and then a streaming torrent. Then the waters of the deep erupted. From within the earth the great underground rivers burst forth upon the land, and where they broke through the earth collapsed into the void they opened. And still man waged unrelenting war.

Atlan was utterly seared with fire. It was a weapon fashioned by the Bhāratan League, an iron thunderbolt that shattered the restraints of nature and loosed fire from the center of the earth. This they launched in the air from a vimana of great power. In one night the kingdom of Kronos ceased to exist, the flood of waters mercifully ending the suffering of those caught up in the burning time. The foundations of the kingdom collapsed, Atlantis sank into the depths of the ocean, a flood of waters rising up leaving nothing but muddy shoals and sea. And so it was the land of Atlan once a shining light in the earth, was lost to the memory of waters.

Still it was not done. Caught up in the wake of the stella nova, the old sun stripping atmosphere from the earth in a fearful field of fire, were it not for the broken mantle of waters thrashing rains upon the earth, there should no flesh survive. And it was these rains continuing unabated forty days, covering the scorched earth with healing waters that allowed some flesh to be saved.

Magda huddled within the Watcher's cloak as if to shelter from the rains she saw, though no rain or any harm fell upon them. But there were tears. She sobbed and wept for mankind lost, whimpering like a small creature of the earth, huddled within its rocky den, seeking safety from the thunder, lightning and wrath of the storm. In her hurt came Irkala whispering insinuation in her heart, that except man learn to be as god, he was ever a victim in the hands of an angry God.

The Watcher stood with her in the pre-dawn chill of the morning silently facing what must inevitably come, and come it did. "What must I do," she asked, "that the likes of this comes nevermore?"

"A simple choice," the Guardian said. "We have set before you blessing and cursing, life and death. Wherefore, choose life."

38

The Choice

She could not see, but hear the sound of waters near and far. Magda was utterly alone in the dark. By touch alone she guessed she was on a rough, narrow ledge of stone, and would not move for fear of what lay beyond. She willed it change for her and it would not, so she sat silently gathering what little wit she had remaining.

She had been taught to first calm the waters of the heart before attempting to shape anything beyond, and when she did it all began to change. It began with the first flush of dawn on the horizon of her mind. She forced nothing but simply rested in the realization and she began to see.

The sounding waters fell from a high ridge encircling a half moon caldera. On the crest of the ridge the waters parted into seven heads, falling over rocky terraces of fire burned rock where channels shaped and cooled in the once molten mass. Each stream parted into veins, some cascading in rugged flumes, erupting in spouts, pooling and falling to the next plateau in white veiled falls. Under the force of the water spectacular fountains arose pulsing with invisible currents as trees in the wind. The whole cliff face of terraced ridges, outcrops and plateaus was a cacophony of waters; falls and fountains gathering at last into the caldera and vanishing.

Her own position was precarious. She was on a narrow ledge at the head of a roughhewn path that only a mountain goat would willingly attempt, descending from the crag to the edge of the caldera. But it was the way she must go, and for what seemed an hour in eternity she picked her way down the cliff face to the great caldera. When she reached the water's edge, she realized how desperate her cause. It was beyond her art to calm this flood of waters. "What do you want of me?" Magda shouted into the waters. There was no reply. She needed something more; influence on a scale she'd only imagined, and must insist.

"Yield me the sun-stone, and I will master the waters and the way we must go." Still there was no reply. She wondered after those who had gone before, who despite the promise of a new day were left in darkness how to master the chaos of the world.

At Green Chapel she was taught to begin transit of the sun-wheel through the force of water. She suffered the Masters citing the impetuous nature of her desire. She was counseled to wait until the waters within stilled and insight came, to be at rest in action and realize action at rest. Truth was when she followed their instruction she found the water vibration a misting fountain on a hot day, easing the mind and opening the soul to contemplation. Still action not contemplation was her nature. "You are always trying to push the river," Blaise rebuked her. "Surrender your will to the flow of life. Let the spirit create pattern and outcome perfect to purpose."

"Silly old man," she shouted into the thunder of waters. "You never warned me." Then she bit her tongue, for it may be all gathered to Caer Myrddin were party to this spectacle of her ineptitude. But did Blaise not understand her nature? Had God not made her this way? Full of ire she lamented how Caron used and abandoned her.

At length worn with emotion she wept for her condition, and purged returned to the task at hand. This was more than image. She was in an elemental field of flowing forces beyond her own powers, and very real. She felt the mist on her face, saw sunlight play in the waters, and her gown was damp with spray. On the shore of the caldera was a rock worn with time and there she sat, as those who came here before her must have. It was beyond her strength to shape the waters to her will, and so finally she did what she was taught to do, and let the waters still in her. As she did her peace came upon her, and from the rock she began to see ephemeral patterns in the waters. In the confluence of forces shapes appeared momentarily, sustained until the pulse of the flow changed, dissolving to let another shape emerge.

It was like looking at clouds and seeing patterns in changing shapes, now and then something distinct emerging, until the winds shift and the patterns change. In these waters she saw repeating patterns. First she discerned the shape of a woman with sweeping wings unfurled that fluttered as the currents shifted and was gone. The waters flowed, the fountains surged, the falls intermingled and all changed, until in time the image came again: the artist's work written in water, in pattern, and in time.

She was in a vast field, a water garden of forces, ever fluid, moving in cycles, revealed in patterns that passed and came again inexorable as day and night. Underlying these recurring ciphers of creation was design, and those who shaped this place must have come here to remind themselves, that beyond the show of forms in the world there were limits to power and influence to shape the world. Perhaps they had made this place to contemplate those forces, knowing that enduring change must first be wrought in essence. But how does one write ones will in water, so that what is made endures?

She had no ready answer, but felt she was on the path of an ancient knowledge, and use of power once known to the Blood Royal. Then the thought that knowledge of that mastery was held by others to whom the Domina was subject entered in and troubled her deeply. She would not be beholden to the Guardians whoever they were, for now she believed Caron was among them and they had led her into this absurdity. Men always wanted the mastery, and she was full of fear what these might demand of her.

No, she would fight tooth and nail with the weapons she knew to rule her Order. She was sure the temporal lords would find this chicanery nonsense and embrace her pragmatic rule by wealth and power to secure their sovereignty to stand with her. Even those who might observe this now would see the sense of her way and the relegation of this ancient rite to a world and time long past.

She was discouraged at the magnitude of the problems she faced, but the woman she glimpsed in the waters appeared to come in answer, and Maia's image emerged. "They have given you an elemental garden to master," she said gently. "They would have you discover what is within you to shape a cycle to the purposes of the Blood Royal."

"You promised to guide every step of the way," Magda accused. All this had come of some betrayal of trust.

"There is a power beyond my own I slept, but awakened come to you."

"Am I beguiled to think the Guardian other than Caron?" Magda asked. "If it is he to whom I must give myself, it ends here. I will not serve or subject myself to him or any who stand with him."

"Be still," Maia insisted. "When we possess the stone of sovereignty nothing will be restrained us, which we shall imagine to do. The stone is the key to the shaping of the waters. Fulfill this cycle and we shall have no need of Irkala or any of these archaic masters."

"Irkala fills me with fire to endure," Magda said. "I need her fierceness of passion to govern."

"In the power of the stone star fire will inform our designs. Irkala is not to be trusted; she will destroy you with the same fierceness of purpose to accomplish her aims as she informs our own."

"Men lay waste the earth for their ideals and desires. If I am to stand up to these, I must be steeled to this savagery."

"Do you think our sex guiltless? This rage to impose order is rooted in our insecurity. Look what Irkala has wrought of the realm under her hand. She entreats you with soft words but loosed in the earth she wreaks havoc."

"You have turned against her?"

"I have slept and am awakening."

"Well, then, what am I to make of this trial? I am told I must ask a question unknown to me, and answering choose whether life or death shall come. How am I to riddle this?"

"This rite of passage is overseen in the presence of a Watcher, one who did not fall but abides for the spiritual regeneration of the human race. Perhaps you might begin by asking what this means to you."

"I thought first he had some semblance to Caron, and it revolted me to think him come into such power. I think now this is another. Who is the Watcher? What is he to us?"

"Master of the arts of shape shifting and in possession of powers beyond my own, a master of the In-world."

It struck her that Maia was conflicted. "I am Domina of the Blood Royal," Magda insisted. "How should I yield myself to another? Are we not one in this?"

"Let us face the waters together," Maia said, "and conceive in our heart of hearts what we would bring forth for the springtime of the world."

"A new Atlantis," Magda said, and Maia agreed. As one they turned to face the tumult of waters and under Maia's hand they stilled as a mirror, first reflecting what was in Magda's heart, then opening as if a window onto something beyond.

"Let me shape this to our purpose," Maia said. And what they agreed to conceive in the waters was a world restored to the order and beauty of a time before the angry ones lay waste the earth. "Concentrate on the image I shall give you," Maia continued. "Free your mind from any thought but that, and let the image of it grow in you, visualizing every detail to perfection. Let nothing trouble the waters, and I shall bring forth our vison of what may be, give shape to what is wrought here today."

Magda gave herself utterly to what Maia envisioned, until heart and mind were alive with the detail of the world of her heart's desire. In that moment the waters mirrored the essences and Magda glimpsed the pattern of what might be. What followed was beyond comprehension, for she saw in an instant the restoration of a world the Watcher gave but glimpses of, in a time when it ceased to be.

"Vision is one thing, fulfillment another," Maia said. "Too often it ends with visions writ in water. To establish this pattern in the earth, in your time you must complete the cycle of the sun-wheel, until a foundation wrought in water, air, earth and fire is fulfilled in you and all gathered to you."

"I understand," Magda said, though she did not. "But the question I must answer. What is the question?"

"Your Order answers to the Guardian. I think you must answer to what the Guardian means to you. It is an answer we must have to hedge what is wrought in your heart."

"Means to me?"

"It is the task at hand. Do what it takes to acquire the stone. Then we shall see what we shall see."

Maia was gone and Magda stood alone facing again a commotion of waters. She would but could not move on, so she sat upon the rock gazing into the waters, questioning the question to which Maia believed she must give answer. A single passage of the sun-wheel was to be the ceremonial fulfillment of her right to rule. Entering a field of forces drawn about Caer Myrddin to keep the sanctity of the rite, she assumed it was her Masters of Hallows who wrought this of their arts. Instead, she found them solicitous of Bran, lord of Caer Myrddin, and he in turn deferential to the Guardian who came to judge of her competence to govern the Blood Royal.

What she experienced under his hand exceeded all expectations. As a daughter of the Blood Royal she was taught the order descended from holy blood to keep true the way of the eternal feminine, but none spoke of its genesis in the world that was. She never dreamed it had come down from a time when the way of all flesh was perverted in the earth. What was made to endure tides and times was hers to hold true to purpose, but she erred in Caron. He irked her as all men irked her. Full of the pretense of love but wanting only its fruits, they plucked the souls of women like ripe fruit from the tree, and when they had sucked the juice of life discarded the bitter husk. There was no security in them but the liberty of making one's own way was exhilarating, even if at every turn she faced the brute force of male domination.

With that she'd opened the Pandora's Box and her mind filled with a litany of complaints. It was men who loosed an apocalypse of ills upon the world, men who heeded not the quiet counsel of women. She knew it. All ills came of this bondage of superior to inferior being, and so a world turned upside down.

She pondered and thought and wrestled with the turmoil in herself in this rock barren elemental wilderness, until the sound of many waters broke in upon and washed over her. Tired of chasing one errant thought after another, her heart grew weary of the effort to evade the issue. Inevitably, she came again to the question she must pose and answer.

Exhausted with the effort the waters stilled within her, and the question that troubled her from the day of her coming to Caer Myrddin broke surface. If there was authority over her investiture, authority to judge her fitness to rule, who granted that authority? In whose name did the Watcher come? She knew the purpose for which the Blood Royal was made, but if not her whom did the Blood Royal serve?

She panicked for it implied service to someone beyond herself. The question once posed she knew she must answer true or fail. She feared the answer was Caron, whom the Cailleach acknowledged Grail King. Taking her flesh in her she hedged the asking of it. "Who, then," she posed, "do the grail maidens, the daughters of the Blood Royal, serve?"

And she received the beginnings of an answer. An image appeared in the falls and fountains, fluid but taking on subtle form of three women. The image materialized in the weave of waters, until shining they emerged in white robes mounting the stairs from three pools into which the falls plunged. First was Siduri and she held at her breast the vessel of the grail and within the radiant jewel of sovereignty. At Siduri's right hand was the Lady Abbess Aletheia of St. Odile, and to Siduri's right Constanza, the fair. They approached together with ceremony in their step, the stone of sovereignty shining with an inborn light, enveloping them in a cool, blue radiance.

Magda could not take her eyes from the vision. In their presence she felt all was coming together and her trials near done; the authority of her office was come upon her and she addressed them forthrightly as if solely for her. "When he lived your father was master of the Grail Hallows; did you know that Siduri?"

"I know something of it."

"And now your duty is done and the Blood Royal is become the setting for the jewel of sovereignty on earth."

"Seed of a new beginning," Constanza said.

"You have learned much in your short stay with us," Magda said, covering her vulnerability with authority: "Perhaps before your return there will be time to instruct you more."

"I long for the teachings of the Masters."

Magda scarcely heard, for she could not leave off gazing on the shining of the Grail and radiant like a sun the stone of sovereignty within. "How apt, Grail maidens bearing the Grail," Magda said, "come to acknowledge my sovereignty. Welcome." It was brash but Siduri answered sweetly.

"It is not yet done, Lady Madelon, for we are come to bring you to the place where you may give answer and be it true receive sovereignty of the Order."

"Have you all seen what I have seen, accomplished with me what I have accomplished?" Magda challenged. "I have affirmed our ancient past, shaped a pattern afresh in the waters, and initiated a new cycle of creation for the Blood Royal. Is it not wonderful the way that is open to us?"

"It is," Aletheia answered, "but do not we women love the appearance of achievement. So like Martha we are busy about many things, contemptuous of those who are not, and miss the better part.

"For as women led in the way of the fall, so must we reveal the way of return. But scattering influence lo here and lo there to distraction, our hearts are never a setting for the jewel.

"There is work to be done but more the truth of womanhood is that we should be as Mary, sat at the feet of the lord of love, awake to the deeper needs of being."

There was authority in their presence and there was no denying it. She would deal with this later. "How then shall we now fulfill this cycle?"

"Turn," Aletheia said frim as the dawn.

"Turn?" Magda was surprised at her tone, but she could not resist, and turning around found herself again in the midst of the sun-wheel of Caer Myrddin, the morning sky a pale rose with hints of first light.

Wary, she looked about the circle, fearing what lay ahead. Aletheia stood still at her side; Siduri and Constanza seated at the altar before the fifth gate. Telgesinus caught her eye and dark fire moved between them, rousing passion and encouragement in Magda. Blaise stood stable, impassive, unjudging as ever. At his side was the Master Origen, whom she could not read. But it was the Master of the first gate that astonished her. Expecting Falconieri in his stead she saw Flegetanis of Alexandria, no more the ragged player but radiant as clear shining after rain; the accounts of his death apparently a gambit to bring him here unawares. And in him she felt not only inspiration and vitality but, indeed, encouragement.

There was no sign of Caron or the Guardian who watched over her rite of passage and in her that raised suspicion. But Bran of Caer Myrddin was present, and he alone stood before the fifth gate beyond the obelisk and altar stone. "To complete the initiation of this cycle," Bran said, "it remains but for you to enter in through the fifth gate."

"The fifth gate," Magda demurred. She knew she was being manipulated into something not of her own choosing. "Why must I enter the fifth gate?"

"To come into the power of the stone of sovereignty, you must offer yourself to the one within who grants sovereignty or the vessel of your heart shall be unclean, your authority a mockery of life."

Aletheia took Magda's arm in support. "Enter in, cross over and come before one who dwells," she said. "In spirit bear the vessel and the stone, and for one and all offer these hallows to him. So shall you ascend into governance of the Order."

They drew near until they stood before Bran, and Magda asked, "Who is the one who dwells within?"

"It is the Aton-Re, lord of the crossing, who keeps the way of the wonderful one that dwells in the realms of light. Yield the stone of sovereignty in him and let the way be revealed in the light."

"Is he the Guardian?" She felt Irkala stir and whisper warning in her, but Maia was silent as if she slept.

"In measure to the yielding of your heart you will receive power, and know even as you are known."

Irkala rose up and with her came dread. Magda feared the one whom she had condemned to death, and set the creatures of the world upon, was none other than he who would now sit in judgment over her in some ethereal realm beyond the fifth gate.

They conspired against her. This was all a game of the mind. Led by the Abbess Aletheia it was a scheme of those daughters of the Blood Royal on whom Squin inflicted his madness and for which they blamed her. Yes, it was so. On the twilight edge of the circle lurked the temporal lords, many of them fathers to the very daughters that conspired against her. These had come to humiliate and subdue her to their purpose.

Was that not Roland on the inner circle and beside him the Lady Gwen watching over this moment of truth? They were laughing at her caught up in a mirage world of their contriving, wrought with the assistance of the traitor Caron, who under Flegetanis' tutelage was become a mage of greater power then she imagined possible. What of her Masters of Hallows, had they also betrayed her for her failure to honour them? And now all gathered to have their revenge upon her, by forcing her to worship at the feet of one she reviled, when all she desired was to serve her Order.

Enough, she would give nothing more to those who would humble her to their cause. Irkala agreed: no more. Burning with ire, resolved to assert her right to rule, Magda called up fire from the center of the earth. She turned away from the fifth gate, turned aside to Telgesinus, and summoned Irkala to bear witness to her need to bond with that master of hallows in the fire.

The link was made. Taken by *Sham-she-el,* Telgesinus was overwhelmed by force that obliterated sense. And in a moment he who was Morgon Kara possessed another fit to his purpose. Feeding the flame in her heart Telgesinus summoned up the currents of the dark wind, as Magda raised hands over the assembled host.

"You contrive to humiliate, to strip my power, to impose your will upon me: Here then is my answer."

It began as a rumor of something yet to come, the rumble of something afar off gathering strength, driven before a tumult of churning, dark cloud converging on Caer Myrddin.

"Be my altar in the earth," Irkala whispered, "and when you call, I will loose the image of the beast and rider of the storm."

Driven by the dark wind of the Shades, a surging mass of vapors coiled serpentine throughout the sanctuary of Caer Myrddin, weaving in and out among the dolmens. The fiery mass gathered into the shape of a lurid, red dragon clasping everything in its coils. And in her ire Magda was taken. All others unseen, she found herself alone in a maelstrom of flame and feared for her life.

"Do not fear the fire born of the rider of the storm," Irkala said. "You are safe in me. Ask and I will destroy those who are anguish in your path and distress you in the way."

"Destroy all those gathered here?"

"Do you wish it?"

Magda reached out for Maia but found her not, and Irkala felt it. "This world is taken by fire and fury," Irkala said. "Maia is nothing but the twitter of sweet imaginings that shall never be. Deny her. Abide in me, and the earth is yours and everything that is in it.

"Did she tell you that ages upon ages ago it was nothing like this; that man fell into this bestial state and there is a way of return to the First

Time? Were that true long before now the state for which she yearns would have been restored.

"No, what is lost is forever gone. Evermore, there is only blood and gold and steel; the will and force of fire to forge what we can of this waste world among the stars. Take my hand. Be my altar in the earth. All these things shall hunger to come to you."

Irkala put out her hand, but Maia whispered, "No." Magda listened and drew back.

"Do it," Irkala insisted. But with remembrance of Maia's caution and now conviction, answered: "No." And as if her words had opened the doors of a great furnace, the heat bore down upon her so that her clothing smoked and her flesh felt like to melt upon the bone. Her heart filled with acid resentment of all that beset her in the way. But part of her would not give way. All the years she craved the left hand path of passion, and she would now give her life for the healing touch of cool water. And it came.

In the midst of the flame Aletheia came to her with open hand outstretched, and with fingertip touch enveloped Magda in fountain cool mist. With dragon's breath on the dark wind Irkala came on with fierce insistence, but could not penetrate the hedge Aletheia drew about them. Irkala raged but to Aletheia she was nothing, and taking Magda's outstretched hand led her out from the dragon's wrath.

"Mining the hurts of the heart, she conjures with the hurt of things past, "Aletheia comforted Magda. "She exploits grievance, manipulates through fear, greed and shame, and deceives the world with her wiles. In time all she has contrived, all she has exploited, will be cleansed from the earth.

"Do but enter in through the fifth gate," Aletheia counseled. "You must transcend the delusions of this world to know what is wrought in the heavens of this earth, and what is ordained in Eden for us in all the days of our tomorrows."

But it was not to be. Stripped of her will to go on, Magda faltered on the brink of an abyss of nothingness. In that moment everything seemed utterly meaningless but to cling to her ruling passion.

Her force exhausted, the very life drained from her, she sank slowly to her knees facing oblivion. "I am Domina of the Blood Royal," she insisted, clinging to her fleeting identity. "By right of birth and blood the sovereignty is mine.

"I will not yield to one utterly unknown to me."

Telgesinus would come to her but could not. He was paralyzed in place by the very power loosed, turned back upon him.

The sun yet unrisen, russet sky gave way to the beginnings of a daffodil dawn.

39

The Fifth Gate

Flegetanis and Blaise came to Magda to hedge what would possess her soul. "Be at peace," Flegetanis consoled her. "You are not the first to walk this way and front the beast. A day will come when the dragon shall nevermore steal the flame of life to empower the rulers of the darkness of this world."

Bran beckoned the four who manifest the influences of the Hallows - paten, spear, cup, and sword maidens - to come to him. And with Aletheia, Constanza, and Siduri, who still held the jewel of sovereignty safely to her breast, they were in number seven who stood with Bran before the fifth gate.

"Never alone did Magda journey, for you have followed precisely in the way of the Watchers. You, Siduri, to whom the sun stone was given, you Constanza who keep the way of the heart, and you, Aletheia, who knows what is needful to consummate lest this cycle fail: you three shall lead in this. Radiant with influence the Hallows shall uphold you in the way."

So it was the seven who bore the essence of the Hallows in the earth entered in through the fifth gate. Aletheia led. Siduri followed, hands outstretched in offering, bearing the stone of sovereignty, with Constanza at her side. Immediately after the handmaidens of the Masters of Hallows crossed the threshold of the fifth gate to whatever lay beyond, and were gone.

Magda tried to rise but could not, falling back again upon her knees. Flegetanis rested hands upon her shoulders; Blaise knelt with her, clasping her hands in his own to uphold her heart. The circle of Caer Myrddin was wholly still in the first light of morning and silent it remained, until at last it seemed it was finished and nothing more was to come. Even so no one moved or spoke, but the circle of stones answered.

A rising mist gathered about the arc of standing stones, sifting through the gateways and mounting the columns, enveloping all in a pearly essence, the stones began to shimmer with a golden glow and the stones began to sound. Each vibrated with a timbre of its own and true, gathering in consonance until a single pure tone resounded from the sun-wheel of Caer Myrddin, rousing a current of answering life in all it touched.

Among those was Bran who stood before the fifth gate. The old Guardian raised his arms in joy with the lightning of his heart. "The Lord is in His holy temple," he avowed. "Let all the earth keep silence before him."

At his word all eyes lifted to an unseen point high above the open temple. From there the one tone emanated, raining down in a shower of light. Emptied of herself, even the Lady Madelon could not but lift her head to see. The very stones were awake, transformed in the radiance as if to evanesce into the heavens, until all that remained were crystalline pillars glowing with blue flame within; towers of force enshrining the shining firmament of the sun-wheel.

Like windows opening on a darkened room, light at the five gateways shone through to drive away the shadows. Out of the light through those radiant portals the maidens returned, each through the gate of her hallows, to form an arc facing the fifth gate. Like the heart a mirror of the world, except it be a window of heaven, through the fifth gate the three returned where they had begun. Crossing over they emerged appearing nothing had changed, but radiant with the light of life that illumines all who come into the world, within changed utterly.

Aletheia came first, Constanza and Siduri at each and, and it was now she who bore the stone sovereignty. Aletheia stood before the maidens at the center of the arc they formed and with Siduri and Constanza affirming, turned to face the fifth gate. On the threshold of the worlds the light intensified, until within the limen of the arch it gathered to a sun with radiant corona. And in the midst of the flame a man appeared, and the lord of the crossing, the Aton-Re, crossed over into the sanctum of Caer Myrddin.

Aletheia knelt offering in upraised open hands the stone of sovereignty to the one who dwells, entering into the world through the fifth gate of life. All gathered together, taken up in the effulgence of the union of the worlds, rose on an ascending current so they were one in Aletheia in her offering. For a moment it seemed all flesh must simply dissolve into morning dew, leaving only a being of light. But Aletheia spoke for them and to the cause for which long ago to this hour some flesh was saved.

"We are your bone and your flesh," she affirmed. "Thou in us, we in thee, and in us the heavens and the earth are one."

As she spoke a graceful form of subtle flesh infused with light emerged, revealing a man of stature, full of grace, and truth be told too beautiful to look upon through eyes of corrupted flesh. He stood within a cloven flame, its arc peaking above him like wings yet to be unfurled. Free from a shroud of fallen flesh he was a splendid being, full of light and air, and the pure joy of angelic life; the very likeness of what was, and is, and is to be manifest in man's true flesh.

In this wise he would come into the world, but little time there was to sustain this revelation of the transmutation of the flesh. To this end, if but for a moment, he took on the appearance of a man without fault or flaw in form and promise that what you saw without was but perfection shaped from within. Without guile, irresistible in force, and pure of intent, he shone steady as the sun in a cloudless sky, and to that one Aletheia offered up the stone of sovereignty.

At her back with Constanza at her side Siduri remembered - so long ago now it seemed – how on Nile bank below her father's villa she rose to greet the dawn. *"Your dawning is glorious in the House of Heaven, O living Aton, beginning of life."* She remembered the morning sun of red, hammered gold rising on the Nile, as she spoke softly to the god-like sun words of an ancient hymn her father Flegetanis taught her, come down he said from the *Na-Akhu-El* sages, the deathless ones of the First Time. *"O living God whose powers none other possess, you created the world according to your heart."* And one with Aletheia it was her heart now she offered without reservation, even as Aletheia offered the Aton-Re the sun stone. "Your rays encompass all the lands, even all that you have made; you bind them to you with your love."

The Aton-Re took the stone from Aletheia's outstretched hands, held it a moment to his forehead and returned it to her. He smiled on Siduri, eyes resting a moment upon Constanza, then returning to Aletheia, he reached out and touched each in turn upon the forehead. And when it was done he drew back within the arch of the fifth gate, blazed up a moment and was gone.

But the evidence of his presence remained within each one, touched and transfigured in the light. All in appearance returned to what it had been but a perfect flame was lit within the purified hearth of the heart that this new cycle of creation should not fail. Each alone with his own thoughts, all stood silently letting the moment settle in the soul, until the sun of hammered gold rose on the horizon of the world among the standing stones of Caer Myrddin, casting before its rising shadows of a day that was yet to be.

Only then as sunlight filled the circle did Magda raise her head, and looking for pity into Blaise' eyes, her own filled with pleading, asked, "The one who came forth through the fifth gate, was it Caron?"

Demetrius brought the Ariadne about in calm sea and flutter of wind, easing her beneath the shadow of the cliffs into the harbor of Caer Myrddin. With its six hundred stairs through the crags from the sea to the meadows above, it made no sense as a commercial port; that was in the great bay where the town had grown up. But it was the swift way to the sea from the old stronghold on the sea cliff. Even in ruin one must marvel at what was wrought among the crags. So it was Shirazi saw the woman on the cliff's edge among the ruins, and even from afar felt her distress. He waved to her as they made landfall, as if to one who needed to know others there were in the world who cared she existed. She saw him but did not return his greeting, backing out of view among the stones of the old fortress.

Straightway Shirazi came ashore and began the climb. His charges

Robert Hode come home at last and with him Freischütz Marcus Veidt, his sight much improved, close behind. Hode could not restrain himself. When at last they reached the meadows above the sea, the sweetness of the very earth rising up to greet him, unrestrained he ran circles though the long grass, like a puppy ecstatic to find its master home. When at last he settled they walked the half mile together, away from the shore ruins toward the castle mount, a rocky outcrop in the midst of autumn meadows.

They announced and were expected. "Hugues Caron," Shirazi said, "he was to have come before us." The castle was sleepy, a few about their business, but much of it had the feel of the damp of a morning after the night fires are extinguished, the stones have cooled and only cold ashes remain.

When they were admitted to the great hall everything changed. Though it was near empty, tables were set and a group of elderly men gathered about a fresh fire upon the hearth. They were in cautious conversation one with another, and halted at once when Shirazi, Hode and Veidt entered. If one were sensitive one might almost feel a mild annoyance at the interruption, but it passed at once.

Out of the number Flegetanis greeted Shirazi with a simple: "Good, you are come; you are needed." As if no time had passed, and no need to address the small matter of his supposed death or disappearance to reconcile, Flegetanis took up where they left off with a dismissive, "Later." And Shirazi must take it in his stride for he knew his father's manner, and it was clear Flegetanis wanted none of it here.

Flegetanis rose to embrace his son, but checked himself, turned and to the little congress of elders confirmed, "We are decided then," he said. "I have given my reasons and we do agree, do we not?"

There was no dissent. "We do," one said for all. "You will speak to the Lady Madelon for us."

Flegetanis nodded and turned to his son.

"Siduri is she here; is she well?" Shirazi asked.

"I think very much in love," Flegetanis said.

"Presently, you will tell me with whom," Shirazi said, "and I have a few stories of my own: this is Sir Robert Hode and here Conrad Veidt."

Flegetanis passed his hand over Veidt's eyes. "We can do something more about this, I believe," he said, "if you will stay with me awhile."

"And is Hugues Caron here?" Hode asked. "We owe him our lives. He bade us come on this day to meet him, and we were expected."

"He is not here but in sanctuary on the Holy Isle of Lindisfarne, where he will for now abide."

"It is the way I must go," Hode said.

"And I know one who would journey with you," Flegetanis said. "We shall speak of travels presently, for there is a gathering storm and we must take the winds favorable."

Hours Magda stood and watched the halcyon sea looking for some answer in it but it gave up nothing. It was at odds with what she felt within. It should rage, thunder with high winds and waters, rise up in tornadic spouts and overwhelm the earth and sky, for what she felt within. But it did not. Instead, as she watched from the cliff's edge she saw it bore a graceful sail under light air to safe harbor within the crags below. And a sailor on the foredeck waved cheerfully to her with the joy that must come from making safe landfall after a long sea voyage.

Her shame was complete. Before all who gathered to watch her investiture she failed. It was entirely because she feared the humiliation of what lay beyond, and that humiliation she feared had come upon her. She pondered throwing herself off the cliff face onto the rocks below to spite them. There was no way forward but an affront to her pride. If she was not Domina of the Blood Royal she was nothing. Lifelong she prepared in expectation and in a moment it was wrest from her; all the more humiliating for the neophytes who passed beyond her through the fifth gate, and what was loosed in the world by reason of them.

It was too much to bear and thinking on it she cursed them and she cursed her fate. Even Maia shunned her now that she was of no use in her grand schemes for a world to come. Telgesinus alone stood with her, but how long before he sought his own advantage. Beyond wrath she was caught up in a conflagration of the heart not even an ocean could extinguish, and through the burning time Irkala came to comfort her in the midst of the fires.

"What did I tell you of these," she chided. "You would not listen. The left hand path," she insisted, "walk the left hand path into the fire, and master the world they have denied us in the waters."

She was deep into the mystery of the meaning of this when Flegetanis came to her. He laid hands on Magda's shoulders to comfort her, and Magda hid the meditations of her heart in darkness too deep for light to enter. In his presence she let herself know nothing but the longings of a fall day, the rustling of long grass in the wind that rose from the sea, and the smell of ripening apples on the air. She knew why he had come. With his touch, at that moment she knew she was dead to the world. Flegetanis felt it in her and said nothing until Magda uncomfortable with his compassion asked again.

"Was it Caron?"

"It was Caron came to Sainte Odile in the guise of John of Oxford."

"And you Signor Falconieri."

"It is an old art. The Master Origen taught him well, and he has become skilled in the arts of shaping to shift his appearance with ease."

"How is this done?"

"By reading and assuming the pattern of another," Flegetanis said. "Actors have some minor talent in this wise – an outer imitation of an inner gift - but none so skilled to vanish into the part and take the appearance of another."

"Then I was right, he did come to Caer Myrddin," Magda said, "and by reason of him it has come to this."

Flegetanis was not about to commiserate. "These trials did not unfold in the mundane world. And the one who came to Caer Myrddin to guide you through your trials was greater by far than the man you know as Caron."

"Is Caron dead?" Flegetanis said nothing. Perhaps he didn't know. "I thought to throw myself into the sea," she confided, "but these several hours I have relived all that has befallen me and decided no."

"It would be a great loss."

"The shame is too much to bear. Aletheia, Siduri, even the Lady Constanza who knows nothing of our Order have entered in through the fifth gate, crossed over into the presence of I know not who or what and are glorified in it. And I could not find it in me but supported by you and the Master Blaise only watch my failures unfold and made complete. I know not what or whom it is the Blood Royal serves. I failed in my trials and all who witnessed this dishonor me."

"The Grail serves the Grail King; the Blood Royal the one who dwells in the realms of light. You know this of old, from the first day of our counseling in the way."

"And yet I do not know what dwells within."

"You were there when he took flesh, uplifting all in radiant life. It is the Aton-Re, lord of the crossing, who dwells in the light of the wonderful one as so should we.

"And to bear his burden of light and life we do leave the world, for those realms enter into the world through us, even as the seven maidens bore his presence when they came forth through the fifth gate."

"What is to become of me? Aletheia is forgiving. May I take sanctuary with her at Sainte Odile, while I ponder my fate? Give me time to let my vision restored be, for I know nothing more than this path I have walked."

"You may take sanctuary with Aletheia as ever you wish to focus the meditations of your heart," Flegetanis said. "It is well you should from time to time, for mostly I suspect you will be very busy bearing the burden those duties the Na Akhu-El purpose for you."

"You have devised some heavy penance. Say and I will do it."

"No more than your path demands, Lady Madelon, for this night you will prepare for the celebration of the investiture of a Domina of the Blood Royal."

"Is it Aletheia or Siduri, for Siduri is your daughter by Aletheia, is she not?"

"Who told you this?"

"One who failed me at the last."

"Maia, who weaves water into knots," Flegetanis said.

"How do you know?"

"Lady Madelon, hear me true. The Elders will confirm you Domina, not by right of flesh and blood alone, but for what you have and may yet fulfill sovereign of the Order."

Magda felt her heart surge like an ocean swell. "But my failure was seen by all."

"Each sees only what he can bear. Those who were able to witness the consummation of these trials saw only you kneel between myself and

Blaise. The revelation at the altar of the fifth gate, fulfilling the cycle you had borne through the four, was seen in fulfillment of your rite. Your tears they saw as tears of joy, our encompassment reverence and respect for what you had accomplished. Let it be that."

Her heart was full and her breath came with sighs. "Then the Watchers embrace my vision."

"They would see a world restored in a new order of the ages through the spiritual regeneration of the race. And to that end they have initiated in you a cycle of creation, to let the influences and ordinances of that world to come inform the purposes of the Order of the Blood Royal."

"But I failed."

"Not if you learned. The days are long until all shall be fulfilled, and you will not see the consummation in your life time. But you may labour in the field, tending and keeping this new garden of creation. The Hallows yielded in essence, the seed of the cycle is sown, engendered of the radiance of the lords of light. In season that new heaven shaped this day in essence will flower in a new earth."

"And shall the stone of sovereignty come to my hand?"

"Sovereignty shall remain in the hands of the Guardian watchers. In measure the virtues of the stone will be released, the seals of creation loosed, according to times and tides in the affairs of men true to its season. There will be no sovereignty of orders or nations that endure. Only when the setting comes true to the powers it must accommodate shall sovereignty be given.

"Shall we walk together milady?" Flegetanis said, taking her hand. "The lords are concerned for your presence and I am to bring you to them." Magda took Flegetanis' arm and together they turned toward the castle of Caer Myrddin.

"That the stone of sovereignty shall have its true setting," Magda said, "Aletheia shall redouble efforts to teach the daughters of the Blood Royal to walk the Right Hand Path."

"Do so," Flegetanis agreed.

"But I shall master the Left Hand Path," Magda silently vowed: "master it to put the Masters of Hallows to shame."

She said not a word but Flegetanis sensed it in her. It was as they supposed, Magda had turned humiliation into resolve to prevail. They had spoken to the opening of the seals, of difficult days to come, the four horsemen loosed upon the earth. With famine, plague, war and death, man's reaction to the intensification of life, it needed strength of purpose to endure the purification of the heart.

"It is a long journey home, Magda," Flegetanis said, walking the path across the autumn field with the Lady Madelon on his arm. "There are difficulties to come, yet sweet they are the uses of adversity."

40

Sovereignty

Maia awoke from deep sleep with no memory of having gone to rest. She remembered being troubled by her refusal to meet with Innkeeper, awakening to find herself in the heights of Whiter Morn in the presence of the Aton-Re. And she remembered, disavowing the limits set upon her, she had gone in search of Morgon Kara in Irkala's realm of Shades.

She communed with the Aton-Re, met with the Fates, forged an agreement with Irkala, and guided Magda through her trials, until they stood together facing the resolution of waters. That was their moment of truth, framing a question to confirm her Domina of the Blood Royal, and curiously Maia had no idea what came of it.

Now it all seemed a fading dream with some conclusion that posed her a question she could neither grasp nor remember. It all distilled into an uneasy feeling that someone more skilled than she had taken possession, and authored the shaping of her consciousness to this end.

The more she thought on it, the more she wondered after it, for she feared the powers of her sister, Irkala. So, rising she called her Chamberlain to her. "Have you yet set the bar I directed against passage from these realms to Whiter Morn?" she asked.

"Mistress, what bar? Have I forgotten to do what you ordered?" He saw her confusion.

"No matter, only what day is this? I must journey this night to meet with Innkeeper."

"Your maidens cautioned you were in deep sleep, so none would approach too close but to watch over you. Well we know what this means; for us it is a watch in the night, but for you a journey of shaping, its demands great upon you."

"My good Chamberlain," Maia said, "how long did I sleep?"

"A night and two days, and now night comes on again."

"From the hour Innkeeper bade me come to him?" Her Chamberlain looked puzzled, and she did not wish to engage him further. "Near three days then. So it is timely, and I have not over slept his invitation."

"No mistress," he replied, but concerned: "May I know what you dreamed?"

"A dream so vivid I thought myself awake," she said. "And now awake I wonder if that was real, and this my dream."

It made no sense but it was not for him to interfere. This shaping of the vibratory patterns of the Archaeus to inform the outer realms was beyond his art. "She is a mistress so subtle," the Chamberlain whispered when they parted, "I wonder that she does not sometime deceive even herself."

Maia was expected. On this night the Inn at the Parting of the Ways offered a silent and cozy sanctuary. Innkeeper by his fire awaited her coming, and this time he rose at once to his feet to greet her. "You were right to come to me, Maia," he said, warmly extending his hand to her, "tell me what you have seen."

He said no more for he saw she was troubled. "I have matters within to resolve," Maia began, "influences and cross-currents that need reconciling. So I entered as we are instructed into vibrational-repose, that I might be at rest in Whiter Morn to enter into the action of the world.

"And then, unaccountably, I fell into a trance-like sleep," she said, sitting beside him, "and now am overwhelmed by what I must resolve."

He settled her before the fire and she opened her heart on all that unfolded, from sleep to awakening and communing with the Aton-Re, to her parting moments with Magda, who wrestled with the framing of a question she must answer to live. He listened, saying nothing. On edge for his reply, she looked about and noted the absence of his chessboard, the impersonal divide he usually put between himself and all who came to trade a question for a question. This was far more intimate, and she felt his concern for her.

"I believe I have seen the shape of things to come," Maia said, "the beginning of the end of this sad interlude. But whether it will be an end of sorrows or of mankind I cannot say."

"And your concern is whether or not the pattern you have touched and wrought is real or illusion?"

"Am I dreaming I am awake, or am I awake, dreaming? It was so real I wonder now if I am here with you or only dream I am. I fear I have become so entangled in my own gifts that what I thought real is illusion, and what I thought illusion, real."

"Master, I fear what is wrought in me is an empty dream; that nothing touched was true, though some of it I would as well it were not."

"You are not alone in coming to me in this," Innkeeper assured her. "And what you have seen I have seen, even before you told me."

"And what have I seen?"

"The parting of the ways, the beginning of a day that will end this interval of fallen man, and come the dawn of a new heaven and new earth."

"Then it was not a dream, and man must now once and for all choose?"

"What you have known is vision in repose. Because of your obsession for Morgon Kara, what was done could not be done in any other way without our loss of you."

She knew she must be careful, but it troubled Maia something should be wrought in her unawares. "Who are you that I should sleep and dream to let you shape your will through influences that are mine?" She spoke mildly to appear curious, not contentious, and deliberately he took her that way.

"There is no power you and I possess but hold in trust, Maia," he replied. "Nothing was done in violation of what you are, but all fit to shaping the purposes of Whiter Morn. You do agree to those purposes do you not?"

"I, too, serve the wonderful one," she said, a hint of frustration in her voice.

"I know it, and to your everlasting credit. For in repose you repented of those influences that would warp your will, and at the last sought to turn Magda from Irkala."

"But why do I not know what all has become of it, for I was awake to the shaping of it."

"Like a shining jewel the pattern wrought has many facets," Innkeeper replied. "There are dimensions to this we know nothing of. But each one need only play his part true to the light given him, so what is conceived in time will manifest to perfection in the cycle of creation."

Again she protested. "Who are you to have taken me unawares and wrought all this in my substance?" Truth be told it was now less that she unwittingly played a part beyond her arts, but wonder at the mastery that wrought it.

"Not I alone," Innkeeper said. "When you refused to come to me the matter passed to another. The magnitude of this is beyond my art, and like you I simply played my part.

"In vibrational-repose you awakened in spirit to commune with the Aton-Re. He it was who caused a deep sleep to fall upon you. He it was who shaped these patterns in the vibrational substance of your influences. And as it is his creation conceived in you, you may rest assured in him, for he will see it through to fulfillment be it a thousand years or a day."

"He has the power to enter into and know the essence of each one of us?"

"And as if midwife to what is conceived vibrationally in you, he has given me to watch over you to its fulfillment."

"A world restored?"

"Were that not the commission, we should all have crossed over long ago."

"I can come and see you anytime?"

"Yes, but you will find a limit set upon your powers until certain matters are resolved. Morgon Kara, the fallen watcher *Sham-she-el*, dwells now in the person of the Master Telgesinus. What is more, the Lady Madelon, who has become Domina of the Blood Royal, has opened her heart to Irkala, and together they will increase him in his way mightily in the earth."

"And I have done this."

"No, it is what it is. All this was present in the world of illusion from of old, and you have now taken it upon yourself to resolve and lead out of the mirage world.

"And so you shall as your heart is given to the one whom we serve. Hold with me in these matters, Maia, and it shall all be used to advantage.

"For now we let what is sown, the wheat and the tares, grow together. But in an hour to come, we shall all come forth in our strength to gather the wheat to harvest, and let burn the tares in the fires of creation."

"So, you have seen it all."

Caron sat on the foreland of Holy Isle looking out over the morning sea, when the Aton-Re appeared to him. He turned to see the voice that spoke, and there was one seated in repose beside him, alike enjoying the tranquility of a new day. No blinding apparition like the sun, but sheathed in soft light, Caron met eyes radiant with understanding. That one might well have been a mirror image, but for the weathering of the world imprinted in his own flesh.

"I have given my substance to your use and you have taken me to yourself," Caron said. "In your presence I have seen through your eyes what you would have me see. And now I see you as my very self. Even so I know you are far more, and I do not understand as you understand."

"One may know who and what he is," the Aton-Re said, "but given the dissonance of the world, cloaked in flesh there are necessary limits, and not for one's own sake alone.

John of Oxford was gone, leaving Caron wondering if he had ever existed. From that hour he had borne the burden of light with reverence, but in the silent aftermath of Caer Myrddin, after weeks of isolation on Lindisfarne, Caron felt very much alone. Drained, disheveled, and unsure for wondering what was to come, he felt altogether unworthy of the presence that manifest beside him. Yet the Aton-Re's manner was so mild Caron's shame at his wretched state simply dissolved, and he dared asked questions yet troubling his soul.

"I do not understand why the Lady Madelon is confirmed Domina of the Blood Royal, while others more worthy are passed over. Irkala of the Shades is increased in her; so also Morgon Kara in the Master Telgesinus.

It seems a path to disaster. If the seals upon those powers of the deep are loosed in creation, these parasite powers shall be loosed to intensified destruction in the earth."

"One way or another we will have an end," the Aton-Re said. "The universe unfolds, the cycle moves on, and the fallen state of man cannot long endure. A limit is set to the time remaining, and in thought, word, and deed man must choose whether life or death shall come."

"Irkala is the distillation of ancient evil," Caron persisted. "She exploits the longings of the heart, perverts all that is made, and looses streams of witchery in the earth."

"In the time given we shall try the spirits in the hearts and minds of man that a clear choice is set before him."

"Under Magda's influence, I fear the Blood Royal will no longer serve its ordained purpose."

"We have withheld the stone of sovereignty, and set a bound to their powers."

"Magda will turn the more to Irkala," Caron said.

"It would be a great victory for her to reject that brew of bitterness, and be a blessing," the Aton-Re answered.

"She is willful and will have her way."

"We have set the seed for what is to come, and for the moment accepted these limitations. Whatever the appearance, all things will be used to advantage."

It seemed he took his flesh in his teeth to ask for pressing all he dared, but the Aton-Re seemed unconcerned and so ask he did. "In the last of days to come… how shall it be?"

"Do you truly wish to hear it?" the Aton-Re answered. "Very well, know then that in those times the children of men will multiply greatly in the earth. The world will swarm with populations that devour its sustenance, all green things and living ravished, so it seems a plague of locusts has descended upon the land.

"Driven to exalt himself over God, in the last days men will worship forces at their command to wrest from the earth what they will to build Mammon's kingdom. In those days the wealth of the earth shall fall into the hands of a few, who believing themselves its masters will exploit the masses, demanding bondage for survival.

"To that end all peoples of the earth shall be enticed and drawn, or resisting driven into slavery to serve the mind-made world the merchants of the earth have wrought. In thrall they will sacrifice the flower of their lives to uphold the gods of force and industry. And all shall seem to have come of necessity for the greater good.

"In those last of days, believing they have defeated God and established the kingdom of man in His stead, consciousness shall fail them. And in the dying of the light, man shall forget the way of the wonderful one to whom the whole, holy world belongs.

"In darkness they will not see they have but retraced a path trod long ago, and come again to where all this began. For in those days as in days of yore, man will again have learned to loose fire from the center of the earth, and nothing changed he will turn it upon himself in a final deluge of flame."

"All men held in bondage, how then could it be otherwise, for those enslaved have no choice," Caron said.

"In a time to come, the way to transcend this vicious cycle imposed on life will be offered one and all from within. Then shall it be seen who is the free man and who the slave, for the spirit shall try the hearts and minds of all men, whatever their station, to find them true or false, perverse or pure. And so will the end come, for there will be time no more."

All the miles and memories distilled into a single moment, realizing the way he had come. Given all in all, it seemed petty to ask but if he was to continue he must. And so his breath scant and heart aching for release he simply asked, "How long?" He could say no more.

"I have set a task for you while there is yet time," the Aton-Re replied.

"Lord, what task," he whispered.

"To begin, rest here a season; the monks will take you into their labours. You have seen things they have not yet seen for what they are, but keep their simple order. Concern yourself only with being here and now, and it will be healing to your flesh and health to your bones."

"Irkala is ancient evil," Caron insisted. "She will pervert all that is made." He at once regretted the unintended outburst, but the Aton-Re agreed.

"She is distilled wickedness in the heart of darkness, putting on a face in the world to masquerade as virtue. Even so, despite the impure heart, there are powers must be loosed and mastered."

"She will pervert life to turn those powers to destruction."

"If she is indulged," the Aton-Re said, "but there is more to this than Irkala. From the time of the great transgression, when man hid himself from the light of the wonderful one, there has distilled an essence that perverts the way and leads forever to destruction.

"In the fallen state there are many who rule the darkness of this world, but there is always one, deep hidden though he may be from light of day, in which the essence of that false identity comes to focus.

"And therein is the task I set you. We would see the dissolution of that focus of spiritual wickedness that it possesses the human heart no more."

Caron heaved a sigh, almost a sob, for his breath failed him. It was too much. He fought back a rising wave of world sorrow and found his voice. "I do not know how to do this… or where to begin," he said, mastering himself.

"It always begins with oneself, and always it is the same story," the Aton-Re said. "Whenever a focus of love comes into the world, a focus of wickedness intensifies to overwhelm it. At the heart of this perversion is hatred of God. In it is the will of fallen man to be as god, imposing the dark designs of the fallen mind on creation.

"It is as was with the magicians of Egypt sent by Pharaoh against Moses. For all their efforts to match and defeat the word of God there was a point beyond which they could not go, and all their arts failed them. Their conflict brought deadly plagues upon the land, and in the end Pharaoh must let the people go.

"There is one law, Caron, steadfast and true in all the realms of creation: Only what is wrought in spiritual expression, in the radiance of divine being, endures and prevails.

"If you will hold steady and true in the power of love, you will come to a place where the rulers of the darkness of this world cannot go. Then shall the focus of wickedness be exposed in the light for what it is, and dissolved in its shining.

"In all this keep faith with your brethren, the shining ones of the First Time, and let the increase come. Though now few in number they are abroad in all the earth, bearing the burden of light for the spiritual regeneration of the human race, and they will stand with you in this."

It was the simple rebuke, more a reminder of duty, and he knew it. But drained of all the passion that brought him across a wilderness of years, he felt if just for a moment the unbearable loneliness of a world bereft of its Creator. "Stay yet a little while with me," he urged, "even in silence, if you will."

"A little while, then, for the tide withdraws and across the waters some of your brethren wait to come to you. My cycle of action in the earth ends and yours begins anew, for like the tide I must withdraw and you take up the cloak and firmament of this world."

Caron looked where he pointed and, indeed, on the tidal flat some half dozen figures made their way across the barren strand to Holy Isle.

"You have never been alone in the earth, nor ever shall be," the Aton-Re said. "She who abode with me to shape your path dwells now with the Master Flegetanis in Crete. Seek her out on the rising tide of spring."

The sun rose. The tidal waters mingled with celestial fire, marking a shining path across the sea. Caron lifted his head and looked into the sun, and when he looked again beside the Aton-Re was gone, leaving him alone with the earth, the wind and the sea. Yet in Caron's heart the presence of the one who dwells rose like a sun, filling him with love's radiance, and whispering in the light of morning, "Closer than breathing, nearer than hands or feet, I Am."

Archangel

Perrin, the poet, was among those who came in search of Caron at Lindisfarne. And when Hugues had told his story so far as he might, Perrin set down these words for remembrance.

> You come as the sun
> Casting your shadow of light
> Before you.
> Your wings unfurled
> Are dawn and dusk, and night
> A cloak you gather round you
> Like peace,
> Starlight shimmering in the
> Folds.
>
> You have made your temple
> Of our hearts:
> Drawn, we are become your altar,
> Kindled in your embrace
> We unfold,
> Wonder in the cloven Flame.
>
> Closer than breathing,
> Nearer than hands and feet,
> We honour your return,
> Remembering
> The feathered-glory of sunlit
> Flight.
>
> Now we know as you have known,
> And welcome you,
> Home to our heart's silent ease -
> Soft as dusk,
> Firm as a summer's dawn.

Made in the USA
Monee, IL
22 November 2021